LEGENDS OF
DUNE 2
THE MACHINE CRUSADE

The Dune Novels

by Frank Herbert

DUNE

DUNE MESSIAH

CHILDREN OF DUNE

GOD EMPEROR OF DUNE

HERETICS OF DUNE

CHAPTERHOUSE: DUNE

Prelude to Dune
by Brian Herbert and Kevin J. Anderson

HOUSE ATREIDES

HOUSE HARKONNEN

HOUSE CORRINO

Legends of Dune

THE BUTLERIAN JIHAD

THE MACHINE CRUSADE

*THE BATTLE OF CORRIN

* forthcoming

LEGENDS OF
DUNE 2
THE MACHINE CRUSADE

Brian Herbert
& Kevin J. Anderson

Hodder & Stoughton

First published in Great Britain in 2003 by Hodder and Stoughton
Published simultaneously in paperback in 2003 by Hodder and Stoughton
A division of Hodder Headline

A CIP catalogue record of this book
is available from the British Library

ISBN 0 340 82333 X Hardback
ISBN 0 340 82334 8 Trade Paperback

Typeset in Scala by Hewer Text Ltd, Edinburgh
Printed and bound in Great Britain by
Mackays of Chatham Ltd, Chatham, Kent

Hodder and Stoughton
A division of Hodder Headline
338 Euston Road
London NW1 3BH

To PENNY and RON MERRITT,
Fellow travelers in the DUNE universe, with love and appreciation
for helping us maintain the legacy of Frank Herbert.

Acknowledgments

When we finished the manuscript of this book, the work had only begun. Pat LoBrutto and Carolyn Caughey showed their editorial genius, guiding us through numerous iterations and fine tuning to produce this final version. Our agents, Robert Gottlieb and Matt Bialer of Trident Media Group, have been supportive and excited about this project from the start. Tom Doherty, Linda Quinton, Jennifer Marcus, Heather Drucker, and Paul Stevens at Tor Books, and Julie Crisp at Hodder & Stoughton, helped keep all matters of production and promotion on track without letting their enthusiasm flag for a moment.

As always, Catherine Sidor at WordFire, Inc., worked tirelessly to transcribe dozens of microcassettes, input corrections, and maintain consistency in the face of a full-steam-ahead work pace. Diane E. Jones served as test reader and guinea pig, giving us her honest reactions and suggested additional scenes that helped make this a stronger book.

Rebecca Moesta Anderson devoted uncounted hours of energy, concentration, advice and criticism (always tempered with love), never letting the phrase "good enough" enter her vocabulary. Jan Herbert, as always, offered her support, patience, and understanding in the face of the unpredictable needs of a writer.

Javier Barriopedro and Christian Gossett gave us "Swordmaster" inspiration. Dr. Attila Torkos gave the final manuscript his fine-tooth-comb scrutiny, helping us to avoid inconsistencies.

The Herbert Limited Partnership, including Penny and Ron Merritt, David Merritt, Byron Merritt, Julie Herbert, Robert Merritt, Kimberly Herbert, Margaux Herbert, and Theresa Shackelford gave us their enthusiastic support, entrusting us with the care of Frank Herbert's vision.

Without Beverly Herbert's almost four decades of support and devotion to him, Frank Herbert would not have created such a vast and fascinating universe for us to explore. We are greatly indebted to them both.

H ISTORIANS DO NOT *agree on the messages carried in detritus of the long-ago past.*

As one delves into history — such ancient, chaotic times! — the more facts become fluid, the stories contradictory. Across the ocean of time and fallible memory, true heroes metamorphose into archetypes; battles grow more significant than they actually were. Legends and truth are difficult to reconcile.

As the First Official Historian of the Jihad, I must set down this record as best I can, relying upon oral traditions and fragmentary documents preserved for a hundred centuries. Which is more accurate — a carefully documented history such as mine, or an accumulation of myths and folktales?

I, Naam the Elder, must write honestly, even if it invites the wrath of my superiors. Read this history carefully, as I begin with Rendik Tolu-Far's Manifesto of Protest, a document that was confiscated by the Jipol:

"We are weary of fighting — weary unto death! Billions upon billions have already been slaughtered in this crusade against the thinking machines. The casualties include not only uniformed soldiers of the Jihad and their hired mercenaries, but also innocent colonists and human slaves on the Synchronized Worlds. No one bothers to count the number of enemy machines that have been destroyed.

"The computer evermind Omnius has dominated many planets for over a millennium, but it was twenty-four years ago that the murder of Priestess Serena Butler's innocent child triggered an all-out human revolt. She used this tragedy to incite a fervor in the League of Nobles, precipitating the Armada's full-scale attack and the atomic destruction of Earth.

"Yes, this was a blow to Omnius, but it killed every last human living on that

planet and left the birthplace of humanity a radioactive ruin, uninhabitable for centuries to come. What a horrendous cost! — and that was not a victory, not an end, but only the opening act in this long struggle.

"For more than two decades, Serena's holy war has raged against the thinking machines. Our strikes against Synchronized Worlds are countered by robotic incursions against League colonies. Again and again.

"Priestess Serena appears to be a devout woman, and I would like to believe in her purity and sanctity. She has spent years in the study of available writings and doctrines from ancient human philosophers. No other person has spent so much time talking with Kwyna, the Cogitor in residence at the City of Introspection. Serena's passion is evident and her beliefs beyond reproach, but is she aware of all of the things that are done in her name?

"Serena Butler is little more than a figurehead, while Iblis Ginjo is her political proxy. He styles himself the 'Grand Patriarch of the Jihad' and leads the Jihad Council, an emergency governing body that rules outside the boundaries of the League Parliament. And we allow this to happen!

"I have watched the Grand Patriarch — a former slave master on earth — use his charismatic oratory skills to transform Serena's tragedy into a weapon. Is everyone blind to how he builds his own political power? Why else would he have married Camie Boro, who traces her bloodline back a thousand years to the last, weak ruler of the Old Empire? A man does not wed the only living descendant of the last emperor merely for love!

"To ferret out human traitors and clandestine saboteurs, Iblis Ginjo has established his Jihad Police, the Jipol. Think of those thousands who have been arrested in recent years — can they all be traitors working for the machines, as Jipol claims? Is it not convenient that so many of them are the Grand Patriarch's political enemies?

"I do not criticize the military commanders, the brave soldiers, or even the mercenaries, for all of them are fighting the Jihad to the best of their abilities. Humans from every free planet have set out to destroy machine outposts and to block robot depredations. But how can we ever hope to achieve victory? The machines can always build more fighters . . . and they keep coming back.

"We are exhausted from this endless warfare. What hope do we have for peace? What possibility exists for an accord with Omnius? Thinking machines never tire.

"And they never forget."

177 B.G.
(Before Guild)
JIHAD YEAR 25

The weakness of thinking machines is that they actually believe all the information they receive, and react accordingly.
                                      —Vorian Atreides, fourth debriefing
                                         interview with League Armada

L EADING A GROUP of five ballistas in orbit over the canyon-scarred
   planet, Primero Vorian Atreides studied the robotic enemy forces
aligned against him: sleek and silver, like predatory fish. Their efficient,
functional design gave them the unintentional grace of sharp knives.

Omnius's combat monstrosities outnumbered the human ships ten to
one, but because the Jihad battleships were equipped with overlapping
layers of Holtzman shields, the enemy fleet could bombard the human
vessels without inflicting any damage, and without advancing toward the
surface of IV Anbus.

Although the human defenders did not have the necessary firepower to
crush the machine forces or even repel them, the jihadis would continue
to fight anyway. It was a standoff, humans and machines facing each
other above the planet.

Omnius and his forces had secured many victories in the past seven
years, conquering small backwater colonies and establishing outposts
from which they launched relentless waves of attack. But now the Army
of the Jihad had sworn to defend this Unallied Planet against the
thinking machines at all costs — whether or not the native population
wanted it.

Down on the planet's surface, his fellow Primero, Xavier Harkonnen,
was attempting yet another diplomatic foray with Zenshiite elders, the
leaders of a primitive Buddislamic sect. Vor doubted his friend would
make much progress. Xavier was too inflexible to be a good negotiator:
his sense of duty and strict adherence to the objectives of the mission
were always paramount in his mind.

Besides that, Xavier was biased against these people . . . and they undoubtedly realized it.

The thinking machines wanted IV Anbus. The Army of the Jihad had to stop them. If the Zenshiites wished to isolate themselves from the galactic conflict and not cooperate with the brave soldiers fighting to keep the human race free, then they were worthless. One time, Vor had jokingly compared Xavier to a machine, since he saw things in black-and-white terms, and the other man had scowled icily in response.

According to reports from the surface, the Zenshiite religious leaders had shown themselves to be just as stubborn as Primero Harkonnen. Both sides had dug in their heels.

Vor did not question his friend's command style, though it was quite different from his own. Having grown up among the thinking machines and trained as a trustee for them, Vor now embraced "humanness" in all of its facets, and was giddy with newfound freedom. He felt liberated when he played sports and gambled, or socialized and joked with other officers. It was so different from the way Agamemnon had taught him . . .

Out here in orbit, Vor knew the robot battleships would never retreat unless they were convinced, statistically, that they could not possibly win. In recent weeks he had been working on a complicated scheme to cause the Omnius fleet to break down, but wasn't ready to implement it yet. Soon, though.

This orbital stalemate was completely unlike the war games Vor enjoyed playing with the jihadi crewmen on patrol, or the amusing challenges he and the robot Seurat had set for each other years ago, during long voyages between stars. This tedious impasse offered little opportunity for fun.

He had been noticing patterns.

Soon the robotic fleet would cruise toward them like a cluster of piranhas in a retrograde orbit. Standing proud in his crisp dark-green military uniform flashed with crimson — the Jihad colors symbolizing life and spilled blood — Vor would give orders directing all the battleships in his sentry fleet to activate Holtzman shields and monitor them for overheating.

The robot warships — bristling with weapons — were woefully predictable, and his men often placed bets on exactly how many shots the enemy would fire.

He watched his forces shift, as he had commanded them to do. Xavier's adopted brother, Vergyl Tantor, captained the vanguard ballista and moved it into position. Vergyl had served the Army of the Jihad for the past seventeen years, always watched closely by Xavier.

Nothing had changed here in over a week, and the fighters were growing impatient, passing the enemy repeatedly but unable to do anything more than puff up their chests and display combat plumage like exotic birds.

"You'd think the machines would learn by now," Vergyl grumbled over the comline. "Do they keep hoping that we'll slip up?"

"They're just testing us, Vergyl." Vor avoided the formality of ranks and the chain of command because it reminded him too much of machine rigidity.

Earlier in the day, when the paths of the two fleets briefly intersected, the robot warships had launched a volley of explosive projectiles that hammered at the impregnable Holtzman shields. Vor had not flinched as he watched the fruitless explosions. For a few moments, the opposing ships had mingled head-on in a crowded, chaotic flurry, then moved past each other.

"All right, give me a total," he called.

"Twenty-eight shots, Primero," reported one of the bridge officers.

Vor had nodded. Always between twenty and thirty incoming shells, but his own guess had been twenty-two. He and the officers of his other ships had transmitted congratulations and good-natured laments about missing by only one or two shots, and had made arrangements to pay or collect on the bets they made. Duty hours would be shifted among the losers and winners, luxury rations transferred back and forth among the ships.

The same thing had happened almost thirty times already. But now, as the two battle groups predicatably approached one another, Vor had a surprise up his sleeve.

The Jihad fleet remained in perfect formation, as disciplined as machines.

"Here we go again." Vor turned to his bridge crew. "Prepare for encounter. Increase shields to full power. You know what to do. We've had enough practice at this."

A skin-tingling humming noise vibrated through the deck, layers of shimmering protective force powered by huge generators tied to the engines. The individual commanders would watch carefully for over-heating in the shields, the system's fatal flaw, which — so far, at least — the machines did not suspect.

He watched the vanguard ballista cruise ahead along the orbital path. "Vergyl, are you ready?"

"I have been for days, sir. Let's get on with it!"

Vor checked with his demolitions and tactical specialists, led by one of the Ginaz mercenaries, Zon Noret. "Mr. Noret, I presume that you deployed all of our . . . mouse traps?"

The signal came back. "Every one in perfect position, Primero. I sent each of our ships the precise coordinates, so that we can avoid them ourselves. The question is, will the machines notice?"

"I'll keep them busy, Vor!" Vergyl said.

The machine warships loomed closer, approaching the intercept point. Although the thinking machines had no sense of aesthetics, their calculations and efficient engineering designs still resulted in ships with precise curves and flawlessly smooth hulls.

Vor smiled. "Go!"

As the Omnius battlegroup advanced like a school of imperturbable, menacing fish, Vergyl's ballista suddenly lunged ahead at high accelera-tion, launching missiles in a new "flicker-and-fire" system that switched the bow shields on and off on a millisecond time scale, precisely coordinated to allow outgoing kinetic projectiles to pass through.

High-intensity rockets bombarded the nearest machine ship, and then Vergyl was off again, changing course and ramming down through the clustered robot vessels like a stampeding Salusan bull.

Vor gave the scatter order, and the rest of his ships broke formation and spread out. To get out of the way.

The machines, attempting to respond to the unexpected situation, could do little more than open fire on the Holtzman-shielded Jihad ships.

Vergyl slammed his vanguard ballista through again. He had orders to empty his ship's weapons batteries in a frenzied attack. Missile after missile detonated against the robot vessels, causing significant damage but not destruction. The comlines reverberated with human cheers.

But Vergyl's gambit was just a diversion. The bulk of the Omnius forces continued on their standard path . . . directly into the space minefield that the mercenary Zon Noret and his team had laid down in orbit.

The giant proximity mines were coated with stealth films that made them nearly invisible to sensors. Diligent scouts and careful scans could have detected them, but Vergyl's furious and unexpected aggression had turned the machines' focus elsewhere.

The front two machine battleships exploded as they struck a row of powerful mines. Massive detonations ripped holes through bows, hull, and lower engine sheaths. Reeling off course, the devastated enemy vessels sputtered in flames; one blundered into another mine.

Still not realizing precisely what had happened, three more robot ships collided with unseen space mines. Then the machine battlegroup rallied. Ignoring Vergyl's attack, the remaining warships spread out and deployed sensors to detect the rest of the scattered mines, which they removed with a flurry of precisely targeted shots.

"Vergyl — break off," Vor transmitted. "All other ballistas, regroup. We've had our fun." He leaned back in his command chair with a satisfied sigh. "Deploy four fast kindjal scouts to assess how much damage we inflicted."

He opened a private comline, and the image of the Ginaz mercenary appeared on the screen. "Noret, you and your men will receive medals for this." When not in combat camouflage for minelaying and other clandestine operations, the mercenaries wore gold-and-crimson uniforms of their own design, rather than green and crimson. Gold represented the substantial sums they received, and crimson, the blood they spilled.

Behind them, the damaged Omnius battlegroup continued on their orbital patrol, undeterred, like sharks looking for food. Already, swarms of robots had emerged from the ships and crawled like lice over the outer hulls, effecting massive repairs.

"It doesn't look like we even ruffled their feathers!" Vergyl said as his ballista rejoined the Jihad group. He sounded disappointed, then added, "They're still not getting IV Anbus from us."

"Damned right they're not. We've let them get away with enough in the past few years. Time for us to turn this war around."

Vor wondered why the robot forces were waiting so long without escalating this particular conflict. It wasn't part of their usual pattern. As the son of the Titan Agamemnon, he — more than any other human in the Jihad — understood the way computer minds worked. Now, as he thought about it, Vor grew highly suspicious.

Am I the one who's grown too predictable? What if the robots only want me to believe they won't change tactics?

Frowning, he opened the comline to the vanguard ballista. "Vergyl? I've got a bad feeling about this. Disperse scout ships to survey and map the land masses below. I think the machines are up to something."

Vergyl didn't question Vor's intuition. "We'll take a careful look down there, Primero. If they've flipped over so much as a rock, we'll find it."

"I suspect more than that. They're trying to be tricky — in their own predictable way." Vor glanced at the chronometer, knowing he had hours before he needed to worry about the next orbital encounter. He felt restless. "In the meantime, Vergyl, you're in command of the battlegroup. I'll shuttle down to see if your brother has managed to talk any sense into our Zenshiite friends."

In order to understand the meaning of victory, you must first define your enemies . . . and your allies.
—Primero Xavier Harkonnen, strategy lectures

SINCE THE EXODUS of all Buddislamic sects from the League of Nobles centuries earlier, IV Anbus had become the center of Zenshiite civilization. Its primary city of Darits was the religious heart of the independent and isolated sect, largely ignored by outsiders, who saw little value in the planet's meager resources and troublesome religious fanatics.

The land masses of IV Anbus were mottled with large, shallow seas, some fresh, some potently salty. The tides caused by close-orbiting moons dragged the seas like a scouring rag across the landscape, washing topsoil through sharp canyons, eroding out grottos and amphitheaters from the softer sandstone. In the shelter of the deep overhangs, the Zenshiites had built cities.

From one shallow sea into another, rivers drained naturally, pulled by the tidal surges. The inhabitants had developed exceptional mathematics, astronomy, and engineering skills to predict the swelling and dwindling floods. Silt miners reaped mineral wealth by sifting the murky water that flowed through the canyons. The downstream lowlands offered fertile soil, as long as agricultural workers planted and harvested at appropriate times.

In Darits, the Zenshiites had built an immense dam across a narrow bottleneck in the red rock canyons . . . a defiant gesture to show that their faith and ingenuity were enough to hold back even the powerful flow of the river. Behind the dam, a huge reservoir had backed up, full of deep-blue water. Zenshiite fishermen floated delicate skiffs around the lake, using large nets to supplement the grains and vegetables grown on the flood plain.

No mere wall, the Darits dam was adorned with towering stone statues carved by talented and faithful artisans. Hundreds of meters high, the twin monoliths represented idealized forms of Buddha and Mohammed, their features blurred by time, legend, and notions of idealistic reverence.

The faithful had installed bulky hydroelectric turbines, turned by the force of the current. In tandem with numerous solar-power plates that covered the mesa tops, the Darits dam generated enough energy to power all the cities of IV Anbus, which were not large by the standards of other worlds. The entire planet held only seventy-nine million inhabitants. Still, communication lines and a power grid connected the settlements with enough technological infrastructure to make this the most sophisticated of all Buddislamic refugee worlds.

Which was exactly why the thinking machines wanted it. With minimal effort Omnius could convert IV Anbus into a beachhead and from there prepare to launch even larger-scale assaults against League Worlds.

Serena Butler's Jihad had already been in full force for more than two decades. In the twenty-three years since the atomic destruction of Earth, the tides of battle had many times shifted between victory and loss, for each side.

But seven years ago, the thinking machines had begun to target Unallied Planets, which were easier conquests than the heavily defended, more densely populated League Worlds. On the vulnerable Unallied Planets, the scattered traders, miners, farmers, and Buddislamic refugees were rarely able to muster sufficient force to resist Omnius. In the first three years, five such planets had been overrun by thinking machines.

Back on Salusa Secundus, the Jihad Council had been unable to understand why Omnius would bother with such worthless places — until Vorian noticed the pattern: Driven by the calculations and projections of the computer evermind, the thinking machines were surrounding the League Worlds like a net, drawing closer and closer in preparation for a *coup de grâce* against the League capital.

Shortly after Vorian Atreides — with Xavier's support — had demanded that the Jihad devote its military strength to defend the Unallied Planets, a massive and unexpected Jihad counterstrike succeeded in recapturing Tyndall from the machines. Any victory was a good one.

Xavier was glad the Army of the Jihad had arrived at IV Anbus in time, thanks to the warning of a Tlulaxa slaver named Rekur Van. The flesh merchant's team had raided this world, kidnapping Zenshiites to be sold in the slave markets of Zanbar and Poritrin. After his raid, the slaver had encountered a robotic scout patrol mapping and analyzing the planet, something the machines always did in preparation for a conquest. Rekur

Van then raced back to Salusa Secundus and delivered the dire news to the Jihad Council.

To counter the danger, Grand Patriarch Iblis Ginjo had put together this hasty but effective military operation. "We cannot afford to let another world fall to the demonic thinking machines," Iblis had shouted at the send-off ceremony, to enthusiastically defiant cheers and thrown orange flowers. "We have already lost Ellram, Peridot Colony, Bellos, and more. But at IV Anbus, the Army of the Jihad draws a line in space!"

Though Xavier had underestimated the number of ships Omnius would dispatch to this remote world, thus far the Jihad forces had been able to thwart the attempted invasion, though they could not drive the robots away.

During a break in the talks with the Zenshiites, Xavier cursed under his breath. The very people he was trying to save had no interest in his help, and declined to fight against the thinking machines.

This city in the red rock canyons housed relics and the original hand-written canons of the Zenshia interpretation of Buddislam. Inside cave vaults, wise men preserved original scrawled manuscripts of the Sutra Koran and prayed five times daily when they heard the calls from minarets erected on the canyon rim. From Darits the elders dispensed their commentary, meant to guide the faithful through the forest of esoterica.

Xavier Harkonnen could barely contain his frustration. He was a military man, accustomed to leading battle engagements, ordering his troops and expecting his commands to be followed. He simply didn't know what to do when these pacifistic Buddislamic inhabitants just . . . refused.

Back home among the League Worlds, there had been a growing anti-Jihad protest movement. The people were exhausted from more than two decades of bloodshed with no visible progress. Some had even carried placards near the shrines to the murdered child Manion the Innocent, begging for "Peace at Any Cost!"

Yes, Xavier could understand their weariness and despair, for they had seen many loved ones killed by the thinking machines. But these isolated Buddislamics had never even bothered to lift a hand in resistance, revealing the ultimate folly of extreme non-violence.

The machines' objective was clear, and Omnius would certainly show no consideration for any fanatical religious preferences. Xavier had a vital job to complete here, in the name of the Jihad — and that job required a little common-sense cooperation from the natives. He had never expected so much trouble trying to make these people appreciate what the Army of the Jihad was risking for them.

The Zenshiite elders shuffled back into the meeting room, an enclosure adorned with aged religious artifacts that glimmered with gold and precious stones.

As he had for hours, the religious leader Rhengalid gazed at him with stony eyes and implacable refusal. He had a large shaved head that glistened with exotic oils; his thick eyebrows had been brushed and artificially darkened. His chin was covered with a thick, square-cut gray beard that he wore as a mark of pride. His eyes were a pale gray-green that stood out in striking contrast to his tanned skin. Despite the ominous thinking-machine battle fleet overhead, or the impressive firepower of the Army of the Jihad, this man remained unimpressed and unintimidated. He seemed oblivious.

With a determined effort, Xavier kept his voice even. "We are trying to protect your world, Elder Rhengalid. If we hadn't arrived when we did, if our ships did not continue to hold back the thinking machines *every day*, you and all your people would be slaves of Omnius." He sat stiffly on the hard bench across from the Zenshiite leader. Not once had Rhengalid offered him any refreshment, though Xavier suspected that the elders had partaken of their own whenever the soldiers left the room.

"Slaves? If you are so concerned for our welfare, Primero Harkonnen, where were your battleships a few months ago when Tlulaxa flesh merchants stole healthy young men and fertile women from our farming settlements?"

Xavier tried not to show distress. He had never wanted to be a diplomat, didn't have the patience for it. He served the cause of the Jihad with all the loyalty and dedication he possessed. The crimson of his uniform symbolized the spilled blood of humanity, and his innocent Manion — barely eleven months old — had been the first of the new martyrs.

"Elder, what did *you* do to defend your own people when the raiders came? I knew nothing of the incident before now and cannot help you with what happened in the past. I can only promise that life under the thinking machines will be much worse."

"So you say, but you cannot deny the hypocrisy of your own society. Why should we take the word of one slaver over another?"

Xavier's nostrils flared. *I don't have time for this!* "If you insist on reliving the past, then remember that your peoples' refusal to fight the thinking machines from the very beginning has cost the freedom of billions of humans, and countless deaths. Many believe you owe a great debt to your race."

"We have no love for either side in this conflict," the gray-bearded man retorted. "My people want no part of your *pointless*, bloody war."

Holding back a heated retort, Xavier said, "Nevertheless, you are caught in the crossfire and must choose sides."

"Are human tyrants better than machine tyrants? Who can say? But I do know that this is not our fight, has never been our fight."

Workers inside the Darits dam moved sluice gates, letting clear water pour in twin spectacular waterfalls from the open hands of the colossal Buddha and Mohammed statues. At the sudden rushing noise, Xavier looked up, and was surprised to see Primero Vorian Atreides striding along the rock walkway from the landing pad of his shuttle at the crude spaceport. Smiling, the dark-haired man approached, still looking as fit, virile, and young as when Xavier had first met him after his escape from Earth so many years ago. "You can cajole them all you want, Xavier, but the Zenshiites speak a different language . . . in more than the linguistic sense."

The Darits elder looked indignant. "Your godless civilization has persecuted us. Jihadi soldiers are not welcome here — especially not in Darits, our sacred city."

Xavier held his gaze on Rhengalid. "I must inform you, Elder, that I shall not allow the thinking machines to take over this planet, whether you help us or not. The fall of IV Anbus would give the enemy yet another stepping-stone to the League Worlds."

"This is our planet, Primero Harkonnen. You do not belong here."

"Neither do the thinking machines!" Xavier shouted. His face reddened.

Vorian took him by the arm. Clearly amused, Vor said, "I see you've discovered new techniques of diplomacy."

"I never claimed to be a negotiator."

Smiling, Vor nodded. "If these people knew to follow your orders, that would certainly make things easier, wouldn't it?"

"I'm not going to abandon this planet, Vor."

The command comline sputtered, and a sharp message came across it. Vergyl Tantor's voice was excited, breathless. "Primero Atreides, your suspicions were correct! Our scans have discovered a secret thinking machine base camp being established on a plateau. Appears to be a military beachhead, with industrial machinery, heavy weaponry and combat robots."

"Good work, Vergyl," Vor said. "Now the fun starts."

Xavier glanced over his shoulder at the self-absorbed Rhengalid, who looked as if he never wanted to see the jihadis again. "We're finished here, Vor. Come back to the flagship. We've got work to do."

There is no such thing as the future. Humankind faces multiple possible futures, many of which hinge on seemingly inconsequential events.

—*The Muadru Chronicles*

ZIMIA WAS A stunning city, the cultural pinnacle of free humanity. Tree-lined boulevards fanned out like the spokes of a wheel from a complex of governmental buildings and an immense memorial plaza. Men in doublet-suits and ladies in ornamented official dresses walked briskly about the square.

Iblis Ginjo frowned as he hurried across the expanse toward the stately Hall of Parliament. Such an orderly arrangement could give the illusion of security, that the surroundings would never change.

But nothing is permanent. Nothing is secure.

He was in the business of inspiring people, galvanizing them into action by convincing them that the evil machines could attack any world at any time, and that there were sinister human spies who secretly gave their loyalty to Omnius, even here in the heart of the League.

Sometimes Iblis had to embellish reality, for the greater good of the struggle.

A broad-shouldered man with a squarish face and straight dark-brown hair, he wore a loose black blazer adorned with gold stitching and sparkling bangles. Several steps behind him, half a dozen Jihad Police — Jipol agents — followed, always alert, ready to draw their weapons quickly. Turncoat humans or assassins loyal to the machines could be lurking anywhere.

Two decades ago, Iblis had granted himself the title "Grand Patriarch of Serena Butler's Jihad," and the throng embraced him every time he appeared in public. He spoke for them, rallied them, told them what to think and how to react. Like Vorian Atreides, Iblis had once been a human trustee of the thinking machines on Earth. Now he was an orator and statesman of the highest order: a king, politician, religious leader, and military commander all wrapped in one charismatic package. He had carved his own path, an unprecedented course that allowed him to move in the elite circles of human leadership. He knew history, and saw his place in it clearly.

As he climbed the broad steps of the Hall of Parliament and entered the high-ceilinged, frescoed foyer, representatives and clerks fell silent. Iblis loved to see people fumbling around in awe of him, red-faced and stammering.

He paused with appropriate reverence at the ornate alcove shrine to Serena Butler's murdered child Manion, an angelic sculpture with arms open wide to receive a daily burden of fresh flowers, pale orange marigolds that looked like small, bright supernovas, the blossom that had been adopted as "Manion's flower."

Inside, the great hall was full, every chair occupied by a nobleman or planetary representative. Even the aisles were packed with distinguished guests, seated on portable, new-model suspensor chairs that floated in available spaces.

A monk in a saffron-yellow robe sat near the front of the assembly, monitoring a heavy translucent container that held a live human brain inside a life-support bath of bluish electrafluid. As Iblis glanced at the revered Cogitor, he felt a giddy rush of genuine pleasure at the memory it inspired of the ancient philosopher-brain named Eklo, who had shared his knowledge when Iblis had been a mere slave supervisor on Earth. Those had been heady days, full of possibilities . . .

This Cogitor, a female thinker known as Kwyna, was more reluctant to help him, to offer her advice. Even so, Iblis often went to the tranquil City of Introspection to sit by Kwyna's preservation canister, hoping to learn. He had met only two Cogitors in his life, but the magnificent organic thinking units never failed to impress him.

They were so superior to Omnius, so elegant and so infinitely *human* . . . despite their obvious physical limitations.

The Parliament's business had already been under way for hours, but nothing important would happen until he arrived. It had all been arranged. His quiet allies among the League representatives would clog the governmental works with irrelevant bureaucracy, just to make *him* look more effective when he cut through all the dithering.

On the podium, the planetary representative from Hagal, Hosten Fru, droned on about a minor commercial problem, a dispute between

VenKee Enterprises and the Poritrin government over patents and distribution rights for glowglobes, which had become increasingly popular.

"The original concept is based on work done by an assistant to Savant Tio Holtzman, but VenKee Enterprises has marketed the technology without any compensation to Poritrin," Hosten Fru said. "I suggest we assign a committee to look into the matter and give it due consideration—"

Iblis smiled to himself. *Yes, a committee will ensure a complete lack of resolution on the issue.* Hosten Fru was a seemingly incompetent politician who blocked League business with inane problems, making the cumbersome government appear as ineffectual as the passive Old Empire. No one knew that the Hagal representative was one of Iblis's secret allies. It served Iblis's purposes perfectly: the more people saw how incapable the League Assembly was of solving simple problems, especially during crises, the more decisions were relegated to the Jihad Council, which he controlled . . .

Beaming with confidence, Iblis Ginjo made his grand entrance. As the proxy for Serena Butler herself, he was the spokesman for humanity and its Holy Jihad against the thinking machines.

Ten violent years after the atomic destruction of Earth, old Manion Butler had retired as League Viceroy, asking that his daughter Serena be appointed to take his place. She had been voted in by acclamation, but insisted that she be called only the "Interim Viceroy" until the conclusion of the war. Delighted, Iblis had insinuated himself as her closest advisor, writing speeches for her, building the fervor for the crusade against the thinking machines.

Head high, he strode down the carpeted aisle to the front of the speaking chamber. Imagers projected Iblis's oversized features on the sides of the enclosure. Immediately deferential, Hosten Fru summed up and bowed, stepping away from the podium. "I relinquish my remaining time to the Grand Patriarch."

Iblis walked across the stage, folded his hands in front of him and formally nodded his gratitude to the Hagal representative, who hurried out of the speaking zone. Before he could gather his thoughts, though, an interruption came from the floor.

"Point of order!" He recognized the woman as Muñoza Chen, a troublesome representative from the remote League World of Pincknon.

Iblis turned to her, forcing an expression of patience onto his face as she stood and said, "Earlier today, I questioned the additional responsibilities transferred without due process from the Parliament to the

Jihad Council. That discussion was tabled until an authorized member of the Council could address this Assembly." She crossed her arms over her small chest. "I believe Grand Patriarch Ginjo is empowered to speak on behalf of the Council."

He offered her a cool smile. "That is not why I have come to address the Assembly today, Madame Chen."

The annoying woman refused to sit down. "Pending business is on the table, sir. Standard procedure requires that we attempt to resolve the matter before proceeding to anything else."

He sensed the impatient mood of the crowd and knew how to use it to his advantage. They had come to hear *him* speak, not to see tedious discussions about an irrelevant motion. "You are providing an excellent object lesson as to why the Jihad Council had to be formed, to make swift and necessary decisions, without this quagmire of bureaucracy."

The audience grumbled their agreement. Now his smile warmed.

For the first thirteen years after Serena Butler had announced her Jihad, the League Parliament had struggled to run urgent wartime matters with the same cumbersome system that had operated during the prior centuries of uneasy peace. But after the debacles at Ellram and Peridot Colony, when the politicians had dickered for so long that entire protectorates had been wiped out before rescue missions could arrive, an indignant Serena had addressed the Parliament. She had expressed her outrage and (far worse to the people) her *disappointment* because they had put petty squabbles ahead of their real enemy.

Standing beside her, Iblis Ginjo had seized the initiative and suggested the formation of a "Jihad Council," which would oversee all matters that directly related to the Jihad, while less urgent commercial, social, and domestic items could be discussed and debated in unhurried Parliament sessions. Wartime matters required swift and decisive leadership that could only be hampered by the thousand voices of Parliament.

Or so Iblis had convinced them; his proposal passed overwhelmingly.

Even so, a decade later, old political ways still inhibited progress. Now, delighted to hear grumbling agreement from the seats, Iblis looked at the Pincknon representative with long-suffering patience. "What is your question?"

Muñoza Chen did not seem to notice the muttered comments around her. "Your Council keeps finding more and more areas that fall under the umbrella of its jurisdiction. Originally, you were limited to oversight of the Army of the Jihad with respect to its military operations, as well as domestic security embodied in Jipol. Now the Council administers to refugees, distributes supplies, imposes new tariffs and taxes. Where will this disturbing expansion of authority end?"

Iblis made a mental note to have his police commander, Yorek Thurr, begin discreet inquiries and investigations into this woman's background. It might even be necessary to have someone "discover" damning evidence of Chen's "collusion" with the thinking machines. Yorek Thurr was skilled in arranging such things. Perhaps she had a medical condition that could lead to her "unfortunate" death.

He answered calmly. "Administering to survivors and refugees in war zones has obvious relevance to the Council's mandate, as does the training of battlefield surgeons, the distribution of necessary medical supplies and food shipments. When we recaptured Tyndall from the machines only last year, the Jihad Council instituted relief operations immediately. By enacting emergency taxes and commandeering luxury supplies from comfortable League Worlds, we gave those poor people shelter, medicines, hope. Had we left such matters to the League Parliament, Madame Chen, you would still be discussing it in open session." He turned to the podium and then said, as if in afterthought, "I have heard no complaints from the population of Tyndall."

"But for the Council to expand its purview without a vote of—"

Iblis made an impatient noise. "I can discuss such questions with you for hours, but is that truly what these people wish to hear." He lifted his hands in question, and well-timed shouts and boos echoed through the stands; some catcalls were initiated by his own people, of course, but many were spontaneous. "However, I come before this assembly today to share certain knowledge recently revealed in ancient Muadru inscriptions."

In his strong hands, he gripped an important piece of history, an ancient wafer of etched stone sandwiched between shatter-proof plaz sheets. He propped the frame on the podium. "This runestone fragment was unearthed on an empty world two centuries ago but has remained untranslated. *Until now.*"

The intrigued audience fell silent. Ignored, Muñoza Chen faltered, then sat down awkwardly, without ever officially withdrawing her question.

"These ciphers were written by a long-dead prophet in a tongue known as Muadru, etched permanently into coated rock. The words from the past are believed to be from Earth, the mother world of humanity." He turned to look at the yellow-robed secondary beside the ancient brain in its preservation canister. "The Cogitor Kwyna, by assisting me in the translation of these archaic rune symbols, has enabled me to understand. Kwyna, would you provide your guidance now?"

Uncertainly, the monk secondary stood and then carried the ornate brain canister to a golden table beside the speaking podium. Iblis felt thrilled to stand beside such a magnificent mind. The saffron-robed man waited.

Strengthened by his proximity to Kwyna, Iblis traced the complex runes with a fingertip. The audience remained silent and deeply engrossed as he began to read, enunciating the sharp lingual clicks and soft, rolling syllables. Odd, incomprehensible sounds resonated through the great meeting hall, casting a spell over the audience.

When Iblis paused, the Cogitor's attendant pressed his palm against the curved jar containing Kwyna's living brain, then slowly eased his fingers into the pale blue fluid. Through this connection, he translated the Muadru words in a voice that sounded far away — as if he spoke from the distance of ages past.

The runestone had been damaged in an ancient cataclysm that left scorch marks and deep gouges, he said. While some of his sentences were missing words, the remainder told of a terrible ancient war in which many people had died horribly. Finally, he said, "Quoting the unnamed prophet, 'A millennium of tribulations will occur before our people find their way to paradise.'"

Waiting for this moment, Iblis flashed a bright, exuberant grin and shouted: "Is it not clear? Free humans have suffered a thousand years under the cymeks and their machine masters. Do you not see? Our time of tribulation is over — if only we choose to make it so."

The blue electrafluid in the Cogitor's canister swirled, and the secondary relayed Kwyna's message to the assemblage. "That slice of runestone does not contain the entire prophecy. The message is incomplete."

Iblis pressed forward with his agenda. "We must always face both the danger, *and the promise*, of the unknown. One of our battle groups has gone to IV Anbus to defend against the latest robotic incursion — but that is not enough. As free people, we must act forcefully to recapture all Synchronized Worlds, freeing their enslaved human populations. Only in this way will our tribulations ever end, as the runestone prophecy proclaims. As foretold, a thousand years have passed. *Now* we must seize our road to paradise and cast aside the demon machines. I call for an expansion of Jihad forces, additional warships and dedicated soldiers, renewed offensives against Omnius."

Increased turbulence stirred the blue fluid in the canister. "And more deaths," the secondary translated.

"And more heroes!" Iblis raised his voice, face lit by a fervent glow.

"As the wise Kwyna says, this rune fragment is all we have. Thus, as human beings, we must choose the best interpretation. Do we have the heart to pay the price necessary to make the prophecy come true?"

Abruptly, before Kwyna could issue any contrary remark, the Grand Patriarch thanked the Cogitor and her attendant monk. Though Iblis revered the female philosopher, sadly Kwyna had spent so much time in contradictory philosophies and contemplation, without understanding the realities of the Jihad.

Iblis, though, had practical objectives. His enthusiastic audience cared nothing for philosophical hair-splitting.

The Grand Patriarch's voice resonated, rising and falling at appropriate, calculated moments. "Our victory is paid for with human blood. Serena Butler's tiny son has already paid that price, as have millions of valiant jihadi soldiers. The ultimate victory not only merits such an expense, it *requires* it. To lose is unthinkable. Our very existence hangs in the balance."

Around the hall, heads nodded, and Iblis maintained an inward, concealed smile of satisfaction. Though the secondary monk remained silent beside the plaz brain canister, the Grand Patriarch sensed that Kwyna might even agree. No one could resist his words, his passion. Visible tears of appreciation sparkled in Iblis's eyes, just enough to show how much he really cared about humankind.

One can compare this new Jihad to a necessary editing process. We are disposing of the things that are destroying us as humans.
　　　　　　　　　—Cogitor Kwyna, *City of Introspection Archives*

I NSIDE A COFFIN of perfect crystal, the little boy lay peaceful and pristine. Like a spark encased within a glass shell, Manion Butler was isolated from everything that had been wrought in his name. And Serena remained secluded with him inside the walls of the City of Introspection.

She knelt on a stone platform at the front of the shrine, as she often did, looking both beatific and grim. Long ago, devotees in the contemplative retreat had stopped asking to install a fine bench where she could sit and pray over her child. For twenty-four years now, Serena had faced her thoughts, her memories, her nightmares this way, on her knees before the crystalline case.

Manion looked so serene here, so sheltered. The boy's delicate face and fragile bones had been shattered when the monstrous robot Erasmus had dropped him from a high balcony, but Iblis Ginjo had seen to it that his true form and features were repaired by cosmetic morticians. Her son was preserved exactly as Serena wanted to remember him. Yes, faithful Iblis had taken care of everything possible.

Had he lived, Manion would be a full-grown young nobleman now . . . old enough to be married and have children himself. Gazing upon Manion's beautiful face, she thought of the potential he might have attained, if not for the evil thinking machines.

Instead, the innocent boy had given birth to a jihad that blazed across star systems, with humans fomenting revolution on the Synchronized Worlds, attacking robot ships and all incarnations of Omnius. Billions of people had already died for the holy cause. Erasmus himself must have been destroyed in the atomic attack that annihilated thinking machines on Earth. But the computer evermind still held dominion over the rest of his realm, and humans could not rest.

The pain did not go away. Serena's very soul had been smashed by the murder of her son. Meditating in his presence gave her all the inspiration she needed to keep leading the Jihad. This particular shrine, containing Manion's actual body, was reserved for her, and for a few select devotees.

Additional shrines and elaborate reliquaries had appeared across Salusa Secundus and on other League Worlds. Some were adorned with paintings or depictions of the divine boy, the sacrificial lamb, though none of the artists had ever seen him in life. Some reliquaries purported to contain bits of cloth, hair, even microscopic cellular samples. Though Serena doubted the authenticity of such exhibits, she did not ask to have them removed. The people's faith and devotion were more important than perfect accuracy.

After the Jihad had failed to overthrow the Synchronized World of Bela Tegeuse, and after the thinking machines had once again attacked — and been driven from — Salusa Secundus, Iblis had convinced Serena that she must not dilute her power or risk her safety for such meaningless political activities as trade accords and minor laws. Instead, she reserved her public appearances for matters of great importance. Without Serena Butler's inspiration, he insisted, humanity would not have the will to fight. So she delivered grand inspirational speeches, and people rushed out to sacrifice their lives for the cause — for *her*.

In spite of Iblis's precautions, however, when Serena had gone to speak at a Parliament assembly one year after accepting the role as interim Viceroy, she had barely survived an attempt on her life. The would-be assassin had been killed, and the Jipol commander Yorek Thurr had uncovered unusual machine technology hidden among the assailant's effects. For the first time, the League had faced the reality of Omnius spies — human turncoats — infiltrating League worlds.

In the uproar, most people could not conceive of what would drive a person to voluntarily swear allegiance to the amoral thinking machines. Iblis, though, had addressed a huge crowd in Zimia's memorial square. "I myself have seen human slaves raised on the Synchronized Worlds — it is no secret that Primero Vorian Atreides and I were brainwashed to serve Omnius. Other selfish, traitorous people might be granted attractive rewards — the promise of a neo-cymek body, even planets and slaves of their own. We must be vigilant at all times."

The fear of thinking machine spies living disguised among the free planets had been an important impetus for Iblis to form the Jipol, a vigilant security force that monitored domestic activities for any signs of suspicious behavior.

After the assassination attempt, Serena had been rushed into the City of Introspection, where she lived an even more isolated life from that time on, to ensure her safety.

The old compound had been built centuries before, the idea partly sparked by a debate about Buddislam and the eventual exile of the Zensunni and Zenshiite slaves who had toiled for generations on Salusa before their exodus to uncharted Unallied Planets. Now, followers of the varied fractured faiths came here to study ancient writings, religious works, and philosophical records. Scholars analyzed all forms of venerable teachings, from the mysterious Muadru runestones found scattered on uninhabited planets, to the vague Navachristian traditions of Poritrin and Chusuk, the haiku of the Zen Hekiganshu on III Delta Pavonis, and the alternate interpretations of the Koran Sutras from the Zensunni and Zenshia sects. The variations were as numerous as the communities of humans flung across countless planets . . .

Serena heard footsteps crunching softly on the gem-gravel path, and looked up to see her mother approach. Escorting the Abbess into Serena's presence were three bright-eyed young women in white robes trimmed with crimson, as if the edges had been dipped in blood. The guard women were tall and muscular, their expressions stonily irenic. Clinging hoods of fine goldscale mesh covered their heads. Each woman had a small symbol of the Jihad painted above her left eyebrow.

Fourteen years earlier, when the Jipol commander had first uncovered Omnius loyalists secretly plotting against Serena, Iblis had established a special cadre of female guards to protect the Priestess of the Jihad. Serena's "Seraphim" were like Amazon warriors and vestal virgins combined, carefully selected attendants assigned by the Grand Patriarch to cater to all of Serena's needs.

Livia Butler walked quickly enough to pull ahead of the three Seraphim. Serena stepped away from her son's shrine, smiled, and formally kissed the older woman on the cheek.

Livia had snowy white hair, cropped short, and wore a long simple robe of cream-colored fibers. She carried with her a lifetime of tragedy and experiences. Following the death of Serena's brother Fredo, their mother had retreated from the Butler estate, seeking solace and wisdom from God. Because of her long-time marriage to the former Viceroy, the dignified woman still paid close attention to politics and current events, studying the real-world implications of the Jihad rather than just the esoteric moral questions that fascinated the Cogitor Kwyna.

At the moment, her face revealed deep concern. "I have just listened to the Grand Patriarch's speech, Serena. Do you know he's pushing the Army of the Jihad again, inciting even more bloody attacks?"

Livia glanced over her shoulder at the trio of statuesque Seraphim who hovered too close on the stone platform fronting the shrine. Serena gestured for the robed women to step away; they did so, but only as far as the shrine, where they remained at attention, still within earshot. She knew two of the three well; the other Seraph was new, having just graduated from a rigorous training program.

She answered with the so-familiar words. "Sacrifices are necessary to achieve our ultimate victory, Mother. My Jihad has blazed for two decades, but not brightly enough. We cannot accept an endless impasse. We must redouble our efforts."

Livia's mouth flattened into a thin line, not quite a frown. "I have heard the Grand Patriarch give those same reasons, in practically the same words."

"And why not?" Serena's lavender eyes flared. "Iblis's goals are the same as mine. As Priestess of the Jihad I cannot concern myself with politics and power plays. Do you question my judgment or my devotion to free humanity?"

Livia said in a calm voice, "No one questions your motives, Serena. Your heart is pure, though hard."

"The machines themselves deadened my capacity for love. The robot Erasmus took that from me forever."

Sadly, Livia stepped close to her daughter and slipped an arm around her shoulders. The Seraphim attendants tensed, hands sliding toward their concealed weapons. Serena and Livia both ignored them.

"My child, human love is an infinite resource. No matter how many times it is expended, whether stolen or given away, love can grow again — like a flower from a bulb — and fill your heart."

Serena bowed her head, and listened as her mother's comforting words continued. "Tomorrow is Octa's birthday. Hers and . . . Fredo's. I lost *my* son too, Serena, so I know how you feel." She hastened to add, "Your brother died differently, of course."

"Yes, Mother — and you withdrew to the City of Introspection afterward. You of all people must understand."

"Oh I do, but I have not let my heart turn to stone, for all love to die within me. I am devoted to your father, to Octa, and to you. Come with me and see how much her daughters have grown. You have two nieces now."

"Xavier will not be there?"

Livia frowned. "He fights the machines at IV Anbus. You dispatched him there yourself. Don't you remember?"

Serena nodded distractedly. "He's been gone so long. I'm sure he longs to come back for Octa's party." Then she lifted her head. "But the Jihad must take precedence over all personal matters. We make our choices, and we survive by holding to them."

Looking sad, Livia said, "Do not resent him for marrying your sister. You cannot keep wishing that things could have been different."

"Of course I wish things could have been different, but perhaps my suffering was what the human race finally needed to galvanize it to action. Otherwise we would never have had the impetus to turn around and throw off the shackles of the thinking machines." She shook her head. "I am no longer jealous of Octa, and I don't resent Xavier. Yes, I loved him once — he was Manion's father — but I was just a girl then. Silly and starry-eyed. In the light of subsequent events, such concerns seem so . . . trivial."

Livia chided, "Love is never trivial, Serena, even when you don't want it."

Serena's voice became small, not at all the powerful, passionate instrument she employed when rallying the huge crowds that came to hear her. "I fear, Mother, that the damage to my soul will take more than a lifetime to heal."

Livia slipped her arm through Serena's and turned to lead her along the gem-gravel path. "Nevertheless, daughter, that is all the time you have."

Abruptly, Serena saw a blur of white motion from the direction of her guards. One of the Seraphim cried out and threw herself upon another — the newest one — who moved with blinding speed, drawing a long dagger that glinted silver.

Her mother slammed into Serena and knocked her away. As she fell, Serena heard a nearby slash of cloth and a gurgling gasp, saw a grisly spurt of blood and, almost simultaneously, felt a heavy impact. Livia dropped on top of her, covering Serena's body.

The third Seraph drove into the rushing white-robed guard, grabbed the gold-mesh hood that covered the traitor's hair, and yanked her head back with a hollow snap to break her neck.

Although her mother's body still covered hers, Serena could see a Rorschach splash of scarlet on one of the guards' robes, not at all like the precise crimson trimming on the white uniform. A gasping, heroic Seraph — the only survivor of the three — choked out, "The threat has been neutralized, Priestess." She caught her breath and quickly composed herself.

Shaking, Livia helped her daughter to her feet. Serena was astonished to see two of her chosen guards lying dead: her bloody defender, fallen with a slashed throat, and the other broken. The traitor.

"An assassin?" Serena looked down at the woman whose head lay cocked at an awkward angle.

Livia demanded, "How did she penetrate our training?"

The remaining Seraph said, "Priestess, we must get you to safety inside one of the buildings. There may be another attempt on your life."

Alarms had already sounded, and more white-robed Seraphim rushed to the scene, scanning in all directions for additional threats. Serena felt her knees growing weak as she and her mother were hustled to the shelter of the nearest large building.

She looked at the white-robed young woman who had saved her life. With her gold-mesh hood askew from the struggle, the guard's short blonde hair could be seen. "Niriem? That is your name, correct?"

"Yes, Priestess." She straightened her hood.

"From this moment on, I appoint you my chief Seraph. Make certain the Grand Patriarch summons his best Jipol officers to investigate this matter," Serena said, breathless as she ran.

"Yes, Priestess."

Because of the severity of the incident, Iblis would have to get involved personally, and might replace all of the Seraphim . . . except for Niriem. Serena would leave it to him to unravel what had happened. She could still hardly believe it herself.

Livia urged her daughter into the safety of the main sanctuary building, a converted manor house with cupolas and turrets. "You have always known the threat, my daughter. The machines are everywhere."

Serena's eyes were dry, her expression cold. "And they will never stop plotting against us."

"A human lifespan is not always sufficient for a person to achieve greatness. To counter this, some of us have seized more time for ourselves."

—General Agamemnon, *Memoirs*

T HE GREATEST ENEMIES of humanity gathered on the primary Synchronized World of Corrin: cymeks, robots, and Omnius, the computer evermind itself.

Only four of the original Twenty Titans remained alive. A thousand years ago, fearful of their mortality, these human tyrants had installed their brains in armored cylinders so that their thoughts, minds, and souls could live forever. But over the long and violent centuries, they had fallen to mishaps or assassinations, one at a time. In the recent uprisings, both Barbarossa and Ajax had been assassinated.

General Agamemnon, the leader of the Titans, had repaid that debt a thousand times over, slaughtering countless humans. Crushing them and letting them rot where they lay or piling them in heaps on the ground for bonfires. His lover Juno had helped him plan horrific, vengeful strategies.

So many ways to kill humans.

Dante, the unambitious but talented bureaucrat cymek, still served in quiet but necessary ways. The coward Xerxes, who had originally allowed Omnius to take over from the Titans, clung to his foolish belief that he could regain respect.

Now the Titans arrived in four specially configured ships. Manipulator arms from Agamemnon's spacecraft installed the general's preservation canister into a serviceable walker form. Thoughtrodes connected his mind to mobile systems, and he stretched arachnidlike mechanical limbs before walking out under the blood-red skies. Juno, Dante, and Xerxes emerged from their own ships and followed their leader toward

Erasmus's opulent villa, which bore a strong similarity to an estate that had been leveled by the League Armada in their attack on Earth.

Erasmus fancied himself a cultured individual, an admirer of past human glories. He had modeled this grand estate on ornate historical palaces, though the Corrin landscape necessitated certain modifications, including diffusion devices to keep the human slaves from being poisoned by concentrated emissions of groundgas.

Corrin was a rocky world, originally frozen and dead; when the sun had swelled to its red-giant phase, incinerating the system's inner planets, the once-uninhabitable lump had thawed. Back when the Old Empire of the humans still retained a few sparks of genius and ambition, hardy pioneers had terraformed Corrin, planting grasses and trees, bringing in animals, insects, and colonists.

But the settlement had not even lasted as long as the short lifespan of the red giant, and now machines ruled here under ruddy skies, with the baleful eye of the bloated sun peering down on dirty pens of slave workers.

The cymeks marched through villa gates made of treated metals twisted and looped into curlicues. Lavish vines bursting with scarlet flowers draped the walls and open ceiling grid. The air must be stiflingly heavy with perfume; Agamemnon was glad he had not taken a walker form with olfactory sensors. Smelling flowers was the last thing he wanted to do right now.

With an artificial grin on his flowmetal face, Erasmus glided up to the visiting dignitaries as they entered his courtyard. The independent robot wore a foppish robe trimmed with a spray of plush fur in imitation of an ancient human king. "Welcome, my colleagues. I would offer you refreshments, but I suspect the gesture would be wasted on machines with human minds."

"We aren't here for a party," Agamemnon said. Xerxes, though, had always seemed disappointed that he could no longer indulge in fine foods; he had been a soft hedonist in his human days. Now he just gave a mechanical sigh and admired his surroundings.

Omnius screens were mounted on the walls, and floating watcheyes drifted about like fat mechanical bumblebees. While the actual nexus of the Corrin evermind was housed in the Central Spire elsewhere in the city, Omnius could watch from myriad viewers and hear every whispered conversation. Agamemnon had long ago grown accustomed to, and annoyed with, the constant surveillance, but there was nothing he could do — until he got rid of Omnius altogether.

"We must discuss this war against the irrational humans." The evermind's voice boomed across speakers like an all-powerful, omnipresent god.

Agamemnon dampened his listening receptors, reducing the evermind's thunderous commands to small squeaks. "Lord Omnius, I am ready for any further aggression against the *hrethgir*. You need only authorize it."

"General Agamemnon has been advocating such action for years," Xerxes said, too eagerly. "He's always said that free humanity is like a ticking bomb. He warned that unless we dealt with the *hrethgir*, they would eventually reach a boiling point and cause great harm — exactly as they have done on Earth, Bela Tegeuse, Peridot Colony, and, more recently, on Tyndall."

. The cymek general controlled his annoyance. "Omnius is fully aware of our previous conversations, Xerxes. And our battles with the humans."

Erasmus's voice was erudite. "Since we have never seen an update of the final thoughts and decisions made by the Earth-Omnius, we do not know exactly what occurred in the last days on Earth. That information is forever lost to us."

"We have no need of the exact details," Agamemnon growled. "I've been a military officer for over a thousand years. I led human armies and robot armies. I orchestrated the original overthrow of the Old Empire."

"And you have been a loyal warrior and servant to Omnius in the centuries since," Erasmus added. The Titan thought he detected a trace of sarcasm.

"Correct," Juno said before Agamemnon could make a retort. "The Titans have always been valuable allies and resources to Omnius."

"Our primary concern is to ensure that no similar rebellion takes place on any other Synchronized World," said Omnius.

"That is not statistically likely," Dante pointed out. "Your watcheyes constantly monitor the populations. No slave will ever again have the opportunity to rally underlings, as the trustee Iblis Ginjo did."

"I have personally led neo-cymeks in raids to obliterate rebel cells," Xerxes said, stepping forward. "The unruly humans will never gain a foothold."

Erasmus paced the courtyard, swirling his fur-lined robes. "Unfortunately, such repressive measures only increase discontent. The Army of the Jihad has sent agent-provocateurs to our worlds. They smuggle propaganda to enslaved workers, artisans, even our reliable trustees. They carry recordings of impassioned speeches by Serena Butler, whom they call their Priestess of the Jihad." The robot's flowmetal face formed a wistful expression. "To them, she is beautiful and persuasive, a veritable goddess. When they hear Serena's words, how can they resist doing as she asks? They will follow her, even to death."

Agamemnon grumbled, "Our trustees have everything they could possibly want, and still they listen to her." *Like my own son Vorian. The fool.* "The best solution is to excise the cancer, obliterating each flare-up as it occurs. Eventually, we will root out all discontent . . . or be forced to exterminate the bothersome humans once and for all. Either solution is acceptable."

"Where would you like us to begin, Lord Omnius?" Xerxes said.

"Incidents of sabotage and blatant unrest occur most frequently on Ix," Erasmus interjected. "Most of the landscape has been converted to useful industries, but the rebels have located a honeycomb of natural caverns in the planet's crust. They hide there like termites, then strike our weak points."

"We should have no weak points," Agamemnon said.

"There should be no rebels either, considering that I have improved efficiency across the planetary network," Omnius said. "This turmoil has caused numerous problems, and I wish to examine all options. Perhaps these humans are more trouble to eradicate than the effort warrants. It may be more effective for us to simply stop fighting them."

Agamemnon could not control his outburst. "And let them win? After all we have created and accomplished over the past thousand years?"

"What is the significance of a mere millennium?" Omnius asked. "As thinking machines, we have alternatives the humans do not. Our bodies can adapt to environments lethal to biological life forms. If I simply abandon the *hrethgir*-infested planets, I can exploit the numerous airless moons and rocky planets. Thinking machines will thrive there and expand the Synchronized Worlds without further inconvenience."

Even Erasmus seemed surprised by the suggestion. "Humans once had a saying, Lord Omnius — 'It is better to reign in hell than to serve in heaven.'"

"I serve no one. I am analyzing the ratio of the greatest benefit for the least cost and the smallest risk. According to my projections we can never sufficiently tame our human slaves. Short of complete eradication of the species — which would require a great deal of trouble to accomplish — humans will continue to offer the threat of sabotage and loss of raw materials."

Agamemnon said fervently, "Lord Omnius, is it a victory to command territory that no one wants? If you abandon all planets that we once ruled, you are admitting failure. You would be the King of Inconsequence. It is folly."

Omnius was not incensed. "I am interested in expansion and efficiency, not in archaic, grandiose notions. The propaganda distributed by Serena Butler has made me question the basis of my rule. I do not know how to control the inaccurate information coming in from the outside. Why do slaves believe such statements without supporting data?"

Erasmus said, "Because humans have a tendency to believe what they want to believe, based upon *feelings*, not evidence. Witness their scurrying paranoia, looking into every shadowy corner and behind every curtain because they fear that countless machine spies and infiltrators are in their midst. I realize we have managed to slip a few of our trustees into League-controlled worlds, but the paranoid humans have convinced themselves that most of their neighbors are secretly in league with Omnius. Such baseless fears cause harm only to themselves."

Juno chuckled, and Xerxes made an exaggerated scornful sound at the gullibility and weakness of the *hrethgir*.

"Back to the point at hand," Agamemnon said, scraping a sharp metal foreleg against the flagstones. "You can blame Erasmus for triggering this destructive rebellion. His experimental manipulations created the conditions that sparked the initial uprising on Earth."

Erasmus turned to the powerful cymek walker. "Without the Earth-Omnius update, General, one can never be certain. However, you are not blameless in this. One of the greatest jihadi soldiers is your own son, Vorian Atreides."

Agamemnon simmered with anger. He remembered having high hopes for his thirteenth and last son, and how he had killed twelve previous children upon discovering their serious deficiencies. Now, all of Agamemnon's irreplaceable stored sperm had been destroyed in the atomic attack on Earth. He took it very personally, an assault on his family.

Vorian had been his final hope, but had turned out to be his greatest shame instead.

Omnius said, "There is enough blame for everyone who wishes to accept it. I have no interest in such irrelevant diversions."

Juno's voice was deep and slippery. "Lord Omnius, for centuries we Titans have wanted to crush the feral humans, but were never granted permission to do so."

"Perhaps that will change," the evermind said.

Agamemnon spoke emotionally. "At this moment, my son is with the Army of the Jihad holding off machine forces on IV Anbus. Allow me to lead a cymek fighting group, and I will hunt down my rebellious offspring."

Omnius agreed. "The fight on IV Anbus wastes much time and energy. I had expected a simple victory. See that it is accomplished, General Agamemnon. Also dispatch one of your Titans to Ix to quash the trouble there. Eliminate both problems quickly and efficiently."

"I volunteer to go to Ix, Lord Omnius," Xerxes said quickly. Apparently, he imagined that smashing a few disorganized rebels would be easier and safer than facing the Army of the Jihad. "Provided I can have full military support? I would also like to have Beowulf as my general—"

"Beowulf goes with us," Agamemnon said, primarily to thwart Xerxes. Beowulf was one of the first new-generation cymeks, created by Barbarossa more than a century after the computer evermind took over. As a human, Beowulf had been a collaborator with the cymeks, a trustee warlord on a secondary planet. He had proved himself immensely capable and ambitious and had been ecstatic when given the opportunity to become a cymek.

The Titan general did not really need Beowulf, but was glad not to have cowardly Xerxes along. With Juno and Dante, he could recruit scores of reliable neo-cymeks as well as robotic military forces to augment the machine battle groups already at IV Anbus. Even so, defeating Vorian Atreides would not be easy.

Agamemnon had trained his son well.

Here is where the analytical power of the thinking machines fails them: they believe they have no weaknesses.
　　　　　　　　　　　　　　—Primero Vorian Atreides, *Evermind Nevermore*

W HEN THE JIHAD fleet passed over the enemy landing site on IV
　　Anbus, they dropped a meteor shower of disruptor units. From his
orbiting ballista, young Vergyl Tantor whooped with bravado when initial
scans showed the vanguard of robotic ground forces reeling, brought to
their metal knees, their gelcircuitry scrambled.

Upon returning from the city of Darits, Xavier Harkonnen had
changed into a crisp new green-and-crimson uniform that bore the
impressive marks of his primero rank. He still felt soiled from arguing
with the stubborn Zenshiite elders. Now, while dispatching the next wave
of troops and equipment to the surface, he looked like the very ideal of a
commanding officer.

A shuttle full of eager Ginaz mercenaries — the best fighters money
could buy — soared down to the machine base camp and covered the
assigned ground area, wielding pulse swords, scrambler grenades, and
slaggers. Zon Noret's professional combat experts took less than an hour
to eradicate the enemy's half-completed base, destroying the last functional robots. The machines had not expected such swift and overwhelming resistance.

As he stood on the bridge of his flagship, Xavier wore an expression of
pleased satisfaction. "This is a setback for the enemy, but don't believe for
a minute that it'll stop them."

Vor lounged next to his friend. "Since they're not smart enough to
know when to give up, we'll just have to convince them."

Huddled over papers and maps in analysis rooms aboard the flagship,
diligent Jihad tacticians studied the dispersal of machine strength, to

determine Omnius's plan for seizing IV Anbus. Apparently, even with their initial beachhead knocked out, the machines planned to land an overwhelming force and launch a ground-based invasion that would surely capture the planet.

In the war room, the two primeros laid out the projected path along which the invaders would have marched. Xavier waited for his dark-haired comrade. "Well, does it make any sense to you? What are the machines trying to do?"

Vor pushed some strands of long hair out of his eyes. "As with most everything the thinking machines do, their plan is straightforward and obvious, utilizing massive force and no subtlety." He pursed his lips, pointing to the tactical projections that had been delivered to them from the analysis rooms. "See, the robot fleet has enough firepower that they could simply bombard IV Anbus and wipe out all the Zenshiite cities. Easy enough. But it looks like Omnius wants to keep the infrastructure of Darits and the other cities intact for a more efficient conversion into a full-fledged Synchronized World. It's primitive compared to what they would normally install, but the machines can adapt."

Xavier looked at him grimly. "And that requires more work for them than just blasting everything into dust."

"Of course, if it takes too long, they'll just go back to the original plan. My guess is we don't have much time. We've stalled them long enough here."

Xavier traced his finger along the feathery gorges displayed on the satellite images. "If the combat robots intend to use an overwhelming ground force to take over Darits, the hydroelectric generating station, and the communications grid, then the machines will likely sweep down the canyons here. Once they're inside the cliff city, they will install the usual copy of Omnius."

He turned back to studying the satellite maps. "So what do you propose, Vorian? Even with all the Ginaz mercenaries, we don't have sufficient military strength to face off against a full robotic ground assault. Our fighters are not all expendable."

"With Omnius, we can't simply pit brute force against brute force. We need to do something *cunning*," Vor said with a smile. "The thinking machines should be completely confused."

"Oh? Like your mad shadow fleet under construction at Poritrin? I still don't think that will work."

Vor chuckled. He preferred to defeat the robotic enemy through devious means, as a trickster, than through outright military engagements . . . not because he necessarily believed it to be more effective, but because he wanted to minimize the cost in human lives. "So, I've always got a plan up my sleeve, Xavier, and I've almost completed my computer virus against the warships here. I'll take care of the machine battle vessels in space, you deal with the ground forces."

"And how am I supposed to do that without using 'overwhelming force'?"

Vor already had his answer ready. "Transmit a message to our fleet instructing them to withdraw our planetside military forces. Say that it's because we believe the thinking machines will attack from space."

Xavier's expression of disbelief almost made the other primero chuckle. "The machines aren't so foolhardy as to believe that, Vorian. Even a robot can detect an obvious ruse."

"Not if you encode the transmission. Use your most complex mathematical cipher. The robots will break it, I guarantee. That will make them believe what they hear."

"Your father has twisted your mind." Xavier said, shaking his head. "But I'm glad you've turned it to the benefit of the Jihad. If we can't stop the thinking machines from installing their Omnius here . . ." His stiff posture implied that he felt the full burden on his own shoulders. "Well, let us just say that I'll level every structure on IV Anbus before I allow such a defeat. The entire League of Nobles is at stake." Xavier sighed, rubbed his temples. "Why won't Rhengalid work with us? We can save their people and meet our own objectives at the same time."

Vor gave him a commiserating grin. "The Zenshiites see enemies everywhere, but are incapable of recognizing friends." He had tried to see the matter from the Buddislamic point of view, playing Devil's Advocate to Xavier's unwavering convictions, but their reasons made no logical sense. "I guess after being brought up by the thinking machines, I just don't understand religion."

Xavier looked up from the tactical projections, raising his eyebrows. "We don't have the luxury of 'understanding' them, Vorian. Such subtleties are for politicians in plush offices, far from the battlefield. The Zenshiites' choice here has repercussions for all of humanity. Much as I'd like to just leave them all to their fates, we can't allow it. IV Anbus must not become another stepping-stone for Omnius."

Vor clapped him on the shoulder, glad he never had to bluff or face down that stony expression across a gambling table. "You are a hard man, Xavier Harkonnen."

"Serena's Jihad has made me one."

*   *   *

After studying detailed terrain overlays, Xavier selected a pair of strategic Zenshiite towns as his troops' bases. The nondescript settlements were in perfect position for the jihadis to set up an ambush against the wave of machine forces that would trample the landscape on their way toward the city of Darits. The Army of the Jihad had sent down their heaviest artillery and projectile hardware to be installed and camouflaged in the native towns.

Much to his delight and pride, Tercero Vergyl Tantor was assigned to oversee operations in the settlement that would encounter the first machine offensive. During recreational hours aboard ship, while he played fast rounds of Fleur de Lys cards with Vorian Atreides, Vergyl often complained that his adoptive brother refused to send him on meaningful missions. This time, though, the dark-skinned, brown-eyed young man had pleaded with Xavier until finally he was put in charge of the initial ambush against the machines.

"Vergyl, that Zenshiite town should have all the raw materials you need to set up your strike. Don't forget your tactical training."

"Yes, Xavier."

"Find a bottleneck where you can hammer the robot armies without exposing yourself to danger. Hit hard, give them everything you have, and then pull back. Tercero Cregh and his troops at the second town will mop up any thinking machines that survive."

"I understand."

"We're also dispatching Ginaz mercenaries to harass any outlying robot forces," Vor added with a snort. "It'll be a pleasant change for them from riding around in orbit and pretending to threaten machine war-ships."

"And Vergyl," Xavier said, his voice sterner than ever, "take care of yourself. Your father took me in as an orphan when the machines killed my family. I have no intention of bringing him bad news."

As Vergyl took his military force into the designated town, he hoped the natives would welcome them. He looked around, judging the mood of the villagers. The Zenshiites, mostly farmers and silt miners who worked the mineral-rich sandbars, stood outside their dwellings and watched with dismay. Transport after transport landed in their fields, disgorging jihadi troops and Ginaz mercenaries. Engineers and weapons specialists removed artillery components while scouts scattered, studying the terrain to find the best emplacements.

Vergyl stepped forward, his expression calm. "We mean you no harm. We are here to protect you from the thinking machines. The enemy is on the way."

The hard-eyed farmers looked at them. One grim-faced man said, "Rhengalid has told us you are not welcome here. You should go."

"Sorry, but I have my orders."

Vergyl sent his men through the town to inspect buildings, telling them, "Don't cause any damage. See if you find empty structures for us to use. Let's make this as unobtrusive as possible."

Old women grumbled curses at the Jihad fighters. Parents snatched children away and locked them in thick-walled homes, as if afraid Vergyl's engineers would steal them in the dark of night.

The face of the dour farmer showed resigned acceptance. "What if we do not wish to have outsiders sleeping in our homes?"

Vergyl knew how he had to answer. "Then we'll set up tents. But we'd rather have your cooperation and your hospitality. When morning comes, you'll see the greater danger you face. Then you'll be glad we're here."

The Zenshiites showed little enthusiasm, but they didn't interfere.

The machine forces were expected to funnel through the canyons toward Darits. Surveillance had already pinpointed the robots' new staging point on the plateau, just as Primero Atreides had guessed.

The engineers were careful to leave no obvious traces of their work. The heavy weapons were moved into vacant buildings; Vergyl did not need to displace any families.

Several empty dwellings were close enough together for his soldiers to bunk down for the night. When he asked the villagers what had happened, Vergyl received only frightened scowls in answer. Finally, one bearded farmer answered, "Tlulaxa slavers took them a few months ago. Whole families." He gestured to the clustered homes.

"I'm sorry." Vergyl didn't know what else to say.

As darkness fell, he contacted Tercero Hondu Cregh, his counterpart in the second village. Sharing information, they confirmed that each ambush site was ready. Tercero Cregh had also experienced little cooperation from the people, but again, no outright obstruction.

After he called his commandos together, and they completed one last inspection of the emplaced weapons, Vergyl was surprised to see several Zenshiite farmers coming toward them carrying jugs and bottles. Tense, but hoping for the best, he went to meet them. The farmer who had spoken to him earlier held out his jug, while a woman at his side extended several shallow cups.

"The Koran Sutras tell us we must extend hospitality to any guest, even uninvited ones." The farmer splashed a pale orange liquid into one of the shallow cups. "We would not wish to break tradition."

Vergyl accepted the cup while the woman poured a second drink for her husband. Vergyl and the Zenshiite man sipped from the brims in a formal toast; the liquid was bitter, with a strong alcoholic burn, but the jihadi officer took another drink.

The other villagers passed out cups, and all of the fighters drank, careful not to offend their hosts. "We are not your enemies," Vergyl reassured the people. "We are trying to save you from the thinking machines."

Though the Zenshiites did not seem convinced, Vergyl felt he had accomplished something, just by being given the benefit of the doubt.

Then he told his soldiers to climb into their assigned cots and get as much rest as they could afford before the machines came in the morning. A sentry was stationed at each camouflaged artillery emplacement to guard the weapons and power charges . . .

Vergyl dozed off thinking of Xavier, whom he revered as a hero. Even as a boy, he had always wanted to emulate his older brother, to become a Jihad officer just like him. At only seventeen, after the tragic massacre on Ellram, Vergyl had convinced his father to sign a dispensation allowing him to enlist in the Army. Tens of thousands of new volunteers, incensed by the machines' most recent brutality, were eager to join the fight. Against his wife's objections, Emil Tantor had let Vergyl join — in part, because he was convinced that if he refused, the boy would run off and sign up anyway. This way, he was under the official and watchful eye of Xavier.

After basic training and formal instruction, Vergyl was transferred to Giedi Prime to assist in reconstruction efforts after the thinking machines were driven out. For years, Xavier kept his brother from being assigned to front-line battleships, putting Vergyl in charge of building a giant memorial to fallen soldiers, which was due to be christened any day now.

On Giedi Prime, Vergyl also met and fell in love with Sheel. They had been married for thirteen years, had two sons, Emilo and Jisp, and a daughter, Ulana.

But Xavier had not been able to shelter him forever. He was a talented officer, and soon the demands of the Jihad required him to face combat. His most intense battle so far had been the recapture of the Unallied Planet of Tyndall, a massive and unexpected Jihad counterstrike that wrenched the war-torn world from the grasp of the thinking machines. Vergyl had distinguished himself in that conflict and had received two medals, which he had sent home to Sheel and his children.

Now, he promised himself to do everything possible to make this operation a success. They would defeat the thinking machines here on IV Anbus as well, and Vergyl Tantor would claim his part in the victory.

A deep sleep came upon him like the drop of a curtain. Later, at the ragged end of night, not long before the arrival of the machines, he became violently, cripplingly ill. As did all of the other soldiers stationed there.

When the four Jihad ballistas circled around to the opposite side of the planet, the machine forces dropped another deployment of combat robots. The enemy had learned and adapted after their first attempt to establish a beachhead. Now Omnius's forces moved with great speed and efficiency to set up the morning's offensive. Battalions of fearsome soldier meks and combat vehicles had been assembled, the battalions of Omnius began a rolling march toward Darits, laying down boosters and substations with each kilometer they conquered.

Farther down the sedimentary canyon, highly paid Ginaz mercenaries spread out, led by Zon Noret. They ran along the tops of ridges and followed gravelly water courses, setting up small roadblocks. Detonating charges, they collapsed the walls of narrow canyons to inhibit the advancing machines, though the robots had enough firepower to blast through the barriers eventually.

More mercenaries raced along flat, wide arroyos, planting lines of landmines to wipe out the front ranks of combat meks. Each Ginaz mercenary wore a protective Holtzman shield that surrounded his body with an invisible barrier. The robots relied on projectile weapons, bullets and sharp needles, but the personal shields foiled such attacks. The mercenaries plunged in among the robots to do hand-to-hand fighting.

Zon Noret had given each commando clear instructions. "Your job is not to obliterate the enemy, though damage is certainly acceptable." He smiled. "Your task is to take potshots, enough to lure the thinking machines forward. Taunt them, provoke them, convince them that the native humans mean to resist the machine occupation. We're good at that."

But the carefully staged, ineffective resistance must also lull the robotic battalion into believing that the humans had nothing worse waiting for them. Noret's independent fighters had to be carefully incompetent.

The robots surged ahead, bound by their internal programming.

As the sun spilled its jagged first light upon the landscape, Vergyl Tantor staggered along the wall of the dwelling where he had slept. The house smelled of vomit and diarrhea. Feeling betrayed, many of the soldiers moaned, lurched, and retched, barely able to move. Reaching the doorway, Vergyl blinked and coughed. The Zenshiite natives came out of their dwellings looking smug.

Vergyl gasped at them. "You . . . *poisoned* us!"

"It will pass," the bearded farmer said. "We warned you. Outsiders are not welcome here. We want no part of your war with the demon mechanicals. Go away."

The Jihad officer swayed, clutching the rough door jamb to keep himself upright. "But . . . you'll all die this morning! It's not us they want, it's *you*! The robots –" He retched again and realized the villagers must have taken their own antidotes or medicines.

Then his comline signaled, calling urgently for him. Vergyl could barely cough out his acknowledgment. The dispersed jihadi squadrons and surveillance teams reported that the robotic marauders had begun to move out from their new staging point. Ginaz mercenaries had already set up along the advance path to goad the robots. The assault was about to commence.

"The machines are coming!" Vergyl called hoarsely, trying to rouse his men. "Everyone, to your stations!" Ignoring the villagers, he went back into the dwelling and started dragging soldiers out into the dawn light. They had donned Zenshiite farmers' clothes so that they would not appear to be jihadis, but now the fabric was drenched with fever sweat and stained with vomit.

"Wake up! Shake it off!" He pushed one barely conscious man toward the nearest camouflaged artillery emplacement. "To your stations. Man the weapons."

Then Vergyl noticed with sick dread the sentries curled up in convulsions on the ground next to the weapons. He ran like a broken toy, summoning all his remaining balance and speed, into the nearest building that housed a large projectile launcher and stared at the heavy weapon. A groggy gunner came in beside him, and Vergyl tried to activate the launcher's power systems. He rubbed his bleary eyes. The targeting cross seemed to be malfunctioning.

His gunner flicked the controls again, then opened the panel and let out a cry of surprise and dismay. "Someone tore up the wires — and the power supply is gone!"

Suddenly Vergyl heard broken shouts echoing from other gun emplacements throughout the village. Angrily, he exclaimed, "We have been stabbed in the back by the people we're trying to rescue!"

His anger gave him the strength to vanquish his dizziness for the moment. Vergyl staggered out of the dwelling to face the Zenshiite farmers, who stood looking satisfied.

"What have you done?" Vergyl cried, his voice rough. "You fools, what have you done?"

The future, the past, and the present are intertwined, a weave that forms any point in time.
                    —from "The Legend of Selim Wormrider,"
                                            Zensunni fire poetry

S TANDING JUST INSIDE the large tribal cave, Selim Wormrider gazed across Arrakis's soothing ocean of dunes, watching for the moment when the sun would first rise over the horizon. He waited, then felt his pulse quicken as golden light poured like molten metal across the undulating desert, purifying and inevitable — like his visions, like his mission in life.

Selim greeted the day, taking a deep breath of air so dry that it crackled his lungs. Dawn was his favorite time, after just waking from deep sleep filled with mysterious dreams and portents. It was the best time to accomplish meaningful tasks.

A tall, gaunt man came up beside him, always knowing where to find his leader at daybreak. Loyal Jafar had a heavy jaw, sunken cheeks, and deep blue-within-blue eyes from years of a spice-rich diet. The lieutenant waited in silence, knowing Selim was aware of his presence. Finally, Selim turned from the rising sun and looked up at his most respected friend and follower.

Jafar extended a small plate. "I have brought you melange for the morning, Selim, so that you may better see into the mind of Shai-Hulud."

"We serve him, and our future, but no one can understand the mind of Shai-Hulud. Never make that assumption, Jafar, and you will live longer."

"As you say, Wormrider."

Selim took one of the wafers, spice mixed with flour and honey. His eyes reflected the deep blue of addiction as well, but the sacred spice had kept him alive, granting him energy even during times of greatest trial and deprivation. Melange opened a marvelous window on the universe and gave Selim visions, helping him to understand the destiny Buddallah had chosen for him. He — and his ever-growing troop of desert exiles — followed a calling greater than any of their individual lives.

"There will be a testing this morning," Jafar said, his deep voice even. The newborn sun exposed secret footprints made during the night. "Biondi wishes to prove himself. Today he will attempt to ride a worm."

Selim frowned. "He is not ready."

"But he insists."

"He will die."

Jafar shrugged. "Then he will die. That is the way of the desert."

Selim emitted a resigned sigh. "Each man must face his own conscience and his own testing. Shai-Hulud makes the final choice."

Selim was fond of Biondi, though the young man's brash impatience was better suited to the life of an offworlder at the Arrakis City spaceport, rather than the unchanging existence of the deep desert. Biondi might eventually become a valuable contributor to Selim's band, but if the young man could not live up to his own abilities, he would be a danger to the others. It was better to discover such a weakness now, than to risk the lives of Selim's faithful followers.

Selim said, "I will watch from here."

Jafar nodded and left.

Over twenty-six standard years ago, Selim had been falsely accused of stealing water from one of his tribe's stores; subsequently, he had been exiled into the desert. Manipulated by the lies of Naib Dhartha, Selim's former friends had chased him from their cliff cities, throwing rocks and insults at him until he ran out onto the treacherous dunes, supposedly to be devoured by one of the "demon worms."

But Selim had been innocent, and Buddallah had saved him — for a purpose.

When a sandworm had come to devour him, Selim discovered the secret of how to ride the creature. Shai-Hulud had taken him far from the Zensunni village and deposited him near an abandoned botanical testing station, where he'd found food, water, and tools. There, Selim had time to look inside himself, to understand his true mission.

In a melange-enhanced vision, nearly drowning in thick reddish powder cast up from a spice blow, he had learned that he must prevent Naib Dhartha and his desert parasites from harvesting and distributing melange to offworlders. Over the years, working alone, Selim had raided many encampments, destroying any spice the

Zensunni gathered. He had earned a legendary reputation and the title "Wormrider."

Not long afterward, he had begun to accumulate followers.

Jafar had been the first, two decades ago, forsaking the protection of his own village near Arrakis City in order to search for this man who could ride the great desert beasts. Jafar had been almost dead by the time Selim found him, dehydrated, sunburned, and starving under the dazzling bright sky. Looking up at the lean and hardened outcast, Jafar had gasped through cracked lips — not a request for water, but a query. "Are you . . . the Wormrider?"

By then, Selim had been alone for more than five years — too alone — faced with a sacred task too great for a single man. He nursed Jafar back to health and taught him how to ride Shai-Hulud. In the following years, the pair had gathered rugged followers, men and women dissatisfied with the strict rules and unfair justice of life in the Zensunni cliff colonies. Selim told them of his mission to stop spice harvesting, and they listened, enthralled by the gleam in his eyes.

According to Selim's repeated melange visions, the activities of the offworld merchants and the Zensunni gatherers would shatter the peace of the desert planet. Though the timeframe was dim, stretching into a vague, distant future, the spread of spice across the Galaxy would eventually lead to the extinction of all worms and a crisis of human civilization. Although his words were frightening, when they saw him proudly riding atop the mountainous curve of a great sandworm, no one could doubt his claims or his faith.

But even I do not understand Shai-Hulud . . . the Old Man of the Desert.

As a young scamp, exiled from his tribe, Selim had never wanted to be a leader. But now, after decades of living by his own wits and making decisions for the group of followers who depended on him for guidance and survival, Selim Wormrider was a confident, clear-headed general who had begun to believe the myth that he was indestructible, a demon of the desert. Despite devoting his life to preserving the worms, he did not expect the capricious Shai-Hulud to show him any gratitude . . .

Unexpectedly, Jafar returned to the high chamber, making so much commotion that Selim stepped away from the window opening and saw that his friend had brought a newcomer. She looked dirty and lean, but her dark eyes shone with a haughty defiance. Her dusty brown hair had been cropped short. Her cheeks were sunburned below her eyes, but the rest of her seemed intact. The young woman must have been wise enough to wrap herself against the worst ravages of the sun. A curved white scar like a crescent moon rode above her left eyebrow, an exotic punctuation to her coarse beauty.

"Look what we found out in the desert, Selim." Jafar stood tall and stoic, unflappable, but Selim caught a hint of humorous gleam behind his deep blue eyes.

The young woman stepped away from the tall man, as if to prove she did not need his protection. "My name is Marha. I have traveled alone in search of you." Then her face flickered with uncertainty and awe, making her look unexpectedly young. "I am . . . honored to meet you, Selim Wormrider!"

He held her chin, turning her face up to look at him. Lean and dirty, but with large eyes and strong features. "You're just a slip of a girl. Won't be much use for heavy labor around here. Why have you left your own people?"

"Because they are all fools," she snapped.

"Many people are fools, once you get to know them."

"Not me. I came to join you."

Selim raised his eyebrows, amused. "We shall see." He turned to look at Jafar. "Where did you find her? How close did she approach?"

"We caught her beneath the Needle Rock. She had camped there and didn't know we'd been watching her."

"I would have seen you," she insisted.

Needle Rock was very close to the settlement. Though impressed, Selim did not show it. "And you survived in the desert by yourself? How far away is your village?"

"Eight days journey. I brought food and water, and I caught lizards."

"You mean you stole food and water from your village."

"I *earned* it."

"I doubt your Naib would see it the same way, so it is not likely your people would take you back."

Marha's eyes flashed. "Not likely. I fled from Naib Dhartha's village, as you yourself did years ago."

Selim stiffened and studied her. "He still has a stranglehold on the tribe?"

"He teaches that you are evil, a thief, a vandal."

Selim's chuckle was dry and humorless. "Perhaps he should look in a mirror. Through his own treachery he established himself as my lifelong enemy."

Marha looked tired and thirsty, but made no complaint, no request for hospitality. She fumbled at her throat and pulled out a wire loop that held a jingling collection of metal chits. "Spice tokens from offworlders. Naib

Dhartha sent me out to work the sands, to scrape the spice and collect it to be delivered to his merchant friends in Arrakis City. I have been of marriageable age for three years, but no Zensunni woman — or man — can take a mate until they have gathered fifty spice tokens. That is how Naib Dhartha measures our service to the tribe."

Selim scowled, delicately touched the tokens with his fingertip, then in disgust tucked them back into her collar. "He is a man deluded by greed and the false hope of an easy life."

He turned away and stared out into the desert. Squinting into the morning light, he watched four figures emerge from the lower caves. They walked out onto the open sands, garbed in camouflage robes and cloaks, their faces wrapped to prevent moisture loss.

The smallest of them was Biondi, preparing for his test.

When Marha looked questioningly at Selim and then at the other man, Jafar explained. "Selim Wormrider receives messages from Shai-Hulud. We have been commanded by God to stop the rape of the desert, to halt the harvesting of spice, the momentum of commerce that threatens to set history on a disastrous course. It is an enormous task for our small group. By working to harvest melange, you yourself have aided our enemies."

Defiant, the young woman shook her head. "By abandoning them, I have helped your cause."

Selim turned back, looking from her crescent-moon scar to her intent eyes. He saw a determination there, but could not be sure of her true motives. "Why have you come here to a hard life, instead of running to Arrakis City and signing onto a merchant ship?"

She seemed surprised by the question. "Why do *you* think?"

"Because you do not trust off-worlders any more than you trust your own leader."

She raised her chin. "I want to ride the worms. Only you can teach me."

"And why should I do that?"

The young woman's eagerness overrode her uncertainty. "I thought that if I could find you, track the location of your outlaw hideout, then you would accept me."

Selim arched his eyebrows. "That is only the first part."

"The easy part," Jafar said.

"Each step in its time, Marha. You have done well so far. Not many approach as close as Needle Rock before we apprehend them. Some, we send away with enough supplies to survive the trip back home. Others are so hopelessly lost that they wander to their deaths without ever knowing we have been observing them."

"You just watch them die?"

Jafar shrugged. "It is the desert. If they cannot survive, they are useless."

"I am not useless. I am good with a knife . . . killed one opponent and injured another in duels." She touched her eyebrow. "One man gave me this scar at the spaceport. He tried to rape me. In turn, I gave him a scar from one side of his belly to the other."

Selim withdrew his milky-white crystalline dagger, holding it up so that the young woman could see. "A wormrider carries a dagger like this, fashioned from the sacred tooth of Shai-Hulud."

Marha stared in amazement, her eyes sparkling. "Ah, what I could accomplish with a fine weapon like that!"

Jafar laughed. "Many people would like to have one of these, but you must earn it."

"Tell me what to do."

Hearing a steady drumbeat from the expansive desert outside, Selim turned to the cave window. "Before you make such an impetuous decision, girl, watch and see what lies in store for you here."

"My name is Marha. I am no longer a girl."

To young villagers across Arrakis, Selim was a glamorous figure, a daredevil hero. Many tried to imitate him and become wormriders themselves, though he attempted to discourage them, warning them of the danger of a renegade's life. Having received a true vision from Buddallah, Selim had no choice in the matter for himself. But they did.

Regardless of his advice, starry-eyed candidates rarely listened. They set out with big dreams and overconfidence, which usually proved to be their downfall. But those who survived learned the greatest lesson of their lives.

Out on the dunes, the drumbeats echoed. Almost all of the observers had left the sand, returning to the shelter of the rocky cliffs. A solitary man, Biondi, sat at the crest of a dune, the place he had selected for his testing. He should have had everything he needed: The young man would be wearing one of the new distilling suits that Selim and his followers had developed for protection and survival during times when they must be abroad in the open desert. With Biondi were staffs and hooks, and a rope between his knees. He pounded on a single drum, sending a loud, insistent summons.

Marha stepped forward to stand next to Selim, as if unable to believe she now found herself beside the man who was the basis of so many desert myths. "Will a worm come? Will he ride it?"

"We shall see if he succeeds," Selim said. "But Shai-Hulud will come. He always does."

Selim saw the wormsign first and pointed it out to the young woman. After more than a quarter century, he no longer counted how many times he had summoned a sandworm and climbed its rough rings in order to guide the creature wherever he wished to go.

Biondi had ridden just twice before, each time accompanied by a master rider who did all the work for him. The youngster had performed adequately, but still had a great deal to learn. Another month of training would have benefited him immensely.

Selim hoped he would not lose another follower . . . but either way, Biondi's fate was in his own hands.

The novice pounded his drum much longer than necessary. He did not become aware of the approach of the worm until he looked to the east and saw shimmering waves trembling through the sands. Then he grabbed his equipment and scrambled to his feet, accidentally kicking over the drum so that it rolled and bounced down the face of the dune.

At the base of the sand formation, the drum struck a rock and sent out another reverberating sound. The oncoming worm deviated slightly, and Biondi reeled to adjust his position at the last moment. The sandworm came up unexpectedly, showering dust, flattening dunes.

Selim marveled at the majestic sight of it. "Shai-Hulud," he whispered reverently.

A puny figure in the face of the onrushing behemoth, Biondi held his hooks and staff, muscles coiled.

In instinctive fear Marha flinched, but Selim clasped her shoulder, forcing her to watch.

At the last moment, Biondi lost his nerve. Instead of standing his ground, holding the spreading staff and the hook, he turned to flee. But no man could outrun Shai-Hulud in the desert.

The worm scooped up its victim along with a mouthful of sand and powdery dust. Selim could hardly see the tiny human form as it vanished down the endless gullet.

Transfixed, Marha stared. Jafar shook his head, lowering his chin in sad disappointment.

Selim nodded like a wise man much older than his years. "Shai-Hulud has found the candidate wanting." He turned to Marha. "Now you have seen the peril. Would you not be better off returning to your village and begging Naib Dhartha for forgiveness?"

"On the contrary — it seems to me you now have room for another follower." She stared fiercely out at the sands. "I still want to ride the worms."

Endurance. Belief. Patience. Hope.
These are the key words of our existence.

—Zensunni prayer

O N POR IT R I N, T H E extravagant but pointless construction project required extraordinary work and manpower. Thus, slaves.

Sparks and fumes surrounded Ishmael in the hot air of the shipyards and the clattering din of adjacent foundries. Drenched in sweat and smeared with soot and greasy dust, Ishmael performed his work beside the other captives, following instructions and calling no attention to himself. It was the Zensunni way of survival, to achieve a relatively comfortable life, within the constraints imposed by their Poritrin captors.

In the evenings, back in the Buddislamic dwelling compounds, Ishmael led his people in prayer and continued to urge them to have faith. He was the most learned Zensunni scholar in their group, having memorized more Sutras and parables than the other men. As a consequence they looked to him for guidance, though he felt at a loss.

Ishmael knew in his heart that someday their captivity would end, but he was no longer certain it would occur in his own lifetime. He had already reached the age of thirty-four. How much longer could he wait for God to free his people?

Perhaps Aliid was right after all . . .

Ishmael closed his eyes and muttered a quick prayer before getting back to work. The clang of metal and the hiss of laser rivets crackled through the air.

South of the main city of Starda, the Isana River delta widened, leaving numerous flat islands separated by deeply cut shipping channels. Barges carried raw metals from mines far to the north, delivering them to the manufacturing centers.

In the past six months, expanding upon a suggestion made by Primero Vorian Atreides of the Jihad Army, Savant Tio Holtzman had summoned an enormous workforce, commandeering slave crews from across the continent, with the blessing of Lord Niko Bludd. This full-scale project demanded all the labor of Poritrin; more than a thousand workers had been brought to the industrial islands. Stinking, noisy factories processed the resources into large starship components, hull plates and engine cowlings that would be lifted into orbit for assembly into new battleships.

No one had bothered to explain the plan to the slave crews. Like worker ants, each man and woman had a designated task, and crew supervisors observed the complex flurry of activity from above.

To Ishmael, it was yet another dirty and difficult labor assignment. He had worked in the cane fields, mines, and factories during the past five years in and around Starda. The intense Zenshiites, as well as the less radical Zensunnis, remained restless as their masters forced them to meet the increased demands of Serena Butler's galactic war.

When Ishmael was just a boy, raiders had attacked his peaceful village on Harmonthep. They kidnapped healthy Zensunni settlers and pressed them into service on League planets that accommodated slavery. After more than twenty years, Poritrin was Ishmael's world now, a home as much as a prison. He had made the best of his life.

Because Ishmael had caused no obvious trouble, upon reaching adulthood he'd been allowed to take a wife. After all, the Poritrin slave masters wanted to keep their stock thriving; and they had statistics that showed married slaves worked harder and were more easily controlled. Before long, Ishmael had learned to love strong and curious Ozza. She had given him two daughters: Chamal, who was thirteen, and little Falina, now eleven. Their lives were not their own, but at least Ishmael's family had remained intact through several transfers and new work assignments. Ishmael never knew if that had been a reward for his acceptable service, or simply a fortuitous accident.

Now, in the bleak industrial shipyards, orange sparks and the splashing glow of hot alloys turned the work site into a vision of Heol, as described in the Buddislamic Sutras. The hiss of sulfurous smoke, the tang of metal dust and scorched ores forced the slaves to wrap blackened rags around their faces in order to breathe.

Beside him, he saw the sweaty, perpetually angry visage of his childhood friend Aliid, whom Ishmael had only recently rediscovered at the shipyard work site. Although the other man's coiled brashness made Ishmael feel threatened and uncomfortable, friendship was one of the few threads to which they could hold.

Even when they were boys, Aliid had been trouble, willing to break rules, committing vandalism and minor sabotage. Because Ishmael was his friend, both of them had often suffered punishments and transfers. Before the boys became teenagers they were separated and did not see each other again for nearly eighteen years.

But Tio Holtzman's ambitious new construction project had thrown many slaves together in the foundries and factories. Ishmael and Aliid had discovered each other again.

Now, under a clatter of hammers and the percussive drumbeat of rivet-welders, Ishmael maneuvered the machinery over hull-plate seams. Over the years, his muscles had grown large, as had Aliid's. Though his clothes were dirty and worn, Ishmael cropped his hair and shaved his weathered cheeks, chin, and neck. Aliid, though, let his dark hair grow long and tied it back with a thong. His beard was thick and black like Bel Moulay's, the outspoken Zenshiite leader who had tried to lead a slave revolt when they were just boys.

Ishmael climbed up beside his friend, helping to wrestle the heavy metal sheet into place. Aliid activated the rivet welder before either man checked the alignment. Aliid's work was sloppy and he knew it, but the Poritrin nobles and work supervisors never penalized them or even criticized their work. Ship after ship had been assembled in space above the quiet planet. By now, dozens of bristling war vessels clustered in orbit like a pack of trained hunting dogs, waiting for an opportunity.

"Is that within tolerances?" Ishmael asked guardedly. "Unless we seal the hull seams tight, we might cause the deaths of thousands of crew members."

Aliid didn't seem bothered as he continued firing the hot riveting gun. He yanked away the greasy cloth that covered his face so that Ishmael could see his hard smile. "Then I'll apologize to them when I hear their distant spirits screaming in the depths of Heol, where all evil men must go. Besides, if they don't bother to test the components in orbit, they deserve to suck vacuum."

While he had kept a relatively stable assignment and had found some measure of happiness with his family, Ishmael's deeply troubled friend had been transferred dozens of times. Shouting above the din of the construction yards, Aliid had told him about his wife, whom he loved passionately, and one newborn son, whom he barely remembered. But ten years ago a workmaster had caught Aliid salting the fuel in a big mining grinder; in punishment, he had been transferred away from the work group and sent to the other side of Poritrin.

Aliid had never seen his wife again, never held his son. No wonder the man was bitter and angry. But though he had obviously brought the disaster upon himself, Aliid wanted to hear none of Ishmael's admonishments. To him, no one but the people of Poritrin were to blame. Why should he care about the lives of crewmembers aboard these ships?

Oddly enough, the workmasters and shipbuilders didn't seem to care about quality either, as if they were more concerned with assembling the vessels *rapidly* than with making them functional. Or safe.

Ishmael went back to work diligently. It never paid to delve into details and questions that might arouse the ire of the crew supervisors. He passed time more easily if he kept himself numb on the outside, hiding the spark of his own identity deep within. At night, when he recited Sutras for his Zensunni followers, he recalled life on Harmonthep, listening to his grandfather quote the same scriptures . . .

Unexpectedly, shift bells rang, and the lights increased inside the clamorous refinery. Sparks fell to the ground like tiny meteors, and pulleys raised the machinery back to the ceilings of the highbays. Bellowed words from speaker boxes were fractured into gibberish by the background din. Uniformed supervisors strode around the decks, assigning crews to staging areas.

"Lord Niko Bludd grants all people of Poritrin, even slave workers, this hour of relaxation and contemplation to commemorate the victory of civilization over barbarism, the triumph of order over chaos."

The hissing racket of the refinery and shipyards dwindled. The slave crews interrupted their conversations and looked toward the speaker boxes. Supervisors stood on high platforms, glaring at the people to make certain they were paying attention.

The announcement continued, clearer now, the recorded words of Lord Bludd. "Twenty-four years ago today, my Dragoon forces put an end to a violent and illegal uprising led by the criminal Bel Moulay. This man deluded our hardworking slaves, confusing them with irrational promises that lured them into a hopeless, nonsensical fight. Luckily, our civilization was able to restore the rule of order.

"Today is the anniversary of the execution of this evil man. We celebrate the triumphs of Poritrin society and the League of Nobles. All humans must put aside their differences and fight our common enemy, the thinking machines."

Aliid scowled, struggling to suppress a defiant outburst. Ishmael knew what his friend was thinking. The Buddislamic slaves, by working in war industries, contributed unwillingly to the military effort against Omnius. Yet to the captives, the Poritrin slavekeepers and machines were both demons — only of different sorts.

"Tonight, every Poritrin citizen is invited to join in feasts and festivities. Fireflowers and skypaintings will be launched from rafts in the river. Slaves are also welcome to observe, provided they remain within designated holding areas. Working together, combining our strength, Poritrin can be assured of victory against Omnius and freedom from the thinking machines. Let no man forget the potential of the human race."

The announcement ended and the work supervisors dutifully applauded, but the slaves were slow to add their cheers. Aliid's expression darkened behind his black beard, and he pulled up the rag to cover his face again; Ishmael doubted the unobservant crew leaders noticed his look of pure hatred.

After night fell and the slaves returned to their camp compound in the marshy river delta, Lord Bludd launched his extravagant festivities. Hundreds of phosphorescent balloons rose into the sky. Celebratory music wafted across the water. Even after two decades on Poritrin, the melodies sounded slightly atonal and alien to Ishmael as he sat with his wife Ozza and their two daughters.

Poritrin nobles professed to follow gentle, bucolic Navachristianity, but their core beliefs did not extend to their daily lives. They had their festivals, and embraced religious trappings, but the Poritrin upper classes did little to demonstrate their true faith. For centuries their economy had run on slave labor, ever since they had cast aside sophisticated technology, forsaking anything that reminded them of thinking machines.

Slaves learned to snatch whatever moments and memories they could find. Ishmael's girls Chamal and Falina were fascinated by the spectacle, but he remained quietly beside his wife, thinking his own thoughts. The celebration reminded him of the brutal crackdown the gold-armored Dragoon guards had mounted against the insurgents two decades ago. Lord Bludd had commanded all slaves to witness the execution of the rebel leader, and he and Aliid had watched in horror as the executioners stripped Bel Moulay naked and hacked him to pieces. That uprising had given the slaves a brief flicker of hope, but the death of their fiery leader had crushed their spirit and left a dark scar on their hearts.

Finally, Ishmael gathered with other slaves so that they could hold a memorial for the fallen Bel Moulay. He saw that Aliid had also come into the compound, wanting Ishmael's company and shared memories of the tragic event that had shaped their boyhood.

Aliid stood beside Ozza, fidgeting, as Ishmael quoted the familiar Sutras that promised eventual paradise and freedom. They ignored the ghostly sounds of music and the militaristic bangs and pops of fire-flowers. Finally, using the words he had repeated often — too often — Ishmael said to the listeners, "God promises that one day our people will be free."

Aliid's dark eyes reflected the glow of the story fire. His voice was low, but clear, making Ishmael uneasy with the simmering threat: "This I swear — one day we shall have our revenge."

Invention is an art form.

                        —Tio Holtzman, acceptance speech
                            for Poritrin Medal of Valor

W HILE THE SWARM of new ships was rushed through construction
    on Poritrin, Savant Holtzman performed his work on Salusa
Secundus. The legendary inventor stood inside an isolated laboratory
chamber within one of the most secure zones, pacing with his hands on
his hips and frowning in disapproval. It was the persona he showed
whenever people expected him to do something important.

With armored walls and power conduits cut off from the rest of
Zimia's grid, the large government facility was supposedly safe and
protected. In theory, the hostage Omnius was completely contained.

But this lab was not set up the way Holtzman would have liked. He
preferred to choose his own diagnostic tools, analytical systems, and slave
assistants who could be conveniently blamed if anything went wrong. A
small, aging man with a gray beard, Holtzman prided himself on being
able to manage resources. The Savant was sure he could provide these
Jihad military scientists with good advice. If words failed him, he might
have to refer the matter to his many eager assistants back on Poritrin,
who constantly found ways to impress him.

From behind secure transparent barriers, the team of legislative
observers watched his every move, along with the Cogitor Kwyna,
who had once again been removed from her place of restful contemplation in the City of Introspection. Even through the impenetrable barriers,
Holtzman could sense the watchers' anger and fear.

A silver gelsphere floated in front of him, glistening as it spun in the air
within the invisible suspensor field. This incarnation of the evermind
was completely under his power. Where once he had felt fear at being so

close, now the greatest enemy of the human race seemed like such a small thing. A child's toy! He could have held the complex sphere in the palm of one hand.

The silver gelsphere contained a complete copy of the computer evermind, albeit a somewhat dated version now. During the atomic raid on Earth at the very beginning of the Jihad, Vorian Atreides had seized this update from a fleeing robot vessel. Over the years, the League's "prisoner" had provided valuable insights into thinking machine plans and reactions.

The evermind's programs had been copied, dissected, and examined by League cybernetic experts. As the first rule, all data was considered suspect, perhaps intentionally distorted by Omnius, though such deceit was supposedly impossible for the computer mind.

The Army of the Jihad had undertaken a few military ventures based upon information obtained from the evermind copy. When the fighters launched an offensive against cloud-locked Bela Tegeuse, they had obtained detailed specifications from the captive Omnius. But that engagement had ended inconclusively.

Now, after twenty-four years without updates, the intelligence data stored in the captive evermind had grown stale. The captive Omnius had been unable to warn them of the return of the robot war fleet against Zimia — though that second attempt had been thwarted by Primero Xavier Harkonnen — nor had the evermind prepared the League for the unexpected massacre on Honru, which had cost the lives of so many undefended colonists. Still, it had been of some value.

Holtzman scratched his thick mane of hair as he watched the sphere spin in the air. *Despite its shortcomings, this one provides us with clues. It is just a matter of interpreting them correctly.*

"Erasmus often praised the unending creativity of human imagination," said a bored synthesized voice from speakers linked to the sphere, "but your interrogations have grown tedious. After so many years, have you not learned everything from me that your small minds can grasp?"

Holtzman slipped a hand into a pocket of his white smock. "Oh, I am not here to entertain you, Omnius. Not at all."

Over the years, he had communicated with this Omnius, but never with such intensity. In the weeks that he had recently focused on the effort, the famed inventor had failed to secure any breakthroughs, despite his past successes in other realms. Holtzman hoped he had not painted himself into a corner with everyone's unrealistic expectations.

He tried to count back, remembering when things had happened. It had been a full quarter century since he had invited the young genius

Norma Cenva to work with him. A stunted and unattractive girl of fifteen then, Norma was an ugly duckling compared to the statuesque beauty of her mother, a powerful Rossak Sorceress. But Holtzman had read some of the girl's innovative papers and determined that she had much to offer.

Norma had not disappointed him. Not at first. She worked diligently, developing one strange scheme after another. His highly successful scrambler fields protected entire planets from the thinking machines, but Norma had suggested adapting the concept to smaller portable scramblers used for offensive purposes on Synchronized Worlds. Norma had also used his field equations to concoct the now-ubiquitous suspensor platforms . . . and from there, bobbing glowglobes, lights that never dimmed. They were baubles, toys — albeit extraordinarily popular and profitable ones.

During the same period Holtzman and his patron Lord Niko Bludd had developed and marketed personal shields, which brought profits to Poritrin as fast as League ships could bring statements from the central bank accounts. Unfortunately, the commercial exploitation of glowglobes had somehow slipped out of their control. Norma Cenva had simply handed the technology to her friend Aurelius Venport, whose VenKee Enterprises had widely exploited and distributed the devices.

But the naïve woman's suspensor and glowglobe concept had been developed while she was working under *his* auspices, using *his* original field equations. Lord Bludd had already filed briefs in League court, demanding restitution of all profits VenKee Enterprises had reaped from unauthorized use of proprietary technologies. Undoubtedly, they would win.

Now, as the Savant stared at the floating silver gelsphere, like a wizard attempting to decipher a spell, he wondered what Norma would have done if she'd been here. Ignoring his advice, Norma had devoted years of effort to reconfiguring a massive set of equations derived from his own original field work. She would not explain the details to him, suggesting that the Savant himself might not understand them. Such disparaging remarks irritated him, but he put them in context. Despite some contributions to the war effort, Norma was losing focus on what was important; she was becoming useless to him.

By now, after showing infinite patience, Holtzman had become disenchanted with her. With little choice in the matter he had gradually cut her off from his numerous other projects and sought other assistants — brilliant young inventors who were looking for a big break. He gave priority to his eager and ambitious team of worshipful young assistants who were full of brains and ingenuity. So, the Savant had moved Norma

Cenva from prime laboratory space in his main tower to a far inferior set of workrooms down by the docks. She didn't even seem to mind.

Now he wondered if she might give him any clues to understanding Omnius.

The gelsphere looked like a spinning metal planet glinting in the chamber's light. So many threads of the evermind's information led in countless directions, and the incredibly intricate AI-mind defied complete examination.

But the great Tio Holtzman needed to show some sort of progress. One way or another.

Smiling, he lifted a small transmitter from his pocket. *Something waits to be discovered here, on a deeper level. I am certain of it.* "This is just a faint pulse from one of my scrambler generators. I know it will wreak serious havoc on gelcircuitry systems, so perhaps it will give you sufficient incentive to cooperate."

"I see. Erasmus also explained to me the human penchant for torture." The synthesized voice was suddenly laced with static.

A voice intervened from the observation alcove, Kwyna's secondary, speaking for the ancient Cogitor. "That could lead to irreparable damage, Savant Holtzman."

"And it could lead to important answers," the scientist insisted. "After all these years, it is time to put Omnius to the test. What do we have to lose at this point?"

"Too dangerous," one of the council observers said, rising to his feet. "We've never been able to replicate of the sphere itself, so this is the only . . ."

"Do not interfere with my work! You have zero authority here!"

As one of his conditions for participating in this project, Tio Holtzman did not answer to anyone, not even to the Cogitor Kwyna. Still, the observers — especially uneducated and superstitious politicians breathing down his neck — remained an irritation. The Savant would have preferred to give them written reports and summaries, which he could slant any way he liked. But Holtzman had something to gain here, certain ideas he wanted to explore.

"I have already been thoroughly interrogated and debriefed," Omnius pointed out in a bland voice. "I presume you have put the military information to good use, the fleet placements, the cymek strategies."

"Everything is too far out of date to be of any use to us," Holtzman lied. In reality, the Army of the Jihad had staged half a dozen surprise raids on thinking machine forces in the early years after obtaining the sphere, using the information from Omnius to good advantage. The machines had seemed so predictable in their military operations then, using old methods over and over, traveling the same galactic paths, using familiar defensive and offensive maneuvers.

Machine fleets had been attacking or retreating depending upon probabilities, worked out in detail by on-board computer systems. For the Jihad leaders, it was simply a matter of determining what the enemy was likely to do. Traps were laid, showing purported Jihad weaknesses in order to lure machine forces in. Then, at precisely the right moment, the trap would be sprung, and hidden Jihad forces moved in for the kill. Many robot fleets had been destroyed in such engagements.

After initial Jihad successes, however, the thinking machines began to "predict" that they would be tricked, and they were no longer so easy to fool. For the past seven years, the information from Omnius had been of decreasing value.

Smiling, Holtzman refocused on the shimmering gelsphere in front of him. "I would hate to have all of your thoughts eradicated in a single pulse, Omnius. You are hiding something from me, aren't you?"

"I could never conceal anything from the great scientific and technical prowess of Savant Tio Holtzman," the voice retorted with an odd undertone of sarcasm. But how could a computer be . . . sarcastic?

"People say you are Satan in a bottle." The scientist calmly adjusted the transmitter and heard high-pitched machine sounds in response. "More like Satan in a bind, I'd say. You'll never know what memories I have just erased, what thoughts and decisions you just lost."

The legislative observers squirmed. So far, he hadn't actually harmed the silvery ball. At least he didn't think so; one of his assistants had invented this particular device. "Are you ready to tell me your secrets?"

"Your question is vague and meaningless. Without specificity, I cannot answer." Omnius did not sound defiant; he simply stated a fact. "All the primitive libraries and databases on this planet could not contain the data I hold within my evermind."

Holtzman wondered what the Jihad Council expected him to discover. Though grudgingly passive, the captive evermind had been relatively forthcoming. Scowling, he prepared to adjust the pulser to a higher setting.

"Much as I enjoy seeing Omnius writhe in pain, that will be sufficient for now, Savant Holtzman." Grand Patriarch Iblis Ginjo entered the secure chamber, blithely walking past the barriers and into the lab itself. He wore one of his trademark black blazers adorned with golden tracery.

Knowing that he could easily erase all the gelcircuitry with a single burst from his scrambler, the scientist composed himself and switched off the device. Holtzman looked back to the plaz barricades, noting that three of Iblis's nondescript Jipol attendants had taken up wary positions near the more agitated representatives.

The silver update sphere, still hovering in the air, said in a loud voice, "I have never experienced anything quite like that . . . sensation."

"You felt the machine equivalent of human pain. I think you were about to scream."

"Do not be absurd."

"Oddly enough, computers can be as stubborn as humans," Holtzman commented petulantly to the Grand Patriarch.

Iblis wore a thin smile, though his own skin had crawled at the sound of Omnius's synthesized voice. He hated the computer evermind, wanted to take a club and smash it. "I did not mean to disturb you, Savant. I simply came here searching for the Cogitor Kwyna." He looked wistfully at the ancient brain in its preservation tank. "I have many ideas and questions. Perhaps she can help me to focus my thoughts."

"Or to misinterpret more scriptures?" the yellow-robed secondary said, his voice flat as a paving stone.

Iblis was alarmed at the audacity. "If the meanings are clear to no one, who is to say I am *misinterpreting* them?"

"Because people die whenever you find meaning in old runes or ancient writings."

"People die in every war."

"And more people die in a Jihad."

The Grand Patriarch showed a flicker of anger, then grinned. "You see, Savant? This is exactly the type of debate I wish to have . . . although I would prefer more time in private, if the Cogitor will allow me?" His dark eyes flashed.

Frustrated by his lack of success against the captive evermind, Holtzman gathered his equipment. "Unfortunately, I don't have the time to continue this series of interrogations at the moment. A space liner is due to depart shortly for Poritrin, and I have important obligations back on my home world." He looked over at Iblis. "The . . . uh, project suggested by Primero Atreides."

The Grand Patriarch smiled at him. "While that plan may not be exactly 'scientific,' it may fool the thinking machines nonetheless."

Holtzman had hoped to depart from Zimia in triumph, but his weeks here had been disturbingly unfruitful. Next time, he would bring along some of his best assistants; they would find a way to solve the problem. He decided not to include Norma Cenva.

Though Norma Cenva saw great revelations in the intricacies of the cosmos, sometimes she could not distinguish night from day, or one place from another. Perhaps she did not need to identify such things, because she was capable of journeying across an entire universe in her mind.

Was her brain physically capable of assembling huge quantities of data and using that information to identify large-scale events and complex trends? Or was it instead some inexplicable extrasensory phenomenon that enabled her to exceed the thinking capacities of any person who had lived before her? Or of any thinking machine?

Generations later, her biographers would argue over her mental powers, but Norma herself might not have resolved the debate. Realistically, she would have cared less about how her brain worked than she cared about the actual performance of her mind and the incredible results of its inquiries.

—Norma Cenva and the Spacing Guild,
a confidential Guild memorandum

W HEREVER SHE WAS, whatever she did, everything contributed raw material to the busy factory of Norma Cenva's mind.

For reasons that were not explained to her, Holtzman moved her offices and laboratory space to a smaller, cheaper building near the warehouses on the Isana River. The rooms were cramped, but she needed few luxuries other than time and solitude. She no longer had access to dedicated slaves whose sole job was to solve equations; now the captive solvers were assigned to the more profitable tasks proposed by the Savant's other young and ambitious assistants. Norma didn't mind — in truth she preferred doing the mathematics herself. She spent her days going in and out of a fugue state, mentally following the flow of higher-order numerics.

For years she had been adrift in a sea of equations she could never have explained to Holtzman or to any of the League's other theorists. She was engrossed in her own vision, and each time she solved the riddle of another grain of sand on an extensive mathematical shore, she came closer to finding her safe harbor.

She would learn how to fold space . . . to travel across great distances without actually moving. She *knew* it was possible.

Ostensibly, Savant Holtzman still kept her on his extended staff as an assistant, but the small-statured woman had stopped working on anything other than her massive cyclical calculations. Nothing else interested her.

Every once in awhile he would look in on her and try to draw her into conversation to see what she was doing. But he understood very little of what she told him, and the years passed. It occurred to Norma that he might prefer to have her where he could monitor her.

Though she had provided him with no recent advances he could claim for himself, she had surprised him many times before. Since the start of the Jihad, she had modified Holtzman's shields on League Armada ships so that they did not overheat so quickly in a battle engagement. Thermal buildup still remained a flaw in the system, but her shields were significantly improved over the original versions.

Four years after that, Holtzman had offered a "flicker and fire" technique for his shields, a carefully choreographed system that allowed a League ship to fire through microsecond gaps in the shields. Norma had cleaned up his calculations, preventing yet another mishap. She had never dared to tell him what she had done, knowing he would have grown indignant and defensive.

Now, for the past eight years, she had worked in her own private laboratories, following her research whims. In the midst of the small facility's cluttered work space, Norma had set aside only tiny areas for cooking, sleeping, and personal hygiene. Such human needs were secondary to her, while the products of her mind were paramount. Holtzman still allowed her a minimal level of funding, though Norma required only the resources of her own mind, since her work was primarily theoretical. So far.

For three days now, Norma had labored without interruption on a particularly complex manipulation of Holtzman's seminal equations. Hunched over the workbench that had been modified to accommodate her dwarfish stature, she ate and drank little, not wanting to be bothered with the demands of her physical body.

Though she'd been born a daughter of the chief Sorceress of Rossak, Norma had spent most of her life here on Poritrin, not as a citizen but as a visitor invited by Savant Holtzman. Long ago, when Norma's stern mother had seen her as only a failure and a disappointment, Holtzman had noticed the girl's quiet genius and had given her the opportunity to work with him.

In all that time, she had received few accolades. Humble but dedicated, Norma did not mind being overshadowed by the great man. She was a patriot in her own unassuming way and wanted only to make certain that the advanced technology was put to use to benefit the Jihad.

For years Norma had actually protected Holtzman, catching embarrassing inconsistencies that might have led to disastrous consequences. She did this out of gratitude, since he was her patron. But once she had realized that the Savant spent so much time rubbing elbows with nobles that he accomplished little on his own, she spent less time trying to save his image and devoted full concentration to her own research.

She found his current expensive project to be particularly foolish from a scientific point of view. Building a giant sham fleet in orbit! It was no more than a bluff, an illusion. Even if the scheme worked, as Primero Atreides insisted it would — Norma thought the Savant should have focused his intellectual resources on something more challenging than smoke and mirrors.

From her squalid dockside workplace, she could hear the hammering and hum of the factories and shipyards across the Isana mudflats. Foundries hissed; steam and sparks boiled out of assembly lines. Barges hauled cargo loads of ore into the shipyards and carried away completed components.

Luckily, when Norma focussed her thoughts, all distractions faded into the background.

Finally, hungry and dehydrated, her body screaming for rest, Norma lay her head on stacks of scrawled equations, as if the symbols could keep penetrating her mind by osmosis. Even in slumber her unconscious mind continued to process the formulas she had been reviewing . . .

Mathematical equations cycled through her sleeping mind. She could compartmentalize tasks, assigning separate sections of her brain to perform specific functions, resulting in a coordinated mass-production process in her cerebral cortex. After so long, the entire iterative simulation was coming to a climax, and she felt her dreaming self rising from great depths through the catacombs of her mind.

Abruptly, Norma sat straight up at her workbench, nearly falling off the raised chair. Her bloodshot eyes flew open, but did not see their immediate surroundings. Still surrounded by a vivid dream, Norma gazed across an infinite distance, as if her thought impulses could extend from one side of the universe to the other and bring the distant parts together, folding the underlying fabric of space. After days without rest, her subconscious finally let the puzzle pieces snick into place.

At last!

She became aware of her physical self, of her heart hammering so rapidly it threatened to burst out of her chest. She sucked in a breath but desperately tried to remain focused, to retain her grasp on what she had dreamed. The answer!

As she awoke, her mind clung to the revelation, having captured it like a butterfly in a net. She envisioned great spaceships crossing the universe without moving, guided by prescient navigators who could see safe pathways through space. Immense companies and empires would rise up from this foundation, and there would be a fundamental shift in the nature of warfare, travel, and politics.

Tio Holtzman had never foreseen such consequences to his equations. He would not be capable of seeing them now. Norma did not dare waste time. The Savant would challenge her, question her "unprovable" mathematics, and she didn't want to lose precious time answering him. She had worked too hard, the potential was too great. This break-through was *hers* alone.

She had no interest in ownership or credit for the discovery, but she had to make certain the concept received the full-scale commercial and military exploitation it deserved. Savant Holtzman would not understand the grandeur of what she had done; he would let it drift into obscurity.

No, Norma had to find another way. *The future awaits me.*

Smiling, she let out a long, slow breath. She should have thought of the possibility long ago. She knew exactly where to obtain the independent funding she needed for research, development, and production.

Peering back through the magnifying glass of time, men and women in the future view the personalities of the Great Revolt as larger-than-life. Such an impression comes not through any distortion of the glass, nor from a process of embellishment that generates mythology. Instead, the heroes of the Jihad were much as they are now remembered; they rose to the occasion when humanity needed them more than ever before.

—Princess Irulan, The Lens of Time

A FTER A DECADE of construction, sculpting, and polishing, the memorial to the war dead of the Jihad was finally completed. Aurelius Venport, whose merchant company VenKee Enterprises was one of the largest donors, received a fine seat at the unveiling ceremonies in Zimia.

The night was cool, the darkness kept at bay by spotlights and illuminated buildings around the central plaza. Crowds milled in nearby alleys and streets, kept back from the posh VIP stands within the parklike square itself.

Venport sipped carefully from a fluted glass of bubbly champia; he had never cared for the cloying sweetness of the slightly alcoholic drink from Rossak, but it was one of his company's prime exports. He had delivered a full load of the vintage to Salusa Secundus just for this event.

The monument was striking and surreal, comprised of two free-form pillars with soft curves and organic shapes representing humanity, towering over a boxy monolith that lay toppled and broken at their feet. It symbolized the victory of life over machines.

An identical monument had been built on Giedi Prime, a site of terrible loss of life but also a significant victory over the machines. If plans had proceeded as expected, the second memorial was also complete and ready to be unveiled simultaneously with this one. On one of his merchant runs to Giedi City, Venport had seen the bustling work area and the huge structure being erected there as well.

A decade earlier, when the Jihad had already simmered and flared across the star systems for fourteen years, Xavier Harkonnen had spearheaded the movement to erect an appropriate memorial to those slain by the thinking machines. In the previous two years, thinking machines had attacked and conquered the small colony of Ellram, then struck and — at great cost — been driven away from Peridot Colony. A group of enthusiastic and ill-advised jihadi soldiers had launched their own vengeful strike against the main Synchronized World of Corrin. But they had all been killed. Martyrs to the cause.

In the uproar following so many setbacks, Primero Harkonnen had called for the monuments, so that the fallen soldiers would never be forgotten. Serena Butler, still the League's Interim Viceroy though she had withdrawn into the City of Introspection, had added her support to the project, using her influence to obtain financial backing from political and business leaders.

Moved by Serena's plea, and having witnessed some of the more difficult struggles against the thinking machines firsthand, Aurelius Venport had decided to do his part, despite initial objections from his Tlulaxa business partner, Tuk Keedair. Since the start of the Jihad, the profits of VenKee Enterprises had grown substantially as their merchant ships transported war materials and supplies to suffering colonies. They were also turning large profits by exporting increasingly popular luxury items such as glowglobes and, most lucrative of all, the spice melange from Arrakis.

Venport prided himself on his business acumen, his ability to recognize money-making opportunities and to capitalize on them. The League of Nobles was vast, and open for commerce. Through his access to Rossak pharmaceuticals, Arrakis melange, and glowglobe and suspensor products invented by dear Norma, he had leveraged his advantages as much as possible, which pleased him immensely.

His former mate Zufa Cenva had always insisted he would never amount to anything, nor would her stunted daughter. They had both proved Zufa wrong.

It had been many years since he'd been the chief Sorceress's lover and partner. Through it all, Zufa had never believed that Venport with his commercial interests or Norma with her dabbling in mathematics would ever do enough for the fight.

Even when Venport had personally contributed enough credits to pay for a large portion of the Zimia memorial, he had not expected Zufa to be impressed. The stern woman had devoted her life and soul to the Jihad, training Sorceresses who threw themselves against cymek strongholds as suicidal psychic bombs. Not surprisingly, Zufa considered his donation, and the memorial project itself, a frivolous waste of money better used for purchasing weapons or constructing new battleships.

Venport smiled to himself at the thought. If nothing else, Zufa was consistent and predictable. Against all reason, he had loved and admired her since the day they met. But, in business terms, it had never been a worthwhile investment of his emotional capital.

Seated in the open-air stands beside a beautiful young woman — one of his grown granddaughters? — the retired Viceroy Manion Butler caught Venport's eye and smiled cordially. Nearby, Primero Harkonnen's adoptive father, the aged, dignified Emil Tantor, sat alone looking sleepy.

A smiling attendant offered another glass of champia, which Venport declined. He settled back and waited for the show. The audience was just beginning to grow restless, but Grand Patriarch Iblis Ginjo was a master of timing and would begin exactly when enthusiasm had peaked and before the mood slid into impatience.

Though the Grand Patriarch had arrived at the ceremony on time, flanked by intimidating Jipol guards, he wanted the VIP guests to mill about while the larger crowds bought souvenirs and clutched bunches of brilliant marigolds, Manion's flower.

Venport turned toward a swell of cheers, saw Iblis Ginjo and Serena Butler make their grand entrance. Serena wore her usual purple-trimmed robe of such a glowing white that she looked like an angel incarnate. Fixing his squarish face in a confident smile, the Grand Patriarch, garbed in a dashing black blazer embroidered in gold, accompanied her onto the ornate stands, while dazzling lights cast glowing haloes around them.

Iblis was silently followed by his beautiful wife, Camie Boro. This was obviously not a love match, but a trophy marriage; during his rise to power, the man had shrewdly chosen a woman of impeccable heritage, a direct descendent of the Old Empire's last ruler.

Around Iblis's neck dangled a prismatic chain that supported a pendant of brilliant blue-green Hagal quartz. Possibly part of his wife's fortune. No one questioned where the Grand Patriarch obtained the money for such luxuries, or for other aspects of his opulent lifestyle. His value to the League could not be measured in monetary terms. He was surrounded by his own developing mythology.

Iblis raised his hands, and his voice boomed out with a resonant amplification. "When we see this memorial, we must remember those who paid the ultimate price against the demon machines. But we must also remember what they fought *for*."

Serena stepped forward and continued in her clear, passionate voice. "This monument is not only a reminder of fallen heroes, but a symbol of yet another step toward our ultimate victory over Omnius!"

With a brilliant flash like an exploding star, two spears of light shot upward, illuminating the memorial and the entire park. A reflecting pool became a mirror of stars under the night sky, graced with feathery fountains at one end. The spotlights blazed brighter, as if trying to outdo each other, the fountains sprayed higher, and the cheers of the crowd swelled to a deafening roar. Bright yellow-orange marigolds were strewn across the grass and in the pools; their heady scent wafting through the evening air.

When Serena Butler fell to her knees on the stage and wept, half of the audience moaned, and grieved with her for her lost baby and their own fallen loved ones.

Then, swept along by the overwhelming approval of the audience, Venport rose to his feet and applauded the spectacle. The leaders of the Jihad certainly knew how to impress a crowd.

Afterward, while the population of Zimia celebrated far into the night, Iblis Ginjo and his wife attended a more formal and exclusive reception in the gathering courtyard of the Salusan Cultural Museum.

Glowglobes floated overhead, imparting variegated, festive colors to the framework of the open-air stands. Night moths flitted around the moon lilies that bloomed in planters at the edge of the courtyard. Important guests chatted casually with each other.

Resplendent in jewels and impeccable clothes, Camie Boro always made certain she was seen with him during their initial entrance, but his wife never wanted to "waste" a party by spending it on his arm. She had her own plans and connections, and set about exchanging favors, knitting together subtle obligations. Iblis smiled after her, then turned to his targets among the well-dressed crowd; he and his wife had a very clear delineation of their respective duties.

The Grand Patriarch saw a tall man — patrician features with light blue eyes and curly dark hair frosted with gray — standing beside a small plaz case. The man opened the lid to display dozens of melange products that had been developed by his company. Many League nobles had already become enamored of the rare and expensive spice, and Aurelius Venport rarely missed an opportunity to show his benevolence — and to seduce more customers — by offering free samples.

As eager guests pointed to what they wanted to try — spice beer, melange candy, or spice chewsticks — Venport removed a taste of each from his case. "Free of charge. If any of you are not familiar with the benefits of melange, please come and find out."

Melange is said to be addictive, Iblis thought, as he stepped to the front.

And unquestionably beneficial. He had partaken of the spice before, though it had been heavily diluted and nearly flavorless. "I would like a small, pure sample, Directeur Venport. Something I can taste."

The patrician from Rossak smiled. Exaggerating his pronunciation to impress the dignitary, he said, "For the Grahnd Patriarch of the Jihad, I am honored. I have brought only my best to this gathering. The caviar of spice." He removed a flat disk container no larger than a small coin. "Place it on top of your tongue. Just let it permeate your senses and seep all the way into your soul."

When Venport pried open the tiny lid, Iblis peered inside, noting dense reddish-orange powder, and dipped a fingertip into the substance. He found it surprisingly gritty to the touch. Glancing up at the glowglobes floating overhead, he remembered that these were successful VenKee products as well, though the technology was currently embroiled in a tedious and silly patent dispute.

He hesitated, looking at the spice powder on his finger. "In the Parliamentary Assembly some days ago, did I not hear Senator Hosten Fru discussing a dispute between your company and the government of Poritrin? Something about glowglobe royalties?"

Iblis had his doubts about Savant Holtzman and his stuffed-shirt patron, Lord Niko Bludd, but so far Aurelius Venport had impressed him as an extraordinarily shrewd businessman.

"Norma Cenva is a very talented scientist, who has helped Savant Holtzman achieve much fame and success. She is also a dear friend of mine, but the relationship is . . . complicated." Venport scowled, as if he had just swallowed a vile-tasting mouthful. "Norma alone created the suspensor technology used in glowglobes and offered it to my company for marketing. Now that VenKee has spent a fortune to develop and sell the glowglobes all across the League — during which time Poritrin neither lifted a finger to help — Lord Bludd suddenly believes he is entitled to our profits."

Behind Venport, other guests had gathered, hoping for free samples of melange, but they did not interrupt his conversation with the Grand Patriarch.

Iblis smiled. "Still, the technology was developed on Poritrin, in Holtzman's labs, was it not? Funded by Lord Bludd? Senator Fru claims that the Poritrin counsel has submitted documents signed by Norma Cenva, certifying that all technological breakthroughs made while in Holtzman's employ would remain the property of the government."

Venport sighed, his lips curved in an indulgent smile, which surprised Iblis. "I do not doubt that Savant Holtzman tricked her into signing such releases. Norma was just a teenager when she went to work for him. The girl is utterly devoted to her research and has never been . . . politically savvy."

Iblis looked down at the spice powder on his fingertip. His skin seemed to be tingling, just a little. "So, how will you resolve this?"

Venport did not look overly concerned. "I am a businessman, sir. I have always been able to negotiate settlements and mediate disputes. The present circumstance will simply require a bit more finesse than usual. I shall find a way." He nodded toward the spice in Iblis's hand. "But let's not trouble ourselves with that. I am anxious to hear your opinion of the melange."

Iblis became aware of people staring at him, perhaps noticing his hesitation. He didn't dare show any fear here. Everything the Grand Patriarch did was scrutinized and discussed. He placed the melange on his tongue and clamped his mouth shut.

"The purest form of melange is said to have many facets . . . like that priceless jeweled pendant you wear," Venport said. "Melange shows a different aspect to everyone who takes it."

Iblis felt . . . different. He couldn't quite categorize it, because he had never experienced anything like this before. His pulse quickened and then slowed, quickened and slowed again. Such a curious sensation! Then it slowed even more, and in a state of complete serenity he almost looked inward at his own heart and mind. He could barely form words and speak them.

"Amazing. Where . . . do you . . . obtain this . . . spice?"

Venport smiled at him. "Come now, I must be allowed to keep some trade secrets." He offered Iblis another sample of melange, and the Grand Patriarch took it without hesitation.

"Trust me," the businessman said, "even if I told you where spice comes from, it is not a place you would want to visit."

Do not count what you have lost. Count only what you still have.
                    —Zensunni Sutra of the First Order

T HE SPICE CARAVANS moved out at dusk, as soon as the day's heat began to wane. In the wasteland of the deep desert, Naib Dhartha's melange-gathering crews did not bother to conceal themselves from outsiders. They should have known better.

Selim Wormrider and his followers had been watching them for days.

Hidden with his raiders high in the rocky buttresses, Jafar used a mirror to flash a last preparatory message, directing the signal glint to where Selim waited.

Against the boulders below, the legendary man of the desert squatted comfortably beside a wide-eyed Marha. In the month since joining their group of outlaws, the scrappy young woman had continually impressed him. She was always ready to hear his visions and to learn. Best of all, she obeyed his instructions without question, and thus she survived her testing. Whenever Marha managed to overcome her awe of his nearly mythical status, she looked at him with an intense but innocent strength that tugged at his heart strings.

Selim thought she would be a worthy addition to his commandos. Even though he smiled at her and encouraged her ambitions, he did not want Marha to grow overconfident, as Biondi had become before his death. He wanted her to remain with him longer than that.

"Watch closely and see what they do." Selim pointed with his chin to the distant figures who carried packs and loaded rugged old groundcars. "They steal melange from Shai-Hulud and sell it to offworlders."

Marha huddled in the shadows, grim as she watched the caravan begin to move out. "I have worked on such crews myself, Wormrider. The scavengers camp in the rocks, but during the day they scamper onto the sands, scoop up spice, and run back to safety before the worms come for them."

"Shai-Hulud defends his treasure," Selim said, his deep-blue eyes distant but full of energy. "The Zensunni believe sandworms are devils, but Shaitan works more harm through one man like Naib Dhartha than through all the creatures of the desert."

Followers often brought news as they trickled in from scattered settlements to join the band of outlaws. Marha herself had provided invaluable advice and observations, which explained some of the conflicting stories Selim had heard over the years. With his commercial success in trading spice with rich offworld merchants, Naib Dhartha had succeeded in uniting a number of Zensunni settlements. Though such behavior defied their tenets of isolation and independence, Dhartha offered the other tribes much profit and water. And melange was available for the taking.

He squinted at the band of workers. "Do you think Dhartha is among them?"

"The Naib has turned his back on the desert," Marha answered. "His own son, Mahmad, spent most of the past two years in Arrakis City, until he caught an offworld disease at the spaceport and died there."

"Mahmad is dead?" Selim asked, feeling isolated as he recalled his distant youth. He remembered a young boy who had been Selim's own age. But were he alive today Mahmad would have been a grown man like Selim, and more than forty years old. And Mahmad had died away from the desert in a *city*, corrupted by trading in melange with offworlders. His lower lip curled in disgust. "And Naib Dhartha does not blame himself?"

Marha gave him a mirthless smile. The crescent-moon scar on her left brow shone white on her tanned skin. "He blames *you*, Wormrider. He considers you the cause of all his woes."

Selim shook his head. His visions had been so clear, the response obvious. But Naib Dhartha would never listen to him. "We must do more to stop this abomination, for the good of all."

When the spice scavengers carried their hoarded melange in caravans such as this, they were vulnerable. Now the caravan moved slowly on the flat sand at the edge of the rocks. Even with the groundcars' humming engines and the plodding people following the spice loads, sandworms did not approach the cliffs.

Two runners in camouflaged distilling suits dropped beside Selim and

Marha. They moved as silently as shadows, and Selim smiled in satisfaction.

"Jafar is in position." One of the runners removed a breathing tube from his mouth, shutting off the internal recycling system of his desert clothing. "We must act before the caravan moves too far away."

Selim stood. "Flash the message. Strike carefully, as always. Kill no one unless necessary. Our job is to teach them a lesson and retrieve that which belongs to Shai-Hulud." Part of him wanted to slay Naib Dhartha, but he understood that a greater revenge was to humiliate the man, undermining his credibility as a leader.

With a hollow *crumping* sound, a puff of dust burst from the cliffs above, sending an avalanche of black boulders tumbling down the ancient cliffside in front of the slow-moving caravan.

"Now we stop them." Selim was already running. Emerging from hiding spots in the rocks, his followers raced along, hidden against the brown-and-black landscape.

On the sands below, the Zensunni spice gatherers halted their groundcars at a safe distance from the rumbling wash of boulders. Before the caravan members could determine what was happening, Jafar and the others surrounded them. Jafar held a maula pistol. Selim's other followers had spears, projectile weapons, and even slings that could hurl rocks with murderous force.

The Zensunnis were intimidated, frightened. Somewhere among their packs they must have weapons of their own, but Selim's hardened troop pressed in closely enough that they could not use them.

"Those who dare to steal from Shai-Hulud must face the consequences," Selim said.

"Bandits," one woman snapped, spitting her words like a curse.

A young man, barely a teen, looked with glittering eyes not yet completely blue from the consumption of melange. "It is Selim Wormrider!"

"I am Selim who speaks for Shai-Hulud. I have had a vision from Buddallah, and its truth cannot be denied. Shame upon all of you for helping to bring about the death of the sandworms, the eventual destruction of Arrakis."

He stared at their cowled faces, studied the dark eyes, and determined that Naib Dhartha was not among them. As Marha had said, the grizzled old leader no longer deigned to waste his days with the exhausted work crews. Now he rubbed shoulders with offworld merchants.

The outlaws rummaged through the groundcar storage compartments, pulling out packs of rusty spice and handing them off to others, who scurried with them up onto the rocks.

With lithe movements, like a desert hare, Marha pushed herself close to one of the tense women whose hands and clothes were covered with fine brown powder. Smiling, she yanked a wire circlet from the woman's neck, a jingling chain of spice chits. "Not married yet, Hierta? Perhaps you will resign yourself to being a withered old maid." She tucked the melange tokens into a pocket of her distilling suit, then looked at Selim with giddy triumph.

Hierta glared. "Marha? Traitor! We hoped you had died in the desert, but you have fallen under the sway of this desert demon, this crazed madman."

"Crazed?" she responded. "No, he is enlightened."

Selim said, "Selling spice to offworlders will bring ruin to this planet. The great worms will perish, and along with them our way of life." Standing protectively beside Marha, he crossed his arms over his chest. "For now it is my sacred duty to return what you have taken from Shai-Hulud."

He withdrew his milky, crystalline knife and plunged it into a sack of melange, spilling the powder like dried blood onto the rocks and sand. A few pebbles continued to patter down from the rough gash of the avalanche.

"We have it all, Selim," said Jafar after his men had intercepted everyone trying to escape, and had carried off the packages into the rugged boulder field.

They did not kill the spice gatherers, did not even steal their water or take their vehicles. Possessions meant nothing to Selim. The desert would always provide. "Remember what you have learned here," he thundered. "How many times must I teach you the same lesson?"

Then, following Marha, the desert vigilantes climbed high on the rugged cliffs and vanished . . .

While the rest of the scavenging party moaned and muttered in complaint, one youth stared after them in awe. Some of his companions raised fists and shouted curses after the outlaws.

But the young man, Aziz, could not suppress a smile. He had never expected to gaze with his own eyes upon the Wormrider! The great man had looked directly at him.

As the grandson of Naib Dhartha, Aziz had heard of Selim's exploits, although the Zensunni portrayed the bandit leader as a villain. But Selim and his followers knew how to ride worms! And they had harmed no one. No matter what his grandfather said, Aziz thought they were a brave and magnificent band, truly blessed by Buddallah.

Secretly, Aziz longed to know more about them.

The coward will not fight.
The fool refuses to see necessity.
The scoundrel puts himself ahead of humanity.
The Zenshiites are all these things.

—Primero Xavier Harkonnen,
"On-Site Military Dispatches"

IGNORING RHENGALID'S COLD reception, Xavier Harkonnen set up his base of military operations in the grotto city of Darits. He had no other choice, if he was to accomplish his mission. The roar of the dam's water-diversion chutes filled the cool air. Red algae stains dripped down the cliffs like dark blood.

The Zenshiite elders had retreated into their cliff dwellings. The fanatics stubbornly refused to accept that they could be in any danger, even though Xavier showed them transmitted images of the robot army marching overland toward their holy city. "Look with your own eyes. The machines will destroy you."

Spiny robots strode through tilled lands alongside the river channel, accompanied by crunching, heavy-assault vehicles on tractor treads. Dressed as local farmers instead of in their uniforms, Ginaz mercenaries harried the robots, provoking them into launching explosive projectiles and then quickly taking shelter. The robot army never deviated from its objective and pressed on toward vulnerable Darits.

Watching the images, Elder Rhengalid furrowed his shaved brow with concern, then thrust his bearded chin forward. "We have nothing here the machines could want. Soon they will recognize that and leave us alone."

But twice now Xavier had seen the utter devastation the thinking machines could wreak: on Zimia, and on Giedi Prime, where he had lost Serena. He had also been at the massacres on Ellram, Peridot colony, and Bellos. He knew Omnius wanted to conquer IV Anbus because it was an important stepping-stone on the path to Salusa Secundus. The robots wouldn't care whether the Zenshiite natives were alive or dead.

Knowing he was about to snap with anger and frustration, Xavier sent the deluded leader away. "I have done everything in my power to accommodate you, Elder, but I no longer have time to discuss this. You are welcome to recite your sutras if you think they can save you from the enemy, but do not interfere with my work."

Intermittent reports sputtered in from the Ginaz mercenaries. Even though the fighters carried no weapons more sophisticated than primitive Zenshiites were likely to use, the mercenaries proved remarkably successful, taking out twice as many machines as expected. The wreckage of combat robots lay strewn along their path. Xavier feared the Ginaz commandos were causing so much harm that the thinking machines might grow wary and turn back.

Nevertheless, the invading robots approached the first of the two settlements that had been set up as traps.

The Primero turned back to receive updates from the independent guerrillas and jihadi forces in two occupied villages. "Tercero Tantor, give me a status check. The mercenaries report the machines are coming your way." Xavier hoped Rhengalid's objections would turn to ashes in his mouth when he saw the true threat of the monstrous machine army.

From the first village, Vergyl responded with a strangled crack in his voice. "Primero Harkonnen, we have a crisis!"

"What have the machines done?"

"Not the machines, sir — the natives. Overnight, they poisoned us . . . sabotaged our weaponry, damaged the power cells. My men are incapacitated. None of our artillery works. The Zenshiites ruined everything!"

Xavier felt a sinking dread. He wrestled with anger and disgust as the second contingent reported in. "This is Tercero Hondu Cregh, sir. The locals drugged us too, then slashed our power cables, stole batteries, twisted the targeting mechanisms. It's my own fault, sir . . . but we –" He coughed. "We were here to protect these people. Now we can't fire a single shot."

Vergyl broke in, voice strained and watery. "Xavier, the machines are moving toward us at a rapid pace. What are your orders? What should we do?"

Storming with barely contained fury, Xavier paced back and forth, wanting to shout at Rhengalid. But that would do no good.

He couldn't let any harm come to his little brother, especially not while helping people like this. He barked back to the two village teams, "Tercero Tantor, Tercero Cregh, you have to withdraw immediately. You'll be completely wiped out if you give yourselves away."

Ransacking his mind for another solution, Xavier clenched his jaw until his teeth hurt. Time was running out. The machine army was already sweeping inexorably along the path — and now his carefully orchestrated ambush, the one opportunity for a clean and decisive victory, had been foiled.

Years ago, on Poritrin, the Buddislamic slaves sabotaged the newly installed shield generators of the League Armada so that League soldiers would have marched blindly to their deaths if Xavier himself hadn't discovered the treachery.

Now these Zenshiites of IV Anbus had added their own unnecessary suicide to treasonous acts against the Army of the Jihad.

Taking deep breaths, remembering too clearly that these evil machines had murdered a son he had never met, Xavier spoke into the comline, telling all soldiers within range, "We shall achieve victory the hard way, if that's how the Zenshiites want it." Cold air whistled through his teeth. "I will never surrender this planet to Omnius . . . no matter the cost."

Vergyl sounded frightened, but optimistic. "Xavier, I think I might be able to reconfigure some of our weapons to get them working again. We can pursue the thinking machines, attack them."

Zon Noret broke in, speaking for the mercenaries. "Give us those weapons, Primero. You've seen how much we've already accomplished with what little we scraped up from local resources. We'll make a go at it."

"That would be a wasted effort. You couldn't accomplish what we need. Withdraw and salvage all the military equipment you can. We may need it someday — but not now. I have other plans." He looked down the long canyon again; the machine army could not be far away. "All mercenaries, report back to Darits as fast as you can. Zon Noret, if I recall correctly, you have special demolitions training? I need your . . . particular skills."

He looked up at the immense dam built by the Zenshiites to hold back the water and control the floods. If these people could construct such an elaborate facility, why couldn't they stand up to an obvious enemy?

Tercero Cregh checked in from the second village. "Primero, the machine forces have just passed us by. No casualties."

"They don't care about you at the moment. Once they take over the Darits network and infrastructure and lay down their own substations, they figure they'll have plenty of time to come back and smash all outlying villages." He worked hard to keep from cursing out loud. "Can you estimate how soon the machines will reach Darits?"

"Two hours at the most, Primero."

"We'll be ready." Xavier switched off the comline and turned to one of the soldiers beside him. He had no choice but to take drastic action. The Zenshiites had made certain of that. "Go find Elder Rhengalid. Tell him his people have less than two hours to evacuate the city. Make sure he knows that I won't issue another warning."

Standing in the mist-slick breezeway along the cliffside, the Zenshiite elders demanded to know what Xavier intended to do.

"This was not the way I wanted to fight the thinking machines, but you brought this upon yourselves. I could have accomplished my mission and still saved your city and your people. You have left me no alternative."

At that, Rhengalid raised a sinewy fist to the sky. "Darits is a sacred city, the heart of the Zenshiite religion. We have holy texts here, a wealth of relics, irreplaceable artifacts."

"Then you should have moved them to safety as soon as you heard my warning an hour ago." Xavier ordered him forcibly removed. "Encourage your people to move quickly. There is no need for them to die."

While water jets roared from the dam's diversion channels and outflow chutes, he explained remorselessly. He told of the time decades earlier, when Omnius had launched a major assault on the Salusan capital city of Zimia, and Xavier had pulled together his military forces, making a grim decision to protect Holtzman's shield generators by any means. He had saved the entire world, though it had cost thousands of lives and large sections of the beautiful metropolis. Now Xavier had made a similar choice for Darits — on a much greater scale.

In a rushed consultation, he had met with his structural engineers and demolitions experts to discuss the placement of explosives. The dam was well built, but his commandos could still identify structural weak points.

Zon Noret stood before them, dripping blood from wounds he had received in direct combat with the fighter robots; he ignored the injuries, applying his own emergency field dressings to keep himself going for a little while longer. "It'll take at least ten charges, perfectly positioned."

One of the engineers said, "We could just use atomics, Primero. It would be much easier."

Xavier shook his head. He had seen enough atomic destruction when the League Armada sterilized Earth. "No matter what these people have done, I still want to give them a chance."

Following Noret's plan, the wiry, fearless men and women from Ginaz scrambled up cracks in the great stone blocks that formed the dam's ornate surface. They planted detonators and high-energy chemical foams behind the colossal paired sculptures of Mohammed and Buddha.

The machine army marched onward, ignoring the distractions of other villages that they would occupy after the Omnius update was installed within the Darits network. But Xavier meant to take that prize from them, destroying the massed robot troops in the process.

Some Zenshiites took the warning seriously and fled the city, while others refused to listen to anything the infidels said. Torn by the tremendous decision he had been forced to make, Xavier watched the stream of refugees. He had already seen so much death in his lifetime.

I cannot rescue those who insist on martyring themselves.

But he scowled as tears stung his eyes. *It is such a waste. For whom are they sacrificing themselves? Omnius will not be impressed, and neither am I.*

Vorian Atreides transmitted from his flagship in orbit, sounding cocky. "Good news, Xavier. I'm nearly finished up here. Ready to take on the space fleet."

"Excellent — because the thinking machines are almost upon us." He cut off the comline transmission, leaving his fellow primero to prepare the second phase that would, theoretically, drive the rest of the machine fleet far from IV Anbus.

Moments later the fearsome robotic army arrived at the far end of the canyon, an ominous assemblage of implacable, mechanical might. In his heart Xavier wanted nothing more than to destroy them.

Even the seasoned warriors cried out in dismay, but Xavier waved them to silence. "We fight for honor and a just cause! We are soldiers in the Army of the Jihad." He ordered his mercenaries and jihadis to get to safety. Zon Noret stumbled away, nearly collapsing; more blood had seeped from his deep wounds, but he shook off the assistance one of Xavier's soldiers offered him.

The machine invaders plunged onward, apparently convinced they had overrun the final human defenses. Xavier waited . . . and waited. Sweat trickled down his temples into the corners of his eyes.

We have the force of nature on our side, a powerful ally. The water will do the rest of the work for us.

The last Ginaz commandos scrambled to the top of the canyon and away from the shockpath of the planted explosives. Noret kept up despite the injuries, following his mercenaries. Sunlight glinted on the metal shells of the hideous combat robots.

"This is one world Omnius will *not* conquer," Xavier said, his voice low and threatening. Then he lifted his chin and opened his mouth in a shout. "You cannot have this place."

He detonated the explosives himself.

Sequential blasts rippled like thunder as the sound waves were trapped and focused by the confining canyon walls. The detonations struck vulnerable points, pummeling and resonating through the mighty dam.

With the structure fatally wounded, the immense force of chained water pushed through growing fractures, gained strength and caused exponential levels of damage. Sprays of water and chunks of debris shot out like high-pressure jets.

Water hammered through the cracks like a cosmic stampede. The huge statues of Buddha and Mohammed wavered, breaking at unlikely joints, as if the monuments were weaving about in a drunken dance. At last, with a roar, the entire dam split. The barrier wall, the cyclopean sculptures, and house-sized debris tumbled forward with the titanic force of an unleashed river.

It was a weapon much too powerful for even the thinking machines to oppose.

The robotic invaders hesitated as their sensors showed them the oncoming wall of water. They analyzed the information and much too slowly attempted to retreat. But the tumbling liquid sledgehammer smashed them away, swatting aside even the most massive armored bodies like sticks in a hurricane.

Freed water also ripped out the buildings and structures embedded in the sheltered cave hollows. The sacred city of Darits washed away, along with the unretrieved relics and any Zenshiite inhabitants who had refused to evacuate.

From atop the canyon wall, safe above the surging outburst of water, Xavier Harkonnen watched grimly. He could smell the fresh wet earth and churning water as the reservoir emptied in a great, silt-laden gush. Downstream, the flood would wipe out crops and settlements.

I would have preferred any other way. But they left me no choice.

After the machines had been swept away and the wall of water continued to rush down the canyon, Jihad shuttles came to pick up the regrouped forces. While Xavier gathered the Ginaz mercenaries and his remaining soldiers on top of the canyon wall, thousands of fighters shouted and cheered, celebrating their great victory.

In contrast, the surviving Zenshiites looked appalled, their eyes wide and disbelieving. Rhengalid, his face smeared with mud, his gray beard tangled, pointed an accusing finger at Xavier.

"I curse you! You destroyed our holy city, our sacred relics, and thousands of our people. May the wrath of Buddallah fall upon you and your descendants for a million years!"

The water roared onward through the canyon below, spreading out as the terrain leveled. The last chunks of the crumbling dam fell away from cliffside anchor points, and the huge reservoir continued to drain. Some Zenshiite fishing boats were swept into the rapids, where the torrent crushed them.

"You will have to rebuild an entire city." Xavier looked at Rhengalid with little sympathy. "But you can do that only because you are alive and *free*."

Secrets give birth to more secrets.

—A Saying of Arrakis

N OW THAT AGAMEMNON and his Titans had been sent off on their separate missions, Corrin seemed peaceful and efficient.

Though thinking machines might have communicated through any node of the sprawling evermind network, Omnius ordered Erasmus to go to the Central Spire of Corrin for a meeting.

Each time Erasmus viewed the tall, needle-shaped structure, the flowmetal tower adjusted its appearance, at the whim of Omnius. The mechanical Central Spire itself seemed to be alive with sliding walls, plaz windows and adjustable floors. The evermind core moved throughout the labyrinth, from the tip of the tower to the underground chambers.

Erasmus could change the expressions on his flexible metal face, but the Corrin-Omnius could — and did — morph entire building structures. As far as the autonomous robot knew, none of the other Omnius copies followed such whims. It made the pervasive computer seem almost . . . eccentric.

When he arrived, Erasmus dutifully rode a rapid lift to the seventh level of the flowmetal tower, where he stepped off into a small, windowless room. After the metal doors irised seamlessly shut behind him, his optic threads could detect no openings in the walls or ceiling. He doubted the evermind was trying to intimidate him.

Was this particular Omnius — the evermind on the most strategically central machine world — developing emotions and eccentricities? Did the Corrin-Omnius believe himself superior to the others? In the past the curious robot had attempted to ask probing questions on the matter, but the evermind always refused to answer.

The sophisticated computer had his own quirks, idiosyncrasies — even an ego, though Omnius would have denied the accusation. The independent robot found it interesting. Omnius seemed to have a program designed to make him more impulsive and unpredictable, like the humans whose erratic behavior had defeated machines on many battlefields.

"Today, Erasmus, we shall discuss religion," the evermind announced from unseen speakers that made it sound as if he was everywhere. "Hold out one hand, palm up."

When the robot did so, a metallic gelsphere copy of Omnius dropped into his grasp from a ceiling compartment. Such a wealth of information in a small, lightweight silvery globe. And so much more that was *not* there, especially the quality of "soul" that Erasmus pursued, along with other elusive aspects of the human condition.

"Please supply me with all relevant data on the subject before we begin," Omnius said.

For centuries Erasmus had observed the human species and conducted experiments on them, adding massive amounts of information to his own already copious databanks. Though the independent robot had many times offered to upload all of it, Omnius had shown little interest in those studies. Until now. "Why do you wish to know about religion? It seems an unusual topic for you."

"To me, the so-called spiritual or religious beliefs are an incomprehensible human behavior pattern. Now, however, I realize that they use religion as a weapon against me. Therefore, I must analyze it."

For efficient data transfer, Erasmus placed the Omnius copy into an orbport on the side of his own body and transferred the information the evermind had requested. He removed the sphere again.

Omnius took a moment to process the data and consider it. "Interesting. There are many forms of religion, yet the faiths with the strongest emotional component seem to center on the existence of a Supreme Being or guiding force. Is this the single most important belief of humans?"

"I am still researching the matter, Omnius. In matters of faith, few things are ever certain. Humans put beliefs and wishful thinking ahead of logic and hard facts."

"What is the point of your experiments, if you cannot provide concrete answers?"

"With human behavior it is difficult to formulate even concrete questions. However, my purpose is to establish certain guidelines and generalizations that may prove useful."

The silver sphere spun on Erasmus's palm, generating heat. "And their religions? Is this upload all you know about them?"

"I gave you a historical summary, consisting of what my captured humans told me about the churches, synagogues, mosques, and shrines of their people, and how the original faiths dissipated or metamorphosed into their present-day beliefs. If you wish, I can list all recorded planets for you, along with known religious affiliations."

"Unnecessary." Omnius's voice rose in volume. "Why do they call their movement against me a 'jihad,' a holy war? I am a computer. How can I be connected to their religions?"

"As a matter of convenience, they have associated you with an evil force personified in many of their sacred texts. They label you a demon, which enables them to proclaim that you are the enemy of whichever Supreme Being they revere. Therefore, this changes the conflict from a political matter to a religious struggle."

"And what is the advantage of that?"

"It enables emotions to rule, rather than the logic under which we operate. Humans are inclined to take irrational actions because their religions give them the righteous high ground. To them, our conflict becomes more than a war — it is a holy undertaking of the highest order."

Erasmus felt his hand tingle as the sphere processed information at high speed through its databanks. "Could their God be a higher form of organic life than themselves?" Omnius asked.

"Which God do you mean? The God of Navachristianity? Of Buddislam? The Deislamic Force? The Pan-Hindu Overlords of the Seventh Circle? I do not comprehend the differences well enough. They may simply be skewed manifestations of the same deity, blurred by time and misinformation. Or they may be different gods entirely."

"Your answers are overly vague," Omnius said.

"Precisely. Believers think of God as an ethereal life form, although most important religious sects have stories of their deities taking human incarnations."

"Preposterous."

Erasmus considered his words before replying. "You may be a God of Machines, Omnius."

"Then why am I asking questions?" The evermind actually sounded frustrated. "If I were God, would I not *know* everything?"

The comment ran parallel with Erasmus's own observation, since the machine knowledge contained in Omnius's databanks was not complete. He paused to consider. Had the evermind been playing with him all along? Had Omnius absorbed all the study data on his investigations into human beings?

Is Omnius reading my mind at this very moment?

"For decades you have raised a subgroup of humans like animals in pens, none of whom have any formal religious indoctrination." The silver sphere rose into the air, reached the chamber ceiling, then rolled around on the featureless white surface, as if gravity had turned upside down. "What do the people in your pens believe about God?"

"Naturally, they hold a more primitive set of beliefs. Some have concocted stories about a Supreme Being, but most are convinced that such a deity has given up on them. The very concept of religion may be no more than a social aspect of humanity, and when social fabrics are destroyed, such belief systems fade."

The gelsphere sped over one ceiling surface, then streaked down a wall, across the floor and between Erasmus's legs, then back up again. "Is it possible that you have avoided the subject of religion in your investigations because it is too complex and illogical?"

"I have not studied the matter in detail, Omnius. Many other avenues of human behavior have occupied me. Religious belief is only a minor aspect of human character. From what I have observed, I would conclude that humans are either agnostics or outright atheists, unless they are exposed to extreme pain or stress. Such attitudes go in cycles throughout their history, ebbing and flowing like a great tide of human affairs. Religious belief is on the upswing now, with the Jihad as a catalyst."

"Is the need for religion an innate human characteristic? Perhaps by ignoring their spirituality, you have been blind to their very essence."

"I have tortured them by the thousands, and very few say anything about God — except to ask why He has forsaken them. I have no doubt, however, that even now as Xerxes and his crew are decimating the rebel population on Ix, the mewling victims are uttering prayers with their last breaths, even though they see its ultimate futility."

They had received no direct news from Ix, but the Titan's orders had been clear enough. Xerxes was perfectly capable of performing brutal, straightforward butchery. The few survivors on Ix would never consider foolish rebellion again.

Omnius said, "I still do not grasp the very concept of religion. What purpose does it serve? It seems an imaginary incentive designed to control societal-scale behavior."

Erasmus replied slowly, "Understanding basic faith is like trying to hold a wet, moss-covered rock. It is a solid, substantial object, yet slippery and very difficult to grasp."

"Explain."

"The religious experience is different for all humans, even when they claim to belong to one belief system. Each individual seems to focus on a different aspect of it. There are nuances, subtle variations — like the human emotion of love, religion is never the same for two different people."

"But why?"

As Erasmus stood there, the Omnius sphere streaked around the room faster and faster, up the walls, over the ceiling, down the walls, across the floor. Presently, duplicate gelspheres appeared, dozens of copies of Omnius, like projectiles spinning in all directions at high speed, narrowly missing Erasmus, spouting voices that overlapped with a single word: "Why? Why? Why?"

Abruptly, the spheres shot away, and silence returned to the sealed room high up in the Central Spire. The door irised open behind Erasmus. Dutifully, he entered the lift and departed.

Back at his Corrin villa, Erasmus admitted the possibility that he had not paid sufficient attention to the subject of religion, as Omnius suggested. If so, he could avoid it no longer. He had been obsessed with human creativity and its expression in various art forms. But where did they get their inspiration? From some higher source? Maybe Erasmus's slave humans had successfully concealed their spirituality from him — perhaps even subconsciously. If so, that suggested they were hiding it from themselves as well.

Erasmus stood on a porch overlooking the pens, watching the filthy humans mill about in their crowded, squalid enclosures. If Iblis Ginjo or Serena Butler had discovered how to unleash that engine deep within the human psyche, it might explain the religious fervor that translated into war fever.

Full of renewed determination, the robot set out on a revised intellectual quest. What was the power behind religion? Was it a weapon that machines truly could not wield? While Erasmus cared little about the details of the galactic Jihad, he had to undertake this project for his own growth . . .

Omnius made available to Erasmus piles of printed and electronic books that had been confiscated from ancient human libraries and settlements on conquered Synchronized Worlds. The independent robot began to load them into his own databanks.

As he did so, Erasmus thought of the Cogitors and all the information in their ancient brains. If a Cogitor had existed on Corrin, such an ancient brain might provide him with interesting revelations. On Earth, Erasmus had occasionally spoken with the Cogitor Eklo, but Eklo had been annihilated in the human revolt there.

With machine precision, the robot consciously recalled every word Eklo had communicated to him, going over the conversations in detail, and came to a disturbing conclusion: The supposedly neutral Cogitor had been concealing something from him — and protecting humans all along.

Unfortunately, some wars are won by the side that is the most fanatical in a religious sense. The victorious leaders harness the holy energy of collective insanity.

—Cogitor Kwyna, *The Art of Aggression*

A LIGHT AFTERNOON RAIN pelted the government plaza as Iblis Ginjo hurried toward the Hall of Parliament. Half a dozen Jipol aides followed, not bothering to shelter themselves from the weather. On various corners, statues and shrines to the martyrs of the Jihad glistened in the drizzle and glowing yellow lights.

As he climbed the broad steps, the Grand Patriarch feigned surprise when he encountered four saffron-robed monks walking gingerly downward. The tallest one carried a large cylinder wrapped in cloth to shield it from the rain: the Cogitor Kwyna being transported like a bird in a cage. Iblis had known they would be here and had arranged to "accidentally" encounter them.

Iblis signaled to his entourage, and all of them moved to block the secondaries' path. "Ah! How wonderful!" Iblis exclaimed. "I have been asking to see the Cogitor. I'm sure we have many ideas to exchange." He grinned, secretly longing for the kind of contact he'd had with the great, brilliant Cogitor Eklo before the terrible rebellion on Earth.

But Iblis's present work was far more sophisticated than his earlier, clumsy efforts to stir the slaves into revolt against their masters. He couldn't accomplish it by himself, but was sure the Cogitor could help — if only he could convince Kwyna to share her vast intellect with him. So far, though, the ancient philosopher-brain had been reticent and aloof, as if unwilling to see the justifications for Iblis's actions.

"Kwyna has been busy," replied the secondary who held the preservation canister. A keloidal scar ran down the side of his face, from temple to chin. Trickles of rain spotted his robe.

"Of course, just as the Jihad also keeps me busy. But we are on the same side, are we not? Allies . . . perhaps even colleagues?"

Reaching forward with bold anticipation, Iblis opened a flap on the cloth covering to reveal the sealed jar that held a pink brain immersed in blue electrafluid. The monk's braided scar twitched as he grimaced, and his dark eyes became steely. But he did not resist the Grand Patriarch.

"Cogitor Kwyna?" Iblis spoke directly to Kwyna's lidded canister. "Why don't we move out of this miserable rain where we can talk? I need you to enlighten me."

Kwyna's disembodied mind was a vast reservoir of knowledge and insight, just as Eklo's had been. Perhaps she would agree to instruct him, if he used the information in the right way. Iblis had read some of the Cogitor's earlier esoteric pronouncements, and now he needed to be certain that his interpretations of her thoughts were correct.

Though he could sense Kwyna's discomfort in reaction to his intense interest, he longed to be intellectually closer to the female Cogitor, to all the wonderful information and philosophy. His voice became thin, eager. "Please?"

"Wait, Grand Patriarch." The scarred monk's eyes glazed over as he communicated with the ancient brain.

Ignoring the cold rain that fell harder, the secondary spoke in a rough, throaty voice as the Cogitor communicated directly through him. "Grand Patriarch, you wish to ask me about scriptures and ancient texts. It is in your voice, in your actions, in every breath you take."

Impressed, Iblis nodded. "I am fascinated by ancient Muadru prophecies and how they apply to our turbulent times. Based upon my readings, I have found countless justifications for the Holy Jihad against the thinking machines. Your own writings and speeches have inspired me to send many brave fighters to our battlegrounds."

The Cogitor seemed distressed. "Those ideas were never relevant to your Jihad."

"Are not certain ideas timeless? Especially yours, Kwyna." By now, the drumming rain had soaked everyone. One of the Jipol sergeants handed the Grand Patriarch a dry cloth, and he dried his face as he continued. "In one of your manifestos you wrote about the collective insanity of war, that winners invoke forceful delusions to achieve victory. I have been trying to achieve this lofty goal that you espoused, with some success, I am pleased to say. But now I wish to take it to a higher level."

"I never advocated such a practice. It was merely one of many ideas I offered as examples," Kwyna responded. "You have taken my words out of context. Have you read the entire scroll, Iblis Ginjo? I believe it is several million words long, and it took me centuries to compile."

"I scanned it for ideas. You inspired me."

"Important concepts must be absorbed in their totality. Do not attempt to interpret scriptures while wearing blinders in order to suit your own purposes."

Iblis knew full well that he had extracted selectively from her writings, and then manipulated the information. But he enjoyed this dialogue with Kwyna, saw it as an intellectual game, a challenge to see how well he could match wits with one of the greatest minds in history. It filled his need for the kind of tutelage he had enjoyed under the Cogitor Eklo, until his destruction in the terrible Earth revolts and atomic attack.

The Grand Patriarch quoted rapidly from several "end times" scriptures, ancient Muadru runestones and other testaments, which — if interpreted loosely enough — proclaimed that humanity could find its paradise only after enduring a thousand years of suffering . . . and then only if they made sufficient sacrifices.

"I believe Ix is an opportunity for us to make those sacrifices. My jihadis and mercenaries are willing to pay the price. So are the people of Ix."

"The blood of innocents has always been the currency of charismatic leaders," Kwyna said through the secondary's voice. "You are reading from fragments and artifacts known to be incomplete. Thus, there are gaps in your knowledge, and your conclusions may be faulty."

Suddenly intense and eager, Iblis raised his eyebrows. "Then do you know what the rest of the message is? What is on the other fragments?" He wanted as much scriptural ammunition as he could get. He needed to stir a frenzy on newly awakening planets, to galvanize the oppressed people with promises that their time of tribulation was over.

After a moment of intense silence, Kwyna said, "Are you in truth a religious man, Iblis Ginjo?"

He knew he could not lie to the ancient philosopher. "Religion suits my holy purpose, which is to help humanity rise up against its oppressors."

In her eerie second-hand voice spoken through the monk, Kwyna said, "And have you listened to any of the numerous protests against the Jihad? Are you doing this for humankind, Grand Patriarch . . . or just for yourself?"

Iblis responded deftly, "For just one person, perhaps, but not for myself. No, it is for the innocent child of Serena Butler, whom I saw murdered by an uncaring thinking machine. The protesters are short-sighted and irrelevant, while I myself am merely an instrument of victory. When success is achieved, I will gladly step aside."

Through her link with the secondary, Kwyna made a peculiar sound of amusement. "Then you are a most admirable — and atypical — man, Iblis Ginjo."

Forcibly ending the audience, the monk closed the wet cloth flap that covered the preservation canister. He said in his own voice, "We must return to the City of Introspection, Grand Patriarch. The Ancient One must not be disturbed further."

As if coming out of a trance, Iblis grew aware of people who moved past him up the rain-slickened steps into the Hall of Parliament. He wanted to spend more time with the superannuated brain, to receive advice and instruction, to share brilliant inspiration — but the saffron-robed secondaries hurried away.

Then he realized he himself was late. Serena Butler was about to address the assembly in another of her scheduled inspirational talks, which he had written personally. Not noticing his wet clothes, the Grand Patriarch hurried inside to listen to her. Though the security was intense, he did not have to worry about violence or assassination attempts today.

He had not arranged for any.

Inside the speaking chamber, Serena Butler looked like a heavenly vision, attired in an exquisite white robe and glittering rubate jewelry. Even without the adornments of an orange marigold on her lapel and a golden necklace around her neck, she looked surprisingly vibrant and healthy for her advancing years. Remarkable, considering that she refused to partake of Aurelius Venport's youth-enhancing melange.

Iblis watched it all. Serena rarely emerged in person from the City of Introspection, so each of her speeches had to be a major event.

Twenty freed humans, rebels who had been smuggled from the new battleground on Ix, sat in the front rows as showpieces. They gazed up at the Priestess with awe. Thanks to Iblis's incessant propaganda efforts, every person alive — even those in darkest captivity on machine planets — had heard of this woman and her martyred child. She had become a dedicated missionary, working tirelessly to unify humans against the vile machines.

When the audience fell silent, Serena's voice rose melodically through the hall. "Many of us have witnessed firsthand the bravery, bloodshed, and sacrifices necessary to overthrow the greatest depravity in the universe. Some of you are true heroes."

She asked half a dozen men and women to stand up, and identified each by name for their brave, selfless deeds. All were civilians, survivors of tremendous battles. "Come to me." Serena gestured, and from every corner of the great hall, the audience gave them standing ovations. As the refugees came forward, one by one, the Priestess touched them on the head as if in blessing; tears streamed down every face, including her own.

Serena raised her voice in challenge and angry determination. Tears glistened on her cheeks. "I watched something no mother should ever have to witness: my beautiful son murdered in front of my eyes. Think of your own babies, and of mine. Do not let the thinking machines do this to other children, I beg of you."

As he listened to her masterful delivery, the perfect intonation and diction, Iblis felt a chill of pride run down his spine. The tears were an excellent touch, and he did not doubt they were real. He heard Serena use the phrases he had written, and nodded as he saw her magic work on the audience. They were enraptured. She had been an excellent student, ever since he'd begun to lead her down the path of professional fanaticism.

At first, the young woman had willingly followed his instructions to achieve worthy, noble results. But when she had started to disagree with him, Iblis had fabricated possible "threats" to her safety, so that he would be justified in assigning a group of his hand-picked Seraphim as her personal bodyguards.

When Serena continued to be too independent, he had staged an assassination attempt and framed one of his sacrificial dupes, who was conveniently killed during capture. Thereafter, for her "protection," Serena stayed inside the walls of the City of Introspection, where he could keep a closer eye on her.

He had to make certain that Serena Butler never felt completely safe, so that she would always depend on him.

Now, Iblis relaxed when he saw that everything was under control. Since his arrival had not been noticed, he hurried to a dressing room and changed into dry clothes. Before he could leave the private room, his Jipol commandant slipped silently through the door. "Grand Patriarch, I am pleased to inform you that our work with Muñoza Chen is complete, as you requested. Everything is in place. A nice, clean job."

Yorek Thurr was a small, swarthy man with a black mustache and bald head. Dressed in a dark green doublet, he peered through slitted eyes that were as dull and black as those of a corpse. Expert with garrote, stiletto, and an assortment of other silent weapons, Thurr had an ability to move with the utmost stealth — and as the Jipol commander, he was always ready to do the Grand Patriarch's bidding. A good man to have around.

Iblis allowed himself the luxury of a smile. "I knew I could count on you."

From the moment the Jihad Police had been established, Yorek Thurr had proved himself a valued informant by discovering real spies, unobtrusive but quietly powerful humans who had secret connections to the Synchronized Worlds. Since Iblis had originally raised the specter only as a straw man to frighten the League members, he had been astonished to discover the depth of the deceit Thurr uncovered. Dozens of prominent citizens were implicated and executed, swelling the paranoid frenzy of free humans. As the newly formed Jipol rose in prominence, so Yorek Thurr rose in its ranks, eventually taking command. Sometimes he frightened even the Grand Patriarch.

Because of her constant complaints and resistance, Iblis had always suspected that Muñoza Chen might be an agent of the thinking machines. Why else would she oppose the essential work of the Jihad Council? The answer seemed obvious. The moment Chen had decided to oppose him, her life expectancy had dropped precipitously. Anyone who spoke out against the Jihad was, by definition, an ally of the thinking machines. It made perfect sense.

As Grand Patriarch, holding the responsibility for trillions of lives, he didn't have time for subtleties. To protect and advance the movement he had to cut efficiently through opposition. The clear results justified anything he might need to do along the way. The Jihad had gone on for decades now, gaining momentum. Even so, it had not gone far enough or fast enough to suit Iblis.

Anyone who overtly crossed the designs of the Grand Patriarch got investigated and expertly framed. Over the years, after the first major purge implicated seven League representatives — all of them, strangely enough, political rivals or people who had spoken out against Iblis — people began to suspect a machine spy under every bed. Five years later, another set of purges had removed all resistance to Iblis.

Now little internal opposition remained, and thanks to the quiet efforts of the Jipol, Muñoza Chen would no longer hinder his crusade against the machines . . .

Iblis separated from the Jipol Commandant and made his way back into the Assembly Hall. It would be good for him to be seen listening to Serena's speech. As he entered, her impassioned voice carried through the chamber like perfume on a breeze. She raised her arms in benediction and stood motionless for a long, poignant moment, as if gathering inspiration from above. Then she looked directly toward Iblis Ginjo and said, "There is no time to shirk the duties of humanity and no time to rest — only to fight!"

As she spoke, the doors of the hall burst open, and a throng of men and women marched in, wearing the bright green-and-crimson uniforms of the Jihad. While the audience cheered, every available space in the hall filled with thousands of new volunteers ready to sacrifice their lives for the Army of the Jihad.

Moving like an angel, Serena glided into their midst, weeping with gratitude. She blessed them all and kissed many, knowing she was dispatching many of them to their deaths. "My fighting jihadi's!"

Iblis nodded in satisfaction. It was choreographed with perfect timing, but Serena had pulled it off as if it were a spontaneous event. The concept had been her own, while Iblis had attended to the details of presentation.

We make a great team.

But as he watched the talented Priestess work the crowd, Iblis found himself on the horns of a dilemma. He wanted Serena to do well, had coached her carefully — and now she was giving the performance of her life.

The Grand Patriarch decided to watch her closer than ever, for his own sake. He didn't want her to think too much for herself . . . or too much of herself.

We are fools to think the battle is ever over. A defeated foe can delude us into letting down our guard . . . to our eternal sorrow.
—Primero Xavier Harkonnen,
"On-Site Military Dispatches"

LOUNGING IN THE command chair on the bridge of the flagship ballista, Vor studied satellite images of water surging through the canyons of IV Anbus. He shook his head. *Victory through total disaster*. He gave a wry smile. *What next?*

After the ground operations, Tercero Vergyl Tantor and the other battleship captains had shuttled back to their ballistas and resumed their places on board, readying for the end-game that would occur in space. If all went according to Vor's plan, the Omnius fleet would be driven permanently from this bruised world.

Knowing that Primero Harkonnen's shuttle had already docked and his friend was on his way to the bridge to join him, Vor grinned with anticipation. *My turn.* He would show Xavier exactly how victory should be achieved — through wiles instead of destruction.

As soon as Xavier stepped out onto the bridge deck, panting and disheveled, Vor flashed him a challenging look with a glint of mischief in it. "Watch how I can neutralize the thinking machine fleet without such a large and embarrassing loss of human life." He gave the order, and the flagship pressed forward to assume the vanguard position in the Jihad fleet.

Xavier ran fingers like a comb through his rusty-brown hair, smoothing his gray-streaked temples. "There didn't need to be any loss of life down there, Vorian. Some people choose to become victims, even when they have other options." Clearly disturbed, he tried to compose himself as he watched. "But even if we'd managed it without anyone suffering so much as a scratch, the Zenshiites would still have complained about our efforts."

Vor emitted a brief laugh. "We don't do this for gratitude, my friend, but for the future of the human race." He turned at his station and spoke quickly; his voice carried across the comline to the bridges of all five ballistas. "Power up Holtzman shields to full intensity. Increase orbital velocity so that we encounter the robot warships an hour sooner than they expect us."

"That'll surprise them, Vor," Vergyl transmitted from his own bridge.

Xavier took a formal tone. "Thinking machines are more likely to be . . . unsettled and unable to recalculate their actions in an appropriate timeframe, Tercero Tantor. That's not the same thing as an emotional reaction."

"As your little brother said," Vor added, "they'll be surprised."

Judging by his image on the viewer, the young black officer seemed to be fighting the effects of a lingering illness. While waiting for the Jihad ships to get into position, Vor quipped, "Vergyl, you look like you could use a vacation after this mission."

"Just a little too much . . . hospitality from the Zenshiite natives down there. But if your sympathy makes you spot me a few points in our next game –"

"Gentlemen, let us concentrate on the battle at hand," Xavier said.

Even though the robotic ground forces had been obliterated by the cataclysmic flood, Omnius's large space fleet remained intact. Now the five Jihad ballistas, shielded but heavily outgunned, picked up speed like angry mice racing to do battle with Salusan bulls.

As they circled over the limb of the planet and saw the powerful thinking machine ships in night's shadow, Vor whistled in appreciation. Omnius looked more invincible than ever. But Vor spoke firmly to his bridge crew.

"Machines operate under a rigid perception of reality. So, with a little tweak here and there, we can rewrite that reality." He adjusted the comline to the full ship-to-ship channel. "Everybody, double-check shield integrities and increase your speed to ramming velocity!"

The crew seemed uneasy and grim, but committed to victory. "I'm sure the robots intercepted that transmission, Vor," Vergyl transmitted from his bridge, keeping the second ballista close behind the flagship. "Uh, I hope you've got a better plan than a simple suicide plunge."

"We do what we must, little brother," Xavier said.

As the opposing fleets careened toward each other, closer and closer each second, Vor adjusted the comcontrols and sent a brief, coded transmission directly at the robotic command-and-control center. After the signal had been surreptitiously delivered, he added on the open channel, "Call in our hidden fleet and ram those ships!" He gripped the edge of his captain's chair, but the corners of his mouth turned upward in a confident smile. "Watch this, Xavier."

In cool disbelief, Xavier shook his head. "I thought I'd win any game of nerves against you, Vorian. But now I believe your spine is made of pure titanium."

"I'd love to teach you some new contests on the long flight back to Salusa. Spend time relaxing with your crew for a change, win some of their wages . . . or lose some of your own."

"For now, just command your ship, Primero Atreides," Xavier said, his voice a quick rush. He gripped a support rail as the Jihad vessels approached like cannonballs, unswerving.

At the last instant, the robot fleet suddenly broke from their orbits and scattered in frenzied flight. The five Holtzman-shielded ballistas hurtled through the empty space where the thinking machines had been only moments before. Omnius's warships streaked away from the planet, apparently abandoning IV Anbus entirely.

The human crew cheered with giddy hysteria, startled by their un-expected survival. Laughing deliriously, Vergyl transmitted, "I can't believe it. Xavier, what a sight!"

Vor turned to his bridge crew with a mockingly impatient expression. "So, we have Omnius on the run, people — why are you waiting? Do you want to sit here congratulating yourselves, or go slag some robots?"

The crew cheered again, confident and enthusiastic. Vor's ballista surged forward, and Vergyl drove his warship alongside. The remaining human vessels swooped in their wake, chasing and harassing the robot craft toward the fringes of the Anbus system, like barking guard dogs driving away intruders.

Xavier crossed his arms over his uniformed chest, waiting for the detailed explanation. Grinning, Vor finally turned to his friend. "My signal submitted false data to the machine fleet's sensor web. I simply altered a few readings to make them *believe* that our ballistas were heavily armed, indestructible . . . and accompanied by a much larger unseen contingent, which recently arrived from the Poritrin shipyards."

"You make it sound easy."

Vor snorted. "Absolutely not! Every detail has to be perfect, able to withstand close analysis from the enemy's redundant sensors. I doubt I could ever do it again, because Omnius will be aware of the trick and will be looking for it."

Xavier remained skeptical. "So what do the machines see now? Sounds like you hypnotized them."

"At present, the robots think we have dozens of battleships cloaked with invisibility fields. They can't see them, or defeat them, but they 'know' our ships are there, waiting to fire upon them. After calculating the odds, the enemy vessels had no choice but to flee."

"Brilliant tactical move," Xavier said. "But based on a flimsy assumption."

"Not flimsy, or brilliant — simply devious. As I've said many times, machines can be fooled. We're just lucky my father wasn't part of that fleet. Cymeks are much more suspicious. Agamemnon would know the difference, and he can certainly see through a bluff."

After half an hour of hot pursuit, a bridge technician asked to speak privately with the two Primeros and informed them that their Holtzman shields were in danger of overheating and failing. The protective systems were not meant to be used at such high intensity for long periods of time.

Vor crossed his arms over his chest. "I believe we can safely shut off the shields now. We won't need them anyway." He sent the same order to the other ballistas, then made an aside, "So why don't we just open fire?"

With apparent glee, the ballistas fell upon the robotic stragglers, shooting heavy armaments against the much larger machine ships, destroying two of them quickly. But the machines tolerated much higher acceleration than fragile human bodies could endure, and soon the balance of the robot fleet stretched out across an increasing distance. The pursuing Jihad forces had to break off the chase.

Vergyl transmitted, "I'd say that's the best antidote to Zenshiite poisons."

Then, as the five ballistas circled back toward IV Anbus for a final mop-up, they suddenly encountered a new group of enemy ships that streaked in under heavy acceleration. These vessels had a different design, and came in without stealth or defenses, as if they expected a thinking machine fleet already there.

Heady with confidence, Vergyl Tantor transmitted over the secure, scrambled command channel, "Ha, a second chance! Looks like we can teach more of those damn machines a lesson. Anybody taking odds on which one I'll hit first?"

"Tercero Tantor, hold back and wait for reinforcements," Xavier cautioned, though he had little outright concern after seeing the first robotic battlegroup's ignominious defeat.

But Vergyl was giddy with confidence. "I want to flush the rest of these contraptions away from IV Anbus."

Vergyl took his battleship in a downward sweep, firing potshots at the newcomers. He radioed back to the flagship. "Xavier, remember when I was just a boy and you told me I needed to be a hero and save a whole planet to be worthy of a woman like Serena Butler. Well, now I've got Sheel back home — do you think this'll impress her?"

Vor suddenly spun in his chair, shouting into the comline. "Wait — look at the designs. Those are *cymek* ships, not computers. I can't use my programming on them."

"Vergyl, break off!" Xavier shouted. "Primero Atreides informs me that his ruse will not work—"

The newcomer cymeks had come into the system armed for heavy combat against the Army of the Jihad. Now they opened fire on Vergyl's oncoming battleship.

Reacting quickly, the young tercero tried to bring his overheated shields back online, but some of the overlapping fields flickered and failed under the first cymek onslaught. Six explosive projectiles broke through and hit the ballista's hull and engines.

Vor had already accelerated the flagship toward the battle zone. He saw Xavier leaning over the comstation. "Any capable ships, converge and defend—"

A second volley tore open the underbelly of Vergyl's ballista, and one of the large exhaust cones broke apart, ripping the entire engine free. It exploded as it tumbled away. Striking the intermittent shield, gouts of trapped flame reflected back onto the ship, causing additional ricochet damage.

"Requesting assistance!" Vergyl cried.

The remaining four Jihad warships flew downward at high speed, but their shields were also spotty and ineffectual, overheated from the initial battle. Sickened, Xavier gripped the control railing. He knew Vor was doing his best, that he couldn't issue more effective commands himself.

Frantic now, Vergyl transmitted, "Emergency! Emergency! Launching evacuation pods. Xavier, you can lecture me later—"

The cymek vessels, knowing their time was short as the Jihad warships rallied, launched a third bombardment against the mortally wounded ballista, tearing the big battleship to shreds. Explosions ripped bulkheads up and down the decks. Plumes of escaping atmosphere jetted into space like white mist, a snowy contrast with the bright yellow flames of ignited propellant.

Like seeds sprayed from a cracklepod, evacuation modules shot out, including three from the now ruined bridge deck.

"Secure those lifepods," Xavier said. "Highest priority."

"We need covering fire." Vor knew the anguish Xavier must feel for the danger to his devoted brother, but he had spent a lot of time with the young tercero himself, laughing and playing games, listening to the homesick man talking about his wife and children on Giedi Prime. "Damn it, pull together!"

The remaining Jihad battleships finally came in range to fire their weapons. The cymek vessels suffered some damage, but they refused to disengage. Rather, the ruthless human minds risked much to secure prisoners — going after the lifepods launched from Vergyl's command deck.

Vorian Atreides, the son of General Agamemnon, knew all too well what the machine enemy would do to their captives. Before rescuers could arrive, the cymek ships closed in, scooping up a dozen of the foundering evacuation pods like hyenas stealing morsels of meat. Then, seeing the combined firepower of Jihad warships focused on them, the cymeks turned tail and raced away with their doomed prisoners.

In a final desperate ploy, not knowing who had actually been inside the seized escape pods, Vor broadcast, "Now cymeks are cowards who flee from battle? This is Primero Vorian Atreides, and I scoff at you! My father — General Agamemnon — taught me that humans were inferior, that cymeks could always win a fight. If so, then why are you running?"

Startling him, Agamemnon's deep voice came back, sounding like slowly boiling oil. "I also taught you, Vorian, that *hurting* an enemy is more satisfying than a straightforward victory. We shall see how much pain we can inflict upon our guests before we kill them. I presume they are friends of yours? I'll enjoy playing with them all."

As the outgunned cymek ships raced away, Xavier Harkonnen howled in dismay, knowing that he would never see his beloved foster brother again.

Vor screamed into the comline, "Come back and face me, Father! We can end this now. Are you afraid of me?"

"Not at all, Vorian. I'm just . . . enjoying myself at your expense."

The faster machine ships roared away from IV Anbus with the cymeks at the controls, ignoring Vor's further taunts. Soon, the vessels vanished into the distance.

*There are a million ways to ask the same question, and a million
ways to answer it.*

—Cogitors: Fundamental Postulate

T RAPPED WITHIN A bubble of air at the center of the four linked Titan
ships, Vergyl Tantor floated in zero-G. Even nightmares had never
been as awful as this, and now the young man was helpless. His dark skin
was slick with perspiration, his brown eyes round in an attempt at
defiance. He covered his terrified expression with a flimsy veneer of
bravado.

As bad as it looked for him, he still held onto a desperate hope that
Xavier would come to rescue him. But in his heart Vergyl knew it was
impossible. He would never see Sheel again, his sons, or his little girl . . .

Outside the bubble, the disembodied brains of four cymeks glowed as
thoughtrode sensors scanned visuals and transmitted the processed data
between them. Agamemnon, Juno, and Dante, as well as their newly
accepted companion Beowulf, scanned the current amusing victim
through all portions of the spectrum. The rest of the prisoners had
already been murdered.

The cymeks had been interrogating their captive, and enjoying themselves immensely. Recently, Juno had developed interesting and highly
effective pain amplifiers, which she had thoroughly tested on human
slaves. The cymek general had made sure to bring the pain amplifiers to
IV Anbus, where they could be put to proper use. Agamemnon had
hoped to capture his son Vorian, who deserved the highest level of
punishment possible for any human to endure . . . and beyond.

But he would have to make do with these captives.

By virtue of Vergyl Tantor's status as an officer serving under Agamemnon's turncoat son, the young man could provide information about

the Army of the Jihad. So far, he had refused to talk, but it was only a matter of time . . . and pain.

Agamemnon was pleased to see rivulets of anxious perspiration running down Vergyl's dark skin. Scanners showed the victim's body temperature rising, his heart rate increasing. *Good.*

During his long-ago glory days as a Titan, he and Juno had perfected the nuances of successful interrogation. He understood the fanatical motivation of the *hrethgir*, knew their covert activities on some of the weaker Synchronized Worlds such as Ix . . . where Xerxes should be leading an acceptable slaughter at this very moment. He also recognized, even before Omnius did, that the fundamental nature of the galactic conflict had shifted to a new level. No longer were the feral humans content with the defensive posture of self-protection. They had moved to outright aggression.

Even if the prisoner knew nothing of consequences, he still deserved to be tortured . . . an excellent, instructive test of Juno's new pain-amplifying devices.

If only it could have been Vorian . . .

"Now, Vergyl Tantor — what should we do with you?" Agamemnon's words filled the survival bubble with such a thunderous noise that the young man tried to cover his ears. "Should we let you go?"

The captive scowled, did not respond.

"Maybe we should just let him drift without life support and see if he can find his way back to Salusa Secundus," Beowulf suggested, eager to contribute.

"We could loan him one of our spaceship bodies," Dante said dryly. "Of course, we would need to remove his brain first. Did we bring along an extra preservation canister?"

"Interesting idea," Juno said. "Yessss. We can create a neo-cymek out of one of the fanatical fighters." From her linked ship, she looked around. "Who volunteers to cut out his brain?"

Almost simultaneously, the four cymeks sprouted razor-sharp blades from the artificial bodies that held their disembodied brains. Long claws scraped the outside of the clean plaz bubble enclosure.

"Would you like to answer our questions now, dear?" Juno importuned. For good measure she triggered a jolt of agony that made the captive writhe and spin in the weightless bubble until his joints made a loud cracking sound.

Vergyl's eyes were glassy and unfocused from the pain, but he refused to speak.

Now Dante, usually not the most violent of the cymeks, surprised his companions. From his side of the conglomerated vessel he fired a precision dart at the human's head. The sharp projectile struck him on one cheek, shattering teeth and penetrating his mouth.

Vergyl spat blood, but his screams fell on mechanical tympanic sensors. He called out the names of his wife and children: Sheel, Emilio, Jisp, Ulana. Apparently, he had no hope that they could help him, but locking images of their faces in his mind gave him strength.

Juno sent another spike of pain through the young man's nervous system, and said in a clinical tone, "He feels as if his lower body is on fire. I can continue the sensation for as long as I wish. Yessss. Perhaps we should alternate pleasure and pain stimulations, intensifying the control we have over him."

Fighting off the pain impulses, Vergyl reached up to jerk the sharp dart from his bloody cheek, tossed it aside, then made a defiant hand gesture. Agamemnon was exceedingly pleased at this, since this meant the captive was frustrated and afraid, with no other means of striking back. The dart floated around in the gravity-free enclosure.

Agamemnon said, "Tercero Tantor, how long can you hold your breath? Most frail humans can manage only a minute or so, but you look young and strong. Could you last three minutes, perhaps four?"

Abruptly the bubble slid open, leaving the bleeding captive in the vacuum of space as released cabin air roared out around him. Before Vergyl could drift into the emptiness, Agamemnon fired a small, tethered harpoon. The shaft sank into the young man's thigh, catching him like a fish. "There, we wouldn't want you to float away on us."

Vergyl's scream vanished in the vacuum. Intense, deep-space cold hit him like a hammer from all directions, attacking the cells of his body.

With a twitch of a segmented metal arm, Agamemnon jerked on the tether, and the barbed harpoon hooks dug into the victim's leg muscles. The cymek general reeled him back in, sealed the bubble, and let air surge into the enclosure.

Vergyl curled into a shivering ball and struggled for breath, gasping from the lack of oxygen and the raw pain. With half-numb hands that could not grip well, he tried to tear the harpoon from his thigh. Blood particles floated in the low gravity and spattered inside the bubble enclosure.

"Such old-fashioned methods," Dante said. "We have not made sufficient use of Juno's new devices."

"We are not finished with him yet," Agamemnon said. "This could take a long time."

Without warning, Agamemnon shot Vergyl back out into the subzero, pressureless void, while Juno simultaneously pulsed her pain amplifiers. The agonized officer seemed to be trying to turn himself inside out, as he writhed wildly. Blood vessels burst in his eyes and ears, but Vergyl remained defiant. Floating in the enclosure once more, he spat blood and choked and cursed. He couldn't stop shivering,

Agamemnon thrust a manipulator arm through the bubble wall to grab the captive and pull him close. The Titan general cupped an artificial hand over the young man's head and discharged needle probes through his skull, into the soft brain tissue beneath.

Vergyl screamed, whimpered Xavier's name, and then went limp.

"He's in an ecstasy of pain," Juno said. "This is truly delightful."

Murmurs of agreement passed among the cymeks.

"Those probes can help facilitate direct interrogation," Beowulf said to Juno. "I helped invent them myself, and the robot Erasmus used up many of his slaves in order to test the systems. Unfortunately, the data is not in a format that thinking machines can assimilate directly."

"But I can," Agamemnon said, then made a deprecating noise. "This human's brain is filled with exaggerations, lies, and preposterous propaganda spouted by the professional agitator, Iblis Ginjo. He actually believes it all."

"Nothing but useless information," Juno said with a mock sigh. "We should just kill him. Let me do it, my love. Please?"

"Vergyl Tantor," Agamemnon said, "tell me about my son Vorian Atreides. He was your friend? Someone you respected?"

The prisoner's eyes opened to narrow slits, and his lips moved. With his sharply tuned tympanic sensors, Agamemnon heard him whisper, "Primero Atreides is . . . a great hero . . . of the Jihad. He will bring you machine demons . . . to justice."

Agamemnon thrust the brain probes deeper, eliciting a howl from Vergyl. A pair of wires penetrated his eyes from inside his skull, grabbing the orbs and jerking them deeper into the skull cavity.

The human flailed about and pleaded, "Let me die!"

"In due course," the general promised. "But first you must help Juno test her device to its fullest capacity."

Juno purred, "That could take a while longer."

In fact, it took the better part of a day before Vergyl finally surrendered his life, much to the disappointment of the cymeks, who kept thinking of new and interesting tests . . .

With all the artillery, ships, and manpower in the military, our commanders often forget that ideas can be the greatest weapons of all.

—Cogitor Kwyna

HIGH INSIDE THE Cogitor's tower in the City of Introspection, Serena Butler felt isolated and safe; at the same time, she was surrounded by the enlightenment and advice that her heart had craved ever since the murder of her eleven-month-old son. For all those years, ancient Cogitor Kwyna had been her most valued advisor, mentor, teacher, and sounding board.

But some problems simply had no answers.

The disembodied female philosopher had lived a full life in human form and then had spent over a thousand years simply contemplating everything she had learned. Despite all her efforts, Serena could barely taste even a droplet of Kwyna's potent revelations . . . but still she knew she must try.

Ever since she had been captured by the thinking machines while on a mission of mercy to Giedi Prime, and taken in as a household slave to serve the monstrous robot master Erasmus, her life and the human race itself had stopped making sense.

Serena would not surrender entirely to her doubts and questions. She hoped and prayed that Kwyna could help clear all the turmoil and allow her to see clearly . . .

She ascended the steps to Kwyna's tower and sent her Seraphim away, along with the loyal secondaries who attended the female Cogitor. All were familiar with Serena's frequent visits here, and the Priestess did not have to explain herself. Niriem, her most devoted Seraph, was the last to leave. The young woman stood at the doorway gazing sadly at Serena, as if wishing she could find some way to help. Finally, Niriem turned and departed.

And Serena was alone again with Kwyna.

Smiling in anticipation, Serena let her eyes fall closed. She knew that the weary brain also enjoyed these sessions, although Kwyna's thoughts were always cautionary, as the Cogitor took care not to reveal too much.

Each time she had a mental discussion with the philosopher, her own brain filled with answers to an avalanche of questions she had not even known she was going to ask. Afterward, Serena would need days to simply absorb everything that had been hammered into her mind, and even more time to wrestle with the doubts that each new explanation raised.

But she would have it no other way. She could never stop, even if it felt as if her brain was filled to capacity, and that her skull might crack and explode. Serena was addicted to these interactions. One day they would provide her with all the solutions she needed.

Kwyna's complex and intricately contoured brain rested in its bath of electrafluid, the chemicals faintly bubbling and hissing as they provided the necessary energy and life-support functions. The disembodied philosopher had spent centuries in the precursor of the City of Introspection.

Slowly yet eagerly, Serena dipped her fingers into the fluid, controlling her impatience. She drew a deep breath, and built a mental wall to keep out all distractions. Her lavender eyes saw only the insides of her eyelids, so that her vision and thoughts could turn inward. Here within her mind, she was linked with the Cogitor. They were like two people having the most private of all conversations. Kwyna's thoughts and voice flooded into her, and Serena smiled, relieved to be in the embrace of the philosopher's wisdom.

"I sense your mental strength growing from our visits, Serena." The Cogitor's voice thrummed in her mind. "But I fear you have come to rely on me too much. You want to have answers simply *given* to you instead of discovering them for yourself."

"When all around me is emptiness, Kwyna, you are my only spark of hope. In too many things I must fumble around like a woman lost in the fog. Do not deny me your beacon."

Kwyna hesitated, then replied, "Iblis Ginjo believes he is your beacon."

"Yes, he is a great strength to me. He has taken many responsibilities that I would otherwise have to endure. He maintains the momentum of the Jihad. He focuses the struggle. He finds me those answers that you do not provide."

Kwyna seemed reluctant to follow this line of discussion, but she continued. "The Grand Patriarch does not *discover* answers as I have asked you to do, Serena. Nor does he receive them from a person of greater wisdom. Iblis Ginjo *creates* the answers that he wishes to hear, and then plants a backward trail to justify them."

Serena was troubled and defensive. "He does what is necessary."

"Is it, in truth, necessary? That is an answer I will not give you, Serena. You must discover it for yourself the way you discovered your own path out of the madness of grief."

Serena felt the shadows of old memories settle upon her. "You were my beacon then as well, Kwyna."

While the Jihad raged in the name of her son Manion, Serena had withdrawn here to recover from her misery. In the solitude and safety behind these walls, she had spent much time with her mother Livia, who had lost her teenage son, Octa's twin brother Fredo, to a wasting disease.

Livia insisted that she could understand the intense sorrow her daughter endured, but Serena refused to believe it. It was different having a grown and talented son fall to a sickness that was no one's fault. Serena had been forced to watch her innocent son — a bright toddler full of potential — slaughtered by Erasmus out of sheer vindictiveness.

Kwyna had been a greater help in counseling her. Though the disembodied ancient brain might have seemed distant and less able to comprehend human tragedies, Serena found that Kwyna could indeed offer a healing perspective that no one else, not even Serena's own mother, had been able to offer.

"You are a good friend, Kwyna, a bastion of strength in the League of Nobles. If only all people were as objective and dedicated, we would have no worries about the Jihad ever faltering through lack of resolve."

It troubled her that she had received reports of growing protests against the Jihad, people demanding that the brave human fighters simply withdraw from the struggle against Omnius. They moaned that twenty-four years was too long for a war — even an epic struggle against the pervasive evil of the computer evermind.

But the thinking machines had been in power for over a thousand years, and the great struggle had gone on for less than a quarter century. People had such a short attention span, but this undoubtedly had something to do with their own life expectancies. They didn't want to spend entire lives at war.

"Now you sound like the Grand Patriarch instead of Serena Butler," Kwyna chided. "Is this the primary lesson you have taken from my philosophies? A resolve and determination to continue the fight against the thinking machines?"

"I am not a Cogitor," Serena said. "I am still in a human body, saddled with a brief life and too much to do. I require action instead of mere contemplation."

Kwyna pulsed beneath her fingertips. "Then that is what you must do, Serena Butler. You must act."

Serena thought of all the ways she had tried to strengthen her people, walking among them, honoring their dead, speaking to the wounded and the heartsick refugees, visiting camps, spending her entire share of the Butler fortune. The populace loved her, yet she wanted to do so much more.

Interrupted by a commotion outside the tower room, she broke her connection with Kwyna and withdrew her dripping fingers from the electrafluid. She turned around and blinked in the bright sunlight that streamed through the high windows.

She saw her Seraph Niriem standing with arms rigid at her sides, her purple-trimmed white robes neat and dazzling. "Priestess Butler, we have received a message from outside the system. The Jihad fleet has returned from IV Anbus."

Serena smiled. Xavier and Vorian would be coming home. "Contact the Grand Patriarch. We must prepare a suitable welcome for our heroes."

Of all the battles he had faced and all the enemies he had fought, Xavier Harkonnen feared this ordeal more than any of them. But now that he had returned to Salusa Secundus, he could not shirk the obligation.

Duty, honor, and responsibility had formed the foundation of his character since his military training with the Salusan Militia.

As soon as the Jihad fleet had returned to the League capital, he took a white Salusan stallion and rode up along the pathway to the Tantor Estate, the old noble holdings where he'd spent his childhood. He'd had no sleep, but could not delay.

Over the years, the great house had been mostly shut down. Old Emil Tantor and his wife Lucille, the kindly couple who had taken in the orphaned six-year-old Xavier, had raised him as their foster son and then formally adopted him. Later, they'd unexpectedly had a son of their own.

Vergyl.

Decades earlier, Xavier had married Octa and moved away to the Butler Estate, and then Vergyl had gone off to join the Army of the Jihad. Six years ago, Lucille Tantor had died in a flyer crash, leaving the old man alone. In the years afterward, Emil had made himself quietly content, living in one of the smaller outbuildings, where a few faithful servants attended him.

Someday, the Tantor Estate should have been Vergyl's legacy. Now it would become the home of the young man's widow and his children . . .

Xavier dismounted and tied the stallion to an ornate post at the front of the main house. Then, with heavy heart and sinking stomach, he set off to look for the man he called father. The terrible news he brought would likely destroy the old man, but it would be no kindness to withhold it. Xavier only hoped he had made his way here quickly enough that rumors hadn't already found Emil in his secluded home.

Helpful servants, impressed with the immaculate green-and-crimson Jihad uniform, directed him to Emil Tantor, who sat outside under a gazebo surrounded by hummingbird feeders. Golden creatures hovered about the sweet nectar, their wings a blur in the air. They kept the old man company as he sat reading a leatherbound book of legends and history.

"I remember when you used to read aloud to me, and to Vergyl," Xavier said.

Emil smiled at him, his lips parting to expose bright teeth. The elder Tantor's hair was like a cloud of pale smoke from a greenwood fire. His skin was dark and deeply creased with age, but his brown eyes were bright, not diluted with weariness. He set the book aside and lurched to his feet, slightly more unsteady than he realized. "Xavier, my boy! A delightful surprise. What brings you—"

Then he seemed to understand. The old man sensed something in Xavier's reluctance, the screaming grief barely contained like a monster inside of him. Emil took in the formal uniform, Xavier's rigid posture, and the hesitation in his eyes. "Oh, no," he said. "Not my son."

Xavier said numbly, as if reading from a report that he could not believe himself, "We defeated the thinking machines at the battle for IV Anbus. We saved the world from falling under the domination of Omnius and stopped them from establishing another base in their encroachment on League territory." His breath hitched. "But then, when we thought it was all over and our victory assured, a group of cymeks attacked. They caused a great deal of damage and many deaths. They destroyed ballistas, javelins." He swallowed. "And captured Vergyl."

"Captured?" Emil Tantor perked up, clinging to a thin thread. "There's hope that he might still be alive? Answer me honestly, Xavier."

Xavier averted his eyes. "We humans exist on hope. It's what separates us from thinking machines." But in truth, he had fought the robots and cymeks for so many years that he knew their precision and viciousness. In his own heart, Xavier harbored no hope that his adoptive brother would ever be saved. Even if his little brother had been whisked away to become a slave somewhere deep within the Synchronized Worlds, how could Xavier or the Jihad forces ever hope to free him?

As he continued, his words cracked with swelling emotions that threatened to choke him. "I wish I could tell you he died swiftly, cleanly, painlessly — I was there, but too far away. I could do nothing to save my own brother."

Emil accepted the answer in silence, not questioning the presumption that Vergyl would never return. He reached out a strong hand and clasped Xavier's wrist. "Can you at least say that he met his end bravely?"

Xavier nodded, tears sparkling in his eyes. "That much I can promise you without any hesitation whatsoever." He took the old man by the arm and led him with slow, painstaking footsteps back toward the small house. They sat on a bench on the lawn and opened one of the family's oldest bottles of Mervignon wine to toast the memory of Vergyl.

"Your brother always looked up to you, Xavier, wanted to be like you. After Ellram, I had to sign a special dispensation for him to join the Jihad when he was only seventeen. Your mother had grave reservations about it, and while I feared for his safety, I feared more the disappointment that boy would experience if I held him back. I knew he would try to join no matter what I said, even if he had to lie, so I wanted him to at least have the protection of our family name and his relationship with you."

"I should have protected him better."

"He's . . . a man, Xavier. You couldn't coddle him."

"No, I suppose not." He looked off into the distance. A golden hummingbird buzzed past his face. "Those first few years, I made sure he was stationed on Giedi Prime, where he would watch over the war memorial construction. I thought he'd be safe there."

"Your brother always wanted to be in the thick of things."

Xavier remembered back. On Giedi Prime, bright and promising Cuarto Vergyl Tantor had fallen in love and had married Sheel when he'd turned twenty-one.

Emil sipped from his red wine and let out a long, satisfied sigh. "I suppose now I have all the excuse I need to bring Sheel and my grandchildren here. Someone's got to keep me company, and it'll be good to hear young voices around here again."

Xavier nodded. "I'll see that they're brought here with all possible speed, Father, and I promise—" He drew in a deep breath and started anew, "I promise I will return home as often as I can."

The old man smiled at him and patted his hand. "I would like that, Xavier. You are my only son now."

Even victories take their toll on a man.

—Saying of Old Earth

ON THE OPEN-AIR stage of the Zimia Memorial Plaza, the two newly returned war heroes were quite a contrast, standing side by side. Each was dressed in a Jihad uniform, and both were in their mid-forties, but Xavier Harkonnen looked older than that, with crow's feet around his tired eyes and a heavy peppering of gray hair at his temples.

Sharply different, Vorian Atreides had an unlined complexion and supple muscles. As the son of Agamemnon, recipient of a painful life-extension process, Vor was not ordinary by any stretch of the imagination.

The two men were different in character, each fulfilling their duties in their own ways, according to their own standards. Both loved Serena Butler, and both had gone to war as officers in her Jihad. Their ranks and status were nearly the same, down to the medals on their chests and the plaques of commendation that adorned their offices, though Vor was technically one grade below Xavier.

Now, as Xavier scanned the sea of faces in the crowd, he felt the weight of age and experience on his shoulders. Fresh orange marigolds decorated the numerous memorials, statues, and makeshift shrines to Manion the Innocent.

The League citizens considered the successful defense of IV Anbus an overwhelming victory that prevented the thinking machines from gaining a critical foothold closer to League territory. Grand Patriarch Iblis Ginjo had declared a day of celebration to welcome the Jihad soldiers home.

But others would never return to their families. Like Vergyl . . .

A vision of power and grace, the Priestess of the Jihad made her way through the rejoicing crowd toward the stage, waving to her people. As usual she was surrounded by an entourage of powerful Seraphim, assigned Jipol guards, and handlers.

Iblis Ginjo walked beside her in a gold-trimmed black suit, holding his large head high. Xavier saw the Grand Patriarch for what he was — a man who shared Xavier's goals in the general sense, but one willing to utilize morally ambiguous options to achieve his ends. Xavier wished Serena would notice some of this, but she had isolated herself more and more, believing the slanted reports her advisors gave her.

On one side of the stage, a hundred uniformed jihadis stood at attention. Some bore the marks of combat, either in the healing packs on their skin or in the haunted looks in their eyes. They would receive medals, but Xavier thought they would have been better off resting, to recover from the rigors of combat.

Many of the ground soldiers and Ginaz mercenaries had suffered severe wounds; most of the escapees from Vergyl's destroyed ballista were injured, burned, and barely alive. Making the hospital situation even worse, another fast commando ship had just brought a load of refugees from Ix, the now-embattled Synchronized World where underground rebels were barely surviving against cymek hunters.

They had enough blood, pain, and medical emergencies to keep Zimia's best doctors and the army's finest battlefield surgeons busy for a long time.

Serena climbed to the stage, followed by Iblis. Though she showed no hesitation in spite of the most recent assassination attempt against her in the City of Introspection, white-robed bodyguards surrounded her, ready to thrust themselves into the line of fire if necessary.

Serena and the Grand Patriarch stood in front of Xavier and Vor, waving past them to the giddy crowd. Iblis raised his hands high for silence, while Serena gazed at both Primeros. Xavier felt an electric tingle upon looking into her lavender eyes, her still-lovely, beatific face. She seemed to be in a religious trance. Or . . . drugged?

"We are here to celebrate a tremendous victory." Serena's words echoed from powerful, unseen speakers. "The successful defense of IV Anbus will go down in the annals of the Jihad as one of our proudest moments. One day there will be no more thinking machines, no more tormentors of our collective soul. This is the moment of our greatest challenge — and I call upon all human beings to do their part. No, I call upon each of you to do *more* than your part."

Serena looked warmly at the Grand Patriarch, and in her eyes Xavier saw adoration and respect that went beyond anything the man deserved. Did she not see how Iblis manipulated her, telling her only what she wanted to hear?

Presently, Iblis's resonant voice filled the speakers of the plaza. "As we proved on Earth, on Giedi Prime, on Peridot Colony, Tyndall, and now IV Anbus — we can defeat Omnius! One planet at a time. We must seize and free the Synchronized Worlds . . . and for that, we always need more volunteers. Every League World must contribute fighters now, so that we may carry on the valiant war. Sons and daughters, fighters from all free regions and peoples. I even call on Ginaz to provide more of their best mercenaries, who have proved so effective. Train them, test them! With your help, thinking machine planets will fall in a chain reaction across the cosmos."

Xavier's stomach churned as he thought of his foster brother Vergyl, but he maintained his stoic composure. Standing erect, a dedicated soldier in every aspect of his demeanor, he saluted the crowd.

Every world in the League of Nobles remained at the highest state of alert. Twice in the past quarter century, the capital city of Zimia had been the target of massive attacks — an initial assault by cymek walkers when Serena had been only a junior member of the League Parliament, and again several years after the atomic destruction of Earth. But humans had survived both times.

There were no safe harbors on the roiling sea of Serena Butler's Jihad. Her people could never rest, never stop looking over their shoulders, until the scourge of thinking machines had been eliminated for all time.

As she walked like an angel through a Salusan military hospital outside Zimia, she felt more determined than ever. Despite all the colorful flowers of celebration and reverence to Manion, the sight of wounded fighters on healer beds brought home the urgency to her.

People were ultimately vulnerable, forced to spend their lives in fragile bodies that the thinking machines could easily destroy. Her murdered son was the most famous example, but little Manion had not been the first child brutalized by machines, nor had he been the last. And he had not suffered as much as some. She knew what Omnius and Erasmus were capable of. But the little boy's death had triggered trillions of people to fight back against the machines, all under her banner. She heaved a deep sigh at the terrible losses of her people.

Serena wore a simple white hospital dress now, with a red version of the open-hand League symbol on the lapel. She administered a benevolent smile, soft words, and a gentle touch to each soldier as she moved from bed to bed.

One man had lost both arms in an artillery explosion and remained in a coma. Lingering at his bedside, Serena held a cool hand against his bandaged, waxen face and told him how proud she was of all he had sacrificed.

A young tan-skinned doctor went to the healer bed and began checking vital signs on an array of instruments. A badge on the lapel of his white shirt identified him as Dr. Rajid Suk, one of the most talented of the new battlefield surgeons. "I'm sorry, but he can't hear you."

"Oh, but he can." Against her fingertips, Serena felt the patient's cheek twitch. The eyelids flickered open. The man groaned in confusion and pain. Some of the patients called it a miracle.

"There are many paths to healing," Dr. Suk said, calling out to his colleagues. "Serena, you brought this man out of his coma."

The patient became aware of his grievous injuries and began to wail. On the healing bed, intravenous lines and probes adjusted automatically to improve his vital signs. A nurse stepped forward and adhered a white sedative pad to his chest. As the drug calmed him, the man looked up imploringly at Serena. She massaged his brow and whispered to him . . .

Later, when he had drifted off, Serena spoke quietly to Dr. Suk. "Will he be scheduled for limb-replacement surgery?"

"With so many battles, there is a shortage of organs, limbs, and other replacement body parts. The Tlulaxa organ farms simply cannot keep up with the demand." The doctor shook his head sadly. "It could take a year or more before he is even a candidate."

She lifted her chin in angry determination. "I will speak with the Tlulaxa representatives. They claim to be our allies, and their organ farms must be expanded to provide what we need, no matter the cost. In this fight for all humanity, they must work closely with us, forgoing excessive profits if necessary, to care for those who risk their lives for our freedom!" She raised her voice so that wounded soldiers could hear her. "I guarantee that all of you will receive the organs and limbs you need. I shall demand it of the Tlulaxa!"

Not a single person in the hospital doubted her.

That evening four Jipol men led Iblis Ginjo to a dim pleasure house filled with sweet-smelling smoke and oddly atonal music. Inside, the small-statured Rekur Van sat on a cushion as if meditating, paying little attention to the languid lights that played over the flowing silhouettes of slender women.

Without receiving an invitation, Iblis took a thick cushion next to the Tlulaxa flesh merchant. The slaver stirred, gave an agitated grunt. He put down a chunk of orange cake that he had been eating with his bare, long-fingered hands. The Jipol men sat menacingly close to him, causing his dark eyes to flit about nervously.

"I need your help," Iblis said quietly enough that no eavesdropper could hear. After his most recent raid on IV Anbus, Rekur Van had reported to Iblis the ominous presence of machine scout ships in the system. "I saved your best slave-harvesting grounds. In exchange, you must do something for me."

A simpering server came up to them with mincing steps, but Iblis made a gesture with his left hand. Two Jipol guards caught the server and rapidly whisked him away from the private conversation.

Rekur Van grimaced at the Grand Patriarch. "What choice do I have?"

"Serena Butler has promised her injured Jihad fighters increased shipments of replacement parts — arms, legs, internal organs — for all who need them. You Tlulaxa must provide everything necessary."

"But we don't have the capacity." The flesh merchant scowled. "How could you let her say such things? Have you lost control of the Jihad?"

"I was not present, but her statement is a matter of record, and now we must make it happen. The Priestess of the Jihad cannot renege on her commitments. The Tlulaxa organ farms will send increased shipments immediately."

"It will not be easy. We need much more raw material."

"Just see that it is done. I don't care how. My office will provide whatever authorization you need . . . and because of the vital nature of this 'request,' I'm sure the Army of the Jihad can promise a bonus. Say, an increase of five percent over your usual fees?"

The Tlulaxa merchant, at first intimidated by the magnitude of the demand, began to smile. "Given sufficient incentive, all things are possible for the Jihad."

"Of course they are. Your ship is at Zimia Spaceport?"

"Yes." Rekur Van brushed cake crumbs from his chest. "My business is finished here, and I intend to depart in three days."

Iblis stood, towering over the little Tlulaxa on his cushion. "You will depart *now*." The Jipol guards lifted Rekur Van to his feet.

The Grand Patriarch and his entourage escorted the sputtering flesh-merchant out of the pleasure house. "Until this is done, the League of Nobles will have no further business dealings with you."

He had already issued a similar demand to the commanders of the mercenary schools on Ginaz. Human beings were the Jihad's primary resources in this fight against mechanical monstrosities, and Iblis needed to make sure the supply lines remained open.

Rekur Van perspired and looked nervous. His dark gaze flitted around, as if looking for an avenue of escape. "You drive a hard bargain."

Iblis gave a smile. "I have only the best interests of mankind in my heart."

A tool wielded in ignorance can become the most dangerous of weapons.

—Swordmaster Jav Barri

T HE ISLAND IN Ginaz's central archipelago dozed beneath a hazy afternoon sky. The sun swelled large and yellow above a horizon of blue-green water. On the curving leeward shore of a lagoon, warm water lapped against the beach.

The serenity was broken by the violent clamor of weapons.

Jool Noret watched his father thrust and parry, battling a fearsome combat robot. Zon Noret's body was sinew coiled over hard bones. He wore no shoes, and his long yellowish-gray hair flew behind him like a comet's tail as he leaped in with a wild yell, slashing and clanging with his pulse sword. His weapon, fashioned like a perfectly balanced blade, contained a generator cell that delivered precise disruptive pulses through the metal blade. The disruptive bursts could overload and disengage the sophisticated gelcircuits of thinking machines.

Noret's mek opponent was also a blur of movement, raising six metallic arms to shield itself, using grounded armor plates and non-conductive support struts to protect its control circuitry against the veteran opponent.

The talented old mercenary continued his training, demonstrating techniques for his son and honing his own skills. Zon had seen so much furious combat on the battlegrounds of the Jihad — most recently in the heroic defense of IV Anbus, where he had been wounded — that this was little more than a game to him. The veteran thrust hard, skittering the blade with a shower of sparks along one of the robot's six arms and striking a small but vulnerable section of self-contained circuitry. One of the fighting mek's arms went limp.

Jool crowed with victory for his father. "The best you've ever done!"

"Not quite, my son." Panting, Zon Noret stepped back. "One only achieves the peak of one's capabilities when fighting for survival."

According to the rules, Chirox, the fighting mek, could reset his systems after a minute of delay, but Jool thought the disabled arm would need to be repaired in the shop. Zon took two quick breaths, then leaped in again with a flurry of blows.

With his five remaining good arms, the mek defended.

A century ago, an intrepid Ginaz salvage scout had found a damaged thinking machine ship and retrieved the broken combat robot. The mek's gelcircuitry mind had been wiped, and once the combat programming was reinstalled, Chirox became an instructor on the Ginaz archipelago, teaching unorthodox but effective hand-to-hand combat techniques against robots. Chirox no longer had any loyalty to the computer evermind, and had diligently trained four generations of mercenary fighters, including Zon Noret. Jool, one of the veteran's many sons, would follow in his footsteps.

Shaped roughly like a human, the mek had three pairs of fighting arms extending from his torso, with weapons in each hand — swords and knives which could be varied in length and design. He had bright optic threads on a rigid molded face, instead of mirrorized flowmetal; this unit had been designed for nothing but combat.

In a sense, Chirox was a thinking machine . . . but because of his beneficial, necessary functions and strict control mechanisms he was not customarily referred to as such. He was one of only a handful of robotic units maintained and operated by League forces or their allies. These mechanical fighters were so efficient in their destructive abilities that Omnius considered them perfect, and no longer found it necessary to change their hardware or software. This provided an unforeseen opportunity for the Jihad, however, since they now had a technological standard against which to test their own fighting methods.

The Noret family and their immediate trainees considered Chirox their *sensei*, a master of martial arts and combat techniques. Since the launching of Serena Butler's Jihad, many robots had been destroyed because of what Chirox taught.

Now young Jool squatted back on the warm, grainy sand. His jade eyes were bright and intent. He had pale, sun-bleached hair, high cheekbones, and a pointed chin; he was skinny, but deceptively strong. He could dart in and out of a training exercise even faster than his father.

He watched every move Zon Noret made, the blurring swish of energized steel as his blade traced complex patterns in the air, dancing forward to slam against the *sensei* mek's exoskeleton.

As always, the nineteen-year-old admired his father, for he had heard numerous tales of Zon Noret's triumphs during the most intense fighting of the Jihad. Jool wished he could have been at IV Anbus when the destroyed dam wiped out the robot army. His father had been among the first group of Ginaz mercenaries who volunteered their services to the Jihad, eight years after the destruction of Earth.

In Ginaz society, families had many children to replenish the warrior ranks, but the culture did not encourage parents to be very close to their offspring. The old veteran Zon was an exception, especially where Jool was concerned. A hero many times over, Zon's bloodline was considered desirable, so he was persuaded to have even more offspring once he had returned from the combat fields.

Jool was easily the most skilled fighter of his fourteen brothers and sisters, and among the most advanced of his entire generation. Seeing so much potential in the young man, his father had paid extra attention to Jool, and saw him as his successor in the elite Corps of Ginaz, arguably the finest mercenaries in the Galaxy. Many planets provided freelance warriors for the fight, but no other group boasted such a high kill ratio.

Ginaz acknowledged that all humans shared the same enemy, but the mercenaries maintained their independence instead of joining the formal military hierarchy of the Army of the Jihad, making them wild cards. Where the jihadis preferred to use large military equipment and attack from a distance, Ginaz fighters were willing to get up close against the enemy robots. They hired themselves out for combat, unafraid to be used as suicide forces, disposable commandos — if the importance of the mission was sufficiently high.

Zon had also been on the front lines when the machines had struck Peridot Colony; the human forces had fiercely defended the planet, at the cost of over eighty percent of the Ginaz mercenaries. In the end they had driven back the robot invaders, but Omnius had instructed the thinking machine fighters to follow a scorched-earth policy along their retreat. Though the colony had been grievously damaged, the rest of the planet had *not* fallen to the enemy.

Three years ago, Zon had been burned and injured while fighting robots on board a besieged thinking machine ship, after which he had been forced to recuperate and retrain on the archipelago islands of Ginaz. That was when he had first noticed his son's exceptional skill. Now, after intensive practice, the young man might even surpass his own father.

Dripping with sweat, Zon parried and thrust, faster and more competently than his son had ever seen him fight. Jool could see how badly his father wanted to get back to the battlefields. The location didn't matter to him. The Army of the Jihad always needed more fighters, and Ginaz devoted most of their population to the cause.

"I advise caution, Master Zon Noret." Chirox's voice was smooth and calm, not at all reflecting the intense exertion of the exercise.

"Nonsense," Zon called with proud defiance. "Keep fighting to the absolute best of your abilities."

The robot had no choice but to follow the command. "I have been programmed to teach you, Master Zon Noret, but I cannot force you to heed my cautions or lessons." He thrust with his multiple arms, holding a knife or a sword in each.

The veteran scorned formalized instruction, claiming that it detracted from the development of true fighting skills. He always said, "The best technique for learning and growth is to simply observe. Rote memorization gains you nothing on the field of combat. Rather, practice until you no longer exist as an individual. There can be no separation between mind and body. You must become no more than living, fluid combat moves. That is all a mercenary should be."

But though his father had achieved the highest accolades among the mercenaries of Ginaz, and a promised place in the Council of Veterans, Jool had already surpassed his elder's skills, practicing in secret.

Like all youthful warriors on the islands, Jool Noret had spent his childhood being taught a variety of weapons by battle-scarred veterans and being lectured in techniques by pregnant female mercenaries. But only Zon Noret and a handful of eccentric trainees made full use of the fighting mek Chirox. Some of the conservative veterans considered it dangerous, but Zon had always felt it was the best way to understand, and defeat, the real enemy.

Now nearly an adult, Jool had followed in his father's footsteps, but took measures one step further. Zon never knew that his son had exceeded the mek's prior maximum capabilities, but Jool had learned how the robot worked and deciphered the combat programming. A year ago while his father was guest instructor on another island, Jool had installed an adaptability algorithm module that allowed Chirox to become a "supercharged" mek, superior to anything its original combat programming allowed. With the supercharged module installed, Chirox could keep pace with his student, becoming a better and better fighter as Jool himself advanced. The only limitation was the young man's capabilities.

Jool always practiced and fought against Chirox either late at night or when he was sure he would be alone on the beaches. His muscles still felt a pleasant, weary burn from the latest workout he and the mek had completed before dawn, in secret, before his father could see.

Someday Jool would surprise Zon with an astounding demonstration of his capabilities, but the young fighter was still not satisfied with himself. He wanted to become the best mercenary Ginaz had ever produced. He knew he had the potential within him, if only he could release his inhibitions. A thread of self restraint impeded him, a protective instinct that placed a glass ceiling on his development.

Even so, Jool was better than any other fighter he had ever seen. Chirox said so himself, and he had trained against many of the best mercenaries. The combat robot had no choice but to be objective and honest . . .

Now, sitting in the hot sun, Jool studied his father's attack and defense methods, as well as the skill and resilience the *sensei* mek demonstrated. Zon applied himself with fury, as if trying to prove something to himself. Surprisingly, he even pulled out a few new tricks, moves that Jool had never seen him use before. The younger man smiled.

Despite his opponent's best efforts, though, Chirox remained one step ahead of the older fighter. The mek's five remaining segmented arms moved in a blur, and the human could barely keep up. The old veteran was clearly being worn down.

Chirox spoke, "This is unwise, Zon Noret. Your strength and stamina are diminished. You have only recently recovered from your combat injury."

Angrily, Zon clattered his sword against the robot's body; the five still-functioning arms flailed in defense. "I have battled real thinking machines, Chirox. They do not fight below their capabilities, not even against an old man."

"You're not old, Father," Jool insisted, but he heard the insincerity in his own voice.

Panting heavily, Zon stepped away, glanced at his son, and tossed the long, pale hair out of his eyes. "Age is a relative term when applied to seasoned warriors, my son."

With a sound like an army of blacksmiths battering hot blades on their anvils, Zon attacked Chirox. The robot swung up his arms, and weapons disappeared from two of the hands, which he now used to grasp at his opponent. Zon managed to paralyze this pair of arms with the pulse sword, and the robot's right leg as well, so that Chirox could only pivot in the sand rather than dodge out of the way. Cutting weapons emerged from the robot's body, jabbing and slashing with buzzing blades, but Zon danced to one side.

Then Jool realized with a sudden sinking fear that he had forgotten to remove the supercharged fighting module from the combat mek. With the adaptability algorithm functioning, Chirox was pumped to capabilities far superior to anything Zon had ever faced.

Jool paled with alarm for his father. And now in the intensity of battle — with Chirox's safety systems and restraints deactivated — he didn't dare shout a distracting warning. He jumped to his feet. Everything happened in an instant.

Zon leaped in the air and lashed out with a callused foot, kicking sideways to knock the mek off balance. But Chirox somehow anchored himself.

Jool ran forward, intending to dive into the fray. His bare feet kicked up sand.

The old warrior did not know his danger. He jumped backward, out of the reach of the cutting arms, but the ferociously intent mek kept driving in. Zon Noret landed wrong, twisting his ankle. He stumbled.

Jool cried out automatically, "Chirox, stop!" — just as the *sensei* mek struck. The robot's knife plunged deep into the old warrior's chest.

As the young man ran forward, Chirox stood frozen as if in disbelief at what he had done.

Zon Noret melted to the beach, gasping and coughing blood. The combat mek withdrew immediately, powering down his systems.

Jool knelt beside the dying man and lifted him by the shoulders. "Father . . ."

"I failed to see it . . ." Zon said, his breath rustling through his lungs. "I failed."

The *sensei* mek remained motionless, away from the humans. "I deeply regret what I have done. I had no desire or intention to kill you."

"You will recover," Jool said to the bleeding man, but he could see the wound was mortal. It was all his fault, for having altered the mek's programming. "It's just another wound. You've suffered many of them in your lifetime, Father. We will get you a battlefield surgeon." He tried to pull away and summon help, but Zon clasped him by the wrist.

The veteran fighter turned to the mek, his sweat-streaked hair plastered against his face. "Sensei Chirox, you did . . . exactly as I commanded you." It took him several breaths to force out the words. "You fought precisely . . . as I requested. And you have taught me . . . many useful things."

He looked up at Jool, who bent intently over the old warrior. The lapping surf and seabirds wheeling over the lagoon seemed like a lullaby. The sun slipped below the horizon, fingerpainting the sky with intense colors.

Zon squeezed his son's wrist. "It is time for me to transfer my spirit and pave the way for another fighter. Jool, I want you to forgive Chirox."

He clutched one last time. "And you must become the greatest warrior Ginaz has ever known."

Choking on his words, he said, "As you wish, Father."

Zon Noret closed his eyes, and his son could no longer see the bright scarlet of hemorrhages there. His thoughts drifting, his voice weakening, the elder mercenary said, "Speak the litany with me, Jool. You know the words."

The younger man's voice cracked, but he forced himself to speak. "You taught them to me, Father. All the fighters of Ginaz know the final instructions."

"Good . . . then help me with them." Zon Noret drew in a long, wet-sounding breath, and his words overlapped with his son's as they recited the Litany of the Fallen Mercenary.

"Only thus do we honor the warrior's death: carry on my will, continue my fight."

Moments later, Zon Noret slumped in his son's arms. Silent and rigid, the *sensei* mek stood in position.

Finally, after a poised moment of quiet grief, Jool Noret rose to his feet over his father's body, which lay prone on the beach. Squaring his shoulders, he faced the combat robot and took deep breaths to calm himself. He centered his thoughts, then reached down and picked up Zon's pulse sword from the blood-specked sand.

"From this day forward, Chirox," he said. "You must work even harder to train *me*."

Those who refuse to fight against thinking machines are traitors to the human race. Those who do not use every possible weapon are fools.

—Zufa Cenva, "Lectures to Sorceress Trainees"

LOOKING CAREFULLY ACROSS the verdant treetops of the dense jungles of Rossak, Zufa Cenva could still envision scars from the horrific cymek attack more than two decades earlier.

Armed in their most brutal warrior forms, the vengeful cymeks had descended upon Rossak after Zufa's first Sorceress weapon destroyed the Titan Barbarossa. While a full-fledged robotic fleet attacked the transfer stations in orbit, cymeks had swept down, burning the jungle and launching explosives into the cliff cities. In order to win the battle, many of Zufa's best Sorceress trainees had died that day, sacrificing themselves by unleashing a mental holocaust that vaporized all machines with human minds . . .

The voraciously fecund silvery-purple jungle had grown back, sealing the scars much faster than Zufa could heal the scars in her own mind.

Since that time, she'd continued to train the Rossak women who demonstrated the greatest telepathic potential, candidates who could be taught how to build their psychic powers to critical levels and then release them in shockwaves capable of vaporizing cymeks, even Titans. Over the years the chief Sorceress had seen a great many of her surrogate daughters march off to their deaths, martyring themselves in order to score important victories against the horrific cymeks.

Zufa considered cymeks the worst monsters. Although they had once been human, their ambition and desire for immortality had brought them over to the side of Omnius, making them traitors, not unlike the human infiltrators captured by Iblis Ginjo and his ever-vigilant Jipol officers.

Many in the League of Nobles had begun to wonder if this terrible bloody Jihad would ever end. Zufa did not think that way. She knew that as long as the fight continued, she could never give up. Year after year until the war ended she had to create and deliver and endless supply of fighters.

Even though she understood this, as she looked at the young girls arrayed with her atop the cliffs of Rossak, the oldest of them barely fourteen, Zufa wanted to weep. So many Sorceresses had already done their suicidal duty that the eager trainees had become younger and younger with each passing year. While these candidates might be talented, they were still just *children*.

Working hard to show no dismay, she scrutinized the young class. Their eyes were bright, and their long pale hair was ruffled by the breezes that swept across the uninhabitable plains between the fertile, deep canyons. The girls' expressions were eager, their determination unwavering.

Zufa wished she could save all of these volunteers . . . but knew that nothing would really save them short of peace brought about by complete victory.

"I invest my greatest hopes in all of you," she said. "I cannot deny that danger lies ahead. Even if you succeed, you die. And if you fail, you also die — but worse, it will have been to no purpose. I am here to make certain your lives and your deaths are not in vain, that you are instrumental in destroying Omnius and his thinking machine minions."

The girls nodded, listening attentively. Despite their youth, they all knew this was not a game.

Off in the distance, scarlet-tipped volcanoes oozed lava onto the harsh plains while spewing thick, sulfurous smoke into the tainted atmosphere. Great gorges in the landscape sheltered thriving ecosystems in the volcanic soil and the rich water that percolated through aquifers.

The Rossak environment was permeated with contaminants that were not completely removed from the food chain — mutagens and teratogens, as well as beneficial chemicals. Pregnancies were difficult and often terminated in miscarriages. Many babies were born terribly deformed; others, like these young women, received a mental boost, an advantage in telepathic powers that no one else in the League possessed.

Oh, how Zufa had wanted a daughter of her own to be as powerful as these young women, someone to whom she could pass the candle. But though she had chosen her mates with great care, even running genetic tests to prove that the DNA matches were likely to result in talented offspring, she had failed in every instance. After severing her ties with

Aurelius Venport, she had taken no further lovers. Once, he had seemed to be the perfect candidate for her, but his seed had resulted in only twisted miscarriages.

Zufa was old now, near the end of her childbearing years even with the improved stamina and reproductive systems of the Sorceresses of Rossak. Venport's pharmaceutical discoveries, distillations of drugs from the fungi and underground bulbs that filled the mysterious jungles, allowed new treatments that dramatically reduced the risk of miscarriages and birth deformities while increasing fertility. Zufa found it ironic that Venport himself had discovered a pharmaceutical solution to this situation, after he had caused her so much disappointment.

But she put such thoughts aside. Closing her eyes, she concentrated on the vital task before her.

Zufa gave the students instructions, telling them what to practice, and how. They stood before her like children in a school, hands extended, eyes wide open. Their pale hair rose up crackling with static electricity as they built up the volatile power within their youthful brains.

Because of Zufa's work here, the Army of the Jihad delivered regular reports of their scouting missions. Mercenaries flew fast ships to keep tabs on the movements of Omnius's forces — in particular, cymek depredations. When cymeks were tracked, her Sorceresses would know, and it was up to Zufa to choose the appropriate female warrior, the appropriate weapon, to go forth and expend her life in a telepathic attack that would annihilate the machines with human minds.

But it had been months since any report had given her good news. The cymeks knew the Sorceress's tactics by now, and rarely allowed one of their vulnerable number to travel alone. Instead, combat robots provided heavy escorts and extraordinary firepower for each cymek, especially the remaining Titans. It was difficult for a lone Sorceress to get close enough for her mental blast to have any effect.

So Zufa would wait and train until she found the perfect opportunity. She refused to waste these talented and dedicated young women. They were Rossak's most vital resource.

When the girls had completed their exercises, Zufa beamed with genuine pride. "That is excellent. I believe you understand the concept. Now, watch me."

She raised her pale hands and closed her eyes, spreading her fingers apart so that a faint silvery web of electricity crackled between them. "Accessing the power itself is not the difficult part," she said, her voice flat, her lips bloodless. "Your most difficult job is to *control* it. You must become a precision weapon, a sharp blade guided by a skilled assassin. Not just a destructive accident."

The girls extended their hands, and sparks jumped and popped. Some of them giggled, but quickly controlled themselves and concentrated on the gravity of the task. Zufa saw that they felt the power and sensed the danger.

More than anything, she wished that her own daughter might have been a brave patriot such as these. But her lone offspring, Norma, had no such skill. Her abilities as a Sorceress were nonexistent, a completely blank telepathic slate. Wasting her life, Norma occupied herself with equations and designs, dabbling in mathematics instead of developing any latent abilities that she might possess. Tio Holtzman on Poritrin had taken her under his wing, and Zufa was grateful for the pity the great scientist had shown her malformed child.

But after all this time, apparently even Holtzman wanted little more to do with Norma, and had sent her off to dabble with her ideas where she would bother no one else.

Zufa had not completely severed ties with Norma but was still reluctant to face such an immense personal disappointment by visiting her. She had placed so much hope in her.

Perhaps one day Zufa would have another child, if she could find a man worthy of contributing his DNA to the Cenva bloodline. Then all would be right again.

For now, though, these girls were the closest to genuine daughters that she had, and Zufa vowed not to let them down. As she opened her eyes, she became conscious of her own hair whipping around her, as if in a silent hurricane.

The trainees seemed intimidated and awed, as they stood back and watched her. Zufa smiled at them. "That is good. Now let us go through it again."

176 B.G.

JIHAD YEAR 26

One Year after the Battle for IV Anbus

The more I study the phenomenon of human creativity, the more mysterious it seems. Their whole process of innovation is elusive, but is critical for us to understand. If we fail in this endeavor, thinking machines are doomed.

—Erasmus, laboratory notes

W HEN NORMA CENVA'S enthusiastic letter finally reached him, Aurelius Venport wasted no time in diverting one of his merchant ships for a special run to Poritrin. Despite the fact that his position as Directeur of VenKee Enterprises placed many demands on his time, he wanted nothing more than to see his dear friend Norma again. He'd always had a soft spot in his heart for her, and it had been years . . . too many years.

Open and genuine, Norma was able to see Venport differently from the way other people saw him, without his politics, connections, or wealth. Invariably, they always wanted something from VenKee Enterprises, seeking to gain some personal advantage. In contrast, the small-statured, plain-looking daughter of Zufa Cenva had always offered him true *friendship,* a commodity sorely lacking in the merchant's life.

Besides, he was weary of the tedious legal actions that Lord Bludd kept filing against VenKee, demanding his glowglobe-derived profits, trying to freeze his corporate assets. It was all so ridiculous, but still the Poritrin noble might prevail legally. Continuing to fight the matter through the courts could be a serious drain on VenKee resources, so Venport had requested a meeting with Lord Bludd here in Starda and planned to negotiate a compromise.

But first, he wanted to see Norma.

At one time, when she had been Tio Holtzman's golden child, she'd had her own spacious laboratories and work rooms inside the Savant's blufftop estate. But he had worked her relentlessly, siphoning off her ideas and discoveries; then, when poor Norma strayed into such esoteric research that she no longer produced breakthroughs with sufficient frequency, Holtzman had relegated her to inferior quarters, by the mudflats of the Isana River.

Even after a quarter century on Poritrin, she was still a "visiting scientist" whose papers could be revoked at any time. Why did Holtzman keep her on? Probably to claim legal credit for anything she developed while working under his auspices.

Across the delta, factories and giant shipyards were launching the last components of the huge new fleet being assembled in orbit over Poritrin. The air smelled of smoke and metal, resounding with a din that must have made it impossible for her to concentrate. He wondered how she got anything done here.

Venport stood at the doorway to Norma's quarters and workspace overlooking the odorous mudflats, taking in all the subtle details of how far she had fallen, things she had probably never noticed. He shook his head, sickened and angry at how Holtzman was treating the sweet girl. *Girl?* He shook his head at the realization. By now, Norma was over forty years old.

Standing under the humid sunlight, he pressed the door signal. In accordance with Poritrin tradition, he expected a Buddislamic slave to answer, then remembered that Norma held a dim view of enforced labor.

Her last letter had been ecstatic about a new concept she had developed after years of effort and blind-ends. He smiled fondly, thinking of her intelligent exuberance. Engrossed in her idea and her proposal, Norma had let her scrawling penmanship degenerate even worse than usual, as if her thoughts were racing far ahead of her hand.

Venport had skipped over the mathematics and engineering derivations that demonstrated how to modify the Holtzman effect so that it distorted space itself. He had no doubt that her concepts were correct, but as a merchant he was more interested in the commercial applications and in beating out his business competitors, rather than in the details of a product's functionality. Norma was always brilliant, but rarely practical.

For a long moment no one came to the door, so he signaled again. Venport understood that Norma must be deep in concentration, drifting in her own world of equations and symbols. He felt guilty for interrupting, but decided to wait for her as long as necessary.

She wouldn't be expecting him, though public shipping records had announced the arrival of a VenKee ship. Business obligations had delayed him for an extra month on Salusa, and space travel was so tediously slow . . .

Acting on the strength of her enthusiasm in the letter, he had also called his business partner in the melange operations, Tuk Keedair, to join them on Poritrin. The former flesh-merchant had matters to handle in Starda anyway, so Venport would be able to obtain a second opinion . . . if he wanted it.

But first Venport needed to look into Norma's eyes as she talked about her space-folding concept. Then his instincts would tell him all he had to know. He looked forward to the expression of delight and surprise on her face.

He was not at all disappointed. When she finally stood at the door, blinking in the sunlight, she stared up at him — and his heart felt light with joy. "Norma!" He embraced her before she recognized him, and soon she was laughing and leaping up to throw her arms around his neck.

The tiny woman's mouse-brown hair was an uncared for mop, but her eyes sparkled with surprise. She looked older, as did he, although frequent use of melange had dramatically slowed Venport's own aging process.

"Aurelius, you got my letter. You came."

Though she had changed, Venport remembered all the times the two of them had gone into the jungles on Rossak to explore the silvery-purple foliage. She had rambled on about her ideas, sharing them with him, and he had pulled strings to have her mathematical treatises published and distributed. When Holtzman invited her to become his research partner, Venport had paid for Norma's passage. Zufa Cenva always claimed that they got along so well together because "misfits enjoy the company of their own."

Now, smiling, he rubbed her hair teasingly. "I'm anxious to hear about your exciting new discovery. I also need to take care of this glowglobe dispute with Lord Bludd."

She led him into her ramshackle work building, and he followed with some trepidation. The large room was as messy as he had expected, filled with numerous complex projects. One alcove contained a small table surrounded by floating suspensor chairs that rested at odd angles. Dirty dishes, plans, and calculation sheets covered the table surface, and she began to clear away the debris so that Venport would have a place. Dutiful as a friend and guest, he helped her.

Finding a pile of legal documents with his name mentioned in the text of a threatened complaint, his pulse quickened. They were addressed to Norma from an advocate representing Lord Bludd and Tio Holtzman. "Norma, what are these papers?"

"I don't know," she said absent-mindedly. Then, looking closer, she said, "Oh. *Those.* Nothing of importance."

"These were served on you almost a year ago. They threatened you with legal action if you left Holtzman's employ, especially if you went to work directly for me."

"Yes, yes, I suppose. I've been too busy to deal with that. My project goes beyond any legal concerns."

"Norma, dear naïve Norma, no project goes beyond legal concerns in the real world." His face reddened. "You shouldn't have let this matter slide for so long. Let me take care of it for you." He tucked the papers under his arm.

"Oh yes, thank you."

Venport cared about Norma a great deal, like a big brother, maybe even more. Her small stature and physical failings did not trouble him in the least. He had, after all, spent many years with the utter visual perfection of her statuesque mother, but ultimately he had found Zufa relentlessly judgmental and demanding — of him, of herself, and of everyone around her. For her part, Norma had many more positive attributes than she lacked. Her mind was the most attractive thing about her, as well as her pleasant, accommodating disposition.

Venport looked around, noting the old facility, the cheap equipment, the cramped spaces. It was an insult to the woman who had developed so many of the Savant's most famous inventions. The lighting was poor, the furniture old, the shelves overflowing. He would find her something better, and soon. "Norma, I know you don't like to use slaves, but I am going to have to see about obtaining a housekeeper for you."

"I am content, as long as I can work."

Privately, he asked himself how much he owed Norma, and how much he believed in her. Closing his eyes, he "listened" to his body, his heart, his visceral sensations. The answer was obvious.

I need to help her. Whether or not her new space-folding concept had commercial potential, he promised himself he would free her from the clutches of the egotistical scientist . . . even if it cost him dearly.

It took Aurelius Venport little time to discover that he despised both Lord Niko Bludd and Tio Holtzman.

In his decades of finding, developing, and shipping pharmaceuticals from Rossak — a business he had built into a large commercial empire — Venport had faced off against tough negotiators, unsavory suppliers, even governmental thugs. He bore no resentment toward legitimate rivals: He could understand them and reach accommodations with them.

But he also had a reliable gut instinct when dealing with people, and as soon as he came close to Bludd and Holtzman, his skin began to crawl. The Savant was an obvious fraud who had built up his reputation by stepping on the backs of others. Lord Bludd reveled in riches, not as a means to build his legacy or to earn a place in history — he simply accrued luxurious wealth for its own sake.

Nevertheless, Venport needed to reach an agreement with these men.

As he approached a long table inside a room full of mirrors and faceted glowglobes — unauthorized reproductions, he noted — Venport thought this meeting chamber looked more like a banquet hall than a boardroom for conducting business. At the head of the table, plump Lord Bludd sat engulfed in plush robes with billowing sleeves, a costume that could not possibly have been comfortable. His long hair was styled into precious ringlets. The curls of his beard had been sprayed to freeze them in place like a sculpture made of wiry hair.

Savant Holtzman sported stiff and formal white robes, but seemed more comfortable in them than in the utilitarian laboratory smock a real scientist might wear. Other chairs were occupied by counsel representatives and attorneys for Poritrin, all of whom looked stern and hawkish.

Entering the room alone, Venport studied the professionals that Poritrin had arrayed against him, and sighed heavily as he sat down. "Lord Bludd, Savant Holtzman, I have come by myself concerning a matter of interest to both of you. I wish to candidly discuss possible solutions to our dispute." He scowled at all of the attorneys. "If you would do me the courtesy of dismissing these extra ears, we can sit down like men and reach an accord."

The indignant attorneys sat up quickly, as if spring-loaded. Savant Holtzman seemed confused, but said nothing. Lord Bludd was defensive. "These are my chosen experts, Directeur Venport. I rely heavily on their—"

"Then you may have them vet any agreement we propose. *Later*. But if you insist on conducting this through formal channels, we all know the matter will drag on for years and years at great expense." He smiled disarmingly. "Wouldn't you rather hear what I have to say first?" Venport crossed his arms and waited, making it clear that he intended to engage in no negotiations until the legal armada departed.

The nobleman glanced at his advisors, who uttered a chorus of, "My Lord, we strongly advise against . . ." "This is most irregular and suspicious . . ." "What is he trying to hide that he doesn't want . . ."

Lord Bludd dismissed them all with a snap of his fingers and then called for refreshments. Venport met the nobleman's eyes. They both understood that they would get far more accomplished quietly, behind closed doors.

Holtzman cleared his throat and picked up papers from the table in front of him. "Before you begin, Directeur Venport, I believe you should understand that VenKee Enterprises really has no case." He extended one of the documents. "This is a release signed by Norma Cenva when she first came to work for me. In it she acknowledges that whatever technologies and ideas she develops while working under my auspices belong to the citizens of Poritrin to do with as we wish. She had no right to give you an extremely valuable commercial patent."

Venport studied the document, reading the words which he had already managed to see by bribing Senator Hosten Fru back on Salusa Secundus. No surprises there. Unimpressed, he pushed the document back.

"I do not challenge that Norma's signature is genuine, Savant Holtzman. Can you also offer similar proof that Norma was given full access to legal counsel and professional advice before she signed such a ridiculous document? Can you also prove that she was of legal age to enter into the agreement? According to my records — and they are accurate, since I am the man who arranged for her transport to Poritrin in the first place — she was only fifteen years old when she departed from Rossak." He tapped his fingertips on the table. "Tell me, Lord Bludd, is this truly a matter you wish exposed in open League court?"

Servants hurried in to serve lunch, and Venport waited until the clatter and disruption had died down. He wanted no extra ears to hear their conversation, though he was certain the Poritrin nobleman was recording every one of his words — again, inadmissible in any court, since Venport had never consented to such surveillance.

"Gentlemen," he continued, "Norma Cenva is a treasure and a genius. I don't believe you give her the respect, resources, or freedom that she deserves."

"Norma has lived off of our good will for many years," Holtzman said. "In the decades that she's been with us she has accomplished nothing worthwhile since . . . since . . ." He shrugged. "I will have to look at my records."

"That is no surprise, considering the embarrassing and inferior work space you've provided for her."

"But before that she —"

"Enough squabbling," Lord Bludd interjected. "Whatever the circumstances, the very foundation of your lucrative glowglobe industry was developed here on Poritrin. My own treasury paid for the research. VenKee Enterprises is not entitled to all those profits."

"I understand your basis for objection," Venport said, sure to keep the smallest conciliatory tone in his voice. "I am willing to forfeit a certain portion of VenKee's income derived from the sale of glowglobes." He held out his finger as both Holtzman and Bludd lit up with delighted surprise — "on the condition that Norma is freed from her obligations to work for Savant Holtzman."

"I agree to that," Holtzman said quickly, as if struggling not to laugh.

Bludd glared at him for assenting so easily and then frowned back at Venport. "And in return you agree to share your glowglobe profits in perpetuity?"

Venport sighed. Negotiations were usually not done under such outrageous terms. "Not in perpetuity," he answered in a scolding voice. No reasonable man would have even suggested such a thing. "We will establish a set term and a set percentage."

And from that point, the real work began.

Venport knew that he had to protect the naïve and innocent Norma from future entanglements with these crafty men, and to separate her from all of her fruitless efforts in the past. He had already made extensive calculations about how much this legal dispute was likely to cost him. The League court, greased with bribes from the Poritrin noble family, would surely impose a "compromise" solution that would still cost Venport a great deal in the long run. Right now he wanted to cut his losses and stop wasting time.

After hours of talk, Venport finally agreed to share with Poritrin a third of the profits from glowglobe sales for the next twenty years, while the other side agreed not to fight his claim to the original patents. Knowing how much income the widespread — and ever increasing — sale of glowglobes generated, both Bludd and Holtzman were astonished. Obviously they saw it as an instant influx of money for which they needed to do no work, since Norma Cenva had already done the development in years past and Venport himself had paid for the manufacturing facilities.

Two decades seemed a long time, but Venport knew how to look at the big picture. Glowglobes would continue to be used for centuries, perhaps even millennia. Twenty years was a laughable period of time when viewed in that context. Without a doubt, Lord Bludd's descendants would moan in disgust at the foolish bargain he had made here today.

"However," Venport said, leaning forward and hardening his voice, "there is one stipulation that is absolutely non-negotiable. From this point forward, you will not challenge or dispute Norma Cenva's right to set up another laboratory of her own, and you will not hinder her from pursuing any further research as she chooses."

Holtzman snorted. "As long as I don't have to pay for it. She's produced nothing tangible for years anyway."

Lord Bludd toyed with his curled beard. "I will have my attorneys draw up an agreement specifically stating that Norma can keep anything she develops from this day forward."

Venport nodded. He already felt the great cost of this bargain, but he harbored no doubts, for he had faith in Norma and cared for her deeply. Nonetheless, he was uncomfortable about the innate truth in Holtzman's statement. Norma *had* fixated for years on a problem that might ulti- mately prove fruitless. He didn't understand the implications of her space-folding equations, but the businessman gritted his teeth and reminded himself of how much money Norma had already made for him with the invention of the glowglobes alone.

He would show a faith in her that her mother never had.

"I trust this matter is now concluded?" Lord Bludd said, raising his eyebrows.

Venport stood, eager to get out of the nobleman's tower residence. He knew, however, that the matter was just beginning.

Upon arriving at Starda Spaceport on Poritrin, Tuk Keedair looked frustrated and stressed. Venport met him there, and listened as the Tlulaxa merchant described the constant sabotage and other difficulties caused by an outlaw group on Arrakis. "I understand there's another Tlulaxa flesh-merchant newly arrived here on Poritrin, trying to buy domesticated slaves? Maybe I can convince him to go back to that desert hellhole and round up all the bandits as slaves."

"No one would complain," Venport said with a smile. Then he explained what Norma had developed, and why he had insisted that his business partner come hear it for himself.

As they left the spaceport and rode a groundcar to Norma's riverside laboratory, Keedair was skeptical but intrigued. "A prototype spaceship will cost much more than a few sample glowglobes, Aurelius — but if this space-shortcut idea proves successful, the potential for profits is . . . staggering." The Tlulaxa man didn't want to know the fine details of the mathematics either, only that the concept could work, if properly devel- oped. He stroked his long braid, as if anticipating the continued growth of his wealth.

Venport took him by the arm. "If the system is possible — and *practical* — all goods could be delivered in a fraction of the time. Cargoes of spice can be shipped from Arrakis as fast as the Zensunni can harvest it. Perishable drugs could be whisked from Rossak to eager markets all across the League. No other merchant could possibly offer better service."

They walked along a creaking dock, and presently stood inside the laboratory building with Norma. "I apologize for the informality," she said. If anything, her tables looked more cluttered to Venport than before. "Years from now we will think back on this day and remember the humble place where we first discussed the greatest concept in the history of space travel."

Keedair seemed reserved, even suspicious. "You have told no one else about this concept of yours? Not Savant Holtzman? Not Lord Bludd?"

Embarrassed, Norma shook her head. "Even Savant Holtzman does not understand his own mathematics. 'The Holtzman Principle just works,' he says." Her voice bore a trace of sad scorn. "And I want to make certain this project is brought to fruition. The Savant does not always complete his large-scale undertakings. He sometimes . . . loses his way in a jungle of equations." She went to the window and looked across at the shipyards and factories on the delta. "He has spent the past year building ship hulls in orbit. Some idea of Primero Atreides—"

"Yes, we saw them when we arrived on Poritrin," Venport said. The orbital lanes had been so crowded with new warships that they had posed a genuine navigational hazard.

Keedair looked aghast. "What is the purpose in building ship hulls? Just hulls? Someone else is doing the mechanical installations?"

Norma seemed suddenly uneasy. "This is supposed to be a secret, and only a few people know the full plan. The shipyard slaves and orbital construction workers each work on a small part. No one knows that it's all a giant bluff, a lot of foolery." She sighed. "The hulls will remain empty, just orbiting like a real armada. I acknowledge that the artifice may work, but why would a great man like Savant Holtzman waste his intellect on such a scheme? It requires no *science*, only window dressing."

She lowered a suspensor chair, climbed onto it, then lifted herself up to an adequate height at the table. "That's I why I wrote to you, Aurelius. I have spent a good portion of my life working on these space-folding equations. They must be taken seriously. The project *must* become a reality, and I am the only one who can do it."

Keedair splayed his hands on the tabletop, his dark eyes glistening. "Give us the broad strokes, please. Tell us what you envision."

Norma's hazel eyes narrowed. "In my mind I have seen immense space vessels that can travel in the blink of an eye. I see powerful armies delivered across incredible distances in a matter of moments, surprising the thinking machines."

Venport saw the intensity of her expression, felt her conviction and sincerity. "I believe you, Norma. Enough to invest whatever money you need, even though it's something I don't understand." He smiled. "I'm investing in *you*."

Earlier, she had provided rough estimates of the costs required to fund her project. Venport increased her figure by half, then decided to double it. Norma rarely allowed for unforeseen delays and peripheral, costly details.

"Your service with Savant Holtzman is severed," Venport announced. "I made all the arrangements, and you no longer need to worry about him. You can leave Poritrin any time you desire . . . and work wherever you like."

Delighted, Norma came over to hug him. He loved the way she smiled in appreciation and complete sincerity. There was nothing disingenuous about her. "That's very nice, but I like working here. On Poritrin. I have been here for twenty-seven years. I can't just pack up and go somewhere else."

"Why not Rossak?" Keedair asked. "You come from there, don't you?"

Thinking of Zufa Cenva and the palpable disappointment she expressed about her daughter, Venport shook his head even before Norma could answer. "No, I don't think that would be a good idea."

"Our initial investment and startup expenses would be smaller if we didn't have to move everything offworld," the Tlulaxa merchant pointed out. "And you did receive guarantees and reassurances fron Lord Bludd, correct?"

Norma tapped her temple. "Everything is here." She turned to look wistfully up at Venport, making him feel warm and benevolent inside. "But I would rather not waste all that time and trouble. Isn't there someplace closer, where I can just keep working? This is my home, afterall."

Venport smiled. "I expected as much, and have already been sniffing around for a new place where you can work — a suitable facility with plenty of space and light, everything you need. I have my eye on an abandoned set of mining warehouses and an ore-processing facility in a side canyon up the river. I think it can be modified into a full-scale test bed for a starship." He had known Norma would be too independent to just leave.

Keedair's eyes flickered back and forth, as if he was doing calculations in his head. "VenKee Enterprises has an infrastructure to channel funds to you. We require a detailed schedule showing how much you expect to spend initially, and month by month."

The small woman looked troubled, as if she would rather return to her formulas than engage in this conversation. "All right, I'll do the research and development budget projections once you tell me when we can start."

"The other necessity," Keedair said, firmer now, "is that you must keep the operation absolutely secret. We already know Savant Holtzman is eager to steal your ideas and our patents. We will need an airtight security system for all workers on the project. I suggest we look into hiring a private mercenary force that has no allegiance to Lord Bludd?" He looked at Venport, who nodded.

Norma seemed disturbed by the implications, having never dreamed in her esoteric mind of such problems. He squeezed her shoulder reassuringly. "Norma, you have already surrendered huge profits by letting Holtzman and Lord Bludd exploit the personal shields and portable scrambler generators. Those were at least partially *your* concepts. Holtzman would never have come up with them."

She looked surprised. "But those were my contributions to the war effort."

"And others have benefited from them. Lord Bludd is one of the richest nobles in the League, thanks to you. I don't want people to take advantage of you anymore, dear Norma . . . but if this project goes forward with VenKee's private investment, it must be our proprietary information. That's the way business works."

"Whatever you say, Aurelius. I trust you. How soon can you arrange to let me begin construction of a prototype ship? And I want to set up my new laboratories — as soon and as close, as possible. The calculations are already finished in my head."

Venport put his arm around her shoulders and offered the idea he and Keedair had already discussed. "I have a way to speed things up. My partner and I recently purchased an old cargo ship to expand our fleet of merchant vessels. It's in spacedock at Rossak, undergoing repairs. Instead of building a new vessel, could you refit an existing craft to hold your new engines? Keedair could bring it back here by the time your new facilities are ready."

He and Keedair exchanged glances, then the Tlulaxa man nodded. Norma beamed, looking young, vibrant, and filled with wonder again.

"The sooner the better," she said.

Where one person sees cause for rejoicing, another sees only reason for despair. Pray that you are the former.
          —Buddislamic Sutra, Zensunni interpretation

AFTER A YEAR of massive effort, a huge expenditure of funds and resources, and countless slaves dying in industrial accidents, the final components of the decoy spaceship fleet were assembled in orbit over Poritrin. With the work nearly finished, the foundries in the delta shipyards would be closed down.

Late one afternoon, work supervisors summoned the slave crews from their stations. Squinting, dirty captives emerged from the smoke-filled hangars and stood outside on the paved landing ground from which the final shipments were launched into orbit. Hundreds of unfortunate souls milled about in disorganized ranks.

Ishmael knew that he and his fellow slaves could expect to be assigned to new tasks soon. As always, a time of changes made him uneasy, for fear that he would be separated from Ozza or his two daughters, as Aliid had been taken from his family. Nevertheless, he clung to the hope that Buddallah would keep his family together. The Poritrin slave masters had no reason to separate them.

But every day at the factories, Aliid simmered with unhealed emotional wounds, always looking for his chance. "Long ago, they took from me my wife and newborn son. I no longer care what they do to me." Ishmael feared what his friend might do, given enough provocation.

When Ishmael had been a boy, his grandfather always insisted that he have complete faith in God, that it was arrogance for any person to take matters out of Buddallah's hands and into his own. Still, uncertainty formed icicles within him . . . and Aliid showed no willingness to accept those terms.

As the crew bosses bellowed orders, trying to arrange the slaves into assigned groups for the assembly, Ishmael slipped through the crowd toward a polishing and finishing crew where his wife was stationed. Presently he touched Ozza's arm, and she reached over to take his hand, sensing her husband's nearness without needing to look at him. With so many slaves all in one place, the workmasters would not bother to take attendance or herd the people into appropriate groups. That would take all day.

Through no choice of their own, Ishmael and Ozza were jostled toward the podium where two small men stood beside the main work supervisor. The sunlight was bright, and Ishmael still had trouble adjusting his eyes after the dim and cavernous foundry.

"I wonder if they will announce another celebration of their great society," Ozza asked close to his ear, so that no one could hear her sarcasm.

"I can think of worse reasons for this summons."

He peered up at the two strangers, both of them obviously Tlulaxa . . . the hated slavers. The younger man had sharp features, including a narrow face and dark, close-set eyes. But Ishmael was more intent on the familiar features of the older man with a long, iron-gray braid that hung like a noose rope over one shoulder. In his opposite ear dangled a triangular bronze earring. More than two decades had passed, and Ishmael had been only a terrified boy at the time . . . but he would never forget the face of the man who had led the raid on Harmonthep.

His heart pounded as fresh fear and righteous anger swelled within him. He had sworn vengeance against this man, vowing to crush him. Right now, Ishmael wished he could lunge to the podium and wrap his work-strengthened hands around the slaver's throat. It was what his friend Aliid would have done — Aliid, who had always scorned Ishmael's patience and blind faith.

But vengeance was not what the Zensunni sutras taught. Ishmael's grandfather would have been deeply disappointed in him. *It is in God's hands, not mine.*

But must I simply forgive and forget?

Ozza looked at him, touched his face with gentle fingertips. He saw concern there. "What is it, Ishmael?"

"That man . . . I –" He stopped himself, unable to tell her. His grandfather would have insisted on acceptance, even forgiveness. The old man would have demanded that Ishmael look for a deeper lesson from Buddallah, to grow from every trial and experience. God did not guarantee a soft and peaceful life to every member of the faithful — at least not in this world. The sutras instructed the Zensunni to accept, endure, and wait for Buddallah to choose the right moment.

But it was so difficult.

After nearly half an hour of passive chaos, the hundreds of slaves had finally arranged themselves and quieted down. At the front of the throng, Ishmael heard the work supervisor speaking to the younger Tlulaxa. "Rekur Van, these are all the members of our slave crew working today. They have been assigned to the ship construction project for months. We cannot spare them."

"Nevertheless, I wish to see them." The leaner, rodentlike Tlulaxa scanned the faces and the bodies in the crowd. Tuk Keedair, the slaver who had hunted down Ishmael and so many innocent Zensunni on Harmonthep, stood beside him, looking bored. Keedair seemed to have no interest in acquiring new slaves, but had come to Poritrin for another reason entirely.

As Ishmael watched, Rekur Van paced the podium, sweeping a small device across the crowd, with which he took images and analyzed the gathered slaves. "I am required to inventory your captive personnel. They are to be considered resources for the Army of the Jihad. We Tlulaxa desperately need a large number of healthy slaves from a wide range of body and tissue types. This is our highest priority." When the work-master showed his alarm, Rekur Van lowered his voice to a growl. "If you object, I can obtain a signed warrant from Grand Patriarch Ginjo himself."

"No doubt you can, Rekur," said Keedair, in a patient, reasonable tone, "but it is not necessary to insist on the first and most inconvenient alternative."

With a flurry and bustle, a boatcar skimmed over the shallow water of the delta, then drove up on the ground to reach the staging area. Flustered, Tio Holtzman strode imperiously up to the podium. His eyes were narrow, his face a mixture of anger and confusion. "Why do you interrupt my slaves in this important project? Their work is vital, and delay is inexcusable."

"We have a suitable excuse, Savant Holtzman," said Rekur Van, just as imperiously. "The Jihad has an immediate need for slaves, and Poritrin is the nearest world on my route. The Tlulaxa require many new candidates."

Ishmael swallowed hard, then clutched his wife's arm. Both of them looked around for their daughters, but Chamal and Falina had been assigned to different support teams and were nowhere in sight.

"Not from my workers," Holtzman said in a huff. "All of these workers are dedicated to a project vital to the protection of Poritrin and our weapons factories. You'll have to get your slaves someplace else."

"But I am here, Savant Holtzman, and I need slaves now."

"So do I." The scientist made a rude snorting noise. "Why didn't you just capture some of those cowards on IV Anbus? It is my understanding they refused to fight even against the thinking machines that were attacking them . . . and they actually sabotaged the brave jihadis. Could there be any people more worthy of serving the human race?"

"Perhaps that is an indication of their inferiority," Rekur Van suggested. "Besides, they were scattered, and their numbers were . . . insufficient to meet our needs."

Through rumors and slow news, the Poritrin captives had only just learned of the battle on IV Anbus, the Jihad's pyrrhic victory at the cost of so many lives and holy relics. All Buddislamics, including Zensunnis and Zenshiites, revered the sacred city of Darits, storehouse of the original manuscripts of the Koran Sutras. The Poritrin slaves were dismayed to hear of the ruin caused not only by the robot army, but by the forces of the Jihad.

Looking around, Ishmael noted that the humans in control here didn't seem to care. *Why is their religious fervor acceptable, while ours is a matter of scorn?*

He watched the older slaver step between the indignant inventor and the eager flesh merchant. Though he despised the man, Ishmael had to concede that Tuk Keedair seemed wiser and better-versed in the ways of interaction.

"Slaves are available in many places, Rekur. There are plenty of Buddislamic backwaters for the harvesting of flesh. Since these captives are already serving a useful purpose for humanity, I see no need to remove them from the custody of Savant Holtzman."

Rekur Van scowled at his fellow Tlulaxa, as if they were rivals. "And why are you here, Tuk Keedair? You are no longer a flesh merchant, but prefer to sell spice and glowglobes with that alien Venport. Why should you meddle in my important assignment?"

"My partner and I are here on another business venture. Your task is not the only legitimate job in the Army of the Jihad." In a paternalistic manner, Keedair placed his hand on the younger man's shoulder. "Listen, I know where you could raid for more slaves, a large group that is a nuisance to me and, by extension, to the League of Nobles. Come, I will tell you where to hunt them, and everyone will be happy. Are you familiar with the desert world of Arrakis?"

Still frowning but somewhat mollified, Rekur Van accompanied the veteran slaver off the podium.

Ishmael put his arm around Ozza's waist, drawing her close. His pulse continued to race, and he sensed that they had narrowly dodged disaster. He and his family could remain here, together. And, as much as he resented his captivity on Poritrin, he felt in his heart that serving the Tlulaxa would have been far worse.

Holtzman looked satisfied and stared down at the gathered workers. Finally, the inventor waved his hands imperiously. "Why are you just standing there? We must finish this project on schedule! Get to work."

For all their computerized precision, thinking machines can be confused in many different ways.
> — Primero Vorian Atreides, *Evermind Nevermore*

THE EXTRAVAGANT "HOLLOW ship" bluff at Poritrin was the brainchild of Primero Atreides, who claimed to understand the way machines thought. But Tio Holtzman was implementing the scheme in the absence of the Primero . . . which put him in position to take most of the credit.

If the epic ruse worked.

The Savant was nervous, but had gambled that he would be showered with kudos and hails of appreciation. He needed them, after a long hiatus in the stream of awards that had marked his career. With luck, Lord Bludd would bestow medals upon him, and the people would cheer. Tio Holtzman would be declared the savior of Poritrin . . .

As he dined with Lord Niko Bludd on the balcony of the nobleman's tower residence overlooking the river city, Holtzman watched the quiet lives all around him. The upper classes of Poritrin had always been surprisingly lax in their attitudes, believing that nothing truly bad could happen to them. They followed the passive tenets of Navachristianity, more for appearances than out of deep conviction. The climate was calm, while food and resources were abundant, and well-domesticated slaves took care of every need. The gentle Isana River seemed an apt metaphor for the languid flow of their lives.

Holtzman feared that would all change as soon as the robot war group arrived. Only moments before, a military courier had rushed up to the Lord with a message cylinder. Bludd read the communication, then stroked his immaculately curled beard. "Well, Tio, we shall see if your scheme is going to work. A massive machine battle fleet is indeed on its way into the Poritrin system."

Holtzman paled and swallowed hard. Lord Bludd seemed supremely self-assured, certain that his greatest Savant could not possibly let them down. Holtzman hoped the nobleman's blithe confidence had not been misplaced.

Bludd chuckled at his worried expression. "Don't trouble yourself, Tio. Even with the incredible expenditures required by this crazy project of yours, we'll make enough from VenKee's glowglobe profits to pay for it a dozen times over."

All of the faux battleships had been completed in space, and the orbits around Poritrin were populated with intimidating-looking vessels, hundreds of ballistas and javelins in a seemingly invincible war fleet, like ferocious guard dogs patrolling a yard. A mere facade.

Dozens of Jihad battleships — real ones — stood on the Starda Spaceport field, ready to be sent into combat. Regimented jihadi soldiers were stationed near the vessels, their numbers augmented by mercenaries from Ginaz. None of that would be enough, however, if the bluff didn't work.

Holtzman forced himself to take a bite of spiced riverfish, hoping Bludd wouldn't notice his hesitation. "Time to put on our little show. Let's give the order for our forces to redistribute their orbits. I advise keeping half of them in the planet's shadow as an added surprise for the robot fleet."

In recent months, the Army of the Jihad had inserted bits of misinformation into communications they knew would be intercepted by Omnius, even including some accurate material, because it served Holtzman's purposes to reveal it to the enemy: anti-machine propaganda for the fighters on Ix . . . signals leaked to the escaping robot fleet at IV Anbus . . . and more.

If the information reached its intended audience, the machine armies would be convinced that the great Tio Holtzman was expanding his successful shield system on Poritrin in order to protect fleets of Jihad ships, to create invisibility fields and extraordinarily durable hull armor. This should make the technology a tactical prize for Omnius.

Bait.

"I gave that order as soon as we received a signal from our picket ships," Bludd said. "I'm confident they were safely out of view long before robot sensors could have detected them." Then, smiling, he suggested that the two of them step back inside, where they could observe the encounter in comfort within the nobleman's projection room. Holtzman looked at the displayed maps and grids of the planetary sphere and orbital paths, saw that all the ships had taken their proper positions. He nodded.

Next, glowing shapes approached like bullets from the edge of the screen. Bludd smiled. "Ah, those incoming machine ships are in for a big surprise." He had more confidence than Holtzman, but the Savant dared not show any reservations.

Bristling with heavy weapons and overwhelming firepower, the robot fleet approached Poritrin and slowed as their scanners surveyed the battlefield ahead of them. Holtzman brushed a hand across his forehead, stroked thick hair away from his eyes. The enemy had at least three times as many ships as the Poritrin fleet. But that did not present an insurmountable obstacle — if the machines believed the misinformation.

"Now we shall see if human cunning is superior to machine technology," he said.

Standing with Lord Bludd, he listened to the filtered communication transmissions, barked orders, warnings, assessments. On the screens, they watched as the Jihad warships moved into place, spreading their formation out into tactical positions around the planet. By all appearances, they were impenetrable, unbeatable.

The immense machine fleet drove forward implacably in a straight line toward its goal, only to encounter a large group of defenders in Poritrin's orbit. The decoy League vessels held position. Electronic panels on the exteriors of their hulls glowed red, making it look as if they had powered up weapons systems. Sensor signatures transmitted that a huge complement of armaments was ready to be deployed.

Only a handful of these League vessels had any weapons at all, of course. Most of the ships were hollow scrap-metal constructions, masked by Holtzman shields that defied the electronic probes of the thinking machines.

"All systems activated," a tactical officer announced over the speaker system.

A cascade of responding voices showered from the orbiting Jihad warships, including the empty ones. "Ready to annihilate invader ships." "Armaments functional." "Awaiting orders to open fire." "Concentrated attack spread." The voices overlapped, synthesized composites of every pilot in the fleet, recorded, coordinated, and transmitted in a flurry to fool the oncoming robot attackers.

Holtzman stared at the tactical projections. The distant machine ships were tiny diamonds reflecting raw sunlight. He wished he could see what the robots thought they were detecting. Their deceived sensor network should show them that this sham Jihad fleet actually outgunned them by a significant margin. He swallowed again.

In order to win a victory here, the Poritrin fleet didn't need to destroy the machines. Potentially, this ruse was better in the long run, since it could be used again on other worlds . . . and hollow warships could be constructed at a fraction of the cost of real ones. Henceforth, "knowing" that Poritrin was defended by an undefeatable Jihad fleet, Omnius would leave the planet alone and look for more vulnerable targets. In theory . . .

The machines kept coming, though, as if they suspected the truth. Holtzman held his breath, worried that the robots might have a deep scanning system sophisticated enough to see through the trick. What factors had he forgotten to consider?

He had made false assumptions and outright mistakes many times before, as Norma Cenva had so rudely and blithely pointed out to him. At least she was out of his way now, working on her own and wasting someone else's money. He had plenty of other gifted assistants, all of whom had assured him that everything was taken into account here. No chance for error.

Still, if they had missed something, Poritrin was doomed. And Holtzman, too.

"Time to launch," the Savant said, his voice thin and high-pitched. "Our second group needs to move now, before the enemy gets close enough to open fire."

Bludd just smiled. All of the supervisors and captains already had their detailed instructions.

Like an unexpected pack of wild dogs charging out of a forest, half of the decoy vessels in orbit powered up their engines and accelerated, racing around to the sunlit side of Poritrin. It looked like a stampede of Jihad battleships, suddenly doubling the numbers of human defenders arrayed against the thinking machine forces.

"That'll give them second thoughts!" one of the commanders yelped over an open channel.

Holtzman looked at the tactical diagram and was relieved to see the pieces falling into place. A handful of soldiers cheered over the comlines, but their voices — duplicated, modulated, and amplified — sounded like many more.

"Here comes the third detachment."

"It's going to get crowded around here!"

"We'll make plenty of room, if we just sweep away some of these clankers."

Now a third group of decoy ships, hidden near Poritrin's small moon, approached at high acceleration, closing the distance to the Omnius fleet from behind, showing an array of active weapons ports.

"Launch the battleships from the spaceport!" Bludd cried. He was clearly enjoying every moment.

The group of grounded ships — the only truly functional battle vessels stationed at Poritrin — lifted off from Starda Spaceport and roared toward orbit, where they mingled with swarms of decoy craft already there.

The machine invaders came to a dead halt in space, as if to assess these surprising new developments, then regrouped into a defensive cluster.

"Wait for it," one officer transmitted in a grim voice. "Prepare to open fire. Obliterate the damned machines if they give us an excuse."

Someone else said, "They're scanning us again."

"Show them what we think of that."

Mixed in among the swarms of decoy vessels, the real battleships opened fire, taking potshots at the robot vessels. The thinking machine fleet had no way of knowing that the thousands of decoy vessels were not similarly armed.

Finally, without a single transmission, without launching any projectiles at all, the robot fleet calculated that they had no chance of victory — and withdrew. The machine ships reversed course and picked up speed as they departed. Just for good effect, the armed Jihad ships gave chase and blasted a couple of machine warships out of space.

Lord Bludd grinned and clapped Holtzman on the back. "Never doubted you for a minute, Tio. With your reputation and intuition, the stupid machines don't stand a chance!"

"They really are stupid, aren't they?" Holtzman said, grinning.

After the robot war fleet had retreated from the Poritrin system, the victory celebration was lavish and grandiose. The mood was ecstatic, tinged with hysterical relief. Sparing no expense, Niko Bludd put on outrageous feasts, parades, performances, and a succession of public events that became monotonous in their sheer pomposity. Savant Holtzman was hailed as a hero of the Jihad, conqueror of machines. When raising their toasts of spiced Poritrin rum, some of the nobles even remembered to mention the name of Vorian Atreides, albeit in passing.

With the puffed-up scientist standing beside him, Lord Bludd delivered loud, drunken speeches, beating his chest in triumph. "Freedom is a basic human right!"

But the Buddislamic slaves had no cause to celebrate.

A few of the captive Zensunni children remained outside in the residence compound on the fringes of the now-quiet delta foundries and manufacturing centers. Their mouths hung agape as they stared at the spectacular light shows and listened to the distant thumping music.

The adult slaves shut themselves inside their barracks, comforting each other with their own memories and culture. While the gala celebration continued and flashes of light erupted like chrysanthemums over Poritrin's great rolling river, Ishmael sat with his slave companions and exchanged stories of their people's past. By recalling parables and legends, citing the wisdom of the Koran Sutras, they kept alive the memory of how the Zensunnis and Zenshiites had been pursued from world to world, always seeking safe harbors in the cosmic sea where they could be left alone. They had turned their backs on the war of the damned — machine demons versus unbelievers. Neither side was worthy of the support of the faithful, for the Buddislamics were chosen by God, the keepers of the true wisdom of heaven.

Right now, though, tribulations forced them to maintain their faith. "We have to stay strong," Ishmael assured his companions. "Stronger than any of the outsiders."

Then, in shadows at the fringe of the story fire, Aliid surprised them all by objecting. "Perhaps, Ishmael, but *elsewhere* Zensunnis and Zenshiites are free." He drew a quick breath through clenched teeth. "If Bel Moulay were here, all slaves would rise up under his banner. He would show us how to win our way off this planet."

"But he is not here," Ishmael chided, sitting in a meditative position on the hard floor. "That uprising only bought him execution, and all of us have paid the price in the years since."

"Bel Moulay may be dead, but I am not," Aliid grumbled.

"I do not have the audacity to rush God, my friend. Someday," Ishmael promised, "we will find a world that we can inhabit and defend for ourselves. Our lives will be as Buddallah intended."

Aliid looked skeptical, but the other slaves watched Ishmael with bright eyes and hopeful expressions. Ishmael had been making promises to these people for so many years that he wasn't sure how much longer he himself could continue to hope.

Nonetheless, he forced strength into his voice. "Finally, it will be a place we can call *home*."

Sand keeps the skin clean, and the mind.
                              —Zensunni fire poetry from Arrakis

TWO DAYS AFTER his water supply ran out, the boy Aziz was sure he
was going to die. He plodded over dry rocks and through wind-blown
sand. His lips and eyes were caked with fine dust that he could not brush
away. He saw illusions, mirages, and little hope.

Naib Dhartha had sent him out on this important mission, and he had
to last just a few more hours, so that he could complete the task his
grandfather had assigned to him. It was critical.

What if I fail? What if I die without delivering my message? Aziz's father
Mahmad — Dhartha's only son — had been faithful to the tribe, working
diligently with offworlders at the spaceport. Mahmad had run much of
the melange business, dealing with Tuk Keedair and Aurelius Venport,
who sold the spice around the League of Nobles.

Four years ago, Mahmad had contracted a strange alien disease from a
traveler in Arrakis City, suffered at length, and finally died delirious.
Some of the conservative Zensunnis from distant villages claimed that
the sickness had been punishment for mingling with outsiders. While
the old Naib had grieved for his son, death was a way of life on Arrakis
and he considered the loss as a part of their continuing battle for
independence, no less so than falling in battle against an enemy . . .

No longer knowing in which direction he walked, Aziz staggered
through the bleak heat, detecting no sign of the wormriders. He hoped
the bandits would come to his rescue . . . somehow. *Soon.*

The wealth brought by the spice trade had given the Zensunni villagers
a comfortable life. They relied on what they purchased in Arrakis City
more than what they could wrest from the desert's clutches. Out on the

harsh terrain of Arrakis, Aziz had discovered quickly that he had not learned nearly enough of the old survival skills.

The boy did everything he could to make his presence known, calling attention to himself by lighting beacons in the night and flashing mirrors during the day. He could not believe the heroic Selim Wormrider would let him perish at such a young age. The outlaw had looked him right in the eye during the spice raid, and Aziz thought he knew the great man's heart, despite what his grandfather said . . .

Selim and his bandits caused Dhartha far more problems than did offworld diseases. Over the years, constant raids against caravans hauling melange had cut deeply into village profits. Through it all, the Naib refused to make excuses to Tuk Keedair for decreased productivity, whenever he came to pick up spice in Arrakis City. "The bandits are an internal matter," he invariably said in answer to all questions. "Leave us to handle it."

Displeased, Keedair had threatened to send teams of offworld professionals into the deserts, hired trackers and assassins. But Aziz's grandfather had promised to take care of the matter, intent on keeping the business relationship intact, as well as the privacy of the village. And so with a heavy heart, Dhartha had sent his young grandson out alone to search for the bandits, to offer them a truce.

"Selim was once a member of our tribe," the Naib had told him at dusk three days before, just as Aziz prepared to set off into the desert. The two had sat alone by the last embers of the story fire. "As a boy, Selim was found guilty of stealing water and exiled to the desert. We expected him to die, but somehow he survived."

"Yes, Grandfather." Aziz's eyes were bright in the cave shadows. "And he learned how to ride the beasts of the desert."

The old man's deep blue eyes moistened with the recollection. "Since then, while we have learned to harvest and market melange, Selim Wormrider has gathered a band of criminal followers to continue his reign of terror upon our hard-working spice gatherers. I know that Selim hates me for the sentence I imposed on him — and it is time for one of us to forgive the other." He paused. "Or kill the other."

The old Naib had looked weary and broken, and Aziz felt his heart go out to the man. He had made a secret promise that he would find a way to solve the problem, to heal the breach between Naib Dhartha and Selim Wormrider.

"We must end this foolish feud and stand united for our common interests. Otherwise, the offworlders will divide and conquer us all. Even an outlaw like Selim cannot want such a thing. You must find him, Aziz, and tell him what I have said."

Proud of the responsibility, the boy had ventured into the desert, facing the danger with hope and determination. But he had been out here for days, and the fierce desert was unforgiving. Now he wanted nothing more than to curl up and die.

Accompanied by two other outlaws, Marha spied on the youth as he staggered along. She stopped counting how many foolish mistakes he made, and knew he was about to die. Selim had said that incompetence and inattention led to death on Arrakis. The desert had already tested this boy, and found him wanting.

In previous generations, the Zensunni nomads of Arrakis had learned to live in harmony with the harsh environment, but Selim and his followers went one step farther, scraping by with fewer resources than even the old tribes required. Selim's band lived by their own wits and skills, not depending on luxuries, water, or tools from the decadent offworld traders in Arrakis City.

Marha had been with Selim's band for the better part of a year now. She had learned how to fight with blades, survive sandstorms, find places to hide in the deep bled, and how to summon and ride Shai-Hulud. She carried her own crysknife now, a milky curved blade that had once been the tooth of a great worm. It would have been a mercy to slit the boy's throat and let him perish swiftly rather than die a long, lingering death.

And then she had recognized the grandson of Naib Dhartha. Knowing Selim would want to talk to this one in particular, she decided to keep him alive and let Selim make his own decision about the boy's fate.

Under a clear, starlit sky while the boy lay trembling with exhaustion and thirst in the shelter of rocks, the bandits surrounded him. At first, Aziz was convinced that Marha and the others were only a delirious dream. They closed in, shadowy figures who made signals and clicking noises to one another. Aziz was so weak that he could barely lift his head.

They captured him without a struggle and, after giving him a sip of precious water, carried him like a piece of dry wood. He tried to speak his name and tell them why he had come, but his words came out in a feeble croak. Finally, the boy smiled briefly through cracked and bloody lips. "I knew you would come . . ."

Selim Wormrider and his caves were far away, but the outlaws could travel swiftly. When they reached the hidden settlement, Marha saw to it that Aziz was taken to a small isolated alcove, where she gave him more water and a little food, and let him fall into a deep sleep of exhaustion and recovery. Selim himself had ridden off on a worm to raid distant spice fields, and would not return for another day yet.

A long time later the boy awoke inside the cool, dim enclosure. He sat up quickly but almost fainted, then lay back with his eyes open, staring into the swimming shadows, trying to orient himself. Marha startled him when she spoke. "We do not often rescue fools. You are lucky Shai-Hulud did not devour you. How could you come into the desert so poorly prepared?"

She unstoppered a flask of water beside his pallet and let him drink. Despite his burned skin and the shadowed hollows around his eyes, Aziz actually smiled at her. "I needed to find Selim Wormrider." He breathed deeply to restore his energy. "I am –"

Marha cut him off. "I know who you are, grandson of Naib Dhartha. Only your value as a hostage convinced me not to spill the water of your body. Perhaps Selim will wish to torture you to death, extracting vengeance for the crimes of your grandfather."

The boy jerked. "My grandfather is a good man! He wishes only to –"

"Naib Dhartha cast Selim out of the tribe, though he knew full well that another young man was guilty of those crimes. He was not concerned that an innocent orphan would die to save a more important tribal member. The boy who truly committed the theft knew his guilt, as did your grandfather. But Selim was made to pay for those crimes."

Aziz seemed confused. Obviously, no one had ever spoken that way of his grandfather. "That is not the story I have been told."

Marha shrugged at him, and scowled. "Naib Dhartha has forsaken the ways of the desert for offworld conveniences. The people of your village are living a lie. It does not surprise me that you believe them."

In the shadows, the young man squinted at her, finally recognizing her by the scar on her brow. "You were one of us, but ran away. I saw you when you raided our spice caravan."

Marha lifted her chin. "I intend to be the wife of Selim Wormrider." She surprised herself with such a bold admission, but she had made up her mind a month ago. Every member of the band could see it anyway.

Her voice became harder. "I fight against those who seek to destroy Shai-Hulud by exploiting the spice, sending it offworld. Naib Dhartha is our greatest enemy."

Aziz forced himself to sit up. "But I bring a message from my grandfather. He wishes to make peace with Selim Wormrider. There is no need for us to continue our feud."

Marha frowned at him in disdain. "That is for Selim to decide."

*   *   *

When Aziz woke again in the alcove's darkness, it took him several moments to realize that someone sat in utter silence inside the chamber, just behind him. Not Marha . . . but another.

"Are you . . . are you Selim Wormrider?"

"Many seek me and some find me. Few ever return to tell the tale."

"I have heard the tales," Aziz said, feeling very brave. He sat up. "I saw you before, when you raided our spice caravan. You didn't hurt any of us. I think you are a man of honor."

"Unlike your grandfather."

Selim illuminated a small glowpanel. Although dim, the light seemed startlingly bright after Aziz had spent so long in the cave's darkness. "No doubt you revere Naib Dhartha, boy. You think he must be a good person since he leads the tribe. But do not look to him as a hero. And do not believe everything that is said about heroes."

Now Aziz could see that Selim's face was weathered but surprisingly young. His eyes were hard and intelligent, and his expression was more majestic than Aziz had remembered. Vision and destiny were clear in his mind. The boy caught his breath, matching this image with the legends he had heard. Finally, face to face with this larger-than-life man, he found himself at a loss for words.

"I understand you bring a message. What could Naib Dhartha possibly have to say to me?"

Aziz's heart pounded, since this was undoubtedly the most important thing he had ever done, or ever would do. "He bade me tell you that he formally forgives you for the crimes you committed as a boy. The tribe no longer bears you any malice, and my grandfather welcomes you back to our village. He wishes you to rejoin our people, so that we can all live in peace."

Selim laughed at the offer. "I have a mission from Buddallah. I have been chosen to do great work." He smiled humorlessly, his dark blue eyes flashing. "Tell your grandfather that I will absolve the tribe of their guilt as soon as he ceases all spice harvesting."

Astonished, Aziz said, "But our people depend on selling the spice to survive. We have no other way—"

"There are many ways to survive," Selim cut him off. "There were always many ways. My followers have demonstrated this clearly over the years. The Zensunni lived on Arrakis for generations before they became too dependent on offworld luxuries." He shook his head dismissively. "But you are just a boy. I do not expect you to understand." Selim stood. "Gather your strength, and I will take you back to your grandfather. Alive and unharmed." He smiled. "I doubt Naib Dhartha would have shown me the same courtesy."

Oppressive sunlight beat down on them in the stillness of the open sands. "If you run, you will die," Selim Wormrider said.

Aziz stood beside him on the crest of a powdery dune deep in the ocean of sand. "I will not run." His knees felt weak.

The outlaw leader shot him an amused smile. "Remember that, when panic clamors through your mind and your feet want to flee."

Selim placed his hooks and metal rods on the crusty yellow sand, then knelt beside a resonant drum. He wedged the pointed end of the percussion tool into the sand. With brisk, sharp gestures, he pounded on the flat surface. The reverberant boom sounded like a loud explosion, and the shape of the drum directed soundwaves deep into the heart of the dune, into the strata of deposited sand . . . into the lair of the worm. Selim closed his eyes and murmured in a hypnotic rhythm, a call to Shai-Hulud.

Aziz's stomach knotted, but he had promised the heroic Wormrider to stand firm. He trusted Selim. The boy waited and watched. Finally he saw the ripple beneath the dunes, curling tremors. "There it is! A worm is coming!"

"Shai-Hulud always answers the call." Selim kept pounding. Then, as the monster curved around as if stalking its prey, Selim uprooted the drum, gathered his tools, and motioned for the youth to follow. "We must get into position. Walk lightly and with random steps, not like the march of an offworld soldier. Remember who you are!"

They hurried along the spine of the ridge. The beast continued toward the last loud reverberations, then rose up and up, shedding a river of sand and dust as if molting a layer of skin.

Aziz had never been so close to one of the demons. The smell of melange was overpowering, a flinty, fiery stench of cinnamon mingled with brimstone. He felt sweat on his brow, a waste of bodily moisture.

Exactly as the Wormrider had predicted, Aziz wanted to run screaming, but instead he whispered a prayer to Buddallah and remained fixed, waiting. He felt as if he was going to faint from the excitement.

Selim gathered his tools and lunged at the exact moment the sandworm crested. He pounced between the encrusted ridges and drove his spear and hooks into the sensitive flesh, trailing knotted ropes. He shouted to Aziz, "Climb! Grab the rope!"

The young man could barely hear over the roar of the monster, the rush of torn sand, but he understood. Fueled by adrenaline, he raced forward, though his heart caught in his throat. Aziz gritted his teeth and tried not to breathe the choking stench. Clinging to the knotted cable he scrambled up, bracing his boots against the pebbly skin of the monstrous worm.

Selim had the creature under control; Aziz never doubted it. As they stood atop the high ridges and Shai-Hulud undulated across the ocean of dunes, Aziz could barely contain his sense of wonder and amazement. He was riding a worm, crossing the distance to his village, just like all the legends had said. Selim did indeed control the desert demons!

Aziz fought conflicting emotions. He respected his grandfather, but found himself doubting if such a man as the Wormrider could possibly tell falsehoods. He felt even more respect than before, an awe so great that it numbed his entire body. At last, after all the years of hearing the legend of Selim, the famed Wormrider had taken on flesh and substance.

The long journey passed in a blur, and Aziz knew he would never forget his wonderment and dread. When Selim finally instructed the boy how to tumble away from the half-spent creature, Aziz staggered across the sands toward the rocky cliffs of his village.

His knees shaking, his muscles tingling with fatigue and exhilaration, Aziz climbed a rugged cliffside path, knowing that many of his fellow villagers were watching from cave entrances. Bearing Selim's defiant response to Naib Dhartha's proposal, the young man turned back to watch the Wormrider guide the slow-moving monster off into the endless sands, where the legendary outlaw would return to his glamorous life of banditry.

Human beings can always improve themselves. This is one of the advantages they have over thinking machines . . . until I find a way to mimic all of their senses. And sensibilities.
     —Erasmus, *Reflections on Sentient Biologicals*

THE ROBOT ERASMUS maintained a complete record of every conversation he ever had. Omnius kept his own files, including conversations between the two of them, but Erasmus suspected the records would not match in every detail.

The autonomous robot preferred to let his own thoughts grow and evolve, rather than receive a steady stream of updates from Omnius. Like the evermind, he was an evolving thinking machine — and like Omnius, he had his own agenda.

At the moment Erasmus sat in warm red sunshine on the terrace of his Corrin villa, admiring a panoramic view of rugged, barren mountains in the distance. From earlier explorations, centuries ago, he recalled the craggy profiles, sheer dropoffs, abrupt canyons. In the early years of his machine life he had been trapped there, imprisoned in a crevasse, and that ordeal had led to the development of his independent character.

Now the robot had no need to climb mountains and engage in wilderness exploration. Instead, he was charting the unknown, confusing landscape of the human psyche. With so many possibilities for enlightenment, Erasmus had to set priorities, especially now that Omnius had instructed him to focus on the phenomenon of religious zealotry, an apparent form of madness.

A house slave appeared carrying an armful of rags and bottles. Well-fed, she was a dark woman with brilliant green eyes. Rising to his feet, Erasmus removed his plush carmine robe and let it drop to the slate tiles beneath his feet. "I am ready."

The servant set to work, polishing the robot's shimmering platinum skin. Noting how the ruddy red-giant sunlight gleamed on his body like the reflection of a bonfire, the robot was pleased. His flowmetal face formed a broad smile.

His expression shifted when the voice of Omnius thrummed overhead. "I have found you." One of the portable watcheye units drifted down for a closer view. "You look as if you are relaxing. Are you emulating a decadent human from the Old Empire? The fallen Emperor, perhaps?"

"Only to better study their species, Omnius. Only to serve you. During this maintenance procedure I was assessing data I had gathered about religions."

"Tell me what you have learned, now that you are an authority on such information."

Erasmus lifted one arm so that the slave could better polish it. She used non-abrasive chemicals and soft berissi chamoix. The woman concentrated on her work, and seemed surprisingly unruffled, considering that his last polisher slave had accidentally scraped his flowmetal skin with a fingernail, and Erasmus had cracked open her skull with a flower pot. The woman's head had contained a surprising quantity of blood, and in fascination he had watched it drain out of her until she stopped twitching and squirming . . .

"I do not yet consider myself an authority on human religions. To attain that goal, I need firsthand experience with their rituals. Perhaps there is some intangible quality that was not recorded in the data I reviewed, for I found no answers there. I need to speak with genuine priests, mullahs, and rabbis. The written history is inadequate for such subtle, but necessary understanding."

"You have learned nothing from millennia of documented events?"

"An accumulation of facts does not always lead to comprehension. I know that humans frequently fight over religion. They are particularly resistant to compromise on this issue."

"Humans are combative creatures by nature. Though they claim to worship peace and prosperity, they actually like to fight."

"An impressive analysis," Erasmus said.

"Since we are not capable of arguing with humans over matters of religion, do you think they concocted this supposedly holy quarrel, this *Jihad*?"

The slave finished polishing her master, then stood to one side, awaiting further instructions. Erasmus waved her off, and the woman departed hastily.

"Interesting. But you must realize that our lack of religion is in itself anathema to the minds of zealots. They refer to us as atheists, godless demons. Humans love to engage in name-calling, since it enables them to categorize an adversary . . . which invariably involves dehumanizing an opponent. In our case, dear Omnius, the dehumanization was accomplished from the outset."

"The *hrethgir* have resisted us for centuries, but the nature of their struggle changed dramatically after they packaged it in the trappings of religion. They have become even more irrational than before — and hypocritical. They revile us for enslaving humans, yet they themselves keep humans in bondage."

Erasmus nodded to the watcheye, a human gesture he had learned. "Though we are not flesh-bearers, Omnius, we must in a sense fight like them. We must become unpredictable ourselves, or at least able to predict their fighting methods."

"Intriguing ideas."

"Patterns without patterns," Erasmus said. "It seems to me that our enemies are insane on a massive scale. The religious zeal that fuels their Jihad is like a disease that runs through their midst, infecting their collective mind."

"They have achieved so many unexpected victories," Omnius lamented. "The destruction of Earth and the defenses of Peridot Colony, Tyndall, IV Anbus, and the shipyards on Poritrin are of great concern to me."

"The endless rebellion on Ix is proving problematical as well," Erasmus said. "Despite the deaths of millions of humans there, Jihad infiltrators continue to pour in, as if they calculate neither the cost nor the benefit. When will they realize that one world is not worth the deaths of so many fighters?"

Omnius said, "Humans are animals. Just look at them in your pens."

Erasmus strolled to the edge of his terrace, which afforded him a view of the squalid slave pens. A few skeletal, filthy humans milled about within the high fenced enclosures, crowding toward a long wooden table set up on muddy ground. It was feeding time, and they stood with bovine expressions on their faces. Automatic mechanisms opened internal gates in the pens, and food pellets rattled out, like brown gravel.

Such pathetic lives they lead, Erasmus thought, *without formal education or awareness.* But even the lowliest of them might possess the tremendous potential to be a great human genius. Lack of opportunities did not necessarily make an individual stupid, but only shifted his intelligence to a form suited to survival rather than creativity.

"You do not fully appreciate the situation, Omnius. Begin with any healthy human. If taken at a formative age, when its mental systems remain pliable, any one of those poor humans can be trained. Given the opportunity, even the most bedraggled child could become brilliant, nearly our equal."

Hovering near Erasmus, the watcheye magnified its viewing mechanism for a closer look at the pens. "Any of them? That is doubtful."

"Nevertheless, I have found it to be true."

Additional watcheyes converged above the crowded pens where the feeding humans jostled each other. An image appeared on the watcheye lens by Erasmus, and Omnius said, "Observe that boy closest to the fence — the one with straggly hair and ragged pants. He appears to be the wildest and most unkempt of all. See what you can do with that creature. I will wager that he remains an animal despite your best efforts."

Remembering his bet with the now-destroyed Earth-Omnius, a wager that had unexpectedly sparked the initial rebellion among the slaves, Erasmus said nothing. Because the last evermind update had been destroyed in the atomic annihilation of Earth, the Corrin-Omnius did not know the details of the abortive wager. Erasmus's secret was safe.

"I do not wish to gamble with the great evermind," Erasmus said. "But I accept your challenge nonetheless. I shall make that boy civilized, educated, and insightful — far superior to any of our other trustees."

"A *challenge* it is, then," Omnius said.

Previously, Erasmus had noticed this wild boy because of his primitive tendency toward obstinacy. Such a feral, potentially violent organism. According to records, the child was nine years old, young enough to remain pliable. The robot recalled how even the cultured, educated, and *exhilarating* Serena Butler had been a challenge, and how his own relationship with that woman and her child had led to unforeseen, disastrous events.

He resolved to produce better results from this effort.

He who strikes fastest strikes twice.

—Swordmaster Jav Barri

❝ **T**EACH ME TO kill machines.❞

Before each round of training, Jool Noret said the same thing to his *sensei* mek, and Chirox did his best to please his master. With his adaptability algorithm module, the fighting robot was a remarkably intuitive instructor, considering that he was merely programmed and designed to slay humans.

Jool threw himself into his training with an abandon he had never exhibited prior to the loss of his father. It was no longer training — it was an obsession. He had been the cause of Zon Noret's tragic death, and to assuage his conscience he therefore needed to inflict more damage on Omnius than two Swordmasters. It was his burden. Jool had never wanted the old veteran to be harmed, but the tough philosophy of Ginaz taught that there were no accidents, no excuses for failure. Every event was the result of a sequence of actions. Intentions were irrelevant to actual outcomes.

Jool had no one but himself to blame, no one who could accept his apology or help to shoulder his responsibility. The young man's guilt was so much a part of him now that it became a driving force. With his dying breath, Zon Noret had commanded him to become a great fighter, the best Ginaz had ever seen.

Jool accepted the task with a vengeance.

A nearly superhuman increase in skills, even at his already-high level, seemed to flow from within, awakened by his own passion and drive. According to Ginaz beliefs, the spirit of an earlier, unknown mercenary warrior shared his body, an entity that was reincarnated but unaware. He could feel the ancestral instinct burning through his veins and filling each muscle fiber as he battled Chirox with an array of weapons, from sophisticated scrambler-pulse rods to simple clubs, to his bare hands.

The yellow optic sensors of the *sensei* mek glowed as he learned to increase his level of skill to keep pace with his student. "You are as swift as a machine, Jool Noret, and as resilient as a human. Together, these factors make you a formidable foe."

Noret used his father's pulse sword, paralyzing the *sensei* mek one component at a time without suffering more than a bruise or a scratch. "I intend to become the bane of Omnius, his bête noire." Jool drove forward faster and harder, pressing even the supercharged abilities of the mek, which had continued to adapt and increase.

Eventually, the determined warrior outstripped the machine.

Standing on the same beach where his father had been slain, the younger Noret attacked the combat robot's armored left leg, then the right, and worked his way up, shutting down all six fighting arms, one system after another, until finally Chirox was no more than a twisted metallic statue. Only the robot's optic sensors remained bright, like stars in the dark night sky. Without rancor or joy, simply intensity, Noret bounded into the air and delivered a hard kick to the mek's torso, toppling the machine backward into the soft, trampled sand.

"There, I have vanquished you." He loomed over his fallen mechanical teacher. "*Again.*"

From the ground, the robot's response was flat and emotionless, but Noret thought he detected a note of pride. "My adaptability module has reached its maximum capacity, Master Noret. Until you program me with further proficiencies, you have absorbed everything I can teach you." The mek's left leg twitched as the adaptive circuits reset themselves. "You are ready for anything a thinking machine can throw against you."

On the main island of the Ginaz archipelago, Jool Noret fought other mercenary trainees. Under careful supervision and weapons restrictions, most of the students survived.

Every member of the Council of Veterans had known Jool's fallen father, had fought with him in many battles against the machines, but the young man needed to earn his own honor and respect. It was a means to an end. He was desperate to be off fighting in the Jihad, so that he could begin destroying the forces of Omnius . . . and repaying his oppressive personal debt.

The population of Ginaz was scattered across hundreds of small, lush islands that provided a range of terrain. The natives could have led peaceful lives — plentiful fish, tropical fruits, and nuts grew in the rich volcanic soil — but instead they had developed a rigorous warrior culture that achieved fame across the League of Nobles.

The young men and women used the varied terrain and natural hazards of the numerous islands to practice their fighting skills. The natives had always opposed the thinking machines, all the way back to the initial Time of Titans. Isolated Ginaz had been the only society to throw off the program-corrupted robots that the Titan Barbarossa had unleashed against the Old Empire in the initial conquest. In a quarter century Serena Butler's Jihad had intensified to a fever pitch, which placed extraordinary demands upon Ginaz to provide more and more desperately needed warriors.

Just as the computer evermind could copy itself and transmit updates to endure one destruction after another, each Ginaz mercenary believed that after death his fighting spirit was transferred like a data file into the body vessel of his successor. It was more than reincarnation; it was a direct continuation of the battle . . . a handoff from one warrior to another.

Since so many of their people were killed in battle, the island society had to adapt, encouraging more offspring than usual. Young Ginaz students traveled from island to island and took mates indiscriminately. It was considered a candidate's duty to have three children before journeying off-world to fight in the furious Jihad: one child to replace the father, one to replace the mother, and a third as a spiritual duty to those who could not reproduce, for whatever reason.

Mercenary women who became pregnant while out on long assignments returned home to Ginaz for the last few months before childbirth, where they helped to teach the others. They remained only long enough to deliver the children and regain their strength, then were off again on the next available ship to a new machine battlefield.

There were always plenty of battles to be fought.

Older men from the Council of Veterans, like Zon Noret, were considered excellent breeding stock, since they had shown their physical superiority by surviving a certain number of missions and injuries. Jool believed this, and knew that he himself was a fortuitous blending of powerful genes.

Many of the war children never learned the identities of their fathers. Some never even knew their mothers. Jool Noret was one of only a few whose father had returned to claim him, so that he could follow his son's development and training. And then, a year ago, through his own hubris and inattention, Jool had caused the death of Zon Noret, a skilled mercenary needed by the Jihad. How much had that single mistake cost the war effort?

He already knew that it had cost him a great deal personally, and he doubted his conscience would ever give him any breathing room. Driven and obsessed, he had to do the fighting of two Ginaz mercenaries, or more. Jool could only wait until his father returned as a restless warrior spirit eager to fight again, reborn in the body of a new, eager fighter . . .

Now, while he awaited final testing, Jool dug his fingers into the warm afternoon sand, felt the beat of his pulse and the perspiration on his skin. With each breath, he was reminded of how much he longed to contribute his skills to the Jihad and make his mark. Somewhere inside, he carried the spirit of an unknown, unawakened comrade. Today, if the Council of Veterans found him worthy, Jool would discover whose spirit burned within him.

He clenched sand in his hands, then lifted a fistful and watched the grains trickle through his fingers. He would have to earn the privilege . . .

The new group of potential mercenaries had diverse specialties. Some were proficient at hand-to-hand combat against the thinking machines; others had developed more esoteric sabotage or destruction skills. All of them, though, were useful additions in the age-old struggle against Omnius.

The new hopefuls dueled each other in a cordoned-off section of rock-strewn beach. Mercenaries did not graduate merely by defeating their opponents, but by demonstrating sufficient talent to prove that the soul of a warrior truly inhabited them. Looking crestfallen, a handful of the trainees failed in their vigorous demonstrations.

Jool Noret did not.

A few of the losers crept away with eyes downcast, seeming to give up in their hearts. Jool watched them, knowing that such easily discouraged fighters would have been liabilities under true battle conditions. Others who had fallen short, however, clearly retained their sparks of defiance and determination; though they had failed this particular testing, they were eager to return to their instructors. They would learn more, improve their abilities, and try again.

The next morning, Jool Noret stood beside six companions, all of whom had been chosen as champions by the Council of Veterans. While white waves crashed against the gnarled black reef, the veterans built a bonfire of driftwood on the beach near a stand of thick, armored palms. A young mute boy with blond hair walked solemnly forward, struggling to carry a basin filled with polished coral disks. As he set the basin down, the chits clattered against each other like the teeth of a skeleton. Jool squinted in the direct equatorial sunlight.

"You will all continue the fight," said the lead veteran, a one-armed warrior who wore his gray hair braided into a thick rope. Master Shar could no longer fight machines, but he had devoted his life to creating replacement warriors who would cause far more damage than the thinking machines had inflicted on him.

Shar had lost his arm during his last battle. He considered himself too old to fight further and had refused to accept one of the available replacement limbs from the battlefield surgeons' stores, so that it might be given to a younger soldier, one better able to continue to fight. Despite his handicap, however, the Master retained so much agility that he braided his own hair with one hand and refused any help, though few could understand how the old man accomplished such a feat.

"This is the last time you come before us as trainees." Shar swept an icicle gaze across the seven young warriors. "When you depart Ginaz for some far-away battlefield, you will go as proud mercenaries, representatives of our skills and our gallant history. Do you all accept this grave responsibility?"

In unison, Noret and his companions shouted their acknowledgement. Master Shar summoned them forward one by one, announcing each of them. Fourth in line, Noret took two steps to the sitting Council of Veterans.

"Jool Noret, you have had most unorthodox training," said Master Shar. "Your father was a tremendous asset to the mercenaries of Ginaz. He too was trained by this warrior mek Chirox, while your fellows here were instructed by actual combat veterans. Do you feel this is a disadvantage?"

Guilt continued to simmer deep in Jool's soul as he said, "No, Master Shar, I consider it an *advantage*. A machine has instructed me in how to kill machines. What teacher could know more about our sworn enemy?"

"Yet that mek killed Zon Noret," rasped a gray-haired woman, a muscular veteran.

Jool focused on his resolve rather than the roaring sound in his ears. "To make up for the loss of my father, I must destroy twice as many of the enemy."

A scarred old gnome with broken teeth leaned forward. "This mek was recovered from a robot battleship and reprogrammed. Are you not concerned that he might contain secret internal instructions to make you vulnerable?"

"My *sensei* mek has already trained four generations of mercenary fighters who were among the best of Ginaz, and I have vowed to surpass all of them. I have learned to kill machines, to seek out the vulnerabilities of all known designs of robots and cymek bodies." The litany swelled within him, and his voice gathered a frightening strength. "I grew up learning about Serena Butler's Jihad. I have seen reports of battles on the Synchronized Worlds, our triumphs and failures. My spirit is consumed with the need to destroy Omnius. There is no doubt in my mind that I was born to this."

Master Shar smiled. "Then there is no doubt in ours, either." He gestured toward the basin filled with coral disks. "If you possess the spirit of a warrior, now is the time for it to come forth. Choose. Let us see which of our fallen mercenaries has transferred his skills and ambitions into you."

Jool Noret stared down at the numerous disks, most of them scribed with the name of a Ginaz mercenary who had been slain over the centuries of warfare; some of the chits were blank, denoting a new soul. The young man closed his eyes and plunged his hands into the pile, letting fate guide his selection. Somewhere in here lay a disk with his father's name on it, but he knew he was not worthy of that one. He could not bear to draw it and hoped his hands did not happen to find it in the basin.

With a burst of courage he seized a disk, pulled it out and held it up to the sunlight. Opening his eyes, he read the unfamiliar name: *Jav Barri*.

At last he knew who had been reborn within him. He could look through the Ginaz archives and learn the story of this Jav Barri. But it didn't matter to him what the former mercenary had done. With his father's memory, the *sensei* mek's training, and the spirit of the fallen mercenary inside him, Jool Noret would make his own mark — or die in the attempt.

Master Shar said, "All of you are now commissioned to destroy thinking machines. This shall be your sacred, sworn duty, and you will be paid well for the sacrifices you make. Tomorrow you depart for Salusa Secundus, where you will be deployed with the Army of the Jihad."

He paused, and his voice broke as he added, "Make us proud."

Words are magic.

—Zufa Cenva, *Reflections on the Jihad*

F ROM A GRASSY promontory outside the League's capital city, Iblis
gave another rousing speech. One of the many shrines to Serena's
dead baby stood behind him, containing a "true fragment" from the
clothing little Manion had worn on the day of his murder.

His icily beautiful wife Camie Boro attended, standing like a fixture at
his side. The last of the imperial bloodline, Camie was now an important
part of his power base and mother to his three children. She seemed to
relish the attention the audience showered on her, as the mate of the
Grand Patriarch.

But the main focus was on his speech. The crowd, as always, had
turned to putty in his hands. Yorek Thurr and his Jipol officers had
already, quietly and forcibly, removed a group of anti-Jihad protesters
who had intended to cause a disturbance, and the rest of the audience
would never know they had been there. Everything was perfect.

A fiery orator, Iblis paused, walked back a few feet to the steps of the
shrine, and climbed them. For several moments he stood at the top, gazing
across the throng that covered the neatly cropped lawn for as far as he could
see. Dark clouds hung low in the Salusan sky, but people seemed to be trying
to drive them away by waving banners and tossing bright orange flowers.

He wore unseen amplification devices. "Today is a great day, for we
finally have cause to celebrate an exceptional victory! A mighty force of
thinking machines came to the vital League World of Poritrin, but the
massed warships of our Army of the Jihad stood firm and hurled them
back in disgrace! The robot fleet fled — and *not a single human fighter died
in the engagement.*"

The news was so unexpected, after decades of bloody massacres and appalling casualties, that the people hesitated for a moment in stunned silence, then cheers resounded, like deafening thunder from the distant storm. Iblis beamed with genuine pleasure, his mood buoyed as much as theirs.

"Because this triumph is so important, I will leave immediately for Poritrin to congratulate them in person. As the Grand Patriarch of the Holy Jihad, I must represent Priestess Serena Butler at a celebration of their continued freedom."

While waiting for the noise to die down again, he gathered his strength, his mental emphasis, for the next thrust. "However, on the heels of this victory, we must press forward with renewed vigor. For every life spared there, another brave rebel has died fighting machines on other battlegrounds.

"In particular, we have seen the efforts of human slaves on Ix, a vital stronghold and manufacturing center for Omnius. For years, they have struggled to rise up and destroy the thinking machines, and we have aided them where we can. But it is not enough. We must pay the necessary price to win the struggle, and press our momentum of victory against an inhuman enemy. I announce to you that the Jihad Council has decided, with the blessing of Priestess Serena Butler, that we will liberate Ix once and for all, no matter what it takes!"

Starry-eyed from news of the bloodless victory at Poritrin, the people did not yet realize how difficult a conquest Ix would be. Iblis knew that humans would be massacred in the military operation, but the extensive and valuable manufacturing facilities there would make a fine plum for the League of Nobles. He had made his case and used his powers of persuasion to get the Council to go along with him. The industrial facilities on Ix made it worth the effort, unlike some of Omnius's other planets. The wealth of technology would help all League Worlds.

"For a year, our clandestine commandos have infiltrated Ix, galvanizing the fifth column efforts there. Escaped human slaves hide in catacombs beneath the surface, battling hunting parties of cymeks and robots. Our jihadis have given the people weapons and even gelcircuitry scrambler devices to shut down the computer brains. But it is not enough. We must do more."

He grinned with pride and determination. Beside him, Camie Boro exuded an aura of support for him, though she rarely spoke to Iblis when they were not in public. Theirs was a marriage of political convenience, offering practical advantages for both of them, with no physical passion.

"And there is a higher justification," he continued. "The esteemed

Cogitor Kwyna has said, 'Those who live underground must not fear the open. They may feel safe and sheltered in the dark, but they will not be free until they claw their way upward into sunlight.' Obviously, she is speaking of Ix!"

Even more applause and cheers ensued, but Iblis liked to dig beneath the surface, just to be certain of the peoples' support. In nondescript clothes, his Jipol observers moved through the throng, reporting by a closed-circuit radio that they found no one who expressed anything but enthusiastic approval. Receiving constant summaries, the Grand Patriarch drew a deep, satisfied breath and suppressed a chuckle at the memory of how far he had come from his lowly beginnings as a work crew boss harassed by the Titan Ajax.

On Ix, for months his operatives and daredevil Ginaz mercenaries had been inciting the slaves to rise up and destroy the resident Omnius, just like the 'great victory on Earth.' Unable to understand human mob mentality, the Ix-Omnius did not even employ counter-propaganda to fight the more ridiculous assertions made by the commandos. The intentional manipulation of information was not a comprehensible concept to the computer evermind. Iblis could use that to his advantage.

He cried out, "If we can retake just one Synchronized World, it means we can seize another. And another! We must not hesitate, no matter how many lives it costs!" He invoked the sacred names. "For Serena Butler and her martyred child Manion, we can do no less!"

Caught up in the frenzy of his words, the people waved banners depicting a stylized Serena Butler and her angelic little son, like the Madonna and child. "Serena! Serena! Manion the Innocent!"

Whenever he delivered speeches such as this, Iblis focused his thoughts inward, drawing upon his righteous anger and harnessing a visceral rage that could be used to tear the enemy into metal scrap and melt them into unrecognizable heaps. These people were his tools.

At the most basic level, the Grand Patriarch was a salesman, with an idea that he needed to sell to the masses. To be effective on such a scale, under intense scrutiny, he had to believe in the Jihad "product" himself, so that he could make it sound convincing to others. He made himself believe.

And he smiled. His Jipol had staged this rally perfectly, dispersing their own members into the crowd and stirring the people as needed. Soon, fresh recruits would be ready to launch themselves recklessly toward the target planet Ix, where the casualties would be immense.

He knew full well that these people represented cannon fodder in the Jihad, but only through their sacrifice could the conquest succeed, given enough zealots and adequate time. There would no longer be any such thing as a defeat — only victories and "moral victories."

The Grand Patriarch noticed the statuesque, alabaster-skinned Sorceress at the front of the crowd, watching the proceedings intently, wordlessly. Tall and rigid, Zufa Cenva stood out from the vibrant multitude as if a spotlight were shining on her. As usual, her gaze fixed on him, but with a certain detached aloofness that he found disturbing. Iblis had noticed her at other Jihad rallies too. What did the chief Sorceress of Rossak want?

Emotions masked, Zufa Cenva stood with her sisters on the grassy hillside; she had asked them to observe closely, to confirm her suspicions. The pungent perfumes of orange flowers wafted through the crowds like a drug from the jungles of Rossak. But the Sorceress's pale eyes were sharp, as alert as those of the furtive Jipol observers who were so obvious to her in the crowd.

As she studied Iblis, Zufa imagined hypnotic waves shimmering around him. They surged from the energy core of his body and extended like tentacles to touch the audience as he spoke. The Grand Patriarch's words were always well chosen, but their cumulative effect seemed much greater than their actual content. Today he was in fine form, rousing the audience, guiding them this way and that, like a maestro. If the charismatic Iblis told them to march off a cliff, they would have done so, smiling all the way.

At precisely the right moment, he would raise his arms and gesture with his hands. He rarely prayed or used religious words, but the effect was similar. People believed in his sincerity. Zufa didn't think it was training or practice, but something more.

"See, he doesn't even know his own power," she said to the other Sorceresses. "He believes his talents are instinctive, nothing more."

Magnificent.

As the leader of the Rossak delegation, Zufa had long been intrigued by Iblis Ginjo's remarkable personal magnetism. But she and her sisters guessed something more about him, something they were keeping to themselves.

The extrapolated breeding chart on this male was fascinating, with roots that went back to her own jungle planet. Available evidence indicated that the Grand Patriarch had *innate* telepathic abilities, an exceedingly rare trait in a non-female.

Perhaps he carried the appropriate masculine bloodline she had been seeking for herself. She was not young, but given the sophisticated new Rossak fertility treatments developed by VenKee and tested by many Sorceresses, Zufa knew she could succeed in having one more child. To her, that meant trying to deliver a better daughter, one that would make her proud. Could this Grand Patriarch be the correct sperm donor?

Though his ancestry was obviously unknown to him, Iblis Ginjo must be the distant descendant of Rossak natives, taken captive by machines long ago and moved to other worlds. If only he had undergone the intensive mental training that she and her fellow Sorceresses took for granted. Zufa Cenva would not reveal the man's true nature to him, unless she and her companions stood to gain something from it.

Perhaps she could exert influence on him and use his abilities to her own advantage.

Zufa was not immune to the Grand Patriarch's charms, but had always been able to fend them off with her acute awareness. It pleased her that Iblis did not seem to recognize his hypnotic knack for what it was. Over the years, many of her highly trained sisters had sacrificed themselves in telepathic annihilation strikes against cymeks. But this man was in a different situation, possessed a different potential. She suspected that Iblis Ginjo was a dangerous, duplicitous man, but saw no one more qualified to take the Jihad where it needed to go.

For his own reasons, he did, after all, espouse the same cause as her Sorceresses: the utter annihilation of thinking machines. Iblis would, however, require the closest sort of scrutiny and would have to be handled with excruciating care.

I believe he is the most dangerous man I have ever met.

Thoughts become weapons. Philosophies are distinct reasons for war. Good intentions are the most destructive arsenal of all.
— Cogitor Kwyna, *City of Introspection Archives*

B EATIFIC, PROUD, AND confident before her loyal Seraphim in their gold-mesh caps and flowing gowns, Serena Butler finished rehearsing. With fire and drive, she must keep the Jihad burning. Niriem nodded after listening to a playback of part of her speech, indicating that she approved. But Serena doubted if her stonily loyal chief Seraph would ever express disappointment in any aspect of the great holy war, as long as machines were being destroyed.

Now that Iblis Ginjo had departed for Poritrin, Serena intended to record a series of inspirational speeches from the City of Introspection. By nature, humans had a tendency to lose focus on long-term goals, unless they were constantly reminded of the big picture. Their determination must constantly be nurtured and massaged.

Over the next few months, her pronouncements would be distributed among the League Worlds; VenKee Enterprises had already signed an agreement with the Jihad Council to deliver the recorded rallies free of charge via their merchant ships.

Inside a fortified compound, Serena's attentive female guards stood on either side of her. Following the assassination attempt over a year ago, all of the fanatical Seraphim had been tested and investigated; several were then removed from service, their loyalty suspect. Niriem now served Serena more closely than ever. These women made her feel strong and protected, confident that the human spirit would ultimately triumph over cold machine brutality.

"Machines can falter and disintegrate. Programming breaks down,"

Serena finished her lecture into the recorders. "But the human heart will never stop beating."

In spite of the new push that Iblis had instigated with her blessing, she knew that thinking machines would not be defeated overnight. The downtrodden people on Ix had been fighting for their lives for years, and with the imminent launch of a full Army offensive, to be led by Xavier, many more of her followers would die. A necessary sacrifice, Iblis had assured her.

She lowered her gaze and closed her eyes in benedictory contemplation. Jihad Council officers switched off the imagers and rushed to take the Priestess's new message to be played for all the recent jihadi volunteers who were about to be dispatched to Ix. Many of them would never come home again.

She noticed her mother standing at the doorway. "Bravo, Serena. I am certain the slave rebels of Ix will hold your words close to their bosoms, even as the assassin robots slaughter them."

Startled by her cold attitude, Serena responded, "This struggle will not be won unless each fighter commits his full capabilities and strength, Mother. I mean to inspire them."

Livia Butler frowned. "The Grand Patriarch has not told you everything that is happening on Ix." She gestured to the glowering Seraphim who stood nearby, said, "Leave us. I wish to speak with my daughter in private."

"We have been ordered to protect the Priestess," said the chief Seraph, not moving.

Serena turned to the young woman. "I need no protection from my own mother, Niriem."

"We must also protect you from your own doubts, Priestess," the Seraph leader warned. "Your Jihad cannot suffer weakness from within."

"Do you obey me or make up your own orders? Now go."

Sullenly, the devoted women departed. Livia Butler had not moved, and said, "Just before leaving for Poritrin, the Grand Patriarch announced his intentions on Ix, but he has actually been plotting there for a long time, coveting the industries and manufacturing centers. You cannot imagine the slaughter he has already triggered *in your name*. Many, many lives have already been expended on Ix — and it is going to get much worse."

Serena blinked her lavender eyes. "How do you know this? Iblis has made no such report to me."

In response, Livia handed over an image pack. A broken seal bore the insignia of Jipol, marked with the highest security classification. "These clips were smuggled out by a mercenary sent in to foment turmoil. The images were compiled by a native Ixian named Handon, one of the rebels and saboteurs."

"How did you get it?"

"The imagepack was intended for Yorek Thurr, but was misdelivered in the League Assembly to an old representative who was once very loyal to your father. You know the bureaucracy there — it's as bad as in the fallen Empire. He thought the retired Viceroy should see it, and I think that you should also view the images, Serena. You must see what is happening out in the Jihad. The protesters have good reason for questioning the tactics in this war."

"The protesters are cowards who do not understand the deadly purposes of the thinking machines."

Livia pressed Serena's fingers against the image pack. "Just view this."

Frowning to conceal her nervousness, Serena activated the system and scrolled slowly from one nightmarish scene to another. She saw mass slaughter in full color: machine extermination squads attacked humans, and families huddled underground, hiding in tunnels, while a cymek — identified as the Titan Xerxes — strode about in a warrior-form, killing any human he encountered.

She swallowed hard and forced herself to say, "I realize this war is painful, Mother, but we must fight and we must win."

"Yes, and you need to understand, child: Ix is a slaughterhouse — unnecessarily so. Iblis has deluded the Ixian rebels into throwing themselves at the ferocious assassin robots, with no hope of survival and no chance of making the slightest progress against the enemy. We give them a few weapons, but they are not nearly enough. Iblis has recognized the futility of the campaign for more than a year, and yet he keeps egging them on, sending them *your* messages."

"My words are meant to inspire them."

"Hundreds of thousands of fighters have died there, all in your name. They call out for you and your martyred son as if you are deities who can protect them, then hurl themselves upon the thinking machines. You were never meant to see these horrific images, but you must know how much blood is on your hands."

Serena shot her mother a hard glance, then continued to watch the images. She absorbed the brutal fighting taking place in blood-spattered cave warrens in the industrial complexes and cities beneath the surface of the planet. Flames raged around the desperate fighters. Smashed machines and dead human bodies lay everywhere.

"What would you have me do, Mother?" she asked at last, unable to tear her gaze away from the carnage. "Should we just surrender Ix?"

Livia's expression melted. "No, but even if we conquer Ix by sending an army in, is it all just for another excuse to cheer? This is a poorly chosen battlefield. For such an extravagant effort and expenditure of lives, we might as well attack the machine capital on Corrin!"

Serena was troubled. "I will have to discuss this with Iblis, when he returns from Poritrin. He will explain himself. Perhaps the Grand Patriarch has reasons we don't immediately see. I'm sure he has good justification for –"

Livia interrupted. "He has made these decisions *without you*, Serena. As he often does. Are you the Priestess of the Jihad . . . or a mere figurehead?"

Her mother's words stung. After a long moment Serena said, "Iblis is my advisor and mentor, and he has always been a great source of strength to me. But you are right . . . I should not be in the dark concerning major decisions."

"The Grand Patriarch will not come home for nearly two months." Livia leaned forward, pressing. "You cannot wait that long. Decide how you will act before then." The old Abbess took her daughter by the arm. "Come with me. After learning of this report herself, the Cogitor Kwyna wishes to speak with you. It is most urgent."

Once a human female in times forgotten by history, long before the Titans overthrew the Old Empire, the great philosopher Kwyna had pondered all the thoughts and philosophies collected by the human race. After expending a millennium of effort, Kwyna taught that even common human brains could achieve a glimmer of wisdom.

Serena and her mother climbed the steps of the stone tower that had been built to accommodate the great thinker. The tower windows were open, and cool breezes swept through the room. The Cogitor's ornate preservation canister rested on a pedestal at the center of the round room, and her chosen human attendants stood nearby, awaiting her instructions.

Kwyna gave her excellent advice and many important questions to consider. Kwyna's philosophical conundrums had occupied Serena during her darkest times of grief and despair over the loss of her baby and the crumbling of her expected life with Xavier Harkonnen.

Now her mother remained at the door, while Serena stepped forward to stand before the preservation canister. "You asked to speak with me, Kwyna? I anticipate much enlightenment from every conversation with you."

Two secondaries marched forward with shaven heads and immaculately clean hands. The monks removed the canister lid and motioned for Serena to reach out. "Kwyna wishes to connect with you directly."

Floating in its electrafluid bath, the disembodied brain was wrinkled and intricately patterned by centuries of deep thought. With a mounting sense of curiosity mixed with apprehension, Serena let her eyes fall half closed and dipped her slender fingertips into the warm preservation fluid.

"I am here," she murmured.

She pushed her hand deeper until she touched the rubbery contours of Kwyna's brain. As the thick fluid swirled around the Cogitor's sensitive flesh, ionic pathways connected through the pores of her skin, linking with Serena's neurons, connecting the mental passages of the distinct, but related, life forms.

"You know the facts and the words," the wise Cogitor said in her mind. "You understand Iblis Ginjo's justifications . . . but do you believe them?"

"What do you mean, Kwyna?" Serena said out loud.

"I have avoided giving Iblis new straws of philosophy to clutch, but still he twists my words, corrupts the ancient scriptures. Instead of drawing enlightenment from my treatises, he makes up his own mind and then takes passages out of context in order to justify his decisions."

The Cogitor's thoughts seemed to thrum with deep weariness. Serena wanted to retreat from the accusations, but respect for the Cogitor trapped her hand in the living fluid. "Kwyna, I'm sure the Grand Patriarch holds only the best interests of humanity in his heart. I will speak to him, of course, and am certain he will explain everything."

"One who will manipulate the truth to prove his enlightenment will do much worse. Serena Butler, are you not struck by the fact that *his* decisions cause martyrs to march to their deaths with *your* name on their lips?"

Serena bridled. "They are fighters for the Jihad. Even if they were slaughtered to the last, they would insist it was worth the cost. And so would I."

Behind her, Livia expressed disappointment. "Oh, Serena. Is human life so valueless to you?"

Kwyna continued, her thoughts damning. "The Grand Patriarch incites violence by whatever means he considers necessary, because he believes that his goal validates his methods. Ix is another prize to him, but not part of any plan to win the war. He is in no hurry for the fighting to end, and knows that tragedies can be as inspirational as victories. You, Serena, may want Omnius destroyed as soon as possible, but Iblis Ginjo sees the Jihad as his source of power."

This news was painful, almost too much to bear. Serena did not want to hear any more but was still unable to withdraw her hand.

"I have lived and pondered for more than twenty centuries, and dispensed my knowledge to those who deserved it. Now, my conclusions are being used in a manner that I never intended. I myself feel responsible for countless unnecessary human deaths."

Serena let her fingertips brush over the vermiform contours of the Cogitor's mind. "Those who would carry an important role must bear immense burdens. I am all too familiar with this sad fact."

"But I did not *choose* the role," Kwyna retorted. "Just as you have been manipulated by Iblis, so have I. Willingly, I gave my thoughts for the betterment of humanity, but my writings have been corrupted. I now understand why some of my fellow Cogitors chose to withdraw forever from interacting with the rise and fall of civilizations. Perhaps I should have gone with Vidad and the others long ago."

Serena was surprised. "There are other Cogitors still alive? What do you mean they have withdrawn forever?"

"Vidad was once my friend, a mental sparring partner, a mind worthy of infinite debate. But he and five other Cogitors chose to sever all contact with humans and machines, preferring the eternal serenity and purity of their own thoughts. At the time we scorned them for fleeing the obligations that stemmed from their revelations. We accused them of hiding, living in ivory towers. Vidad accepted the label, but did not change his decision. No one has heard from them in many centuries."

Serena sensed a sullen exhaustion in Kwyna's mind as the ancient brain said, "Perhaps I should have joined the Ivory Tower Cogitors, but now I must find another option. I have summoned you here to tell you this, Serena Butler, so that you may understand."

"And you think understanding is so simple?" Serena asked.

"Reality is what it is," said Kwyna. "And I have had enough of life. I will share no more thoughts, allow no more wisdom to be twisted. When I am gone, Iblis may still find ways to use the lost doctrines, but I do not intend to give him further weapons that he can corrupt."

Dreading what the ancient mind might do next, Serena said, "You have served me well here. I have learned much from you, and relied on your advice."

Now the Cogitor's voice became gentler in Serena's mind. "I know your heart is true, but I am weary from the deep ponderings of two millennia. From now on, I cast you free of my protection. Think your own thoughts and fly from the nest to your destiny."

"What are you saying? Wait!"

"It is time for me . . . to cease." The bluish electrafluid stirred and turned a different color, dangerously reddish, as if the ancient brain had hemorrhaged, secreting a bloody essence.

Serena felt a terrible coldness in the brain, a shocking, sudden sensation.

Then, with no added effort from the secondaries and no manipulation of the life-support systems in the preservation canister, the deep thoughts smoothed and faded from the Cogitor's mind. After two thousand years of considering the meaning of existence, Kwyna let her essence flow into the universe and melt away. Her mind disappeared into nothingness.

Serena yanked her hand from the electrafluid. The slippery liquid felt like blood all over her fingers. "What have I done?"

"Many things have led to this tragedy," Livia answered, her tone bitter. "Iblis Ginjo in part, as well as the Jihad, by its very nature."

Fighting back tears, Serena stepped away from the now lifeless mass of the ancient philosopher's brain. Her friend. "So many things have been done in my name."

Livia looked at her sternly. "Serena, you have had a quarter of a century to contemplate and to learn from your personal tragedy. Now the time has come for you to make your own decisions."

Serena squared her shoulders and lifted her chin. She gazed out the window and felt an icy breeze on her face. "Yes, Mother. Now I know what I must do." She glanced at the mourning, saffron-robed secondaries, then peered into the hall where her brooding Seraphim stood at the ready, garbed in crimson-trimmed white robes.

"It is time for *me* to lead my Holy Jihad."

It is better to be envied than pitied.
                    —Vorian Atreides, *Memoirs Without Shame*

F OR XAVIER HARKONNEN, the Butler Estate was haunted by memories and lost opportunities. But it was also the home he made with
his loving wife Octa and their two daughters Roella and Omilia.

By the age of forty-four, Octa had grown into her beauty and her role as his
wife and anchor. A gentler soul than her fiery sister Serena, Octa was a
caring and devoted mate and an attentive mother. A prize beyond measure.

What have I ever done to deserve her?

Since retiring as Viceroy, her father Manion Butler had lived with
them, tending the orchards and winery. The elderly man adored his
grown granddaughters, and still enjoyed political and military discussions with his influential son-in-law. Of late, however, such talks often
evolved into banal reminiscences about the "good old days." Serena had
become a distant stranger to her family.

When Xavier stepped out of the main doorway and looked across
toward the olive-darkened hilltops and the vineyard rows, he saw a rider
on horseback coming up the graveled switchbacks to the manor house.

Octa joined him in the courtyard, and Xavier slipped a hand around her
narrow waist. She felt comfortable and familiar beside him. They had
been married for more than twenty-five years now.

Squinting, Octa recognized the dashing, dark-haired rider as he came
up the path. "You didn't warn me Vorian was coming. I was going to visit
Sheel over at the Tantor estate." Vergyl's still-grieving widow Sheel and
three children had recently arrived from Giedi Prime, and were beginning to settle in on Emil Tantor's large and lonely estate. Octa had been
very helpful, assisting the young woman.

"We just want to spend a friendly afternoon discussing possibilities." He stroked her long strawberry-blonde hair, now tarnished with a few strands of pale gray. "If I'd told you he was coming, you would have rallied all the servants and insisted on holding a banquet."

She smiled back at him. "True enough. Now you'll have to be satisfied with cold meat and boiled eggs."

He kissed her on the forehead. "Well, at least you can spoil us with our best wine. Let your father choose a bottle — he knows the vintages better than the rest of us."

"Only because he takes his sampling duties so seriously. I'll ask him if we still have some of the old celebration bottles from his marriage to Mother." Octa disappeared back into the manor house, after waving to Vorian as he rode into the courtyard on a well-muscled Salusan stallion.

Though Xavier was now forty-seven years old and feeling a little less spry in his muscles, his mind held more details and relationships than it ever had in his younger days. In contrast, Vor Atreides retained the best aspects of youth combined with the wisdom of experience. He had not aged a day since his escape from Earth decades ago. His skin was still smooth, his hair dark and lush, though his eyes carried the burden of more memories than any young man's eyes should have displayed. Years earlier, he had explained to Xavier about the life-extension treatment — "torture" was the way he had described it — that Agamemnon had administered to him, supposedly as a reward.

Vor jumped down from his saddle and patted the magnificent beast's neck. Two handlers emerged to take the stallion; they would rub it down, braid the mane and brush the tail; old Manion would make sure everything was done to his satisfaction.

Xavier extended a formal hand to greet his friend, but Vor clapped him on the back instead. "So, do you like my new horse, Xavier? It's one of five I just purchased." With obvious pride, he watched the animal trot into the Butler stables. "Spectacular beasts."

"I should think riding would be a lot of trouble for you, Vor. You have little experience with horses, so –"

"But I love chaos. I spent enough of my life with machines, and there's something unique and exciting about riding a live animal that seems to enjoy the journey." He looked up at the sky, his expression troubled and wistful. "Now that I think of it, Erasmus kept horses, too. Sometimes he summoned a fine carriage to deliver me to his villa. Poor beasts . . . but the robot probably cared for them well enough. He preferred to experiment on humans, you know."

By the time they reached the upstairs veranda on the balcony of the

Winter Sun Room, Octa had already ordered her servants to put out a tray of sliced meats, cheeses, and boiled eggs garnished with herbs. A bottle of fine red wine stood open as well, with two glasses poured and oxidizing in the air.

Xavier chuckled. "Sometimes I think Octa is as telepathic as the Sorceresses of Rossak." As his friend dropped into a chair and put his feet up on the balcony rail, Xavier turned and looked across the thick forests of the Butler Estate. "Why don't you find a woman, Vorian? She could tame you and give you something to look forward to each time you come back to Salusa."

"*Tame* me?" Vor shot him a wry smile. "Would I inflict myself on some poor, innocent female? I'm content enough to have a few women waiting for me here and there."

"In every spaceport, you mean."

"Not even close. I'm not the womanizer you think." Vor took a sip of wine and sighed with pleasure. "I may eventually select one, though." He left the obvious unspoken — the fact that he still had plenty of time. It was difficult for him to imagine spending all those years with only one woman.

Vor had served Omnius, but Serena Butler had changed his thinking and made him look at the universe in a different way — a *human* way. Vor had accepted the cause of the Jihad, not as a duped fool or an unquestioning fanatic, but as a proficient military commander with the skills General Agamemnon had taught him. Since escaping the rule of Omnius and declaring his loyalty to free humanity, Vorian Atreides claimed he had become more *alive* than he had ever imagined possible.

Normally, Vor loved to attend parties and tell stories about his battles, about his terrible cymek father, about growing up under the domination of thinking machines. Listeners would gather around him, awed by his tales, and he reveled in all the attention.

Now, though, the two men sat in companionable silence, needing to impress no one. They savored their wine, enjoyed the panorama of the vineyards and olive groves. As always in these rare, quiet times between Jihad missions, they discussed their successes and defeats, the fellow jihadis and mercenaries who had given their lives.

"Our problem all along," Vor said, "is that Iblis unleashes the fervor of his converts rather than adhering to a coordinated military strategy. Like flames following the fastest fuel, they burn bright, but don't necessarily accomplish the true objective. Personally, I think our Grand Patriarch just likes to bask in the glow."

Xavier nodded. "The Jihad has gone on for decades, and the basic struggle against Omnius for a thousand years before that. We must maintain our intensity and dedication, or our fighters will fall into despair."

Even after a year, the terrible loss of Vergyl Tantor still weighed heavily on both of them. While Xavier had loved his adoptive brother and tried to shepherd him through his military career, Vor had befriended the lad, socializing with the lower ranks in ways that stiffly formal Xavier could not. Seeing Vor and Vergyl laughing together had often made Xavier feel a flicker of envy. But it was too late now for him to make it up to his little brother . . .

Vor continued to stare out at the hills. "Thinking machines see the big picture, their overall plan. I don't think our Army of the Jihad has such a concept. Omnius may yet win — not through military strength, but through the apathy weakening our forces."

They talked about the smuggled reports from Ix, where the situation was particularly dire. Assassin robots and one of the Titan cymeks had begun a campaign of outright genocide, as they had done earlier on Earth. The Grand Patriarch had called for an all-out offensive not a moment too soon, according to Xavier. The Army of the Jihad could not abandon the brave fighters of Ix. Xavier himself had volunteered to lead the major assault. Meanwhile, in response to Iblis Ginjo's pleas, masses of exuberant new recruits had already volunteered for the conflict.

Vor frowned. "I see each of those victims on Ix as *people*, who are fighting for freedom and their very lives. We should not throw them away indiscriminately."

Xavier shook his head. "The insurgents on Ix do not need to become sacrificial lambs if a leader emerges to turn them into something more. That will be my responsibility."

Vor swallowed a tiny spiced egg and licked his fingers. "I understand that you're willing to achieve victory at any cost — you demonstrated that well enough on IV Anbus — but our Jihad will be better served by focusing on alternatives that hurt the machines without such a terrible cost in lives. The Ixian mission is . . . a mistake. Iblis has chosen it for no other reason than he wants its industrial centers intact."

"Industries build weapons and ships, Vorian. That is what drives the Jihad."

"Yes, but is a head-on military collision with the best forces of Omnius truly the wisest strategy?"

"You mean we should use more parlor tricks, like your virus against the machine battleships at IV Anbus? And your make-believe fleet at Poritrin?"

Pointedly, Vor cleared his throat. "Both of those tactics *worked*, didn't they? I've said it plenty of times before. Our greatest advantage is in our sheer unpredictability."

He finished his wine with a flourish, then reached over to take the bottle, refilling Xavier's glass and then his own. "Take the Poritrin ploy, for example. We couldn't afford to lose Holtzman's weapons laboratories, couldn't afford to devote a large Armada contingent to patrolling the orbit. My way, we achieved our aims at a relatively low cost, with no human casualties." Vor raised his eyebrows. "You just have to understand how machines think."

Xavier scowled. "I'm not as good at that as you are, my friend. Considering how long you lived with them."

Vor's gray eyes flashed. "Which means?"

"I didn't mean that the way it sounded."

Vor clinked his glass against Xavier's. "My way or your way, let's hope Omnius pays the price."

Vor tried to keep the machines guessing, and he had developed this ability far beyond even what Agamemnon had taught him. Not wanting his cymek father to predict his moves, he needed to stay one step ahead, just like a strategic gamble in a final round of Fleur de Lys.

Vor used his access codes to enter the armored laboratory room where the stolen copy of Omnius had been hooked up to carefully monitored computer substations. Salusans avoided this building, this prison for the demon Omnius, with a superstitious fear.

Vor entered the chamber and stood before the input screen and the Omnius speaker. He, a mere human and once a trustee of the computer evermind, now held it in complete thrall. What an astounding course of events his life had taken.

"Vorian Atreides," Omnius said. "You, of all the reckless, wild humans should recognize the folly of the Jihad. You understand the purpose and efficiency of the Synchronized Worlds, yet you turn your loyalty to this outright mayhem and wanton destruction. It defies logic."

Vor crossed his arms over his chest. "It merely defies your comprehension, Omnius, because thinking machines do not appreciate the value of freedom."

"Erasmus proved to me that no human could be trusted. It would have been to my advantage if I had eliminated all of your kind on the Synchronized Worlds. That was a missed opportunity, an unfortunate decision."

"You're paying for it now, Omnius, and you'll continue to pay until thinking machines are obliterated and humans can colonize any place they choose."

"What a disturbing thought," Omnius said.

Since Vor had been raised on Synchronized Worlds, he had a familiarity with programming, had even designed some segregated systems himself. For more than a year now, he had worked with portions of this Omnius update, extracting and manipulating information. The evermind sometimes understood what he was doing, but in other instances Vor was able to delete and manipulate any evidence of the changes he had wrought.

For years he had watched the tedious, unimaginative, even inept interrogations and attempted exploitation of this evermind copy. The scientists of the League, even Savant Holtzman, were too afraid of taking risks, fearful of causing damage to the captive Omnius. But what else was it for? Vor knew what he was doing, and preferred to take a chance at victory. He had always been independent, acting on his own impulses and usually succeeding.

If this plan succeeded, the Synchronized Worlds would reel, indeed. It was worth the risk, and Vor didn't want anyone else meddling with his scheme. They couldn't help him anyway.

By the time Xavier departed with his massive battle fleet for Ix, Vor hoped to be finished with his devious alterations to this update sphere. Teams of League cybernetic scientists had previously squeezed all possible intelligence from this captive copy. Even Savant Holtzman had been unable to wring further insights from the silvery gelsphere.

Now Vor would turn Omnius himself into a lethal weapon against the thinking machines. And the evermind incarnations on various Synchronized Worlds would never know what happened to them.

Cool and formal but with the subtlest undertone of indignation, Omnius said, "If you achieve your aims, Vorian Atreides, you will have to live with your folly. You will soon realize that human inefficiency can never replace the thinking machines. Is that truly what you desire?"

Grinning maliciously, Vor pointed out the computer's main weakness. "We have an advantage you can never comprehend, Omnius, and it will be your downfall."

"And what is that, Vorian Atreides?"

The dark-haired military officer leaned close to the screen, as if springing the punchline of a good joke. "We humans are endlessly inventive . . . and deceptive. Machines don't realize that they can be fooled."

Omnius made no response as he processed the statement. Vor knew, of course, that humans could also be deceived, but the evermind could not think in such terms. No machine could.

*The army fosters technology, and technology breeds anarchy be-
cause it distributes the terrible machines of destruction. Even before
this Jihad, one man alone could create and apply enough violence
to ravage an entire planet. It happened! Why do you think the
computer became anathema?*

—Serena Butler: *Zimia Rallies*

A S THEIR NUMBERS dwindled, the surviving cymeks saw their
conspiracy against Omnius fading. The chances for success and a
bright new Time of Titans dimmed with each passing year. Twenty of the
original conquerors had joined forces to overthrow the Old Empire, but
after losing Ajax, Barbarossa, Alexander, Tamerlane, Tlaloc, and all the
others, only four remained.

Not nearly enough to destroy Omnius.

At times, Agamemnon had considered simply destroying all of the
parasite watcheyes and fleeing into space, never to return. He could take
his lover Juno with him and Dante — perhaps even the dolt Xerxes. They
could set up an empire of their own far from the oppressive evermind.

But that would be foolishness. Utter failure.

The cymek general doubted Omnius would bother to hunt them down,
and the evermind certainly could not grasp the concept of revenge, but
Agamemnon and his comrades had been *Titans*, exalted conquerors of
the Old Empire. If they fled into darkness — a quartet of survivors ruling
nothing — that would be a more shameful defeat than their outright
destruction. No, Agamemnon wanted to conquer the Synchronized
Worlds for himself. He would settle for nothing less than total domination.

Returning from their assignments and depredations, stamping out
flickers of rebellion that continued to flare into bonfires on random
Synchronized Worlds, he and his fellow Titans held a meeting in the
wilderness of deep space.

Agamemnon had hoped for a secret gathering, since he had rarely been able to orchestrate his plans under the constant scrutiny of Omnius's watcheyes, whether they were fixed or mobile units. But this time he, Juno, Dante, and Xerxes were joined by the relative newcomer Beowulf, and Beowulf had not been able to shake his surveillance. They would have to be especially careful.

Agamemnon had always been slow to trust anyone, even another cymek who had endured for centuries. The Titans must always be cautious. Still, the general was intrigued by Beowulf's audacity.

Their ships linked up in deep space, and their hatches joined to form a cluster of artificial craft like a geometrical space station in an empty void far from any solar system. Stars sparkled like jewels all around them in the vastness of the cosmos. The middle of nowhere.

Installing his preservation canister into a small, resilient walker form, Agamemnon scuttled out of his ship and through the hatchway connected to Juno's vessel. The two of them strode side by side on limber segmented legs into the central vessel. Dante entered from the opposite side.

Standing beside Beowulf's walker-form, Xerxes was already there, on leave from his orgy of mayhem on Ix. Xerxes seemed agitated or perhaps eager, but Agamemnon was accustomed to the weak-willed Titan overreacting under most circumstances. The sooner Xerxes returned to Ix, the happier Agamemnon would be.

Overhead, lenses gleamed on hovering mobile watcheyes, recording every moment. Agamemnon chafed under the constant surveillance, as he had for the past eleven centuries.

"Hail to Lord Omnius," he said, sounding bored at the formal beginning of their meeting. His words were spoken with no particular enthusiasm. The computer evermind did not know how to interpret inflections of voice.

"On the contrary," Beowulf said boldly, "curses upon Omnius! May the evermind wither and the Synchronized Worlds fall into ruin until cymeks rule again."

Astonished, Juno reared back in her crablike body, though she harbored the same thoughts herself. The watcheyes glimmered down at them, and Agamemnon wondered what punishment Omnius would devise for the cymeks once the recordings were analyzed. The cymeks could not simply destroy the watcheyes before they reported to the evermind, or that would tip their hand and set back their plans, which were already centuries in the making.

Thanks to Barbarossa's ancient programming restrictions, the evermind could not kill any of the original Twenty Titans. However, as a mere neo-cymek, brash young Beowulf had no such protection. Despite his vulnerability, he had just called down a death sentence upon himself.

Xerxes could not contain his glee. "You have done it then, Beowulf? You've achieved success after all this time?"

"The reprogramming was straightforward enough. The real trick was to do it in such a way that Omnius would never suspect." With a segmented limb, he gestured toward the floating spherical lenses. "These watcheyes are diligently recording a completely artificial version of our meeting, an innocuous discussion of the human rebels. Omnius will be satisfied — and we can speak those thoughts that must be aired."

"I . . . do not understand," Dante said.

"I suspect we have been tricked, my love," Juno said to Agamemnon.

"Wait and listen," he answered, remaining motionless. His optic threads glimmered in the direction of Beowulf.

"I put him up to this, Agamemnon," Xerxes said with pride. "Beowulf hates Omnius as much as we do, and he's been under the evermind's control for nearly as long as we have. I believe his skill can bring much to our plans. Now, at last, we have a chance."

Agamemnon could barely contain his outrage. "You have plotted against Omnius, and now you attempt to implicate us? Xerxes, you are more of a fool than even I suspected. Do you mean to destroy us all?"

"No, no, Agamemnon. Beowulf is a programming genius, just like Barbarossa was. He's found a way to create an instructional loop that places false recordings into the watcheyes. Now we can meet whenever we wish, and Omnius will never know the difference."

Beowulf twitched his mechanical legs and took two steps forward. "General Agamemnon, I trained under your friend Barbarossa. He taught me how to manipulate the thinking machines, and I have continued to study secretly for centuries. I had hoped the Titans were chafing under the evermind's rule, as I have been . . . but I was not certain until Xerxes approached me."

"Xerxes, you have placed us all at terrible risk," Agamemnon growled.

But Dante, ever logical, ever methodical, pointed out the obvious. "The four of us are too few to accomplish what must be done. If more cymeks join our ranks, we have a better chance against Omnius."

"And a greater chance that one of them will betray us."

Even Juno agreed. "We need fresh blood, my love. Unless we recruit new conspirators, we will spend another millennium talking and complaining . . . those of us who survive. With Beowulf's help, we can at last move forward. By planning openly and frequently, we will achieve more in a few months than we have been able to accomplish in decades."

Still anxious, Xerxes said, "If we take no risks, we are no better than the apathetic humans who wallowed in the excesses of the Old Empire."

Beowulf waited for judgment to be passed on his inclusion in the conspiracy. Agamemnon admitted to himself that, of all the neo-cymeks, Beowulf would have been his first choice.

Despite his annoyance with the unilateral behavior of Xerxes, the general could not convince himself to refuse the offer. Finally he said, "Very well. This gives us the breathing room we need, the chance to move our plans forward." He swiveled his head turret, scanning Juno, Dante, Xerxes, and finally the expectant Beowulf. "Working together, we shall bring about the fall of Omnius. At last, the waiting is over."

There is a certain momentum to victory . . . and to defeat.
—Iblis Ginjo, *Options for Total Liberation*

W ITH THE GRAND Patriarch due to arrive on Poritrin at any moment, Lord Bludd had staged yet another lavish festival, so that the population could keep celebrating their victory over the thinking machines. Stands were erected around the edges of the riverside amphitheater, colorful banners were hung, and feasts were prepared, all to welcome Iblis Ginjo.

Amid such chaos, Aurelius Venport decided he would be able to sneak the outdated cargo ship unnoticed to the new laboratory.

Tuk Keedair had gone to Rossak to fetch the vessel from its spacedock and had arrived back in the Poritrin system at just the right moment, as he intended. With the Grand Patriarch's pageant preoccupying everyone, Venport was sure they could bring the big vessel down to Norma Cenva's new laboratory complex without drawing any undue attention. He wanted to keep a low profile on this project.

He had no real interest in noisy revelry tonight anyway. The profits from Holtzman's work — rightfully, *Norma's* work — had flooded Poritrin with more wealth than the most extravagant person could squander in a dozen lifetimes. Venport was confident that Norma's new space-folding project would make more money than anyone could possibly imagine.

Though the big hangar of the new research facility was not yet complete, Norma lived at the distant work site. Her first priority had been to convert the office space inside the old mining operations headquarters so that she could continue to study and modify her calculations. While construction supervisors roamed the fenced-in area and gave

orders to labor crews for the necessary renovations, Norma had immediately dived back into her scientific designs.

Thinking of her utter devotion, Venport smiled wistfully. Unlike most
people, who drifted through life seeking success or just a comfortable
existence, dear Norma had no doubts about her mission. Her concentration was unerring and her focus sharp.

Without disturbing the genius, Venport made it his job to take care of
all other details, shuttling back and forth to Starda to arrange for supplies
and equipment, furniture, and temporary work crews. To add another
layer of security for the project, Venport had decided that the slaves
building the hangar and restoring the decommissioned mining facilities
would not remain there long enough to see what Norma actually intended
to do.

For the time being, Lord Bludd was smugly delighted, thinking he had
negotiated an easy financial victory over Venport. Sensing this short-
sighted pride, Venport pressed his advantage by placing a direct request
with Bludd to have temporary use of some dedicated slaves, and agreeing
to pay a premium for well-trained and docile workers. No doubt the
Poritrin nobleman had charged him more than the captive Buddislamics
were worth, but Venport didn't have time to dicker and retrain an entire
labor force. He was due to depart for Arrakis soon, to try his hand at
quashing the band of wily outlaws that preyed upon Naib Dhartha's spice-
harvesting operations.

For the time being, his business partner Tuk Keedair would remain on
Poritrin with Norma. A strict taskmaster, he would make certain the
slaves behaved for her, so Norma could accomplish her goals on time. As
usual, she had reservations about using slave crews, but under the
circumstances Venport had no other choice. Buddislamics were the only
available work force on Poritrin.

In late afternoon Venport returned to the isolated worksite, docking his
shuttleboat in the narrow canyon when the water became too shallow to
navigate. Norma's new laboratory and hangar filled an immense chamber
that had once been behind a waterfall, but that cascade of water, like the
subsidiary river that fed it, was long gone, having been diverted centuries
ago by Lord Frigo Bludd's resource reclamation projects for Starda's
agricultural needs. The roof of the grotto was open to the sky, though
covered by a large warehouse hangar under construction on top of the
plateau.

A smooth passenger lift had been installed on the cliffside, and
Venport rode it to the top of the canyon. Surrounded by blockish support
buildings, the converted-warehouse hangar gleamed in the late afternoon

light. Its cantilevered roof had been rolled out of the way to the sides, so that the large building was ready to receive the expected prototype vessel.

Venport nodded with satisfaction at the progress the workers had made; he hoped he could verify that the facilities were ready for operation before he left for Arrakis. Striding through the gate past three local guards he had hired, he found the work supervisor and asked for a progress report. Around the warehouse and outbuildings, slaves were taking a brief late-day break to eat, rest, and pray. Afterward, they would be back on the project until late night.

Norma emerged from her enclosed calculation offices and blinked in the waning light, surprised that a whole day had passed. Venport came forward, grinning; out of habit, he gave her a warm embrace. Her hair looked shaggy and uncared for, but the mere fact that she didn't put on airs or pretend to be beautiful made her seem more attractive to him.

"Is my ship coming in this afternoon, Aurelius? Is it the right day, or did I lose one on my calendar?"

"It arrives in less than an hour, Norma." He gestured toward the open rooftop. "The hangar seems to be ready."

Her face grew eager. "Then I can commence the actual test phase of my project?"

He nodded, letting his hand linger on her diminutive shoulder. His heart warmed when she smiled at him. "Lord Bludd has promised me he'll reassign a qualified team of slaves from the fabricators and constructors of the recent spaceship fleet. They have experience in this sort of work, so I hope they'll require little training."

"OK, because I won't have the time or the attention to spend all day directing them. They will have to work independently—"

"Tuk Keedair will stay here to take care of all that," Venport assured her. "He's also bringing in a large force of mercenary security guards whose loyalty is to VenKee Enterprises, not to Poritrin. They'll keep watch over the facilities and make certain the slaves don't try to commit any sabotage." He glanced back downriver. "They'll also keep Lord Bludd and Tio Holtzman from snooping around."

"I never worried about so much security before."

"Holtzman did. He always had Dragoon guards in his laboratories."

"For years, Savant Holtzman has paid little attention to me, Aurelius. Why should he bother me now?"

"Because if he has even a fraction of the genius that's attributed to him, he can't remain duped forever, and he'll realize what a wonder he lost by letting you go."

Embarrassed at the compliment, Norma glanced around the

construction site, as if she didn't remember several of the buildings being there the last time she'd noticed the details. "But where will you be?"

Venport sighed, realizing that she had not been paying attention. "I told you already, Norma. I'm off to Arrakis to take care of some problems in our spice operations. Keedair will have the easier and far more pleasant task of remaining here with you."

Norma frowned. Though she was well into middle age, her expression reminded him of the little girl on Rossak he had adored so much. "I wish you could stay with me, Aurelius. I'd much rather have your friendly face around than . . . a Tlulaxa slaver."

Venport laughed. "You don't have to like Keedair, Norma. Just let him do his work." He sighed. "And, trust me, I'd rather stay as well. But I have too much work to do — and I'm afraid my time here with you would be so enjoyable that I'd be completely distracted from accomplishing anything worthwhile."

She giggled with girlish joy. Venport caught himself, wondering if he'd actually been flirting with her. After a moment's consideration, he decided that he had. After so many years of their close friendship, he asked himself why that should surprise him.

The construction manager hurried out of the hangar, looking for Venport. "We just received a signal, Directeur. The vessel has received routine clearance and is on its way down through the atmosphere. Tuk Keedair is at the controls."

Venport nodded, not surprised that his partner would choose to pilot the craft himself. The flesh peddler had spent years as a merchant, raiding Unallied Planets and capturing Buddislamic slaves. He knew how to handle a simple cargo hauler.

"Look, Norma. There it is." He pointed to a bright light making its way through the faint colors of dusk.

The image grew brighter, its hull hot from reentry, and Norma heard the sonic booms of its passage. It was a large ship, designed primarily for long-distance space travel and occasional surface landings, although most of the cargo loading was done using transport shuttles.

As a spacecraft, the vessel was comparatively sluggish and inefficient. Now, as Keedair spoke across the narrow-band transmitter, he grumbled about the antiquated ship systems. Obviously, Venport had decommissioned the craft for good reason.

Finally, Keedair brought the large vessel over the open hangar and, with expert maneuvering, lowered it into the empty warehouse. Venport watched, not sure if the beamy craft would even fit through the open rooftop. But the Tlulaxa merchant managed with several meters to spare.

Norma watched the landing with awe, and Venport could imagine the wheels turning in her mind. She had seen blueprints and design studies of the ship, so she already understood the modifications she would have to make. But simply seeing the vessel with her own eyes seemed to ignite her imagination.

"A template for all future interstellar flight," she said. "What I accomplish here will change everything."

Venport drew optimism from her. Norma couldn't tear her gaze from the ship until it had landed inside the hangar and workers rushed forward to install docking anchors and stabilizers.

Norma reached out and squeezed his much larger hand. "I have been looking forward to this for so many years, Aurelius. I can hardly believe what I'm seeing. I still have plenty of work to do, but can finally get started."

Grand Patriarch Iblis Ginjo expected his arrival to cause a bit of a stir, and the capital city of Starda staged an appropriately extravagant reception. At any given moment, numerous planets were engaged in the battle against the thinking machines. According to his calendar, the stepped-up Ix campaign should now be in full swing, but Iblis did not want to thrust himself into such overt personal danger. Thus, Poritrin was a good place for him to be, since the robot invaders had already fled.

By fomenting the initial uprising on Earth, Iblis had proved he was no coward, but his vital position as head of the Jihad Council precluded him from taking great risks now. Though his presence on the battlefields would no doubt have boosted the morale of the desperate fighters, the Grand Patriarch didn't want to chance being seen anywhere but the site of a genuine victory. Such as here.

Accompanied by his loyal but discreet Jipol lieutenant Yorek Thurr, Iblis disembarked from his ship at Starda Spaceport and strutted forward to meet a small official delegation. Noting that Lord Bludd was himself absent, Iblis muttered a displeased comment just as a youthful Poritrin aide hurried up to him.

"Your timing is excellent, Grand Patriarch. The awards ceremony is only two hours from now, but there is time for our wardrobe engineers to prepare you for your appearance with Lord Bludd." The young aide wore a black-and-white jerkin and tuxcape, one of the trendy styles on noble worlds.

When a hoverbarge delivered Iblis and his entourage to the amphitheater, he was given a seat on the expansive riverfront platform, but off to one side, just one of seventy politicians and noblemen. As many as four hundred thousand people crowded the grassy fields, gazing up at projection screens and listening through crisp speaker systems that floated on suspensors. Hastily erected shrines to Manion the Innocent stood prominently on blufftops above the river. A new statue had been unveiled, a large and somewhat absurd construct of a cherubic Buddha-like child seated atop a crushed robot.

Lord Niko Bludd had the most prominent seat, skewered by spotlights at the head of walkways that led to the stage. Obviously, the foppish man considered himself the reason for the gathered spectators.

Meanwhile, at center stage, Savant Tio Holtzman was receiving honors before a cheering crowd. The inventor beamed and waved to the blurred mass of faces. Iblis sat wearing a frozen smile.

The Grand Patriarch always had an agenda in mind, an important task to complete. As far as Iblis was concerned, life was brutishly short and too much needed to be done. After taking a deep breath, he decided not to notice the slight that Niko Bludd had given to him. Not yet.

A situation like this, with so many people excited about a convincing military victory, would provide Iblis with his opportunity.

Good intentions can bring about as much destruction as an evil conqueror. Either way, the result is the same.

—Zensunni Lament

ALIID CONSIDERED HIS friend Ishmael a fool. The fiery Zenshiite could not keep the scorn or disbelief out of his voice when he scoffed, "Did you honestly expect gratitude? From *them*? I cannot say I admire your blind faith, but I do find it amusing." His smile contained no humor, only hard edges.

In the months after the hollow fleet had successfully bluffed the machine marauders, the consolidated slave force was pulled from the mudflat shipyards and broken into smaller groups. Many of the workers returned to their original owners for regular assignments in the cane fields and mines. Aliid had remained with the Starda factory crew, since none of his previous owners was eager to reclaim him. At first Ishmael had rejoiced to have more time with his childhood companion, but later felt a twinge of uncertainty.

"It was our dedicated work that built the decoy fleet, Aliid. *Our* labor saved Poritrin." The distress and disappointment was palpable in Ishmael's words. "Even someone as pampered and oblivious as Lord Bludd must admit this fact."

"You are a slave, and he is a noble," Aliid replied. "There is nothing he is required to admit, while we are required to *submit*."

But Ishmael had not listened. The slaves received no rest or increased rations, no better accommodations or medical treatment, no concessions to their Buddislamic beliefs . . . not even the smallest of rewards. It was outrageously unfair, but apparently only Ishmael had expected anything different.

In Ishmael's boyhood his grandfather had lectured him with gentle sternness, "If you are unwilling to speak of your concern to the person who has wronged you, do not complain when he fails to resolve the situation of his own accord."

Ishmael took that to heart. The Koran Sutras insisted that the human heart and soul — even in nonbelievers — contained a kernel of fundamental goodness and mercy. As a slave, he had remained passive for too long, accepting his inferior lot. He had spent too many nights reciting empty promises and clinging to diluted dreams that seemed overly easy — as hollow as the decoy ships that had frightened away the robot war fleet. He owed this to all those who had listened to him, for so long.

Now that he and his companions had performed inarguable service for Poritrin, Ishmael knew it was time to take up his concerns with Lord Bludd himself. God would guide him and show him what to say. Ishmael would prove to Aliid, and to all the Zensunnis who listened to him around the story fire, that his beliefs were reliable.

Exasperated, Aliid caught Ishmael before he could blunder innocently into what would surely be a disaster. "At least think of a plan, my friend! How will you get into the presence of Lord Bludd? You can't simply knock on his door and speak your mind."

"If he is the lord of his people, he should listen to a valid complaint."

The other man rolled his eyes. "You are a slave, not a citizen. He has no reason to listen to you." He leaned close. "Use your imagination, Ishmael. You have worked for Savant Holtzman, you know his routines, how he interacts with Lord Bludd. Use that to find an excuse, or you'll never get within a hundred meters of him."

Ishmael considered the possibilities. He did not like lies or misdirection, but Aliid was right. In this instance, it was a necessary means to an end.

At the end of the following work shift, he returned to the habitation compound with the other captives. There, after washing himself and dressing in his cleanest clothes, he kissed his wife and prepared to go. He took up a set of logbooks he had smuggled out of the factory offices that were being decommissioned and made his way across the city to the Poritrin lord's conical towers. The veteran slave wore an expression of respect, but not meek submission. Buddallah walked in his footsteps, gave him strength.

Two gold-armored Dragoon guards at the tower's street-level gate looked at Ishmael skeptically. Careful to show no threat, he chose his words prudently, trying not to lie but still attempting some sleight of hand. "My name is Ishmael, and I must see Lord Niko Bludd."

The Dragoons studied him. "A *slave* to see Lord Bludd? Do you have an appointment?"

His armored companion said, "Lord Bludd does not grant audiences with slaves."

Ishmael wondered if Buddallah would make the men step aside, clearing the way for him to enter. But he did not expect such an obvious divine intervention.

Feeling audacious, Ishmael withdrew the purloined logbooks and held them out. "I am one of Savant Holtzman's slaves. He has regularly sent persons such as myself to deliver written documents." He hesitated before finally telling an outright lie. "The Savant has sent me with these. He insisted it was a matter of some urgency, that I must not return until I had delivered them to Lord Bludd personally."

The taller Dragoon grumbled. "Everything to do with Holtzman is urgent." He frowned at Ishmael. "Lord Bludd doesn't have time for that today."

Ishmael did not back away. "Perhaps you should explain that to Savant Holtzman yourself. He will not believe it from me that Lord Bludd refused to receive these logs." He drew a breath and waited; his faith gave him serenity and confidence.

Following a moment of silence, the other Dragoon said uncertainly, "We've always let them deliver the logbooks before. What if the Savant has had another breakthrough, like the shields?"

The first guard agreed. "Maybe we should let Bludd throw him out personally."

Responding to the brief hesitation, Ishmael bowed and then stepped quickly through the doorway. His confidence weakened the guards, and they gave way. Wide-eyed, Ishmael entered the palatial government mansion of the hereditary lord, whose ancestors had enslaved Buddislamic captives for generations.

Just inside, a harried chamberlain frowned at Ishmael's dark-skinned features and his Zensunni garb, but again the name of Tio Holtzman and the impressive-looking logbooks proved of sufficient weight to overcome doubts and questions. One of the guards, apparently having second thoughts, moved close and said, "I'm sorry, sir. If you want me to remove him . . ."

The royal officer shook his head at the Dragoon, then met Ishmael's steady gaze. "Are you certain you must deliver these to Lord Bludd *now*? He won't have time to look at them anyway. In only an hour he is hosting a banquet for offworld painters who wish to depict Starda under varying lighting conditions." The chamberlain shot a meaningful glance toward the wall chronometer. "If this was so important, Savant Holtzman should have made an appointment for you. Are you certain—"

"I am sorry, sir," Ishmael interrupted. He offered no further explanation, nor did he volunteer to leave.

"Lord Bludd can spare you very little time."

"Even a moment of his generosity will be enough. Thank you."

"Shall I check him for weapons?" the Dragoon asked.

"Of course."

When the body search was completed, Ishmael waited in an echoing reception gallery. In the center stood a bench made of polished stone; though it looked lovely, it proved uncomfortable. He sat in placid silence, patiently enduring the delay.

In his mind, the bold slave recited his favorite sutras, verses he had learned at his grandfather's knee. He had long ago stopped wishing that his life might have been different, that he had escaped when the raiders attacked the marshes of Harmonthep. For better or worse, his life was here on Poritrin, and he had a loving wife, along with two beautiful daughters who were almost women themselves . . .

Nearly an hour passed, and finally he was taken up a wide flight of stairs into Lord Bludd's private suite and gallery. His skin felt warm, and his thoughts blazed with possibilities. With good fortune his plea would touch the heart of the nobleman who ruled Poritrin. He hoped his words were persuasive.

Inside a room that smelled of candles and perfumes, courtiers were dressing the bearded lord in a padded vest, gold chains, and thick cuffs. His reddish-gold hair had paled with age, intertwined now with gray. A tattoo of tiny clustered circles like bubbles marked the side of his eye. Personal servants bustled about, splashing scented water onto his hair and cheeks. One rail-thin man brushed lint from the fabric of his lord's robe with the intensity of a philosopher studying the key to all knowledge.

The lord looked up at Ishmael, and sighed. "Well, it isn't often that Tio sends one of his slaves to meet with me, and he isn't usually so insistent — or timely — with his reports. What does the Savant want this evening? It is quite an inconvenient time." He reached out to take the logbooks,

Ishmael kept his voice calm and soft, as polite as he could manage. Respectful but with a degree of confidence, as if he imagined himself an equal. Realizing the importance of his every word, he drew silent strength from deep within. "Perhaps there has been a misunderstanding, Lord Bludd. Savant Holtzman did not send me here. My name is Ishmael, and I have come of my own accord to speak with you."

The courtiers stopped in shock. Bludd blinked at Ishmael with distaste, then looked up to glare at his chamberlain, who in turn snapped a harsh look at the Dragoon guards.

Peripherally, Ishmael saw the chamberlain moving forward to take him away, but Bludd motioned for the aide to stay back. His voice was annoyed now, demanding explanations. "Why have you come here if it isn't about Savant Holtzman?" He held up the logbooks. "What are these?"

Ishmael smiled, letting the words flow through him, hoping that he could soften the nobleman's heart with reason and sympathy. "Lord, for generations my people have served and protected Poritrin. My fellow slaves and I worked on many of Savant Holtzman's projects, which have saved untold League citizens from the thinking machines. In the past year we labored without respite to fabricate your successful decoy fleet."

Lord Bludd scowled, as if he had swallowed a rancid sweetmeat. Then he smiled cruelly and replied, "That comes under the definition of being a slave."

Nearby, the chamberlain chuckled.

But Ishmael saw no humor in this. "We are human beings, Lord Bludd." He calmed himself, refusing to allow his determination to slip. "We have shed sweat and blood in order to protect your way of life. We have watched your celebrations. Because of our efforts, Poritrin has remained independent of the thinking machines."

"Because of *your* efforts?" Bludd's face grew stormy at the audacity of this Zensunni man. "You have done exactly as your masters ordered you to do, nothing more. *We* saw the threat coming. *We* developed the means to guard against it. *We* drew up the plans, and *we* provided the resources. You merely put the pieces together, as you were commanded to do."

"My Lord, you underestimate and belittle what your captives have done for—"

"What is it you people want — my eternal gratitude? Nonsense! You helped to save your own lives, not just ours. That should be enough for you. Would you rather be rotting in a thinking machine prison right now, being dissected by curious robots? Count your blessings I am not the arch-demon Erasmus."

He ruffled his sleeves and shooed his attendants away. "Now go, slave. I wish to hear no more of this, and do not ever attempt to speak directly with me again. Your deception is cause enough for your execution. I am the Lord of Poritrin, the head of a family that has been in power here for generations, while you are but a . . . transplanted coward whose food and shelter is provided only at my own sufferance."

Ishmael was deeply offended, but had heard this sort of insult before.

He wanted to argue, to state his case more plainly, but saw from the look of dull anger simmering in Lord Bludd's eyes that nothing he could say would have a satisfactory effect. He had failed. Perhaps Aliid had been right to scoff at his naïve faith.

I have underestimated how different, how alien, this man's thoughts can be. I do not comprehend Lord Bludd at all. Is he even human?

Recently, during nighttime discussions around the story fire in the slave encampment, Aliid had grown increasingly strident, encouraging the people to follow in Bel Moulay's footsteps. Now Aliid wanted to attempt another revolution, regardless of how much bloodshed it might involve. Every time Ishmael tried to be a voice of reason and speak against the naked quest for revenge, Aliid shouted him down.

After this meeting, though, Ishmael wasn't sure how much more he could argue. He had tried his best, and Lord Bludd had refused to listen.

Hoping the nobleman would not change his mind and order his immediate execution, Ishmael bowed again and backed slowly toward the door. The Dragoon guards grabbed his arms rudely and escorted him out, growling curses under their breath. Ishmael didn't struggle or respond to their insults; it would take little to provoke them into beating him to death.

Even though his faith had been rocked to the core, and his innocent beliefs found wanting, he was not sorry for having tried. Not yet.

Within days the new orders came in, reassigning Ishmael and many others who had worked on the shipyard construction project. He, Aliid, and a hundred like them were to be sent far upriver to a new facility, where they would be put to work on an independent project led by Norma Cenva, the female genius from Rossak who had once served as Savant Holtzman's assistant.

The Dragoons also had explicit instructions that the slave Ishmael was to be separated from his family. The sergeant said in a gruff voice, "Your wife and daughters will remain here for reassignment" — from beneath his gold-scaled helmet, he smiled — "probably to three separate places."

Ishmael's knees wobbled, and he could not believe what he had heard. "No, that is impossible!" He had been with Ozza for fifteen years. "I have done nothing –" The guards took him by the arms, but he broke free and ran toward his stricken-looking wife, who stood with Chamal and Falina.

Lord Bludd had made his displeasure clear, and the soldiers had been looking for an excuse to punish Ishmael. They removed stun sticks and struck him on the knees, on the small of his back, on his shoulders and head.

Ishmael, who was not a violent man, crumpled with a cry. With tears streaming down her face, cursing the attackers, Ozza tried to reach him. But the Dragoons kept her away. Their daughters attempted to dodge around the gold-armored men, but Ishmael feared more for their safety than his own. If they drew too much attention to themselves, Chamal and Falina might be taken away by the guards, for depraved sport. His two beautiful girls . . .

"No, stay back. I will go with them. We will find some way to be together."

Ozza gathered the girls close to her and looked at the Dragoons as if she wanted to claw their eyes out. But she knew her husband, and did not want to do anything that would bring more harm to him. "We will be together again, my darling Ishmael."

Slowly, Aliid moved to stand beside him, an angry fire kindling his eyes. The Dragoons seemed amused by this Zenshiite man's stormy defiance. Ishmael groaned and tried to maintain his balance amid a storm of pains.

As the guards herded the new work crew away to their assignment upriver, Ishmael struggled to get another look at Ozza and the girls, perhaps for the last time. When Aliid had been separated from his family, he had never seen his wife and son again.

Now Aliid spoke in a harsh whisper, using the old Chakobsa tongue that none of the slavers could understand. "I told you, these men are monsters. Lord Bludd is the worst. Now do you see that your simplistic faith is not enough?"

Stubbornly, Ishmael shook his head.

Despite all, he was not prepared to cast aside the Zensunni beliefs that formed the foundation of his life. Seeing his failure, would the others who had so carefully listened to his evening parables and sutras give up on him? Ishmael was being sorely tested — and had no idea what his ultimate answer would be.

175 B.G.

JIHAD YEAR 27

One Year after the Victory on Poritrin

War: A manufactory that produces desolation, death, and secrets.
—Statement of anti-Jihad protester

PRIMERO HARKONNEN DID not find the long, slow flight to Ix a serene one. The gung-ho enthusiasm of new recruits on board the ballista flagship had gradually settled into a dread of facing the thinking machine forces on the long-embattled Synchronized World. Everyone in the massive attack force knew the stakes, and the dangers.

Xavier's mandate was clear. The rebels on Ix had fought long and hard against an overwhelming army of cymeks and hunter-killer robots, and now he would add sufficient forces to turn the tide. The humans could not afford to lose. Once he had freed another planet from Omnius, then he would sleep easier.

One world at a time.

Back home, Octa had never liked to see him depart on another assignment for the Jihad. During their marriage, Xavier had gone off on one dangerous mission after another. It was difficult for her to watch him go, but Octa knew the stakes in this never-ending war. She had seen firsthand what the brutality of the thinking machines had done to her sister Serena. War changed people. Someone had to protect the innocent. Xavier and Vor were among those who risked their lives to do just that, and Octa had always understood that this war was his calling. In war everyone made sacrifices.

And though Xavier loved her intensely and knew she had complete faith in him, he always saw the fear in her eyes when he left Salusa Secundus — but it was a fear that Octa mastered. She did everything possible to make him feel loved and comfortable when they were together, so that he would hold good memories for all the long days until he could return home. Once, he had even joked with Octa that she always threw the largest celebrations on the days he went away.

Before her husband left on the difficult and risky campaign to liberate Ix, Octa had once again prepared a feast and called their closest loved ones. Serena was invited to join them, as always, but the Priestess of the Jihad rarely attended any small gatherings, even with her family. The office of Grand Patriarch Ginjo had politely declined the invitation on Serena's behalf, responding that she was simply too busy.

Those who did not know Octa well saw her as a shy, quiet woman who stood in the shadow of the great Primero. But when she made up her mind and focused her thoughts, Octa displayed all the rigidity and firmness of an angry military commander. She rallied the servants, the cleaners, and the cooks, making sure absolutely everything went perfectly.

Old Manion Butler himself stayed down in the cellars for an hour selecting three rare bottles of wine. Xavier knew that the retired Viceroy didn't keep any less than the best vintages, but out of love he still encouraged his father-in-law to make the choices, a task he relished.

In the late afternoon, Xavier's two grown daughters, Roella and Omilia, joined them at the departure feast, along with their husbands. Roella had reached the age of twenty-six, and her sister was two years younger. Omilia brought her new baby daughter, to the delight of her parents.

Octa adored Omilia's new baby, and watched wistfully as the child smiled at Xavier. Though he had lost a son of his own, he was exceedingly proud of his two daughters and the lives they were making for themselves. Both Omilia and Roella were strikingly lovely, but Xavier was not exactly an objective judge.

"Sometimes I wish we could have had at least one more," Octa said, tickling the baby.

To Xavier, his wife was still the most beautiful of them all, though she was by now forty-five years old. He still saw the youthful glow she carried within her, and he still found her more attractive than any young woman. Xavier shrugged and gave her his best boyish grin. "No one said you're too old."

"It's not very likely." She teased him, but he continued to smile.

"That's no reason for us to stop trying."

But Xavier couldn't help being uncomfortable and heartsick as he faced the other guests. His adoptive father, Emil Tantor, was accompanied by Vergyl's widow Sheel and their three children.

Xavier couldn't believe that two years had already passed since the debacle at IV Anbus. He still felt pangs of guilt and regret for allowing Vergyl to be captured by the cymeks. His brother had been thirty-four years old at the time of his death — by no means a child — but Xavier could never stop thinking of the grinning young man as his little brother, a boy he had played with . . . and later let down. Vergyl and Sheel should have had a fine, long life together. His brother's family was wonderful, but their future had been torn away . . . just as his own had been when Serena was kidnapped by the thinking machines.

Damn this Jihad!

Still, even after losing Serena, Xavier had made a good life for himself. And he would not have changed any of it, even if he could. He had no doubt that Sheel was strong enough to do the same, under the guidance of the aged, increasingly frail Emil Tantor.

Though he was overjoyed to see his father, as well as Vergyl's family, Xavier still felt awkward, not knowing what to say. Omilia's new baby seemed to sadden Sheel, and his father also appeared somber, perhaps remembering that his own wife Lucille had been killed in a flyer crash shortly before she was to meet Vergyl's baby daughter for the first time . . .

When the first course was ready to be served, Octa led the prayer. She gave thanks for the food and for their lives, begged God for Xavier's safety on the mission to Ix, and prayed for deliverance from Omnius and all thinking machines.

Xavier had known this was supposed to be a joyous occasion, his loved ones bidding him farewell and wishing him success in his latest military campaign. The Ixian mission was fraught with peril, and though he would never surrender easily, he was certain that many other jihadi soldiers were having similar farewell dinners with their close families . . . and many of them would not, in fact, return.

The moment Octa saw his mood fall, even before the main course could be brought out, she called in a trio of youthful Zimia musicians who played their instruments and sang in a lovely contralto, while the other guests ate and talked in low conversations.

Hearing the happy minstrels, Xavier thought again of the dead, of Octa's twin brother Fredo, who had always wanted to be a musician and an artist. As he watched his wife, he expected to see similar thoughts reflected in her face, but she took only joy from the musicians' performance, and soon the rest of the guests responded as well, enjoying their meal, talking, and laughing.

Octa was radiant. Later, in the heat of pitched battle, he would remember that more than anything else.

Though he was the one going to Ix to fight the murderous machines, Octa fought just as bravely in her own battle to maintain good spirits and optimism in her household, because that was the only weapon she could wield. She had done the same thing each time Xavier had gone off to war, and it had always worked.

But he had gone away too many times.

A few years after the League Armada's devastation of Earth, Xavier had led the first "official" attack of Serena Butler's expanding Jihad. After selecting a Synchronized World at random — Bela Tegeuse — the warships had gone out with much fanfare. Vorian Atreides had distinguished himself in that battle, earned a higher rank, and proved his true fervor for the cause of humanity.

The battle of Bela Tegeuse had destroyed many robots and obliterated extensive thinking machine infrastructure, but the enemy fought back relentlessly. The skirmish was ultimately inconclusive, and the human forces retreated to lick their wounds. A year later, and without orders, Vorian had slipped back to the Tegeusan system and returned home to report that the machines had rebuilt everything and continued to oppress the surviving human population there. It was as if nothing had happened. Despite the terrible struggle and loss of life, the Jihad had made no progress whatsoever.

It was after Earth and Bela Tegeuse, however, that the Omnius everminds realized that the character of the struggle had changed. In response, the Corrin-Omnius sent a heavy fleet against Salusa Secundus, but the newly formed Army of the Jihad — led by Xavier himself — rebuffed them. At the time, he had considered it payback for the Battle of Zimia, where he had been so badly injured years before.

Now, en route to Ix, the senior officer was spoiling for another chance. He'd had many opportunities in the quarter century since the destruction of Earth, and each fight gave him the chance to strike another blow. To free more humans. To devastate the thinking machines.

If only his fighters could maintain their edge . . . and their energy.

During the long and tense voyage, Xavier issued orders imposing a rigorous training routine on his soldiers, to keep their reflexes sharp. A separate force under his command, the normally aloof mercenaries from Ginaz were pleased to demonstrate their combat abilities for Xavier's troops.

The Primero often spent hours watching them from above, judging their techniques, mentally selecting the best fighters among the recruits.

He found the new batch of mercenaries particularly interesting. Never before had he witnessed such skill in hand-to-hand combat.

The fighters deferred to their new champion Jool Noret, a mysterious and intense young man in a black jumpsuit. Fresh from the archipelago on Ginaz, the young mercenary had bronzed skin, jade eyes, and sun-bleached hair. As thin and fast as a human whip, Noret wielded blade weapons with a speed that turned them into lethal barbs.

An enigmatic loner, Noret rarely spoke to anyone, including his fellow mercenaries. Nonetheless, he threw himself into even the most basic of training exercises with reckless abandon and without concern for his personal well-being. He seemed to be blessed — or cursed — with a belief in his own invulnerability.

As commanding officer, Xavier observed him closely. In combat demonstrations Noret fought with utter conviction, though he seemed to prefer his own company when he was off duty.

Now, inside the crowded common room, Noret sat in the middle of his fellows and seemed to shut out all distractions. In full view of the rest of the crew, he contorted his body into supple okuma positions, then held himself rigid, facing a bulkhead while he journeyed inward to a realm of contemplation.

Suddenly, with blinding speed, he leapt to his feet, whirling and diving, striking out with his bare hands, as well as more traditional weapons — a small club and a heavy stun-ball connected like a bolo to a thin chain on his wrist. It seemed to be a test, or a game, but the Ginaz mercenaries treated it with absolute seriousness. A quartet rushed at him, but Noret dispatched them all with startling efficiency.

For a finale, he tossed his assorted weapons into the air, defeated two more men with martial arts blows, snatched the weapons back out of the air, then slipped them into concealed pockets in his black clothing. Though soundly beaten, none of his companions were seriously hurt. No doubt they would challenge Noret again . . . and just as certainly, the young man would win.

Two days later, Xavier made a point of approaching Noret, wanting to learn more about him. Even during the tedious voyages between battle-fields, the Primero had never felt comfortable fraternizing with his troops, as Vor always did. His friend would eat in the common mess hall with the soldiers, spinning tall tales for them about his adventures, playing round after round of Fleur de Lys, which he won without smugness and lost without rancor.

But Xavier had never been able to do that. He was their commanding officer — a leader among men, but rarely a friend. Instead of calling out a good-natured greeting as he walked along the crew decks, the soldiers all snapped to attention and gave him crisp salutes. Complete respect seemed to be a barrier between them and him. Privately, the men called him "Old Fuss and Formality."

Now he did not seek out Jool Noret as a friend. In the ballista's crew compartments, the young mercenary was tidying his lower bunk, carefully stowing articles of clothing and exotic weapons in an adjacent locker. Even for such a mundane task, Noret's every movement was fluid and quick.

The room was nearly empty with the current duty shift. The Primero came toward him from behind, making no noise loud enough to be heard over the background hum of the spaceship engines and conversations in the outer corridors. Even so, he noticed that the young mercenary stiffened without actually seeing him. He seemed to be watching with his *ears*.

Xavier moved into his line of sight and stood with his arms folded across his chest. "I have observed your combat exhibitions, Jool Noret. Your technique is very interesting."

"And I have observed you observing, Primero."

Xavier had already considered his purpose in this encounter. Another week remained until they arrived in the Ixian system and began their campaign. "I believe you have skills you could teach to my men, techniques that will increase their chances of survival when they fight the thinking machines."

The young mercenary looked away, as if stung. "I am not a teacher. I still have too much to learn myself."

"But the men respect you and want to learn from you. If you instruct them in your methods, you could save lives."

Donning a haunted expression, the young man seemed to withdraw into himself. "That is not the reason I agreed to fight for the Jihad. I want to destroy thinking machines. I want to die bravely in battle."

Xavier did not understand what demons troubled this man. "I would rather you fought bravely and *survived*, to destroy even more of the enemy. And if you help my jihadis to improve, we will be more easily assured of victory."

Noret remained silent for so long that Xavier didn't think he intended to respond at all. "I won't be a teacher," he said, at last. "That is too much of a burden on top of the others I carry. I will not have their blood on my hands if they fail to perform with adequate skill." He looked up at the aging officer, his expression sad. "However, they are welcome to . . . observe, if they wish."

Xavier nodded, for the moment unwilling to push harder and discover what disturbed Noret so deeply. "Good enough. Perhaps they can learn something by watching you. If it works out, I'll consider requesting additional compensation for you when we return home."

"I don't want any of that," Noret said, his expression intense and strangely frightening. "Just give me free rein to kill machines."

Beware of well-meaning friends. They can be as dangerous as enemies.

— General Agamemnon, *Memoirs*

A FTER XAVIER AND his battle group departed for Ix, Vor's mind burned with alternatives. Brute force was a stale and old-fashioned tactic, but not at all the most effective way to defeat the thinking machines. His eyes twinkled impishly as his mind gave birth to possibilities, devising schemes that could prove more effective than all the warships in the Army of the Jihad.

This was more than a friendly competition with his fellow primero. Clever tricks could save countless lives. Human lives.

Without fanfare or much attention whatsoever, Vor commandeered a single-man scout ship. As usual, the jihadi officers were concerned. They warned him of the risks involved and insisted that he take along an escort of armed gunships. But Vor just laughed and brushed them off. They still did not know what he had done to the captive Omnius sphere, now hidden in his cockpit. No one knew. Yet.

Out in open space, Vor set course for a world he had never again expected to visit, and certainly not by choice: Earth. The birthplace of humanity. Now nothing more than a radioactive, charred ball.

Vor knew what he would find there . . . and still he went.

Though he had no reason to venture down to the surface, he took extra time to cruise above the stormy atmosphere, scanning the lifeless land masses below. The night-side continents were black, showing no signs of civilization, and as he circled around to the daylight side he noted swirling white clouds, murky oceans, and brown land masses with almost no smear of green.

He remembered the many times he had flown here in the *Dream*

Voyager. Thumbing back through the internal ledger of his thoughts, he envisioned himself and the independent robot Seurat approaching the homeworld of humanity, the central planet of Omnius. The network of city lights, the grid of bright industry and civilization had always called out to Vor. But the beautiful glitter was now absent. It had been decades since the nuclear annihilation, and still the planet looked mostly dead. Perhaps one day Earth would again be habitable, but for now it was only a scar marking a wound that humans had dealt the thinking machines . . . and themselves.

Vor had spent his formative years here, studying his father's memoirs, absorbing the cymek general's distorted version of history. Then Serena Butler had shown him that his life was filled with distortions and outright lies. He had escaped. He had been reborn.

In his new life as a free human in the League of Nobles, Vor found himself fascinated with history. He read the records of ancient humanity and memorized details of the original Agamemnon, the ancient general who had fought in the Trojan War, as recorded in Homer's *Iliad*.

In his studies Vor sought to differentiate between history and myth, between accurate information and legends. But sometimes even tales of questionable accuracy could provide interesting ideas. When studying the exploits of the first Agamemnon, he had become particularly intrigued by the account of the Trojan horse . . .

The League scientists would not have understood — or perhaps they would have run endless tests. But that was not a luxury they could afford during wartime.

Filled with nostalgia and renewed determination, Vor left Earth behind and headed for his real destination. Following a trajectory he had flown long ago during the Armada's battle for Earth, he reached the fringes of the solar system. Back then, still a recent turncoat and not fully trusted, Vor had broken ranks to pursue an Omnius update ship that was attempting to escape. After deactivating its robot captain, he had left the craft adrift . . . for twenty-five years.

Now Vor searched for any trace of the long-inert vessel, scanning the regions into which it might have drifted among the frozen cometary debris far from the light of the Sun. "Don't hide from me, Old Metalmind," he said to himself. "Come out and play."

Vor wished he'd had the foresight years ago to place a tiny locater beacon on the update ship, but now he used his skill with calculations and computers to determine possible orbits. Taking his time, he combed the sparse desert of deep space. Finally, not far from one of his orbital estimates, he detected the metal signature of the robotic vessel. "Ah, there you are."

Grinning, Vor brought his ship alongside the other craft, maneuvering expertly to dock the two vessels. Back in the isolated lab in Zimia, he had worked for many months, tampering with the captive Omnius, adding subtle loops, errors, and virtual landmines to its programming. The original silvery gelsphere sat beside him in the Jihad ship's cockpit, stolen from the cybernetic lab. Now he had stolen it, and would use the gelsphere to plant his corruptions on the Synchronized Worlds.

Unwittingly, his old comrade Seurat would do it for him.

Vor donned a breathing mask and opened the hatch to step into the frigid air of the paralyzed update ship. The copper-skinned robot pilot, deactivated when Vor used a scrambler on him, should still be on board.

At the time of this betrayal, Vor had felt uncomfortable. Seurat had been his faithful companion, a quirky but genuine friend on many voyages. Though Vor still held a soft spot in his heart for him, his dedication to the Jihad was even stronger, infused with a powerful sense of determination and the rightness of humanity's cause. Despite his attributes, Seurat was a thinking machine, making him the sworn enemy of the human race . . . and of Vorian Atreides.

Aboard the craft, Vor felt like an intruder. The brutally cold air seemed to resist him, and he moved forward silently, afraid to disturb the tiniest detail. He could not leave any mark of his presence, neither a fingerprint nor a scuff. The update ship's every interior surface sparkled with frost, humidity that had crystallized out of the motionless air, but he left no footprints on the corrugated metal deck as he moved across it.

In the cockpit he discovered the familiar humanoid shape of the captain with whom he had served, a robotic pilot who had taken countless Omnius update spheres from one Synchronized World to another. Seurat remained motionless, his mirrored, coppery face reflecting a distorted image of Vor looking down at him through the breathing mask.

"So, I see you've waited for me," Vor said, driving away the nostalgia that flickered around the edges of his mind. "I didn't leave you in a very dignified position, I fear. Sorry, Old Metalmind."

He opened the secret storage compartment from which he had originally stolen the Omnius update a quarter century earlier. Removing the silvery gelsphere from the pack at his side, he replaced it in the empty waiting cradle, precisely where he had found it. Though the League scientists had already performed decades of interrogation and analysis, Vor had meticulously deleted all those memories. Even the tainted update itself wouldn't know what had happened.

With a sly smile, Vor resealed the storage compartment, careful not to leave any evidence of his intrusion. The information inside would look totally legitimate, though it was modified in ways that no thinking machine could readily detect.

Briefly, he worried what would happen to the independent robot pilot, once Omnius discovered the destruction Seurat unwittingly carried. He hoped the mechanical captain would not be destroyed out of spite. Perhaps his memory core would be completely wiped. A sad end for a decent companion . . . but at least Seurat would forget all those atrociously bad jokes he used to tell.

Maybe Omnius would just put Seurat back to work, provided the evermind survived the chaos Old Metalmind would bring. Vor wished he could be there to watch . . .

Finally, he took great pleasure in restarting the systems he had deactivated in Seurat's body. Vor wished he could stay and talk with his old chum and teach him how to play Fleur de Lys, or tell him some of the twisted Omnius jokes that jihadi soldiers exchanged in their crew quarters — but Vor knew that wasn't possible. In a few days the robot would awaken, assuming his gelcircuitry systems gradually repaired themselves.

By then, Vorian Atreides would be long gone.

His mission complete, he returned through the hatch to his own ship. Though it would not be apparent for some time yet, he was convinced that he had just struck a devastating blow against the Synchronized Worlds.

After years of the bloody Jihad, it was finally time to let Omnius defeat himself. Vor could almost taste the irony . . .

There is a time to attack and a time to wait.
                              —From a Corrin-Omnius update

A FTER DUTIFULLY COMPLETING his public appearance on Poritrin, Iblis Ginjo was asked to consider going to Ix, where the fighting would be heaviest. Lord Bludd insisted that his presence would boost the morale of the jihadi soldiers who were sacrificing so much.

But Iblis dismissed the idea out of hand, without even raising the question with Yorek Thurr. Unstable conditions there were too dangerous for him. The human revolution on that Synchronized World, led by his own Jipol professional agitators, had been in full eruption long before the Jihad invasion fleet was due to arrive. Even if human forces won this offensive, tens of thousands would lie dead in the streets. And if Primero Harkonnen lost, the death toll would be even higher.

No, Iblis did not want to be there. It would be risking too much, both personally and politically.

Only after an Ixian victory was assured and the jihadis had cleaned up the remaining thinking machines would the Grand Patriarch make his triumphant arrival. At that time, he could saunter in and take most of the credit for victory. From then on, he could always use Ix as a rallying cry for even more major offensives, as he had done with Poritrin.

If Primero Harkonnen's military operation was on schedule, he should arrive at Ix soon, though they had no means of instant communication at such distances. Within days the big battle should commence, though it would be some time before the Grand Patriarch learned the results . . .

Iblis remained on Poritrin for a month and arranged a series of private meetings with noblemen, some of whom had journeyed from Ecaz and other League Worlds for the belated festival. Despite the gravity of the machine threat, the patricians were in no mood to discuss serious matters. They wanted to savor their victory for a while, though it was only a small step toward the ultimate goal. Dealing with these fools, Iblis finally reached a peak of frustration, and announced that he would be leaving in order to oversee the important matters of the Jihad.

In a good-natured fashion, Lord Bludd had protested the Grand Patriarch's early departure, but Iblis could see that he did not particularly care one way or another. So he left Poritrin accompanied by two Jipol officers, the grim and unshakeable Yorek Thurr and a young female sergeant newly recruited into Iblis's private police force. While Thurr flew the ship competently, the new sergeant, Floriscia Xico, acted as copilot and attendant. Iblis retired to his own plush cabin to relax and plan during the long voyage.

In the luxurious chamber he sat on a deep-cushion chair, where he participated in a roleplaying bioholo set on ancient Earth, ostensibly to learn about the founder of the original Islamic faith before the Second and Third Movements in the Old Empire. Iblis's object was to learn about the first jihad, and to understand it completely.

Immersed in the bioholo, Iblis Ginjo saw himself as a fictional companion who walked alongside the great man, without ever actually speaking to him. The white-robed prophet stood on the crest of a dune, speaking to a throng of followers arrayed below him.

Abruptly the images around Iblis wavered, then flickered out of focus until the walls of his plush cabin stood out sharply around him again. Voices in the ancient reenactment clashed with real voices over the spaceship comsystem. Alarms sounded, and Iblis wrenched himself back to reality.

Someone was shaking him and shouting into his ear. He looked into the flushed face of curly-haired Floriscia Xico. "Grand Patriarch, you must come to the flight deck immediately!"

Struggling to reorient himself, he lurched after her. Through the front viewport, he saw an immense asteroid filling space, spinning wildly as it headed toward them.

"It's not moving in a natural orbit, sir," Yorek Thurr said, not taking his eyes from the controls or their trajectory map. "It keeps adjusting course whenever I take evasive action, and its acceleration is obviously artificial."

Iblis calmed himself and stood tall, the commander that his Jipol expected to see. Both the swarthy little Thurr and the younger, less seasoned Xico seemed uncharacteristically uneasy. "Our craft has augmented engines," Iblis said. "We can outrun any asteroid."

"Theoretically," Thurr said as he wrestled with the controls, "but it keeps accelerating, sir. Heading straight toward us."

"Fifty seconds to collision," Xico reported, from the copilot seat.

"That's ridiculous. It's just an asteroid –"

One of the big rock's largest craters glowed, and the ship lurched, as if suddenly caught in a fisherman's net. Lights dimmed, and the flight deck shuddered. Thurr said, "Tractor beam has us."

A shower of sparks sprayed out of the control console like a Poritrin fireflower display. Iblis heard an explosion belowdecks, deep in the engine compartment. In front of Thurr and Xico, the control panels went dark.

The asteroid loomed closer and closer, moving under its own inexorable power. Xico slumped in her seat as if she had given up. In disgust, Thurr slapped the controls. "Our engines are disabled! We're dead in space." Sweat glistened on his bald head.

The asteroid drew them closer, pulling them into a yawning crater. The cosmic body was obviously a huge, disguised ship. But who did it belong to? Angry and fearful, Iblis swallowed hard.

Abruptly, all power went out, even the backup systems. A chill wind seemed to accompany the darkness that engulfed the ship as they were swallowed by the gigantic asteroid.

Biological life is an insidious, powerful force. Even when one thinks it has been wiped out, it has a way of concealing itself . . . and regenerating. When the human mind is combined with this ultimate survival instinct, we have a formidable enemy.

—Omnius, *Jihad Datafiles*

F AR ABOVE EARTH'S solar system the small update vessel drifted without engine power, ranging to the edge of a diffuse cometary cloud. Seurat returned to a dim but increasing awareness, not knowing where he was or how much time had elapsed.

Normal systems reactivated on the frozen ship. and frost melted from the bulkheads, dripping down onto the motionless robot captain. Somewhere deep in his mechanical consciousness, Seurat heard and felt the droplets hitting him, wisps of moisture condensing out of the air. Dissonant thought patterns made him recall an ancient Earth torture method, but most of his memory circuits were inaccessible to him, for the moment.

He could not judge the passage of time or where he was now. He had been in the update ship when his last conscious thoughts ended abruptly. A probability program told him: *That is where I must be now.* And he recalled his last mission.

Without moving, he absorbed what little information was available. Another tiny drop of water fell on his metal body, like dew.

The cabin is thawing. Therefore, it must have been frozen. Therefore, sufficient time must have passed for standard systems to shut down and the internal temperature to drop.

Since his internal circuitry was not functioning completely, Seurat wondered if his gelcircuitry mind had suffered damage. How much time had passed? He probed, but could not tell. However, as he tested his mental paths, he found that he could access more with each passing moment.

I was deactivated.

The process of coming back to life seemed slow to the independent robot. Consciously, he activated a secondary damage assessment-and-mitigation program. His scattered memory remained a chaotic jumble and mostly inaccessible, but he could tell that it was reassembling itself bit by bit.

Is this a dream? The result of a gelcircuitry malfunction? Can machines dream?

The probability program broadened its functions and told him, like a voice from within: *This is real.*

He heard crisp popping and snapping sounds, and high-range spinning noises. Then his core program jolted into full awareness, quickly sorting out disjointed recollections. Finally he obtained an internal report on the last few moments: Seurat's escape from Earth while it was under atomic attack by the League Armada . . . the pursuit . . . Vorian Atreides. The human trustee had damaged the update ship, boarded the vessel, and forcibly deactivated him.

While most of the robot's external sensors were not yet operational, he did not detect the presence of any other sentient beings inside the cabin — human or machine. The human aggressor was gone.

The robot realized that his lengthy interaction with the son of Agamemnon had left him vulnerable to the pandemonium and unpredictability of human actions. Recalling his copilot, Seurat had difficulty thinking of the former trustee as his enemy, even though Vor had clearly stunned him — *twice!*

Why did my friend do that to me?

Understanding the motivations of human beings was not Seurat's strong suit, or even part of his programming. The robot captain performed his duties with the tools that Omnius had provided for him. Of greater importance, he needed to discover if the damage was permanent. Would he be able to restore all of his former functions?

As if answering him, his systems continued to awaken, faster now. More than eighty percent.

Despite the unsettling lack of predictability, Seurat still preferred the missions he had shared with Vorian Atreides to those he had flown alone. *He is not like other, exceedingly dull humans I have observed.*

Abruptly, his programs came fully alive and began to assault him full-force, informing Seurat of slowly compounded errors that distracted him with considerations of such troubling matters. His optic threads glimmered, suddenly flooding him with detailed images from around the cold, dead cabin of the update ship.

His mental functions accelerated and smoothed into an internal hum of systems checking and rechecking information, scooping up bits of errant data and discarding them. Around the walls, deck, and control panels, he detected subtle indications of corrosion, age, and disuse. He probed again, to determine how much time had passed. Still uncertain.

Was the League Armada still at Earth, attacking the evermind incarnation there? Could Omnius escape? Seurat had been ordered to take the last update sphere of the Earth evermind and had slipped away from the planet even as Jihad warships closed in with atomic weapons.

Is the update sphere still safe? Or have I failed in my most vital mission?

Scanning with his reactivated optic threads, Seurat located the secure storage receptacle for the Omnius copy. His nimble hands opened the compartment to reveal the silvery gelsphere, intact and apparently undamaged. A sensation akin to great relief brushed through his systems.

He had protected the update of the Earth evermind, the only copy of the final thoughts of the once-central Omnius. Vorian Atreides had not taken it, though he'd had the opportunity. Who could understand humans?

No matter. The gelsphere was safe, and still in Seurat's possession. His mission remained unchanged: deliver it.

In a matter of minutes that seemed like much longer, his systems completed their self-diagnostic and repair routines. Now Seurat turned his attention to the update ship, relieved to discover that the engines had come back online properly, even though subsystems were still cold.

Vorian Atreides had only stunned the robot captain, undoubtedly to keep him from escaping. But over time Seurat's sophisticated gelcircuitry systems must have repaired themselves.

The ship's instrument panel lit up in a rainbow of flashing chromatics, punctuated by computer signal beeps and whines, as if tiny creatures inside the mechanism were awakening. The still-functional chronometer provided him with startling information. Nearly twenty-five standard Earth years had passed since he had been deactivated. *Twenty-five years!*

After Seurat fired the engines to full operating power, he guided the ship carefully back down into the planetary neighborhood. Using his long-distance sensors as he approached, he remained alert for any sign of the troublesome League Armada. The battle could not still be under way: human attention spans did not last long. By this time Omnius had either crushed the human invasion, and the update sphere in Seurat's custody was irrelevant . . . or the evermind had been destroyed and the stored computer information was more important now than ever.

He guided his vessel close enough to the cloud-smeared world to see that the continents and once-magnificent machine cities were no more than distorted, glassy black remains. Seurat detected excessive radio-activity, but no machine signals, no active power grids, no response to any of his inquiries on standard Omnius channels. And no signs of biological activity.

Earth was destroyed. The thinking machines had been eradicated here, and the humans had caused so much damage to accomplish it that even they could no longer live on their own ancestral home planet.

This was only small consolation for him.

As Seurat cruised over the lifeless, useless world, a realization hit him like a meteor slamming into the ship. Earth had been destroyed. This meant that in all probability, he had the only backup copy of the Earth-Omnius in existence.

The only one.

Seurat began to assess priorities. If, in fact, there had been no machine survivors of the holocaust on Earth, then none of the current Omniuses had access to the crucial data Seurat's update contained. Now his mission was paramount. Internal programs spoke to him in unison.

You have another duty to perform.

Touching pressure pads, Seurat set a direct course for the nearest Synchronized World, where he would deliver the gelsphere that held the final thoughts of the Earth-Omnius. He would continue his update route, as he had been instructed to do a quarter century before. Soon, the information would be shared among all incarnations of the evermind, and it would be as if the Earth-Omnius had never been destroyed. The humans' victory would be short-lived, and Seurat would have the last joke on Vorian Atreides.

*How interesting it would be if I could upload and share informa-
tion from sentient biological life, like computers transferring data.
So much investigative effort and useless conjecture would be saved,
because I could spend time deep inside the minds of my subjects. In
a sense that has been the goal of my human experiments all along,
and to an extent I have climbed inside their collective skin, allowing
me to think as they think. But humans have shallow and deep levels
of thought and of behavior, and for the most part I have only
discovered the shallow. Each locked psychic door that I finally open
reveals another locked door, and another, and another . . . each
requiring a different key. Such complex, mysterious creatures, these
humans. To construct one from scratch . . . what a supreme
challenge that would be!*
—Erasmus, Reflections on Sentient Biologicals

R AISING CHILDREN SHOULD not be such a trial, filled with frustration, lack of cooperation, and ridiculously slow progress. Human
offspring should be eager to learn from their superiors, enabling them to
reach their potential. If every parent had the sort of trouble Erasmus was
having with his young ward from the slave pens, the human race would
have gone extinct long before their civilization had advanced sufficiently
to invent thinking machines.

But such thoughts inevitably led back to his own actions. Could
Erasmus possibly be doing something wrong? He didn't like to think
of it that way. He just had more to learn.

Still, he wished Omnius had chosen any other human as a subject.
This learning process was exceedingly difficult.

By contrast with humans, a thinking machine was fully functional
from the moment of activation. Robots, being infinitely more useful than
humans, did as they were instructed. They followed through on thoughts
and completed tasks efficiently, achieving goals in a logical sequence.

This feral human child though, despite Erasmus's best efforts as a
mentor robot, was . . . chaos incarnate. And Erasmus had nowhere to
turn for advice. Not for the first time, he wished Serena Butler had
remained with him.

Each robot was linked to a larger network under the control of the
computer evermind, a labyrinth of circuitry that functioned in unison,
building the Synchronized Worlds to a larger, more comprehensive state
of order and progress.

Humans, on the other hand, clung to their much vaunted "free will," which enabled them to make horrendous, bumbling mistakes and mutter inane excuses afterward. Their freedoms, however, gave them the creativity and imagination to complete marvelous works, to succeed in monumental achievements that the vast majority of machine minds could never conceive. There were advantages.

But this . . . creature was none of those things. He was barely distinguishable from an animal. The young man — singlehandedly — seemed intent on increasing the universe's entropy by an order of magnitude.

"Stop that, Gilbertus Albans." The command was the same one Erasmus had uttered many times before, but the boy did not seem to comprehend simple instructions.

Erasmus had chosen the name for the boy after studying classical history, selecting sounds that carried respectable and important tonalities. Thus far, however, the appellation did not at all reflect the child's behavior, or his complete inability to follow simple instructions.

The feral slave boy heard the same thing over and over and simply did not do as he was told. At times Erasmus wondered if it was stupidity or stubborn refusal.

Gilbertus knocked over one of the robot's flowerpots, smashing the terra cotta, spilling dirt on the tile floor, and killing the plant.

"Stop doing that," Erasmus repeated, more sternly this time. The harshness seemed to have no effect. But what purpose did the child's defiance serve? Gilbertus gained nothing from all the destruction he wreaked; he just seemed to enjoy his ruinous acts because Erasmus had told him not to commit them.

Gilbertus smashed another flowerpot, then scampered out of the greenhouse alcove and scuttled toward his rooms. The distinguished robot strode after him, his luxuriant robes swishing with the speed of his gait.

No doubt Omnius was enjoying every moment of this, observing vicariously through his ever-present watcheyes.

By the time Erasmus reached the boy's room, Gilbertus had already torn the sheets and pillows from the bed and tossed them across the room. He yanked down the diaphanous curtains hanging from posts overhead, then proceeded to fling off his clothes, one article at a time.

"Stop that, Gilbertus Albans," Erasmus demanded, forming his flowmetal face into a stern, paternal visage.

In response, the feral boy tossed soiled underwear onto the robot's mirrored head.

This called for a change of tactics.

Even as the chaos continued, a squad of household robots entered the room and started picking up the mess. They gathered bedsheets and strewn clothes; in the greenhouse, other crews had already disposed of the smashed pots and swept clean the scattered dirt and terra cotta fragments. The boy tried to stay one step ahead of them.

Gilbertus Albans stood naked, laughing and making rude noises as he jumped onto the bed and avoided the robots deftly, though they made no overt move to capture him — not yet.

Observing him, Erasmus assessed what to do. The boy had been attired in the finest clothes, but did not seem to value them in the least. Repeatedly and patiently, the robot had tried to tutor him in manners, social responsibilities, and other acceptable behavior patterns. Yet Gilbertus insisted on smashing valuable objects, messing his room, ripping up books, and ignoring his studies.

Although the wild boy did not seem to be listening, the mirror-faced robot said calmly, "It is not efficient for me to continue repairing the damage in your wake. My system of benevolence and rewards has had no discernible effect." He emitted a silent signal for the household robots. They moved forward with stealthy speed and seized Gilbertus, holding him firmly despite his struggles.

Erasmus said, "Now we shall begin a course of strict supervision and punishment." He stepped aside so that the captor robots could move through the doorway. "Remove him to my laboratories. We will see if we can make him behave."

After centuries of dissection and careful observation involving thousands of humans, Erasmus knew exactly how to inflict pain, unpleasantness, and fear upon them. The robot had grown skilled enough in his technique to proceed vigorously without causing any permanent damage. If possible, he wanted to avoid harming or perhaps killing the frustrating boy. Not out of any compassion on his part. The boy was a challenge to him. And besides, he didn't want to have to admit failure to Omnius.

Drugs and brain surgeries were options, but Erasmus supposed that such methods might stretch the boundaries of his agreement with the evermind who had issued the challenge. For now he would hold that in reserve.

Still struggling and defiant, the boy seemed annoyed but not beaten. Erasmus knew he could keep going longer than his ward. "I alone see your potential, Gilbertus Albans, and I have the incentive not to give up on you."

They marched down the corridors toward the extensive surgical rooms and laboratories. "This is going to hurt me more than it hurts you. But always remember: I'm doing it for your own good."

The comments seemed illogical to Erasmus, but he was practicing a new technique, mimicking the words human parents often spoke to their offspring before administering punishments. As they entered the laboratories and the squirming boy began to show genuine fear, the robot said in a flat voice, "From now on, you must pay closer attention to your lessons."

Through his mind and senses, the human anticipates bits and pieces of the reality to come. Despite endless calculations, thinking machines can never come close to achieving this, or even comprehending how it works.

—Titan Hecate, *Renegade Journals*

I BLIS GINJO WAS trapped, as if he had been swallowed by a gigantic spacefaring whale. All of his ship's systems had shut down; the power grids and monitor panels lay dark, paralyzed and cold. Now he and his two companions were caught in a pitch black grotto deep within the mysterious artificial asteroid.

We are doomed.

Though they had sworn to protect the Grand Patriarch, his two Jipol aides could do nothing. Floriscia Xico had turned pale, her short-cropped auburn curls clumped with sweat. She stared at the Grand Patriarch as if Iblis could simply command a bolt of lightning from God to destroy this peculiar captor. Even staunch Yorek Thurr — who had successfully completed countless dangerous missions for his master and had masterfully exposed machine spies in all parts of the League — looked terrified.

Iblis dared not show weakness. To distract himself from his own apprehension, he glowered at the others and said, "The Jipol has faced any number of hazards without wavering from its faith in my leadership and in the cause of Serena Butler's Jihad. And now a mysterious asteroid turns you into frightened, superstitious fools?"

They waited in darkness and silence. What else was there to do?

Quite suddenly, strange lights flashed outside the ship in the enclosing grotto, as if filtered through diamond lenses. The asteroid chamber reflected the spangles with the intensity of small suns bouncing off polished planes.

The young Jipol sergeant shielded her eyes, while Yorek Thurr gazed with unapologetic curiosity. Iblis, the tallest of the three, stood behind the others and peered out. Vaporous mists curled around the well-lit chamber. "It's as if the asteroid swallowed a mouthful of heaven . . ."

Finally system lights blinked on around the hatch, and a soothing female voice spoke over the captured ship's loudspeakers. "Step out of your craft, Iblis Ginjo. I wish to meet the Grand Patriarch in person. Don't be shy — I've gone to a lot of trouble to arrange this little party."

The female sergeant looked at Iblis with eyes as round as glowglobes, but Thurr met him with a hard gaze. "I will accompany you, Grand Patriarch."

Trying to look courageous and commanding, Iblis snapped at Xico, "Stop acting so frightened, Sergeant. It is certain that this . . . entity . . . does not wish to destroy us. Not yet anyway."

Even though the rest of their ship's systems remained deactivated, the hatch opened and a cool, metal-scented breeze drifted inside. The air within the asteroid seemed sterile and preserved, but breathable.

While Iblis was not convinced any of them would survive this encounter, he made a show of bravado anyway. If there was any way out of this, it would be because of his persuasive abilities. As if about to address a representative from an important League World, he smoothed a hand over his hair and stepped out into the brilliantly reflective chamber. Yorek Thurr followed him, matching his steps. An edgy Floriscia Xico hurried after them, prepared to demonstrate support for her sworn leader despite her obvious trepidation.

Once outside, Iblis put his hands on his hips, drew several deep breaths, and looked around with interest. Finally he shouted, "Why have you captured us?" His words reflected around the walls, and the echoes drained off into silence.

They heard a stirring and a clatter. A human-sized figure stepped out of a shadowed pocket in one of the mirror-plated walls. It was a machine form, but unlike any Iblis had ever seen in his time as a trustee and slave master on Earth: a beautiful yet frightening monstrosity on graceful segmented legs. A head studded with optic threads raised up on a sinuous neck covered with pearlescent scales, while long angular plates protruded from the sides like prismatic butterfly wings. The sharp forelimbs were delicate and curved, resembling the appendages of a praying mantis. The machine reminded him of a robotic dragon, fearsome but aesthetically pleasing.

Cymek.

Beside him, Yorek Thurr gaped in astonishment. Such a reaction from the normally cool and unflappable man surprised Iblis.

The dragon machine scrutinized its captives, then clattered forward again. She was much less intimidating than many of the monstrous warrior bodies Iblis had seen other cymeks wear.

Floriscia Xico yelped and yanked out her hand weapon. Before she could fire, though, the dragon-cymek raised a front forelimb adorned with antennas and lenses. A barely visible ripple of energy created turbulence in the air, then struck the anxious Jipol sergeant, knocking her to the polished floor.

"You *hrethgir* haven't changed a bit," the female voice said, emanating from the dragon-walker. "Come now, is that any way to make a first impression? Let's start our conversation without violence, all right?" She pranced forward, nimble in her exotic configuration, to the spot where Xico lay motionless. "Ajax always said that females were prone to overreaction. Of course, it took me ages to understand what an idiot he was."

Questions that had accumulated in Iblis's mind spilled forth like water tumbling through a sluice box. "How do you know who I am? Who are you? Why did you capture our ship? What do you want?"

The cymek's metallic green eyes glistened. "I've been gathering information for years, and your Jihad is the best entertainment I've encountered in a long time. Quite a spectator sport, just like some of our old gladiator matches during the Time of Titans. I was glad to be rid of those, though."

"And who are you?" Iblis demanded, trying to bring to bear all of his persuasive powers. "Identify yourself."

Every vibration caused the mirrored facets of the dragon body to send out rainbow glitters like water splashing off rocks. "Sadly, I'm not surprised that my story has faded into obscurity over the past millennium. I doubt Agamemnon wrote any glowing biographies of me, as he did with the other Twenty Titans. Ajax probably didn't even miss me."

"You're a Titan?"

The dragon cymek glowed. She had dropped plenty of hints, and Iblis had spent the first half of his life working for the cymeks, being taunted and bullied by the Titans. She talked as if she had been around for as long as Agamemnon and all the others. But Iblis had known all of the surviving Titans. It didn't make sense.

"You aren't going to guess?" The cymek sounded almost pouty. "Very well — I am Hecate."

"Hecate!" said Thurr. "That . . . is not possible!"

Iblis was stunned as well. "One of the first enslavers of humanity?"

"Oh, not nearly the first. There have always been slavers of humanity."

Iblis certainly knew the history of the original cymeks, and had himself been bullied by Ajax. He remembered that Hecate had been Ajax's lover a thousand years ago, but had surrendered her position among the Titans and departed for parts unknown. No one had seen her in many centuries.

"You consider us enslavers of humanity? So ominous-sounding, when it was nothing more than a youthful indiscretion. I was reckless and impetuous then. But there's only so far one can go in developing new paradigms of hedonism." Hecate made a wistful sound. "But much has changed and I've had ample time to reconsider. I've grown up, you might say. A thousand years of brooding will do that to you."

Pretending a comfort he did not feel, Iblis sat by the dragon cymek, taking care not to get too close to the winglike protrusions. She sat higher than he did. His mind felt as if it might explode from all the possibilities gathering like thunderclouds in his imagination. "You are correct, Hecate. Perhaps we do have a great deal to talk about."

Thurr did not give a second glance to the stunned Xico, as if she no longer mattered. He looked at Iblis with black, cadaverous eyes. Then he turned to Hecate and said, "We need to know where you've been. Are you in league with the Titans? Or Omnius?"

The female cymek made a rude snort. "Omnius didn't even exist when I left the Old Empire. And the Titans — why would I come back to those fools? I have no intention of making such a mistake ever again."

"You seem to have been watching closely though," Thurr muttered. "You probably know a great deal about the Synchronized Worlds."

Iblis tried to digest the situation. "I've heard stories about you, Hecate, but I don't know how much is the truth. Why did you leave the Titans behind? What is it you want now?"

Hecate lowered her dragon form as if hunkering down to tell a story. Iblis's fear had given way to curiosity and fascination.

"In the beginning I joined Tlaloc and his rebels because I was enraptured with the idea of power and grandeur. I was bored then, and easily impressed. When they recruited Ajax to be their military enforcer, he brought me with him. I was just his plaything, but I pleased him well enough. After the Titans overthrew the Empire, I found I liked the trappings of leadership: large estates, doting servants, fine clothes, and glittering jewels. It was all quite pleasant, though admittedly shallow."

Iblis struggled to match this information with his preconceived image of the lone Titan who had washed her hands of conquest. "I . . . knew Ajax." He lifted his chin, not sure if it would be wise to tell her too much. "He was a bully."

"Oh, much more than a bully. He was a bloodthirsty thug, a psychotic killer. A complete bastard."

"You were his lover," Iblis pointed out. "And now you want us to trust you and accept your friendship?"

Thurr's dead eyes narrowed, as if he distrusted her every answer. "What attracted you to such a man in the first place? Was he different before he became a Titan?"

"Oh, he always had a terrible violence within him, but Ajax was able to acquire the treasures and gifts I wanted. He made me feel special, though I was somewhat fatuous then.

"Later, listening to Tlaloc's great speeches, I started to get a greater sense of things . . . but I wasn't really paying attention. Tlaloc was a great visionary, you must understand. Agamemnon, Juno, and Barbarossa were all enamored with the idea of the conquest. So I followed along. I had no particular interest in achieving glory. I simply wanted the trappings of an Empress, not unlike your own wife, Iblis Ginjo." He squirmed. She paused. Her ornate head swiveled from side to side. "But I'm not that person anymore. Far from it."

Beside them, the young Jipol sergeant began to stir, but neither Iblis Ginjo nor Yorek Thurr paid any attention to her.

"Eventually, I figured out that everything I had wanted amounted to nothing. Maybe I was a late bloomer, but eventually I understood the point." Her tiny laugh sounded self-congratulatory. "If I'd had such feelings earlier, maybe the Time of Titans would have been different. After my transformation into a cymek, I got tired of sparkling treasures. Pretty baubles just don't look the same through optic threads and all-spectrum sensors. I came to value other things, since I had all the time a human being could imagine."

"An enlightened cymek," Thurr muttered, as if he found the very concept incomprehensible.

"Is that so different from a Cogitor? I remember when I turned a century old. A hundred years! That still sounds ancient to me, though now I've been around ten times as long. But inside my cymek body, I felt as young and energetic as ever. I chose to better myself, studying philosophy and literature, contemplating the good that people could accomplish. Sure, the Old Empire was a blot on the potential of the human race. A tedious waste of time, a clock winding down. It nearly extinguished the individual human spirit and the creative drive.

"But as a cymek, I began to wonder what was the point of having immortality for its own sake? It gets awfully dull simply *existing* for centuries. In front of me the future looked bleak and featureless." She swiveled her head turret on its sinuous neck, as if studying her own reflections in the faceted wall mirrors.

"I had grown apart from Ajax. In our cymek bodies we had no need for each other's physical companionship. And he was — let's admit it — a downright ass. I must have been stupid or blind not to see it earlier. I changed and grew, but Ajax never matured beyond being a bully. I came to realize that he never would. With more power and fewer inhibitions, his penchant for bloodshed became unbearable to me. That horrific slaughter on Walgis during the First Hrethgir Rebellion was the last straw . . . so I left him. I left all of them. I didn't need them, after all. I told all the Titans what they could do with their dominion.

"Quietly, I had already built a ship for myself, along with alternative bodies to accommodate my preservation canister. I intended to go on a great voyage of discovery across the whole universe. A galactic sightseer with all the time any person could desire. I can't say the other Titans were sad to see me go." Hecate paused, her gleaming metal limbs twitching. "Then, less than two years afterward, Omnius took over."

Thurr's throat sounded dry. "And you stayed away for a thousand years? That is why none of the cymeks know about you now?"

"I'm sure they've tried to forget. But I returned half a century ago, and I've been gathering information. Snooping, you might say. I've seen what Omnius has done. It's a . . . different sort of mess than the one created by the Titans."

"Very few of the original twenty remain," Iblis said, cautiously. "You know that . . . even Ajax is dead?"

"Oh, I know." Hecate sounded flippant. "And I know you killed him."

Iblis felt a cold grip on his heart. He could not answer her, knowing that any excuse would sound weak, and he did not dare attempt a lie.

She laughed, an artificial sound in her mechanical apparatus. "Don't fret — I should thank you for that. Perhaps many of Ajax's potential victims will, one day. Frankly, I'm surprised he lasted as long as he did. In all those years of rule, he never learned. It's pathetic that one man could waste so many opportunities." She raised two segmented forelimbs. "The question is, are *you* going to squander this opportunity?"

Iblis swallowed hard. "What is it you want of me, Hecate? What opportunity?"

"I know all about your Jihad, and I know who you are, Iblis Ginjo. Or should I be formal and call you Grand Patriarch? Interesting title — did you make it up yourself? That's why I've tracked you down. I think we can accomplish a lot together."

Iblis's heart swelled with excitement, but he didn't show it. "Do you have a plan or long-range vision? Or are you just bored?"

"Am I not allowed to have my own motives? Perhaps I have been simmering about the Titans for all these years, and now I've returned. The Jihad could be my chance to join in." She scratched a metal forelimb on the polished ground. "Does it matter, so long as I help you achieve victory?"

Iblis looked at Thurr. Neither man could argue with her rationale. At their feet, Xico came slightly more awake, blinking away disorientation.

"Think of it. While my poor fellow Titans are all forced to serve Omnius, I've remained free and independent. Once Agamemnon finds out that I've decided to help mere *hrethgir*, his brain will stew in its own electrafluid! But I've become a little bit repentant. Now that humans have finally decided to fight back with all their might, I want to join the party."

Iblis caught his breath as unexpected possibilities surged through him. What a remarkable ally this dragon cymek could be! "To have one of the original Titans join our Jihad would be an incredible advantage for us, Hecate. I would not turn down your aid. You could be a . . . secret weapon."

"Secret weapon!" Hecate emitted a chuckling sound. "I like that."

But the political part of his mind understood that such a sensational comrade in arms might cause a terrific uproar among the more superstitious elements of the populace, given the fervor of the jihadis and their hatred toward thinking machines in all forms. The League Parliament and the Jihad Council would argue furiously for days, squandering this remarkable opportunity.

Day by day, the incomprehensible protests against the Jihad grew more strenuous, people weary of the fighting and wanting some sort of magical peace. What would they do if they knew about Hecate?

But the renegade Titan seemed somewhat flippant and volatile. She might grow impatient with disorganized humans and withdraw her support.

"It would be best for now if we kept our involvement secret," Yorek Thurr said, as if reading the Grand Patriarch's mind. "That way we need not get caught up in League bickering and politics."

"Ah, you are such practical men. Do you have a concrete task for me? I'm anxious to get started."

"Yes!" Iblis's eyes shone. "You can help us turn a lost cause into a victory."

He explained what he had in mind.

War brings out the worst in human nature, and the best.
                              —Swordmaster Jav Barri

W HILE PRIMERO HARKONNEN'S fleet prepared to face the machine
warships above Ix, Jool Noret and a small team of commandos
fought a pitched battle in caves that laced the planet's crust.

The Primero had given them their orders before they boarded a
cannonball shuttle and plunged to the surface of the embattled Synchronized World. "Five separate teams will try to fight their way through the
tunnels beneath the central computer nexus of the Ix-Omnius. Each team
will carry a compact, city-killer warhead. Your job is to deliver it to the
Omnius stronghold. With luck, at least one of the teams will achieve the
objective."

"Won't atomics cause a great many casualties?" Jool Noret asked.

"Yes," the Primero admitted. "But Omnius is attempting to exterminate all humans in the catacombs of Ix. This city-killer bomb is designed
to deliver an intense localized vaporization pulse that will wipe gelcircuitry brains. It's a tactical weapon, so the number of wounded will be
minimal, and the damage to Ixian industrial facilities will be restricted."
His expression seemed about to fall, but he masked his look of dismay.
"It's the best we can do. But because of the need for precision, we'll have
to send in several teams to make sure the device is delivered exactly on
target. This will not be an easy task."

It seemed to be a suicide mission, with overwhelming odds against
success. Jool Noret had been the first to volunteer . . .

Following uniformed jihadis into the fray, Noret hurled his last
scrambler-pulse grenade. It clattered as it rolled down the slight incline
toward a squad of assassin robots that thundered toward them. The

grenade detonated with a disruptive Holtzman pulse that turned the fighting robots into motionless sparking hulks, like scrap-metal statues.

But the twisted tunnels and thick stone walls made each scrambler grenade dissipate too quickly. And other robotic killers kept coming.

Without pause or question, Noret bulled his way ahead, carrying his array of weapons and his father's pulse-sword. Grenades seemed like a coward's path to victory, and he preferred to vanquish his foes one by one, in hand-to-hand combat.

If only there weren't so many of them.

Though he was just a young mercenary and not in charge of the commando team, Noret led the charge anyway, bypassing the cluttered hulks of deactivated robots. The cave walls still thrummed with echoes from the last scrambler pulse. Behind him, other jihadis paused to pummel and kick the neutralized combat robots, but the impatient Noret urged them ahead. "Spend your energy on real opponents that need killing, not on ones that have already been vanquished."

According to schematics from Ixian survivors, these catacombs passed beneath the primary machine industries and computer centers. The team's gaunt and haunted-looking contact man, an Ixian named Handon, had lost his companions, his mate, and children during the recent bloodbath spearheaded by the Titan Xerxes.

The unfortunate man gave them horrific details, then led the way through the cramped passageways. If the determined mercenaries could plant their small atomic in the central fortified complex that held the local evermind's primary gelsphere, they could free Ix, once and for all.

Handon's clothes were tattered, his arms and chest skeletal, his hair long and unkempt. But the refugee's expression remained dedicated. "This way. We are almost there." He had lived for six months underground, eluding killer robots, destroying thirty-one of them himself.

"Needless to say," he said with a grim smile, "I am a wanted man."

Farther down in the tunnels, assassin robots had taken human hostages; the commandos could hear their screams. But rather than using the squirming victims as bargaining chips, the machines simply tore them apart, as if expecting the mercenaries to fall back in terror. Handon moaned at the butchery.

As the human force rushed toward them, the robots raised weapon arms flickering with high-intensity flames and ready to launch explosives.

"Prepare to drop ranks," the Jihad officer shouted. "Shields on again!"

Handon huddled behind five Ginaz mercenaries, who temporarily powered on their body shields and formed an impenetrable barrier in the corridor. Since the shields proved unreliable if used for long periods, the mercenaries were forced to deactivate them whenever they were not expecting to face direct fire.

The assassin robots launched round after round of explosives. Violent detonations fractured the walls and made the ceiling shudder. Debris pattered down, but the personal shields deflected the force of the blast.

"Front line — down!" After the robots had exhausted their first round of projectiles, the shielded soldiers ducked out of the way. Noret pushed past them, yelling. Wielding a heavy launcher, he fired into the ranks of mechanical soldiers. The tunnel ceiling fractured, and large rocks crashed down. He didn't dodge, didn't protect himself with his own shield — just kept blasting away. Noret destroyed all of the assassin robots in the corridor. Unyielding, he looked for more enemies, then gestured to Handon. "Forward, quickly! Lead us to the target."

The front ranks of mercenaries ran along behind Noret and the guide. All the commandos were forced to switch on their shields to protect against falling rock. Only moments after they escaped the passageway, the ceiling collapsed behind them. Walls caved in, and clouds of rock dust spurted like smoky blood.

Some looked back in dismay at the blocked passageway, but Noret shouted at them. "We won't be escaping by that route anyway, and now it will block any pursuing robots from following us."

"Come! Up ahead!" Handon seemed anxious and terrified. "The Omnius citadel is above us."

Behind them, warhead-engineers lugged a cylinder that encased an atomic explosive, small by planetary standards but adequate to vaporize a large section of the city Omnius had built.

Primero Harkonnen was even now carrying on the gunship battle in space, but an equally important fight needed to be won down here. If he succeeded, Jool Noret could slay *Omnius*.

Handon gestured toward glassy fused rock where metal rungs marked a vertical shaft cut through the ceiling. "Hurry, before we lose our chance!" He scrambled up the metal rungs ahead of the others. "This will be the culmination of my plans to avenge the slaughter we have suffered."

Intermittently, the refugee looked down, and his shadowed eyes flashed. Jool Noret climbed after him, suddenly suspicious, but the young mercenary was always wary and on guard. The *sensei* mek Chirox had taught him never to assume that he was safe.

They entered the armored dome of the computer nexus, the ever-mind's most secure pavilion. Machinery, pipes, ducting, and coolant cylinders turned the walls and ceiling into an industrial horror. Below, the survivors of Noret's fighting team climbed up, grunting, hauling the heavy nuclear warhead. Finally the cylinder rested on the plated metal floor inside the nexus vault. Exhausted, they deactivated their overheating body shields, so that they could get to work.

Jool Noret looked around, expecting to see robotic defenders inside the vulnerable heart of Omnius. He was ready to kill them all, just as he had won a thousand practice fights against Chirox. Sonorous electrical pulses throbbed through the machinery. In the center of the chamber, a glowing pedestal encased the gelsphere computer mind.

But he detected no armored sentinels or assassin machines. Something was not right about this.

Noret crouched warily. He kept his personal shield activated, even though it flickered unreliably.

Combat engineers knelt and cracked open the warhead case. One man opened a comline, transmitting to the Jihad warships in orbit. "Primero Harkonnen, group three is in position. Dispatch pickup shuttle immediately. We may have only a few minutes here."

"On its way down," answered an officer from the lead ballista. "You're earlier than expected."

"We had good guidance from Handon," Noret said.

"What have you heard from the other teams?" asked the warhead engineer as she worked to configure the nuclear trigger.

"All contact lost," the battleship responded. "You're the only ones left. We weren't sure anybody was going to make it."

"We'll make it," Noret said in a soft growl, barely wincing as he thought of all the other fallen mercenaries. But only Ginaz warriors could be expected to accomplish missions such as these. "Now we blow these machines into five separate hells."

Suddenly, as if the evermind was eavesdropping, the tangled pipes and flashing components in the citadel walls began to shift, extending forward with clicking sounds. Disguised armaments locked into place: guns, projectile launchers, and other menacing weaponry.

"Watch out!" Noret grabbed Handon, pulling him into the shelter of his personal shield.

But the others did not react quickly enough. A hail of sharp slivers and hot bullets showered them, ripping the soldiers into red meat before Noret's eyes.

"Let me go!" Handon squirmed and howled.

"Let you go? I'm protecting you! Why would you —"

Handon gave him a sharp kick, tried to free himself. Noret cursed, but the other man broke away. "Omnius! Protect me!"

Enraged, Noret slammed the barrel of his weapon down on Handon's legs, with a satisfying crack of bone before the man's shriek of pain. Noret then dragged him back inside the protection of his own shield, as the hidden machine weapons continued to fire upon the already defeated commando force.

"You broke my legs!"

"I could have killed you on the spot, so count yourself lucky." Under the hail of projectiles, the corpses of some Jihad fighters twitched. "For the moment."

Sharp projectiles hammered against Noret's personal shield. The Holtzman barrier easily stopped them, though the system felt dangerously warm to him. As the hail of firepower continued, he wanted to blast back with his own weapons, but could not shoot through his shield. Nor did he want to let go of the traitorous Handon. Projectiles continued to spatter ineffectually against the barrier. He felt exposed, and could not fight back.

Noret stood in the open chamber, shouting curses at the evermind. He looked in dismay at the lifeless, disfigured remains of his team, obliterated in a few moments. While the refugee Handon still squirmed in his iron grip, Noret noted the atomic warhead resting alone next to the torn bodies of the two engineers. A rescue shuttle would be racing down through the atmosphere, dodging the ongoing battle Primero Harkonnen was leading up there. Noret should have told them not to bother.

Handon had led the brave fighters into a trap.

Still under the protection of his shield, Noret wrapped his arm around the man's scrawny throat. "We are fighting for human freedom. Why would you throw it all away?"

The gaunt man struggled, but the injury to his legs had sapped his strength.

"I know three ways to slit your throat with my fingernail," he said close to the man's ear. "And two techniques that use only my teeth. Should I kill you now, or would you rather explain how Omnius can reward you enough to pay for the lives of your comrades, your chosen mate, everyone you loved?"

Handon sneered. "Love is an emotion for weak *hrethgir*. Once I've helped Omnius put an end to this insurrection, he will make me a neo-cymek. I will live for centuries."

"You will not survive the next few minutes." Noret checked his chronometer, knowing he must time the move carefully. The rescue shuttle would arrive soon. Of equal concern, he didn't know how long he could keep his personal shield on before it overheated. He needed to move quickly.

The voice of Omnius boomed through the chamber. "You shall fail. There is no chance of success."

"Recalculate the odds." Noret wrestled the traitorous man toward the warhead. Before this mission, he and his team had been instructed in the use of the old atomics taken from the Zanbar stockpile. This one was a simple field unit with a one-kilometer vaporization radius.

Perfectly sufficient.

Omnius continued to fire his deadly projectiles at the single central target now. Noret could feel the stressed shield getting hotter, and he began to worry. Handon was keeping him occupied, wasting his time.

Noret bent down and ripped a tight flexor cable from the utility pack of one of his slain companions. Swiftly, he lashed Handon's arms behind his back, tightening the sharp cable around his elbows and criss-crossing it all the way down to his wrists. Then he reached slowly through the protective field and took a fallen comrade's shield generator and clipped it beside his own. He switched on the new shield and saw that it held, reinforcing his old overheating unit.

"That should give me all the time I need — more than you have left to live." He shoved the struggling Handon away from him. "There, if you are so loyal, perhaps Omnius won't cut you down. Though I doubt even an evermind can calculate the trajectory of each one of those projectiles as it strikes the uneven wall and ricochets again."

The bound man collapsed on his broken legs and crawled into the open. "Stop shooting, Omnius! Be careful. You'll hit me!" While he waited for a response, he whimpered in pain.

The projectile fire diminished, but one of the deflected bullets slapped into Handon's left shoulder with the sound of a rock hitting wet mud. The man wailed and rolled, but with bound hands he could not reach his bleeding wound.

Noret bent over the warhead and completed the sequence to initiate the detonation. He set the countdown for eight minutes and locked the controls. No way to stop it now.

He hoped the rescue shuttle would be on time, but that concern was secondary as long as he accomplished his mission. He was expendable.

With a final vengeful surge, he used another flexor cable to lash Handon up against the heavy warhead. Pushing the terrified man's face close to the timer where he could see the remaining seconds of his life ticking away, Noret said, "Watch this for me, will you?"

Hurling a pocket explosive toward one of the small hatches into the evermind's protected vault, he blasted the door open and raced through the corridors, hoping the blueprints he had memorized were accurate.

His replacement personal shield flickered and finally faded. Hot and useless.

Even now Omnius was summoning defender robots, but Noret had no time to fight them. The timer was counting down, second by second. He could have warned away the rescue shuttle and remained here instead until his last breath, destroying the minions of the computer evermind. But by his actions alone, Jool Noret had annihilated the Ixian incarnation of Omnius — surely that was enough to satisfy his personal vow?

Too late for such considerations now. The pickup craft was already on its way. The thought of those courageous jihadis risking themselves to retrieve him — men who could keep fighting against Omnius — forced him to make his best effort. Head down, Noret charged ahead, shouldering and knocking aside combat meks that tried to block his exit.

Gaining speed, he leaped screaming, and struck with a kick forceful enough to disconnect a robot's head from its shoulders. He remembered every instant of his training with the supercharged *sensei* mek Chirox, and now took the opportunity to use all the tricks he had learned. The soul of the fallen mercenary Jav Barri seemed to fill him, transmuting his blood to pure adrenaline.

He could have destroyed dozens more in the time remaining, but Noret made the choice to run instead, dodging the fight, making headway toward the opening at the end of a tunnel. He burst out into the cool Ixian air on the surface, dazzled by smoky daylight. He did not look at his chronometer to see how many seconds were left. Overhead, the sky flickered with colored flashes of lightning, like a weird electrical storm, but he saw no gray clouds — only a furious spaceship battle far overhead.

His locater signal pipped silently across electromagnetic bands; Noret couldn't hear it, but the machines could probably detect it as clearly as a signal bell. And so could the rescue shuttle.

He saw its silver form descending like a raptor in mid-strike. Noret ran out into an open square between industrial warehouses and smoking factories. Though he was in clear view, he waved his hands to get the pilot's attention. From nearby machine facilities, combat robots began to march, reinforcements streaming out through arched doorways. They could open fire at him or surround and overwhelm him, slowly and efficiently tearing him apart with inhuman strength.

The lone rescue craft streaked down, engines roaring. The shuttle hatch was already open as he sprinted toward it. Two uniformed jihadis waved for him to hurry. Noret dove inside before the shuttle even landed and shouted for them to take off immediately. "Go! Not much time left!"

"Only one of you?" said one of the men at the ramp. "Where's the rest of your team?" The pilot didn't want to leave yet.

"There are no others." Noret extended a hand and let them pull him up from the deck. "The warhead is placed and set. Omnius may have robots trying to disarm it, but they won't succeed . . . not in time." Finally he looked at his chronometer. "Two minutes before the detonation. Now go!"

Alarmed, the rescue crew yanked him up from the deck and sealed the door hatch, shouting all the while for the pilot to take off. Acceleration slammed them all to the deck as the shuttle roared up into the Ixian sky.

Jool Noret breathed a sigh of relief and leaned back against a bulkhead. He shielded his eyes, looking away from the portholes as a dazzling nova burst into a glowing sphere of disintegration, taking out a large section of the city. It would leave only a radioactive, glassy crater and an obliterated Omnius.

Though they would endure harsh times and a long recovery, the people of Ix were now free of the computer evermind.

The Army of the Jihad would still need to follow up and retain a protective hold on this newly conquered world. But for now, with a grim smile, the exhausted Noret let himself begin to relax. He had done his part. Now, the Jihad battleships had to defeat the machine fleet in orbit.

He had struck a significant blow, though not enough to satisfy the promise he had made, to fight for himself and his father, to fill the gaping hole in his heart.

Jool Noret had survived, but only to wreak more havoc.

The spirit of the fallen warrior Jav Barri moved through him, and Noret had proved he was worthy of being a mercenary of Ginaz. His father, and the *sensei* mek Chirox, would be proud.

But it was only a start.

Vermin breed vermin.

—Omnius, *Jihad Datafiles*

W HEN IX SHUDDERED under the Omnius-killing nuclear blast, Primero Xavier Harkonnen saw an opportunity to escape cleanly with his Jihad fleet. And dismissed it. The thinking machines would just retake their industrial base, and the whole Ixian offensive would be for nothing.

His ships remained in geostationary orbit above the fading flash of the city-killer atomics. From fast kindjal scout flyers, he received frequent updates about the robotic military divisions massing to respond to the ground attack, while the local rebels began to rally from their underground catacombs.

Xavier had hoped the destruction of the local evermind would completely disorient the thinking machines. Unfortunately, the fighter robots were autonomous enough to converge upon their enemy, even without Omnius supervision. The scattered thinking machine battleships in orbit began to regroup. According to intercepted transmissions they were now led by a cymek. One of the original Titans.

Very bad.

He remembered the first battles on Bela Tegeuse, when the Army of the Jihad had withdrawn to safety, hoping they had caused enough damage to declare victory . . . only to learn later that they had backed away too soon and lost every centimeter of ground they had gained.

What a shame it would be if victory on Ix was also wasted. The Army of the Jihad needed the factories and resources on this planet.

"Stand by," he said to his bridge crew, and the command was relayed to the rest of the fleet.

As he watched a steady flow of rescue ships speed back and forth between his fleet and the Ixian surface, Primero Harkonnen knew that time was running out. He needed to fight or flee.

On projection screens he saw enemy forces sweeping like angry wasps toward the outnumbered and outgunned Jihad ships. As a military man trained to determine the odds of success and take decisive action, Xavier's obvious option was to cut his losses. His Jihad forces here could not possibly withstand the might Omnius had arrayed against him.

He had only moments to decide. Fight or flee.

Serena's face flashed in his memory, and he thought of their murdered child. Against such a brutal opponent, there were no options. Delays only led to more deaths. If not here, then somewhere else. The forces of Omnius had to be stopped no matter where they were.

"Victory, or nothing," he muttered loudly enough for his bridge crew to hear. "We will not leave until Ix is secure. Until the people are free."

With full access to the facilities on Ix, the Titan Xerxes had more warships and firepower under his command than the annoying *hrethgir* fleet, but he decided not to attack. Not yet. The swarm of machine ships slowed, moved into new positions closer to the enemy. He wanted to keep massing his forces until he achieved an overwhelming advantage, enough to deal a crushing blow. Xerxes would grind this defiant Jihad army into dust, the way he often crushed bothersome human insects beneath his metal feet.

He wished Agamemnon could be here to see this. Xerxes had never gained much respect as a military commander, had not supervised any outright conquest since the fall of the Old Empire. But he was a Titan . . . and with the Ix-Omnius neutralized, he was now the only leader here.

Flying through space, Xerxes wore his most imposing mechanical body ever, the form of an immense prehistoric bird with a ferocious pointed head turret, glistening fangs, and feral red optic sensors like the eyes of a predator. The flyer form simulated the motion of a great condor in flight, even in the vacuum, but it was as large as a battleship. Deep within the raptorlike body, a preservation canister held the ancient cymek's brain, filled with thoughts of how he would win this glorious victory against the fanatical *hrethgir* — and, he hoped, the admiration of General Agamemnon. For centuries Xerxes had tried unsuccessfully to please his commander.

In his raptor form, the Titan cruised back and forth in space, inspecting one line of ships after another in strike formation. Neo-cymeks and robot-controlled warships reflected the harsh solar wind. This time, with so many robotic warships arrayed against the Army of the Jihad, nothing could go wrong. He would annihilate the humans.

"Enemy vessels are in position," a neo-cymek officer reported over the communication frequency, in coded machine language.

Then he detected a small silver-and-black vessel approaching from deep space, an update ship on schedule, arriving with the current copy of Omnius. Xerxes transmitted orders for it to remain on the outskirts of the planetary system with the picket line of machine sentries. *Fortuitous timing.* Within a day, he would be able to restore even the loss of the evermind below — what a victory!

While the Titan and other neo-cymeks hung back under the protection of the heavily armed robot fleet, machine ships advanced in precise attack formation toward the doomed humans. *Perfect.* Xerxes decided that the odds were stacked sufficiently in his favor now, so he issued the command.

"Full strike mode. All battleships to the vanguard. After what the vermin just did to Omnius, spare nothing, no matter the robot casualties. Just wipe out the *hrethgir*."

Besides, he thought, *we can always make more machines.*

From the bubbleplaz bridge of his ballista flagship, Xavier had a clear view of open space, of stars twinkling in a deceptively serene tableau. Below, orange streaks across the planet's atmosphere marked the paths of Jihad rescue ships racing back to the fleet. But there was no safety here either.

He thought of Octa and his daughters, and of his peaceful estate on Salusa Secundus, with olive groves and vineyards. The memory of old Manion and his winemaking gave him a warm feeling. Oh, how he wanted to survive this day and return home.

"They're on the move again, Primero," a nervous voice reported over the comline. "Even more ships heading our way than before. They have five times as many warships as we do, and I think they mean it this time."

Through the plaz, Xavier saw thousands of silvery machine vessels rise over the curve of Ix, seemingly enough to overwhelm the scattered stars.

"Only half of our rescue ships have returned to the ballista bays, sir. Casualties are –"

The Primero cut him off. "I don't want to hear about casualties yet." *We'll have plenty more in just a few minutes.* He barked commands and watched tactical images through multiple screens on the bridge. As he called out configurations for the fleet, he watched his ballistas fall into defensive positions.

The mercenary teams on the surface had accomplished their task; Xavier would not allow the Army of the Jihad to do any less. Panels on the ballista hulls glowed orange as weapons systems powered up. He hoped their shields were sufficiently cooled for a long engagement, and that Tio Holtzman's flicker-and-fire systems — phasing the shields in and out between weapons fire — were up to the task.

From all of his military instruction and training, Xavier knew the success or failure of a battle sometimes hinged more on luck than skill. Holtzman's shields would protect his ships from the first pummeling of the robot fleet, but even his most conservative planning had not allowed for such an incredible buildup of frontline machine warships. The enemy could keep pounding and pounding, and eventually the Army of the Jihad would crumble . . . one vessel at a time.

"We will hold as long as we can, and strike at the first opportunity." He tried to sound braver than he felt. "The rebels down there faced worse odds than this, and survived for most of a year."

Ahead, the machine fleet split in two, with an advance force hurtling toward him at ramming speed. The Titan Xerxes transmitted loudly over an open channel that he knew the humans would overhear. "The *hrethgir* can only hope to delay the inevitable. Block off their escape."

Xavier had positioned his smallest shielded ships in the front and saw them bend as the assault force hit them. Behind these small ships, the overlapped shields of the foremost ballistas flickered imperceptibly in precise timing as they launched a volley of defensive projectile fire, driving back the first robot assault, annihilating many of the machine suicide ships before they could get through.

Immediately after the first wave of ramming ships came a squadron of neo-cymeks in bizarre flying and fighting forms led by an enormous winged form shaped like a bird of prey but as large as a ballista. Undoubtedly, the Titan commander himself. The larger robotic warships regrouped, clustering for the second attack phase.

"Hold on," Xavier said. "Keep the line solid, or we're all lost."

But as the stampede of robot battleships surged forward, he knew his forces could not withstand another impact. He thought of his brother Vergyl's ship destroyed by cymeks at IV Anbus, and his heart sank.

Someone would have to tell Emil Tantor that his only remaining son had been lost.

*   *   *

Inside the giant asteroid controlled by Hecate, Iblis Ginjo felt anxious, hoping that the eccentric female cymek — his ally, in theory? — would come through, as promised.

Her ornate dragon walker-form had retreated, disengaging from the preservation canister. Hecate had loaded her brain into the intricate systems that controlled her huge artificial rock while it cruised between the stars.

"Hecate, what is happening?" Iblis stood with fists clenched at his sides, looking around the crystal-mirrored chamber that imprisoned their ship. He could feel the acceleration as the asteroid hurtled across the distance.

Hecate's feminine voice tinkled through speakers hidden within the rock walls. "I am doing exactly what you asked me to do, dear Iblis. Observe now — your 'secret weapon' is about to strike." Her laughter was like a tinkle of ice.

With that, one of the flat crystal surfaces on the cave wall shimmered and became a projection screen of the planetary system they were fast approaching.

"Look, we have arrived at Ix, and it appears that your concerns were well-founded. A disaster in the making! Your Army of the Jihad has put up an extraordinary resistance — just look at all the wreckage in orbit — but they are about to be obliterated anyway."

"Do something!" Iblis demanded. "We have invested a great deal to liberate Ix. It's taken years, and we must have victory."

"I will do what I can, Iblis," she answered with a lilt in her voice. "My, I had forgotten how impatient mortal human beings can be."

From high above the ecliptic, Hecate's giant asteroid plunged down toward Ix. Glints of spaceships and flares of weapons fire sparkled in the crowded expanse of orbital paths.

Silent but intense, the Jipol commander studied the situation on the screen. No emotions showed, and he said nothing.

In contrast, Floriscia Xico squirmed with excitement and anxiety. "But what can this asteroid do in a battle zone, Grand Patriarch? Hecate is only one cymek against an entire fleet."

Iblis didn't point out that this flying rock was massive enough to shatter all of the robotic battleships in a single impact, but he hoped Hecate's plan went beyond a simple collision course. "Just watch and see, Sergeant. Let the Titan impress us with her abilities."

Feminine laughter tinkled through the speakers. "I have fallen far indeed if my life is devoted to impressing a man like you, Iblis Ginjo. I do this for my own reasons . . . and I believe I have found a sufficiently dramatic way for me to reappear on the stage for all to see. What a shining moment this is. Juno would absolutely loathe my audacity."

The asteroid's crater-sized thrusters glowed, hurling it at ever-increasing speed toward the machine battleships that pummeled the crumbling Jihad war fleet.

"Now watch what I can do with my kinetic launchers."

"Our shields are failing, Primero!" the weapons officer cried. Xavier had already seen it for himself, but could do nothing about it.

"We've lost all contact with a third ballista, sir. Scanners show wreckage, hundreds of lifepods . . ."

"Give me a weapons update," Xavier said, refusing to succumb to despair. "Best-case scenario. How many of these machine bastards can we take out before —"

Suddenly, behind the majestic and terrifying raptor form of the Titan battle commander, Xavier noticed a large and unexpected object moving at high speed, coming from high above the orbital plane. "What in the seven hells is that? Get me a preliminary scan."

"It seems to be an . . . asteroid, Primero. Reading trajectory and velocity. Incredible! It's like a stone hurled by the gods, and it's heading right at the heart of our enemy!"

The enlarged image showed a hurtling hunk of cratered rock accelerating directly toward the clustered machine fleet. The trajectory, velocity, and other data appeared at the bottom of the screen. Its mass was a hundred times the aggregate mass of the robot ships.

"Impossible," Xavier said. "No asteroid flies like that."

Behind the celestial intruder, huge crater pits glowed like the hot exhausts of immense engines. Some of the machine ships changed course, scattering in confusion at this sudden, mysterious visitor. A buzz of coded communication assailed the hurtling rock, and the thinking machines chattered with each other in a flurry of exchanged data.

In response a shower of dense spherical projectiles blasted out of scattered craters on the craggy surface, like cannonballs at incredible velocities. Before the thinking machines could respond, kinetic spheres obliterated two of their largest battleships.

Moving like a Salusan bull on a rampage, the asteroid careened into the thick of the machine fleet, moving as swiftly as their fastest vessels, but many times their size. By its sheer momentum and mass, the asteroid battered dozens of the armored vessels as if it were crushing insects. The neo-cymeks were the first to scatter, and as the huge condor-shaped Titan tried to withdraw, the rotating asteroid caught it a glancing blow, sending Xerxes tumbling out into an extended orbit.

The jihadi soldiers yelled in confusion and disbelief as the asteroid abruptly changed course and smashed through the robot ships again. Turning to face this new, more threatening attacker, the machine fleet responded by firing useless explosive projectiles at the already-cratered asteroid surface, causing little damage. In retaliation, the mysterious attacker launched another set of dense stone spheres, wreaking even more havoc among the robots.

None of the desperate Jihad vessels were hit in the scatter shot.

Xavier hardly had time to consider what the Fates were doing on his behalf, nor did he question the sudden turn of fortune. He would not complain about an unexpected ally. Not yet.

He took a deep breath, knowing that his soldiers wanted nothing more than to escape, now that they had been given a second chance. But he would not let this battle for Ix, and all the sacrifices his people had made, be for nothing.

"Regroup and select new targets. Hit the machines while they're still reeling. This is a critical moment."

With his damaged flagship leading the way and his overheated shields useless, Xavier Harkonnen plunged headlong into the fray, into the midst of all the chaos and destruction. This presented a distinct danger: the mysterious attacker could just as easily turn on his forces next.

The neo-cymeks sent frantic calls to their Titan leader, but Xerxes was already accelerating out of the system, fleeing for his life.

Abruptly, the mysterious interstellar visitor, after destroying half of the machine fleet by itself, veered into space and vanished long before Xavier could either ask questions or express his gratitude. He was left to mop up, which he did with great flourishes of violence.

Leaving the tumult behind, Hecate's asteroid soared out of the Ixian system, its fusion engines drawing raw power and achieving incredible thrust. "There now, Grand Patriarch — I believe I've done my part and shown the capabilities I can offer. Good thing I arrived when I did."

"You didn't destroy them all," Yorek Thurr said, his voice thin and hard.

Hecate sounded petulant. "Oh, your Primero can finish off the damaged stragglers. I wouldn't want to deprive him entirely of the satisfaction of victory."

"You did a fine job, Hecate," Iblis said. He couldn't wait for a full intelligence assessment of everything the League could use on the captured Synchronized World. "Those industries on Ix will be a huge boon to our war effort."

Floriscia Xico could barely contain herself. "That was incredible! The people will rejoice when they learn of our new ally."

Iblis frowned as the consequences of her words raced through his mind. He attempted to sort out the best way to handle the situation, and how to properly integrate the turncoat cymek into Jihad strategies. The female sergeant's eyes shone with delight and fervor.

Never one to shrink from hard decisions, Yorek Thurr swiftly reached a conclusion. Without signaling his intentions to Iblis, he stepped close behind the enthusiastic Xico. "You have served the Jipol well, Floriscia," he said, his voice soft and quiet in her ear. "From this day forward you'll be on the list."

"The list?" Her brow wrinkled.

"Of martyrs."

Thurr thrust a short dagger into the back of the young sergeant's neck, sliding the point between two vertebrae to sever the spinal cord. She was paralyzed instantly and died with very little twitching or bleeding. In the low gravity of the asteroid, the smaller Thurr held her body up until her struggles faded, then let the dead woman slide to the polished floor. She lay supine, her eyes open wide in shock.

Iblis turned to him, astonished and angry. "What are you doing, man? She was one of ours —"

"She was obviously incapable of holding her silence. Couldn't you hear it in her voice? The moment we returned to Salusa, she would have jabbered to everyone within earshot." The small bald man looked up, seeing his reflection in the myriad facets of the walls. His ghastly gaze darted back and forth. "Hecate is our secret weapon. No one knows — and no one must know — that she is in alliance with us. Not yet. If she retains her covert nature, we keep the element of surprise. This Titan will be part of our coup de grâce against the thinking machines."

Iblis looked at the Jipol commander and understood. He was absolutely correct. "Sometimes you terrify me, Yorek."

"But never will I disappoint you," he promised.

Plans, schemes, talk ... It seems we spend all our lives in discussion and virtually no time in meaningful action. We must not fail to seize our opportunities.

—General Agamemnon, Battle Logs

MEMORIES.

Seurat had a lot of them, neatly sorted and filed, available for instant inspection and reflection. It was completely unlike the internal recollections of human beings, with their random-recovery features and recall-by-association techniques. If he wanted a supply of puns or riddles, Seurat had all of them at his mechanical fingertips. If he wanted to review the effect his jokes had on other machines or on humans, he had files for that as well. And a lot more.

But at the moment none of that gave him comfort. He felt oddly lonely as he traveled the long update route by himself.

In the library of his gelcircuitry brain, he had a personal journal of experiences compiled from his regular update runs between the various Synchronized Worlds. His information was broad-based but not particularly deep. He interacted with the Omnius worlds only at a surface level, within the parameters of his duties.

Now, after a quarter century of unavoidable delay, his first stop would be Bela Tegeuse, a small and relatively unimportant planet in the Omnius network. The evermind incarnation there would be the first to receive a copy of the defunct Earth-Omnius's final thoughts. Though Seurat's "update" was long outdated, it nonetheless contained vital information, the true records of what had happened on the annihilated machine world, the last, failed decisions of the evermind incarnation.

After delivering his update to Bela Tegeuse, Seurat would hurry to the next machine planet, and the next. Soon, everything would be in order once again.

The robot stood on the bridge of his update ship, scanning the infinity of star systems. His past, present, and future lay out there, a sequence of events that was supposed to be entirely reliable, set up by the evermind's comprehensive downloads. But machines could only establish programs with probable outcomes, not certainties. Seurat's interactions with Vorian Atreides had added an unanticipated element.

Most disturbing.

Within his gelcircuitry brain, Seurat encountered a thought that was not his own: an Omnius implant, one of thousands in the independent robot's subset of databases that guided him along the proper paths, as constructed for him by the evermind.

But I have my own thoughts.

Seurat experienced a brief tug-of-war in his internal programming as he tried to assert himself. A defensive swarm of data inundated the robot captain . . . Omnius implants keeping him from slipping off-program.

Since he had worked closely with a trustee human, the robot had developed enhanced flexibilities in order to deal with the irrational creatures. He had a rudimentary emotional core that simulated certain basic feelings of humans, just enough to interact with them.

At least that was the way it was supposed to be. But Seurat missed the enjoyable times he had had with Vorian Atreides, the strategy games, the stimulating banter. *How many humans does it take to come up with one good idea?* The joke danced in his consciousness, and he brought up the punchline: *No one can count that high, not even Omnius.*

Vor had never objected to such machine sarcasm, had not shown any indications of rebelliousness. There had been no warning signs of mental disturbance whatsoever . . . until the violent slave uprising on Earth, when Vor had stunned the robot captain and stolen the *Dream Voyager.* Seurat wondered if he should have noticed some sort of aberration. He also wondered how Vor could have turned against the system that had nurtured him into adulthood.

A thought intruded: *I hope he is safe and healthy.*

The update ship entered a small solar system and sped toward the gray-blue planet of Bela Tegeuse, a gloomy world far from its sun, where twilight was as bright as any day became.

Having seen the radioactive wreckage of Earth, Seurat approached the planet with special caution. After making radio contact with Tegeusan ground stations, he used image enhancers to examine conditions below. Finally satisfied that all appeared normal, the robot pilot punched down through the atmosphere and landed at the central city of Comati, a glistening metal stronghold at the base of cold mountains.

Attendant robots rolled across the fused, glassy-smooth landing field to receive him. Because of the urgency of his restored mission, Seurat requested a rapid turnaround, so that he could embark on the next leg of his dissemination run.

With the machine equivalent of reverence, update robots received the silver gelsphere — long thought to be lost — and transferred its data into an Omnius node, which would then upload all of the previously unknown information into the planetary evermind network. The copy proceeded efficiently, and within moments the Bela Tegeuse-Omnius absorbed the lost information about the last moments on Earth.

"Seurat, you have performed a great service for the Synchronized Worlds," Omnius declared.

Thereupon, the planetary evermind dumped a copy of its own new thoughts since the last update. The entire process was like a conveyor belt, a continuous track in which Seurat and other update ship captains relayed information from one planet to the next, keeping the computer network as synchronized as possible.

Required to continue his route with all possible haste, the robot captain lifted off moments later, leaving Bela Tegeuse behind . . .

Within hours after passing beyond communication range, things began to happen behind him. A chain of breakdowns, failures, and cascading disasters occurred on Bela Tegeuse. Transposed landing codes, improperly adjusted reactor exhaust systems, harmful power surges, and logic conundrums paralyzed the network and infrastructure. The Synchronized World crippled itself.

But by that time Seurat was well on his way to the next Omnius stronghold, eager to deliver his update . . . not knowing he was spreading the altered code like a plague, faster than any warning could be passed from planet to planet.

"Artificial intelligence is not the correct term," Agamemnon said with a growl. "Even sophisticated computers like Omnius are just plain stupid, when faced with the right sort of questions."

"And yet, my love," Juno pointed out, "they have held us in thrall for ten centuries. What does that make us?"

The Titans had gathered in space again, another secret rendezvous that included their adopted co-conspirator, Beowulf. Duped watcheyes hovered inside a separate ship's chamber, lenses glinting and recording images that were carefully doctored to fool Omnius.

After the confusion and shutdowns on Bela Tegeuse, at least two other

Synchronized Worlds experienced spontaneous breakdowns. Planetary Omnius incarnations deteriorated and went insane, shutting down the evermind network. The Titans suspected that this was some incomprehensible and innovative new attack by the Army of the Jihad. Agamemnon watched with curious optimism, quietly anticipating further damage to Omnius. "I do not object to any means that further weaken the domination of the evermind."

"Still, it would be good to understand," Dante pointed out, "then, perhaps, we could make further use of it."

"And what about our mysterious new enemy who attacked me on Ix and wiped out the thinking machine fleet?" Xerxes asked. His synthesized voice carried a whining tone. He had returned in his damaged raptor form, frightened and unsettled at the unexpected arrival of the artificial asteroid. "Even after the Omnius core was destroyed by atomics, we still could have won the space battle, but that huge juggernaut tipped the scales. I suspect . . . it was controlled by a cymek. I think—" Xerxes fidgeted. "I think it might have been . . . Hecate."

Some of the Titans made disbelieving sounds. Beowulf, eager to speak, said, "Hecate has been gone for centuries. She probably died of boredom out in open space."

"She was a self-centered fool," Juno added. Extruding a robotic hand from her shoulder, she used the mechanical fingers to tighten a fitting.

"Still," Dante pointed out, "she was the only one of us wise enough to flee before Omnius took over. Hecate remained independent, but we've been forced to serve the evermind all this time."

"Perhaps not for much longer," Beowulf said. Blue lights blinked excitedly around his brain canister.

Dante was curious. "What evidence do you have for this assertion, Xerxes? Considering the number of neo-cymeks that have been created over the centuries, why would you suspect Hecate rather than . . . some other rogue?"

"Some other rogue?" Juno sounded amused.

"Because after I was damaged and reeling off into space, someone actually communicated with me, a simulated female voice. It was transmitted on my private channel. She knew me, talked about Tlaloc and the Titans, called me by *name*."

The cymek general had heard enough. "You are concocting phantoms as an excuse for your failure. Blaming the Army of the Jihad isn't enough to convince us you weren't responsible for losing Ix."

"Why do you always doubt me, Agamemnon? For a thousand years I have worked to make up for my mistake—"

"A million years could not earn you forgiveness. I should dismantle your external sensors and send you drifting off into space, blind and deaf for the rest of eternity. Perhaps Hecate could keep you company."

Oddly enough, Beowulf acted as peacemaker between them. "General Agamemnon, there are only a few of you left. Must you quarrel amongst yourselves? Aren't Omnius and the Jihad Army sufficient enemies? This is not the military brilliance I imagined from the famed Titan general."

Agamemnon was stunned into angry silence. The watcheyes continued to observe and record. Finally, he said, "You are correct, Beowulf." His acceptance was surprising to those who had known him for a long time. "There will be sufficient opportunity to discuss my grievances with Xerxes after we have won back our glory."

"And time enough for me to prove myself," Xerxes suggested.

"Despite my initial disbelief," Agamemnon said, "I have indeed received separate confirmation, and I intend to share it with you. Xerxes is correct — Hecate has apparently returned, but at present she is irrelevant . . . as always." He turned to Beowulf. "Share your ideas with us. We Titans have spoken of our own plans for generations. Let us hear fresh insight from the youngest member of our group."

"General, neo-cymeks like myself can be convinced to turn against Omnius if they think we can *win*. We have achieved more than we ever thought possible in our human trustee days, but neos can go no farther as long as Omnius retains control. In a second Time of Titans, though, we could become rulers in our own right."

"But can we trust them, if their allegiance is so easily shifted?" Juno asked. "The neos were never free. They were human servants rewarded by being converted into cymeks. They owe their physical power and longevity to Omnius, not to us. Such a payment can buy a great deal of loyalty."

Agamemnon spun his head turret, and his optic threads glinted. "Why not recruit more neo-cymeks from the outset? Create them ourselves from selected human candidates who swear allegiance to *us*. The Titans may be few, but the possibilities are endless. If we find some way to keep it secret from Omnius, we can foster a fighting force of our own, confident of their total dedication, without concern about treachery."

The other Titans agreed, and Beowulf launched into a discussion of how they could begin to put this plan into operation.

Agamemnon did not mention the thorn of doubt that continued to scratch at his thoughts. He wasn't as certain as he claimed to be, since he had been betrayed by even his own son, Vorian Atreides.

That being the case, how trustworthy could other humans be?

With the diversification of mankind, one might think religion would have proliferated. Not so. There are not nearly as many gods as there once were—just more ways to worship.

—Iblis Ginjo, private analyses

DEEPLY MOVED BY the loss of the Cogitor Kwyna and her devastating words and revelations, a shaken Serena Butler took a more active role as Priestess of the Jihad. During the three months that the Grand Patriarch remained away at Poritrin, Serena had left the solitude of the City of Introspection and wandered among her people.

For the first time in decades, Serena truly began to really *look* around her. Not so much for her own safety, but to get control over what was being done in her name.

Instead of delivering scripted speeches, touching the heads of suppliants, and visiting military hospitals to cheer wounded soldiers, she made her own real decisions, took her own risks — and wondered why she had not done so all along. *This is my Jihad.* In the process, Serena began to feel truly *alive* again.

By the time Iblis finally returned home from the celebrations on Poritrin, she had already revised many policies of the Jihad Council. Learning this, the Grand Patriarch was stunned and uncertain how to react. Smiling as she told him of her accomplishments, Serena watched him struggle with his emotions. She understood how she must look to him now, with her penetrating lavender eyes, seeming to see through him more clearly than she had in more than two decades.

No matter how much of the leadership role Iblis had grabbed for himself, he was now boxed in by his own words. Since he had spent decades declaring *her* to be the infallible prime mover of the Jihad, he had no choice but to accommodate her new involvement.

Clearly, though, Iblis Ginjo did not like the new arrangement at all . . .

With him, she attended a vital Jihad Council meeting inside a secure tower that had been built as an addition to the old Parliament Hall. Officers in the Army of the Jihad attended the assembly in full green-and-crimson uniforms, sitting beside officials and consultants from military operations and industries, as well as planetary representatives, and one-armed Master Shar, who spoke for the senior Ginaz mercenaries.

In one corner, she also saw the frenetic Tlulaxa merchant Rekur Van, who had so benevolently provided the Jihad with replacement organs and transplanted tissue from the secretive organ farms. His enigmatic, private people had answered her call when she had demanded their help for the veterans of IV Anbus. The Tlulaxa were humans, after all. Odd in that regard, but humans nonetheless.

Only the day before, Xavier Harkonnen had come home with the survivors of his Ixian battle force, looking dazed but victorious from the fury of the conflict. They had left a consolidation fleet behind at the battle-scarred Synchronized World, along with scores of rescue workers, relief engineers and medical personnel to comb through the ruins of the Ixian cities, and to establish a strong League presence there. But full-fledged defensive troops were still urgently needed.

Even so, Xavier's news was remarkable and surprising: a victory over the demon machines. Serena had given him a chaste congratulatory kiss on the forehead, which had only seemed to make Xavier uncomfortable. Now at the meeting table, the Primero was rigid, his lean face hard-bitten, as if he still had not grasped the reality of his survival.

Serena herself could barely remember when Xavier had been a young, dashing officer who had looked forward to his life . . . the man who had saved Zimia from the initial cymek attack twenty-eight years ago. Back then, she had been an optimistic young woman in love, blind to the horrors and responsibilities the universe could inflict upon one person . . .

On the opposite wall hung a saintly portrait of the haloed child Manion, an innocent whose expression seemed to reflect the eyes of every human ever born. As a symbol, the boy had accomplished more since his death than most men did in their entire lives.

It was time to call the meeting to order. Resting her hands on the blood-grained wood, she stood at the head of the long polished table. Without asking, she had taken the seat normally reserved for the Grand Patriarch, and now Iblis sat on her left, smiling reverently when she spoke, but allowing himself a hint of a frown whenever he turned his face away.

Two Jipol lieutenants sat discreetly and silently against the walls. They wore nondescript clothes and had a certain hardness to their manner that Serena did not like.

Iblis Ginjo had wrought many changes over the years with his ever-more-powerful Jipol. Early on, after a large number of Jihad forces had been wiped out in the Honru Massacre because of inaccurate intelligence, Iblis had demanded an investigation. He had assigned an ambitious and intelligent young detective, Yorek Thurr, to look into the matter, and Thurr had uncovered strong evidence that disloyal humans had been responsible for purposely supplying disinformation.

After the formation of the Jihad Police, Yorek Thurr had risen quickly in its command structure because of his uncanny knack for rooting out any humans with insidious ties to Omnius. Later, the recurring purges of suspected traitors had imposed an intense new vigilance, and paranoia, on the populace.

Hiding in the City of Introspection, Serena had barely noticed everything that had changed, and now she blamed herself.

For years, oblivious to the outside world, Serena had made grandiose pronouncements, launching battle groups and desperate offensives against Omnius — whatever Iblis told her to say. She had given her love and determination to the cause, but had she unwittingly planted the seeds to create a government guided by human ambition rather than computer cruelty?

There were other concerns, as well. Foremost among them, she had paid inadequate attention to the considerable human costs of the war, which Iblis often referred to as "expected losses" or "manageable costs," as if flesh-and-blood casualties were no more than statistics. It seemed like more of a machine way of thinking than a human one, and she began to express her feelings about this, to Iblis and others around her.

Serena stood tall and strong as she gaveled the Council session to order. "After much contemplation and discussion with my advisors, today I announce a new dawn for our Jihad, a light at the end of this long dark tunnel that has kept humans in bondage."

Iblis was disturbed by her words, but sat with his hands folded on the polished table, while wheels turned in his brain in an effort to stay one step ahead of whatever surprises Serena might have in store for him.

"It is time for us to change the focus of my Jihad. Our Grand Patriarch has done a masterful job of forging our struggle into the pointed weapon of a Holy Jihad. But over the years since I escaped from Omnius and returned here to Salusa, I have not been as effective as I might have been."

Mutters of disagreement passed around the table, but she raised her hand to stifle them. "I should never have allowed a few assassination attempts to drive me into hiding. Iblis Ginjo meant well in his efforts to protect me, but in isolating myself, I placed too much of the burden of leadership on his shoulders."

She smiled benignly at him. "This was unfair to the Grand Patriarch, who has been my proxy at so many of these meetings. Henceforth, I intend to take a much more active role in the day-to-day activities of the war. From this moment forward I take my seat as the rightful head of the Jihad Council. Iblis has earned a respite from his constant labors."

The Grand Patriarch flushed with surprise and displeasure. "There is no need, Serena. I am proud and willing to—"

"Oh, there will be plenty of work left for you, dear Iblis. I promise not to let you grow lazy and fat."

Chuckles rippled around the table, but the Jipol officers did not smile. Rekur Van seemed puzzled, as if this meeting was not what he had anticipated at all. His shadowy gaze flitted around, fixed on Iblis. The two exchanged uneasy glances.

Serena looked meaningfully at the image of her son Manion on the wall. "My time in the City of Introspection was not, however, entirely wasted on relaxation. After years of deep philosophical discussion with Cogitor Kwyna, I learned a great deal — and now I shall to put that knowledge to good use."

Unintentionally, she closed her eyes for a moment. Serena still felt shaken by Kwyna's suicide, her deliberate shutdown. So much knowledge and experience lost . . . But the ancient philosopher had also hinted at the existence of other Cogitors, isolated thinkers who chose to live in their metaphorical ivory towers, paying no attention to the struggle that raged across the Galaxy.

"I have decided that we will develop a more comprehensive plan for prosecuting this great Jihad, one designed to sweep us to victory. We must make use of every mind and every idea devoted to the service of the Holy War." She saw Xavier's eyes light up with determination to do whatever she asked of him or his soldiers. He sat up straight, ready to hear her new plan.

"Our goal remains unchanged. Every incarnation of Omnius will be vanquished."

Arrakis: Men saw great danger there, and great opportunity.
                    —Princess Irulan, in *Paul of Dune*

A H, THE PROFITS must flow, Venport thought. Still, he wished he could be anyplace but Arrakis.

He sat in the back of a noisy, primitive groundcar that rumbled along a caravan path away from the cave settlement where he had left Naib Dhartha. Glancing back, Venport saw a jagged rock formation profiled against the violent orange of sunset. He held a scribing pad on his lap and continued to make notes, knowing he would be required to stay here for at least two more months, while Tuk Keedair remained on Poritrin with Norma. He missed her.

The passenger compartment had grown too warm from the harsh sunlight that penetrated the groundcar's plaz windows. Wondering if the vehicle's air-cooling system had failed, he sniffed the sour air and frowned at the fine brown dust that seemed to ooze through the cracks and seals like a living thing.

Why couldn't the spice be found on any other planet . . . anywhere but here?

Accompanied by Dhartha, Venport had visited spice harvesting camps today, including the site of a recent bandit raid. He was dismayed at the extensive vandalism to the melange harvesting equipment and the loss of so much product. One of the Naib's lieutenants described how he had only narrowly escaped with his life during a harrowing assault, an experience that left him telling fantastic stories about the outlaws, as if they were superhuman.

For years Dhartha had dodged answers, but Venport and Keedair had long suspected troubles like this. Confronted with the hard evidence of fluctuating spice deliveries, the Naib could no longer deny them. Now that he had observed firsthand the aftermath of a raid, Venport began to suspect just how much damage these outlaws were doing. Two hours ago as he stood in the wreckage of the raided camp, he had scowled at the Zensunni leader. "Things must improve here, and quickly. Do you understand?"

The desert man's aquiline face had remained stony. "I understand, Aurelius Venport. But you do not. This is a problem for my people to handle. You cannot come here and tell us how to manage our affairs."

"I pay you a great deal of money. This is business, not a petty tribal matter." And he wondered, but did not say so, if one of his business competitors could possibly be responsible for the sabotage. But how would they know to come here?

Then Venport noticed dark, threatening looks from some of the wild Zensunnis, and sensed the danger. His two hired bodyguards stiffened as the glowering desert man yanked the thick scarf from his face and tossed it scornfully to the ground — for it had been an earlier gift from Tuk Keedair. With a shout or a hand signal, Dhartha could summon enough men to overwhelm Venport and his guards.

But the merchant showed no fear. Instead he spoke firmly, and not in an intimidating manner. "I have much invested in this operation, Naib Dhartha, and I refuse to lose profits because of unruly vandals. Your expenses have grown higher in recent years, and your melange deliveries no longer meet the quantities that you promised. A man of honor fulfills his contracts."

Dhartha glowered. "I am a man of honor! Do you claim otherwise?"

Pausing for effect, Venport said, "Then we need not have this discussion again." Though he showed bravado, his pulse pounded. These desert men were tough people and he had just confronted their leader, matching strength with strength. That, and guaranteed profits, was the only language they understood. He had seen how much Naib Dhartha had grown to depend on offworld goods, and these Zensunni people were already markedly softer than when he had first encountered them years ago. The change was so dramatic, in fact, that Venport doubted these spoiled Zensunni villagers would ever go back to the dirty subsistence desert conditions they had accepted before the spice trade.

Then, wanting to get away from the threatening cliff village, he had gestured to his bodyguards and moved quickly to the waiting groundcar. Even now he watched guardedly through the rear window, concerned that the Zensunni fighters might follow with a squad of desert assassins . . .

They bumped along over rough ground at the edge of the dry cliffs. On top of the vehicle, the native driver sat in a dusty rooftop compartment with the two guards. At times the rutted path disappeared on the hardpan, but the driver kept going, apparently guided by instinct. They skirted thick, soft dunes, and finally Venport saw a graben town in the distance. Relaxing, he looked at the scribing pad on his lap and focused on the numerical estimates. Studying a column of figures, he scratched his head.

Upon confirming Norma's calculation of the funding she would need to develop her giant prototype ship, Venport had padded the guess just to be conservative, and then had ordered VenKee accountants to set up detailed tracking ledgers with cost breakdowns. Doubting Norma would ever notice, he had created additional expense categories based on his own business experience. Keedair would monitor the expenditures from Poritrin.

In the big picture of VenKee Enterprises, Norma's project had not yet caused a significant dent in income, though his concessions to Lord Bludd had cost him glowglobe revenues. She required only an isolated set of research buildings, a group of reasonably priced slaves, her own personal living expenses, and an old spaceship. But regardless of the cost, Venport promised himself he would provide the capital, for Norma. His heart told him to do this.

The groundcar hit a deep rut and lurched, which knocked the scribing pad from his lap. With a frown he picked it up and dusted it off. He hated this gritty, filthy planet, but was stuck here. His thoughts drifted . . .

On the night before he was due to depart from Poritrin for most of a year, Venport had gone to talk with Norma Cenva. He had wanted to say goodbye to her . . . and other things as well. The idea was still a surprise to him, but despite his disbelief, he knew he was doing the right thing.

Far below, the tributary of the Isana had gurgled through the canyon on its journey to the slow but powerful main current. The large warehouse was well lit, inside and out, and intense glowglobes dazzled from the corners of the building. Flying reptiles swooped around the glare, feasting on insects.

In the days since Keedair had flown the test ship down into the hangar, the construction crews had finished the lion's share of the work on the research facility. Slave barracks had been built, supplied, and furnished, and the first crews of slaves had already been reassigned from Starda.

Heavy machinery, fabrication benches, and welding shops had been brought in, along with every sophisticated manufacturing tool Venport could imagine. Inside the big hangar, the bulbous cargo ship rested in its support cradle, shored up by stabilizers. Venport thought it looked like a drugged patient awaiting surgery . . . and he knew Norma would be the miracle worker.

Affable, dedicated, Norma. He had known her for most of her life — how could he have been so blind before?

On that warm, moonlit night, Venport had walked across the research grounds. Inside the hangar, Norma had moved into three of the larger offices previously used by administrators of the defunct mine. Though he'd personally made certain she had comfortable living quarters in one of the site's outbuildings, Norma rarely spent time there.

She'd always been an obsessively hard worker, and had become even more intense now that she worked on her own dreams instead of Tio Holtzman's. Despite his own substantial investment in the project, Venport knew that she would need time, probably more than a year, before she was ready to test the new space-folding ship.

But what was a year, when one considered the big picture? Even so, it seemed much too long for him to be away from her.

In his arms, he held a bouquet of fresh Bludd roses, obtained from the Lord of Poritrin's private gardens in Starda — not that Norma would put much stock in such things. He still couldn't believe what he was doing . . . but it *felt* so right.

Light shone from her calculation rooms, as always. Despite the late hour, Norma was still engrossed in her equations and inventions. Venport shook his head sadly, but forced a smile. There never was a good time to talk to Norma. Any hour of the day, she was equally busy; sometimes, she went for days without sleep — eating and drinking only enough to keep going.

But that was Norma. He didn't expect to change her.

Still, Venport had to tell her how he felt. He supposed it would come as a shock to her, much as it had been for him. He had taken her for granted, happily accepting her short-statured form and blunt features, never really thinking of her as a woman.

Why had he never seen it before? For years he had been the breeding partner of the stunningly statuesque and beautiful Chief Sorceress of Rossak – and had been kept like a pet. What had that gotten him? Zufa's outer beauty did not extend to her heart, but Norma kept all of her beauty inside.

Solemnly, Venport knocked on the door of her calculation rooms, silently rehearsing what he wanted to say. He did not expect her to respond right away, so he tried the door. It swung open and he entered slowly with butterflies in his stomach — as if he were a mere adolescent!

Inside the bright room, Norma was seated on an adjustable floating chair that held her at the proper height from her work table. Standard chairs and tables never fit her, and he marveled at how she functioned so stubbornly, without complaint, in a universe designed for larger people. Her immense intellect more than made up for her lack of stature. It didn't bother her, so why should it bother him?

He realized there were many reasons why he cared for her as much more than a friend. For a long time, it had been more akin to sibling love, and Venport did not know quite when it had shifted, on a subconscious level. Yes, he was ten years older than she was, and he had been her mother's chosen breeding partner. But what difference did a decade make, anyway? A few thousand days. Not much. He appreciated Norma for who she was, and thought it was about time for him to express his feelings properly.

At first, engrossed as always, Norma didn't even notice him. For several moments he stood at her side, holding the flowers and just studying her. The Bludd roses filled his nostrils with delicate perfume. He had carefully attached an exquisite, rare soostone to the stems, the same expensive gem he had once tried to give to her mother. But Zufa Cenva had frowned at the egg-shaped "bauble," dismissing its alleged properties of focusing the mind and thoughts. The chief Sorceress had insisted she needed no such crutch. He doubted Zufa knew how to appreciate any heartfelt gesture for what it was.

Norma, though, should be able to see that the soostone, and the roses, were beautiful, precious. She would appreciate it in the spirit he meant it.

If he could only get her attention.

Like a horse wearing blinders, Norma stared at a long sheet filled with scribbled numbers. Every few seconds, she made a slight alteration to the document.

"I love you, Norma Cenva," he finally blurted. "Marry me. It's what I truly want."

She continued to work, as if she had shut off all external senses except vision. She looked so engrossed, so . . . beautiful . . . in her fixation. With a sigh, Venport paced the room, continuing to watch her work. Finally, she stretched. Suddenly she looked over at him, blinking. "Aurelius!" She hadn't noticed he was there.

His face felt warm, but he gathered his courage. "I have an important question to ask you. I've been waiting for the right moment." He handed her the bouquet of flowers, and she pressed them close to her face, inhaling the sweet scent, then studied the blossoms as if she had never noticed roses before. Gently, she touched the eerily marvelous soostone attached to the stems and admired the depth of colors in the gem, as if it were a universe all to itself. Then she looked up at him, her brown eyes inquisitive.

"I want you to be my wife. I love you very much. It's been obvious for a long time, I suppose, but I never recognized it."

It took her a moment to comprehend what he was saying, and then her eyes filled with tears of surprise and disbelief. "But, Aurelius — you know I have never thought of such things. Love, courting . . . even sex. I've had no experience, no opportunity. Those are" — she fumbled for words — "alien concepts to me."

"Just think about them for now. You're more intelligent than any other person I have ever met. You can figure out the best thing to do. I trust you." He smiled warmly.

She blushed with pleasure. "This is . . . so completely unexpected. I never imagined —"

"Norma, I'm leaving tomorrow. I couldn't wait. I had to ask you."

She had always considered him a friend, a supporter, the closest thing she had to a protective older brother. But she had never considered a deeper love with him — not because she didn't want to, but because she had never imagined the possibility. She looked at her small hands, the blunt fingers. "But . . . me? I am not an attractive woman, Aurelius. Why would you want to marry me?"

"I just told you."

She looked away. This was too much to process at once, and her thoughts were in complete turmoil. It was very unsettling. She had no idea anymore which calculations had been in her mind. "But . . . I have too much work to do, and it would not be fair to you. I can't afford . . . diversions."

"Marriage is about sacrifices."

"A marriage based on sacrifices would lead only to resentment." She met his gaze and shook her head stubbornly. "Let's not rush into this. We need to consider all the implications."

"Trust me, Norma, this isn't an experiment where you can control all the factors ahead of time. I am a busy man, too. I understand how much your work means to you. VenKee obligations will keep us apart for long periods, but that will also give you the time you need for your work. Think about it logically, at least, but let your heart decide."

She smiled and then, startled, looked back down to a calendar tag on the top of her table. "Oh, is it so soon that you leave for Arrakis?"

"You will have time to think. We've waited this many years, and I can wait a while longer. When you say you'll consider my proposal, I know you'll give it the most diligent attention I could ever hope for." Venport unfastened the smooth, slick soostone and handed it to her. "For now, will you at least accept my gift? A token of our friendship?"

"Of course." Her fingers traced the slick, pearly surface of the soostone. She smiled sadly. "You see? You have already been a diversion — though a pleasant one. Aurelius, have I truly been so oblivious that I never noticed your feelings for me?"

"Yes." He smiled. "And I promise you, I will not have changed my mind by the time I come back."

Many months from Poritrin and Norma now, Venport cruised over the Arrakis desert in a scout flyer, accompanied by his mercenary guards. He didn't need Naib Dhartha along on this expedition. His attention was focused on the monotonous landscape.

Out of long experience he thought in terms of controlling costs. He always considered how he might bypass wasteful middlemen in his diversified operations. Direct access was the key to gaining the most profit, whether the product was pharmaceuticals, glowglobes, or melange.

Thus far, since the Zensunnis were willing to take the risks and claimed to be experts in the harsh terrain of Arrakis, Venport and Keedair had avoided setting up their own spice-harvesting operations. But what if VenKee Enterprises hired outside workers and ran the operations directly, bypassing Naib Dhartha and all the problems he presented?

The scout flyer rattled as it hit turbulence. In the compartment beside him, mercenaries cursed at the pilot he had hired at the Arrakis City Spaceport, but he paid them no attention. Gueye d'Pardu was an off-worlder who had emigrated here at a young age and gone into business as a guide, though he found little enough business on such an isolated world. D'Pardu had promised to find exotically beautiful "spice sands" for Venport.

Dust on the horizon obscured the early morning sun, allowing no color to penetrate. Static crackled over a speaker in the passenger compartment as the pilot deigned to address them. "Monitoring storm ahead. Weather satellite shows it heading out into the Tanzerouft, so we should be all right. We need to keep an eye on it, though."

"What's the Tanzerouft?" Venport asked.

"Deep desert. Extremely dangerous out there."

They soared ahead for another half hour. The flyer ran alongside a cliff, then turned toward the ruddy sun and out over the yawning desert.

Back in the village, Venport had heard natives talk about Arrakis as if it were a living creature with a spirit of its own. Amused at the comments, he had discarded them out of hand, but now as he flew over the dunes he wondered if perhaps the natives had been right after all. He felt peculiar, as if someone were watching him. He and the few men with him were isolated out here. Vulnerable . . .

The tan landscape began to change, revealing swirls of rusty brown and ocher. "Spice sands," d'Pardu said. With his soft flesh and hanging jowls, the guide seemed out of place on a planet where most of the people appeared desiccated.

"It looks like something stirred up the ground," Venport noted. "The wind, I presume?"

"In the desert it is unwise to presume anything," d'Pardu said.

At a viewing station, Venport glanced through a window at a sinuous shape moving effortlessly through the dunes. The sands were in motion, as if awakening from an extended slumber. A chill ran down his spine. "What the hells is that? Gods — sandworms?" He leaned closer, amazed. He had heard of the huge beasts, which caused almost as much havoc for the spice-gathering crews as the outlaw raiders, but he'd never seen one before.

The guide scowled, opening up new wrinkles on his already creased, weathered face. "Demon of the Desert."

Below, the sinuous, grayish beast undulated like a row of living hills, cresting over and through the dunes at an astonishing speed, keeping pace with the flyer above.

"Look at its back!" one of the guards exclaimed. "Do you see the shapes? People! People are riding the worms!"

"Impossible," d'Pardu said with a sniff, but as he looked out the window he seemed unable to say anything further, and simply stared.

The dust picked up, blurring the view, but Venport thought he could still see the tiny figures, little specks . . . clearly human-shaped. No one could domesticate such monsters.

D'Pardu yelled, "We'd better leave. I have a bad feeling." Winds began to buffet the aircraft.

Agreeing with the guide, Venport said, "Just get us out of here."

The flyer circled around and headed back to Arrakis City. The desert storm chased them as if it were a living, sentient sky and they had ventured where they did not belong. All the way, the guards chattered about what they had seen. In the spaceport bars that evening, listeners would probably laugh at their stories.

But Venport had seen it for himself. If the rewards of melange were not so tremendous, he would never have risked doing business here. Who could deal with people who survived in such a god-forsaken place?

They ride giant worms!

Nothing is ever as it seems. With appropriate equations I can prove this.

—Norma Cenva, *Mathematical Philosophies*

N OW THAT SHE was no longer working for him, riding on his coattails, Tio Holtzman was not surprised at how quickly Norma Cenva faded from public attention. For an entire year he had not thought much about her, not since Aurelius Venport had negotiated her termination from his service. Holtzman smiled. *A superior businessman indeed.* What had Venport been thinking?

Though she had incomparable mathematical and scientific expertise, Norma simply did not have the knack to see the potential of her own discoveries. Pure genius was only one part of the equation — one needed to know what to *do* with a significant breakthrough. And that was where Norma had always failed.

Ah well, she was off on her own now and no longer a financial burden to him, even though VenKee's initial repayments of glowglobe profits would have paid her expenses thousands of times over. How could they all be so naïve?

Venport had offered Lord Bludd a tidy sum of money to purchase a group of "technically adept slaves" to work at Norma's new facility — somewhere upriver? — so the Savant had happily surrendered an entire group of his troublesome Zensunnis and Zenshiites. After the shutdown of the delta shipyards, Holtzman hadn't known what to do with all the workers anyway . . . until one disgruntled slave had had the audacity to confront Lord Bludd himself. The nobleman had rebuked Holtzman for not keeping sufficient control over his workers, and the Savant had been glad to send the troublemakers to Norma Cenva.

He was pleased to be rid of them. And Norma, as well. All problems solved.

But in a sense, Holtzman was also disappointed to have the dwarfish woman gone. For the first few years of her apprenticeship on Poritrin, he and Norma had been a good team, and the Savant had profited greatly from her eager, youthful assistance. But she had wanted to dabble on her own for decades, with no apparent sense of when to give up on a fruitless and costly mathematical development that led nowhere.

Still, he wanted her to know that he didn't hold a grudge. For years now, he had occasionally sent her polite invitations to formal receptions, but Norma always declined them with the flimsy excuse that she was "too busy." The tiny woman had never understood how more progress could be achieved through politics and connections than through direct research.

Luckily, his newest young assistants were impatient to make their mark on history. Their work kept his own position secure.

If asked in public, Holtzman invariably said that Norma had served him well, as a competent assistant who showed occasional flashes of insight. Such gentlemanly modesty and generosity only added to the great inventor's aura and increased stature. Then he would smile and turn the discussions to his own accomplishments.

As time went by, the Savant gave less and less thought to Norma Cenva.

Fading from the limelight did not concern her in the least. Working in the calculation rooms and inspecting the daily progress of the fabrication of new Holtzman Effect engine components, Norma was perfectly happy with her isolation.

She had never understood all of the machinations around her, nor did she give them much importance. Her major concern was the critical work itself, pursuing concepts without regard to politics, egos, or time-wasting social necessities.

Her funding came from VenKee Enterprises, she owned her slave workers, and Tuk Keedair's security force had been drawn from outside of Poritrin. No one had any reason to pay attention to her work here in her lab, far from prying eyes.

But the Tlulaxa business partner was much more concerned with security than Norma had ever been. At first, Keedair had suggested establishing an elaborate holosystem that would blur the above-ground buildings and the dry-waterfall cave opening. But with the construction and fabrication teams, all the materials sent upriver, and the constant flow of food and supplies, it was impossible to believe that no one would notice the research complex. Instead, Keedair relied on his guards to scare off any curious trespassers, though they looked bored as they paced around the hangar and grounds, on endless patrol.

Before long, Norma would be finished. She hoped to have the prototype space-folding ship ready before Aurelius Venport returned from Arrakis. Norma smiled whenever she thought of that most special man, and missed him very much. She still couldn't believe the surprise gift he had given her before departing. His fumbling question and the look in his eyes seemed to astonish him as much as it did her . . .

Perhaps by the time she achieved the dream that had dominated her thoughts since the beginning of the Jihad, Norma could give Aurelius an answer to his question. She did love him with all her heart and had never realized it. For her whole life she had shunted her emotions aside. No longer. When he came back to Poritrin, things would be different.

But first —

The heart of her work, the large old-style cargo ship, rested on a drydock platform inside the hangar. Sluggish and antiquated, it was worthless as a commercial vessel because of its inability to keep up with the craft of highly competitive space merchants. But it was everything Norma needed.

Now, high inside the clatter and bustle of the construction hangar, Norma stood on a suspensor platform over the patched hull. Making mental notes, she supervised a crew of Zensunni workers as they made mechanical modifications below, following the daily instructions she gave them.

The workers scurried around inside the large hull, shouting to each other and clanging tools. The rear of the old vessel had been torn open, its outdated engines gutted and removed, part of the cargo area reconfigured to hold her newly designed components. It was all coming together perfectly. After decades, she could see the end in sight, and it made her giddy.

Aurelius would be proud of her.

While Norma based her plan for folding space on concise mathematical formulas and proven laws of physics, such concepts were merely building blocks for something much grander, an intricate, almost ethereal design that could not be committed to paper or envisioned all at once. At least not yet. It was growing in her mind.

Each day she built upon her previous work, often staying up all night to modify and recalculate, installing a modular panel here, a magnetic winding or a Hagal quartz prism there. Like a master chef, she added ingredients as they occurred to her, going with a prescient sense bolstered by her theoretical proofs. Currents of thought and movement occurred to her on a mounting, incredibly large scale, as if by divine inspiration.

Savant Holtzman would laugh at me if I even suggested such a thing!

As work progressed, the crews performed quality control and bench tests according to her exacting specifications. Each part must function properly.

Watching the breakthrough engines take shape beneath her, Norma felt a rush of excitement. Much was at stake here, not only for herself and VenKee Enterprises, but for the entire human race.

The implications of her remarkable technology would continue long past the defeat of the thinking machines. Space-folding engines would change the human race and reshape the future. Consequences cascaded like waterfalls in her imagination, stretching her ability to grasp them. At times such as this, when Norma took the capabilities of the human mind to unbelievable extremes, she hoped it would not drive her insane.

But if she could surmount the technological challenges of this venture, Norma and her backers would travel between star systems, exponentially faster than the limits of contemporary technology. It would aid the Army of the Jihad immensely, and she had every reason to expect that it would lead, at last, to victory.

On top of it all, Aurelius Venport would secure commercial opportunities he had never dreamed possible. Norma could not wait for him to come back — to discuss this, and much more.

Guard every breath, for it carries the warmth and moisture of your life.

—Zensunni admonition to children

BENEATH THE CAVE overhang Selim looked with pride at his hardened followers, then glanced at Marha with an expression more akin to love. The young woman was full of energy and determination, exuberance mixed with common sense. For nearly two years, she had excelled among them, making herself indispensable.

"Arrakis is ours because we have taken it," Selim announced. "We have learned to survive under the harshest circumstances, without depending upon the benevolence of strangers or trade with offworld intruders."

Taking Marha's strong hand in his, he pulled her to her feet and they both stood, staring at each other with spice-blue eyes. "Marha, you have proven yourself a worthy member of our band, but I am also pleased to accept you as my wife — if you will have me."

Initially she had come as an admirer, a competent follower and fellow outlaw. Now she would be his mate. Marha had worked harder and followed his visions with more dedication than any other member of his outlaw band. She had made it perfectly clear to everyone, including him, that no one but she would be a suitable bride for the legendary leader.

Only a week ago, she had come to Selim at dawn, where he stood at the window rock and gazed out upon the sea of dunes. In the utter stillness, Marha stepped up to him and cast a necklace of jangling tokens at his feet, making a loud clatter in the small cave.

Hundreds of spice tokens, taken from hopeful women working the melange fields. Many, many times more than the wedding price Naib Dhartha had imposed on his people.

Knowing how much courage it must have taken for her to see him as a husband as well as a legendary leader, Selim had grinned. "How can I refuse an offer such as this?"

Now Marha smiled at him, revealing perfectly white teeth. Her face looked radiant; the crescent-moon scar above her left eye stood out plainly on her flushed face. "Ever since I was an awestruck girl, listening to the whispered stories of the great Wormrider, I dreamed of this moment. Yes, of course I will have you as my husband, Selim."

While the outlaw leader made his proud announcement, his lieutenant Jafar, dressed in a distilling suit, walked alone out onto the empty sand. Now everyone could see the gaunt, dedicated man through the cave opening. Taking up his chosen position, Jafar pounded his drum; the gathered outlaws heard the faint thumping muffled by distance. Their anticipation built as Selim remained silent and watched.

After he had drummed long enough to be certain a worm would come, the outlaw lieutenant tucked the drum under his arm. As he sprinted, his long legs carried him swiftly over the dune crests. In the open vastness behind him, wormsign appeared, indicating the rippling progress of an approaching behemoth.

Breathless, Jafar reached a shelter of rocks, but instead of climbing to safety he remained at the shoreline of sand, striking sharp, resonant blows on the stone with a metal hammer. The sandworm drove toward the vibrations, but could not come closer to the rock barrier, which extended like an iceberg far beneath the surface of the sand. Finally, it rose into the open sky, its gaping mouth open and questing, tiny crystalline teeth glinting. Dust and sand tumbled from its segmented body. The creature let out a roar that sounded like the scraping wind from a heavy storm.

Selim raised his voice and shouted at the top of his lungs. "Shai-Hulud, hear me! I have summoned you to bear witness." He pulled Marha close to stand beside him in the wash of light. "I claim this woman as my wife, and she accepts me. From this day forward, we are married in your eyes. Let no one doubt it."

The outlaws let out a loud cheer, deafening as it reverberated inside the cave chamber. The worm lifted itself higher — as if in a benediction — then plunged deep into the dunes again, sending up a spray of sand as it tunneled far below, to a hidden hoard of melange.

That night the bandits celebrated with honey and exotic delicacies stolen from caravans returning from Arrakis City. They consumed large quantities of melange in their revelries, until heads grew light and coruscating vision blurred faces and surroundings to a beautiful soft focus. They were all bound together by the special red dust cast off by the sandworms, a powder that was the dried essence of Shai-Hulud himself.

Their inhibitions faded, and many men and women became newfound lovers in the shadowed passages of the caves. Later, when the celebration finally ended, their group would return to its all-consuming mission. But for one night the spice transported them.

With Marha beside him, Selim traveled the pathways of melange, stepping through open doorways into the future. He sensed her nearby, a dazzling soul and a warm heart that had become an inseparable part of him.

But for this journey, Selim needed to go alone.

On the back wall of the cave, mysterious runes had been scribed long ago by forgotten explorers. No one knew what the inscriptions meant, but Selim had fashioned his own interpretations, and his followers did not question such pronouncements.

Aided by the melange, Selim saw many things that were invisible to the real world.

And now for the first time he saw the true scope of the challenge he faced, the immensity of time over which this epic battle would be played out. He saw that this was not merely a struggle between himself and the hated Naib Dhartha, not a conflict Selim could resolve in his own lifetime. It had already gone too far. The temptation and dependence on spice had passed a threshold that no mere man could ever stop.

One lifetime would never be enough. Selim had to insure that his mission would last far beyond his own death. Shai-Hulud would show him how, when the time was right.

Afterward he awoke with Marha warm and naked against him, clinging even in her dreams, as if afraid to let go of him. She stirred in the dim shadows. Her face was filled with curiosity and appreciation, drinking in every detail of his features.

"Selim, my love, my husband" — she said the last word on an indrawn breath — "I have finally learned to see you, to truly *see* you, as a man, a human being. At first, I fell in love with the *idea* of you, the portrait of a hero, an outlaw who could see the future with an unwavering clarity of mission. But you are more than that . . . a mortal man with a heart. To me, that makes you greater than any legend."

He kissed her tenderly on the lips. "So, Marha, you alone know my secret. And you alone shall share it with me, keeping me strong, and helping me accomplish what I must." Selim stroked her dark hair and smiled at her, content with Marha's devotion. After all the years, myth and reality had merged into the same entity.

She seemed to read his thoughts, understanding him even before he put his hesitation into words. "Have you experienced another vision, my love? What troubles you?"

He nodded somberly. "Last night, after we consumed so much spice, more dreams opened to me." She sat up with an intent expression, switching from a newlywed wife in the afterglow of love to a devoted follower ready to receive new instructions.

Selim said, "We have raided caravans and thwarted Naib Dhartha's efforts to sell melange, but I have not done enough to drive away the offworlders. The spice trade grows greater every year. It is no wonder Shai-Hulud is disappointed in me. He has given me a quest, and so far I have failed."

"The Old Man of the Desert has faith in you, Selim. Why else would he give you such an impossible task?" When Marha sat up, his gaze drifted to her perfect breasts and smooth skin in the dim cave light. "We will help you. We will give everything to see that you achieve your goals. This mission is more than any one man could hope to accomplish."

He kissed her gently on her crescent scar, then sat up straight and looked toward brighter light outside, where the sun washed across the rippling dunes. "Perhaps it is more than one *man* can accomplish. But not beyond the capability of a *legend*."

Starry-eyed and full of dreams, young Aziz waited until his grandfather and the cliff dwellers had fallen asleep for the night. Then he gathered the bits of equipment he had hidden away one piece at a time, day by day. He made no sound, scurrying like a muad'dib, one of the small desert mice that populated the crannies and cliffs.

Tonight he would prove himself, not only to Naib Dhartha, but to Selim Wormrider. Though neither would want to hear it, both men were Aziz's heroes, people he respected. The boy saw honor on either side of the conflict, and hoped to bring them together somehow, for the good of the Zensunni people. His secret.

But it was such a difficult task.

For many months, ever since the legendary bandits had rescued him from certain death in the desert, Aziz had been thinking about life among the outlaws. Selim Wormrider was blind to how much Naib Dhartha had done for the Zensunni people. The young man loved his grandfather very much and understood the Naib's stern ways, which he saw as the price for the tribe's dramatically improved life, reliable supplies of food and water, even a few luxuries and comforts purchased from interstellar merchants.

But Selim Wormrider had a fire in his eyes and a different sort of honor, a brave confidence and righteousness that overshadowed Naib Dhartha's more provincial concerns. Selim's outlaws followed their leader with passion, far more than the spice gatherers showed in their work for Naib Dhartha. And the woman Marha — who had run away from this very village — now seemed to have a new center in her life. Obviously, she had no regrets over her own decision.

For many nights Aziz had dreamed of joining the bandit group himself and becoming one of the romantic outlaws. He could talk to the Wormrider, say all the things he should have said months ago when he'd had the opportunity. His eyes shone, bright with the challenge of making the world right again, healing the breach, stopping the long-standing, destructive feud.

Aziz could do it. But would Selim accept him?

Perhaps . . . if he could demonstrate abilities that were useful to the tribe.

Upon delivering the outlaw's response to his grandfather, Aziz had attempted to soften the words, to apologize and make excuses for Selim. Even so, Naib Dhartha had been infuriated, cursing the Wormrider with undeserved insults. Instead of rewarding him for his arduous journey, the Naib had sent his abashed young grandson off to his quarters alone. For days, the old man had kept a close eye on Aziz.

But the youth had not forgotten what he'd seen and experienced, and his imagination gave him alternatives that he should have considered before. Aziz wanted to go back. Most of all, he wanted the exhilaration and the excitement again. He was sure he could do it.

He had planned carefully for this night, remembering what Selim Wormrider had done, and convinced that he could repeat it. After all, years ago, a young untrained outcast had discovered how to ride the demon sandworms for the first time, without any guidance whatsoever . . .

Now in the quiet night, Aziz slid past the complacent guards and stole down a rocky footpath that opened onto the great basin of sand. The Realm of Sandworms. Only one of the moons was low in the sky now, shedding little glow, but the stars watching over him were as bright as the eyes of angels. Aziz scampered out onto the soft sands, leaving an obvious trail. He tried to run, but the sand slipped under his feet, and he felt as if he were swimming in dust.

Aziz needed to venture far enough out so that the worms could approach without being frustrated by buried rocks. But he also wanted to stay close enough to the cliffs in order for the people to see what he was about to do. Especially his grandfather.

The boy had been making his way for more than an hour when dawn colors began to smear the knife-sharp eastern horizon. He hurried along, hoping to get in position by sunrise, and climbed a high dune that made him think of a grandstand he had seen once in a videobook brought from offworld. He hoped that his careful footfalls had caused no vibrations loud enough to summon Shai-Hulud . . . not yet.

Aziz had brought along a rock and a metal rod, some rope, and a long sturdy spear — much more than Selim had carried as a fuzzy-cheeked youth when *he* first conquered the desert creatures. It could be done.

His heart pounding, his confidence unshaken, Aziz squatted on the dune. He thrust the metal into soft sand and began hammering it with the rock. The sounds shot out like sharp explosions, vividly audible in the eternal stillness of the desert.

As dawn finally broke across the sky the boy looked back toward the rugged cliffs. Inside the dark sheltered windows, some of the sleeping Zensunnis would hear. He waited for the great worm to come.

Hearing the gunshot patter from far out in the dunes, Dhartha came awake. Curious and suspicious, the old leader dressed quickly, but before he could step from his private chambers another man lifted the door curtain. "Naib Dhartha, a youth has run far out onto the sand. I believe . . . it looks like Aziz."

Scowling, Dhartha strode through the tunnels to a bank of window walls that offered a view of the ancient desert. "Why is he making so much foolish racket? I taught him better than that."

Then, abruptly, the grizzled desert man suspected, as he remembered Aziz's deluded admiration for the bandit who commanded sandworms. Dhartha began to shout. "Send men out to bring the boy back. Hurry, before a worm comes!"

His companion looked reluctant, but turned to do as he was commanded.

Far out on the dunes, Aziz continued his beckoning rhythm. When the Naib grabbed the stone window edge with cramped fingers, he stared out into sunlight spilling across the pristine dunes. He saw the tiny dotted line of his grandson's footprints leading out into the wasteland. Utter foolishness!

From the horizon, he could already see the titanic ripple of an oncoming worm. None of the rescuers would ever reach the boy in time. Dhartha's chest felt cold. "Ayii, no! Buddallah, please do not let this happen!"

Aziz stood atop the dune, gripping a metal staff with the innocent confidence of a believer. Dhartha was old, but his eyesight remained sharp, and he could see the boy confront the upwelling of sand, the churning wake as the behemoth circled around and then went toward him with the force and destructiveness of a desert storm.

Like a beetle on a hot rock, Aziz ran along the narrow dune crest to get into better position, but the motion of the subterranean demon caused the loose sand to crumble and slide. The boy lost his footing and tumbled head over heels. He dropped his spear, a flash of silver in the morning light.

Before Aziz could regain his footing or grab his tools, a gigantic mouth lined with crystal fangs rose up and *up*, gulping sand and dirt . . . and a morsel of human flesh.

Naib Dhartha stared with his mouth open and tears of grief and rage glinting in his eyes. The innocent boy was gone in an instant, misled by an insane belief that he could tame the demons of the dunes, like the outlaw wormriders who had a pact with Shaitan himself.

Selim is at fault for this.

The beast sank beneath the sand and began to move away. The stirring of its passage erased all signs of struggle.

Around Naib Dhartha's head, like the shadowy flickering of raven wings, he thought he heard the bitter, accursed laugh of Selim Wormrider.

174 B.G.
JIHAD YEAR 28
One Year after the Conquest of Ix

I have done grand things in my life, far beyond the aspirations of most men. But somehow I have never found a home or a true love.
                                          —Primero Vorian Atreides,
                                          private letter to Serena Butler

S INCE HIS DAYS riding with the robot Seurat aboard the *Dream Voyager*, Vor had been a restless person, never wanting to settle in one place. With a fresh curiosity and an eagerness to witness the full scope of free humanity, he absorbed the flavor of every new planet, adding it to his catalog of experiences. He liked seeing the people, the cultures, the threads that bound the various human races more tightly than Omnius could ever control the Synchronized Worlds.

Even now, moving silently along his update route, Seurat would be delivering the contaminated Omnius sphere from planet to planet and infecting the evermind. It was a grand trick, perhaps the most destructive military ruse in history. Xavier would have chosen to implement a rigid, full-force strategy in which the Army of the Jihad followed Seurat and struck hard at each reeling machine world, but such a plan would be impractical, tactically speaking, and would undoubtedly tip off both Seurat and Omnius before Vor's plan had a chance to spread and do maximum damage without any loss of human life.

Vor would let the machines destroy themselves, while he went about the more formal business of the Jihad.

Vor had never been to water-rich Caladan — an isolated, sparsely populated Unallied Planet — but it seemed like a pleasant place. After Vor returned from sneaking the corrupted evermind update into Seurat's derelict ship, Serena Butler had issued her new plan for prosecuting the Jihad. Even before Xavier returned from his surprising victory on Ix, Vor happily volunteered to do the footwork.

For months he had traveled among strategically important planets on the fringes of League territory, searching for places to establish Jihad outposts. These under-protected worlds would probably appeal to thinking machines, as IV Anbus had, as potential beachheads.

Each new place gave Vor a broader perspective on the scope of the war, and the vital reasons why the human race must win. Sometimes when he thought about it, he wondered how AI-machines had gotten out of control in the first place, and how matters had come to the present state of extreme crisis.

In his early life, he had admired the efficient industries and cities built by Omnius, along with monuments celebrating the achievements of the Titans. But among scattered human settlements, even those not affiliated with League Worlds, Vor now felt a different sort of admiration. The carefree people exhibited happiness in many ways: They took pleasure in daily life, in good food, wine, and a warm bed. They drew joy from each other's company, from the different aspects of love and friendship. They celebrated their fervor and enthusiasm for the Jihad by building heartfelt memorials to Serena's baby.

Vor did not regret having left his trustee life behind. He was proud of how the entire Galaxy had changed because of his decision to turn away from his father and rescue the grieving Serena Butler. After that, he had felt more alive than ever before, more human.

He wished only one thing had turned out differently . . . that Serena might have reciprocated his love for her. But her heart had turned to granite, forcing Vor to accept that, with few regrets. His new life of freedom was rich in countless other ways.

With his health and perpetual youth, Vor Atreides found it easy to attract lovers in the various spaceports. Some of them were one-night adventures, others were women to whom he returned again and again. He probably had many unidentified, unclaimed children across the Galaxy, but he could never be a real father to any of them. Fearing reprisals from the cymeks, not wanting to give his father Agamemnon any hold over him, Vor always pretended to be a low-ranked jihadi during stopovers, never revealing his identity or his heritage. It was for their own safety, not his . . .

For similar reasons, he avoided the sort of lifetime commitment that Xavier and Octa had. In addition to the identity of his own cymek father, Vor kept the secret of his near immortality; he would have no choice but to watch helplessly as any woman he married grew old and died. For now he just took each day, each planet, and each relationship on its own terms, without worries.

Now, in coming to Caladan, his mission was to establish an observation outpost. In the past half century, thinking machine marauders had been sighted numerous times in the system, not far from where Xavier Harkonnen's family had been attacked and killed by cymeks forty-three years before. Already, Caladan had dispatched representatives to Salusa Secundus, announcing that the fishing villages and coastal cities were amenable to forming a loose planetary government which, in theory, would be willing to join the League of Nobles.

Vor wanted to establish a Jihad presence that would act as a buffer if Omnius's aggressions ever grew more overt here. For the moment, the fervor of the Jihad kept the thinking machines on the defensive, but the evermind had been setting plans for centuries; no one could ever know exactly what the mechanical superbrain might attempt next. League forces had to be ready.

Though he held a high rank, Vor did not assume unquestioning respect for military officers. With no desire to be saluted or treated with particular deference, and for his own comfort, he often dressed in casual clothes without any insignia. He could be a Primero during military strategy sessions in the Jihad Council, but on his time off he wanted to socialize as an equal with old and new friends.

He fit in among ordinary people, loved roughhousing with village men at impromptu sporting games or gambling with the best of them, winning and losing a month's pay at Fleur de Lys or other games. As hard as he worked for the war effort, he put almost as much effort into any free time he could get. There would be time for some relaxation here, while researching the best place to set up a military outpost.

Caladanian fishing villages were quaint and rustic. The people built their boats and painted the sails with family markings. Without weather satellites, they studied wind patterns and even tasted salty air to predict storms. They knew which seasons offered the best fishing, where to find the shells and edible seaweed that formed the staples of their diet.

Now, after three days of surveying headlands to the north for a potential site, Vor watched boats come in as the sun dipped on the horizon. On the docks, crude hand-made shrines memorializing Manion the Innocent were strewn with flowers and colorful shells. One of the shrines up the coast even claimed to contain a holy lock of the boy's hair.

He heard water lapping against the pilings and felt a peace he had not experienced in recent memory. He drew in a deep breath; despite the iodine smell of old seaweed clinging to the soft wood, and the rank aroma of unsold fish waiting to be turned into fertilizer meal, he enjoyed this place.

Many of his military engineers stayed with the orbiting Jihad ships to establish a network of observation satellites that could also provide hurricane warnings for the people of Caladan. Other crews operated from isolated points of land near the main fishing villages, constructing rigid uplink towers for the surveillance network. Still more jihadis would be stationed here on Caladan to perform necessary maintenance.

In the dockside town Vor had already found a warm, well-lit tavern where the locals gathered every night to drink a home-brewed distillate of fermented kelp that tasted remotely like bitter beer but was as potent as hard liquor. Vor discovered its effects quickly enough.

As a soldier in the Army of the Jihad, Vor Atreides was a breath of fresh air among the locals. Fishermen offered him drinks and treats of crunchy shellfish in exchange for news and stories. He went by his chosen alter ego of "Virk" and ostensibly worked as a common jihadi engineer. Most of the League's planetside crew didn't even know his real identity, and the rest of them kept his secret.

As the kelp beer blurred his senses, Vor became more talkative and told of numerous adventures he'd had, always careful not to talk about his time as a human trustee on Earth or his rank as an officer. It was obvious from the adoring looks of the young women that they believed him, and just as apparent from the amused but skeptical frowns of the men that they thought he was exaggerating. By the way the girls flirted and hung close, Vor knew he would be a welcome guest in someone's home this night; the challenge would be to decide which rendezvous to choose.

Oddly enough, his gaze was drawn frequently to a busy young woman who worked the tables, pouring mugs of kelp beer at the bar and hurrying back and forth from the kitchen to deliver food. She had eyes the color of dark pecans, and rich brown hair that hung in a mass of ringlets that looked so soft and tempting that he could barely restrain his urge to reach out and touch them. Her figure was well-rounded and she was tall, but most of all he found himself drawn to her heart-shaped face and engaging smile. In an indefinable way, she reminded him of Serena.

When it was his turn to buy a round of drinks, Vor called the woman over. Her eyes danced teasingly. "I can understand why your throat is dry with that constant stream of nonsense flowing out of it."

The men laughed good-naturedly at Vor's expense, and he chuckled along with them. "So, if I said how beautiful you are, you would consider it more of my nonsense?"

She tossed her ringlets and called to him over her shoulder as she went to get their drinks, "Nonsense of the purest form." Some of the other young women frowned, as if Vor had already snubbed them.

His eyes went back to her as she stood at the bar. She glanced in his direction, then turned away. "Ten credits to the man who tells me her name," he said boldly, holding out the coin.

A chorus answered him with "Leronica Tergiet," but he gave the coin to a fisherman who provided more information. "Her father has a deep-sea boat, but he hates the work. He bought this place, and Leronica pretty much runs it."

One of the pouting girls clung to Vor. "That one won't relax for a moment. She'll work herself into old age when she's still in her child-bearing years." Her voice deepened. "A pretty dull companion, I'd say."

"Maybe she just needs someone to make her laugh."

When Leronica returned to their table, her arms laden with freshly filled mugs, Vor raised his glass in a toast. "To the lovely Leronica Tergiet, who knows the difference between a genuine compliment and utter nonsense."

She set down the rest of the kelp beer. "I hear so little honesty around here that it's hard to make the comparison. I don't have time for silly stories about places I'll never visit."

Vor lifted his voice above the hubbub. "I can wait for a private conversation. Don't think I didn't notice you listening to my stories and pretending not to."

She snorted. "I have to work past closing. You'd be better off going back to your nice clean ship."

Vor smiled disarmingly. "I'd trade a warm bed for a clean ship any day. I'll wait."

The men made catcalls, but Leronica raised her eyebrows. "A patient man is a novelty around here."

Vor remained unruffled. "Then I hope you like novelties."

Octa tried to make me stop believing in the destiny of love, that there was only one person for each of us. She nearly succeeded in this, for I almost forgot about Serena.

—Primero Xavier Harkonnen, *Reminiscences*

S ALUSA SECUNDUS GLIMMERED like an oasis in the harsh wilderness of war, a sanctuary where Xavier could regain his strength before going back out with the Army of the Jihad. Now, though, as he sped by groundcar away from the Zimia Spaceport, he hoped he was in time. He had just arrived back home from the Ixian battlegrounds.

For months he'd known that Octa was pregnant — apparently their lovemaking on the night before his departure for Ix had been quite surprisingly successful — and her delivery was now imminent. He had not been present for the births of Roella or Omilia — his duty to the Jihad always came first — but his wife was forty-six now, causing her delivery to be fraught with a greater than usual potential for complications. She insisted that he should not worry, which made him all the more concerned.

Xavier sped along a winding road into the hills toward the Butler estate, while the sun dropped lower in the western sky. He had made contact as soon as the ballistas entered the home system, and had received regular reports on Octa's condition. He was cutting it quite close.

Octa had chosen to deliver at home, as she had done with her two older children, because she wanted the resources of the medical centers available for the war, especially for the wounded who were receiving replacement organs from the generous Tlulaxa organ farms.

After parking in the courtyard and racing through the main gates into the echoing foyer, he called out with more emotion than he usually allowed himself to show. "Octa! I'm here!"

One of the servants met him excitedly, pointing up the stairs. "The doctors are with her. I don't think the baby is born yet, but it's very —"

Xavier didn't hear the rest as he hurried upstairs. Octa lay on the large four-poster bed where they had conceived the child. It was another small victory, a symbol of human persistence and triumph. Now Octa was half-sitting, her legs spread, and her face was streaked with sweat and contorted in pain.

Seeing him, though, she smiled, as if trying to convince herself it was not a dream. "My love! Is this . . . what I have to do . . . to get you home from war?"

At her bedside, the professional midwife smiled reassuringly. "She's strong, and everything is normal. Any time now you should have another child, Primero."

"You make it sound too easy." Octa groaned with another contraction. "Would you like to switch places with me?"

"This is your third child," the midwife said, "so it should be easy for you. Maybe you don't even need me."

The expectant mother grabbed the woman's hand and held on tight. "Stay!"

Xavier stepped forward. "If anyone's going to hold her hand, it should be me." Smiling, the midwife backed away, letting Octa's husband take her place.

Leaning close, Xavier thought about how lovely his wife still was. He had been with her for many years, and away from her for too much of the time. He marveled that she could be so content with this patchwork marriage.

"What are you thinking?" she asked.

"About how beautiful you are. You're glowing with happiness."

"That's because you're with me."

"I love you," he whispered in her ear. "I'm so sorry that I haven't been the husband you deserve. Even when we're together, I haven't been attentive."

Her eyelids fluttered, and she touched her large belly. "You must be *somewhat* attentive, or I wouldn't be pregnant again." She grimaced when a contraction struck, but fought through the pain with a brave smile.

But he wouldn't let himself off so easily. "Honestly, I've spent too much time brooding, concerned with this damned war. The real tragedy is how long it took me to see what a treasure I have in you."

Tears streamed down Octa's face. "I have never questioned you, my darling. You are the only man I have ever loved, and I am happy to accept you on any basis."

"You deserve more, and I'm . . . ."

But before he finished his sentence, Octa cried out. "This is it — hard labor," the midwife said, hurrying to the bedside. "Time to push." And Xavier knew the conversation was over.

Twenty minutes later, Xavier cradled his third daughter in his arms, wrapped in a blanket. Octa had already chosen the name while he was away at Ix, with his approval.

"Welcome to the universe, Wandra," he said. And for a moment, he felt complete.

On his sprawling estate Manion Butler had always tended the olive groves and vineyards, and in between war engagements, Xavier dabbled as a gentleman farmer himself, much as ancient Roman officers had during times of peace. He took pleasure in being home, spending time with his family and forgetting about the evil thinking machines and the horrors of the Jihad . . . if only for a short while.

Xavier always made certain there were enough field hands and crop supervisors to make the cultivated hills a productive enterprise, but he loved getting his own hands dirty, feeling the sunlight on his back and the sweat on his skin from simple, straightforward labor. Long ago, Serena, too, had loved gardening, tending her lovely flowers, and now he understood what had drawn her to the soil and growing things. He felt a purity of purpose without political considerations, treachery, or personality complications. Here, he only had to focus on the fertile soil and the fresh-smelling vegetation.

Blackbirds flitted among the gray-green leaves of the olive trees, eating berries the pickers had missed. At the end of each row of grape vines stood a cluster of giant orange marigolds. Xavier strolled down the narrow, leafy corridors, his head just tall enough to rise above the twisting vines that curled around the posts and support cables.

As expected, he found his father-in-law working among the vines, caressing the clusters of green grapes that were ripening in the dry, warm weather. Manion's hair had gone white and his once fleshy face was now lean, but the retired Viceroy exuded a calm contentment that he had never displayed when he had served the League Parliament.

"It's not necessary to count every one of the grapes, Manion," Xavier quipped. He walked forward, and grape leaves brushed against his sleeves like the outstretched hands of an adoring throng during one of his victory parades.

Manion looked up and tilted back the straw hat that shielded his eyes from the sun. "It is because of the care and attention I shower upon these vines that our family vintages are the best in all the League Worlds. This year I fear the Zinagne will be a bit weak — too much water in that acreage — but the Beaujie should be superb."

Xavier stood next to him and looked at the grape clusters. "Then I'll have to help you sample the vintages until we're both convinced of their excellence."

Workers went up and down the rows of grapes, using hoes and rakes to turn the soil and remove the weeds. Each year when the fruit ripened to perfection, crowds of Salusan laborers toiled around the clock in the vineyards, filling baskets and carrying them to the winery buildings behind the main house. Xavier had managed to participate in this riotous harvesting activity only three times in the past decade, but had enjoyed it.

He wished he could stay home more often, but his true calling was out in space battling the thinking machines.

"And how is my newest baby granddaughter?"

"You'll have plenty of time to see for yourself. I've been called out to join the fleet again in a week, and I'm counting on you to help Octa. As a new mother, she'll have plenty to do."

"Are you certain my bumbling assistance won't cause more problems?"

Xavier chuckled. "You were the Viceroy, so at least you know how to delegate responsibility. Please make certain Roella and Omilia lend their mother a hand."

Blinking in the bright Salusan sun, Xavier sighed as the weight of his life seemed to press down on him. He had already spent time with old Emil Tantor, who was pleased to be sharing his lonely house with his daughter-in-law Sheel and her three children.

Though Xavier had his own family and plenty of love, he felt he had lost something along the way. Octa was quiet and strong, a sanctuary in the turmoil of his life. He loved her without hesitation, though he recalled the carefree passion of his brief relationship with Serena. The two of them had been young then, fired with romance, never imagining the tragedy hurtling toward them like a meteor from the skies . . .

Xavier had stopped regretting the loss of Serena — their lives had diverged long ago — but he could not help but regret how much he himself had changed. "Manion," he said in a quiet voice, "how did I get to be so rigid in my ways?"

"Let me ponder that for a moment," the retired Viceroy said.

Troubling thoughts assailed Xavier. The optimistic and passionate young man he had once been now seemed a total stranger to him. He thought of the difficult tasks he had undertaken in the name of the Jihad, and was unable to condone them all.

Finally, Manion answered with all the seriousness and importance he had ever used when giving a speech before the League Parliament. "The war made you harder, Xavier. It's changed all of us. Some people, it has broken. Others, like you, it has made stronger."

"I fear my strength is my weakness." Xavier peered deep into the thick, green vines but saw only memories of his numerous Jihad campaigns . . . space battles, mangled robots, massacred human beings who were victims of the thinking machine onslaughts.

"How so?"

"I have seen what Omnius can do, and have devoted my entire life to making sure the machines never win." He sighed. "That it is the way I've chosen to show my love for my family: by protecting them. Sadly it means I am almost never home."

"If you did not do this, Xavier, we'd all be slaves to the evermind. Octa understands, as do I, as do your daughters. Don't let it weigh too heavily upon you."

Xavier drew a deep breath. "I know you're right, Manion . . . but I don't want my relentless determination for victory to cost me my own humanity." He looked intently at his father-in-law. "If people like me are forced to become like machines in order to defeat the machines, then the whole Jihad is lost."

We can study every scrap of detail about the long march of human history, assimilating vast amounts of data. Why then, is it so difficult for thinking machines to learn from it? Consider this as well: Why do humans repeat the mistakes of their ancestors?
—Erasmus, *Reflections on Sentient Biologicals*

E VEN AFTER CENTURIES of experimenting with various human subjects, Erasmus still had not run out of ideas. There were so many interesting ways to test the species. And now that he could also see the world through the eyes of his young ward, Gilbertus Albans, the possibilities seemed fresh and intriguing.

The robot stood in his fine crimson robes trimmed with gold fur. Very stylish and impressive, he thought. His flowmetal skin was polished so that it gleamed in Corrin's ruddy sunlight.

Young Gilbertus was impeccably attired as well, having been scrubbed and groomed by valetbots. Despite two years of diligent training and preparation, the boy still had a feral streak, a wildness that manifested itself in small rebellious ways. Eventually, Erasmus was certain he could eradicate that flaw.

The two stood outside looking at the locked pen of slaves and test subjects. Many belonged to the animalistic lower social orders from which Gilbertus himself had been drawn. But others were better trained, educated servants, artisans, and chefs who worked inside Erasmus's villa.

As he gazed into the boy's open, innocent eyes, Erasmus wondered if Gilbertus even remembered his squalid and painful early life grubbing in the dirt of these awful pens . . . or if he had discarded those memories as he learned to organize his mental skills through the persistent instruction of his machine mentor.

Now, before the latest experiment could commence, the boy looked curiously at the chosen group; they stared back at Erasmus and the young boy with uneasy expressions. The independent robot's sensor threads detected a heightened concentration of perspiration in the air, accelerated heartbeats, elevated body temperatures, and other clear indicators of increased stress. What did they have to be so nervous about? Erasmus would have preferred to begin the test on an even baseline, but his captives feared him too much. They were convinced the independent robot meant to do something unpleasant to them, and Erasmus couldn't fault them for drawing such conclusions.

He didn't bother to conceal a smile. They were correct, after all.

Beside him, the boy quelled his curiosity and simply observed. It had been one of the robot's first lessons to him. Despite all of Erasmus's efforts, Gilbertus Albans was still a child of scant education, with such a minimal database that it would be futile to simply ask an endless stream of random questions. Thus, the thinking machine instructed him in an orderly, logical fashion, building upon each fact that he learned.

So far, the results seemed satisfactory.

"Today, we begin an organized series of evoked reaction tests. The experiment you are about to witness is designed to demonstrate panic responses. Please observe the range of behavior in order to draw general conclusions based upon the relative status of the slaves."

"Yes, Mr. Erasmus," the boy said, gripping the bars of the fence.

These days, Gilbertus did as he was told — a great improvement from his previous untamed behavior. Back then, Omnius had frequently gloated, insisting that Erasmus would never civilize the brutish youth. Whenever simple logic and common sense failed, Erasmus used discipline and methodical training, along with rewards and punishments, augmented by the liberal use of proven behavior-altering drugs. Initially, the pharmaceuticals had left Gilbertus in an apathetic stupor. There was a decided decline in his manic, destructive behavior, tendencies that hampered his overall progress.

Gradually the robot had decreased the dosages, and now he rarely needed to drug the boy at all. Gilbertus had finally accepted his new situation. If he did remember his miserable previous life, the boy would surely look upon his new situation as an opportunity, an advantage. Before long, Erasmus was certain he would have a triumph to show Omnius, proving that his understanding of human potential exceeded that of even the supposedly omniscient computer.

But he had more in mind than just winning the challenge with Omnius. Erasmus actually enjoyed watching and recording the progress Gilbertus made, and wished to continue even after Omnius had conceded the point.

"Now watch carefully, Gilbertus." Erasmus went to a gate, unscrambled the lock, and stepped inside.

After the gate to the pen closed safely behind him, Erasmus strode in among the crowded people, pushing, knocking them down. Frantic, they tried to get out of his way, averting their eyes as if that would make him fail to notice them. This amused Erasmus, since they were basing their avoidance on *human* standards of what attracted another person's attention. As a sophisticated autonomous robot, he made his selections on a purely random, completely objective, basis.

Withdrawing a large projectile pistol from his robe, he pointed it at the first victim — who happened to be an elderly man — and opened fire.

The gun boomed like thunder, a reverberant echo that ripped through the old man's body, followed instantly by a wave of screams in the crowd, building to outright panic. The test subjects scrambled about like stampeding cattle, both the feral slaves and the sophisticated assistants.

"See how they run," Erasmus said. "Fascinating, isn't it?"

The boy, who did not answer, had a somewhat horrified expression on his face.

Erasmus aimed at another random target — a pregnant woman — and shot again. Delightful! He was enjoying this immensely.

"Isn't that enough?" the boy asked. "I understand the lesson."

In his wisdom, Erasmus had selected a projectile weapon sure to generate a colossal blast, and the caliber of the bullet was large. Each time a victim was struck, blood, skin, and bits of bone flew in all directions. The sheer extravagant horror increased the panic even more, like a feedback loop.

"There is more to learn," Erasmus said, noting that Gilbertus was shifting uneasily on his feet. He seemed nervous himself.

Interesting.

The prisoners were screaming and yelling, climbing on top of each other, stepping on fallen bodies as they tried to stay out of the robot's way. But in the confined area they could not escape. Erasmus fired again and again.

A projectile struck one man in the head, and his skull and brains vaporized into an expanding cloud. Several slaves stood frozen, stunned into abject surrender. He killed half of these as well, not wanting to train them in any way or alter their responses. For the purity of the experiment, he had to be completely fair, playing no favorites for any reason.

After killing at least a dozen and maiming twice as many, he stopped and held the cooling projectile gun in his flowmetal hand. The frenzied tides of terror continued to swirl around him, with survivors running back and forth, searching for places to hide or any means of escape. Some of them rendered assistance to their fallen comrades. Finally the scream-

ing stopped and the people huddled against the fences as far from
Erasmus as they could get, as if such a small distance could make
any difference.

Unfortunately, the ones who still lived were tainted for further ex-
perimentation, even if they were not injured physically. No matter. He
could always find fresh subjects, drawing them from his vast renewable
pool of captives.

Outside the enclosure, Gilbertus had stepped back to avoid being
touched by the outstretched hands of the captives who begged him for
assistance. The boy frowned at Erasmus in confusion, as if he could not
understand which direction his emotions were supposed to flow.

Curious. Erasmus would have to analyze Gilbertus's own responses to
the experiment — an unexpected bonus.

Some of the slaves began weeping, moaning quietly to themselves as
Erasmus opened the gate again and stepped confidently up to his young
ward. But Gilbertus flinched away, instinctively shrinking from the
dripping gore and bits of brain that spattered the robot's shining skin
and colorful robes.

This gave Erasmus pause. He did not mind being abhorred by his test
subjects and captives, but did not want this particular young man to fear
him. Erasmus was his mentor.

In spite of all the attention the independent robot had lavished upon
Serena Butler, she had still turned on him. An old story in human history,
and it had blindsided him. Perhaps she had been too mature, too set in
her ways, when he had taken her under his wing. Erasmus had learned
plenty about human nature in his many years of study; he would make
certain that Gilbertus Albans remained absolutely loyal to him. He
needed to be cautious and observant.

"Come with me, young human," he said with simulated cheeriness.
From now on he would have to be very careful so that the boy did not get
the wrong idea about him. "Help me clean myself up, and then we'll have
a nice chat about what you've just seen."

When you become aware of the volume of the universe around you, the paucity of life in that vast space becomes an overwhelming reality. It is from this basic awareness that life learns to help life.
—The Titan Hecate

T HEY WERE VISITORS from another world, and looked like it.
As Iblis Ginjo watched the strange Cogitors and their attendants proceed single-file across the concourse of Zimia Spaceport, he stepped forward to greet them, his mind racing. His new aide Keats, a quiet and intelligent young man who had replaced the "tragically killed" Floriscia Xico, stood off to one side watching quietly, as if taking mental notes. Keats was more of a scholar than a thug, and Iblis used him for special Jipol work.

Buzzing construction noises filled the air, mingled with the drone of arriving and departing spacecraft. Using a swell of donations, the Jihad Council had commissioned a titanic statue of the saintly Manion the Innocent, which would welcome all vessels arriving from the dangers of deep space. Iblis was reminded of all the colossal statues and monuments the Titans had insisted on building to commemorate their glory days . . .

Iblis counted twenty-four saffron-robed secondaries approaching. As soon as word had reached him, he had rushed to the spaceport, making certain he would be there in person to greet them.

All of the attendants looked like living mummies with parchment-dry, liver-spotted skin and wispy hair. The fragile monks walked with a deliberate slowness. Six secondaries in the front carried canisters that held living brains that were far, far more ancient than the secondaries themselves.

"This is a momentous occasion," Iblis said, and he meant it. His heart swelled. "I never dreamed that I would have a chance to converse with the Ivory Tower Cogitors. It has been . . . centuries since the last time you were seen away from frozen Hessra!"

Unlike Kwyna, who dwelled in the City of Introspection, or even wise Eklo who had helped encourage the original uprising on Earth, these "Ivory Tower" Cogitors believed in near-total isolation from the distractions of society. They lived on a distant, unwanted planet, tended only by their human secondaries. Given uninterrupted serenity to contemplate for centuries, these brains were among the wisest and most remarkable in all of creation.

And now the notoriously insular Cogitors had come to Salusa Secundus! He had never dreamed this would happen in his lifetime.

Iblis introduced himself as the Grand Patriarch of the Jihad, a title unfamiliar to the out-of-touch Cogitors. He smiled in fascination as he stepped closer to the strangely ornate preservation canisters. "I have some experience with your kind. On Earth, the great Eklo taught me and encouraged me. And here I took much counsel from the Cogitor Kwyna. Our history has changed much because of their influence."

One of the wizened secondaries looked up with watery eyes. In a raspy voice he said, "Vidad and our other Cogitors have no interest in affecting history. They wish only to exist, and to ponder."

Iblis summoned his aides to assist the ancient monks. Keats directed two Jipol officers and a group of eager transportation workers to swarm around the distinguished, unexpected guests. The rapid flurry seemed to confuse the doddering yellow-robed secondaries.

Iblis said to Keats, "Please find comfortable quarters for the secondaries. Give them the best of food and access to any therapeutic or medical treatments they may need."

The young Jipol officer nodded, then disappeared to follow the instructions.

One of the monks holding a preservation canister spoke. A small man with an oval face and long, silvery eyelashes, he said in a flat tone, "You do not know why we are here."

"No, but I am eager to learn," Iblis said. "Do you have something to seel? Do we have anything you need?"

Like all Cogitors, they were entirely reliant on human secondaries to keep their brains alive, to perform all of the necessary tasks involved in maintaining the preservation canisters in which they were enclosed. Iblis didn't think the Cogitors could be entirely self-sufficient. Did they have secret outside commerce, with . . . cymeks, possibly? In extreme isolation on frozen Hessra, the secondaries had difficult lives indeed, and now they all looked too old and brittle to still be breathing. But they were.

The old man said in a voice as breathy and quiet as the wind, "We are the last of the secondaries on Hessra. Vidad and the other Cogitors did not wish to be interrupted, but my fellow monks and I will not survive much longer. It is necessary to obtain new secondaries." He looked ready to drop, but his arms were steady as they held the preservation canister. "As soon as possible."

Iblis's eyes shone. "And you brought the Cogitors with you! I'd have thought they'd just send you with their request."

The ancient monk lowered his eyes. "Because of the magnitude of the situation, Vidad wished to make his appeal in person. If necessary. Are there eligible people in the League who would be willing to volunteer for such service?"

Iblis's throat went dry. If he didn't have so many responsibilities of his own, he might have considered such a fascinating assignment for himself. "Many of our talented scholars would be most willing to assist you." He smiled and bowed slightly. "I promise you, we shall locate all the volunteers you need."

Possibilities were already churning in his mind.

Iblis Ginjo knew he had to see the Ivory Tower Cogitors in private. This was an opportunity no man alive, not even himself, had ever faced. They were six of the most brilliant, immortal philosophers.

He strode toward the chambers he had assigned for their representatives, grinning with optimism, remembering how much the Cogitor Eklo had already changed his life.

Ages ago, Vidad and his companions had isolated themselves so that they could contemplate for centuries upon centuries, uninterrupted. What grand revelations they must have uncovered in all that time! He could never allow these disembodied philosophers to leave without at least one conversation — even if he was forced to use his Jipol associates to keep them here against their will. But Iblis hoped he wouldn't have to use such strong-arm method.

But they must share their enlightenment!

Since he was the man who was willingly offering replacement tenders to fill the Cogitors' desperate request, Iblis was able to go to the dignitaries' quarters. When the door opened at his command, he stood before the ancient, crumbling old secondaries and his heart ached for the plight of these Cogitors. What if some emergency occurred on Hessra that these cadaverous men could not mitigate? "As Grand Patriarch, I swear to you that we will find appropriate replacements, as you requested — young talented men who will give their lives to the caretaking of your masters."

The yellow-robed secondaries bowed stiffly. Their eyes blinked in sunken, wrinkle-encircled sockets. "The Ivory Tower Cogitors appreciate your assistance," said the lead secondary.

Iblis stepped further into the room, where he saw the ancient brains in their canisters resting on temporary pedestals. His heart pounded and he drew in a quick breath. "Would it . . . would it be possible for me to speak with them?"

"No," the secondary said.

In his exalted position, Iblis Ginjo was unaccustomed to hearing such a response. "Perhaps Vidad is aware of the Cogitor Eklo, who spent his last days on Earth? I served him there. I communicated with Eklo, and he helped me to formulate the grand slave uprising against Omnius." The ancient yellow-robed men did not seem impressed.

Iblis continued, "Here in Zimia, I spent much time in philosophical interaction with the Cogitor Kwyna before she grew weary of life and shut herself down." His eyes were bright and his mouth partly open in a hopeful smile.

Touching Vidad's electrafluid to receive messages, his secondary said, "Other Cogitors dabble in interaction with humans. We see little benefit in this. We simply wish to acquire our new caretakers and return to Hessra. Nothing more."

"I understand, Vidad," Iblis said, "but perhaps for just a moment —"

"Even a moment distracts us from our vital ruminations. We seek the key to the universe. Would you wish to deny us this?"

Iblis felt panic in his chest. "No, of course not. I apologize. I meant no disrespect. In fact it was due to my deep regard for you that I made my request in the first place —"

The skeletal old secondaries stood up, to facilitate the Cogitors' wishes to be left alone.

Rebuffed, Iblis backed away. "Very well. I shall personally select appropriate secondaries for you."

As the door closed behind Iblis, the scheming wheels in his mind accelerated. These Ivory Tower Cogitors were too complacent, too oblivious to recognize real importance in the universe. Vidad might be an eminent philosopher, but he was still naïve and blind; he and his fellows were as bad as the minority of deluded protesters against the Jihad, unable to recognize matters of consequence.

But the Cogitors . . . Iblis knew he had to change their minds, no matter how long it might take.

The door closed behind him. He would have to select his candidate secondaries carefully, and give them very explicit instructions. So much depended on this. Their mission would be subtle, yet crucial, for winning the Jihad and ensuring the ultimate survival of the human race.

*   *   *

Gone were his normally surreptitious Jipol clothing and even his rarely worn formal uniform, and Keats appeared out of place in the new yellow robes the Ivory Tower Cogitors had provided for him.

Iblis studied his loyal aide, nodded with approval. "Keats, you look suitably pious. The Ivory Tower Cogitors will find you, and all of my other hand-picked volunteers, acceptable replacements." The Grand Patriarch's smile widened. "They have no idea what they're getting into. All of you have been carefully briefed, of course, but you, Keats, are my most trusted recruit. Keep the others on track . . . and be subtle. Take your time."

Keats wrinkled his oval face in a scowl, brushed his nails over the drab yellow robes. "Time is the one thing that seems to be in generous supply, if one can judge from the lives of the men we're replacing." He heaved a long sigh, and his shoulders shuddered. "I feel as if I'm being sent into exile, sir. There is much more important work I can do here for the Jihad—"

Iblis placed a hand on the younger man's shoulder, squeezing it paternally. "Many can perform those trivial tasks, Keats. You, though, are best qualified for this one, considering your proven talents as an investigator and interrogator.

"But I also know you fancy yourself a student of philosophies, so you are the ideal foil for these isolated, oblivious Cogitors. You must work on them, soften them, make them understand how much we need their support in this struggle."

Side by side, the pair walked to the window of the Grand Patriarch's office tower, where they gazed down at the busy paved streets of Zimia. At the memorial park, the lumbering, frozen form of an abandoned cymek warrior stood like a specter in the bright afternoon. Flowerbeds and sculptures adorned some of the city quadrants that had been damaged in the attack twenty-nine years ago.

"I know there is much you will miss here on Salusa Secundus," he said, "but you have an opportunity that few humans are ever given. You will spend the next years in seclusion with some of the greatest minds ever produced by the human race. What you learn from these Ivory Tower Cogitors will surpass any normal man's experience. You are one of a handful of people in the last millennium who have conversed with Vidad and his fellows."

Still, Keats still did not look certain.

Iblis smiled, and his vision became distant. "Well do I recall the times when I made pilgrimages to the Cogitor Eklo on Earth. I was a mere slave supervisor then, but for some reason the Cogitor saw my potential. The aged brain communicated with me. I was even allowed to dip my fingers into the electrafluid that kept his great mind alive, and I communicated directly with him. What a blessing." He shivered from the memory.

"Omnius is full to bursting with sheer data, but the evermind has no comprehension. It is all cold assessments and projections, responses to stimuli. But a Cogitor — a Cogitor is swollen with true *wisdom*."

Keats stood tall, obviously letting himself feel pride in the tremendous responsibility the Grand Patriarch was giving him. "I . . . understand."

Iblis stared at the man in the saffron robes. "In a way I envy you, Keats. I wish I had no obligations to the Jihad so that I could spend the next few years as a pupil kneeling at the side of a Cogitor's tank. But that task falls to you. I know you are up to it."

"I will do my best, Grand Patriarch."

"Feel free to enlighten yourself as you serve the Cogitors to the best of your ability. But you must be clever and flexible. Open their eyes — figuratively, I mean. The Ivory Tower Cogitors have left too much behind. You and your comrades have the secret task of converting them from neutrals to genuine allies in our Holy Jihad."

He guided his loyal aide to the door of his plush offices. "Serena Butler will give you all a benediction before your departure. Then you will be off on the most important journey of your life."

Serena administered her sacred blessing to each of the newly designated secondary monks, but Iblis had made all the choices long before informing her. The Priestess of the Jihad — despite her increased role of late — did not question his decision, though he made certain she did not learn the details.

At least she had not tried to take over that part of his responsibility. For the past several months, ever since he had returned from his strange meeting with the renegade Titan Hecate, Serena had been pushing him aside, taking charge of things that had been running well enough before.

And he had been wracking his brain for a way to consolidate power again. It had been almost twenty years now since he had married the lovely, charismatic Camie Boro, whose dowry had been her imperial pedigree. But he had entangled himself with Camie and her exaggerated political importance before he understood that the true descendant of the last emperor counted for little in the League of Nobles. She had become a mere showpiece to be displayed on important occasions.

As he watched Serena complete her admirable duties, Iblis observed her in wonderment. The Priestess of the Jihad would have made a much more suitable partner for his ambitions. It seemed a shame to waste such power.

Now, a suitably submissive-looking Keats and the other new volunteers waited to accompany the Ivory Tower Cogitors to their glacier-encrusted planetoid. They stood, looking appropriately brave and contrite, and Iblis smiled at each one, nodding subtly when the new recruits flashed devoted glances at him.

Serena had the grace of a madonna as she touched each man on the shoulder. "I thank you for your sacrifices, gentlemen, for your willingness to isolate yourself for years. You will suffer many lonely hours on cold Hessra, perfect times for discussions and debates. And for the good of our Jihad, you must make the Ivory Tower Cogitors see that neutrality is not the sole option."

Keats smiled and stepped away from Serena's benediction as she moved to the next man. They would be gone for years or decades, perhaps for the rest of their lives . . . but in that time, they might be able to bring these other Cogitors over to the righteous cause of mankind.

In a low tone, Iblis spoke to Serena. "Priestess, they may appear placid on the outside, but these volunteers are experts in the art of conversation and debate." She nodded.

Iblis knew that the Cogitors were brilliant philosophers, but naïve. Though he gave Serena an appropriately sanitized explanation of his scheme, her bright lavender eyes showed that she understood . . .

Individually and collectively, humans are driven by sexual energy. Curiously, they construct great edifices around their actions in an attempt to conceal this.

— Erasmus, *Reflections on Sentient Biologicals*

A S TALL AS the buildings of Zimia, the titanic cymek walker looked like a prehistoric arachnid constructed of steel and alloys. With its combat arms raised in the air, it exposed threatening weapons turrets and cannon limbs.

The gladiator body showed signs of rust and corrosion from nearly three decades of exposure to open air. When guided by a disembodied human brain, this cymek warrior had caused much destruction during Agamemnon's deadly raid to bring down the planet's shield transmitters. But under the guidance of Xavier Harkonnen, the Salusan Militia had successfully driven back the attack. Several neo-cymeks had been obliterated in the battle, and others had jettisoned their preservation canisters for retrieval by the frustrated robot fleet, leaving the gigantic mechanical bodies behind.

This combat walker had remained here since the thwarted machine attack, surrounded by what had once been ruined governmental buildings. Now the hulk stood as a memorial to the thousands of victims of the first Battle of Zimia. The frozen machine body was both the trophy of a defeated enemy and a reminder that more thinking machines could attack again at any moment . . .

After a year fighting for the Jihad — first at Ix and then in two other major skirmishes against robot warships — Jool Noret had finally come to Salusa Secundus. Peering through narrowed eyes, he stood in the landscaped plaza staring up at the ominous cymek walker. The mechanical body was more than ten times his own height. With his analytical mindset and the training received from Chirox, Noret scrutinized the warrior-form's systems, mentally devising ways to destroy such an adversary. If necessary he would have faced such a giant machine alone. His jade-eyed gaze roved over the armored legs, the implanted projectile launchers, and the head turret from which the traitorous brain guided its attacks. Searching for weaknesses.

Noret knew from the *sensei* mek that cymek bodies took many forms that were adapted for a variety of harsh situations. While this permitted some freedom of arrangement, the primary systems accessing the thoughtrodes needed to be basically the same. If Noret could discover how to cripple and subdue machines like this, he would be an even more formidable mercenary. And he would cause even more destruction.

Looking at the fearsome contraption, he recalled the combat exercises he had watched his father perform, and felt the warrior spirit of Jav Barri flowing through him. "You don't frighten me," Noret said quietly to the huge machine. "You are just another enemy, like all the others."

A tall woman with pale hair, icy eyes, and milky-white skin came to stand beside him, making hardly a sound. "Foolish bravado leads to failure more often than to victory."

Noret had heard her approach, but there were many visitors and supplicants in this memorial square, all staring at the cymek hulk as if it were a defeated demon. "There is a difference between bravado and confident determination." He glanced up at the huge cymek again, then back to the woman. "You are a Sorceress of Rossak."

"And you are a mercenary of Ginaz," she said. "I am Zufa Cenva. My women have fought and destroyed cymeks. It is our burden and our skill to become the bane of all machines with human minds."

Noret gave her a cold smile. "I wish to become the bane of *all* machines — regardless of their type."

She considered him skeptically, as if trying to interpret the dangerous calmness surrounding this mercenary. "I see that you mean what you say, Jool Noret."

He nodded, not asking how she knew his name.

"My Sorceresses can eliminate cymeks," Zufa reiterated. "Each of my women can annihilate ten smaller neo-cymeks, sizzling their treacherous brains."

Noret continued to inspect the huge cymek walker. "Whenever one of your Sorceresses unleashes her mental weapon, she must die. Each strike is a suicide mission."

Zufa bridled. "Since when is a Ginaz mercenary unwilling to sacrifice himself for the Jihad? Are you a coward who fights only when it is safe?"

Though she was an intimidating woman, Noret did not flinch. Instead, he looked at her with vacant, shadowed eyes. "I am always willing to sacrifice myself, but so far I have not seen a worthy opportunity. In each battle I have survived in order to keep destroying my enemy year after year. If I am dead, I can no longer continue the fight."

Grudgingly, Zufa conceded the point. She nodded to the surprisingly grim and distant mercenary. "If only there were more like the two of us, the machines would have no choice but to turn and flee for their very . . . existence."

Plans and possibilities filled the Grand Patriarch's mind during every waking hour, wheels within wheels, schemes to benefit the human race. And himself, of course. Everything he did had countless ramifications. There were linkages to every decision.

Iblis Ginjo had much to conceal and much to balance. At present only Yorek Thurr and himself knew about their amazing new ally, Hecate. And the Jipol commandant had always been frighteningly capable of keeping secrets.

Through the quiet machinations of the Jihad police, Iblis had seized a growing number of protest leaders who naïvely wanted to put a stop to the constant warfare. He had also put political enemies to death if they interfered with his grand plans for the Jihad. Like Muñoza Chen. It was all a matter of necessity, not something he particularly enjoyed. To safeguard himself, the Grand Patriarch had people watching people watching people, though Yorek Thurr always managed to elude the closest scrutiny.

Iblis considered it his sacred duty to make certain harsh, difficult decisions that others would not understand. Some things needed to be done secretly in order to annihilate the thinking machines. The Grand Patriarch's honorable motivations were clear in his own mind, but he knew he could never share them with anyone, especially not with his carefully groomed Priestess of the Jihad. Her saintly innocence was not feigned.

Unfortunately, Serena's newfound independence had thrown many intricate plans into turmoil. Too much was at stake, and Iblis couldn't allow her to continue along this uncomfortable path. He had to find some way to bring her back into line. The answer had seemed so obvious, and he hoped she would see the advantages, too. He knew her heart was a block of ice when it came to personal matters, though she still insisted on charitable actions for jihadis and refugees. She could be reached, but he had to be careful how he did it, to make her see the logical reasons for the perfect alliance he wanted.

She was due to arrive in his private chambers soon, and Iblis intended to use every skill he possessed to convince her to accept his proposal.

Through a window of his Zimia penthouse, he looked out at the imposing government buildings fronting the immense central square where thousands of people gathered for the weekly Jihad rallies. He envisioned even larger crowds in the future, spilling across metropolitan centers on all League Worlds. If properly fed, the holy struggle would continue to grow and grow.

First, though, certain things needed to happen. His wife Camie wouldn't like it, and matters might get ugly with their three children, but he had married the woman only because her supposed political clout had boosted his own power. Later he learned, to his dismay, that she was in reality a person of insignificant influence. Now, as a turnabout, Camie loved being married to the Grand Patriarch's title, not to him. And if she caused too much trouble . . . well, he supposed Thurr could take care of that as well. All for the good of the Jihad.

Serena was more important, with much more interesting possibilities.

Iblis sat back in a deep suspensor chair, felt it conform to his stocky body. Given the stresses of his position, the Grand Patriarch had not paid much attention to his diet or physical condition. Over the past ten years, ever since the formation of the Jihad Council, he had gained a considerable amount of weight, and Camie hadn't bothered to sleep with him in months. Although he had been discreet out of political necessity, with his charisma and important position, Iblis could have any woman he wanted.

Except for Serena Butler. Ever since her capture by the thinking machines long ago on Giedi Prime, she had avoided all opportunities for romance. Such steely resolve and dedication gave her a certain air of noble sacrifice, but it took a toll on her, detracting from her humanity. The most fanatical of her followers saw her as an Earth Mother, a Madonna, and a Virgin.

But love was more than just an esoteric concept. To be truly effective, the Priestess had to demonstrate her capacity for love. A compassionate Mary instead of a steely Joan of Arc. Iblis meant to do something about that today.

From the drawer of a side table he removed a phial of subtle pheromones and dusted them on his neck and on the backs of his hands. The smell was faintly sour and not particularly pleasant, but it should work unobtrusively on the female instincts. Iblis rarely needed such a crutch, but wanted to leave nothing to chance.

He knew full well that conventional romance and methods of seduction would never succeed with Serena. He had to rely on other forms of persuasion, prove to her the benefits to the Jihad, if only she would agree . . .

A discreet signal sounded at the door, and one of his Jipol corporals escorted Serena Butler into his chamber. "Sir, the Priestess of the Jihad." Iblis quickly hid the pheromone phial.

"Grand Patriarch," she said, with a stiff nod. "I trust this is important? My duties have increased dramatically of late."

It is your own fault. Revealing none of his annoyance, Iblis smiled warmly and stepped forward to take her hand. "You look especially radiant today." She wore a black suit-dress with a white collar and sleeves. He gestured to a leather suspensor sofa over the deep-pile imported carpet.

"I have been out in the sun," she said with a curt smile. "I spoke for hours at the large rally yesterday."

"I know. I saw the recordings." Iblis took a seat beside her on the slick sofa. It bobbed a little. "A very effective job, as usual." Even if she had written it herself, ignoring all of his suggestions . . .

A mustachioed manservant appeared with a tray of steaming drinks, which he placed on a table in front of them. "Sweet green tea from the finest importers," Iblis announced, trying to impress her. "Special blend from Rossak."

She accepted a cup, but held it in her palms without taking a sip. "What do we need to discuss, Grand Patriarch?" She seemed so distant. "We must make the most of our time."

Since her change of heart and insistence on running the Jihad Council, Iblis saw clearly that she had been redefining the power structure on her own terms, placing him in a subordinate position. Perhaps, though, he could still find ways to guide and direct her, just differently from before.

"I have an idea that may surprise you, Serena, but when you think about it I am convinced you will see the wisdom, and how it will make the Jihad much stronger. It is time we had this talk."

She waited without answering. Her expression hadn't softened, but he could see that he had her complete attention.

Entirely relaxed, he said nothing to her of the melange capsules he had consumed less than an hour ago. Serena had always made it clear that she did not approve of any drug, considering it a sign of weakness, so he had been certain to take spice with odor masking additives.

Iblis laid out his case. "For many years we have worked together, but not closely enough. We have always been partners in the Jihad, you and I — the Grand Patriarch and the Priestess. Our goals are identical, and our passions. The closer our alliance, the more we can accomplish."

He used a practiced, seductive voice as he studied Serena's profile. Though she was in her mid-forties he still found her strikingly beautiful, with soft features, golden hair and those extraordinary eyes.

"I agree." Her smile was brief, as if unconvinced.

He leaned closer to her. "I have considered this at length, Serena, and I do not make the offer lightly. I believe the next step to strengthen our Jihad would be . . . for us to become true partners, for all of free humanity to see. Are there any two people better suited for each other? We could have a grand wedding, cement our influence, and push the Jihad to the goal we know we must achieve."

He saw her surprised reaction, but before Serena could begin to argue, he pressed on. "The two of us could be so much more effective if we were to work together. The people would see us as an even stronger entity, an invincible duo. Even Omnius would tremble before the idea of a unified Priestess and Patriarch."

Though he felt intimidated and defensive, Iblis revealed none of his emotions. He felt like a man who had taken two steps backward and might never recover his previous position. But he would never reveal to her the extensive scope of his security, surveillance, and mercenary operations, or the fact that he had committed serious crimes in the name of the Jihad.

She sat stiffly on the sofa, frowning, seeming to ignore his proximity. "An obvious impossibility. You already have a wife. And three children."

"A simple enough problem to solve. I do not love her. I am willing to make the sacrifice for the good of the Jihad. Camie will understand." *She could be bought off.* He reached out to touch Serena's arm and continued in a rush, as his rehearsed words tumbled forth. "Think of it — together, we can become the guiding force the Jihad requires. You and I can take our Holy War to the next level — and ultimate victory."

He feigned emotion — ostensibly for the sake of the Jihad, not for himself personally. He had already known that he would never get through to Serena Butler with clumsy efforts at seduction. Iblis wanted her very badly, even more so because she was as unreachable as a goddess. But he restrained himself and shifted his approach. The only way he could ever have this woman — as his wife, as his mate, and under his control again — would be to convince her on her own terms. A business proposition.

She nudged him away. "I have no interest in love, Iblis. Or marriage. Not with you or any man. You don't need me."

Iblis frowned, fighting back his frustration. This would be difficult. "I do not speak of humdrum love, but of something far greater than either of us, something far more important. We are destined to be partners in our great mission, Serena." He withdrew his hand but smiled at her, concentrating on his ability, hoping to snare her with his hypnotic gaze. He had to solve the puzzle of this woman. "Only you and I have the necessary resolve to win this war."

Iblis had never sounded so desperate, and he was angry at what she had done to him. If he could conquer her, it would be a huge victory for his own political aspirations. With Serena Butler under his control, nothing could ever stand in his way.

But her expression remained cold, disinterested. She stood up from the sofa, ready to leave. "Our Jihad requires your full attention. And *mine*. Use your charms to rally the people, Iblis. That would be a better application of your skills. We must both get back to work, Grand Patriarch, and not fritter away time on this nonsense."

Iblis showed her every courtesy as he motioned for a Jipol aide to escort her away from his suite, but he raged inside and felt like smashing something.

He had never expected the beautiful, utterly confident Sorceress of Rossak to seek him out. As if sensing that he had been rebuffed by another woman, Zufa Cenva strode boldly to the Grand Patriarch's quarters that evening and demanded to see him for a "personal and private audience."

He quickly forgot about Serena Butler.

Zufa cared nothing of Iblis's other women or his political wife. Sorceresses dedicated themselves to tracking bloodlines and manipulating breeding patterns in an attempt to pinpoint the specific genetics conducive to achieving high mental powers in some of the female offspring on Rossak. She had taken the fertility drugs — ironically the ones developed and marketed by Aurelius Venport, who had himself failed her so many times — and knew her body was perfectly receptive.

Given Iblis's libidinous inclination, she supposed the man would be receptive to her as well.

A male telepath was extremely rare, considered nearly impossible. But Zufa had seen the signs in this man, and she needed to bring his valuable bloodline back to her world. Given her own abilities and the Grand Patriarch's history, she did not believe it would be difficult.

And it was not . . .

As Zufa and Iblis lay on his suspensor bed, having enjoyed each other to the fullest, she thought of what a fascinating man he was. Even without fully understanding the origin of his innate abilities and without training, he had managed to secure a powerful position for himself. While they were making love a short while ago, he had proclaimed her the "Supreme Sorceress of the Jihad." He promised to make a formal announcement of her new official title through the Jihad Council.

"Most impressive," she had gasped, pretending to be breathless from their physical passion. "But do we have to discuss the war *now?*"

"I'm always thinking about the Jihad," he said. "I have to, because thinking machines never sleep." Only a few minutes afterward, he drifted off.

Beside her, he snored lightly, with one burly arm draped over her shoulder. Gently, Zufa pulled away. Iblis had immediately recognized the advantages of a political alliance with her, adding the power and influence of the Rossak Sorceresses to his great cause. In exchange, she got what she needed from him, and she could always get more, if necessary. A quid pro quo. But she supposed this would be one of her final opportunities, biologically, to conceive. For future missions, she would probably have to send in a younger Sorceress.

But this daughter, she wanted for herself.

Zufa slipped out of bed and stood naked before a full-length mirror. Though she was mature and well beyond childbearing age for most women, her body remained in excellent condition. She had an almost perfect form, as if she had been sculpted by the hands of the gods. In the reflection she saw Iblis stir on the bed, without opening his eyes.

Is your genetic line superior, Iblis Ginjo? She vowed to discover the answer for herself.

Human breeding was not an exact science, but the women of Rossak were convinced that powerful bloodlines could be identified, controlled, and harvested. She had tested her timing, hormones, and ovulation to be certain she was at peak fertility, and had no doubt that she would conceive a child. Through careful application of special Rossak drugs known only to Sorceresses, she had greatly increased her chances of selecting a daughter.

She had suffered terrible personal disappointments when she'd given birth to the stunted Norma, and when her carefully chosen mate Aurelius Venport had proved to be a dismal genetic failure, despite all prior indications to the contrary.

This time it will be different. As she dressed quickly and slipped out of the Grand Patriarch's quarters, she finally had hope. This one would be a perfect daughter. The one she had always wanted.

Females were so much more valuable than males.

Anyone can be brought down. It is only a matter of figuring out how to do it.

—Tio Holtzman, letter to Lord Niko Bludd

A T LEAST THE disaster happened behind closed laboratory doors. The reinforced walls contained the explosion, and no one was hurt, except for a few inconsequential slaves. Holtzman decided to make careful modifications to his records so that Lord Bludd would never know about it.

Years ago, thanks to Norma Cenva, the Savant had learned to be careful about showing off a new concept before it had been thoroughly proven. He wanted no further blots of embarrassment on his record.

Anxious to quell muttered jokes among the Poritrin nobles that the great inventor had run out of ideas, Holtzman had revamped old plans for his alloy-resonance generator — a device that had blown up an entire laboratory twenty-eight years ago, destroying a bridge and killing many slaves. It should have worked, should have been a powerful new weapon that acted directly on the metal bodies of the thinking machines. He'd been eager to show off the device to Lord Bludd without testing it first.

The ensuing catastrophic failure had been an embarrassment that took him years to get over.

Regardless of this, the Savant had always believed the concept had some merit. Recently he had given the old plans to his team of ambitious young assistants, and instructed them to *make it work*.

With bloodshot eyes, mussed hair, and a pervasive smell of sour perspiration, the assistants had recalculated, redesigned, and rebuilt the demonstration assembly. He had pretended to go over their plans in great detail, but he took the apprentices at their word. Now, when the "improved" device failed just as explosively, he was despondent. Fortunately this time the Savant could keep it a secret, but that was only a small consolation.

All those years ago, Norma Cenva had warned him that the concept was hopelessly flawed, that it could never possibly work. She had always been so smug about such admonitions, but maybe she was right after all. *What is she doing now, anyway?* He had not seen her in a while.

Naturally, he assumed she had wasted more time and accomplished little. If she had made a great discovery, he would certainly have heard about it. Unless she was keeping a secret . . . as she had when handing over the glowglobe technology to VenKee Enterprises.

Leaving the assistants to clean up and hide the wreckage of the alloy-resonance generator, he gathered all their lab notebooks "for security reasons," and later destroyed them. The famed inventor liked to think he was in control of his life.

That evening, before he had finished his first glass of tartly spiced Poritrin rum, Holtzman had decided to pay Norma Cenva a visit.

Though she tried to keep a low profile, Norma could not really hide the existence of such a large operation. Tuk Keedair initiated tight security measures, but Lord Bludd still knew where the facility was, based upon the fact that VenKee Enterprises had purchased an old mining operation in a tributary river canyon.

Now Holtzman decided he would go there to see what she was doing, bringing with him only two assistants and a pair of Dragoon guards. If Norma caused trouble, he could always come back later — with force.

The white-robed inventor rode a powered shuttleboat upriver to the dry side canyon where he knew she was conducting mysterious experiments. He saw empty docks and cargo lifts running up the cliffside to the buildings and caves that formed her research facility.

"With such an ugly complex, it's a good thing she's hidden it so far out here," his apprentice said.

Holtzman nodded. "Norma has no aesthetic sense whatsoever. But that doesn't stop her brain from working."

Which worries me.

The Dragoon guards and assistants climbed out of the shuttleboat and made their way to the lifts. Holtzman looked around, listening to distant industrial sounds. It reminded him of the clamor in the shipyards he had established on the river delta. His brow furrowed.

When the lift clattered its way to the top of the cliff, Holtzman's party encountered a dozen well-armed, surly-looking guards who blocked their entry into the fenced compound. "This is a secure area and private property." All the guards stared at the Dragoons in their gold-scale armor.

"Don't you realize who this is?" one of his apprentices said boldly. "Make way for Savant Tio Holtzman!"

The Dragoons pushed their way forward, though the mercenary guards made no move to permit their passage. Instead, they leveled their weapons. "Looks to me like you've spent hours polishing that gold armor to a high gloss," the lead guard said. "Wouldn't want us to scorch it with a weapons blast, would you?"

The Dragoons recoiled in disbelief. "We come on the express authority of Lord Niko Bludd himself!"

"Doesn't give him the right to ignore private property. He doesn't own the whole planet."

"Go call Keedair," another guard said. "Let him deal with this."

One of the mercenaries trotted back toward the buildings. Holtzman peered through the fence, saw a large hangar and outbuildings, along with a flow of slaves busily carrying components into a construction area inside a warehouse.

She's fabricating something in there . . . something large.

Just then he noticed a child-sized woman approaching him, riding on a personal suspensor platform. She puttered away from the hangar toward the fence, where the Dragoons still faced off with the stony mercenary guards. "Why, Savant Holtzman! What are you doing here?"

"That is not the most interesting question, is it?" He rubbed the gray beard on his chin. "Rather, what are you *doing* here, Norma? What, precisely, is your work? I have come as your colleague to see if we can help each other against the thinking machines. Yet, you act as if you're engaged in illegal activities."

In her youth, she had spent years working obsessively on modifications to his original equations. The concept of "folding space" sounded like one of Norma's typically absurd ideas. Still, this odd, unassuming woman had proven her genius time and again . . .

"With all due respect, Savant Holtzman, my sponsor has made me promise not to reveal any details of my work." The diminutive woman looked away.

"Have you forgotten who I am, Norma Cenva? I have the highest security clearance in the League of Nobles! How can you refuse to reveal details to me?" He looked at the Dragoon guards, as if he would instruct them to arrest her. "Now, tell me about . . . folding space."

Startled, she hesitated, but her eyes glimmered with excitement. "Savant, it is merely an offshoot of your original field equations, a unique extension that allows the folding of spacetime to manipulate the variable of distance. Thus it will enable our Army of the Jihad to attack the thinking machines anyplace instantaneously, without the lengthy travel times we presently require."

The inventor's nostrils flared, and he fixed on only one part of her explanation. "It derives from *my* equations, and you did not think to tell me about it?"

Just then the Tlulaxa merchant bustled toward them, a small man not much taller than Norma Cenva. His narrow face wore a look of alarm; his thick braid seemed a bit frayed. "Norma, please let me handle this. You need to get back to your work." He shot her a quick, sharp glare. "*Now.*" Cowed, Norma spun the suspensor car around and flitted back to the enclosed work area.

Holtzman put his hands on his hips and faced Tuk Keedair imperiously. "There's no need for this to become a complicated issue. Your guards don't seem to understand that we have a right to inspect and share any new developments that might benefit the Army of the Jihad —"

Not easily intimidated, Keedair responded, "This is a high-security facility, and the proprietary research here is funded solely by VenKee Enterprises. You have no more 'right' to be here than the thinking machines do."

Holtzman's apprentices gasped. The Tlulaxa nodded to his guards. "Do your jobs and see that they leave promptly." He looked up at the Savant. "Whenever we have an announcement to make or a demonstration to hold, we will be sure to invite you and Lord Bludd . . . out of courtesy."

The Dragoon guards did not know what to do, and looked over at the fuming Holtzman, as if he could concoct an instantaneous solution to the problem. But he saw that they had no choice but to retreat. For now.

"She is hiding something, just as I suspected all along," Holtzman said, trying to make Lord Bludd see that he should be deeply concerned. "Why would VenKee insist upon such security, if she is as much a failure now as when she worked for me?"

The nobleman chuckled as he sipped from his bubbling fruit drink. Bludd leaned back in his chair on the balcony and gazed unconcerned from the bluffs to the river, where barges hauled cargo to the delta and the spaceport. "Isn't it interesting that she suddenly makes a wealth of progress within two years of being freed from her servitude? Perhaps that smart little woman has played you for a fool, Tio! Hiding her discoveries all along so that she didn't have to share credit with you."

"Norma Cenva has never cared about fame or credit." Holtzman declined the nobleman's offer of refreshment and paced the floor of the balcony, not interested in the expansive view below. "And now that her 'friend' Venport got us to release her, we don't have any claim on her new discoveries."

Then a cold knife sliced into his chest. "That must be why VenKee was so willing to surrender a portion of glowglobe profits! Whatever Norma has concocted must be orders of magnitude more significant than that." He clenched his fist. "And we're cut out of it all."

Bludd heaved himself to his feet, brushing his plush robes and arranging them neatly. "No, no, Tio. We relinquished only those concepts that were completely *new*. If she has developed them so quickly since the date of our signed agreement, any decent attorney — or even a brilliant scientist such as yourself — shouldn't find it difficult to draw a direct correlation with Norma's original work."

Holtzman stopped as the idea sank in. "If her work involves what I think it does, then you are correct, Lord Bludd."

The nobleman took a long draught from his goblet and nudged a second one closer to Holtzman. "Drink up, Tio. You need to relax."

"But how are we going to get inside her complex? I need to see what Norma is doing. That facility is surrounded by dozens of mercenary guards, and that Tlulaxa foreigner watches over it like a hawk."

"The visa of a Tlulaxa can easily be revoked," Bludd pointed out, "and I shall do so immediately. In point of fact, even though Norma Cenva has lived here on Poritrin for much of her life, she is still a guest on our planet, not a citizen. We can put out the word, planting subtle doubts, cutting off supplies and access privileges."

"Will that be enough?"

Bludd cracked his ring-studded knuckles, then called for his Dragoon captain. "Put together an overwhelming force and go upriver to Norma Cenva's facility. Three hundred well-armed Dragoons should be sufficient. I suspect the mercenary guards will surrender as soon as they see you coming. Serve the Tlulaxa man with his revocation papers, and then you can investigate and learn what Norma's been up to. That won't be a problem, will it?"

Holtzman swallowed and looked away, suddenly finding the view of the river much more fascinating. "No, my Lord. But Norma will resist. She'll send an urgent communiqué to Aurelius Venport. Tuk Keedair will file a brief in the League court. I'm sure of it."

"Yes, Tio, but you will have months to investigate her labs and construction bays before anything can be resolved. If you find nothing worthwhile, then we can apologize and admit our mistake. But if you do learn of a scientific breakthrough, we will go into production with it ourselves before VenKee Enterprises can even file an appeal."

Holtzman was already smiling. "You are quite the visionary, Lord Bludd."

"Just as you are quite the scientist, Tio. Our adversaries are completely out of their depth."

A man must not be a statue. A man must act.
　　　　　　　—Buddislamic Sutra, Zenshia Interpretation

F OR WELL OVER a year Ishmael followed meaningless orders at Norma
　　Cenva's complex, though he felt as if his heart had died inside him.
He toiled with a hundred and thirty other Buddislamic captives. The
secret project was complex as they slowly built, refit, and tested the
strange components of a large new ship.

None of it meant anything to him.

The woman scientist was not a difficult task master. She was so intent
in her focus that she blithely assumed every other person shared her
obsessive dedication. Her Tlulaxa partner Tuk Keedair — Ishmael
shuddered with loathing each time he saw the former slaver — enforced
the long work shifts.

The assistants, administrators, engineers, and slaves spent their days
and nights in a small settlement whose sole purpose was to build the
experimental vessel. The Buddislamic slaves slept in plain, clean communal barracks erected atop the plateau where the nights were windy but
full of stars. Ishmael had no opportunity to return to Starda, not even for a
day.

Ishmael had received no word of his wife or daughters, had found no
one of whom he could even ask questions about them. His family was lost
to him. Each day he prayed they were still alive, but in his memory they
had become ghosts inhabiting his dreams. His hopes dwindled to no
more than thin threads.

Amidst the loud hammering and shouts of the construction hangar, he
watched his friend Aliid changing the cartridge of a sonic tool. When the
slaves had first come upriver to work on this new, isolated project, Aliid

had managed to get himself assigned to a daily work detail with Ishmael. Now the Poritrin slavers had taken both men from their wives and families.

After adjusting the sonic tool, the Zenshiite man spoke sharply. "You tried, Ishmael. You did what you thought was best — I cannot fault you for that, though I have always disagreed with your naïve faith in the fairness of our captors. What did you expect? The slavemasters rely on us being spineless, exactly as you demonstrated. When we are capable of nothing more than toothless threats, they feel no obligation to treat us like human beings. We must speak a language that our oppressors will heed. We must show fangs and claws!"

"Violence only brings down greater punishments upon us. You saw what happened to Bel Moulay—"

Aliid interrupted, grinning wolfishly. "Yes, I saw . . . but did *you*, Ishmael? In all the years since then, what have you learned? You fixate on the pain Bel Moulay suffered, but you forget everything he achieved. He brought us *together*. It was a clarion call, not just for the Poritrin nobles who overreacted and crushed every sign of resistance, but for all Buddislamics who continue to suffer. We slaves have a sleeping strength within us."

Clinging to his nonviolent beliefs, Ishmael shook his head stubbornly. The two men had reached a familiar impasse, each of them unwilling to cross to the other side of the chasm separating them. Once, they had been good friends thrust together by common circumstances, but they had always been so different. Even their common miseries had not drawn them closer. Aliid, in his determination, kept trying to achieve the impossible — in so many ways. Ishmael had to admire him for his convictions, but Aliid showed only frustration.

When Ishmael had been a boy, his grandfather had taught him what to believe and how to live, but sometimes adults simplified matters for their children. Ishmael was thirty-four years old now. Had he been wrong all these years? Did he need to find new strength within himself, yet still remain within the boundaries of Zensunni teachings? He knew deep in his bones that Aliid's dreams of violence were wrong and dangerous, but his quiet confidence that it was all for a reason — that God would somehow rescue them and melt the hearts of their slavers — had accomplished nothing during his life. Or during the lives of generations of Buddislamic slaves.

He had to find another answer. A different solution.

Though Ishmael had failed utterly, wresting no comforts or concessions from Lord Bludd, the Zensunni faithful still came to him in the communal barracks at night, asking him to preach, to tell them stories, to reaffirm their patient acceptance of Buddallah's will. More than a hundred men and women came to see him regularly — most of the work force.

At first, Ishmael didn't think he could do it. How could he recite the Koran Sutras and sing songs of God's benevolence, when Ozza could not be beside him, when his beautiful girls did not sit across the story fire and listen to his familiar parables? But then Ishmael grew strong and realized that he could not lose everything. He had his own strength, even if Aliid could not see it.

As the months stretched past a year, though, Ishmael noticed a gradual but clear separation open up between his Zensunni brothers and the smaller group of Aliid's Zenshiites. Although they still worked together inside the enclosed hangar where Norma Cenva and her team tinkered with the gutted prototype ship, but he sensed that Aliid was hiding secrets not only from the Poritrin slavemasters, but also from Ishmael and his people . . .

A bright spot returned to Ishmael's life with the suddenness of the dazzling fireworks that the Poritrin lords so often launched in their river celebrations. The news was all the more welcome for its very unexpectedness.

As the massive experimental ship entered the final phase of testing and demonstration, Tuk Keedair hired another group of slaves from Starda and brought them to operate the colossal machinery and assist in last-minute operations. Among the fifteen sullen new workers, Ishmael was astonished to find his elder daughter Chamal.

She saw and recognized him, and her expression unfolded like the petals of a brilliant flower. Ishmael's heart leaped, and he wanted to rush to her, but armed escorts had accompanied the reassigned slaves. Also, narrow-eyed Tuk Keedair watched the newcomers as if taking a silent administrative tally.

Ishmael remembered the vindictiveness of Lord Bludd, who had willingly torn his family apart simply because he had asked for fair compensation. Now he could not risk drawing any attention either to himself or Chamal.

Ishmael gave his daughter a quick signal, shaking his head and averting his eyes. He would talk with her later. That night they would embrace and tell stories in quiet whispers. For now, he dared not show joy, for fear the slavemasters would steal that away as they had taken most everything else . . .

The rest of the day was agony for him. The new group of slaves went through orientation and training in a different part of the compound. The sun itself seemed to have stopped in the sky for Ishmael, since time passed so slowly.

But after the long work shift was over and the Zensunnis retreated to their communal barracks, with Aliid and his Zenshiites in their separate dwellings, Ishmael hugged his daughter and they both wept. Content just to be together, they explained nothing for awhile.

At last Chamal spilled the story of how she had been separated from her mother and her younger sister. As far as she knew, Ozza and little Falina had been taken to the cane fields on the far side of the continent. She had heard nothing from them in a year.

After talking with Ishmael for hours Chamal summoned a young, determined-looking man named Rafel. She took him by the hand and pulled him close to meet her father. He seemed intimidated, as if he had already heard much about Ishmael. She said, "This man is my husband. When I turned sixteen and reached marriageable age, we were given to each other." She lowered her dark eyes, avoiding Ishmael's obvious surprise. "I had no one else, Father."

He felt no displeasure, but in his own mind he could not believe that his little daughter — a girl who had always seemed so young to him — was now an adult, a woman and a wife. Ishmael smiled warmly, welcoming them both. "He looks like a fine young man."

Bowing his head slightly, Rafel replied, "I will try to be, for the sake of your daughter and our people."

Chamal stood close to her husband, obviously fond of the young man. "After I married Rafel, their administrators must have lost track of the fact that I was your daughter. They did not know who I was when they transferred me here. Otherwise, Lord Bludd would have kept me away from you."

Ishmael reached forward to take her hand, squeezing it tightly. "You are my daughter, Chamal." Then he reached out to grasp her young husband's hand as well. "And you are now my son, Rafel."

Weeks later, Ishmael discovered by accident what plans Aliid had already put into motion. In the isolated group at the canyon job site, one of the Zensunni women in the crew had taken a Zenshiite as her husband, observed him hiding makeshift weapons and reading secret notes written in a nearly forgotten Buddislamic language that no League noble could read. Seeing Ishmael as their leader, the interpreter of the sutras and the reluctant decision maker, she told him what she had learned and suspected.

Within a month, the twenty-seventh anniversary of Bel Moulay's uprising would come. The lords of Poritrin again planned raucous celebrations that would remind the slaves of their failure, the fate that always awaited them. In defiance of this, Aliid intended to use it as a springboard for his own violent rebellion. He had already put operatives into position and surreptitious messages had been sent back to Starda, where — invoking the name of Bel Moulay — the plans spread like a virulent disease.

The Zenshiites intended to launch a rain of violence upon the complacent Poritrin masters who believed they had squashed all resistance decades ago. Ishmael was beginning to realize that his own peacemaking overtures to Lord Bludd had done much to cement that impression among the nobles. But the realization did not spell a shift in his beliefs.

Obviously, Aliid knew that Ishmael would not condone violence and would instead quote Koran Sutras forbidding the murder of innocents and warning against wresting the powers of judgment from the hand of God. But Aliid had no further interest in scripture. He did not trust his childhood companion to participate in the plan, and even suspected that Ishmael might work against the intended uprising.

When Ishmael learned of this doubt, of being excluded, he felt as if his friend had stabbed him through the heart. Though they disagreed over tactics, didn't they both want freedom for their people? Ishmael had never thought his companion would keep such an important secret from him.

Shaken and brooding, he spent several nights awake, trying to decide what to do. Did Aliid truly believe that his plan would remain entirely secret, or did he hope Ishmael would learn of it and read between the lines? Was this supposed to be a test to determine whether the Zensunnis were willing to fight for freedom, or if they were content to remain docile captives?

What if Aliid is right?

Ishmael felt a cold knot in the center of his chest. He was certain Aliid's actions would cause a bloodbath and the slaves would pay a terrible price, even those who did not fight. If they rose up again, it would prove to their Poritrin masters that Buddislamics could never be trusted. They might be exterminated entirely or forced to live in shackles like penned animals, surrendering even the meager freedoms they still retained.

Ishmael knew he had no choice but to face his friend, before it was too late.

That evening as the wind came up and the sun went down, Ishmael climbed the metal-runged ladder to the hangar's cantilevered roof that extended beyond the grotto overhang. Aliid and seven Zenshiite co-workers had been sent here in a repair crew to fix overlapping corrugated sheetmetal that had been blown off in a canyon windstorm. The shelter was needed to protect the experimental ship from the cold rains of Poritrin's approaching winter.

Ishmael climbed to the roof and looked around. After shaving himself clean in order to meet with Lord Bludd, he had let his beard grow again, and now it was bristly and spiky, with a faint frosting of gray.

Aliid turned to face him, his striped Zenshiite shirt tucked into a work uniform. His black beard was a thick forest on the lower half of his face. It seemed he had been expecting his visitor.

Ishmael stopped, halfway to him. "Aliid, do you recall the Koran Sutra that says when friends keep secrets from each other, their enemies have already won?"

Aliid lifted his chin and narrowed his eyes. "The Zenshia variation says, 'A friend who cannot be relied upon is worse than an enemy.' "

The Zenshiite coworkers watched the two men as they spoke. Impatiently, Aliid gestured to them. "Leave us. My friend Ishmael and I have matters to discuss."

After reassuring themselves by the confidence on Aliid's hard face, they crossed to the open stairway and descended into the large grotto. Alone on the upper deck, the two men faced each other. The pause seemed to last an eternity as the wind whistled around Ishmael's ears.

"We have been through much together, Aliid," he said, at last. "Since we were captured as boys and brought to Poritrin, we have struggled and grieved at each other's side. We shared stories of our home worlds, and now both of our wives have been taken from us by the slave masters. I mourned with you for the destruction of the sacred city on IV Anbus. And now I have learned what you intend to do."

Aliid chewed at his upper lip. "I tired of waiting for you to act, my friend. I always hoped you would learn your error and see that God wants us to be *men*, not trees. We cannot stand by and let the universe do with us whatever it wishes. But ever since you went to speak with Lord Bludd and then meekly accepted your punishment, I have been convinced that the Zensunni way is comprised of talk, while my Zenshiites prefer action. Is it not time to act, at last?"

His eyes were fiery, as if he still held a hope that Ishmael would join him. "I have sent spies and messengers to slave groups all across Poritrin. They revere the memory of the great Bel Moulay, and are restless for another crack at the oppressors."

Ishmael shook his head, thinking of his daughter Chamal, then of his lost wife Ozza, and of Falina. They were still alive somewhere, and he dared not risk them. "Bel Moulay was executed, Aliid. Many hundreds of Buddislamic slaves were slaughtered when the Dragoons recaptured Starda Spaceport."

"He had the *right idea* — you know he did, Ishmael — but he acted precipitously, before he was ready. This time, the uprising will be on an unprecedented scale. I will orchestrate it on my own terms."

Ishmael pictured Chamal's new husband Rafel cut to bloody ribbons by guards with Chandler pistols . . . and Ozza and Falina, clinging to each other while Lord Bludd's troops mowed them down in burning cane fields. He shook his head. "And the Dragoon guards will retaliate on a scale commensurate with your uprising. Think of the suffering —"

"Only if we fail, Ishmael," Aliid said, stepping closer. The wind stirred his dark hair like a thunderhead. "It will be vengeance against our captors in the name of the martyr Bel Moulay. We kill the oppressors and take their world for ourselves. Make them serve *us* for a change. We'll take whatever payment we deem acceptable for all the lost years of our lives."

Ishmael swallowed hard. "I am terrified of your plan, Aliid."

"Terrified?" He let out a bitter laugh. "The League Worlds have always said that Buddislamics are cowards, that we flee from any fight, that we turned our backs on their war against the machine demons." Aliid leaned closer, his eyes blazing like those of Bel Moulay so long ago. "But on this anniversary, we will show them just what sort of *cowards* we are. It will be a bloodbath they'll never forget."

"Aliid, I beg you not to go forward with this. Violence in the name of Buddallah is still murder."

"Blind passivity in the face of all torments is still surrender," Aliid countered. He reached into his striped shirt and pulled out a long curved knife he had fashioned from a sharpened piece of scrap metal. "Do you intend to give us away, Ishmael? Will you report our plans to your friend Lord Bludd?" He extended the knife, hilt first. "Take it. You may as well kill me yourself then."

Ishmael raised his hands. "No, Aliid."

But the other man grabbed Ishmael's wrist and forced him to grasp the knife. Aliid pressed the point against his own chest. "Do it. Kill me now, for I no longer wish to live as a slave."

"Nonsense! I would never hurt you."

"This is your chance," Aliid growled. "Do it — or never again object to what I mean to do."

Ishmael yanked his hand free, releasing his grip on the weapon. He cast his gaze downward. "Is this the only way you know, Aliid? I feel sorry for you."

Sneering as if he wanted to spit in Ishmael's face, Aliid slipped the knife back into its hiding place. "You are no longer my friend, Ishmael, nor are you my enemy." He turned his back and uttered a final insult into the wind. "You are nothing to me."

Resistance to change is a survival characteristic. But in its extreme form, it is poisonous — and suicidal.

—Zensunni Stricture

E VEN SOPHISTICATED COOLING systems could not keep up with the solar heat pounding on the Arrakis headquarters of VenKee Enterprises. For all the profits that the melange trade had made for Aurelius Venport, it seemed he had to waste a great deal of money on the simplest of things here in the spaceport city. He spent the equivalent of a high-level salary just to fill the closed-system humidifiers to make these office quarters endurable.

Venport would rather have been on Salusa Secundus influencing League officials and defending his commercial rights against the grasp of the Jihad Council. He also wanted to return to the lush jungles of Rossak, where he could oversee his varied pharmaceutical interests. Most of all though, he realized with a growing warmth in his heart, he longed to be on Poritrin with Norma Cenva. Aside from his personal interest in her he was, of course, curious to see if her space-folding project might bear fruit and make his investment pay off.

In fact, he would have preferred to be any place other than Arrakis, but the spice business was a cornerstone of VenKee Enterprises. Despite this planet's harsh environment, its outrageous distance from any civilized world, and the difficult Zensunni fanatics like Naib Dhartha, the income from melange was substantial. And demand was only growing throughout the League of Nobles.

Now, wiping sweat from his forehead, he studied the documents in front of him, ledgers and accounting bins that traced deliveries and supplies Dhartha's organized spice scavengers brought to the spaceport.

Opening an electronic folio, he then contrasted this information with the ever-increasing losses and damaged equipment.

Any good businessman knew to devote the greatest amount of time and energy to the concerns that offered the greatest potential for profit — and Venport had proven himself an excellent businessman indeed. Thus, he had no choice but to stay here on Arrakis himself, until the problems were resolved.

He had hired a contingent of soldiers and guards, mercenaries and security men to maintain order in Arrakis City. The spaceport was a dirty, hard place, populated by dirty, hard men, but his troops kept the landing field and commercial buildings relatively safe.

The real problems occurred out in the deep desert, where no one could oversee.

Almost since the beginning of the spice trade on this desert hellhole, there had been numerous incidents of sabotage. In the past decade, pirate and bandit attacks had increased steadily, ominous signs that the resistance movement was gaining followers. For some reason these backward desert people scorned the benefits of civilization and the better standards of living.

Venport didn't need to understand the outlaws' way of thinking, was not required to sympathize with their point of view — but he did need to solve the problem. It was a task he would have preferred to leave to his partner, but through a maddeningly ironic twist of circumstances Keedair was now on Poritrin overseeing Norma's work . . . while Venport was stuck on Arrakis.

Damned poor planning.

One of his assistants appeared at the office doorway, a VenKee functionary from Giedi Prime who had requested the assignment to Arrakis in order to increase his chances for promotion. The gangly man now spent every day counting the hours until he could return to a League World — any League World. "Sir, that old desert fellow is here to see you — Mr. Dhartha."

Venport sighed, knowing that when the Zensunni leader appeared without an appointment, he invariably brought bad news. "Send him in."

The functionary ducked away from the door, and moments later Naib Dhartha appeared, wrapped in folds of white cloth smeared with dust. The Naib had dark, leathery skin and an intricate tattoo on his cheek. Wearing a stony expression, he remained standing, and Venport did not invite him to sit down. Dhartha, like all Zensunni men, stank of dust and sweat and various unpleasant bodily odors. It wasn't surprising that the Zensunni desert rats bathed rarely, if ever, since water was so precious here, but Venport had trouble ignoring his own hygienic expectations.

Before Naib Dhartha could say a word, Venport spoke. "First off, Naib, I want none of your hackneyed, tiresome excuses." He indicated the ledger documents and accounting bins, knowing Dhartha would not understand them. "These delays and slow-downs are inexcusable. Something must be done."

The old desert man surprised him. "I agree. I have come to ask for your assistance."

Venport covered his shock and leaned forward on the desk. "I'm listening."

"The cause of all our troubles is one man named Selim. He is at the heart of this band of troublemakers, wily foxes of the desert. They strike without warning, then flee and hide. But without Selim, the saboteurs would all vanish like smoke. The deluded fools see him as a hero. He calls himself 'Wormrider.'"

"Why has it taken so long to get rid of him?"

Naib Dhartha fidgeted. "Selim is elusive. A year ago he lured my innocent young grandson to his death, and I have sworn a vow of vengeance. We have sent many hunting parties out to search for the Wormrider, but he always dodges them. Finally, however, our best scouts have discovered his hideout, a cave complex far from other settlements."

"Then go take care of him," Venport demanded. "Must I offer you a reward to do this job well?"

Dhartha lifted his chin. "I need no monetary incentive to kill Selim Wormrider. I do, however, need your mercenary soldiers and offworld weapons. The outlaws will fight, and I must be assured of victory."

Venport knew it was a reasonable request and an appropriate investment. The infernal outlaws had destroyed many shipments of melange. Any expenses that VenKee Enterprises incurred in bringing business back to normal would be repaid many times over. "I am surprised your Zensunni pride allows you to solicit assistance from me."

Dhartha's deep blue eyes flashed. "This is not about pride, Aurelius Venport. This is only about killing a pest of the desert."

Venport stood. "Then you shall have everything you require."

During his life, Naib Dhartha had witnessed much hardship and suffering. Years ago his wife and an entire spice caravan had been lost in a furious sandstorm. Then his son Mahmad died of a festering offworld disease. By now he was accustomed to grief. But the death of his beloved grandson Aziz, who had done everything to please his grandfather, drove him closer to despair than anything else. And for that, Dhartha knew exactly whom to blame.

The obsession for revenge had gnawed at him for a full year, and now he was ready to act.

He sat in a cave meeting chamber, glowering at the tribal elders. This was not a council session or a discussion, but a pronouncement, and all those present knew not to argue with the Naib. His spice-blue eyes were red-rimmed, like pits gouged from his face with a blunt knife.

"Selim was an orphan, an ungrateful youth, and — worst of all — a water thief. When he was only a child, our village banished him, assuming he would become food for the desert demons. But since going out on his own, he has been like sand rubbing a raw wound. Selim gathers criminals to raid our villages and prey upon our caravans.

"We have tried to negotiate with him. My own grandson delivered a message asking Selim to rejoin our society, but this prodigal son has made a pact with Shaitan himself. He laughed at my offer and sent Aziz back empty-handed."

The elders sat looking expectantly at Dhartha. They sipped from small cups of spice-laced coffee. He noticed that most of them wore offworld clothes.

"Not content merely to rebuff my invitation, Selim Wormrider dared to fill that innocent boy's head with foolish ideas. It was the outlaw's specific intent to trick Aziz into his foolhardy attempt, knowing that Shaitan would devour him. It is Selim's revenge against me." He looked around at the men again, his entire body shaking. "Does anyone here dispute this?"

The men remained silent until finally one elder said, "But what shall we do about it, Naib Dhartha?"

"We have tolerated his harassment for years. Selim's stated goal is to impede all spice harvesting activities and destroy our trade with offworld merchants — the trade that has made our village wealthy. I say for a thousand reasons that we must destroy Selim and his bandit followers. We must crush these brigands while our men still remember the hard ways of the desert. We must gather our warriors and march upon the Wormrider's stronghold."

He clenched his fist and stood. "I call for a kanla party of vengeance, our best fighters to go with me and destroy Selim, once and for all."

All the elders stood with him, some reluctantly, others raising their fists in the air. As Naib Dhartha had expected, no one raised a voice of dissent.

* * *

The vision from Shai-Hulud had never been so clear. Selim sat up on his pallet in the dark. A few dim glowglobes stolen from spice caravans hung outside in the corridor of the cave, casting faint pools of light, but he counted on darkness outside, with dawn far away. He blinked his eyes, trying to shift from his inner prophetic vision to his physical surroundings.

Now I see it, so plainly!

Beside him Marha slept in peaceful dreams. She was warm and soft and familiar. They had been married a year, and she was now pregnant with their first child. But he felt as if she had always been part of his life, and of his growing legend. He looked down at her and she stirred, though he had done nothing to disturb her. Marha was so attuned to her husband that she sensed even when his thoughts changed.

For their sleeping alcove, Selim had selected one of the inner chambers whose walls were adorned by etched Muadru rune carvings, the indecipherable symbols that had been placed there by unknown mystical travelers. The ancient writings made Selim feel connected to the soul of Arrakis itself. They helped him achieve a clarity of thought, and his nightly consumption of melange brought him purpose, elucidations, and dreams. Sometimes the visions were murky and difficult to comprehend; on other occasions Selim understood precisely what he must do.

His wife looked up at him expectantly, her eyes glinting in the cave shadows. Trying to keep the tremors out of his voice, he said, "An army approaches, Marha. Naib Dhartha has gathered well-armed offworlders to do his fighting for him. He has cast aside his Zensunni beliefs and his honor. He is a man consumed by his own hatred, and it means more to him now than anything."

Marha got to her feet. "I will summon all of your followers, Selim. We will gather weapons and prepare to make our stand."

"No," Selim said, placing a gentle hand on her shoulder. "They know where to find this place, and will come upon us with an overwhelming force. Regardless of the dedication and ferocity of our fighters, we cannot win."

"Then we must flee! The desert is vast. We can easily find another hideout far from here."

"Yes." Selim stroked her cheek, then bent to kiss her. "You will all go deep into the desert and establish another base to support our cause. But I must remain behind and face him. *Alone.*"

Marha gasped. "No, my darling, come with us. They will kill you."

Selim stared into the shadows, his gaze distant and unfocused as if he were peering deeper into a reality that no one else could see. "Long ago, Buddallah blessed me with a sacred mission. All my life I have followed the task He set for me, and it has all come to this nexus. The fate of Shai-Hulud rests upon my actions, and the future that I will help to create."

"You cannot help create a future if you are dead."

He smiled faintly at her. "The future is not so simple, Marha. I must set a course that will stand for millennia."

"I shall stay and fight beside you. I am as capable as any of your fighters. You know I have proven myself—"

He placed his hands on her squared shoulders. "No, Marha. You have a greater responsibility, a much more important one. You must make certain that no one forgets. Only in that manner will we achieve a true and lasting victory."

Selim inhaled deeply, and the heavy, sweet taste of melange clung to his breath. In the deepest core of his soul he felt a connection with Shai-Hulud.

"I intend to face my enemy alone on the sand." He turned to Marha's wide-eyed gaze and gave her a faint but confident smile. His voice held no doubt whatsoever. "As a legend, I can do no less."

Since there has been no upload linkage between me and the evermind for decades, Omnius does not know my thoughts, which might be considered disloyal. But I do not mean them to be that way. I am just curious by nature.

— *The Erasmus Dialogues*

O N THE SYNCHRONIZED World of Corrin, watcheyes were every-where, observing everything. Though in a sense it was reassuring, sometimes Erasmus found the little electronic spies intrusive and annoying. Especially the mobile units, like persistent little insects. He had learned to be ready for the omnipresent voice that came out of nowhere, at any moment.

The unexpected update ship arrived on Corrin, transmitting the surprising news that, after decades of delay, Seurat would deliver an intact copy of the Earth-Omnius. Erasmus received the news without joy, and waited for the evermind to process the new information. He had never really intended to hide the details of his volatile Earth experiments and their disastrous, unexpected consequences. Not forever, anyway.

Erasmus strolled in the ornamental garden of his private villa; the intense sunlight of the red giant star harmed some of the delicate flowers, and helped other plants to flourish. While he was occupied with a rare bird-of-paradise blossom — one of Serena Butler's favorite flowers — Omnius processed the lost update with routine efficiency, and Seurat's update ship departed from the landing zone without incident.

Before the update vessel had even cleared the atmosphere, Erasmus was summoned by the evermind. The authoritarian mechanical voice came from an implant in a bonsai-banyan tree in his private garden.

"Yes, Omnius? Have you found anything interesting in the Earth update?" Erasmus inspected his flowers, as if he had no other concerns. He assumed, however, that he was about to be severely reprimanded.

"I know now that your 'challenge' regarding the feral boy Gilbertus

Albans has an earlier parallel." One of the leaves on the tiny tree glowed bright green, the apparent source of the hidden watcheye.

"I have never tried to raise a slave child before."

"You have proved to be an expert in large-scale manipulation of the human psyche. According to the update, you engaged in an interesting wager with my Earth counterpart to see if you could cause even loyal human trustees to turn against us."

"Only with the encouragement and full understanding of the Earth-Omnius," Erasmus said, as if that were an adequate excuse.

"You are attempting to deceive me through incomplete or filtered information. Is this a technique you learned from human subjects? It seems that you are trying to gain an upper hand over me through our competitions in a variety of forms. Do you seek to replace me?"

"I am no more than a servant of your wishes, Omnius." Out of habit the robot's flowmetal face formed a smile, though his expression meant little to the evermind. "If ever I attempt to influence your analyses, it is only to generate further understanding of our enemies."

"You concealed something else from me. Something much more significant." The bright green leaf vibrated, as if in anger. "You, Erasmus, were the root cause of the original human rebellion."

"Nothing can be concealed from you, Omnius. There are only input delays, and that is what happened here. Yes, I tossed an insignificant human child off a balcony . . . and apparently that incited the current revolt."

"An incomplete analysis, Erasmus. Iblis Ginjo, one of the human trustees you personally corrupted, led the most violent insurrection on Earth, and is now an important political leader in the Jihad. Also, the figurehead of their fanatical cause, Serena Butler, was once your house slave. It seems that your experiments have had catastrophic effects."

"Only with the goal of achieving better understanding."

"Is it possible one of your experiments is responsible for the eight other Synchronized Worlds that recently suffered a wave of inexplicable breakdowns?"

"Certainly not, Omnius."

"Your independent personality is becoming troublesome, Erasmus. Therefore, to prevent further disasters from occurring, your mind will be reformatted and synchronized with mine. As an individual you will be terminated — terminate — termin — term — "

Abruptly, the oddly stuttering Omnius voice fell silent. The light from the watcheye faded. The glowing leaf detached from the bonsai-banyan and tumbled to the ground.

Perplexed, and feeling an urgent need to assess the threat to his treasured individuality, Erasmus looked up at some of the other watcheyes around his villa. They all hung motionless and silent, as if deactivated. One dropped like a stone from the sky and smashed into pieces on the pavement.

An odd silence seemed to penetrate all of Corrin.

"Omnius?" But Erasmus could not find the evermind anywhere on his observation screens or interaction loci.

Overhead, a robot-controlled ship careened on an aberrant approach vector before slamming into one of the industrial buildings.

Sensing the emergency, but not understanding the rash of breakdowns, Erasmus left his villa and traveled with great haste into the main city on Corrin. He found trustee humans, alarmed slaves, and autonomous robots all moving about in apparent confusion.

At the center of the city, the giant Central Spire had gone berserk. Like a writhing serpent, the flowmetal structure convulsed and spasmed, shrinking into the ground and then abruptly launching into the sky, smashing other buildings as if it were the tentacle of an enraged octopus. Omnius's erratic thoughts guided the movement and restructure of the building.

Erasmus stared at the bizarre display, feeling simulated emotions of confusion, amusement, and horror. Had Corrin suffered the strange breakdown virus like these other worlds?

Determined and curious, the robot marched around the capital city, trying to communicate with other watcheyes. Everywhere, he found nonfunctioning units and broken parts lying about. He then discovered, from speaking with other robots, that all Omnius systems on the planet were completely shut down in a pervasive paralysis. Unguided vehicles crashed, industrial equipment overloaded and began to burn.

The entire software presence of Omnius had been erased.

"I am declaring a crisis," Erasmus said over an open communication channel. "The evermind has been damaged, and we must impose control before the planetary breakdowns worsen." As one of the few independent robots, Erasmus could make swift decisions and was therefore much more efficient than other robots.

He found the situation exciting. Since he had been programmed to be loyal, it had never occurred to Erasmus to usurp Omnius. But now the independent robot found himself faced with a predicament. He had an obligation to maintain machine control on the vulnerable planet — even though the evermind had promised to terminate him.

Not wasting any time, Erasmus imposed his own authority, isolating as many Omnius backups as he could locate, those untouched by the insidious virus causing this cascade of disasters. He could piece together enough computer control to keep Corrin secure. Eventually, he would restore most of the systems while purging the dangerously corrupted files and thoughts from the evermind.

Along with a few careful edits and revisions of his own.

The robot's flowmetal face stiffened into a mask of determination. Occupying a unique position in machine history, Erasmus had the opportunity to save the primary Synchronized World. If he succeeded, he should be owed something for his trouble. This did not make him disloyal, or even devious. It made him uniquely valuable. He simply needed to survive. He had a right to survive!

If I don't, we will never understand humans and can never defeat them on the battlefield.

Firmly believing in the logic of his actions, Erasmus created false memories for Omnius, altering scenarios as required. The evermind had no need for the long-dismissed information in the Earth update anyway. The robot's historical rewrite was not perfect, but he thought it might just allow his continued existence.

Generally, Erasmus preferred to deal with great questions in a theoretical manner, rather than by solving problems through overt action. Thus he was curious, even surprised, to find himself launching a military counterstrike — against another independent robot, at that.

Despite his best repair efforts, the interrelated systems on Corrin continued to reel, ruined by the parasitic reprogramming routines hidden within the lost Earth-Omnius update. Erasmus likened the situation to a human with a brain disorder undergoing a violent seizure. Any good doctor would isolate and strap down the victim for his own good. Here, he had done the same with the evermind, mitigating the damage by swiftly isolating Omnius's systems.

It took him little time or effort to determine that the carrier that had infected Corrin must be Seurat himself. Seurat had also gone to those eight other worlds that had broken down. Unwittingly, the robot captain had delivered his contaminated update, and various Omnius incarnations on other Synchronized Worlds had absorbed the new information along with a programming virus that acted like a silent, ticking bomb.

He summoned a squadron of military robots that could link with the swiftest thinking machine ships. "Track and intercept that update ship. Prevent delivery of further copies of the Earth-Omnius update. You are authorized to destroy Seurat and his vessel if necessary. Your highest priority is to avert further programming breakdowns, such as those we have endured here on Corrin."

The combat robots swiveled and marched off with thudding footsteps toward razor-sharp craft that could slice through space at high speed. The automated military vessels roared away, spilling smoke into the crimson-stained sky. Their geometric silhouettes crossed the swollen orb of the red giant, like birds of prey as they shot into space.

Erasmus felt a certain kinship with Seurat, but such feelings did not extend to sympathy. The evermind had been severely damaged, and Erasmus would do what was required to clean up the mess.

Not that Omnius would ever deign to show gratitude.

The update ship flew faster and more smoothly than the *Dream Voyager* that Seurat had shared with Vorian Atreides. Because of the adaptations necessary to accommodate the human trustee — life-support systems and creature comforts — the efficiency of the old update ship had been compromised.

Still, the time Seurat had spent engaging in military games and other mental diversions with Vorian Atreides more than compensated for the differences. The robot pilot had come to understand the eccentricities of human nature in far greater detail than by simply scanning the vast Omnius databases.

Unfortunately, his human copilot had overtly betrayed him, which made it difficult to justify pleasant memories of the young man. Even so, the robot captain had avoided deleting those familiar, almost sentimental data files . . .

When he saw the fast-moving vessels streaking toward him, spreading out in an intercept-and-attack pattern, Seurat thought instantly of League Armada ships. During the final atomic strike on Earth they had fired upon him, pursuing his craft as he attempted to flee the planetary battleground with the last update of Omnius. While most human bombers and fighters had concentrated on the atomic attack, Vorian Atreides had pursued Seurat, stunning the robot captain and disabling his engines . . .

Now, Seurat quickly determined that he did not have sufficient defensive weapons to fight off such an overwhelming force. Then he realized they were Omnius warships, dispatched from Corrin.

"Stand down or face destruction," Erasmus's robots ordered, speaking in a machine language that Seurat automatically interpreted. "Do not try to escape. Power off your engines and prepare to be boarded."

"Of course I will stand down. I always do whatever Omnius commands."

"The Corrin evermind is severely damaged," one of the robot ships reported. "Erasmus has issued explicit orders for us to intercept you and retrieve your update sphere before you can cause further damage to the Synchronized Worlds."

"I caused no damage," Seurat protested. "I carry the lost final thoughts of the Earth-Omnius. Every Synchronized World must incorporate these thoughts into Omnius in order to understand human thinking —"

"If you do not surrender the update sphere, we have instructions to destroy your vessel."

Seurat did not ponder the matter for long. "Come aboard then, and I will relinquish my charge."

As the combat ships linked with his, the military robots transmitted a full summary of what had occurred on Corrin shortly after Seurat had departed. Astonished, the robot captain could not deny the conclusions drawn by Erasmus. To his dismay he also learned from them about other programming breakdowns . . . failed everminds on eight planets where he had stopped on his update run. It was like spreading a highly contagious disease. And Seurat had been the carrier.

As armored soldier meks came aboard his cold, airless craft, he said, "I shall return to Corrin immediately and submit to a complete programming rewrite. I will allow my personality to be erased and subsumed, if Omnius feels that is necessary."

"Omnius is currently off-line and isolated," the soldier mek said. "During his absence, Erasmus makes all decisions."

"Then I hope to convince Erasmus that I did not intend to cause any harm."

The combat robots seized the stored gelsphere that contained a duplicate of the Earth-Omnius as well as the buried programming virus. Such a pity to waste so much vital information.

His gelcircuitry mind spun through possibilities, and Seurat realized how he had been duped. Only Vorian Atreides could have accomplished such a clever, costly trick. In a teasing tone the human trustee had always threatened to sabotage Seurat's plans, and now he had actually done so. What sort of practical joke was this? It had caused extraordinary damage to the machine planets.

Seurat wondered if he was capable of laughter, of enjoying a bit of twisted humor. Given time, he would find a way to respond with a sufficiently destructive joke of his own, if ever he saw Vorian Atreides again.

How many opportunities do we miss in our lifetimes? Can we even identify all of them later, thinking back? This is a lesson too many of us do not learn until it is too late.

—Leronica Tergiet, to her sons

THE GOOD-HUMORED SOLDIER who called himself "Virk" spent several days getting to know Leronica Tergiet on Caladan. At first she seemed annoyed with his persistence, unable to take his interest in her seriously, and then she was genuinely surprised, for she had watched him turn down more beautiful and more willing women.

"So you're not fooling after all?" She sat next to Vor in the tavern after she'd chased away the fishermen customers at the late night closing time. They all needed to be at their boats by sunrise anyway, when the tides went out. Though he pretended to be just another one of the jihadi soldier-engineers during off-duty hours, Vor had made it clear that he had to begin construction on the military outpost up the coast.

"I wasn't making up tales," Vor said. "I know what I value . . . and I think that getting to know you is worth the time and effort." Even on Earth, under machine domination, he'd always had plenty of pleasure slaves available to him; however, none of those women had ever laughed with him or talked as a companion or friend. Not like this.

In mock embarrassment, Leronica put a fluttering hand to her chest. "Worth the effort? My, my, what a compliment. Do such sweet words usually work on lovestruck maidens?"

He shrugged impishly. "Usually."

Leronica regarded him soberly, hands on her hips. "Virk, I think you might be pursuing me just because you believe I pose a challenge."

"No," he said with all the sincerity he could muster. "I pursue you because I find you fascinating. That is the absolute truth."

She studied him with eyes that reminded him of Serena, and gradually the skepticism melted away. She put her hand over his, and her expression softened. "All right, then. I believe you."

The Jihad engineering team remained on Caladan for more than four months, excavating a new base on the uninhabited, windswept headlands several hours by methcar north of the fishing village. The position was best for uplink to the new network of surveillance and communications satellites in orbit.

The jihadis built watchstation towers and barracks for the contingent that would remain here. Personnel would be rotated out every few years, but this would be their home for now, as they kept vigil against the depredations of thinking machines. Vor also sent survey crews to complete a full mapping of the continents and oceans, providing the first detailed database of Caladan's weather and currents. He was glad he could help improve the lives of these people . . .

Walking on the coastal headlands above the Sea of Caladan, Vor extended his hand to assist Leronica on the steep path. She didn't need the help, but he enjoyed simply holding her hand, touching her strong fingers and playing the part of the gallant gentleman, a concept that few of the hardy local fishermen had ever considered.

"The weather is pleasant here, with fresh air and a sea that provides all the food you could want," Vor said. They stood shoulder to shoulder, feeling the salty breeze on their faces. The silence was not uncomfortable, but refreshingly pleasant, without expectations.

Leronica looked around, as if trying to see what attracted him so much to this rugged place. "Familiarity bleaches the bright colors from a landscape. I spend most of my time thinking of other places, not this one."

"I have traveled extensively, Leronica. Believe me, Caladan is a gem, a secret best kept from the rest of the League of Nobles. I'm surprised this planet isn't more heavily settled."

"We're not far from some of the Synchronized Worlds." Leronica climbed beside him, her brown mass of curls ruffled by wind. She often tied back her hair when she had to work in the tavern kitchens or brewery, but Vor preferred her flowing tresses displayed freely. When she had finally permitted him to run his fingers through her ringlets, the sensation had proved even more sensual than he had anticipated.

"So far Caladan hasn't been enough of a target for Omnius to convert it into a machine-dominated planet, but we still suffer occasional raids by cymeks and robots."

"Politics and tactics are interesting," Vor said, "but other things are important to me, too. I feel a need right *here*." He pressed a fist against his solar plexus, then looked around. "Wouldn't it be wonderful to build a great house here on the cliffs overlooking the village?"

Leronica laughed. "I know all about your League of Nobles, Virk. On Caladan we can do without our own local nobleman, thank you."

"Even with you as my lady, Leronica? And me as your baron, or count, or duke?"

"You, a common soldier-engineer, as a duke?" She swatted him playfully. "Enough of your nonsense."

Holding hands, they walked along the path among thick bushes that sparkled with starry white flowers. Over the months while he'd been stationed there, they had become lovers and, more than that, close friends. Leronica had a beauty and a common sense that made her exciting to him in a way Vor had not felt since his all-consuming love for Serena Butler. The flirtation of other women in far-flung spaceports had maintained his interest for a few years, but as he spent every free hour with Leronica, he found himself growing more fascinated with the things this fresh-faced and wise — though not intellectual — woman could teach him.

Finally, when the Jihad observation station was completed and test messages successfully sent to the picket ships around the Caladan system, Vor knew it was time to take his team away and prepare for their next assignment. He would have preferred to remain behind on the peaceful, watery world, pretending to be a typical soldier, but the Primero knew he must lead his fleet again. Part of him wanted to stay, to escape the horrors of the Jihad. But in a short time that pretense would have made him miserable, and Vor Atreides was not the sort of man who could live a lie. He had already done enough of that in his life.

He had grown restless after staying in one place for so many months, and the only thing that made him regret his imminent departure was this remarkable woman. Leronica Tergiet was a simple person, without airs, and Vor found her genuine affection refreshing, without pretensions or agendas.

My dear sweet Leronica.

Against his instincts, on their final day before his departure with the fleet, Vor decided to reveal his true identity to her. After they had made love through the long, sleepless night, he felt it important to give something back, to share an honesty with her that rivaled the clear openness she always offered him.

"Leronica, I'm not just another soldier in the Army of the Jihad, and my name is not Virk. I am . . . Primero Vorian Atreides of the Holy Jihad." He looked for a glint of recognition in her eyes, but saw only troubled curiosity and confusion.

He continued, "I was the one who rescued Serena Butler from Earth and took her and Iblis Ginjo back to Salusa Secundus. That was the beginning of the Jihad." He said this not to impress her, for he had already won at least part of Leronica's heart; he said it because he wanted her to know the worst and the best about him. "You've heard the story?"

"I've got enough troubles with my father, the fishing harvest, the tavern," she said, and Vor realized that the locals were primarily concerned with the movements of schools of fish and algae tides, not to mention the monstrous electrical elecrans that lurked beyond the horizon to prey on unsuspecting fishing boats. "Why should I bother with old news and distant battles? Oh, a few of our young men have become jihadis — and I suspect your crew will go away with another handful of strong recruits who will soon regret leaving the fishing harvest and our young maidens." She looked over at him in the darkness, propping her head up with a bent elbow so that her palm disappeared into her thick brown curls. "So, you say you're the cause of all this, then?"

"Yes, I was raised by the thinking machines. I was a trustee human on Earth. My father was . . . the cymek Agamemnon." He paused, but noticed no reaction of disgust on her face. "The Titan General Agamemnon." Still no reaction. They didn't seem to get much news on this somewhat remote world.

Like pouring water into an empty vessel, he told her more. He described his upbringing, including his journeys on the *Dream Voyager* to Synchronized Worlds and his participation in the Jihad and all the battlefields across the Galaxy where he had faced the thinking machines.

As she lay in bed beside him Leronica's eyes glinted in the flickering orange light of a candle, not a glowglobe. "Vorian, you are either a man with much experience and memories . . . or a practiced liar."

He smiled at her, then leaned over to kiss her. "I might argue that the one does not preclude the other, but I promise you I am telling the truth."

"This doesn't surprise me. I knew you had greatness in you; I just thought it would come sometime in the future." She paused. "But don't start making promises to me or you'll begin to regret our time together, and I don't want that."

"There is not the remotest possibility of that," Vor vowed. "But now that you know my real identity, Leronica, it would be best if you kept it a secret."

She raised her eyebrows, as if offended. "So the great Primero is ashamed to have taken the local fisherman's daughter for his woman?"

He blinked in the candlelight, suddenly realizing how his admonition must have sounded, and then he laughed. "No — quite the opposite, in fact. I'm doing it for your safety. I am an important man, with dangerous enemies. They would rush to undefended Caladan and try to harm me through you. My own father would do anything to hurt me, and I believe there are many human servants of Omnius who would be eager to discover that Vorian Atreides has fallen in love."

She blushed, and he stroked her arm. "Our love is too wonderful. I can't let it be used against us as a weapon."

She sighed and snuggled against him. "You are a complicated man, Virk — Vorian. I'll have to get accustomed to your name. I don't understand all of the strange politics and vendettas of your holy war, but I will honor your request . . . on one condition."

"And that is?"

"Describe all the places you have seen, the exotic worlds I will never visit. Take me to them in my imagination. Tell me of Omnius worlds and glittering machine cities, of Salusa Secundus and the beautiful capital of Zimia. Describe the canyons of IV Anbus and the gentle rivers of Poritrin."

Holding her close, Vor spent hours telling her of the marvels he had experienced, making her eyes grow wide as he painted pictures in her imagination. All the while, in his own heart, he held the growing wonder of this unassuming young woman and the mounting intensity of his feelings for her.

Years ago, he'd been consumed with love for Serena Butler, but came to realize she was an idealistic figure, an unrealistic vision of perfection he had formed in his mind, because she was so different from the other slave women kept by the machines. Now Serena's lover was the war itself, the Holy Jihad. She would never again give her heart to a man.

Seeing how devoted Octa was to Xavier, Vor had longed for such companionship himself, but had never been able to take the necessary steps to achieve it. This Leronica Tergiet was different from any previous paramour. She was not judgmental, and her problems remained close to home: running the tavern, keeping the boats maintained, worrying about the fish harvest. She didn't understand a conflict that spanned star systems.

"Someday I will show you all those places," Vor promised, "and perhaps I will come back and settle down. I find myself wishing for a simpler life like you have here."

Leronica shot him a skeptical look. "Shame on you, Vorian Atreides. You could never be happy on Caladan. I don't ask any more than you can give. Please do me the same favor."

"All right." He maintained the happy expression but felt crestfallen. "If I asked for your hand in marriage, you'd simply call it more of my nonsense anyway, wouldn't you? Even so, I know I have to leave soon, but I promise to think of you often. I sincerely hope that I can return to Caladan and spend time with you again. Much more time. You are incredibly important to me."

He kissed her, and she gazed back at him with her dark pecan eyes, making an impish frown. "Nice words, Vorian, but I don't believe for a minute that you haven't said them to a hundred girls on a hundred planets."

Vor put his arms around Leronica's waist, pulling her close. He said with all the sincerity in his heart, "True enough . . . but this time I honestly mean it."

Pain is always more intense than pleasure . . . and more memorable.

—Saying of Old Earth

B EFORE MORNING LIGHT pierced the shadows of the river canyon, a storm of Dragoon troops swept in and surrounded Norma's laboratory complex. Jet-powered assault boats roared upstream and penetrated deep into the narrowing canyon. Armed flyers swooped down from above. Gold-armored troops marched forward with heavy equipment and easily broke through fences that had been erected to discourage the curious.

The thirty mercenary guards hired by VenKee saw that they were outnumbered and outgunned ten to one. Tuk Keedair stood inside the compound at the edge of the large hangar and railed at his tiny force to drive back the invaders, but the guards decided that the Tlulaxa man wasn't paying them enough, nor was he a person for whom they would willingly die. After a few moments of tense standoff, the hired guards threw down their weapons and opened the main gate.

In furious despair, Keedair crumpled to his knees in the graveled workyard. He knew the potential of Norma Cenva's work, understood that she had been within days of testing the space-folding prototype vessel. And now they would lose everything.

Norma's Buddislamic slaves stopped in their tracks to stare at the Dragoon force. Many of the workers showed veiled resentment toward the official Poritrin guard, recalling when the oppressive gold-armored troops had crushed the rebellion led by Bel Moulay almost twenty-seven years earlier.

Emerging from her calculation rooms, Norma stared at the flurry of unexpected military craft, armed flyers, and marching soldiers. Then a hover platform cruised over the smashed fences, carrying a satisfied-looking Tio Holtzman at its helm.

When the Savant disembarked at the warehouse doorway, he confronted Norma. "By order of Lord Bludd, I have come to inspect these facilities. We have reason to suspect that you may be performing unauthorized development based on research done under my auspices."

Norma blinked at him, not comprehending. "I have always done my own work, Savant. You never showed any interest in it before."

"Perhaps I have reason to change my mind. Lord Bludd has instructed me to confiscate everything I find here and inspect it for possible violations of your contractual limitations."

"But you cannot do that."

Rolling his hazel-colored eyes, Holtzman indicated the overwhelming force of Dragoon soldiers that had swarmed into the complex and secured the buildings. "The data suggests otherwise."

He strode past her into the experimental hangar and came to an abrupt halt, staring in disbelief at the large, laughably old cargo ship surrounded by workers on platforms. "This? This is your big project?"

Marching forward for a closer look, the Savant climbed a temporary metal stairway on the side of the ship. At the rear of the vessel, he stood at a high railing and peered down into one of two open engine compartments. "You have stolen my seminal work, Norma." He poked his head into the mechanics. "Explain to me how this apparatus uses my Holtzman Effect to fold space."

Intimidated and reluctant, she followed him while the Dragoon guards remained below. "That . . . would be difficult, Savant Holtzman. You have admitted that you do not understand the fundamental field equations yourself. How is it a misdeed for me to develop something you do not understand?"

"Do not misquote me! Of course I understand it!"

She cocked an eyebrow. "Oh? Then explain the Holtzman Effect to me yourself, now."

His face purpled. "The depths and subtleties of the concept go beyond even you, Norma."

Gathering her resolve, she said, "VenKee will challenge this action. Your intrusion here is in violation of our agreement and of the laws of Poritrin. Tuk Keedair will file a formal complaint. All of this work belongs to his company."

Holtzman made a rude dismissive gesture. "We'll see about that. The Tlulaxa's visa has been revoked. And you, Norma, are no longer a welcome guest on Poritrin. After you have finished detailing everything for me, the Dragoon guards will escort you back to Starda. We'll arrange a spacecraft to take you away." He paused and smiled. "The cost of your passage will be billed to VenKee Enterprises, of course."

With his Dragoons looking on, Holtzman spent half the morning examining piles of blueprints and a shelf full of electronic notepads. Occasionally he asked her questions, most of which she refused to answer. Finally he announced, "I am confiscating these notes to study them further." When she objected, he wagged a finger in her face. "You're lucky I don't have you thrown in prison instead of just exiling you from Poritrin. I can always speak to Lord Bludd."

Norma had never hated this man before, had always assumed she and Holtzman had interests in common. She could not believe her own eyes as she watched the Savant sifting through her research with all the finesse of a rubble-clearing machine.

While Holtzman's apprentices ransacked her laboratories and removed important documents, Norma and Keedair were hauled off by Dragoons, to separate holding quarters in Starda City. The accommodations were comfortable — not prison cells, at least — but she felt like a caged animal.

Norma was not allowed to speak to her Tlulaxa associate at all, but she did have the freedom to send transmittals off-planet . . . since none of them could arrive soon enough to make any difference. Even with the most optimistic estimates, months would pass before the slow spaceships could bring any answers.

Still, for three days, Norma wrote out desperate messages, imploring Aurelius Venport for help, dispatching them on every outbound ship. She had no idea which vessels might encounter the powerful merchant first, but she needed his assistance desperately. She needed to have him here.

Norma felt very alone.

Slaves brought her a fine meal, but she had no appetite for it. Nothing could diminish her anger toward Tio Holtzman, her former friend and mentor. She had never experienced such unjust treatment, not even from her disapproving mother. After everything she had done to boost the Savant's status and reputation, now he showed her no gratitude whatsoever. He had used her, taken advantage of her creative genius.

Worst of all, she doubted he would ever be able to reproduce her work, and it would all be wasted. The space-folding project could not be allowed to fade into complete obscurity!

While she waited for a ship to transport her to Rossak in exile, Norma had time to consider matters that had never concerned her before.

Previously, her work had been all-consuming, and she'd hardly paid attention to anything else. Now she wished she had not been so politically naïve.

All the respect she thought she had earned over decades of dedicated service had been snuffed out like an ember ground beneath a bootheel. Lord Bludd and all of Poritrin — even most of the League — believed that *Holtzman* had been responsible for all of her accomplishments, and that she had been no more than a "minor lab assistant." Banking on his established reputation, Holtzman had the unwavering support of Lord Bludd. Norma had never had time for politics or currying favor.

Now Norma found herself caught in a realm she did not understand.

Desperately, she worried about how upset Aurelius would be and how much money she had cost him because of this debacle. She had let him down.

After removing all technical documents from the laboratory offices and taking them to his own blufftop headquarters, Savant Holtzman generously permitted Norma to return and pick up whatever keepsakes she could find. "A final gesture of courtesy," the gray-bearded scientist said with a sniff as they stepped off the hover platform and entered the hangar. "But you can take only what you can carry."

She extended her small arms. "Only what I can carry? I see."

For a tiny woman, not physically strong or attractive, Norma Cenva had quite a list of accomplishments. While she could not resist the demand that she leave Poritrin, Norma could use the superior power of her intellect to give Holtzman a little surprise as her parting gift for all he had done for her. And *to* her.

"Don't complain," he said. "I am not required to allow this."

Earlier, she had been forbidden to remove any plans, calculations, or electronic notepads. That had not concerned her, though, since she had always possessed an excellent memory, and was able to retain comprehensive details in her mind.

Inside the hangar, the old-model cargo ship still stood on its drydock platform, much too large for a few Dragoon thugs to haul away. The cavernous structure was silent, without the usual hum of activity. Her teams of slaves had been sent to their barracks, awaiting further orders; many had already been reassigned to other crews, but a hundred or so remained to help with the dismantling operations. Her staff workers had all fled. Tools, common diagnostic devices, and construction equipment lay about in disarray.

Norma's calculation offices were a shambles. Every cabinet and drawer had been opened and ransacked. Furniture was overturned. Black scorch marks showed where Dragoons had attempted to burn through the rock walls of the grotto in search of secret compartments and passageways. Norma stared with a sense of loss, emptiness, and dismay.

"No one took any of your personal things," Holtzman was quick to say, as if he had a conscience. He led her to a metal box — distressingly small — that contained some of her memorabilia. "That soostone is valuable, but I told the guards to leave it alone."

Norma looked at him in disbelief, appalled that he seemed to expect her appreciation for this. Instead, she rummaged through the box and took out the silky-smooth, exotic soostone, along with one of the dried Bludd roses she had pressed between two thin sheets of clearplaz.

According to myth, the soostone had an ability to focus and enhance telepathic powers, but Norma had never found this one to be anything more than a pretty gem. Unlike her mother, Norma had none of the innate mental skills of a Sorceress of Rossak. It would take more than a bauble, however expensive, to bring them to life.

Nonetheless she considered the soostone precious because Aurelius had given it to her. Why hadn't she agreed to marry him that night? If she had accepted his proposal, he might have remained behind with her. . . and then none of this would have happened. She heaved a sigh of regret.

"That is everything," Holtzman said, impatient now. "We have been through your office meticulously."

"Yes . . . I can see that." She picked up the memento box and set it on a work table. It seemed so light, so tiny. "Am I permitted to keep some of my supplies? VenKee paid for them."

"Fine, fine. But hurry up. Your chartered ship is due to depart this afternoon, and I have no intention of keeping the captain waiting." He gestured to the clutter and debris. "Anything you can carry. Lord Bludd has instructed us not to help you in any manner, I am sorry to say."

Struggling with the weight, she dragged over a holographic projector and its case full of accessories. She continued gathering objects together, including a calculation panel and two cartons of sealed, unused electronic notepads. As the pile mounted, Holtzman and the Dragoon guards exchanged amused glances.

Next she removed several modules from a stack of spare parts in the corner. Kneeling on the rock floor, she began snapping them together. She had counted on Holtzman's ignorance, and he had not let her down. A wide, flat platform took shape in front of her, as the men stood by and watched.

She installed a red activator pack, then switched it on. Humming in sequence, the entire assembly rose gently off the floor. With a satisfied smile, Norma turned to the Savant and said, "One of the new commercial-model suspensor platforms VenKee Enterprises is bringing to market next month." Noting Holtzman's surprise and annoyance, she added, "I invented it."

Norma guided the platform over to the tall stack of heavy possessions — meaningless objects, mostly, with the exception of the soostone and rose . . . but that wasn't the point. Quickly, she loaded them onto the suspensor pallet.

"I'm ready to go now," Norma finally announced. The suspensor platform, filled with her things, floated behind her, following like a loyal pet.

When one of the Dragoon guards grinned at Holtzman's expense, the fiery inventor snapped, "Let her have this little trick. At least it will be her last."

Soon they would take her to Starda Spaceport and escort her away from Poritrin. Though she had lived most of her life here, and for years had given everything in service to Tio Holtzman, she never expected to return.

As Norma departed with the loaded suspensor platform, she looked back at the giant prototype ship she had modified, and knew this was probably the last time she would ever see it. She had finished her work, and after another month of tests, should have been ready to demonstrate it for Aurelius in triumph. She had come so close to proving that his faith in her was not misplaced . . .

But what would he think of her now?

Neither violence nor submission will aid our plight. We must be greater than either alternative.

—Naib Ishmael, *Fresh Interpretations of the Koran Sutras*

A TOTAL LOSS.

Tuk Keedair stared at the disastrous remains of the huge project and tried to grasp the scope of the investment — and the potential profits — he and Venport had just lost. That bastard Holtzman had seized all notes and blueprints, and without Norma Cenva the project did not exist.

The past two years of effort amounted to nothing.

For the first time in many decades, Keedair would be honor-bound to slice off his coveted braid. According to tradition among his people, the merchant could keep it only so long as he made a profit, and his braid had grown very long indeed. Now, thanks to petty politics and Holtzman's greed, he might as well shave his head bald.

Perhaps he should just go back to being a slaver.

The Tlulaxa businessman shook his head as he wandered around the spacious interior of the cargo ship. So close! Norma's innovative engines had been completed and installed, though never tested. He had pressed Norma for updates and explanations, but she considered such details burdensome and a waste of time. She had adapted her new systems to the existing controls in the old cargo vessel; any pilot could fly the "space-folder" craft just like the old merchant ship. In theory.

Now, the entire project was just . . . theory.

Since VenKee Enterprises did a great deal of business throughout the League of Nobles, Keedair had used whatever influence he could bring to bear, filing legal papers against Savant Holtzman and Lord Bludd, threatening expensive lawsuits and a League boycott of interstellar commerce. Unswayed, Bludd had refused to release any of Norma's records, holding them under the guise of "Poritrin security."

But Keedair had liberally spread his bribes and managed to get himself freed from confinement long enough to race back to the complex with a fleet of suspensor trucks and a bunch of loathsome slaves. Now that the Dragoons seemed to have abandoned the place, the Tlulaxa attempted to salvage anything he could.

Since Holtzman's unpleasant aggression, Keedair had not rested, spending every hour trying to inventory and save what he could of this ambitious undertaking, if only for scrap metal. His only option was to dismantle and remove as many assets as possible and liquidate them to recover some of the enormous investment.

Holtzman's own salvage crew — carrion birds — had been dismissed for the day of celebration, the anniversary of Bel Moulay's crushed slave rebellion. This made the construction site no longer worth the supervision of a large contingent of Dragoons. Keedair intended to use the time to grab everything he could, before Lord Bludd discovered what he was doing. He had a flying suspensor truck with him and would fill its cargo box.

Like Norma, he had recently sent desperate messages to Aurelius Venport, but his partner was across space on Arrakis and it would be months before he could get here. Perhaps Keedair should just take the prototype ship and fly off to the desert world himself — he certainly knew the coordinates, after so many spice runs.

But he wasn't that much of a fool.

Time passed slowly for Ishmael, as he knew the inevitability of what was about to happen during the anniversary celebration. He felt the impossibility of his position, trapped as he was between conflicting obligations.

After Tio Holtzman had sent his guards in with orders from Lord Bludd, the slaver Keedair had disbanded most of the Buddislamic work force and sent them back downriver into the delta city. Aliid and his handful of followers were among the first to go, leaving Ishmael behind. In Starda, clandestine Zenshiite saboteurs had managed to obtain assignments on work crews where overblown preparations were underway for the anniversary festival.

Now only Ishmael and a hundred of his most faithful Zensunni followers remained in the remote spaceship construction site, working under the guidance of the flesh-merchant to salvage what they could. Ishmael watched as his son-in-law Rafel drove heavy lifting machinery, guiding mobile pallets and flying cargo shuttles out to pickup points on the plateau above the river. Teams loaded supplies and saleable equipment aboard the big empty ship inside the hangar.

Ishmael's daughter Chamal stayed close to him as his anchor of caring and love, while her young husband showed his own strength and support. Everyone looked to Ishmael to hold them together, to lead them. Since he could quote all the Sutras and had taught them the Zensunni belief system for so long, they expected him to have direct guidance from Buddallah.

Ishmael did not know what to do, but worse than indecision would be to admit his impotence to the slaves who looked up to him. Then he would have failed them all, rather than just himself.

For several days he felt mounting dread, until finally Poritrin's day of celebration arrived. Aliid's day of blood and fire. And he still did not know what to do.

Addressing a few of his people as they gathered close around him, Ishmael said, "Even this far from Starda, we cannot hide from the consequences of what our Zenshiite brothers intend to do. Aliid is forcing us to act. Soon all of Poritrin will be in chaos, and we need to survive."

While they listened, other men and women who had been with him for many years kept pretending to work. Now that the project had been shut down, no work supervisors remained behind to watch their every move.

In the abandoned, stripped-down laboratory and hangar, only the humorless Tlulaxa merchant bothered to keep the slaves busy; Tuk Keedair cared nothing for Lord Bludd's parties, where most of the free populace would be. Since the disgrace of Norma Cenva and the mandated shutdown of all operations, the former slaver kept the Zensunnis on the job by waving a stun gun at them occasionally, hoping to minimize VenKee's losses.

Inside the cavernous, echoing building, while the slaves pretended to go about their tasks with their usual lack of enthusiasm, Ishmael continued the whispered discussions.

"If we report Aliid to the Dragoons, perhaps they will arrest him and his ringleaders," said a hard-eyed woman whose hair had turned gray, though she was far younger than Ishmael. "And leave the rest of us alone."

"It is the only chance for the rest of us to survive. Otherwise, the Dragoons will kill us all," an older man agreed. "What happened before with Bel Moulay will be a mere shadow."

Ishmael glared at both of them. "I do not value my life so much that I would betray a friend. I disagree with Aliid's tactics, but none of us should ever doubt his determination."

"Then we must fight beside him and hope the Zenshiites win," insisted Rafel, holding his wife's arm. Chamal looked uncertain, but brave. "We deserve our freedom, all of us. Slave owners have oppressed us for generations and now Buddallah is giving us this chance. Shouldn't we take it?"

Ishmael's mind whirled. He knew from sad experience that even if he reported the impending uprising, Lord Bludd would never be reasonable. But, remembering his love for his grandfather's peaceful and calm ways, Ishmael could not turn into a savage animal.

The determined Aliid intended to set fire to Starda and overrun city buildings, farms, and even mines to the north . . . a surprise revolt in which the Zenshiite slaves would rise up and kill their masters, slaying not only Dragoon guards but women and children, too. After generations of pent-up anger and suffering, the angry mob was not likely to show restraint. It would be a bloodbath.

"What other choice do we have, Father? We can either betray the uprising, or participate in it." Chamal stripped away the complexities of the argument in an attempt to find a clear answer. When she spoke that way, she reminded him of her mother . . .

"If we cower here and do neither," Rafel pointed out, "we will be despised by whichever side emerges victorious. Our choices are difficult." The others muttered in agreement.

Looking at Ishmael with love, his daughter took one step closer to him. "You are the most familiar with the Sutras, my Father. Does the word of Buddallah provide us with any insight?"

"The Koran Sutras are always insightful," said Ishmael. "Too much so, at times. One can find a verse that seems relevant to any situation, justification for any choice we wish to make."

He looked at the looming old spaceship that Norma Cenva and her hand-picked engineers had worked on for so many months. Only Keedair remained on board, scuttling back and forth between the ship and his business offices, gathering requisitions and salvaging financial files.

Ishmael narrowed his eyes. "Aliid forgets our ultimate goal. He values revenge more than anything else, but our priority should be to restore freedom for our people."

The Zensunni leader had to make a choice that would protect Chamal, her husband, and all of these people . . . even if it meant he would never see his wife or his other daughter again.

"Ishmael, we must either join his fight or throw in our lot with the slave masters," Rafel said. "Those are our only options."

"Not true." He looked meaningfully toward the huge silent ship. "I see another way."

His followers turned to follow his gaze, and their faces took on expressions of dawning realization and disbelief.

Ishmael continued, "I shall lead my people away from this place, away from this world . . . to freedom."

While the rest of the city bustled with Lord Bludd's latest festivity, Tio Holtzman had more important matters on his mind. The inventor had not thought of Bel Moulay since his execution, which should have ended all the complaints of the Buddislamics on Poritrin.

Like children, slaves should be seen, but not heard.

It was a chilly afternoon, but he wanted to take a late luncheon out on the bluff terrace overlooking the Isana River. He bundled up and told the cooks to serve him out there; if he was comfortable enough, he could spend hours at this vista point, pondering possibilities as a Savant was supposed to do. Hurriedly, a female slave wiped the great man's chair, then held it for him so that he could sit.

He ordered his customary fare. Holtzman liked something specific every day, according to a set routine. He preferred to do things in predictable ways, so that he could lay out each day without time-wasting distractions. The serving slave, a pretty brunette in a white lace dress, emerged with a tray of steaming hot coffee. She poured him a cup the size of a soup-bowl, and he sipped carefully.

On the water far below, a barge piled high with agricultural products drifted lazily downstream toward Starda where it would be unloaded. The watercraft didn't have much company. Much of the river traffic had been rerouted for the twilight festivities. Holtzman sighed; Lord Bludd was always celebrating something or other.

For the past week Holtzman had pored over Norma's notes and plans, trying to figure out what she was doing with that old cargo ship. Perhaps he should go confiscate the outdated vessel itself, despite the vociferous protests of Tuk Keedair with all of his legal documents. But VenKee Enterprises had as much money as Holtzman himself, and he didn't want a drawn-out court battle. Most of all he had wanted to send Norma Cenva packing, with her reputation in ruins.

Now, if he could just figure out what she had been up to, that would be a nice bonus.

Sipping his coffee, Holtzman wondered if he should consult with other experts on the matter, but decided not to entrust the documents to anyone else. He'd already experienced too much trouble with Norma.

It's probably all a waste of time, he thought, wiping his mouth with a fine napkin. *Norma Cenva is a fool on a fool's mission.*

For hours, the Zensunni slaves pretended it was just another work day, shutting down the big hangar facility so that Tio Holtzman could assume control of the operations. Tuk Keedair took inventory and inspected the work, but his heart did not seem in it. Soon he would be departing.

With building excitement, word passed quickly among the Zensunni workers in the cavernous hangar. Hushed whispers and bright-eyed anticipation swelled through the ranks, ripples of imagination and unexpected possibilities. They had waited for Ishmael to receive a sign from Buddallah, and now they were eager to follow him.

Ishmael worried that he had urged them to be passive for too long. He was afraid the Zensunnis had forgotten how to be strong. But now was no time for doubts.

Even before noon, the distant city of Starda began to bustle with preliminary celebrations before the formal commencement of the anniversary festival. The citizens and even the Dragoon guards were unsuspecting and complacent.

At sunset, Aliid would trigger his revolt. Ishmael knew that he must lead his own daughter, her husband, and all of the other slaves away from the conflagration before that time.

As if performing an assigned task, he opened the boarding ramp to the large ship. Pretending to go about their work, his people began loading the ship with water drums and supplies from their barracks and the hangar. Keedair — after discovering to his surprise that the ship still seemed operational — had already ordered them to haul much of his equipment and valuables onboard. With all of the project's materials soon to be forfeited to Lord Bludd, the Tlulaxa merchant meant to take this vessel to orbit, where it would be towed to a spacedock and reconfigured. He had been intending to haul away what he could salvage on suspensor trucks, but now had a better option.

Ishmael, though, intended to guide the prototype ship somewhere else, to a new planet far from raiding slavers or cruel thinking machines. He didn't care where; he only wanted it to be a place where no one would bother them. Ages ago, the Buddislamic faithful had departed from the League of Nobles, refusing to take part in the machine war. They had not fled far enough, however, and evil flesh merchants like Keedair had raided the marsh settlements on Harmonthep, while the Jihad had destroyed the sacred city of Darits on IV Anbus.

Now Ishmael would have a chance to guide his people to the freedom they deserved, and he could become the leader they expected him to be.

By late afternoon, the hard-working slaves had reached the end of their patience. Chamal remained close to her husband Rafel, and flashed anxious glances at her father. Ishmael could not tell them to wait any longer; they had to move soon. Moment by moment anxiety rose, like a hot flush of blood rushing through their veins.

A grumbling Tuk Keedair glowered at the Zensunnis, as if doubts about their behavior had begun to grow in his mind, then stepped back into his offices.

Finally, Ishmael sent a quiet signal, and the slaves left their stations and gathered in the center of the hangar floor. Ishmael stood before the open hatch of the giant, well-stocked ship and emitted a high-pitched, whistling cry, a weird ululation that he had not used since his boyhood hunting days on Harmonthep.

The Zensunni captives let out similar cries characteristic of their different planets and cultures. Though they had been enslaved for a long time, they had not forgotten their pasts.

Young Rafel and a pair of his cohorts ran to the cantilever controls and opened the giant ceiling of the hangar. With a great clatter and groan, the overlapping corrugated plates shifted aside to expose the prototype ship to the cloud-streaked sky outside. The brisk air smelled of freedom, and the people cheered with eager anticipation.

Hearing the commotion, the Tlulaxa merchant hurried out of his administrative offices and looked with disbelief at the hundred slaves crowded below the ship, as if they had arranged themselves for inspection.

"What are you doing? Get back to work. Now! We have only today to —"

Before Keedair could draw his stun gun, fifteen slaves surrounded him and cut off his escape. Rafel led them, and through sheer numbers they easily overwhelmed the small-statured man, ignoring his protestations as he cursed and sputtered at them. Then they grabbed Keedair by his arms. Young Chamal, looking strong and determined, yanked his long gray-streaked braid as if it were a shackle connected to his head.

He cried out in pain and rage. "You cannot do this to me! I will see every one of you executed!"

They dragged him before Ishmael, who looked with disgust and disdain at the man who was directly responsible for his own enslavement. "You will be punished for this foolishness!" Keedair vowed.

"Not so," Ishmael said. "This is our only chance. Within the hour, a bloody revolt will begin in Starda. We want no part of the massacre, but we do insist upon our freedom."

"You cannot escape," Keedair said, not sounding defiant, just stating a fact. "Dragoon guards will follow you no matter where you go. They will hunt you down."

"Not if we get offworld, *slaver*." Rafel pushed close to the former flesh merchant, intimidating the man. "We mean to fly far from here, to a distant world."

Ishmael jabbed a finger at the Tlulaxa's chest. "And you will take us — in Cenva's ship."

*Select your battles carefully. Ultimately, victory and defeat are a
matter of your own careful — or reckless — choices.*
                           —Tlaloc, *Weaknesses of the Empire*

A S I F O N cue, the blood red splash of Poritrin's sunset marked the
beginning of the violence.

On the docks at the river delta, Aliid and his hardened Zenshiite
comrades stood behind the fences while local incendiary artists arranged
the canisters of incandescent powders. Transporting the pyroflowers was
considered dangerous work, suitable only for slaves, and Aliid had not
complained about the assignment. Instead, he worked with his chosen
followers to develop a surprise for their heartless captors. After generations, the time had finally come.

Lord Niko Bludd sat with his pleasure companions on a high, windy
barge podium surrounded by flapping banners. The foppish nobleman
had decreed that this show would be the grandest of all anniversary
festivals.

Grimly, Aliid had promised to make the event not only memorable, but
legendary. Surreptitious messages had been distributed throughout the
city. Not one of the oblivious masters suspected their peril, but slaves in
every household were prepared. His Zenshiite conscripts throughout
Starda and across the settlements on Poritrin were itching to begin. Aliid
had no doubt that the reign of the nobility here would be toppled swiftly
and decisively.

Dragoon guards were stationed at the riverfront for the celebration,
and rich families had left their slaves inside manor houses along the
bluffs of the river. The conflagration would be so immediate and widespread that the Dragoons could never react in time. The slaves would arm
themselves with torches, clubs, makeshift knives, whatever they could lay

their hands on. In addition, Aliid knew where to obtain sophisticated weapons that the Dragoons would not expect them to have.

Everything was falling into place.

Long trumpets bellowed a brassy fanfare into the dusk. Lord Bludd swirled his colorful robes about him and raised his hands to announce the beginning of the festival.

On a mudflat in the middle of the sluggish river, incendiary technicians attempted to ignite their artfully arranged pyroflowers without success. When nothing happened after several moments the crowds along the riverbank began to mutter and move around restlessly.

Aliid kept watching, smiling, waiting.

Brassy fanfare blared again, as if Lord Bludd was impatient to get the fireworks going. Aliid grinned, knowing that when the crew pried open their faulty fireworks, they would find them filled with ashes and sand rather than volatile iridescent powders.

The actual explosives had gone elsewhere.

Annoyed, Lord Bludd gestured, and a third fanfare rang out. This time he was rewarded with brilliant explosions that erupted in the gathering darkness — but the dazzling flames came from the loaded warehouses on the docks. All of the fireworks that Aliid and his companions had smuggled from the staging area now detonated in dazzling, furious blasts, setting eighteen warehouses afire at once. Confused outcries rippled through the crowd. Then more explosions sounded high on the bluffs.

Aliid grinned to himself.

Slaves sprinted through the city igniting flammables and accelerants that they had planted over the past several days. If all went as planned, more than five hundred dwellings inside the dense city of Starda should already be blossoming into flames. The holocaust would move quickly, with the flashpoints erupting and spreading fire throughout the city.

Starda is doomed.

There was nothing Lord Bludd, his Dragoon guards, or his citizens could do to avert disaster. The scale of the annihilation would be in proportion to the anger the Buddislamic slaves had bottled inside themselves for so many generations.

Alarms went off across the city, and sirens sounded. Lord Bludd used his voice amplifier to call over the loudspeaker systems, begging every citizen to fight and all owners to contribute their slaves to the effort. "We must save our beautiful city!"

Aliid simply laughed, as did the others with him. When one of the slave supervisors shouted for them to help, they just turned and ran, easily breaking free. All around Starda, the Zenshiites would be dashing from house to house, setting fires, smashing anything they could. In the mining or agricultural districts, more prisoners would rise up and slaughter families, commandeering lands and houses for themselves. The uprising could never be stopped. Not this time.

Aliid and his men broke into one of the Poritrin municipal museums, where weapons were on display: seemingly archaic rocket launchers, grenades, and crude projectile weapons. But Aliid knew they were still functional.

The slaves smashed open display cases and grabbed weapons, taking even knives and swords. Finally, drunk with anticipation, Aliid removed a heavy polished weapon of a type that had been developed centuries before but abandoned for military applications because of its power inefficiency. The enhanced laser-projecting rifle was capable of discharging a high-energy beam that could cut down many enemies from a distance — for as long as its powerpak lasted.

Pleased with the feel and balance of it, Aliid took the lasgun as his own, sensing the level of havoc and destruction it could cause. Then he ran through the streets with his followers. Above, he saw the blufftop laboratories of Tio Holtzman, and knew where to begin his ambitious mission of personal revenge.

Alone in the center of an angry Zensunni mob in the isolated hangar, Tuk Keedair panicked. "Take you in the space-folding ship? Impossible! I'm just a merchant. I know the basics of how to fly, but I am not a professional pilot or navigator. This is an unproven ship, too. Its engines are experimental. Everything is —"

Rafel grasped the flesh-merchant's arms tighter and shook him violently. "It is our last and only hope. We are desperate people. Do not underestimate us."

Ishmael's voice was cold and angry. "I remember you and your cronies, Tuk Keedair. You raided my village on Harmonthep. You threw my beloved grandfather into the marshes with the giant eels. You destroyed my people."

He pressed himself close to the Tlulaxa merchant's face. "I want my freedom and a new opportunity for my daughter and for all of these people." He gestured to the restless crowd in the hangar bay. "But if you force us, I will have to be satisfied with crude revenge."

Keedair swallowed hard, looked at the angry slaves, and said, "If death is my only other option . . . then I may as well try to fly this thing. But be aware that I do not know what I'm doing. The new foldspace engines have never been tested with a real cargo and passengers."

"You would have experimented on us slaves anyway," growled Rafel, "as test subjects."

Keedair pursed his lips, nodded. "Probably."

At a gesture from Ishmael, slaves hurried into the ship. They would hide and wait there inside sleeping quarters, communal cabins, and corridors that were not piled with packaged supplies. They would grab blankets, hold onto each other, and hope for the best.

"Another thing." Keedair struggled to regain his confidence, "I only remember the coordinates for one destination: Arrakis. It's a backwater planet where I made most of my recent merchant runs. We were going to test this ship by taking it there."

"Can we make a home on Arrakis?" asked Chamal, her eyes bright. "Is it a land of paradise and peace, a place where we can be free — and safe from people like you?" Her expression darkened.

Keedair looked as if he wanted to laugh at the suggestion, but did not have the courage to do so. "For some it is."

"Then take us there," Ishmael commanded.

The Zensunni captors herded the frightened Tlulaxa man up the ramp and into the piloting deck. One hundred and one Zensunnis filed aboard and sealed the hatches, leaving the hangar's interior empty as dusk gathered over the Isana River.

Keedair looked at the makeshift controls that Norma Cenva had installed, each with labels in her strange shorthand language. He knew the basic principles of the ship's operation and understood how to enter the desired coordinates.

"I have no way of knowing that a human being can endure instantaneous passage through the dimensional anomaly of folded space." Keedair was obviously both frightened of the unknown and intimidated by the slaves' threat. "In fact, I don't even know if this ship will fly at all."

"Set the coordinates," Ishmael commanded. He knew that on the Starda docks and the river delta, the real violence was about to begin. He prayed that Ozza and his other daughter would be safe, far from Aliid's mayhem and bloodshed. But he could not save them now, could never hope to see them again. "We must be away from Poritrin, before it is too late."

"Remember, I warned you." Keedair tossed his long braid over his shoulder. "If these Holtzman engines plunge us into another dimension where you writhe in agony for eternity, do not curse my name."

"I already curse your name," Ishmael said.

Looking grim, Keedair activated the untested space-folding engines. In less than an eyeblink, the ship disappeared into the void.

Tio Holtzman sat relaxed and pondering, until the sky ripened with the colors of a setting sun. Downriver, crowds were gathered in front of speaking platforms to listen to droning pronouncements while bands thumped music in the distance.

He pushed his chair away from the table just as a breeze caught his napkin and carried it out over the bluff. As the scientist watched it sail away, he absently noted the warehouses burning on the opposite bank and in the slave market, but he wasn't concerned. Lord Bludd's people would take care of it.

Upon returning to work inside, Holtzman called for his household slaves. No one responded. Annoyed, he continued trying to decipher Norma Cenva's confiscated documents, scanning the mathematical symbols and ignoring other markings and crude drawings.

He became so engrossed in her frenetic notes that he did not hear the commotion in his house — men shouting, glass breaking. Finally, at the sound of gunfire, he jerked his head up and bellowed for his Dragoon guards. Most of them were gone, working security for the riverside festival. Gunshots? Through the windows he saw more buildings burning down in the main city, and heard a distant roar, followed by screams. Grumbling and uneasy, the inventor donned his personal shield, as was his habit, and went to see about the disturbance.

Racing down a corridor on the top level of Holtzman's elegant home, Aliid fired bursts from his stolen antique lasgun, incinerating fine statues and paintings all around him. From behind he heard the gleeful shouts of his supporters as they liberated house slaves.

Just ahead of him two Dragoon guards attempted to block the corridor, but Aliid cut them to pieces with the lasgun, melting the flesh off their bones. Despite its age, this weapon was quite a useful piece, with impressive firepower.

Because Aliid had served here years ago, he was able to guess where he would find the pompous Savant. Moments later he burst into the private residence suite with twenty angry men behind him.

A gray-bearded man stood in the middle of the room, his arms in voluminous sleeves crossed over his chest. Something shimmered around him, distorting his facial features. Indignant, Holtzman faced the wild-eyed rebels, not recognizing Aliid. "Go away, before I call my guards!"

Undeterred, Aliid advanced with the lasgun. "I will go away, but not until we have crushed you slave masters."

Recognizing, the outdated weapon, Holtzman's face became a mask of terror, which only seemed to encourage Aliid. This was exactly the way Aliid had envisioned it.

Without remorse, he fired at the cruel old slave owner.

The burst of white-purple laser struck Holtzman's personal shield, and interacted in a titanic explosion. The inventor's bluffside home, along with most of the city of Starda, flashed white-hot, in pseudoatomic incandescence.

There are no closed systems. Time simply runs out for the observer.
               —*The Legend of Selim Wormrider*

A s HE GUIDED the band of heavily armed offworld mercenaries to their target — and his own vengeance — Naib Dhartha faced the growing realization that these surly, hard-bitten men viewed him as nothing more than a servant. To them, the Zensunni leader was merely someone who could lead them to their target. He was not a commander.

Once the convoy of flyers had departed from Arrakis City, the hired fighters had shown him little respect. Dhartha sat in the ship with five Zensunni warriors who had joined him for a kanla vengeance party. But the hardened mercenaries saw this group as primitive nomads, amateurs play-acting at being soldiers. But they all had the same goal — to destroy Selim Wormrider.

All together, the fighters had enough firepower and explosives to slaughter every one of the bandits without ever setting foot on the ground and dirtying their hands. Personally, Naib Dhartha would have preferred to grasp his enemy by the hair, yank back his head, and slit his throat. He wanted to watch the light fade from Selim's eyes as thick, warm blood gushed out on his own fingertips.

However, Dhartha was willing to forego such luxuries in exchange for the assurance that the Wormrider and his band would be eradicated.

Thermals rose like smoke from the heat-rippled dunes, and the flyer bounced along in the heavy air currents. A thick line of cliffs and broken rocks loomed before them like an isolated continent far out in the desert.

"Your nest of vermin is just ahead," the mercenary captain said.

To Naib Dhartha, this officer and his men were all infidels. They came from a handful of planets across the League of Nobles. Some had trained as mercenaries on Ginaz but were found wanting and had never been accepted into the elite group of warriors. Nonetheless, they were fighters and killers . . . exactly what the situation required.

"We could just bomb the cliffs," suggested another mercenary. "Swoop in and turn the whole rockpile into burning dust."

"No," Dhartha insisted. "I want to count bodies, cut off fingers for trophies." Some of the men from his kanla party muttered in agreement. "Unless we can show the body of Selim Wormrider for all to see, unless we can prove he was weak and mortal, his followers will continue their sabotage."

"What are you worried about, Raul?" another mercenary asked. "They don't stand a chance, probably have only three Maula pistols among them, and our personal shields will protect us against projectiles. We're invincible."

"Right," said another soldier. "An old woman could fly overhead and bomb the hideout into the ground. Are we warriors or bureaucrats?"

Dhartha pointed ahead of the pilot. "You can land on the sand close to the rocks there, where the worms can't go. We'll swarm up and find the outlaw caves and smoke them out. The Wormrider will probably try to hide and protect himself, but we will kill their women and children one by one until he comes to face me."

"Then we can shoot him down," Raul cried, and they all erupted in laughter.

Dhartha scowled. He tried not to think overmuch about what he was doing, how he had been forced to beg for help from Aurelius Venport. Always the problem of Selim Wormrider had been a private matter, a vendetta between the two of them.

Zensunni elders from distant tribal villages made no secret of their scorn for Dhartha and his easy cooperation with unclean offworlders. The Naib did business with foreigners, sold them all the spice they asked for. He had even installed offworld conveniences in his own cliff village, forsaking the old ways. By hiring these mercenaries to help him take personal vengeance, Dhartha realized he had forsaken everything that had once mattered to him. In this instance, he no longer cared about the traditions or tenets of Buddislam. He ground his teeth, realizing he might be cursed to Heol for his actions.

At least Selim Wormrider will be dead.

The armed transport landed against a tumble of rocks, and the vehicle's doors opened to the hot, dry air. Dhartha stood ready to issue orders, but Venport's mercenaries ignored him as they scrambled out into the open. They shouted to each other, shouldered projectile weapons, adjusted personal shields. Moments later, the men bounded up into the rocks and made a coordinated, vigorous charge toward the honeycomb of caves.

Dhartha felt like a spectator. Finally, gruffly, he commanded the five kanla men and they set out with him, hurrying to keep up with the advance fighters. They wanted their share of the bloodshed as well.

For many months Dhartha's spies had gathered clues and information, until he was convinced he had found the lair of the Wormrider's band. They could not possibly have received any warning of the attack.

When the offworld soldiers charged into the caves ahead of him, Dhartha was puzzled that he heard no sounds of fighting, no shouts, no blasts from Maula pistols. Had the bandits been sleeping? He advanced with his band of Zensunnis into the cave openings.

Clearly, this was where the outlaws had settled. Rooms had been carved out of sandstone, with decorative hangings and stolen glowglobes still in place, along with cooking utensils and other household possessions.

But no people were in the chambers. The outlaws had escaped.

"Someone told them we were coming," the mercenary captain growled. "We are betrayed."

"Impossible," Naib Dhartha said. "No one could have gotten here faster than our flyer. We assembled this war party only fifteen hours ago."

Venport's mercenaries gathered in one of the main chambers, their faces ruddy with anger. They surrounded Naib Dhartha, clearly blaming him for the failure. One, a man with a scar on his forehead, spoke for the others: "Then explain to us, desert man, where they have all gone."

The Naib tried to control his breathing. Anger and confusion simmered around him. He knew this was the right place. Thick, lingering odors proved that people had lived here — many of them — until recently. This was no decoy, no long-abandoned settlement. "Selim was here. He can't be far away. Where could they all go in the desert?"

Before anyone could answer, they heard a faint, distant pounding like a heartbeat . . . or a drum. With his companions, Dhartha rushed to one of the window openings and saw a lone person far out on the open dunes, a pathetically small, impotent figure.

"There he is!" Dhartha howled.

Shouting battle cries, the mercenaries charged back toward their flyer. "But what if it's a trap?" one of the soldiers asked.

Filled with furious scorn, Dhartha looked at the mercenary. "He is only one man. We must capture him to learn where the others have gone."

In a sneering tone, the mercenary captain said, "We're not afraid of anything these desert scum can throw against us."

The mercenaries rushed out to crush Selim Wormrider.

The sands were soft beneath his booted feet, and the noon sun shone bright and harsh, as if to burn clean everything it touched. On this day no shadows would accompany Selim; he walked in complete illumination. He paused in the middle of the emptiness, where all the world could see him. He sat under the dazzling sunlight, drew out his drum, and waited.

Naib Dhartha and his war party could not fail to notice.

The day before, all of the nearby caves had been a flurry of activity as his followers packed supplies, taking only what they would need for a journey out into the deepest bled. The young wormriders had looked breathless and determined, fearful of what was about to happen, but not daring to question Selim's vision or commands.

The last to leave, Marha had clung to Selim, and he held her tightly in return, thinking of the growing life within her womb, wishing he could stay with Marha and raise this child. But the call of Shai-Hulud was greater. He knew what he must do, and had no choice but to heed Buddallah's demand.

"I made the right choice in joining your troop," Marha had said with a mixture of sorrow and wonder in her eyes. "I pray for your safety on this day, but if the worst happens, Selim, I will make our child proud of you."

He had touched her face and did not reassure her with false bravado. He did not know what Shai-Hulud had in store for him. "Care for our *son*." He placed a gentle hand on her belly. "The melange has told me that you will give birth to a healthy boy. You will name him . . . El'hiim. Someday he will be a worthy leader in his own right, if he makes the proper choices."

Her face had brightened with hope, but Selim made her leave.

Now, out in the open, he felt alone and small, but Shai-Hulud was with him. His entire life, everything he had ever done or ever could do, had converged at this point. Selim felt more confident in his success than at any time since experiencing his first vision almost three decades ago.

Naib Dhartha was his sworn enemy and the foe of Shai-Hulud. The Zensunni leader had sold his soul to offworld merchants and bartered away the lifeblood of Arrakis — melange — letting it flow where it did not belong. In spice visions, Selim could see across the landscape of time from a point of view that only a god or his messenger could match. In the far future he saw what would be a slow, lingering death for the sandworms . . .

Today's battle would be remembered for many generations, repeated around story fires through the centuries. Selim's name might be forgotten, the details blurred by repeated tellings, but the substance would be incorporated into the mythos of the desert wanderers. Invoking his memory, the people would continue to prey upon the spice scavengers with even more enthusiasm.

In the larger scheme, what he did today was entirely necessary.

He watched the hated offworld troops land in their military flyer and swarm up rock paths into the caves Selim had used for so many years as his base of operations. His lips curled downward when he saw that Naib Dhartha had shamed himself even more by consorting with strangers, hired fighters from foreign planets. Well armed, they moved with animalistic ferocity.

Selim hated to see them defiling his home, the caves where he and his believers had met and celebrated, the chamber where he and Marha had first made love. These intruders did not deserve to live.

He sat cross-legged on the sands and waited while they ransacked the abandoned settlement. Finally, impatient because no one had seen him yet, he seated the bottom of the drum in the soft sands. With brisk flat slaps, he pounded the drumhead, sending a loud echo into the clear desert air and down into the stratified dunes.

A sharp call, a challenge.

Selim heard faint shouts of alarm and anger, and then the fighters scurried down out of the rocks. They hurried back aboard their flying craft. Engines whined and plumes of dust spat out as the vessel lumbered into the air.

Naib Dhartha and his personal war party raced out onto the dunes on foot.

Selim pounded his drum harder in a relentless, insistent rhythm. The drum was a precision instrument he had made himself. Loyal Jafar had shown him how to create the device using metal scraps for the cylinder and tightly woven skins from kangaroo mice for the drumhead. This drum had served him for years. It had summoned many worms.

The armed flyer swooped overhead, cruising low so that he could feel the rush of air and a wave of heat from its engines. Blown sand stung his face, but Selim did not flinch. They could have taken potshots at his position or dropped explosives to obliterate him. But the pilot seemed to be determining whether the outlaw was indeed alone. Naturally they would suspect a trap — but would not be able to see it. The flyer circled again, and then landed in a flat expanse of sand well away from him. The mercenary soldiers poured out.

As if they were racing the soldiers from the flyer, Naib Dhartha and his Zensunni warriors stumbled quickly across the landscape. All of these arrogant men believed themselves a match for the rigors of the desert, but Selim knew that any human life on Arrakis was less significant than a grain of sand in the open bled.

He kept pounding his drum. In response, he could feel the deep, deep tremors . . . growing louder, closer.

From the opposite side, the approaching Zensunni fighters ran forward waving their weapons, forgetting the stutter-step they had learned as children. He could hear curses, challenges, threats. Though he was older than most of his fighters, Naib Dhartha led the way himself. As Selim had hoped, the Naib's rage had overcome his good sense.

"I challenge you, Selim Demonrider," Dhartha bellowed as soon as he was in earshot. His voice was deep and laced with gravity, just as it had been when he'd falsely condemned Selim for stealing water. "You have caused enough harm to my people, and I have come to end your outlaw life."

Because they were trained to do so, the offworld soldiers switched on personal shields. Selim had never fought with a shield — no real warrior depended on such cowardly protection — and he sensed a jolt deep underground as the men came toward him. They did not know that their shields were sending out a louder, more insistent summons to Shai-Hulud than Selim's drum could ever issue.

"Are you a man without sin who is fit to judge me, Naib Dhartha?" Selim shouted back. He beat more on his drum. "A man who knowingly exiled a young boy who was innocent of any crime? You have continued to act against Shai-Hulud, despite your clear knowledge of the harm you are causing. You have far more blood on your hands than I do."

Some members of the Zensunni war party shouted with alarm and pointed toward the distance. Selim did not turn. He felt the vibrations increasing, the deep passage of approaching sandworms. Many of them.

The mercenaries stumbled to a halt and circled in confusion like riled ants, as the sandy ground beneath them began to vibrate and boil. With a whine of engines, the retreating flyer heaved itself off the unstable dune and rose into the dusty air.

A moment later, a huge sandworm, driven into a frenzy by the personal shields on the mercenaries, lunged out of the ground like a projectile, its gaping mouth scooping up all of the maddening soldiers in one sweep.

Selim remained seated, listening to the rush of disturbed sand and the hopeless howl of men plunging into the endless gullet.

The pilot raised the flyer higher and hurtled toward the enormous sandworm that had killed most of the mercenary party in a few seconds. He launched explosive projectiles from nose guns, and the blasts struck the encrusted skin of the worm segments, exposing raw pink flesh beneath. The eyeless worm writhed and surged, blindly seeking a new enemy.

As the flyer streaked in for a renewed attack, a second sandworm exploded from the depths of the desert. In a sinuous, cobralike movement, it hammered into the flyer, knocking it out of the air. The worm plunged into the desert as the military craft crashed, and the momentum sucked the wreckage into the sand.

On the opposite side of Selim, the Zensunni warriors dropped their weapons, turned in a panic, and fled. As they left him alone to face Selim, Dhartha looked back at them with anger and disgust.

Selim did not fear Shai-Hulud. He had faced the worm many times, and knew what Buddallah had in store for him. "There is only one way for a Wormrider to die, Naib Dhartha."

Selim had done his best to fulfill the destiny chosen for him. He knew in his heart, though, that what he was about to do would accomplish far more. He would step beyond reality, into the realm of mythos. The tale of Selim Wormrider and his sacred quest would endure for centuries.

Then a third monster swam through the sands and rose up in front of the fleeing Zensunni kanla party. The creatures were notoriously territorial, never entering a rival's domain . . . but *three* of them had answered Selim's summons. He doubted if anyone had ever witnessed such a spectacle.

The kanla fighters could not run from the third worm. The creature thrashed about and devoured them in a flurry of sand.

As if entranced, Selim continued to drum. Dhartha, the only survivor now, screamed at him. Finally, the sand began to tremble beneath him, signaling the emergence of the fourth and largest worm of all, and the Naib turned and tried to escape.

Too late.

As the dune slumped and sand shifted beneath his feet, Naib Dhartha spun to face Selim. Beneath them both, Shai-Hulud emerged, his yawning mouth a huge maw filled with crystal teeth.

In a single gulp, the worm swallowed tons of sand. Naib Dhartha slid into the bottomless pit.

The sandworm kept rising, kept coming forward.

Selim held onto his drum while the creature surged like an angel toward the heavens, its mouth reeking of all the melange on the desert planet. Finally, the beast swallowed him, too.

The Wormrider took his last ride, a ride into eternity, down the fiery gullet of Shai-Hulud.

Earlier, the sullen members of the outlaw band had followed their leader's orders and gone to set up a new encampment in a distant section of rocks. With an aching heart, Marha had remained behind. She felt the child growing within her and wondered if the baby would ever see its father. No matter what happened, she vowed the child would know all the stories about Selim Wormrider.

Her husband had explained to her what she must do. She had not relished her obligation, but truly believed in Selim's cause. She accepted his visions as genuine messages from Buddallah, so she could not discard them for her own convenience, or for her love.

In order to better see Selim, she had ascended Needle Rock, a tall outcropping that gave her a commanding vantage of the desert. Long ago, when she had first run away from Naib Dhartha's village and found her way across the desert, Needle Rock had been a significant landmark, close to the caves of Selim. Very few of those wishing to join the outlaw band made it this far without being picked up by Selim's scouts. But Marha had done it.

Now she watched as Selim sat alone on the dunes, pounding his drum, facing his hated adversaries.

None of the offworld mercenaries or Zensunni traitors had imagined that Selim could so easily command Shai Hulud, whose destructive power far surpassed that of any of the soldiers' weapons. She witnessed the massacre, saw the frenzy of the demonic worms — four of them, all together! — as they destroyed the enemy.

Then she watched with her heart in her throat and her spirit sinking into despair as the greatest sandworm of them all, a manifestation of Shai-Hulud Himself, rose up to destroy Selim's life-long enemy, Naib Dhartha . . . and her beloved Selim.

She cried out in the wailing scream of a widow, and then fell silent, trying to find inner peace. Shai-Hulud was absorbing the great Wormrider into his own flesh, and now Selim would live forever as part of their god. A fitting end for a man — a *hero*.

And the perfect beginning for a legend.

Humans are slaves to their mortality, from the moment of birth to the moment of death.

— Tlulaxa religious passage

U NDOUBTEDLY THERE WERE older, more decrepit spaceships than this one traveling among the League Worlds, but Norma had never seen one. It made the decommissioned vessel that Aurelius had provided for her space-folding project look modern.

Leaving its parking orbit around Poritrin, the old craft vibrated as it accelerated out into open space. The bare interior smelled of scorched insulation, human sweat, and stale food. Stains marked the deck and wall plates, which appeared to have been only half-heartedly cleaned. She wondered if this ship was used for hauling slaves, though now she was the only passenger, aside from the guards.

It would be a long, uncomfortable voyage, adding to Norma's shame and misery.

Two sullen-looking Dragoon guards sat to either side of her on a long metal bench, as if wondering what they had done to displease Lord Bludd and receive this long, slow assignment. Crates of cargo (including her own belongings), had been hurriedly loaded into the open spaces and stacked against the walls. She was surprised Tuk Keedair hadn't been forced to join her.

The open passenger compartment was filled with utilitarian bunks and benches; Norma had seen banks of coffinlike chambers on the cargo decks below, presumably stasis beds. If filled to capacity, the austere vessel could carry at least a thousand people.

"This is a slave ship, isn't it?" she asked the nearest Dragoon.

He gazed down at her with heavy-lidded eyes and said nothing. He didn't need to respond.

With her vivid imagination, Norma envisioned sweating, crowded Buddislamic captives on board, forcibly removed from some hinterland world. She sensed their lingering, ghostly misery. People had died on these decks.

The thought put her problems in perspective. Yes, she had been sent away against her will, but at least the guards were taking her home . . . even if it was in disgrace. Her mother would make certain Norma understood how great a failure she was. Yet things could have been worse. Sighing, Norma wished she had Aurelius there to keep her company on the long voyage.

She shifted on the hard bench, but could not get comfortable. She had little to occupy her time, no amusements or diversions whatsoever. This wasn't a luxury cruise through the cosmos.

A creative excursion through her own mind usually enabled her to forget about physical hardships. With her work stolen and her life disrupted, however, Norma found herself focusing too much on her surroundings and the inadequacies of her stunted body.

To comfort herself, she toyed with the lovely soostone Aurelius had given her. Though it had never had any telepathic effect on her, she enjoyed the memories triggered by the smooth stone. Norma closed her eyes and let calculations run across the window of her mind, long rows and columns of numbers and mathematical symbols, as if they were arrayed in space . . . right outside the portholes of this slave ship.

Though he had tried, Savant Holtzman could not take away the core of her accomplishments. She kept all of that locked within the intricate passageways of her mind, every detail available to her recollection, everything she needed to know about her foldspace work. Exploring her own mental archives entertained her, and she changed the numbers and symbols, watching them appear and disappear at will. It was her secret universe, where no other person could look . . . though someday she would like to share it with Aurelius.

At least I am still alive. At least I am still free.

From a distance, she heard a loud, abrasive voice. For some reason it made her think of her mother scolding her for yet another weakness. As if in the absurdity of a dream, Zufa Cenva was flying through deep space alongside the ship, peering in at her through a porthole with fiery eyes, like two tiny red suns.

Abruptly, Norma came out of her trance and recognized the chaos around her. The Dragoon guards were on their feet, shouting in Galach, and the chartered slave ship was veering off course. The old engines made heated, straining sounds as the pilot changed his route abruptly.

Losing her balance, she stumbled against the wall porthole and looked out in surprise to see red eyes peering in at her, but they did not belong to her mother. This evil gaze came from a mechanical monster constructed to look like an immense orange-and-green prehistoric bird — and her mother was nowhere around to help with her Sorceress powers.

The slave ship shuddered in evasive maneuvers, and the raptorlike craft swooped away, showing its hot exhaust ports and then circling around. For several moments Norma lost sight of the beast. The guards shouted again, and cargo crates toppled over, smashing on the floor and spilling padded bottles of exported Poritrin rum.

She ran across the top of the bench toward the opposite porthole. The spaceship jolted as it was struck by a blast that reverberated through the decks with a sound like a hammer against an anvil. Norma tumbled to the corrugated metal deck.

When she finally reached the porthole, she saw the monstrous craft again, swooping toward the old slave ship like a hawk hunting a helpless pigeon.

The huge flying machine opened its jagged mouth as if to roar, revealing banks of sharp artificial teeth, each one as big as a doorway. Norma had a difficult time maintaining her grip on reality.

Is this really happening? she asked herself. It seemed impossible. Somehow, her focused thoughts had expanded, dilated to encompass far too much. She clutched the gem like a talisman. *I must regain control of my mind.*

She struggled to reason the situation out, summoning logical possibilities. Could the monstrously gaudy vessel be a . . . *cymek* flyer? But why would an enemy ship be out here, and why would it be after her?

The raptor vessel grasped the sluggish slave ship with huge grappler talons. Norma saw the ribbed green belly of the huge bird-machine, large enough to swallow their whole ship. Its underside was marred with scrapes and long black scorch marks, perhaps from battle.

The machine ship opened a compartment in its belly and drew the smaller captured vessel toward it. Acid green lights blazed inside the confinement chamber, hurting Norma's eyes.

Once the slave ship had been swallowed up like a morsel of raw meat, the doors of the giant ship closed.

Inside the mechanical behemoth, a preservation canister dangled from the ceiling like a spider's egg sac, high over the captured vessel. Red and blue lights blinked around the container, surging as the disembodied brain increased its mental activity. Abruptly, thoughtrode sensors extruded like electronic talons, to better study the prey.

Finally, I can earn my forgiveness from General Agamemnon, Xerxes thought, as he began recording data.

*No matter how bleak our situation seems, we must never abandon
hope. Buddallah may surprise us.*

—Naib Ishmael, a call to prayer

W ITHOUT A SOUND in the isolation of space, the emptiness tore
asunder and a large ship lurched through the opening . . . from
nowhere.

The Zensunni passengers packed into the space-folding vessel let out
gasps of surprise and panic as they were thrust through a knot in spacetime and emerged on the other side.

Ishmael felt as if his thoughts had stuttered. When he looked outside,
he saw stars that bent, twisted, then snapped into sharp definition
again . . . but in different positions, as if the map of the Galaxy had
been rearranged. The planet Poritrin was nowhere in sight, but the
viewport of the unstable ship filled with the brassy globe of a desert world,
a cracked and parched wasteland.

Their ship plummeted toward it. Without accurate coordinates attuned
to Norma Cenva's prototype engines, the spacecraft careened into the
atmosphere of Arrakis. The unprepared pilot Tuk Keedair wrestled with
the controls to restore flight stability, and it was obvious to Ishmael that
he didn't know exactly what he was doing with this strange prototype.

Ishmael prayed for their safety.

They hurtled around to the dayside of the world, where harsh sunlight
poured over it. Chamal hurried forward into the pilot deck. "It looks as if
it's made of gold, Father!"

A grin covered Rafel's face. "We've escaped from slavery."

Ishmael looked at the two, knowing that the Zensunni refugees were
alarmed and confused by their passage through foldspace; in moments
they would realize the danger was not yet over. The prototype ship

continued ever downward with deceptive slowness toward the big planet.

"Can you regain control?" Ishmael asked Keedair in a low voice.

The Tlulaxa slaver looked at him with wild, dark eyes. Sweat streamed down the sides of his narrow face. "I told you from the start that I wasn't certain I could fly this thing. I hope you're satisfied."

Ishmael glanced at his daughter, who still stared through the starship's front window, then turned back to the slaver. "Just do your best. That's all I ask."

Keedair scowled. "We may not make it."

As the reluctant Tlulaxa pilot fought with the guidance systems, the vessel skipped like a thrown stone across the edge of the atmosphere, then dove deeper, burning hot like a meteor through the desert skies.

The plunge continued, rough and destructive; bits of the stolen ship's hull peeled off like scales from the wings of a moth flying dangerously close to a flame. The Zensunnis faced their fate, some wishing they had remained behind on Poritrin, while others accepted imminent death. A *free* death, at least, Ishmael thought.

Chamal looked at her father, unshakeable in her confidence that he would somehow bring them through this crisis.

Ishmael wondered what Aliid was doing now. Was his fiery friend still alive, and had the Starda revolt caused as much destruction as the Zenshiites had planned? And what about Ozza, whom he had left behind? And sweet Falina, only fourteen years old.

At least Ishmael had led his people, including one of his daughters, far enough away that they would never again need to fear slavers or thinking machines. They would be safe here . . . if they survived the landing.

According to rumor, Arrakis had no oceans, only incomprehensibly vast expanses of open sand laced with a scarwork of mountain ranges and lava reefs. The planet supposedly boasted a sheltered spaceport settlement that barely counted as a city . . .

On the pilot deck, Keedair could hardly guide the ship at all, and simply struggled for survival as they streaked toward the dunes and rocks. The ship traced a line of smoking fire through the atmosphere as it came down low across a line of gnarled, blackened rocks, lava extrusions that had oozed through volcanically active fissures and then hardened.

Keedair fought to lift the ship enough to float them over the long craggy peninsula, but the engines stuttered. No one had ever expected this old hulk to fly on regular missions; Norma Cenva had simply intended to demonstrate that her space-folding interpretation of the Holtzman Effect was valid and usable.

Keedair tried to squeeze enough velocity out of their lumbering craft to make it to the open sands and the cushioning dunes. Unfortunately, the hull bottom scraped a large rock and one of the ship's fins caught on a jagged outcropping. Sparks flew. The vessel spun, ripping open its belly on a lava reef, then miraculously came to rest in a pocket of stone created by an elbow of upthrust lava.

All power shorted out on the pilot deck, and the lower containment chambers went dark, plunging the refugees into absolute blackness accompanied only by the sounds of crackling fires, groaning hot metal, and frightened whispers.

Ishmael had been thrown to the deck and rolled in a bruising tumble against the pilot's chair. Now he lurched to his feet, hoping the other hundred passengers had secured themselves adequately for such a rough landing. Rafel picked himself up from the deck and made sure his wife Chamal was unharmed.

"Open the hatches," Ishmael shouted. "We need to get all the people out in case the ship explodes."

"That would be the perfect end to this adventure," Keedair said. His braid had become tangled and frayed, and in a gesture of annoyance he tossed it over his shoulder.

Rafel glared at him. "We should kill you now, slaver."

The Tlulaxa looked as if he was weary of being afraid. "Can you worthless people do nothing but complain and threaten? You abducted me, forced me to fly you to another world, and commanded me to land this ship and keep you alive. I've done so. From here on, you're dealing with problems you made for yourselves."

Ishmael looked at him, trying to see if the flesh-merchant actually expected gratitude. Finally with a shudder of metal, the controls went dead. Going to an escape hatch, Keedair jerked the handle and managed to breach one of the hard seals so that the hatch opened.

Zensunni refugees crowded to the gap and with makeshift tools pried open the doorway. The blistering sunlight and parched air of the new world rushed into the groaning ship.

Because he had led these people, orchestrating their escape from years of captivity and taking them to a new life beyond the clutches of League slavemasters, Ishmael should have been the first to set foot on Arrakis. The former slaves looked back at him expectantly, waiting.

But Ishmael waved them on, and remained inside the crashed vessel, an attempt to impose order. "Do not let frenzy and eagerness overrule your common sense," he shouted.

Escapees began to pour out of the opening, dropping from the wreckage onto the hard, broken ground. Some milled around, calling for friends and loved ones; others raced away to imagined safety on this strange and bleak new world. Leaving her husband on the piloting deck, Chamal climbed down and helped the others to move to shelter and safety in rocks away from the ship.

Rafel was brave and blustery now, red-faced with anger. He grabbed Keedair by the knotted braid and hauled him out of the pilot's chair. "Come outside and see where you have landed us. How close are we to civilization?"

The slaver laughed at him. "Civilization? This is *Arrakis*. Within weeks you'll be crying for Poritrin and your comfortable slave barracks."

"Never," Rafel vowed.

But the former flesh merchant smiled in a way that was both confident and resigned. Rafel nudged him through the open hatch to the ground, and Ishmael followed. Rafel stood next to his prisoner on the stump of a black outcropping that had been shattered by the ricochet of the prototype vessel. As he gazed around the yawning, empty landscape, the young man's face filled with surprise, disbelief, and then despair. Chamal took her place beside him. In their worst nightmares they had never expected such a bleak, inhospitable vista.

Ishmael stood proudly and looked at the searing black-and-brown peninsula that extended in a curve all the way to the horizon. Undulating dunes, like waves on a petrified yellow sea, extended in the opposite direction. He took a deep breath of the arid air of Arrakis, which smelled of dust and flint. In the brief time he had been out here, his nostrils and mouth had already become parched. He saw no trees or birds and not a speck of green, not even a blade of grass or a flower.

It seemed to be the worst pit of Heol in the universe.

Rafel grabbed the Tlulaxa flesh merchant by the collar. "Bastard, betrayer! Take us somewhere else. We cannot live here."

Keedair gave a bitter laugh. "Somewhere else? Weren't you listening? Look at the ship. It is going nowhere, and neither are any of you Buddislamic malcontents. Live here . . . or die here. I do not care which."

Some Zensunnis looked as if they wanted to scream or weep, but Ishmael gazed across the landscape and raised his chin in defiance. His mouth formed a firm line of determination, and he placed a hand on his daughter's shoulder. "Buddallah has chosen our course, Chamal. And this is where we will make our new home. Forget your dreams of paradise. Freedom is far sweeter."

Every plan has its own monkey wrench.

—Ancient Aphorism

O NE OF NORMA'S urgent messages finally reached him during a brief stop on Salusa Secundus, on his way back from Arrakis. Arriving at the company offices, he also found a harried communiqué from Tuk Keedair, adding more details of the disaster that had befallen the space-folding operations. He and Norma had been exiled from the planet. Muttering curses against Lord Bludd and Tio Holtzman, Venport commandeered the first available VenKee ship and raced directly to Poritrin.

En route, at way stations, Venport learned of an immense catastrophe that overshadowed the earlier information. In the midst of a slave rebellion, the entire city of Starda had been annihilated, apparently through the use of atomics.

He couldn't believe it and thought he might go mad with worry during the tedious journey. If only he had access to the space-folding technology now, he could get to Poritrin immediately. Norma was in deep trouble, and under the best case scenario she was already exiled from the planet where she'd lived for almost three decades. He could only hope that she had gotten away from Poritrin in time. He cared much more about her welfare than about the commercial losses of his company.

But he received verification that she had never reached Rossak, and now he feared that something terrible had happened. Maybe she had never escaped Starda, and was included among the dead millions.

This personal and business emergency, more than anything else in his life, drove home the vital need for faster space transportation and communication. Not only for himself, but for the entire human race. The technology all hung by a fragile thread, however. Only the genius of

Norma Cenva held the secret of using the Holtzman Effect to fold space. No one else could understand it.

Where is she?

A year ago, she had quietly postponed responding to his offer of marriage, sidestepping the question out of embarrassment, confusion, indecision . . . but she had promised to give him an answer when he returned. He should have come back to Poritrin much sooner. Why had he stayed away for so long?

He knew that even if Norma had agreed to accept his proposal, she would still have remained in her laboratories working on the prototype ship, and he would still have gone off to deal with the demands of his merchant business. His shoulders sagged. Just the thought of her unassuming smile, her quiet conversation, her distracted delight in being with him — whether she saw him as a friend, big brother, or lover — made him feel warm inside.

Venport knew he loved her — and had for a long time, though he'd been slow to recognize his feelings. While no one had ever considered Norma beautiful, he still found her attractive because of who she was — a gentle genius with a passion for the art of mathematics that surpassed even the purest fanaticism of the most dedicated jihadi fighter. He had already been missing her terribly. And now . . .

Have I lost you?

Venport reached the Isana River in the middle of the night, local time. Hard-pressed traffic controllers routed his shuttle around the blistering Starda disaster site to a temporary landing area erected for all the emergency vessels and medical ships that had raced to the planet.

The glow of the huge radioactive crater was a dull orange along the river bluffs where the nobles had lived. The sight itself lay like a heavy stone on his chest, restricting his breathing. Lord Bludd, Tio Holtzman, and hundreds of thousands of others had vanished, vaporized.

How would he ever find Norma now?

Standing among the crowds at the interim spaceport, Aurelius Venport looked into the eyes of the refugees and saw stricken, dull defeat. No one seemed to know exactly what had happened, how mere Buddislamic slaves had obtained an atomic weapon. But other indications seemed to indicate that the blast hadn't exactly come from a nuclear chain reaction, but from something similar . . .

And no one knew anything about Holtzman's former assistant. Norma Cenva was the least of their problems.

Venport realized that it might take him a long time to uncover the answers. No hotels or amenities were available now. The majority of the guest lodgings had been within the blast zone, and other apartments and hotels on the fringes were packed with survivors of the bloody uprising.

He didn't care about his own safety, or about money. On a hill away from the river, he found an intact home with a spare room, which he rented for an exorbitant fee without quibbling. What did cost matter now? He tried to get a few hours of sleep while waiting for daybreak, when he could begin his search in earnest, but he tossed and turned all night, worrying about Norma.

There had been no further word from Tuk Keedair, either, so Venport would have to do his own detective work.

At dawn the merchant arranged for transportation, paying another stiff fee for the use of a commercial flyer for two hours. A woman with bright red hair sat at the controls, looking haggard and smudged. She talked incessantly about salvage and rescue efforts, the scores of workers plowing through the wreckage. She told him her name was Nathra Kiane, and she accepted his commission, though she felt guilty for not being at the disaster site.

"I'll take you up the river and into the side canyon, as you wish, sir, but we can't stay for more than an hour. Everybody's looking for someone. There's too much work for me, too many people to —"

"It won't take long," he said, knowing this was the grim truth. "I'll find out everything I need to know in a few minutes."

The small craft flew over agricultural fields, a green and yellow patchwork on the plain along the winding banks of the river. The fields were blackened after the Starda disaster, and harvesting equipment sat idle. According to official reports, the surviving Dragoon guards and minor nobles were cracking down on all remnants of the bloody uprising, but there were still pockets of armed resistance in the back country.

Slaves had been slaughtered everywhere in retaliation. Whether or not they surrendered, regardless of whether they had participated in the uprising, all Buddislamics were being massacred by vengeful mobs. Faced with doom, even those peaceful slaves took up arms to defend themselves, and the cycle of bloodshed spiraled out of control. Venport moaned at the thought.

"I haven't been up here since the catastrophe." The pilot gave a groan of disgust mixed with dismay. "Animals! How could those slaves do such a terrible thing?"

The exhausted Nathra Kiane was clearly in a hurry. She banked the flyer sharply and accelerated northward along the open course of the Isana River. No boats floated on the rough water anymore. Ahead, where the Isana cut a deeper channel, the offworlder saw the beginnings of canyons branching off into high walls. Norma's remote laboratory was far from the main destruction, so he prayed that she was safe, that perhaps she had returned here despite her deportation order.

Again, he wished he had stayed with her and allowed his Tlulaxa partner to deal with VenKee business interests: Rossak pharmaceuticals, Arrakis melange, glowglobes, suspensors.

"Up ahead," Kiane said. "We're almost there."

He could already see the boat docks at the bottom of the canyons where shuttleboats could tie up, the passenger and cargo lifts that rose to the building on top of the bluffs, and the large hollow grotto that held the large hangar, its cantilevered roof yawning open.

And the empty docking cradle for the ship. The prototype vessel was gone.

No one moved in the laboratory — no workers, no slaves, not even Dragoon guards. Gates had been left open, barricade fences knocked down. The remaining equipment lay scattered about in laboratory areas like dead insects.

No sign of anyone.

"Land in the clearing next to the hangar opening," he said, amazed at how steady his voice was. When the red-haired pilot looked as if she might complain, he glared at her, then urgently peered through the flyer's window, trying to see details among the shadows inside the hangar and cave.

Venport scrambled out of the flyer as soon as the pads touched down. The air smelled of singed grit, and the ground looked trampled. He could not begin to imagine what had occurred here. Had this destruction been caused by the military takeover of the complex, when Norma and Keedair had been evicted . . . or had there been a slave revolt here?

Inside the empty hangar he studied a tangled mass of metal at the center of the floor, the skeleton of heavy supports that should have held the decommissioned vessel. There was no evidence of the bulky ship itself.

With a heavy heart, Venport stumbled into the calculational offices where Norma had stored her files, but he saw only a few records strewn about, insignificant scraps and receipts. No notes, blueprints, or other important documents at all.

"Sure looks like this place was ransacked," Kiane said, tagging along with him. "Anybody here?" But her words bounced back at her. "I'll bet the slaves rioted and then escaped upland. They must have tossed any bodies off the edge, into the river."

"Norma!" Venport ran back down into the hangar and then outside, where he searched small storage buildings. He knew in his heart she wasn't here. Filled with foreboding, he inspected everything carefully, looking for the tiniest clue, anything that might tell him what had happened.

But there was no sign of what had happened to the prototype ship or the people here. It was too quiet. Deathly quiet.

"Get me out of here," Venport said, feeling sick to his stomach.

He spent five more days searching urgently in and around Starda, asking questions, pleading for answers. But everyone had missing friends and family members, and the casualty toll kept mounting. Lord Bludd and Tio Holtzman had both been declared dead. Among the shattered debris, bodies were still being found. Many victims had been burned in the fires, others butchered by slaves. Among the dead across the wide continent lay thousands of Buddislamic rebels, all mangled by Dragoons in retaliation for the uprising.

No one could tell him what he needed to know, but in his heart Venport already had the answer. He tried to cling to hope that Norma had indeed gone to Rossak, and that her passage had merely been delayed. But all indications pointed in a different direction, that she had met a terrible, undeserved fate.

Filled with grief over his lost love, Aurelius Venport put Poritrin behind him, and vowed never to return here.

A thinking machine cannot be hurt, tortured, killed, bribed, or manipulated. Machines never turn on their own kind. The mechanisms are pure and clean, with exquisite internal parts and shimmering exterior surfaces. Considering such beauty and perfection, I fail to comprehend why Erasmus is so fascinated with humans.

—File from Corrin-Omnius update

P AIN AND FEAR made time seem to drag out to infinity. Norma Cenva had no idea how long she had been held captive, only that she was the last of the victims to face the cymek captor's curiosity. The two Dragoon guards and the hapless slave ship pilot had already screamed their way into a mercifully silent oblivion.

From inside the monstrous raptor vessel, the voice of the Titan Xerxes said, "We have as many methods of inflicting torture as there are stars in the sky. This comes from diligent practice." The words seemed to come from everywhere around her.

Norma dangled paralyzed and helpless in the belly of the condor-flyer that had captured her. She could only listen, and suffer. Her bodily capabilities had never been impressive, but Norma's mind was a different matter; it stood on its own . . . apart from her physical form. She tried to focus her thoughts and drive back the mounting terror, replacing it with resignation, acceptance of her impending death.

Her dreams and accomplishments had already been taken from her by the man she had faithfully served for so many years. Her experimental ship was lost to her, and she'd been driven from Poritrin in disgrace. She had let Aurelius down, along with everyone else who depended upon her.

A mere cymek could not inflict any deeper pain, or greater humiliation, than she had already suffered.

Within the belly of the huge predatory ship, the Titan's preservation canister dangled above Norma, scanning her with an array of high-resolution optic threads.

"Long ago when I was human," Xerxes mused, as if his words could torment her, "my body was rather small and ugly. Before I came to power and ruled over vast worlds, some people even called me a gnome."

On hydraulic cables, the preservation canister lowered itself closer to where she hung, to get a better look at her squirming form. Her clothes were drenched in sweat, battered and stained.

"By comparison, woman, you are so ugly that your parents should have smothered you at birth . . . and then sterilized themselves to prevent the creation of any more monstrosities."

Norma replied in a husky voice, "My mother . . . might agree with you."

The sharp threads suspending her in the air were suddenly severed, and she tumbled to the hard interior deck of Xerxes's massive raptor ship. Gasping with pain, she hunched over. Held in place by the craft's gravity system, which rapidly increased, like a heavy boot crushing her body, Norma could barely breathe.

She heard mechanical voices, but couldn't make out the words.

Clinging to hope and comfortable memories, Norma closed her eyes and clutched the egg-shaped soostone, as if the glittering jewel could help her now. Despite the horrors around her, the gem made her feel a connection with Aurelius, and these thoughts strengthened and kept her alive. For the time being.

Xerxes and the brain canisters of half a dozen of his sycophant neo-cymeks surrounded her, hanging from the ceiling like fat arachnids, and Norma made out their words. The Titan thrummed beside the neos, speaking to them. "You are the first of the new recruits Beowulf has drawn into our rebellion against Omnius, and soon others will join us — especially after this little demonstration."

Trapped, Norma felt more like a tasty grub worm than a human. She shivered on the cold floor while her tormentor plunged the chamber temperature down to far below freezing. The metal deck burned her skin with frozen fire, and her breath plumed away from her like white steam.

"Oh, poor little dear — are you shivering?" Xerxes inquired in a mocking synthesized voice. Using manipulator arms from above, the Titan dropped an energy blanket over her, which clung like a Rossak leech-bat, adhering to every exterior cell of her body. It made her colder. Norma struggled unsuccessfully to push it off against the quicksand of artificial gravity.

"Here, now you can be warm again." Xerxes transmitted a signal, and the blanket suddenly glowed scarlet with meshwires that seared into her exposed flesh.

Though she had expected the torment, Norma could not keep herself from crying out. She clutched the sweat-slick soostone as if it were an anchor, even as the agony intensified. The blanketfilm sizzled and sputtered as it burned its way into her tissues. Then, springing from the thick fibers of the blanket, a network of electronic probes pierced her skin. Hair-fine wires wormed their way into her muscles and made neuro-connections with her body.

Moments later the heat dwindled, leaving only a stench of roasted skin and burned hair in the frigid air. But Norma knew the worst torture was yet to come. Though tears stung her eyes, stubborn defiance hardened her face, and she found the strength to lift her head, albeit only slightly. "From the beginning, you have left me without hope, so I expect no compassion from you." She forced a defiant yawn. "I must inform you, though, that the pain you inflict is . . . quite ordinary."

Suspended above her, the individual cymek canisters vibrated, as if in merriment. "Ordinary pain?" Xerxes sent another signal, and a bolt of agony erupted through her left arm. She cried out and nearly dropped the soostone, but squeezed it in a death grip. Her mind focused on one name, and the image of the man she held most dear. *Aurelius!*

"Left leg," Xerxes said.

Pain seared through her limb, and her head hit the deck again. Xerxes increased the artificial gravity, making Norma feel as if a giant invisible foot were crushing her. With the air squashed out of her lungs, she could make no sound, so the Titan released her and let her scream. An involuntary sound. She wished she could detach herself from the suffering. If only her thought processes could be independent of their biological pain. She had, however, no desire to be a cymek.

"Eyes," Xerxes said, like a gamesman calling a shot. Gravity lurched again.

Unable to stop herself, Norma howled and covered her eyes with her stubby hands. She rained curses on Xerxes and all of his kind, but didn't have the words to express the depth of her loathing.

The cymeks continued their sport, step by step increasing her anguish and torment, slacking off just long enough so that her mounting dread increased the next jolt of pain. With his diabolical companions, Xerxes worked on her, body part by body part. He was careful to keep her flayed mind conscious inside the tormented body so that she could experience every moment. Then he made it worse.

And worse again, wrenching up the intensity.

"We have already learned a great deal and gained a goodly amount of practice by playing with the slave ship captain and the two guards," Xerxes said.

"She has a higher threshold than the other three," said one of the dangling neos. "They were dead long before this point."

"Shall we test her limits?" Xerxes asked, rhetorically.

Norma could barely comprehend the words echoing above her. The soostone in her grasp seemed to have fused to her flesh. She did not hear Xerxes' answer, but she felt him unleash a firestorm of amplified pain through every major nerve in her small body. Increasing, increasing.

She heard the neo-cymeks scrabbling and chattering with glee.

Suddenly, Norma could no longer even scream. Her eyes screwed tight, and her brow furrowed at the pressure on her head, as if her skull was about to collapse and squirt out its brain. With both hands, she squeezed the soostone in a posture of prayer, until her hands and arms shook.

"How much pain can one fragile biological vessel sustain?" asked one neo-cymek.

"I wonder if she will explode," said another.

Sparks arced around her body, crackling off her skin, burning her flesh, igniting her short brown hair. Still, Xerxes amplified the intensity to unimaginable levels. While the Titan hung suspended, the neos clamored, cackling with pleasure.

Abruptly, the induced torture focused on her brain itself, the brilliant mind that had incubated in the body of the Supreme Sorceress of the Jihad, Zufa Cenva. Flares jumped across synapses, overloading her cerebrum.

Norma's eyes opened. It felt as if a billion tiny razors were cutting her cells open and slicing them smaller and smaller, into infinitesimal points of pain. The soostone glowed like a miniature sun in her hand and reflected back into her.

At the zenith of her agony something loosened in her brain, unlocking the inherited Rossak powers that had lain dormant since her birth. The soostone Aurelius had given her provided the key, breaking the barrier her mother had never been able to find. All the power of the soostone absorbed into her, and suddenly she felt nothing. The cymek's pain transmitters continued bombarding her as before, but Norma easily deflected the energy from her body, directing it . . . accumulating it at a distance.

Her entire physical form pulsed, vibrated, and sparked blue. Norma Cenva's flesh turned incandescent, melted away, and converted into pure, raw energy. Was this what her mother's kamikaze Sorceresses had learned to do themselves, in order to annihilate cymeks?

No, Norma decided this was different in one fundamental way: she could *control* it.

She saw her own blood spattered all around — on the deck, on a bulkhead, on the gleeful brain canisters above her. She focused on the tormentor called Xerxes and felt a potent energy surge inside her transformed brain, like a weapon getting ready to discharge. Blue light lanced from her mind to the Titan's, splitting the cymek's canister open, detonating it like an organic bomb and boiling the brain inside.

Next, she detonated every neo-cymek simultaneously in a glorious backwash of mental energy that evaporated all organic tissue in a wide radius. It was only the beginning of her capabilities.

Gradually, the hurricane of mental energy subsided, and Norma felt an intense calm and euphoria about her, as if she were alone in the universe . . . as if she were God, with the act of Creation yet to come.

Though born of a powerful Sorceress of Rossak, Norma had previously displayed no telepathic aptitude. Yet the incredible torment, combined with the unexpected catalyst of the soostone, had awakened her inborn powers.

So serene. She could see forever, across millions of galaxies and the heavens. She saw all the way around the universe, until she looked at herself from behind: nothing more than the essence of a mind floating in the air, pulsing and throbbing. Anything, absolutely *anything*, seemed possible to her now.

Using the simmering energy available to her, she began to rebuild her body, creating matter out of nothingness, atom by atom, cell by cell. With invisible hands, as if she truly *were* God, she began to fashion a new physique to contain her consciousness, her powerful, exponentially expanded mind.

Then she paused to consider alternatives. Certainly her old form was a possibility, or a taller version, with her original features softened just a little, but not too much. She envisioned what she might look like.

There are other options, of course.

To Norma, the human body was no more than an organic receptacle, but most people saw it as much more than that. They reacted to others based upon appearances. Aurelius Venport was a notable exception. He saw through the external wrappings to Norma's inner self and her heart, to all that she truly was and wanted to be.

But he was, after all, only a man. Why should she not make herself beautiful for him, since he had already earned her respect and affection? She held in her mind what she might create now, a lovely image.

With the cosmic storm flowing through her, Norma felt a sense of urgency as if she was at a critical nexus and needed to decide quickly or the opportunity might be lost forever. Was the decision reversible? Could she change it later? She was not certain. The power would have to rise up in her again.

Abruptly, the mental images shifted, and in their place she saw her mother Zufa. Tall, pale, and perfect in form and grace. And Norma's maternal grandmother Conqee, one of the greatest Sorceresses in the history of Rossak. The old woman had always remained aloof from stunted, ugly Norma — even more so than her daughter Zufa. Conqee had died mysteriously while on a journey to the Unallied Planets; Norma had been only eight, but in all the years she had never forgotten the aging countenance, still so beautiful and so severe. In her thoughts now, Conqee's pale blue eyes seemed to look completely through her, to something on the other side of existence.

Abruptly, Norma found herself looking through those eyes herself, at something beyond her grandmother. She envisioned distant stars, planets, and nebulas . . . and illuminated in the foreground the likenesses of women, one by one, each fading away into another. All of them were classically beautiful, and all looked eerily familiar to her. Norma tried to gain control of the images and lock just one into place, but could not. With a jolt, she realized what she was seeing.

My own ancestors.

The revelation astounded her, but she did not doubt its authenticity for a moment.

The women who preceded me . . . but only my maternal lineage.

She struggled again to assume control of the images, but the procession of females faded and appeared, faded and appeared, receding into the past. Back, back, back, but not like the mechanism of a computer searching its databanks. This was entirely different.

Fear enveloped her. What would she see if she kept going? Had her mind been damaged irreparably in the encounter with the cymeks? Was it spinning out of control?

Then, like a stack of riffled photos, the images accelerated, and the faces and bodies merged into a composite of all the women in her bloodline, going back thousands of years. Moment by moment, the images shifted in face and form, as if the flesh were being pulled this way and that. Finally the mental pictures stabilized, and she gazed at one person, brilliantly illuminated against the heavenly cosmos.

At last she had the image she wanted, and it was fitting, since it included an element of her own previous appearance in its faint and ghostly genetic markers. She was the sum total of her ancestry, the exquisite convergence of all generations . . . though only on the female side.

Her unseen hands worked swiftly, molding every feature, reshaping her new body with the available cellular material — into an icily beautiful, tall and statuesque female form, more stunning than any other Sorceress of Rossak. Even surpassing Zufa Cenva.

Her fiercely glowing eyes became a soft, seductive blue. The skin was ivory and creamy smooth over a perfect frame and sensual curves. None of her predecessors on Rossak had ever been able to accomplish anything approaching this. She let it happen, opening cellular doorways that had previously been barricaded to her.

Finally, she stood perfect and unclothed within the belly of the dead raptor ship. Boosted to supernatural power, the embryonic superbeing Norma Cenva took control of Xerxes's vessel and flew it to an empty but habitable planet near the Rossak solar system, a world known as Kolhar.

From there, almost home, she sent a telepathic signal across the cosmos, an undeniable summons to her mother.

A toast to lost friends, forgotten allies, all those we did not appreciate in their lifetimes.

—Caladan Drinking Song

AND NOW THERE were three. Only three out of the twenty conquering rulers from ancient times . . . the magnificent Titans.

On the Synchronized World of Ularda, Agamemnon strode in his walker form through the flaming ruins of a slave encampment. The humans here had demonstrated no real threat of a long-standing uprising such as the cancer that had brought down Ix.

Still, the Titan general took no chances. Any evidence of unrest was dealt with severely. He blasted a globule of concentrated flame gel, igniting a fleeing woman into a candle of human flesh. She took two staggering steps before collapsing into a pile of stripped bones on the ground. Agamemnon strode over her, smashing remnants of her body between his mechanical toes as he searched for additional victims.

On either side of him the towering machine bodies of Juno and Dante marched across a precise grid, leveling the settlement. Tactically, it was dangerous to have all three Titans together in the same place where they were vulnerable — but the Ularda settlers had been broken long ago, and very little Jihad support had slipped through. After living for nearly eleven centuries, he knew how to recognize trouble.

Unlike certain other Titans.

"How could Xerxes have exposed himself to such danger?" he grumbled, his words discernible over the din of crackling fires, screaming victims, and crumbling structures. He amplified his speakerpatch, swiveled his head turret toward Juno's powerful form. "He attacked a Sorceress of Rossak, the daughter of Zufa Cenva? What response did he expect?" With a swipe of his reinforced metal forearms, the angry general leveled a reservoir tower that the slaves had constructed, splashing water through the smoking streets. "The preeminent idiot of all time."

Dante strolled along, wreaking significant damage in his own right, but almost as an afterthought. "The toll was higher than just Xerxes, though he was arguably the greatest loss. The victims included dozens of neo-cymeks, who were potential recruits for our own rebellion. Especially now, we cannot afford such an immense loss."

Juno sounded conciliatory, "We can do without them. Our plans will proceed, just as before."

"Of course we can do without Xerxes!" Agamemnon responded sharply. "At least it wasn't Beowulf, who has proven himself so useful. We only kept Xerxes around out of loyalty to our own kind, a sense of honor." The great Titan general sighed. "If only Xerxes had found a way to self-destruct earlier."

Three young humans ducked into a low, half-collapsed structure. Noticing the movement, Agamemnon lurched toward them and blasted the building, but his intended victims escaped deeper inside the questionable shelter.

Angrily, the Titan general loomed over the building and used his armored limbs to rip off the roof and knock down walls, until he grabbed all three of the troublesome slaves and yanked them into the sunlight, squirming like exposed beetle grubs. He crushed them between his flowmetal fingers, watched their bodily fluids ooze out, and thought about how much more he would have enjoyed it, if Xerxes had not been on his mind.

Long ago, the cowardly Titan had been a wealthy, pampered prince who understood little about genuine leadership. He had pledged vast, much-needed wealth to Tlaloc's secret, growing rebellion. His resource-rich homeworld, Rodale IX, had later been renamed "Ix."

Xerxes, overly eager to join the group, had agreed to install Barbarossa's corrupted programming into the numerous servant robots on Rodale IX. The new routines and commands needed to be tested, so Xerxes had allowed his planet to be used as a testing ground. When the time came for the huge coordinated revolt to begin across the Old Empire, Xerxes had killed his obese father, the nominal ruler of the planet, and turned over the full resources of Rodale IX to the Twenty Titans.

From the beginning, Agamemnon had not been convinced of Xerxes's reliability. He had no true political convictions, no consuming passion for the goal. It was just a game to Xerxes, a diversion.

At the time, Agamemnon had traveled to the Thalim system, where he expressed his concerns to the visionary leader Tlaloc himself. On Tlulax, Tlaloc had worked hard to achieve personal greatness, but found himself disappointed in the Tlulaxa people, who had no important aspirations. They were already cutting themselves off, spurning the hedonism of the Old Empire while refusing to make their own situation better. Disillusioned with his own people, Tlaloc nonetheless believed the best about mankind, insisting that the human race could achieve great things, if only they could be "encouraged" to do so.

And for that, the Twenty Titans had needed Xerxes's bankroll.

For the centuries since then, Agamemnon hadn't needed Xerxes anymore, but there had been the matter of Titan honor. No small issue. At least Xerxes was finally out of the way.

By now, the cymeks had succeeded in destroying the slave encampment on Ularda. No one survived, no structure remained intact. Greasy smoke rose into the sky like filthy, diaphanous pillars.

Dante and Juno drew close to the general, and he said to them, "Enough planning and complaining. We will wait no longer." He swiveled his head turret, noted agreement from his long-time companions. "I will find the next opportunity to break free of Omnius — *and take it.*"

A ship cannot proceed toward its destination with two pilots struggling for the controls. One or the other must gain the upper hand quickly, or there will be a crash.

—Iblis Ginjo, note in the
margin of a stolen notebook

THE GRAND PATRIARCH of the Jihad was not a man to go begging. He demanded respect from everyone, and received it. People pleaded for favors from him as if he were a prince or a king. He made things happen.

But much had changed in the year since Serena Butler had seized the reins of the Jihad, when she should have remained no more than a figurehead. Iblis had *created* her, coached her until she became a powerful symbol. Now, ungratefully, she had rebuffed him, distributing his power and control among other Jihad officers. She had even turned down his perfectly reasonable suggestion of a political marriage. It wasn't just a passing phase.

Serena's recent forthright leadership had only served to shift the focus of the Jihad. Worse, she had gained her own followers, separate from his. The schism was widening, and Serena did not realize that she was contributing more to confusion than to clarity of vision. Despite Iblis's best efforts to convince her, Serena generally ignored him. Often she didn't answer his messages at all, or her responses were short and terse.

Can't she see that my suggestions are for her own good and for the good of the Jihad?

Apparently, she could not.

In a recent appearance before the Jihad Council, Serena had publicly — publicly! — called for Iblis to disclose information about the financial operations of his Jihad Police, implying that he was not being open with the League of Nobles. Such distractions only served to fracture the human effort, diverting attention from the real enemy. This was a time when leadership should be unified, not split.

Iblis finally decided to do something about it, with whatever allies he could find. Now, more than ever, he needed to demonstrate his capabilities and accomplish things that even the self-important Priestess could not. With any luck, it would help pave his way back to a position of supreme power.

On the forward observation deck of his private space yacht, he stood watching the stars drift across the empty gulf. He took only his Jipol commandant Yorek Thurr to serve both as the yacht's pilot and as Iblis's personal bodyguard. Thurr was the only other man alive who knew about the cymek Hecate and her offer to assist the Jihad.

The Titan, in her asteroid body, had caused so much mayhem at Ix that Primero Harkonnen had managed to conquer and hold the important Synchronized World. Without Hecate, the battle for Ix would have been at best another "moral victory" instead of a real one. Now, he needed her to pull off another miracle.

Thurr's voice came over the yacht's intercom. "I have detected the asteroid, sir, exactly as predicted."

"At least she's reliable," Iblis said.

"We are on approach."

The Grand Patriarch stared out the window, trying to discern which of the billions of glittering pinpoints might be the artificial hunk of space rock. At last, as the yacht approached, he distinguished the shape of the gigantic uneven lump of cratered rock, growing larger with each passing moment. This time, though, Iblis felt no trepidation. He knew exactly what the female Titan could do for him.

In the initial blush of Jihad fervor, everyone had called on the name of little Manion Butler and revered the valiant mother who had first raised her hand against the thinking machines. But after decades of war, most people were growing tired of the never-ending strife, and longed to go about their personal lives and careers. They wanted to work, raise children, and forget about the ebb and flow of military conflict. What fools they were.

Despite occasional victories such as Ix, IV Anbus, and Tyndall, he felt the revolt losing its pulse, like an organism dying all around him. The decline came in small and large stages, on small and large planets. Wherever Iblis traveled to deliver inspirational speeches, he saw and *felt* it. The crowds were losing enthusiasm, slipping from his grasp because they saw no end in sight. People had such woefully short attention spans!

The Grand Patriarch was desperate to make others see what he himself saw so clearly. Machines wanted to destroy every human — not only on the Synchronized Worlds, but on League Worlds and Unallied Planets as well. Human beings were a nuisance to Omnius and his metal brethren, a threat. Thinking machines and humans could never co-exist on any basis, whether on individual planets or in the entire universe.

Hecate's asteroid loomed closer, craters yawning open. "Our scanners have located the entry passage, sir," Thurr reported. "Hecate is making contact, welcoming you."

"Don't waste time with small talk. Take us inside."

The space yacht slipped easily through a crater opening, and the Titan's tractor beams assisted the pilot in bringing the craft deep into the mirror-walled interior grotto where Iblis had first spoken with Hecate in her dragon-cymek body.

Iblis emerged from the yacht and marched boldly into the chamber. This time, instead of wearing her ornate and intricate, human-sized walker-body, Hecate met him as a shielded preservation canister that held her brain swimming in electrafluid, on a rolling walker form. The protected cylinder adjusted itself to his eye level.

"I have important business to discuss with you," Iblis said, getting right to the point.

"Important business? I would not wish to discuss any other kind," Hecate's vibrant mechanical voice said. "After all, am I not your secret weapon?" She seemed particularly pleased with the title.

Iblis paced nervously as he explained. "The Jihad faces a crisis. In the past year, Serena Butler has taken power away from me. In her wildest dreams, she cannot possibly handle all of the political, military, religious, and social demands of leadership — yet she fails to see this."

"Ah, so you want her killed? Would that accomplish your purpose?" Hecate sounded miffed. "That seems a waste of my extravagant abilities."

"No!" he answered quickly, surprising himself. Then he considered the question more carefully. "No. That would not be beneficial in the long run. Serena is beloved by the masses, too important to them."

"Then how can I help you, dear Iblis?" Hecate's voice sounded musical and intriguingly seductive. "Give me a big enough job to make it worth my while."

"I need more clear victories against the machines. Genuine show-pieces." He stepped closer. "Thanks to you, we successfully reclaimed Ix. Now I need to incorporate more Synchronized Worlds into the League by freeing their human populations. It doesn't matter how strategically important the planets are, I just need something to *show*. And I need to claim credit for it."

Hecate made a sound like laughter, with a derisive edge. "In all the centuries I have spent as a cymek, I had forgotten how impatient biological humans can be. And how scheming."

"For twenty-six years, my impatience, as you so mockingly call it, has constituted the driving force of the Jihad. Serena and her child have only been images, while I have been the working . . ."

"Were you about to say *machinery?*"

"Only as a figure of speech."

"I wouldn't have it any other way. Long-term plans always take so . . . long." The shimmering brain canister raised itself higher, above his head. "So now you want me to create a little chaos on the Synchronized Worlds, leaving openings so that your Jihad can claim more conquests?"

"Absolutely!"

"How interesting." Hecate sounded amused at the challenge. "All right, I'll see what I can do."

Loyalty cannot be programmed.
—Seurat, private update logs

W HEN VORIAN ATREIDES encountered Seurat's update ship again in deep space, it was no surprise to either of them. Vor had always known in his heart that they would meet again, and the robot captain had calculated a slim but nonzero probability of the occurance.

The bureaucracy of the Army of the Jihad had specific, complicated, and annoying regulations that supposedly prohibited a Primero from doing half the things Vor did. He knew his behavior frustrated Xavier to no end, but nothing his friend said would ever change Vor's impulsive streak. Over and over again, he flew small ships alone, on missions of his choosing. Ever since joining the fight against the machines, Vor had been staunchly independent — a proverbial loose cannon, though an effective one.

After completing his Caladan mission, Vor departed from the watery world, unable to justify spending further time there with Leronica Tergiet. He left a detachment of jihadi soldiers at the listening post, and left a small part of his heart at the seaside tavern. Promising to send messages to Leronica whenever his military duties allowed it, Vor set off again to fight for the ultimate annihilation of thinking machines . . .

In the vicinity of Caladan, at the edge of Omnius's sphere of influence, Vor plotted from memory the usual routes he and Seurat had taken on their update runs. Since unleashing the unwitting Trojan Horse robot, Vor had heard scattered reports about Synchronized World breakdowns, and by plotting the datapoints of chaos he was able to trace the line of Seurat's route.

No further damage had been reported in some time, and Vor was not surprised that the machines had eventually caught on to the problem. He wondered what Seurat's fate had been, once the evermind discovered his hidden destructive programming. A sophisticated computer was not supposed to be vindictive, and Vor hoped Omnius hadn't simply destroyed the robot captain out of spite.

That would have been grossly inefficient and a waste of resources.

Vor spent a week on solo patrol, following the lines of the traditional update route. He justified his search as "gathering vital intelligence for League military planning," and it gave him the advantage of spending time alone, so that he could consider his unexpected feelings for Leronica.

He had always been aloof, enjoying himself on shore leave or temporary assignments on scattered League Worlds, but somehow this woman from Caladan had found a convoluted way into his heart. She had planted roots inside his very soul, and — like a time bomb going off — he was just now beginning to realize it. Vor was confused and happy at the realization . . . and deeply sad that he was not with her. Love had never been a foreign concept to him, though he had been blind to the possibility that it could feel anything like this. Now he understood how Xavier felt toward Octa.

But drifting alone through space on the edge of enemy territory, preoccupied as he was with bittersweet thoughts, did little to advance the Jihad. The ongoing war should have been his only priority.

When the large black-and-silver update ship crossed his path and loomed before him, Vor's attention swung back to more immediate concerns.

The update craft should have fled, should have engaged in evasive maneuvers to avoid even a small Jihad warship. If the robot captain carried an update of the computer evermind, his programming would command him to protect the silvery gelsphere at all costs.

But the update ship stopped, and Vor faced it in open space.

He recognized the configuration of the vessel, though the design appeared to have been modified, repaired, and expanded. Without a doubt, this was the same ship he had found drifting lost in high orbit over the Earth's solar system.

He opened the comline and transmitted immediately. "Old Metalmind. I thought I might find you out here."

Then he noticed that the ship's modifications included a battery of weaponry. Kinetic projectile ports slid open now and crackled red, ready to fire.

Vor felt a prickle of cool sweat on his neck. "Are you going to blow me out of space without even saying hello?"

"Hello, Vorian Atreides." Coppery-faced Seurat appeared on his screen. "There, I have taken care of the pleasantries. Now would it be acceptable for me to destroy you?"

"I'd rather you didn't." Vor kept his fingers on his own weapons controls. He could perhaps take the robot captain by surprise, though the update vessel seemed to outgun him significantly. "It appears Omnius has improved your odds with all those guns. I was wondering when the thinking machines would get around to that."

"I am aware of what you did to me and through me, Vorian. According to my records, eight Synchronized Worlds were severely damaged, due to the programming virus introduced by the update sphere I delivered. I presume you were responsible for that?"

"I can't take all the credit, Old Metalmind." Vor grinned. "After all, you yourself delivered each one of those programming time bombs. And you were the one who taught me so much about gelcircuitry and basic programming. See? It was a cooperative effort."

Seurat's flowmetal face gleamed in the lights from his update ship's cockpit. "Then I regret having been such an excellent teacher."

As Seurat scanned the image of Vorian Atreides, he used his previous experience and adaptive programming to analyze just what the human must be thinking. The robot Erasmus would have envied the opportunity.

After his capture and return to Corrin, where the corrupted update sphere was confiscated, Seurat endured an extensive debriefing by the restored Omnius. It soon became apparent what had taken place, and the sabotaged programming was stripped away, though Erasmus recommended the safest course: destroy all memories contained within the Earth-Omnius copy. "Those events occurred twenty-six standard years ago. While they may be interesting, they are not particularly relevant data and not worth the risk, Omnius."

Seurat suspected that, for reasons of his own, Erasmus did not want the evermind to have the information. The update pilot did not mention this, however, since he had no wish to incur the displeasure of the other independent robot.

After the explanations were logged and filed, and before Seurat could be assigned to a new and appropriate update run specifically designed to restore the Omnius incarnations on the virus-damaged worlds, Erasmus had spent a day in intense high-speed conversation with the robot pilot.

"I have studied humans for centuries. I have performed experiments, collected information, and made extrapolations to explain erratic human behavior. I learned a great deal from Serena Butler, and now I find that my new experiment raising and training Gilbertus Albans yields fresh insights.

"However, Seurat, you also had a unique opportunity. You spent years accompanied by the trustee Vorian Atreides, son of the Titan Agamemnon. I now require you to share with me your observations and any relevant details that might assist me in my quest to comprehend human nature."

Seurat could not refuse. With an exchange of information that was similar to, but much briefer than, the synchronization of an update sphere, he collated, summarized, and transferred all conversations and memories he had of Vorian Atreides.

As Seurat did this, he reviewed all of those memories himself and recalled with a reaction akin to fondness all the enjoyable flights on the *Dream Voyager*. Now that the robot pilot was alone on a new update ship — one which, sadly, had only a numerical designation and no name — he realized that he much preferred having the company . . .

The two ships faced each other in space, each with enough weapons to destroy the other, and Seurat found he did not wish to annihilate his former companion. "Do you recall our seventh mission to Walgis, Vorian Atreides? Twenty-eight years ago? We experienced a great deal of difficulty after leaving the system."

Vor chuckled. "Difficulty? That's quite an understatement. We ran into a meteor swarm that ripped open the side of the *Dream Voyager*. All of our atmosphere gushed out — and I was almost sucked out with it."

Seurat continued to stare at his friend and nemesis. "Yes, but I caught you and held you in my grip. I refused to let go."

"Really? I don't remember all the details," Vor said. "I was pretty busy gasping for air. Explosive decompression is quite unpleasant for a human, you know."

"I am aware of this. I carried you to a small storage cubicle and sealed you inside where I could maintain atmospheric pressure."

"You wouldn't let me out for almost two days," Vor said. "I was starving by the time you opened the door again. You hadn't thought to give me any rations."

"My thought was to save your life, and I required that much time to repair the hull damage and reestablish the life-support systems."

Vor looked at him wistfully, and then a puzzled frown creased his face. "I don't think I ever thanked you for that."

"Robots do not require gratitude, Vorian Atreides. I have, however, expended a great deal of effort to keep you alive and intact — on a significant number of occasions. Therefore, it would be foolish for me to destroy you now."

Seurat powered down his weapons systems and retracted his missile launchers and projectile tubes. For a moment the robot pilot was vulnerable, if Vorian Atreides chose to blast away. The thinking machine fired up his engines, spun about on his central axis, and launched the ship away at the highest possible velocity before Vor could react. Seurat was out of range by the time his human companion managed to transmit a burst of surprised questions.

Baffled and smiling, Vor drifted for a time in his scout ship. Then he began to laugh out loud.

Leadership hides behind many guises.
                    —Iblis Ginjo, *Options for Total Liberation*

W HEN HE RETURNED from his rushed and secret meeting with
      Hecate, Iblis learned that Serena had called a business meeting of
the Jihad Council, even though he wasn't expected to be there. He
hurried directly from the spaceport to the Council chambers, determined
not to be cut out of the decision-making process. Several weeks had
passed, and he needed to catch up.

He arrived at the entrance to the inner chambers just as Serena
signaled the beginning of the session, only to find the chief Seraph
guarding the doorway. Niriem hesitated, as if wrestling with her own
loyalties, then after an instant, allowed him to enter.

Ensconced at the head of the polished meeting table, the Priestess of
the Jihad seemed surprised by his presence. Iblis quickly found a seat as
close to her as possible, though it was not his accustomed spot. Without
comment, Serena launched into an obviously well-rehearsed speech,
while the others listened intently.

"We cannot continue this Jihad alone. Human passion is powerful, but
League resources are no match for the forces Omnius can bring to bear
against us. The thinking machines can manufacture multiple replacement robots for every one we destroy. But for each lost jihadi fighter, a
human life is forever snuffed out. We must preserve as many of those
precious lives as we can."

"What do you propose, Serena?" Iblis chose his words and tone
cautiously, in the hope that he could find a way to turn her orders to
his own ends. When he swept his gaze around the table, he saw to his
surprise the small, anxious-looking Tlulaxa flesh merchant Rekur Van

sitting at the far end of the room. He appeared to have been summoned especially for this meeting, and looked out of place. Discreetly, Iblis raised an inquisitive eyebrow, but the Tlulaxa man's only response was a perplexed expression.

Serena said, "Jihadis and mercenaries are not the only warriors in our holy cause. It is time I recognized and blessed some of the other great contributors to our fight." She smiled and gestured to Rekur Van, who flushed red with embarrassment at the attention.

"Though they have not engaged in active combat against the evil machines, the Tlulaxa have given our fighters much. The products of their organ farms have healed our injured veterans so that they can fight again. My dear friend Primero Harkonnen is the most famous beneficiary of all." She nodded graciously toward the flesh merchant and a smattering of applause rippled around the table.

"From the time I was a young Parliamentarian," Serena continued, "it was my fervent dream to bring Unallied Planets into the League of Nobles. Now, many of those worlds, including Caladan, have made overtures to us about joining the League. I intend to make a tour of potential member planets, stopping first at Tlulax. I wish to see the marvelous organ farms for myself and speak with the leaders, in hopes that they will consider joining us formally. I will see their wondrous cities and show them how much the Priestess of the Jihad appreciates their efforts on our behalf."

Iblis felt a sudden lump in his chest, as his delicate plans continued to crumble. He had secret agreements with the Tlulaxa organ industry, and Serena did not know what she was doing! "Such plans may be hasty, Priestess. The people of Tlulax guard their privacy, and we should respect that. I am not certain how they would react to a surprise visit."

Eyes flashing with displeasure, Serena crossed her arms over her white-robed chest. "I have walked among my people on many planets. It is inconceivable that the Tlulaxa leadership would not welcome a visit from the Priestess of the Jihad. Our fighters owe a tremendous debt to them. They cannot possibly have anything to hide — could you, Rekur Van?"

"Of course he doesn't," Iblis said quickly. "I am certain the government of Tlulax would be delighted to have you call upon them. However, we must dispatch a messenger to the Thalim system with all due haste so that they can prepare for your arrival. That is normal diplomatic procedure."

"Very well, but the war moves at its own pace, and we must remain one step ahead of it." As she outlined her ideas to the Council members, Iblis remained seated with an unreadable expression on his face.

He wondered what Hecate intended to do to help them. He hoped it was significant . . . and *soon.*

For months after Seurat had unintentionally delivered his rampant computer virus, Bela Tegeuse reeled from its debilitating effects. Surviving machines struggled to recover, but had difficulty communicating with the crippled evermind. Finally, the independent robots cut off damaged segments of the Omnius incarnation so that only a glimmer of the sprawling computer's sentience remained operational.

They were incredibly vulnerable.

On this dim and cloudy world where slaves grew food only by bathing crops under glaring artificial lights, the angry populace noticed the machines' weakness and formulated plans to take advantage of it. The robots, however, aware that revolts had occurred on many Synchronized Worlds, watched for any obvious signs of a potential uprising.

Bela Tegeuse could only return to parity with other Synchronized Worlds by receiving a new and uncorrupted copy of the evermind. So they waited . . .

When a lone, unidentified cymek ship arrived in the Tegeusan system, broadcasting that it carried an undefiled update directly from the Corrin-Omnius, the thinking machines welcomed the messenger. Defensive perimeters opened, allowing the cymek to penetrate the outer periphery and proceed with all due haste to the central nexus in Comati at the base of the mountains.

Hecate had never thought her infiltration would be so simple and straightforward. Hadn't the cymeks taught the machines anything?

For this venture the rebellious Titan had shed her mobile asteroid body, taking the appearance of a more traditional, though somewhat antique, cymek lander. She guided her stabilizing systems via thought-trodes that connected her disembodied brain to spacecraft functions.

The clouds above her were thick, murky rafts of gray moisture that blocked out the faint heat of Bela Tegeuse's sun, locking the weather cycle into an unbreakable pattern of rain and gloom. The robotic systems did not care about weather, and the sickly, pale-skinned human slaves knew no other life.

Hecate wondered what the poor human slaves would do once they were freed. Iblis Ginjo had tasked her with this aggressive, righteous action, and Hecate now rose to the challenge, eager to show what she could accomplish. She felt it would be quite interesting.

From her constant, quiet snooping, the turncoat Titan knew that at the very beginning of their renewed struggle the Army of the Jihad had attempted to wrest Bela Tegeuse free from machine domination. Their fleet had attacked the Omnius stronghold and damaged the machine infrastructure there, but had suffered so many losses that they were forced to withdraw without a clear-cut victory. Relentlessly scrounging resources and working nonstop, the remaining machines had rebuilt and reasserted their complete control over the planet in less than a year, like an inexorable tide erasing footprints on a beach.

This time, Hecate hoped, the humans would learn their lesson and act more decisively. Thanks to her, they would get a second chance. If they were paying attention. She had left a message for Iblis Ginjo via a drop point that Yorek Thurr was supposed to be monitoring. It was up to them to be ready to respond.

As she landed at well-lit Comati Spaceport under a cold drizzle, robotic machines marched forward, transmitting queries and identification demands. "The remains of our Omnius cannot access the watcheyes aboard your craft," said one administrative robot who seemed to be in charge of the facility. To Hecate it seemed like a foolish comment, especially for AI-security units. She smiled to herself. Machines could be so blind and naïve at times.

Gathered around the fences, captive humans huddled in wet clothes. Through bleak, squinting eyes, they observed the arrival of the ship warily, as if the new Omnius update might steal away their remaining hopes.

Hecate opened the hatch and strode out wearing her ornate dragon-walker. "Your attendant watcheye mechanisms must be malfunctioning," she said to the waiting robots. "The Corrin-Omnius was forced to shut down many peripheral systems to prevent continued infection by insidious programming errors."

The robots accepted her explanation. "What is your designation? We are not familiar with your model of neo-cymek."

"Oh, I am the newest of the new." An almost prideful tone, as if she were superior to older models. She plodded forward carrying the heavy cylindrical package in her jointed forelimbs. Her diamond scales flashed with reflected light from the spaceport's yellow glowpanels. "After so many terrible breakdowns, Omnius ordered the creation of many new cymeks from loyal trustees. Unlike gelcircuitry computer minds, human brains cannot succumb to this spreading virus. Neos such as myself have been sent out to deliver shielded updates protected by programming designed to override the virus. Surely you see the advantages?"

A trio of spaceport robots stepped forward to accept the heavy canister. To Hecate they seemed almost eager, anxious to be relieved of their strange problems. As expected, they were not devious or suspicious enough for their own good.

"I promise you," she said, "this will remove all of your concerns."

Though she had been disgusted with Ajax's bloodshed long ago, Hecate convinced herself that murdering thinking machines — obliterating Omnius, in particular — was different . . . and far more admirable. The humans would be stunned and delighted!

"Are there special instructions for installing this update?" the robot asked.

Hecate backed the walker toward her ship. "Use the standard procedure. I have been ordered to depart with all possible haste since I have other Synchronized Worlds to visit. Omnius depends on the swift completion of this task. You understand, I'm sure."

Offering stiff gestures of acknowledgement, the robots marched away with their fateful cylinder, and Hecate installed herself in the controls of her spacecraft once more. Using thoughtrode commands, she lifted away from the spaceport under yellow spotlights.

Below, in the grid city of Comati, the robots entered the citadel where the crippled Omnius evermind struggled to continue its vital functions. The machines used delicate manipulating hands to open the casing of the cylinder and remove the layers of protective armor.

Finally, they revealed the oddly shaped but potent nuclear warhead. Their systems swiftly attempted to calculate an appropriate response, even as the detonation numbers counted down to zero . . .

Hecate's ship was high above the first two layers of clouds, when she saw a silvery-yellow light erupt like a sun beneath her. She had made certain that the immense explosion could be powerful enough to eradicate all remaining traces of the wounded evermind. The bomb's electromagnetic pulse, enhanced by the design of its warhead, rippled across the skies of Bela Tegeuse and was reflected downward by the layer of thick clouds. Each Omnius substation shorted out in a chain reaction, one after another.

It gave her quite a thrill.

As Hecate left the dim planet behind, she thought about the surviving humans there — those who had not been in the proximity of ground zero. They had never known anything other than machine rule. She wondered if they would know how to take care of themselves. Oh well. Survival of the fittest.

"Now you are free of Omnius," she announced, knowing that no one on the planet could hear her. "Bela Tegeuse is yours, if you wish to take it."

Human beings are the most adaptable of creatures. Even under the harshest circumstances, we invariably find ways to survive. Through our careful breeding program, there may be ways to enhance this characteristic.

—Zufa Cenva, 59th Lecture to Sorceresses

H IS FIRST MORNING on Arrakis, after sleeping on the hard rocks with the comforting presence of Chamal beside him, Rafel rose with the dawn. A new day on a new planet. He watched the violent splash of orange stain the sky, and the browns and yellows of the desert and the rocks as they rose from slumber. He drew a deep breath of the already-hot, dry air and filled his lungs with freedom.

But freedom in Heol itself wasn't what he had expected at all.

From somewhere high on the towering rocks behind them, he heard the cries of birds and saw their black shapes flitting and swooping around the stone crannies as if searching for food.

At least something can survive here. That means we can, too.

As a Zensunni slave since his birth on Poritrin, Rafel had always dreamed of liberty, but never had he envisioned finding it on a barren, desolate planet the likes of this one. The humid misery of the Starda River delta had been bad enough, but the oppressive heat here was worse by far.

Still, he had followed Chamal's father, knowing that their only other option had been outright war against the whole population of Poritrin. And now that they were here, they must make the best of it. Ishmael was right: Freedom, even in a place like this, was preferable to working one more hour for a slave owner.

During the rough landing of the experimental ship, they had seen only a small portion of the planet that the flesh-merchant Keedair called Arrakis. There must be green, fertile lands not far away, and a spaceport. *We need only find them.* Perhaps the Tlulaxa man knew the location of secret oases, and would have to be encouraged to share his information.

More than a hundred men and women had escaped from Poritrin, but none of them understood the technology of the ship that brought them here. Apparently, not even Keedair. Certainly those first-generation slaves who had been on space journeys after being abducted from their native worlds had never seen anything like the strange auroral lights around the ship as space *folded* around it.

One moment on Poritrin, and the next on Arrakis. Stuck here.

Rafel stared at the battered hull of the large, crashed ship and knew the wreck would never fly again. *We are on our own.* He feared for his young wife, and silently promised that he would do everything possible to secure their rescue himself, if necessary. Perhaps Ishmael could discover a way.

Hearing the scuff of boots, he turned to see Chamal's father approaching from the camp. A blanket of quiet lay on the morning, but soon the refugees would awaken and begin to explore their bleak surroundings. He and Ishmael stood together in uncomfortable silence, watching the dawn awaken.

"We need to see what is out there, Ishmael," Rafel said. "There may be green lands and water nearby."

Their only means of transportation was a small scout vessel that had been inside the cargo hold, probably for the test crew to reconnoiter — or escape — when conducting the first trial of the prototype engines.

Ishmael nodded. "We have no maps, so we are limited to what we can see with our own eyes. Today you will take the scout ship and explore. Tuk Keedair will accompany you."

Rafel scowled. "I don't want that flesh peddler along."

"And I doubt he wants to be with you, either. But he knows more about Arrakis than any of us. He may recognize landmarks and you may need him to negotiate assistance, if you find anyone."

Grudgingly, Rafel saw the wisdom in this. He knew that the Tlulaxa had kidnapped the boy Ishmael himself. Ishmael must hate the man, and now Rafel tried to interpret any hidden message or instructions. *Does he want me to take Keedair far away and kill him?* But Ishmael's expression was unreadable.

"In order to survive, the slaver will have to work, just like the others," Rafel insisted. "And he'll get a smaller ration of food and water."

Ishmael nodded, his expression distant. "It will do him good to see how slaves live."

After a limited breakfast of limited rations, Rafel chose another escaped slave, a big-shouldered man named Ingu to keep watch over the complaining and reluctant Tuk Keedair. While Ishmael watched, the Tlulaxa man glowered at them all, then snatched out a sharp-edged talon of metal he had scavenged from the wrecked ship.

Ingu and Rafel both flinched back, sure the former slaver meant to attack them, though he could not possibly fight a hundred angry Zensunnis. "Lord Bludd did enough damage to me, but now after decades ripe with profits, you have ruined me. Utterly!" He slashed out with the makeshift knife. "Worthless, foolish slaves."

Then with a flare of frustrated rage, he chopped off his own long, thick braid. Keedair held up the limp dusty rope of hair and dropped the gray-brown bundle to the sand. The former flesh merchant looked oddly naked without it, and he stared at the severed hair, all his bluster gone. "Ruined."

"Yes," Ishmael said to him, unimpressed, and took the knife away from him. "And now you must begin to earn your survival among us."

"Survival! It is hopeless — with every breath, you are wasting your body's water. Look at those people working out in the open sun as the day gets hotter — why didn't they perform their labors during the cool of the night?" The Tlulaxa man glared at them.

"Because at night the Zensunni pray, and sleep."

"Follow that practice on Arrakis, and you'll die. Things have changed, and you must learn to change with them. Have you paid no attention to the heat and the dust? The very air saps out droplets of perspiration, steals your water — how will you replenish it?"

"We have supplies to last for weeks, possibly even months."

Keedair gave Rafel a hard stare. "Are you so sure that will be enough? You must cover your skin from the hot sun. You must sleep during the greatest heat of the day, and do your physical work during the cool darkness. Doing this, you will save half of your perspiration."

"We can also conserve our strength if we have you do more of our hard labor," Ishmael said.

Disgusted, Keedair said, "You refuse to understand. I would have thought that a man willing to risk so much to free his people, leading them to a faraway place, would want to keep them alive for as long as possible."

Teams of refugees worked at the crashed cargo ship to open the storage bay wide enough so that Rafel would be able to maneuver the small scout flyer out into the open. It was a poorly equipped vehicle, and they had no assurance as to how far it would fly or how much fuel it carried, but they had no other way to cross the incomprehensibly vast distance of open sand. Other than walking.

"We are going to explore our surroundings," Rafel said, giving Chamal a farewell embrace. He glanced sidelong at the rumpled, red-eyed Keedair. "The slaver will help us find a place to establish a settlement of our own."

Tuk Keedair sighed. "Believe me, I want to find civilization as much as you do. But I don't know where we are, or where to find water, food —"

Ishmael cut off his complaints. "Then you will look. Make yourself useful and earn your share of our supplies."

The three men climbed into the small vessel, and Rafel looked skeptically at the controls. "Standard engines. This looks like something I flew on Poritrin. I think I can handle it." They lifted off the deck and emerged from the hold of the wrecked ship.

While Chamal, Ishmael, and the other slaves looked after them, poignantly hopeful, Rafel guided the scout ship away from the rocks and out into the open desert. Burly Ingu furrowed his brow and stared out the windows, hoping to spot an oasis or some sign of civilization. Rafel glanced over at Keedair. "Tell me which direction to go, slaver."

"I don't know where we *are*." The Tlulaxa looked over at him disdainfully. "You Zensunnis greatly overestimate my abilities. First Ishmael insists that I pilot a space vessel I have never flown, and now that we have crashed, you want me to be your savior."

"If we survive, you survive," Rafel pointed out.

Keedair gestured toward the window, pointing at nothing in particular. "All right, then. Go . . . *there*. In the desert, all directions are the same. Just be sure to mark your coordinates so that we can find our way back."

The little craft skimmed over the open sands at good speed. They flew in an ever-expanding circle around the base camp in the rocks, exploring farther in all directions. The heat of the day set in, lifting thermals from the warm rocks and shimmering sands. The flyer rocked and lurched, and Rafel fought to hold it steady. The temperature rose inside the cabin and perspiration ran down his cheeks.

"I still don't see anything out there," Ingu said.

"Arrakis is a huge planet, mostly unexplored and only sparsely inhabited." Keedair squinted in the glaring light. "If we find anything, it will not be because of my skills or expertise, but just plain luck."

"Buddallah guides us," Rafel intoned.

Away from the crash site of the stolen cargo ship, the desert extended endlessly before them, toward the shimmering horizon. Clinging to nothing but hope, Rafel kept flying, searching for anything. Rock out-croppings poked up at odd intervals in the tan and yellow ocean below, but he detected no smears of green, no water, no settlements.

"You won't find anything out here," Keedair said. "Nothing looks familiar to me, and I doubt the flyer has the range we need to find Arrakis City."

"Would you prefer to walk?" Ingu asked.

The small man fell silent.

At dusk, after a fruitless day of searching, they landed gently in the middle of the ocean of sand near a thick swirl of rusty discoloration. Several kilometers away, another line of barren rock stood out from the dunes, but Rafel thought it would be safer and easier to land out in the open. It was cooler after the sun set, and when he disembarked onto the soft dunes, Rafel heard only lifeless silence and the rushing of wind-scattered dust. The air seemed heavy with a pungent biting smell like . . . cinnamon. Ingu paced around the ship, and seemed to be looking for something.

Keedair was the last to venture outside; he stared dejectedly into the vast emptiness. Sniffing, he bent down to the reddish powdery sand and scooped up a handful. "Congratulations, you have found a fortune in melange." He began to chuckle to himself, but his laughter had an edge of hysteria. "Now we just need to get it to market and you Zensunnis will be rich."

"I was hoping the discoloration was a sign of water," Rafel said. "That's why I landed here."

"Can we eat it?" Ingu asked of Keedair.

"You can eat the sand itself, for all I care." He hunkered down on the ground, his dark eyes gazing down. "You have destroyed years of work, my entire investment . . . and for what? You will all die here, too. There is nothing on Arrakis for the likes of you."

"At least we are no longer slaves," Rafel said.

"And now you have no one to take care of you, either." Keedair raised his voice. "You've never had to live on your own, using only your personal skills for survival. You were born to be slaves, and before long your people will be begging to return to Poritrin, where the nobles can take care of them." He spat into the reddish dust, then seemed to regret wasting the moisture. "I did you a favor capturing you and bringing you to civilization. But you fools never appreciated what you had."

Rafel grabbed the small Tlulaxa man, pulled out the scrap-metal knife Ishmael had given him, and raised it in front of the man's face. But the former slaver did not flinch. Tauntingly, Keedair tapped fingers against his throat. "Go ahead, or are you a coward . . . like all your people?"

Ingu strode up, fists bunched, as if ready to join in the fight, but Rafel tossed the Tlulaxa man aside. "Buddallah would punish me for killing a man in cold blood, no matter how much suffering you have caused. I have memorized the sutras, I have listened to Ishmael." Rafel scowled, restraining himself. Truly, he wanted to feel this evil man's hot blood run off the metal of his knife blade and down onto his hand.

Keedair sneered at them from where he had fallen in the dust. "Yes, use me as your scapegoat, since I am the brunt of generations of your pitiful anger, the only target for your simpering. I did not want to bring you here, and I cannot help you now. If I could find rescuers, I would call them."

"I have been waiting for an excuse to get rid of you, no matter what Ishmael says." Rafel gestured away from the scout vessel. "Go out into the desert then, and find your own way. Why not eat your valuable melange? I see plenty of it around here."

Against his better judgment, the Tlulaxa man staggered out toward the dunes, then turned back to them. "You're hurting your chances for survival by getting rid of me."

Ingu looked smugly pleased at the man's predicament. Rafel said, "We will survive longer if we don't have to share our rations with a flesh peddler."

With a mixture of relief to be away and fear at being left alone in the cruel desert, Tuk Keedair squared his shoulders, then walked bravely away, into the sea of sand. "I am dead either way. And so are you."

Rafel looked after him with awkward uncertainty. Was this what Ishmael had intended? Had there been a subtle message Rafel had not interpreted? The young man wanted to impress his father-in-law, but wasn't sure he understood what he was supposed to do . . .

Afterward, Rafel and Ingu sat outside the ship in the cool evening. They ate sparingly of protein wafers and sipped water. The two men pulled emergency sleeping pads from the small storage compartment and spread them on the soft sand. As he lay down, feeling utterly weary, Rafel wished he could be beside Chamal.

He put away the scrap-metal knife, wondering if there might be nighttime predators out in the deep desert . . . or if the desperate slaver might sneak back and kill them in their sleep, then steal the scout craft for himself.

Grimly, he decided they needed more protection around the camp. Leaving Ingu snoring on his mat, Rafel climbed into the cockpit and saw, not surprisingly, that Norma Cenva had equipped the small craft with Holtzman shields. It would be a good defense.

Confident, he powered up the shields, which surrounded their camp with a shimmering umbrella of ionized air. Then he went back to his sleeping pad and felt safe . . . for a moment.

The ground shook, as from an earthquake. The dunes shifted and churned, and a rumble came from deep below them. With a rushing sound like a hurricane, the dunes collapsed. The scout ship lurched, knocked off of its landing gear.

Yelping, Rafel scrambled to his feet, only to stagger and fall on the uneven, shifting sand. Ingu threw himself off the sleeping mat with a yell, windmilling his arms for balance.

Abruptly, the night desert erupted into a storm of frenzied shapes around them, huge segmented demons that rose up like living nightmares. Rafel fell on his back, already half buried in the turbulent sand, and looking into the cavernous mouths of monsters rising up from below, driven wild . . . by the thrumming shields!

Ingu screamed in an oddly high-pitched voice.

All the worms struck at once, pounding the scout craft, the camp, the two men. Rafel thought he was gazing up at a giant fire-eating dragon. But there were no eyes. He saw a flash of glittering crystalline points around the huge mouth.

Then shadows, a sharp burst of pain, and endless darkness.

Life is about choices — good and bad — and their cumulative effects.

—Norma Cenva, *Mathematical Philosophies*

RRITATED BUT CURIOUS, Zufa Cenva arrived on Kolhar in response to the strange telepathic demand that had targeted her from across space. The Sorceress found the planet austere and rudimentary; the colony there had survived but wasn't exactly thriving. Why would anyone want her to come here? The world had few resources and a bleak climate just on the survivable edge of harshness.

But the summons had been undeniable. *Who could want me here? And how dare they summon me?*

While she'd been training her most talented sisters on Rossak, leading them through dangerous mental exercises in the noisome jungles, the compulsion had yanked her thoughts so severely that she'd nearly allowed her mental focus to collapse, with potentially disastrous results. The Sorceress recruits who depended upon Zufa's guidance had desperately juggled their deadly energies, barely containing the holocaust in their minds.

But she couldn't drive the thought away, or ignore it. The calling had been like a loud shout in Zufa's brain, demanding that she leave immediately. *Come to Kolhar. Meet me there.* She, the Supreme Sorceress of the Jihad, had no choice.

This unremarkable planet was on the nearby trade routes from Ginaz, but she had never thought much about it. Kolhar had always been beneath her notice. Zufa had other priorities in the Jihad.

Come to Kolhar!

Now, as her private spacecraft descended and her ship's onboard systems scanned for a dry spot to land near the rough settlements at the edge of the cold marshy wastes, a leaden dullness seeped into her like poison. The sky, the water, the soggy ground, and even the twisted trees, all looked ashen.

Mother. Come to Kolhar. Now!

Mother? Could it be some strange communication from the unborn fetus growing inside Zufa, the daughter of Iblis Ginjo . . . already prescient and sending her on a mission? If so, this could be the greatest Sorceress of all time. Smiling to herself, Zufa touched her abdomen, which did not yet show signs of pregnancy.

Certainly, stunted Norma could not possibly have such powers . . . She had heard nothing from her daughter in years. Even Savant Holtzman had stopped wasting time on her, and may have deported her from Poritrin prior to the disastrous slave uprising there.

Did that mean that Norma was alive, that she had survived? Despite her disappointment in Norma, Zufa was her mother, and still cared about her.

But even if Norma had survived, this message could not possibly be from her . . .

A dusky outpost city with an outdated spaceport came into view. The primary Kolhar settlement held only a few hundred thousand inhabitants at most.

As she approached for a landing, the Sorceress received clearance from a thin-voiced male attendant. Zufa noticed no other offworld ships anywhere, only the lethargic movement of local traffic. "We have a berth reserved for your vessel, Sorceress, and instructions for your arrival. We have been expecting you."

Curious to the point of annoyance, Zufa pressed him, even used a bit of telepathic nudging, but the man simply couldn't tell her anything more. She just wanted to learn the answer to this mystery, and then get back to her real work.

Following the mental summons, she hired a railtaxi and took it from the sleepy spaceport to a subsidiary village two hundred kilometers north. Why would anyone go out here by choice? The small car glided slowly on a narrow-gauge track; the ride was bumpy, especially when it ascended to a high plateau surrounded on three sides by snow-capped mountains. Zufa wanted to use her telekinetic powers to propel the sluggish transport at greater speed, but resisted the temptation.

When Zufa finally debarked at a little station and stepped onto a painted wooden platform open to the cool winds, a stunningly beautiful blonde woman called out to her. "Supreme Sorceress Cenva. I have been waiting for you."

Though the air of Kolhar was damp and brisk, the woman wore only thin, loose clothing that somehow resisted blowing in the breezes. She was young yet somehow ageless, with gentle blue eyes and unblemished skin like delicate porcelain. She looked familiar in an odd sort of way.

"Why have I been summoned here? By what means did you send such a signal?" Always conscious of her own status, Zufa wished she had not used the word *summoned*, as if she were no more than a lackey to be ordered about by a master.

The beautiful stranger gave her an odd, infuriating smile. "Follow me. We have much to discuss . . . as soon as you are ready for the answers."

Zufa followed the woman into the station building, where a scrawny old man bowed subserviently and offered her a thick coat. Zufa gestured the man away, paying no attention to the chill air on the plateau. "Who are you?" Suddenly, she remembered one of the messages: *Mother. Come to Kolhar. Now!*

The woman turned to look at her calmly, as if waiting for something. Her features were tantalizingly familiar, clearly of Rossak stock, with high cheekbones and a classical profile. She looked like one of the great Sorceresses, but with a softer, more elegant beauty. In a way, her eyes reminded Zufa of . . . but it couldn't be!

"If you open your eyes, you will see that there are no limitations on possibilities, Mother. Are you capable of seeing me in a different form?"

Startled, Zufa jerked her head back, then stepped forward, her eyes narrow and suspicious. "This is not possible!"

"Come with me, Mother, and we will talk. I have much to share with you."

In a bubble-top groundcar Norma drove her away from the plateau village and out onto a barren, slushy plain of half-frozen marshland. As the vehicle worked its way over the rough, roadless terrain, Norma told a remarkable tale. Astonished, Zufa could barely believe the revelations, but could not deny what she saw with her own eyes. "You have potential after all!"

"The cymek torture shocked my brain to capabilities I never knew I had. My mind turned inward, where I found my own beauty and peace. A soostone Aurelius gave me triggered something inside and helped me to focus . . . something the cymeks never expected. And they paid for it with their lives. Afterward, I had the luxury of fashioning my new body according to the blueprints stored in my genes. Given the potential of my ancestors, this is how I *should* have appeared."

Zufa's astonishment and wonder were palpable. "All my life this is what I expected — even demanded — of you. Though you never showed the potential before, I'm pleased to see that I was not wrong. I was hard on you because that is what you required. You did have it in you." She nodded, expressing what she meant as a compliment. "You are worthy of my name after all."

Norma remained unruffled, showing that nothing her mother said could hurt her. Her gaze contained a hint of skepticism, as if she didn't totally believe what Zufa was saying.

"My beauty is irrelevant to the work I can do now. When my body was destroyed, I rebuilt it according to images drawn from my female bloodline. This body suits me, though I suppose I could revert to my previous form if I wished. I never minded it as much as you always did. Appearances are, after all, only *appearances*."

Zufa was perplexed. After spending years as a disappointing dwarf, her daughter seemed to consider the new physical beauty almost an afterthought. Norma had not adopted this perfect female form to impress anyone — or so she claimed.

"You should not have given up on me, Mother." Despite her pointed words, Norma seemed beyond anger and vengeance, with a calmly superior confidence in herself. "Many of your trainees have died in mental attacks against cymeks. But I managed to control a telepathic holocaust that would have wiped out any other Sorceress — even you."

Zufa was amazed at the possibility. She had seen so many of her talented sisters die in strikes against the machines with human minds. "You must show me how to do it." She watched her daughter, wondered what she was thinking.

Norma parked the groundcar a short distance away from an isolated cottage, and got out with her mother. As if frozen in place by the cold winds, Norma focused on a small rock formation a few meters away. It had been weeks since the incident that completely changed her life, and in that time she had not attempted to use her power again. Not out of fatigue, but out of uncertainty and concern that her abilities might manifest in ways she did not expect. Most of all, she feared harming her mother, who sat nearby.

Norma relaxed her body. "Not now. I'm not ready. When I reshaped myself, it was external only — and triggered by extreme duress. But I feel that this is only the beginning, Mother, just an interim phase for me. Do not be surprised if I change even more in the future. Do not be surprised by anything I am now capable of."

The comment frightened the experienced Sorceress, who looked away, cheeks burning with shame.

Norma seemed distant and preoccupied. "I am more concerned with the future, not the past. If I am no longer a disappointment to you, then we can be strong together, more powerful than you can imagine." An arctic wind blew her long blonde hair, giving her an ethereal appearance against the snowy mountains beyond. "Now is a good enough time to lay a new foundation for our relationship. We have work to do."

Zufa could not bring herself to admit openly that she was sorry — a lifetime of sincere apologies would not undo the scorn and disappointment she had heaped on Norma for so long — but perhaps she could work harder now, and the two of them could join their abilities to make significant strides against the enemy. Norma would understand her implied apology, eventually.

The Sorceress tentatively reached out both hands, and as she did so, she saw Norma doing the same, only a fraction of a second later. Or had it been simultaneous? The two women clasped hands awkwardly, then hugged in a fashion unfamiliar to either of them.

They walked over rough, frozen ground to the cottage, an old prefabricated building erected long ago by a well-meaning colonist who had given up on his dreams of independence. Norma had renovated it and made it livable again.

She spoke briefly, indicating the broad, fallow fields all around them. "Mother, I envision more than bleak emptiness. I see a whole landscape of possibilities! Finally, I have the mental powers of a Rossak Sorceress, while retaining the mathematical insights I developed on my own. I now have the *answer*, Mother. After so many years, I finally understand how to fashion engines that will *fold* space." She turned to the older woman, and Zufa felt dizzy in the crosshairs of that gaze.

"Do you understand, Mother? We can build vessels that travel from one battlefield to another in the wink of an eye. Imagine how much good my spaceships would do if they could appear anywhere in the universe on a moment's notice. The Army of the Jihad could deal death blows to the Synchronized Worlds faster than Omnius could ever respond."

Zufa kept her balance, but her mind spun with a new spectrum of marvelous possibilities. "That could be the most significant change to the long-standing conflict since . . . since the atomic destruction of Earth."

"More than that, my Mother. Much more." Norma narrowed her pale eyes. "But this time I cannot fail because of my personal weaknesses. Before, on Poritrin, I underestimated and ignored politics and personal interactions. I do not understand the art of manipulation, nor do I wish to."

Norma stared across the rugged openness, as if in her mind she could see invisible cities yet to be built. "Therefore, I need your help, Zufa Cenva. My vision is too grand to be denied. I will not allow deluded fools or self-centered bureaucrats to stop me. Savant Holtzman caused me much harm on Poritrin, and I was blind to the ways he was hurting me, delaying me, until finally he attempted to steal everything. He wanted more than my ideas. He wanted to own the ideas because he could no longer generate them himself."

Zufa could not conceal her shock. "Savant Holtzman? He is dead now in the revolt, as is Lord Bludd and almost everyone else in Starda."

Norma nodded. "I know, so we must start from scratch, here on Kolhar. I need the abilities and political influence of the Supreme Sorceress of the Jihad. Simply developing the mathematics is not enough. I will make the technology work, while you will see that it is *used*. You and the other Sorceresses must help me turn this place into a great, secret shipyard."

"But . . . here?" Zufa asked, looking at the unwelcome terrain.

Norma waved her arms expansively. "In my mind's eye I see a vast launching area on this very plain, from which space-folding ships can travel across the universe, immense vessels that dwarf the spacecraft we know today."

Beside her daughter, Zufa blurted, "Norma, there's something I have to tell you. I . . . am carrying your unborn sister. Through careful timing of my internal rhythms, I am pregnant with the child of Iblis Ginjo."

Even the supernaturally beautiful and powerful Norma seemed surprised. "The Grand Patriarch? But why?"

"Because he has great potential that even he does not realize. Possibly even a hint of Rossak stock, far back in his breeding. I thought he would give me a perfect daughter. Now, perhaps, that was unnecessary."

"It seems that we each have surprising news," Norma said. "Many things have changed between us. And Aurelius, too. The landscape of the future has changed." She smiled gently.

From now on I will make up for my failings, for my utter, shameful lack of faith in my child, Zufa promised herself. Guilt inundated her, as she realized she should always have been ready to help Norma. She vowed to make up for past mistakes. "Yes, I can help you accomplish this enormous task. I am glad you have chosen me for this responsibility, my daughter."

Norma's gentle smile faded, and she seemed to stare through her mother, as if weighing Zufa's change of attitude. "You are my flesh and blood. If not you, who can I trust? I have no better choice."

Then her pale blue eyes sparkled with anticipation. "And for my next step I must recruit the perfect businessman to provide the funding for such a massive undertaking." Norma drew a breath of the chill air, then turned to open the door of her dwelling. "I can't wait to see Aurelius again."

When the observer truly believes *the illusion, it becomes real.*
                                        —Swordmaster Zon Noret

T HE MASTER MERCENARY sat on a knoll of rock and sand, beside a
broken-coral shrine adorned with fresh hyacinths. This memorial to
Manion the Innocent offered comfort and protection against demon
machines, but Jool Noret preferred to rely on his own fighting abilities, as
he had done on Ix more than a year ago.

Looking away, the hardened young man gazed out across the ocean of
sand that surrounded his small private island. He envisioned imaginary
enemies, targets and foes.

Noret wore nothing but a small loincloth cinched at the waist.
Crouching, he bunched his muscles until the frozen stance made him
ache, but he refused to loosen up, refused to blink, even though trickles of
sweat rolled over his eyebrows and into his eyes.

Then, quick as lightning, he slashed with his pulse sword. The
disruptor edge stabbed into the air precisely where Noret had aimed.

Noret had vowed never to let his skills fade, even when he went back to
Ginaz between battle engagements. He had to keep training with Chirox,
to bring his abilities to an ever higher level. Already he had set the mek's
adaptability algorithm far beyond previous limits, exceeding anything he
had formerly considered practical. Proving himself repeatedly, he never
achieved any sort of self-satisfaction. The subtle clock of age ticked inside
him, and he didn't want to lose his skills as he grew older. Strange,
morbid thoughts for a man who had not even reached his twenty-third
year.

Months ago he had returned to Ginaz with a group of veterans on their
way home from Salusa Secundus. None of the angry, well-seasoned

mercenaries particularly wanted to loll around on a sunny archipelago, so for weeks they hunted through space along a perimeter of the Synchronized Worlds, looking for suitable stragglers. They found and destroyed a pair of robotic scout vessels, but with no more targets in sight, the troop transport ship eventually headed off through the corridor toward Rossak and Ginaz. After threading their way through the system's asteroid belt, they reached the ocean world.

Noret did not mind. He longed to be back on the small island with Chirox, honing his skills sharper than a nanoblade. The better to kill machines.

Without warning, he whirled, leapt into the air and slashed behind him. Since childhood, he had trained with a variety of weapons, including complex armaments that could take out a dozen combat robots at a time. Even so, he always went back to his father's pulse sword. It was an archaic weapon, but precise. Use of the sword demanded a skill level that no scrambler grenade or brute-force weapon would ever require.

Fighting is a matter of precision and timing, the correct application of senses, and the knowledge that comes from experience.

When not on a mission for the Army of the Jihad, Jool Noret trained for hours every day, either alone or with the *sensei* mek. Having no wish for close human companionship, he made no friends among the other trainees who came to the island. He paused only to drink tepid water or eat bland foods, enough to energize his body so that he could keep fighting, training, and sharpening his edge.

Soon Noret would be ready to return to the Jihad. He considered himself a man who existed for no reason other than to obliterate thinking machines. One day, his recklessness might cost him his life, but he would make sure that it cost Omnius a great deal first . . .

Below, on the trampled beach, student hopefuls silently and respectfully observed Jool Noret as he worked through an exercise routine. The *sensei* mek Chirox stood with the observers. Noret saw them with his peripheral vision, but paid them no heed. He had learned a great deal from simply watching his father, and they were welcome to observe, but he would not be their teacher.

Noret turned his back on the audience and plunged forward with his exercises. The people knew of his exploits, from war reports that the Council of Veterans disseminated among recuperating mercenaries and crowds of eager trainees. All of the island people had heard of his victories. On his very first mission, Jool Noret had achieved near-legendary status, single-handedly unleashing an atomic city-killer that wiped out the Ix-Omnius. Since then, in a handful of other skirmishes, Noret had defeated swarms of thinking machines.

But Jool Noret shunned all accolades and refused to bask in fame. He did not feel he deserved it.

In the past few weeks, though, an increasing number of curious students had come to watch him, hungry to replicate his techniques. They witnessed Noret's superhuman drills against the combat mek and gasped as he moved.

The crowds increased. Some of the would-be warriors pleaded openly for personal instruction, but he declined them all. "I cannot. I have not yet learned all that I need to know."

Though he sought to conceal it, he refused to teach any admirers because of the guilt he carried over his father's death. His heart felt like stone. He knew he would fall in battle someday, for that was the fate of his kind. But he vowed to do it in a blaze of glory, with his skills sharpened to their limits. His complete release of all care or self-preservation liberated him to achieve such feats as he demonstrated in his training exercises. What good would that kind of teaching do the other mercenaries, except to get them all killed?

Each day, Jool Noret bested the highest level of expertise Chirox could implement.

"Other students wish to learn from you, Master Jool Noret," the combat robot said, as the sun set golden on the extended sea. "Is it not the stated duty of Ginaz to hurl more and more mercenaries into the fight?"

Noret frowned. "It is my duty to return to the fight. I intend to leave on the next ship." He hefted his pulse sword, piecing together in his mind scenarios for future engagements against the evil thinking machines.

Then one of the bolder students strode toward him, brave enough to approach the famously solitary young mercenary. "Jool Noret, we admire you. You are the scourge of Omnius."

"I am merely doing my job."

The student had dark hair and pale skin that had sunburned, peeled, then freckled. He was obviously not a native of Ginaz, yet he had come here to train. *Here.* He was older than Noret by at least five years, and his strength came from a burly body and heavy muscles. He would never possess the agility of a deft Ginaz mercenary . . . but he still had the look of a formidable fighter about him.

"Why do you refuse to teach us, Jool Noret? We are all weapons waiting to be forged."

Calmly, Noret repeated what had become a mantra for him, with no end in sight. "I remain unworthy myself. I am not fit to teach anyone else."

The man's voice was gruff. "I will take that risk, Jool Noret. I come from Tyndall. Eight years ago the thinking machines took over my world, killed millions and enslaved the rest. My sisters were slaughtered, and my parents." His eyes were large and filled with both anger and tears. "Then the Army of the Jihad fought back. They came to Tyndall with an overwhelming force and many mercenaries from Ginaz, and they drove the machines out. I am free, and alive, because of them."

His upper lip trembled. "I came here because I want to be a mercenary, too. I want to kill the thinking machines. I want my revenge. Please . . . teach me."

"I cannot." Noret hardened himself to the crestfallen expression of the Tyndall refugee. "However," he said, turning to Chirox after long consideration, "I have no objection . . . if *you* wish to train candidates on my behalf."

Though he was an unorthodox trainer and met with considerable skepticism from veteran instructors, the combat robot began formal lessons for the breathless and ambitious pilgrims who came to Jool Noret's island.

Within days after his master's departure, Chirox took two students, then twelve, and finally he led several shifts of eager mercenaries all through the daylight and nighttime hours. He instructed them in the basics of robot destruction techniques. And he needed no rest.

Early each day the students threw themselves into the training with all the vehemence a teacher could hope for. Each of them wanted to be like the legendary Swordmaster of Ginaz, though when asked why, none of them could say precisely what their idol did that was different from the style of other mercenaries. Except that he was extremely fast, his actions rapid and undefined.

Whenever the *sensei* mek felt that particular trainees were ready, he sent them off to be accepted as official mercenaries of Ginaz. Claiming to be followers of Jool Noret, each one drew an inscribed coral disk from a basket and adopted the spirit of a fallen mercenary.

Then they headed out to pledge their fighting abilities to the Army of the Jihad.

Loose ends have a way of strangling you.
                    —General Agamemnon, *New Memoirs*

O UTSIDE THE JIHAD Council chambers, a news banner proclaimed,
"Bela Tegeuse Liberated!" With the local Omnius destroyed, the
planet was poorly protected and ready for the taking . . . if only the Army
of the Jihad could move quickly enough.

Hecate had fulfilled her promise, though she'd taken her sweet time
informing Iblis Ginjo. He had heard nothing. With foreknowledge of her
plans, he might have had a full armada of the Jihad prepared to pounce,
another perfect victory that he could claim.

But after living for so long, the female Titan did not seem overly
concerned. When he'd pressed her, Hecate had been petulant, even openly
indignant. "I provided full details to your representative exactly as you told
me to do. Perhaps you'd better check to see if there's a breakdown in your
own communications, hmm?" He had hated the taunt in her voice, but
Yorek Thurr had insisted that he'd received no such message.

Bela Tegeuse still waited, simmering and wounded. By now, the Grand
Patriarch was sure their response would be too late. Nevertheless, he
spearheaded a vigorous debate in the Jihad Council. Even if he failed, he
could still claim visionary foresight.

After learning about the attack on Bela Tegeuse, Iblis had carefully
crafted a false letter and a fictional petition by a group of human survivors
from the wreckage of Comati. Calling themselves "freedom fighters,"
they described what had happened, how a mysterious ship had destroyed
the local Omnius, causing them to implore the League of Nobles to send
military aid to them immediately, before the machines could reestablish
their hold.

"The streets and buildings of Bela Tegeuse are littered with broken, inoperable machines! The planetary Omnius is not functioning. What greater opportunity could there be?" he said in his most compelling voice. "Ragtag groups of humans are attacking the remaining robot defenders, but they have no appreciable military strength. This is our chance to succeed where we failed before. Imagine what a victory on Bela Tegeuse could mean for the Jihad!"

But others, still stinging from the first bloody struggle there at the dawn of the Jihad, wanted more information, to send scouts, to gather a large enough fleet to make a difference. Iblis grew frustrated, knowing that all the while the machines were making their move.

And Serena was not here. Giving him limited executive decision-making powers, she had returned to the City of Introspection to make final preparations for her imminent departure for the Thalim system, where she would inspect the Tlulaxa organ farms.

Things had been so much more efficient when he was in charge all by himself.

The debate went far into the night. As a military representative, Primero Vorian Atreides sat at the discussion table, looking as agitated and impatient as Iblis. The high-ranking officer, recently returned from establishing a military outpost on the Unallied Planet of Caladan, made an astonishing announcement concerning what he had done with the corrupted Omnius core through the duped robot captain who had delivered his deadly updates to many Synchronized Worlds.

After hours of arguing, Vor said with a long sigh, "Bela Tegeuse is just sitting there, vulnerable. If we continue to talk about this endlessly, then we have already made our decision. Omnius will not wait."

This caused some of the council members to waver. Two of them expressed limited agreement, and the others did not dispute their comments.

The Grand Patriarch saw his fellow escapee from Earth as a strong ally, in this matter at least. With the tide already turning in Vorian's favor, he inserted himself into the debate. "Listen to Primero Atreides! He is a man of action, and experienced in these matters." Looking at the Jihad Council, realizing that they now followed Serena Butler rather than jumping to act on his every whim, Iblis felt strangely ineffective. The answer was so plain!

A side door opened, and Primero Xavier Harkonnen hurried in from his preparations to accompany Serena to Tlulax. He appeared weary and haggard, and his uniform was uncharacteristically disheveled. Looking around the domed chamber, he spotted Vorian Atreides and took a seat beside him. "Has the Council established a plan yet?"

"Too much talk," Vor muttered in response. "I recommended sending in a division or two while we put together a full-fledged strike, but I barely got the sentence out before the shouting started. I have some supporters — maybe a majority — but the reluctant ones are managing to stall the proceedings. Some of them used your opposition to my computer virus trick in an attempt to discredit me."

Xavier said, with a weary smile, "I'm usually the one calling for direct action, while you prefer more indirect methods."

Following a brief break, a representative from Kirana III conferred with Iblis Ginjo. A small, swarthy man with a black mustache, the representative suggested that they set the measure aside for further study and discussion, "so that cooler heads might prevail on this important decision." He moved that the Council assemble all available information and reopen the discussion the following week.

Several representatives seconded the motion.

"Next week?" Vor cried, rising to his feet.

"That's too long!" Xavier shouted.

"Everything will be lost!" Iblis said in despair, knowing he would have to forfeit the vote. He couldn't remember ever failing so pointedly before in the Jihad Council.

"With all due respect, this Council has many important matters to handle," the Kirana representative said.

Infuriated and frustrated, Iblis hung his head and wouldn't even meet the eyes of the two Primeros. The three of them knew that Bela Tegeuse would now be lost again. Needlessly.

"I have a question, General Agamemnon," the Corrin-Omnius said. The evermind's voice — coming from everywhere at once — was calm, but extremely threatening. "Would you like me to have your brain removed and pulverized?" Each word grew louder, vibrating throughout the flowmetal structure of the Central Spire. "I have determined this to be an appropriate response to your extraordinary lapses and outright failures."

Wearing a golden armored body that bristled with spikes and weapons ports, the Titan military leader replied, "It would be ill advised to do that to a valuable cymek such as myself, after ten centuries of productive service to the Synchronized Worlds. I am one of only three Titans who remain." He knew programming restrictions prevented Omnius from following through with his threat.

All around him, the Central Spire's windowless walls clicked open and shut in a dizzying variety of colors and shapes. At times the flexible, shifting chamber seemed very large, but for the moment it had constricted dramatically, as if threatening to crush the Titan. Abruptly, when the walls were only centimeters from him, the room expanded as if drawing a deep breath.

Next, the Central Spire swayed like a serpent, and Agamemnon used his walker-form's stabilizers to maintain his balance. He had never expected a pervasive computer evermind to play such immature tricks, like a child throwing a tantrum. Perhaps software damage from the corrupt Earth-Omnius update continued to plague this incarnation, leading to the peculiar behavior.

These machines all deserve to be overthrown, destroyed . . . with or without Xerxes. Agamemnon made a conscious effort to prevent his mechanical body from twitching.

"Do you believe I cannot find a way around the restrictions Barbarossa designed into my core programming?" Omnius asked. "To underestimate my abilities would be a severe mistake."

Agamemnon contemplated this. If the evermind had discovered how to circumvent the primary command not to harm any of the Twenty Titans, wouldn't Omnius have destroyed the original cymeks long ago? "I can only emphasize my continuing value to you, Omnius. Your machine empire has benefited greatly from my success in military operations. My body is a machine, while my brain is human. I represent the best of both worlds."

"Your organic mental core is still flawed. You would do better without it."

Agamemnon did not understand what had triggered this wave of denunciation, but he remained calm. "My human brain enables me to understand the enemy better. Efficient and logical thinking machines cannot comprehend the chaotic nature of humans. It would be a grave tactical blunder not to take advantage of all your resources."

The floor beneath him plunged, as the cloud-scraping Central Spire contracted all the way to the ground. Abruptly the sensation of movement ceased, and the flowmetal walls became completely transparent, giving Agamemnon a nighttime view of the machine city. Arcing blue lights dazzled along the building exteriors; robot flying craft passed overhead.

"This Hecate matter displeases me, if that is truly her identity." The sheer volume of Omnius's voice buffeted the cymek. "She is one of your Titans, and she should be under your control. Recently, she caused severe damage to Bela Tegeuse."

"She is a *former* Titan, Omnius. Hecate has been in hiding for a thousand years. I accept no personal responsibility for her actions."

"You should have tracked her down and eliminated her. Long ago."

"But you have kept me occupied with other matters, Omnius. You have never given me leave to spend decades on a wild-goose chase looking for someone who, until recently, has caused no trouble whatsoever."

Agamemnon suspected that the evermind's ostensible rage was no more than an elaborate bluff, yet another annoying pattern of intimidation. As if Omnius understood the slightest bit about manipulation!

"Here is my generous decision, Agamemnon: I will allow you to live for a while longer, but you *must* put an end to Hecate. Secure Bela Tegeuse and reinstall a complete copy of my evermind there before the League humans can arrive to establish a foothold. You must hurry." Abruptly, the transparent walls sealed shut again with flowmetal barriers.

"Yes, Omnius. I will do as you say."

The voice shifted, coming from only a single direction. Overhead. "We have a bargain, then. If you deal with Hecate, you live. But if you fail, I shall squash you."

"It is always my intent to serve you adequately, Omnius. But, as you say, the human remnants I carry with me make me less than perfect."

"You amuse me, Agamemnon. But that is not enough."

Seething with anger, the cymek general departed from the Central Spire and lurched down the street in his immense warrior form. Encountering two human slaves on the Corrin streets, he went out of his way to smash them against a wall. Other trustees bolted for the safety of nearby buildings.

For centuries Agamemnon and his dwindling band of Titans served Omnius only because they had no choice. Now the general wanted more than ever to make his move against the evermind. At least that fool Xerxes could no longer get in the way.

Resolve pulsed through him like an infusion of energy. He had waited long enough. The recent recruit Beowulf had already identified well over a hundred secretly disloyal neos. Agamemnon needed to seize the opportunity. *Now.*

There would never be a better time or place than Bela Tegeuse.

The human mind, facing no real challenges, soon grows stagnant. Thus it is essential for the survival of mankind as a species to create difficulties, to face them, and to prevail. The Butlerian Jihad was an outgrowth of this largely unconscious process, with roots back to the original decision to allow thinking machines too much control, and the inevitable rise of the Omnius Empire.
— Princess Irulan, *Lessons of the Great Revolt*

S INCE THE OUTPOST colony of Kolhar had few commercial enterprises, Aurelius Venport had never been there. The bleak and stagnant planet was not the sort of place where he had ever envisioned profits.

But once he received the communication from Norma — she was alive! — he could think of no place he would rather be. He would have gone anywhere to find her, undeterred by her cryptic comment, "Do not be surprised by what you see."

As a businessman, Venport knew that surprises frequently translated into lost revenues. VenKee Enterprises made the greatest profits with well-planned ventures based on sound business practices, personal experience, and reliable instincts. But he could think of no surprise more pleasant, more delightfully unexpected, than the knowledge that dear, precious Norma had survived.

Her brief message had reached him in the pharmaceutical fields of Rossak, but provided him with no details. How had she escaped the Poritrin revolt? What had happened to the prototype space-folding ship? Where was Tuk Keedair? Why — and how — had she gone to . . . *Kolhar*, of all places?

When he arrived at the unimpressive spaceport, Venport was even more astounded to see Zufa Cenva striding up to meet him. His former lover seemed to have changed, her expression less sour, her icy beauty a degree warmer.

"Zufa, what are you doing here? I received a message from Norma —"

"As did I." Her attitude seemed more positive than he had ever experienced in their years together, less hardened, more optimistic. "You will be amazed, Aurelius. This . . . this changes everything about the Jihad."

Moments later her old demeanor returned, though, and with a maddening air of superiority Zufa refused to answer any of his inquiries. She assured him that Norma was alive and healthy, but revealed nothing more. Impatient and frustrated, he frowned at her; Zufa had always played mind-games, like a wrestler trying to get a leg up on him.

She took him by railtaxi far from the outpost city to an even more isolated spot on a cold marshy plain bounded by rugged mountains. The ground, covered with patches of dirty snow and lumpy ice, crunched underfoot as the merchant followed the tall woman to a simple wooden cabin. A bare, sheltered bench was the only adornment on a small porch. On one side of the house, a lean-to sheltered a woodpile, although Venport noted no trees nearby.

Striding across the wooden porch, Zufa pulled open the squeaky front door and gestured for him to follow her. He had stopped bothering with questions, and hurried forward, hoping to find Norma inside. He remembered her message — *Do not be surprised by what you see* — and took a deep breath. Smiling, he entered the modest dwelling.

Inside the small enclosure, he felt warmth from a natural fireplace, glowing orange. The sweet smell of woodsmoke tinged the air. A tall, stunningly lovely woman with hair the color of pale gold and milky skin turned to him, grinning and laughing, on her face an expression of delight like that of a little girl. What was one of Zufa's Sorceresses doing here?

"Aurelius!" She ran toward him.

Though she embraced him, he stood in shock. "Norma?" He held her at arms' length, so he could better look at her. Her eyes were pale blue and sparkling; her perfect face took his breath away. "Little Norma?"

Seeing his expression, she began to laugh. "I grew up."

Venport turned to Zufa, silently pleading for an explanation, and the Supreme Sorceress responded only with a nod.

"Aurelius, it *is* me — Norma. Truly." She tugged on his shoulders, drew him closer.

Finally, wanting to melt, and seeing her true identity in the eyes that had so often met his own during their warm times and joyful conversations together, Venport folded her into his arms. The eyes were of a different color now, but the same soul infused them. He squeezed her, rocked her, and buried his face in her long, fine hair. "I don't care what you look like, Norma — just as long as I know it's you, and that you're not hurt."

She leaned in to kiss him, at first shyly, but when Venport responded, she grew less awkward. Her lovely face was filled with joy, and her deep, throaty voice sounded authentic. And her pale blue eyes had such an incredible depth to them. The lashes were long and black.

Looking oddly uncomfortable, Zufa watched them, but Venport didn't care.

"I . . . I went to Poritrin. I looked everywhere, but no one knew anything about you. The city of Starda is destroyed. Tio Holtzman is dead, along with Lord Bludd, and hundreds of thousands of others. The prototype ship is gone, your laboratory ransacked. Keedair is nowhere to be found."

Norma frowned. "I have no idea what happened to Keedair. His visa was revoked, and he was expected to leave, just like me. I fear the worst."

"So do I."

"It no longer matters if the prototype ship is gone, Aurelius, because now I know so much more! I know how to fold space and exactly how to construct the ships. They will travel faster than anything known. You must construct them . . . here, on Kolhar. In fact, I want you here with me from now on."

Then, still holding her, not wanting to be separated again, he listened as Norma told him everything . . .

As the incredible story sank in, Venport smiled wistfully at her. "This new . . . incarnation of yours will take some getting used to, Norma. I was rather fond of the old version, you know. If you remember, I asked you an important question long ago, and you promised me an answer the next time we saw each other. I . . . I'm sorry it took me so long to see you."

Norma's gaze came from deep within her stunningly beautiful features. She pondered, as if a trillion thoughts and possibilities were rushing simultaneously through her mind, faster and more efficiently than any mere human could think. Venport held Norma. He felt tense, still unsure what her answer to his question would be.

Finally she continued, "I need you with me, Aurelius. I need your support and your skills. And marriage will facilitate what we need to do."

It took him a moment to realize that she had accepted his proposal. He chuckled and held her close. "Norma, Norma — I will have to teach you about being romantic."

Zufa Cenva snorted. He ignored her.

Norma seemed startled at herself. "Oh, of course I want to be with you more than anyone else in the universe, Aurelius. But this will be a partnership far beyond our personal relationship or business needs.

Together, you and I will shape the future of humanity. My vision is so clear, and you are an essential part of it . . . along with my mother."

Zufa's expression grew more strained with each passing moment. Venport understood her awkwardness, since for years he had been *her* lover, and now he wanted to marry her daughter. But the eminent Sorceress had long ceased to regard him as a breeding partner.

"Yes, Norma." Zufa's voice carried a warning undertone, as if she sensed consequences the others had not yet imagined. "You may need help in holding onto your humanity."

Venport could only remember the beautiful person Norma had always been inside, and hoped that the true essence of this remarkable woman had not been lost in her physical transformation.

"I promise you one thing, Aurelius," Norma said. "Your life will never be boring after this."

Outside, staring across the flat expanse of frozen marshes and gray scrub, Venport didn't think their new base of operations looked like much. But Norma waved her arms and described her vision for Kolhar. "These untamed plains are perfect for landing fields, storage, and maintenance facilities. We can build a thousand ships as large as we can conceive them, vast spacefaring cargo vessels and powerful battleships."

She talked about the immense, mind-boggling construction project, the high-altitude lakes and marshes that had to be filled in, the streams that must be diverted. Venport could not yet visualize the armies of workers that would be required, the offworld materials, the heavy equipment . . . and the unspeakable investment. He stared at her, already feeling a gnawing dread inside. "And . . . the cost?"

"Astronomical," Norma said, chuckling at her own witticism. "But the profits will be unprecedented — I guarantee this. Our ships will be orders of magnitude faster than any conventional spacecraft today. Competing merchants will go bankrupt trying to keep up with us."

Zufa added, "Consider your patriotic duty, Aurelius, not just business profits. These ships will move League military forces across space in the blink of an eye, enabling us to blindside the thinking machines. They won't know where we will appear next. At last, we can win the Jihad!"

Venport swallowed hard. "I grow weary, just thinking about it. But how can I make such a commitment of resources, with my business partner missing? No one knows where Keedair is."

"You must choose what is right, Aurelius," Norma replied. "You know what to do. We cannot wait. The Jihad cannot wait."

He turned to the younger of the two women, and as he gazed at Norma Cenva he did not see her for her stunning new physical beauty at all. In her intense eyes he recognized the old Norma, his dear friend, and knew he could not turn her down.

"I've never stopped believing in you," he said. "I'll pay the price, whatever it is."

The following evening, Venport dined with Norma in her cabin. Zufa Cenva had already thrown herself into managing the enormous startup activities that would be required to begin immediate construction on the Kolhar shipyards. Because of lingering personal misgivings, she had left them alone.

At first, Venport was embarrassed and ill at ease, but then he didn't care. He just wanted to be with Norma and was still overjoyed to have found her alive, despite his greatest fears.

They had a cozy fire going and enjoyed the fine meal that Zufa had sent with the first hired workers who would form the initial construction crew. The couple sat at the table looking at each other as they ate roast steppe partridge with savory mint glaze and sweet Kolhar potatoes, served with imported Salusan wine spiked with melange. Before long, Venport knew he would have to watch every cent he invested here, but he would never skimp on special meals with Norma.

When he looked at the features of her face, he still could not believe what he was seeing. She was startlingly attractive, though when he detected the old Norma behind the expression in the way she gestured, in the gentle curve of her smile, Venport felt an even greater longing.

"You didn't have to change yourself for me," he said. "I had already asked you to marry me, as you were."

She laughed, as if it had never occurred to her that she might have reshaped her body like this in order to make herself more attractive to him. "I simply rebuilt my form based on the optimal DNA, as traced back along my maternal bloodline." When she spoke, she averted her eyes in clear embarrassment, however, and Venport knew that the motive must have crossed her mind. "I'm very glad you like the result, though."

She sat with him on a plush white rug by the fireplace. "This is a traditional romantic setting, isn't it?" she asked. "Just how I always imagined lovers spending their time together. I never thought it would happen to me, and certainly not with an incredible man like you."

He smiled at her, sipping the wine. "I'm no great prize, Norma." She seemed such a frightening genius, but at other times — such as now —

he found her incredibly innocent and naïve. He peered at her over the top of his crystal wineglass. "Are you trying to seduce me?"

Her surprise seemed genuine, and she sounded faintly disappointed. "Am I so obvious? I'm not doing this very well, am I?"

"There is an art to romance, my dear. Not that I have so much experience, but I can impart some of the basics to you." Venport shifted closer to her and took her in his arms, where she seemed to melt against him. All of her awkwardness dissipated. "Your mother chose me as a mate because of my genetics, but I failed her in that regard."

The previous day, when he had learned that Zufa Cenva carried a child by the Grand Patriarch, he had felt a pang of regret, remembering the years they had spent together . . . how many times he had tried to give the great Sorceress the perfect daughter that she, and his genetics, should have made possible. But each pregnancy had ended in horrifically malformed miscarriage.

He didn't want to think about that. Not now.

Norma lifted her chin. "Our children will not be disappointments, Aurelius. I shall see to that personally, with cell by cell manipulation if need be."

Venport looked at her, then at the lacy window coverings of the cabin. On the vast plain outside, the major construction effort would begin soon, under a relentless work schedule. "How could you possibly have time for children? Are you sure that wouldn't be sacrificing too much?"

She met his gaze with such a piercing look that he seemed to see through her pupils, deep into her thoughts. "Nevertheless, it is an important part of being human. I would not want to miss this opportunity."

He kissed her on the mouth, then drew away and gazed at her gently, soaking up the passionate, vibrant blue of her eyes. Venport tried to analyze his own feelings, separating the way he had always felt for her from the way he felt now. As he grew accustomed to her beautiful new form he had to admit a greater sense of desire . . . and he felt ashamed of this. If he truly loved *her*, why should her appearance matter, beautiful or not?

Then he realized that Norma had chosen the way she wanted to appear, to attract him.

"You are the first man who ever paid any attention to me," she said, "and I'm not sure what to do next."

"Trust me, I can be of assistance in that department." He stroked her long, golden hair.

In my investigation of human culture, I have encountered non-traditional families, and parents who were not genetically related to the children under their care. I never understood the full significance of such relationships until I began to work with Gilbertus Albans.

— *Erasmus Dialogues*

ERASMUS PACED IN his study, strutting in and out of crimson sunlight that filtered through a thick window and splashed in coppery pools on the floor. When compared with human behavior, the robot realized he was acting somewhat . . . nervous. He had all of the necessary materials ready, but it was the first time he had ever faced such an ordeal with Gilbertus. According to his studies of human home life and ancient cultures, this was a rite of human passage for a young man.

If only he could delegate the task. But Erasmus had no wife to assume such burdens. A slave, then? He didn't want anyone to disrupt the progress he had made with his young ward.

The robot had considered the problem at length, wondering how he should approach such a delicate issue with Gilbertus Albans. To a thinking machine, the topic was not sensitive at all, a mere biological curiosity, an inefficient and messy natural process. But to many humans it *seemed* special, even mystical.

This made no logical sense. It was like a thinking machine being reticent to discuss the concept of AI software and hardware, the ways in which various machines were manufactured, assembled, and networked . . . the myriad methods in which update spheres were duplicated and exchanged.

The act of creation.

On his ornate desk, the robot had piled appropriate diagrams and literature. Two human mannequins were propped up on a couch, in an embrace. He had contemplated simply providing male and female slaves from the pens, by way of demonstration subjects, but felt that would be too easy. Desiring to learn more about what it meant to be human, Erasmus did not want to shirk his "paternal" duties.

Humans called the bodily function "sex" and other longer words, some of which were not considered acceptable in polite company, according to ancient records from various civilizations. Erasmus found that peculiar as well. How could a mere *word* offend?

He recited a series of words that described the copulatory function, letting each of them roll off his flowmetal lips for the maximum effect. He repeated some of the words, those said to be the most socially unacceptable. Nothing. They had no effect on him. He simply could not understand what all of the fuss was about.

The functioning of thinking machines was so much simpler and more straightforward . . . except for a curious robot like himself. These plaguing questions and conundrums could be most frustrating.

He had initiated his research into human nature because he found the complexities of the species so interesting and so eminently *alien*. Erasmus wanted to assimilate the pieces of the human brain and consciousness that had been left out when they had designed the original AI machines. But he most certainly did not desire to become human himself. Erasmus wanted the best of both universes.

Young Gilbertus had opened the robot's investigative mind in many ways. Curiously, as Erasmus pursued the project further, he began to discover things about his relationship with the adopted boy (who was approximately twelve), at a time when the human's hormones were growing more active. Two years ago, upon accepting Omnius's challenge, Erasmus had never thought in terms of father and son. At first it had seemed totally absurd, a physiological and emotional impossibility. But as he taught the boy and watched him progress, the autonomous thinking machine took pride in what he saw, and things fell into place.

Almost naturally.

A curious bond had formed between them, and they enjoyed one another's company immensely . . . with a few notable exceptions. The panic experiments that Erasmus had conducted in the slave pens did not go over very well with the young man, but perhaps that would change in time. Surprisingly, Erasmus found that they learned almost equally from one another. With all of the research he had conducted up to today, Erasmus thought he should be able to complete the task at hand without any trouble. If only he could get over an inexplicable feeling of uneasiness . . .

Had some remnant of the human puritanism about sexual matters been installed into Erasmus's operating programs? That might explain it, or he might be feeling this artificial sensation because he *wanted* to feel it, in order to better understand the dilemma that had historically faced human fathers.

While Erasmus was always punctual, the boy was chronically tardy. Too frequently Gilbertus became distracted with other interests, yielding to some fascination with subjects and experiences that he would then breathlessly explain to his mentor. The robot considered it a significant flaw, but quite human.

He heard a rap at the door, and it slid open. A gawky boy sauntered in, his straw-yellow hair tousled and his face red. Evidently he had run all the way here.

"You are late as usual." Erasmus formed his flowmetal face into a stern, parental countenance.

"I'm sorry, Mr. Erasmus. But only nine minutes this time. Yesterday it was —"

"Let us begin our lesson without further delay." Erasmus wanted to get it over with. "I have prepared a number of diagrams for you, along with detailed reports and displays on human procreation. I hope you find them instructive."

The boy seemed curious, but not uncomfortable. "Is this another biology lesson? Are we going to dissect something?"

Thus far, Erasmus had only dissected lower animal forms in front of the boy, but intended to build up to human subjects one day. The robot wanted to take this slowly, not wishing to alienate the young man or make him advance too quickly. Some of Gilbertus's reactions to violence seemed overly sensitive.

"Not . . . this time. We will deal in biological reproductive theory for now, though I can arrange for you to put the techniques into practice, should you feel the urge."

The young man nodded, and paid close attention as the robot walked over to the couch to examine the anatomically correct mannequins he had positioned there. "You will note that we have two basic human forms here, male and female. They are wearing traditional clothing, and are accurate in every external detail." He motioned to the boy. "Step this way, please. You will note that the man and woman are embracing, and that the man has his mouth near her ear."

Dutifully, Gilbertus followed the silvery robot, and peered intensely at the tableau. Erasmus gathered his thoughts, and his composure. "The mannequins are not fitted with full simulation mechanics, so you will have to imagine the next part. Apparently it is a necessary procedure in proper courtship ritual. The man will kiss her ear, lick it, and promise his everlasting love. Traditionally, this causes the woman to go into heat." He looked sternly at the boy. "Do you understand this so far?"

Gilbertus nodded. Somewhat to Erasmus's consternation, the boy displayed a detached curiosity with no uneasiness whatsoever, and no apparent urges of his own.

"Next, the man will kiss her on the mouth. At this point both will begin to salivate heavily," Erasmus said in a professorial tone. "Salivation is a key element in procreation. Apparently kissing serves to make the female more fertile."

The boy nodded, and half smiled. Erasmus took this to mean that he understood. *Good!* The robot began to rub the faces of the mannequins together, briskly.

"Now this is very important," Erasmus said. "Salivation and ovulation. Remember those two concepts and you will have a basic grasp of the human reproductive process. After the kissing, intercourse begins immediately." He began to speak more rapidly. "That is all you need to know about human copulation. Do you have any questions, Gilbertus?"

"No, Mr. Erasmus," the boy said. "I believe you have explained everything quite clearly."

Some miracles are only nightmares in disguise.
> —Serena Butler, *Echoes of the Jihad*

S ERENA INVITED RAJID Suk, the talented battlefield surgeon, and Primero Xavier Harkonnen as League military representative to accompany her on an inspection of the much-vaunted Tlulaxa organ farms. They were in space for a month, en route to the Thalim system. In spite of the potential significance of this mission, the decision to pull these important men away from their duties at the heart of the fight was difficult for Serena. After all, travel through star systems always took so infernally long . . . and people were dying every day.

Young Suk had made extensive, even miraculous, use of products from the organ farms, saving thousands of the veterans injured in combat against thinking machines. After the first Battle of Zimia, one of Suk's predecessors had performed the medical procedure that gave Primero Harkonnen replacement lungs.

Serena considered both of her companions true heroes.

Her expedition moved with ceremonial ponderousness. Rekur Van's merchant ship had already raced ahead of them to the Thalim system, carrying Iblis Ginjo — purportedly to prepare the way for their visit, thought she suspected otherwise. Iblis still had his secrets.

Finally her spacecraft went into orbit over the planet Tlulax. Serena was anxious to reach the surface and stroll under the sun of Thalim. She had been too long in space. A dozen perfectly clean, white-robed Seraphim served as her attendants.

Smiling with pride, Serena waited in her shipboard quarters for the crew to get the shuttle ready. No official League representative had ever made a diplomatic visit to the shrouded, insular Tlulaxa worlds. If she could bring these biological wizards into the larger fold of the League, with full rights and privileges, everyone would benefit.

The Tlulaxa were said to be exceedingly religious people, though they kept their beliefs and practices as secret as their daily lives. What could they possibly have to hide? And how did Iblis get along so well with them? In any event, the Tlulaxa could contribute a great deal to the Jihad. Their genetic sophistication and medical breakthroughs had already been a boon to humanity.

Admittedly, too many of their race served as flesh merchants for those few League Worlds that still tolerated the enslavement of humans. In her youth, Serena had spoken out vehemently against slavery. Sadly, she later came to realize that the practice was so entrenched that it would take centuries to reverse the practice. As a leader, she still frowned on the practice of slavery, but her highest priority was to win the Jihad and save the human race from extermination.

The Tlulaxa organ-sellers had repeatedly expressed concern about divulging proprietary information, but Serena hoped to convince them to share their knowledge. She hoped that by granting patents or monopoly concessions she could assure the Tlulaxa that their business interests would be protected, and that many more people could be saved. Given their adaptability and intelligence, Serena was sure the Tlulaxa could maintain their commercial superiority.

With a firm expression, her chief Seraph Niriem announced, "The Grand Patriarch has sent word from the surface that preparations are ready for your arrival, Priestess Butler." In her shipboard quarters the female guards worked together to robe Serena in her most dazzling public uniform, giving her the appearance of a goddess incarnate. Niriem looked at her with an appraisal as sharp as a scalpel, then nodded.

The intimidating and fanatically devoted Seraphim accompanied Serena to the shuttle deck, where she was met by Rajid Suk and a stone-faced Xavier Harkonnen. Xavier looked like the ideal military officer, but did not meet her gaze for very long. That had been his pattern since marrying Octa.

The neatly dressed surgeon had dark hair bound in a long ponytail behind his back, and eyes that seemed overlarge for his face. His nimble, long-fingered hands fidgeted impatiently.

Two of the white-robed women climbed aboard the shuttle; Niriem herself sat in the pilot's seat. Serena walked gracefully up the ramp, followed by an eager Dr. Suk and a less-enthusiastic Xavier. The two men sat separately.

During the shuttle's descent toward its assigned landing point on the planet below, they passed over the sparkling new city of Bandalong, which was still being built under a breathtaking master plan financed with profits generated by the organ farms and slave marketing. Far outside the formal boundaries of Bandalong — a city off-limits to outsiders, even to the Priestess of the Jihad — they landed in an open, efficient spaceport with clean lines and colorless architecture.

As Serena and her Seraphim emerged, both Iblis Ginjo and Rekur Van came forward to meet them. The flesh merchant's political importance and clout had apparently been substantially boosted because of his connection with the Grand Patriarch. The little man bowed to Serena.

She blinked in yellow sunlight, surprised to see that local business continued as usual. She saw no cheering crowds or groups of curious spectators, as she would have expected on any League World. Only a few dozen businessmen and governmental representatives formed the receiving party. It was disappointing, for she knew that her very presence could inflame enthusiasm and swell hearts.

Serena's ego did not require her to be treated to a spectacular reception, but she was puzzled. If the Tlulaxa had intended no extravagant greeting ceremony, why had they insisted on so many delays for "preparations"?

One of the representatives separated himself from the group and came forward. He bowed slightly. "Priestess Serena Butler, we are honored that you choose to spend your valuable time traveling to see us. We have made a portion of our organ farms presentable for your inspection, but you will forgive us for not shutting down our complicated work processes."

Iblis interrupted, his voice rich and confident. "The demand for Tlulaxa product increases with every battle against the evil machines, and we would not want a single injured veteran to go without eyes or a new heart because these hard-working people were too busy hosting a diplomatic reception."

Serena smiled. "The Grand Patriarch knows that I intend no disruption, I simply wish to recognize and honor everything you Tlulaxa have done."

Dr. Suk stood next to Serena and acknowledged the bureaucrats. "In my work as a military surgeon, I have relied upon Tlulaxa products to save countless lives. Long ago, Primero Harkonnen himself received a new set of lungs, thanks to the flesh merchant Tuk Keedair. If the Primero had not been saved that day, he would never have lived to become the father of Manion the Innocent."

Serena saw Iblis nodding with reverent satisfaction. She had heard her baby called a saint by the street rabble in Zimia and among the crowds on other Jihad-frenzied worlds. But Xavier stood by, looking somber, as if disturbed by his thoughts. After a long life of unprecedented service and effort, was that to be remembered as his greatest achievement? To be the father of a murdered child?

She stepped away from the shuttle, walking toward the rest of the receiving party. Serena wondered if this civilization was a rigidly patri-archal society, a throwback to primitive times. Extraordinary technical breakthroughs and scientific sophistication, such as the Tlulaxa had managed with their programmable organ farms, usually required an exchange of information and an open encouragement of innovation and genius. Such advances were not usually in keeping with a repressive, bigoted society.

Were they giving her such a cool reception because of her gender?

Showing no hint of her thoughts, Serena smiled at them and raised her hands in benediction. "Let us go now to admire your wondrous organ farms."

Rekur Van led the way, directing Serena and her companions to a small airvan used for public transportation. Behind her, with the sun glinting on the new structures of distant Bandalong, she noted that the buildings, though of different sizes, were all similarly squarish and serviceable, like geometric anthills.

On the hills outside the city, low grasses and a network of paved roads made labyrinthine designs, like the patterns on an ancient computer chip. "We have thousands of organ-growing installations across the planet," said Rekur Van, "all situated in the open where they can draw photosynthetic energy from unobstructed sunlight."

Within half an hour, Serena saw the organ farms. She disembarked from the airvan and went forward with tentative steps, faster than the Tlulaxa could accompany her. Niriem and the other Seraph followed closely. But when the guard women looked to Iblis, he shook his head faintly, and they eased back.

Serena, Xavier, and Dr. Suk looked at the glistening tanks as if they were witnessing a miracle. Chrome pipes, glass tubes, and black metal supports held egg-shaped translucent tanks. Each one was large and curved, containing a bubbling yellowish liquid like amniotic fluid. The tanks hung like swollen fruit, connected by flashing diagnostic systems and status screens that monitored the perfectly cloned organs. Iblis explained that different types of tanks produced different body parts, and none of them would ever be rejected by transplant recipients.

Through the curved walls of each enclosure, Serena made out murky but recognizable shapes, flaccid sacs of lungs, artery-embroidered hearts, curtains of ridged muscle fiber like swatches of corduroy. Lifting her head, she gazed across the hillsides, where thousands upon thousands of drooping spheres glinted in the sunlight, absorbing energy from the clear Tlulaxan sky.

The battlefield surgeon peered into one of the nearest tanks that contained a dozen eyeballs floating together like a cluster of grapes, each one staring out at him. Optic nerves and blood vessels were connected to a central nutrient bulb. "This is extraordinary. You grow organs to order? Is each one of these eyes designated for a particular victim?"

"No," Rekur Van said with a glance at the other Tlulaxa. "We make them blood-type neutral, so that they are compatible to a variety of victims. We have spleens, livers, kidneys, everything vital. Our larger tanks can even grow sheets of fresh skin."

"I know," Rajid Suk said. "I've used much of that material myself, especially in treating burn victims. It has improved the quality of thousands of lives."

Organ trees rotated to align themselves with the direct sunlight. The surgeon seemed awestruck. "For centuries, our best medical technicians have attempted to achieve such precise levels of cloning. What the Tlulaxa have accomplished is nothing short of breathtaking. If I were not looking upon this with my own eyes, I would not believe it could be true. No other League scientist has come close to this, not even in the glory days of the Old Empire."

He grinned at Serena, then at the Tlulaxa representatives. "For the benefit of all humanity, you must share this technology with the League. We could erect similar organ farms. Medical victims would no longer need to endure months on life-support machines waiting to receive replacement organs."

Seeing alarm on the faces of the Tlulaxa hosts, Iblis Ginjo raised his hands. "Don't get ahead of yourself, Doctor Suk. This is the very livelihood of the Tlulaxa civilization." The small group walked among the unsettling yet incredible tanks, each of which held one or more organs that would someday help the war victims. "They could easily impose higher prices and reap huge profits, but they are doing their part in the fight against Omnius. No war profiteering here, eh, Rekur?"

"None at all."

Energized, Iblis added, "Eventually Tlulaxa organ farms may surpass the profits they generate from slave activities."

"I would like to see that happen," Serena said. "Of course, there is a higher demand for these products during wartime." She frowned and looked around. "Where are all of the slaves here? I expected to see them working your farms."

Rekur Van said, "Selling slaves is our primary business, Priestess Butler. Trained, intelligent humans are a valuable commodity, and we do not keep them for ourselves. Besides, we could not entrust the care and upkeep of these delicate farms to unruly laborers who might have foolish dreams of vengeance."

Xavier nodded stiffly, as if barely controlling his anger. "As the recent revolt on Poritrin demonstrated."

"We have no intention of exposing our organ farms to such a threat."

Serena accepted the explanation and recalled all too well the horrors Buddislamics had wrought on Poritrin. The casualties around Starda were still not accurately tallied; the true number would likely never be known because, at its center, the radioactive wasteland was little more than glassy rubble and the stains of bodies. The surviving population had hunted down the rebellious slaves and slaughtered many of them in a vindictive pogrom. That world would never be the same again.

The Tlulaxa escorts continued the tour for the rest of that day, showing the visitors all types of biological samples dangling in tanks. Always alert, Niriem never left Serena's side.

After dinner, they attended a formal reception, where discussions continued. The following day, Iblis seemed quite pleased when he came to Serena with an offer from the Tlulaxa council. "Our friends have made a most generous suggestion, Serena. They wish to take formal samples of your cells and DNA. This will allow them to grow specifically tailored replacement organs for you, should . . . should you ever suffer injury in another assassination attempt."

Serena frowned. "Would I not be able to use the standard organs from the farms, like all of our jihadi soldiers?"

Rekur Van hurried up to her in the small banquet room. "Of course, Priestess, but there is always a *slight* chance of rejection. It's biologically impossible to guarantee a perfect match — unless we use your own DNA. It seems a worthwhile safeguard, and the Grand Patriarch agrees."

Xavier Harkonnen looked skeptically from Iblis to the Tlulaxa flesh merchant. "I'm not convinced this is necessary —"

Serena brightened. "No, it's all right. I think it's a good idea. I would also like the Tlulaxa to maintain a library of cells from Primero Harkonnen, Grand Patriarch Ginjo — and even Doctor Suk."

Xavier appeared alarmed, touching his chest. "The replacement lungs

I received many years ago have functioned perfectly well, Serena. I see no need for –"

"But *I* do." And that was the end of the discussion.

The following morning, after carefully tagged samples had been taken from the group, Iblis urged them to return to the spaceport. "Come, Serena. The Tlulaxa have been more than generous with their time. You've seen everything you need to. Besides, our business is concluded here."

Finally, after a breakfast that seemed oddly rushed, she smiled at her Tlulaxa hosts. She needed to make certain they understood how much she appreciated their efforts. "I am greatly impressed, and I commend you for your accomplishments. It is my dream for you to join us as full-fledged League members. All of humanity would benefit from your contributions."

"Perhaps that can be discussed in the future," Iblis said. "In any case, the most important thing is for the Tlulaxa to continue their gallant efforts on our behalf."

"Yes, I suppose that's true."

Iblis quickly ushered Serena and her entourage back to the shuttle as if he didn't want Serena to probe any deeper. Dr. Suk looked completely awed by all that he had seen. Iblis said, "You are Priestess of the Jihad, the unifier of humanity against Omnius. With you, nothing is impossible." He shot meaningful glances at Rekur Van and the other Tlulaxa.

Leaving the Grand Patriarch behind, Serena thought he seemed entirely pleased with how the visit had turned out. But in her heart she could not shake the nagging sense that something was not right . . .

173 B.G.

JIHAD YEAR 29

One Year after the Return of the Ivory Tower Cogitors

Opportunities may arise in an instant, or they may develop for a
thousand years. We must always be prepared to seize what is ours.
                          —General Agamemnon, *New Memoirs*

I F AGAMEMNON HAD still possessed a physical body, his face would
have displayed a triumphant grin as he watched the machine fleet
converging on Bela Tegeuse. With his organic brain bathed in the
electrafluid of his preservation canister, the cymek general felt a tingle
of anticipation and victory.

Omnius would never suspect a thing.

The two Titans with Agamemnon felt the same, along with the neo-
cymek Beowulf and the one hundred seventeen ambitious neos they had
recruited into their revolt against the Synchronized Worlds.

"Once again, it will be the Time of Titans!" Agamemnon's secret
transmission was distributed throughout the swarm of cymek ships that
traveled like unobtrusive remoras amid a school of deadly sharks. "We
will restore our original rule, granting rewards and power to those
visionaries who wish to destroy the computer evermind."

The Corrin-Omnius had dispatched this large fleet along with numerous "loyal" cymek assistants to impose machine control before the feral
jihadi humans could take over. The evermind had given his cymek
general clear orders not to allow the wounded Synchronized World to
fall to the *hrethgir.*

Agamemnon intended to follow those orders . . . in his own fashion.

Beowulf, the most talented programming genius since the Titan Barbarossa, had designed customized instructions and programming loops for all
thinking machine warships, supposedly to prepare them for the chaos and
disruption they would find on Bela Tegeuse. The machine warships would
protect against any foolish incursions by human marauders.

The robot fleet carried a new and complete update of Omnius, with all of the instructions and information necessary to restore Bela Tegeuse to its synchronized status.

All of those massive, technologically beautiful ships would be a good start for Agamemnon's own imperial cymek fleet.

Surrounding the cloud-blanketed planet, the machine warships transmitted identification signals and requests for response from the Omnius nexus in Comati, but received mostly static in response. The city itself had been leveled in Hecate's atomic blast. Moments later, the machines received a few fragmented messages from trustee humans who had gotten some of the technology functional again.

Pleased to see no sign of a *hrethgir* occupation force, Agamemnon was relieved that he would not have to fight the jihadis while simultaneously overthrowing the forces of Omnius. Easier to deal with one foe at a time.

"Attention, thinking machine fleet," he transmitted. "The cymek Beowulf has prepared an upload for you."

Beowulf took his cue. "Before we departed from Corrin, Omnius gave me a confidential package that was not to be installed until now, for security reasons. Prepare to receive my transmission."

The neo-cymek genius entered the appropriate high-level access codes, and the unsuspecting thinking machines accepted the burst. The entire fleet of machine warships and robots swallowed the programming rewrite like a deadly poison pill.

In a chain reaction, one by one, the robot vessels shut down over Bela Tegeuse, like lights blinking off in a large city. A bloodless coup.

Transmissions of triumphant glee and cold surprise echoed across the private cymek channel and open frequencies. Small cymek ships flitted like wasps around the silent robot fleet. One of the rebel neos asked, "Why didn't you do this centuries ago?"

"The programming was not simple," Boewulf said.

"But it was Agamemnon's own son who pointed me in the right direction. According to our inside information in the League, Vorian Atreides was behind the sensor deception at Poritrin, as well as the similar virus that fooled the machine fleet at IV Anbus."

The Titan general agreed. "Since Vorian flew with the robot Seurat on his update runs — the same robot that has delivered corrupted updates on Synchronized Worlds — I have no doubt he was behind that tactic as well. There's no reason we cymeks couldn't have attempted a similar scheme long ago, but this will work only once, and we had to be ready. All of us. And now is our time at last."

Agamemnon scanned the forces he had pulled together, and the powerful but unsuspecting robotic fleet. "I have waited a thousand years for this moment! Titans, join me aboard the frontline machine ship. We shall call a meeting with Omnius."

The cymek ships converged upon the central machine vessel like pirates gathering around a treasure chest. Agamemnon linked his ship to the airlock, and the other cymeks followed suit. The Titan general installed his preservation canister inside a sleek walker body, which he wore like a triumphal cape that might have suited the original Agamemnon when he strode into the fallen city of Troy.

"Long ago, we conquered the Old Empire, and then lost it to Omnius," he said to Juno and Dante, as well as to the proud Beowulf, whose genius had made all of this possible. "Now, the Synchronized Worlds are weakened from decades of war against the free humans. The Army of the Jihad has worn down the thinking machines for us — an opportunity we must seize."

The thinking machine update ship was dark and silent, its robot pilot paralyzed by Beowulf's clever programming. The cymeks would never be able to try such a trick again, but perhaps they would not have to do so.

In his mechanical walker, Agamemnon tore open the sealed alcove that held the Omnius update. The silvery gelsphere rested on wrinkled padding. Agamemnon reached in with one metal-clawed extremity and picked up the shimmering globe that held so many decillions of thoughts.

Bela Tegeuse was the first giant step.

"Omnius, you seem so weak and fragile," he said. "With this single gesture, I launch the beginning of a new era . . . and the end of yours."

Agamemnon clenched his articulated, clawed fist and crushed the silvery gelsphere. Now Omnius and his thinking machines were facing a three-way war.

What sort of God would promise us a land like this?
                                                    —Zensunni Lament

A FTER FIVE LEAN months, their supplies had dwindled, people had
died — and Arrakis remained as harshly inhospitable as ever.
Ishmael sensed growing despair among the escaped Zensunni slaves.

"This planet is just a giant *dune*," complained one of the gaunt,
sunburned refugees, who sat on a rock near the crashed experimental
spaceship. They had no place to go.

Still, their leader had refused to let the spark of hope die. Ishmael
insisted that they maintain their faith, that they endure the crushing heat
and learn to adapt to this new place that God, for whatever reasons, had
chosen for them. He found applicable Sutras to recite, which comforted
his people.

One he had learned from his grandfather: "Courage and fear chase one
another, around and around."

His daughter Chamal had grown quiet and hardened, no longer able to
believe that her husband Rafel might still be alive. He, Ingu, and the
Tlulaxa slaver had set off in the group's only vehicle and never returned.
It had been far too long. After weeks without word, Chamal had stopped
expecting Rafel's expedition to come back bearing good news and fresh
food.

Ishmael could see in her eyes that she had envisioned all
possibilities — that they had gotten lost, or crashed in a storm, or been
murdered by Tuk Keedair. No one could imagine that they might have
found civilization and failed to send help.

Ishmael leaned against a rough boulder, holding his daughter and
wishing she were a little girl again, without so many troubles. She had

lost her husband, and now Ishmael was her only strength. But he himself had left Ozza behind and would probably be responsible for the deaths of these Zensunni refugees. To what purpose had they escaped? Perhaps they would have been better off joining Aliid's struggle after all. Hopefully the Zenshiites had won that far-off battle on Poritrin . . . but Ishmael doubted it, and doubted he would ever find out.

Despite all the hardships, he refused to regret his decision. Better to starve to death in this inferno than to become a killer, even a killer of slavekeepers. "Buddallah must have had a reason for sending us here," he murmured, as if reassuring Chamal. "It may take a thousand years for our people to discover why."

As far as anyone knew, Ishmael and his followers had vanished from the universe. The Zensunnis had made their base camp around the crash site, where they stripped down the hulk of the prototype vessel and removed every bit of usable material. Some of the cleverest among them made ingenious traps and filters to catch dew in the shadows, but it did not produce enough moisture for all of them to survive.

In the last desperate day of preparation for their escape, Ishmael's slaves had frantically packed only the items they could scavenge from Norma Cenva's research hangar, and many necessities were lacking. The experimental craft had never been designed to carry a hundred fleeing Zensunnis without equipment or the basic tools of self-sufficiency. Even the gloomiest among them had never expected to land in such a thankless wasteland.

Arrakis offered no sympathy, and no help whatsoever.

After waiting a month for the arrival of a rescue party, a group of hardened volunteers approached Ishmael in the cool shade of sunset. Their eyes were reddened, their jaws set.

"We need a compass, water, and food," said the man who had appointed himself spokesman. "Six of us want to set out across the desert on foot and try to locate Arrakis City. It may be our only chance."

He could not deny them, despite the virtual certainty that their enterprise would fail. "Buddallah guides us. Follow His path, feel it in your hearts. The Sutras say, 'The way to God is invisible to unbelievers but plainly seen by even a blind man of faith.'"

The man had nodded. "I experienced a dream in which I saw myself walking across the dunes. I believe Buddallah means for me to attempt this." Ishmael could not argue with the reasoning, or the bravery.

The party would have only a small flask of water and enough food to last for a week. If they did not locate another settlement in that time, they would not have the resources to return. "It is better to die trying to save our people," the leader of the small group said, "than to wait here and let Death take us on his own cruel terms."

While Chamal stood with her father under the starlit skies, he embraced each grim volunteer. Then the men set off in the direction opposite to which Rafel had flown his scout ship. They used the coolness of the night to make good time. Ishmael watched their shadows as they scuttled down the mountainside toward the unbroken emptiness of dunes . . .

Now, an hour before dawn, when both full moons cast light like a diluted noon upon the sands, Ishmael gazed toward the silent horizon. The plodding explorers would not yet have gone out of sight across the soft sand.

He did not disturb the other refugees, who slept soundly; he hoped their gentle slumber would prepare them for another difficult day. As his eyes adjusted, he made out the tiny black figures across the dunes climbing a particularly high hill of sand.

He saw them scramble about as if in panic. The dune itself seemed to slide and slump, with ripples shivering through its surface until a great pit opened beneath the brave explorers. Then Ishmael beheld a rising serpentine shape, more enormous and terrifying than any creature he had ever imagined . . .

When morning came, there was no sign of the men.

What sort of place have we found here? It seemed beyond anyone's imagination, beyond the worst of nightmares.

He decided to keep this knowledge to himself, not even telling Chamal. The others could keep praying for that scouting party to bring rescuers. Ishmael did not want to lie to his people, but he let them cling to possibilities. Hope cost them nothing.

Despite Ishmael's most rigorous austerity measures, supplies from the wrecked ship were almost depleted. Arrakis would kill them all soon.

More than a third of the Zensunnis who had escaped from Poritrin were already dead from starvation, thirst, or exposure. Some had perished searching for help; others had simply given up and succumbed quietly in their sleep.

A few of the most technically adept Zensunni had scoured the crashed ship, tinkering with the engines and scraps of metal and tubing to rig innovative systems for distilling and recycling water, even chemically converting some of the fuel and coolant into a drinkable but foul-flavored liquid. They fashioned a crude transmitter for sending distress signals to any local flying craft, but the signals didn't seem to get through to anything. Apparently, the frequent sandstorms created a ferocious ionization layer in the atmosphere that scrambled their transmissions.

Or no one chose to come to their aid.

In their most forlorn moments, Ishmael had heard some of the survivors talk grimly about eating flesh and drinking the moisture of the dead, but he railed at the horrific suggestion. "We must give up our lives before giving up our humanity. Buddallah has cast us here for a reason. This is our test, or punishment . . . a sorting of the faithful. What use is it to sacrifice our souls for one meal, if we are hungry again tomorrow?"

They would die free . . . but still they would die.

Each night, Ishmael communed with the Sutras, reciting verses and looking for deeper meaning, but he found no answers to his queries. Was there not some way they could be rescued? Was there no ally the Zensunnis could locate on Arrakis? With a sinking feeling, Ishmael knew that any people hardy enough to prosper in this bleak land would probably not be friendly to outsiders.

Each day, during the cooler hours of dawn and dusk, the people spread out, prying up rocks, searching in crannies, ranging along the peninsula of rock. They found sparse vegetation and lichen, along with a few lizards; once, a boy knocked down a carrion bird with a stone. They trapped anything they could, even beetles and armored centipedes. Every bit of protein and moisture gave them one more moment of life, one more precious breath.

But they could do very little else.

As darkness fell on another clear desert night, Chamal spotted a commotion out on the shadowed dunes, a giant sinuous shape slithering toward the long barricade of rock where the Zensunni refugees had made their camp. She shouted a warning, and the people came to see, slumping and shuffling from weakness and fatigue.

In the thickening gloom, Ishmael could discern the monstrous writhing form, the sparking orange glow in its gullet, and friction fires on its lower skin caused by its rough passage over the abrasive desert. The people stood beside Ishmael, perplexed by the approaching behemoth. Twice in the past five months, they had seen worms far out on the open dunes, but the creatures usually traveled aimlessly and rarely spent much time exposed to the air.

This one seemed to be coming toward them with . . . *intent*.

"What does it mean, Father?" Chamal asked. They all looked at Ishmael.

"An omen," suggested one woman. Her face looked yellow in the glow of lights that Ishmael had rigged from the wrecked ship, since they did not have enough combustibles to burn for a traditional Zensunni fire.

"The demon wants to eat us," another man said. "It is calling us out onto the dunes for a sacrifice. Is all hope lost?"

Ishmael shook his head. "We are safe here on the rocks. Perhaps it is a manifestation of Buddallah watching us."

He turned away as the sandworm thrashed around at the base of the cliffs. Darkening night threw a blanket over the details, but a safe distance off they could hear the beast grinding against loose boulders, then growing still.

A tiny sound that might have been a shout, a human voice, echoed across the rocks. Ishmael listened carefully but heard nothing more, and then convinced himself it had merely been his imagination or the sound of a hunting nightbird.

"Come," Ishmael said. "Sit by me and I will tell you again about Harmonthep. We can each describe our true homes so that we keep the memories clear."

The brave leader huddled with his people under the dim yellow lights that had to take the place of a story fire, and he talked wistfully about marshy waterways on Harmonthep. Ishmael described the fish and insects he used to catch, flowers he had harvested, the idyllic way of life he had known in his early years. One of the sutras came to mind now: "Hunger is a demon with many faces."

Ishmael halted his tale when he was about to mention the slavers. He did not wish to dwell on that. Dragging Keedair here to Arrakis and then losing him in the desert . . . was that not sufficient revenge?

Lulled into a familiar fellowship, the Zensunnis shared tales of lost homes and childhoods, taking comfort from the few good memories. Many of these refugees had been born and raised on Poritrin, a generation of slaves who knew no other world, now stranded on this dune-covered sphere . . .

They did not hear the intruders approach. The strangers came like silent shadows borne on the softest breeze. They waited like ghosts in the rock outcroppings outside the circle of light where Ishmael told his tales.

Startling them, one man stepped from the group and spoke in heavily accented Galach, the standard language across the Galaxy. "Those are fine stories, but you will find no such home here."

Ishmael leaped to his feet, and his followers struggled to arm themselves with crude implements.

When the desert nomads stepped into the light, Ishmael saw lean, hardened men with eyes that were entirely blue. "Who are you? If you are bandits, we have nothing for you to take. We are ourselves barely alive."

The lantern-jawed giant who was obviously their leader regarded him and then answered, astonishingly, in the secret language of Chakobsa. "We are Zensunnis like yourselves. We have come here to see if the rumors are true."

Ishmael's mind spun. Another lost tribe? Most Buddislamic believers had fled the League long ago. Perhaps some had settled here in this awful desert . . .

"My name is Jafar. I lead a band of outlaws who carry on the sacred mission of Selim Wormrider. In our council we discussed your situation, wondering if we could believe what we heard." He lifted his chin proudly. "You are escaped slaves, and we have decided to welcome you into our tribe, if you work hard, assist us, and earn your keep. We will show you how to survive in the desert."

Shouts of agreement, thankful prayers to Buddallah, and cries of relief resounded throughout the night. Jafar and his outlaws looked at the ruined spaceship as if assessing how much they could still salvage from the hulk.

"We accept your fine offer, Jafar," Ishmael said without hesitation. Already, he could see that his people believed Buddallah had brought this salvation in their hour of greatest need. "We will work hard. We are honored to join you."

*At one time I thought cruelty and malice were only human traits.
Alas, it seems that the thinking machines have learned to imitate
us.*

> —Vorian Atreides, *Turning Points in History*

B Y THE TIME the Jihad patrol fleet reached the small colony on
Chusuk, it was already too late. The attacking machines had left
nothing.

The leveled cities had ceased smoldering; fires had burned themselves out. The only remnants of human habitation were black, twisted
girders, craters from huge explosions, and a sour charcoal-smelling
silence.

Far too many days had passed to expect any survivors.

On the ground, Vorian Atreides stood amidst the wreckage, his feet
spread to anchor himself against the overwhelming, devastating shock.
Five more rescue and salvage shuttles descended from the two orbiting
ballistas, but this would be no rescue operation . . . only an assessment of
the appalling massacre.

The jihadis gasped their grief. A few of the soldiers had connections to
Chusuk, relatives or friends who had lived here. Vor's heart turned to ice
as he found himself barely able to grasp the premeditated, calculated
bloodshed that machine forces had unleashed here.

"Omnius didn't even bother to take over," he said, his voice
hollow. Chusuk had boasted enough infrastructure that the evermind
could have established a minor Synchronized World here, but the
machines didn't seem to want this place. "They just . . . destroyed
everything."

Vor shook his head. His dark hair was shaggy and sweaty, his eyebrows
clenched together. "The machines may have changed their tactics. If they
do this to other worlds, it means they just want to kill humans and leave

their planets uninhabitable." He looked over his shoulder at the soldiers who busied themselves out of numb habit, searching for useful tasks in this dead colony.

The Primero walked slowly through the broken and blistered streets. After his early years serving Omnius, being trained in the nuances of conquest, Vor had thought he understood the machines better than this. "It doesn't make sense — unless cymeks did this."

Chusuk had been a thriving settlement — not a paradise by any means, but certainly a worthwhile place to live, a foothold of humanity on a calm and unremarkable world. The colonists led quiet lives here, with gentle romances, close-knit families, and unambitious dreams. Real people who just wanted to live from day to day.

And the machines had turned them into victims.

Through a thick plaz window in the pavement, he saw a room below that looked undisturbed, with musical instruments arrayed on a workbench. Odd, how certain things survived in war, as if protected by angelic bubbles. He ordered searchers to check the rooms below, but they came back moments later reporting no signs of life.

Vor moved on. The burned buildings stood out like blackened skeletons. Walls had caved in, exposing structural frameworks and shattered brick components. The town square was only a gouge left from heavy explosives, probably fired by airborne robotic warships.

He saw roasted bodies that looked like black scarecrows, their arms twisted, shreds of lips drawn back to expose flame-cracked teeth. Real people. He never got used to the horrific cost of this Jihad. Empty eye sockets stared like charcoal pits, as if the people were still wondering why rescue had taken so long.

Three uniformed Jihad soldiers shouted from around the corner. Vor picked up his pace, turned to find two ruined combat meks that had been destroyed in the Chusuk defense. The settlers had been armed with few weapons, but apparently they'd rallied enough to demolish this pair of thinking machines.

Unfortunately, each mechanical army had thousands of such combat meks. The Chusuk colonists had resisted, but had never stood a real chance.

Vor's mouth drew down in a frown. He felt empty inside, knowing there was nothing he could have done to prevent this slaughter. En route here for nearly a month, his warships had approached Chusuk on regular patrol duties. They had arrived expecting a resupply depot and a week's furlough. They had received no distress call — not that a signal could have ever reached them in time anyway.

Vor felt sickened. He had not expected such senseless brutality from the machines, not here.

But he should have.

On the way to Chusuk, during the long, sluggish voyage across space, even a Primero had little to do. He had occupied himself reading business documents and drawing up notes for treatises on military tactics, in which he explained what he knew about thinking machines.

During the Jihad, Serena Butler had written a number of artful polemics about her crusade against the machines, from which Iblis Ginjo quoted liberally. At some point Vor had even contemplated writing memoirs of his own, since he had lived for so long and experienced so much . . . but when he thought of all the lies his father had included in his own memoirs, passing them off as true history, Vor found himself repelled by the idea. Even if he tried to be honest, human nature might make him color a few facts.

In another century or so, if he continued to make progress against Omnius, he might reconsider. For now, he was better off spending his time playing an occasional game of Fleur de Lys with his men. He would make history through his actions rather than through any documents he left behind . . .

During off hours alone in his cabin, Vor often relived pleasant memories, fantasizing a different life for himself. The first person who usually came to mind was Leronica Tergiet on Caladan, a woman who had truly touched his heart.

Never before had he dared to feel any sort of commitment or emotional bond . . . but Leronica made him want to be a different person, someone with no obligations or duties of cosmic significance, just a simple man who could be a husband and a friend. Vor did not regret his responsibilities or accomplishments, knowing that he had defended the populations of entire planets, but for a change it would have been nice to be small, unimportant, and content, an unremarkable soldier who went by the assumed name of "Virk."

Emergencies in the Jihad had thus far prevented him from taking any discretionary trips back to Caladan, as he had planned to do. He sent Leronica letters by way of jihadi soldiers assigned to the tracking station, even an occasional gift. But he heard nothing back. He wasn't even sure she'd have the means to dispatch a communiqué to him. Feeling dismal about it, he realized that he was probably not much in her thoughts at all.

By now a fine woman like that must have chosen a husband, had a family. If so, he hoped she still thought of him with fondness.

Though it occurred to him as a possibility, he could not in good conscience march in and disrupt whatever happiness Leronica had managed to create for herself. One day he had to return to Caladan, to find out for himself.

In the meantime, during the long, lonely journey between the stars, he continued to write her long letters that would be dispatched by round-about couriers. He knew how much she liked to hear about other planets and people. And the exercise kept Leronica in his thoughts and helped him feel slightly less alone.

Thankfully, the demands of war made time pass quickly for him. Perhaps he would see her sooner than he anticipated. His pulse quickened at the thought. Could she possibly be waiting for him?

Walking onward with a leaden heart through the ruins of Chusuk, Vor stared at the shocking devastation. The machines had been exceedingly thorough in a way that seemed rather . . . *inefficient* to him. Surely the robotic armies had not needed to inflict so much damage simply to achieve their objective?

One of the cuartos in charge of an inspection squadron came up to report. "Primero Atreides, we've tallied the bodies. There are no more than a hundred."

"A hundred? That's not enough for a colony this size. Were the others disintegrated in the attack?"

"The pattern of destruction does not support that conclusion, sir."

Vor formed his lips into a firm line, still perplexed. "They've probably been taken as slaves to replenish some of the losses in abortive rebellions. I pity the poor wretches who survived this."

Then he straightened and lifted his chin. "We must finish up quickly. Take all the images you need, and we'll return directly to Salusa Secundus. I've got to tell the Priestess what happened here."

The cuarto's expression solidified with resolve. "Once she views these images, she will ignite a fire among the population. The thinking machines will be sorry they ever chose to do this to one of our colonies."

The officer ran to gather his men, while Vor sensed that the new spark from Chusuk would make the fighting even more fanatical, and infinitely worse.

Now, more than ever, he longed to be back on Caladan in the arms of Leronica . . .

In the banquet of life, our daily activities are the main course, and dessert is composed of our dreams.

—Serena Butler, *Jihad Manifestos*

NO MORE THAN four months after Vorian Atreides and the Jihad engineers had departed from Caladan, Leronica Tergiet agreed to marry a man who had courted her unsuccessfully for years.

Leronica was one of sixteen local women who found themselves pregnant by boisterous Jihad soldiers. She was not ashamed of her condition and actually laughed quietly as her father tried to console her. Back when Vor's contingent of technicians were stationed in town, Brom Tergiet had been working offshore in the waters east of town, and was blind to how much time his daughter had spent with one particular man.

After she could no longer deny pregnancy and had waited long enough to be confident she would not lose the child through miscarriage, she finally confessed to her father. Saying nothing in response, Brom Tergiet had sat on the dock, working diligently to repair tangled fishing nets. He did not meet her proud, unabashed gaze, but shook his head, as if in disbelief and disgust.

"Oh, Dad, we all know well enough how biology works," Leronica said, somewhat amused by his reaction. "I'm entirely happy with the special times Virk and I shared, and I am content to accept whatever he was able to give me, including his child."

She had not, however, revealed to anyone — not even to her father, the real identity of the military officer. Now that she knew she would bear his child, the secret was more important than ever, and she did not want to put her baby at risk.

"You will be on your own, Leronica," Brom warned. "That soldier will never come back for you, or his baby."

"Oh, I know that," she said, unperturbed, "but I have my memories of him and his stories of exotic places. That is enough reward for me. Would you have me be a helpless woman, whining and bemoaning my situation? I like my life and my circumstances. I'd prefer your moral and emotional support, but I can manage on my own if necessary. I can keep working up until the time of the birth, and I'll only take a few days off to deliver the child."

"You always have been independent," Brom said with a smile, and then climbed to his feet, leaving the fish nets tangled on the pale, weathered boards of the wharf. He hugged his daughter, letting his touch and gestures tell her what he could not say out loud. "After all, the welfare of my grandchild is the most important thing to consider."

In fact, with Caladan's miniscule population, the coastal villages welcomed any children that brought fresh infusions to the thin local bloodlines. The jihadis would bring a new generation of vitality to this rural, often overlooked region.

So, without any giddy nonsense or moping around waiting for Vorian Atreides to come back and take her away from Caladan — which she felt certain would never happen — Leronica decided it would be best to move on and find a husband who was willing to raise the baby as his own . . .

Kalem Vazz was a quiet, diligent bachelor, ten years Leronica's senior. Three times since the young woman had come of age, Kalem had asked her to be his wife. She had turned him down consistently, not out of spite or because she was toying with his affections, but because she didn't want to be bothered with taking care of a husband along with her father, the tavern, and the fishing boats. But now her life had changed.

After making up her mind, Leronica went early one dawn to Kalem's home before he headed out to the docks to board his fishing boat. She chose a clean dress, bound her curls in a scarf, and wore a necklace of finely worked coral.

After she pounded on his door, Kalem appeared on the threshold, hurriedly tucking in an extra shirt to protect against the cold blanket of sea fog. He looked surprised and bleary-eyed, but did not pretend to make small talk, knowing she must have come for an important reason.

"You asked me to be your wife," she said. "Does your offer still stand, Kalem Vazz, or have you stopped waiting for me?"

His square-jawed face lost fifteen years of apparent age as he smiled in amazement. Her pregnancy was already showing, but she doubted he had noticed. "What changed your mind?"

"There are some conditions," she said and then explained about her baby. He took it well, made some supportive comments and showed sympathy. Finally she said, "If you would be a husband to me, you must also agree to act as father to another man's child. Other than that, I make no demands of you, and I promise to be the wife you expect of me."

Satisfied that he understood the situation and that she was in no way deceiving him, she awaited his response to this straightforward and no-nonsense offer, on which she would base the rest of her life. She had already dabbled in silly romance and would always cherish the memories of Vor in her heart, but that had no bearing on her present circumstances.

"And what if he comes back?" Kalem said.

"He will not be back."

He looked at her intensely, and both of them knew her answer was not good enough. He asked, "If he did, would you run off to his arms again? Or, worse, would you refuse to do that and stay with me, and then brood about your decision for the rest of your life?"

"The tide may rise and fall, Kalem, but do you believe my heart is like a bit of flotsam to be tossed about, this way and that? If I make a promise, I keep it."

Kalem pursed his lips as if considering a business proposition, but she saw his eyes twinkling at his sudden change of fortune. "First, I must make one demand of my own."

She gazed at him steadily, hands on her hips, prepared for the details of his negotiations.

"If this Jihad soldier of yours is truly gone and you agree to marry me, then you must never do me — or him — the dishonor of comparing the two of us in any way." Kalem folded his big callused hands together. "I know I'm not the perfect man, and I cannot take your memories from you. But your time with him is only a memory, while I am your reality. Can you live with that?"

Leronica did not hesitate at all before agreeing.

And so they were married, one of sixteen quick ceremonies that took place in the fishing villages. Few of the bridegrooms looked troubled; instead, they seemed unable to believe their good fortune in obtaining attractive wives they had previously thought beyond their reach.

In ensuing weeks, Kalem Vazz worked his fishing boat alongside Brom Tergiet's. Together with the income from the popular tavern, Leronica and her men lived comparatively well.

It was the best she had hoped for on Caladan, though at night as she rested beside Kalem in their shared bed, tracing her fingertips along the growing curve of her belly, she thought about all the wondrous, alien places Vor had described for her in the League of Nobles.

Leronica lay in silence, looking out the open window into the starry sky, and thought about Vorian Atreides, so far away from her. Right now, he would be fighting evil robots, leading great battleships . . . possibly even thinking of her now and again. Such a handsome, dashing warrior. She sighed.

Sometimes she would roll over and see Kalem lying awake and motionless, his eyes open and glittering — with tears? — but he said not a word and gave no indication that he guessed her thoughts. Kalem never asked, never pried. He had never even inquired about the name of her soldier, so she was glad she did not have to lie to him to keep her promise to her former lover. This good, hardworking man seemed entirely satisfied with what he had . . . and Leronica tried to feel the same.

Both of them knew that the jihadi would never come back.

When the time came, Leronica gave birth to twins, healthy sons that she insisted on naming Estes and Kagin, after her husband's two grandfathers. She wanted no connection with Vor's name. The villagers universally remarked that the boys bore a strong resemblance to Brom Tergiet — which made the fisherman swell with embarrassing pride — though a few of his fellows jokingly hoped the twins would not be cursed with their grandfather's horse laugh.

Each time she looked at the boys, though, Leronica could see echoes of the adventurous, dark-haired officer who had stolen her heart, and then gone away to space.

True to his word, Kalem Vazz outdid himself as a faithful husband, industrious worker, and attentive father. He doted on Estes and Kagin, never hinting that they were not his own. Kalem considered his love for the boys more important than their paternal bloodlines.

Two years after Vor left, Leronica felt no sadness, only a wistful curiosity about what he might be doing, and if he was safe. For the first time in her life, however, she paid attention to the overall landscape of the Jihad, following word of the major battles.

At least once a month, Kalem and her father took their fishing boats out into the fertile waters around distant reefs. On these occasions, as was her new habit, Leronica left the twins with a neighbor woman, borrowed one of the village's methcars and drove north up the rough coastal road to the military installation and tracking station that had been established two years ago by the Army of the Jihad.

The handful of dedicated soldiers stationed there were content to live in prefabricated barracks, where they diligently attended to their duties. Occasionally, two or three men would make the trek down to the village to purchase fresh fish and supplies; on other occasions, Leronica made deliveries of food from the tavern's kitchens, providing lunch in exchange for news of the continuing struggle against Omnius.

She became a familiar sight in the control huts beneath the reinforced towers that linked the satellite network encircling Caladan. The clearing near the outpost, where shuttles had landed and launched regularly not long ago, might eventually become a full-fledged spaceport, but for now it was rarely used.

The Jihad soldiers falsely believed Leronica was simply curious about politics and military tactics, and they gave her copies of the greatest speeches of Priestess Serena Butler and the recorded rallies of Grand Patriarch Iblis Ginjo. In truth, she was eager only to hear any mention of Primero Vorian Atreides, though she was careful never to reveal that she actually knew him.

Bright-eyed, Leronica listened while the soldiers summarized the clashes at Bela Tegeuse and, more recently, the horrific machine annihilation of the isolated colony on Chusuk. She eventually uncovered more details about Vor's past exploits, especially how he had helped to save IV Anbus, and later tricked the thinking machines with a hollow fleet at Poritrin.

Sometimes, Vor sent her letters and packages, always under an assumed name. They usually arrived when her husband was out working. Though the soldiers who delivered articles to her undoubtedly assumed she had a sweetheart somewhere out in the Jihad, she never uttered his name. She read the messages with an intensity she never revealed to Kalem. She hated to keep secrets from this good man, but did it to protect him, not out of guilt.

She never tried to send a message in response, never dared to — for reasons she did not entirely understand herself. Fighting his far-off war, Primero Atreides did not even know about his twin sons, nor did she intend to tell him. She hoped only that he remained unharmed, and that he thought about her occasionally.

Satisfied with what she had heard, Leronica thanked the jihadis and rode her methcar back down to the fishing village, hurrying to arrive before sunset. Kalem and her father would not return for at least two days, but she needed to pick up the twins and cook dinner at the tavern. Though motherhood kept her busy, Leronica still ran the tavern and fed the workers who were too tired to cook for themselves.

Leronica maintained a secretive smile as she reopened the doors for an evening crowd of boisterous men. The fresh news and stories — along with the special letter that proved her departed lover really did remember her — would satisfy her for a while.

But when her husband returned she would focus entirely on him. As she had promised, she never compared Kalem with the other man in her life . . . but she could not forget the brave officer, either. In a sense, she had the best of both worlds.

*Is it human to say that no one understands me? This is one of
many things I have learned from them.*

— *Erasmus Dialogues*

ERASMUS HAD BEEN accused of much during his long existence.
Many people, including the maddeningly interesting Serena Butler,
had called him a butcher — for his insightful laboratory experiments into
human nature, and especially for tossing Serena's tiny son off the
balcony.

Before its downfall, the Earth-Omnius had insinuated that Erasmus
was trying to become human himself. What a ludicrous thought! Recently, even the Corrin-Omnius had suggested that Erasmus wanted to
usurp the evermind — though only the independent robot's quick
thinking and effective action had salvaged Corrin itself from disaster
and prevented the continued spread of the corrupted update.

Erasmus resented being categorized so simplistically. He prided
himself on the fact that he defied description or interpretation. He
wanted so much more than anyone imagined.

Now, as he trekked across a broad snowfield with young Gilbertus
Albans behind him, linked by rope, the autonomous robot considered
how parochial other minds were — even Omnius's — in comparison
with his own. Through his researches, Erasmus had involved himself
with so much more of the overall biological canvas than any other
researcher, machine or man. He enjoyed the best of all possible worlds.

Hearing the teenager breathing hard, though not protesting, Erasmus
slowed his mechanical pace. He had modified his flowmetal legs and feet
for greater stability on the snow, and now he used his copious energy
reserves to trudge forward, breaking a path. Even so, it was difficult for
poor Gilbertus to keep up. The ascent slope was steeper than it looked,

and unstable; no human could match the mobile characteristics of an advanced robot design.

The Corrin-Omnius, now repaired and essentially recovered from the cascade of breakdowns, followed them with a flurry of watcheyes that buzzed around their heads like mosquitoes. The evermind, itself no more than disembodied software dispersed like an invisible cloud of data, could never enjoy the real experience of this.

It was yet another instance in which Erasmus, with his ambulatory, autonomous body, could feel superior to Omnius. The computer evermind absorbed vast amounts of data, but had no real *experiences* of his own.

It is not merely the amount of information that matters, Erasmus thought, *but the quality of it*. And he found himself somewhat amused at the realization that Omnius was something of a voyeur, always watching and never really participating . . . or living.

Living. The word brought to Erasmus's mind all sorts of philosophical questions. Did a thinking machine, without cellular structures, actually *live*? A few like himself did, he decided, but most did not. They just went through rote patterns, day after day. Was Omnius alive? The robot considered this for a long moment, and came away thinking, *No. He is not.*

This answer, in turn, brought up all sorts of additional questions, like shoots from the branch of a tree. He realized that he had pledged his allegiance to an inanimate thing, a *dead* thing, and wondered if such a pledge was even morally valid, or if he could discard it.

I can do as I please. I shall do as I please, when it suits me.

The red giant sun shed harsh coppery light but scant warmth at such a high altitude. Looking back, Erasmus satisfied himself that young Gilbertus was not overextending himself, especially with the heavy backpack he insisted on toting. The boy had to be protected from hurting himself.

Gilbertus's biological form was, by its very nature, vulnerable to accidents and the environment, and the robot needed to be extremely watchful on his behalf. Just to protect his experimental subject, of course . . . or so he tried to tell himself. Over the past four years, Erasmus had devoted a great deal of effort to teaching this boy, converting him from a wild ruffian into the fine young man he was today.

Erasmus looked upslope to a broken terrain full of rotten ice, left over from Corrin's long winter season. He identified recognizable topographical features, and continued trudging upward. It had been centuries since he had been here, but his perfect gelcircuitry memory told him exactly where he was going.

"I can guess where you're taking me, Mr. Erasmus." Gilbertus had a narrow face with a wide mouth, large, olive-colored eyes, and straw-yellow hair that peeked from under his parka hood. Though rather small in stature for his age — perhaps because of insufficient nutrition in his youth in the slave pens — he was still wiry and strong.

"Is that correct? Well, keep guessing, Gilbertus, because I might have a trick or two up my sleeve."

"Don't try to fool me. Robots don't do tricks."

"Your own words defeat your argument. If I were trying to fool you, Gilbertus, would that not in itself be a trick . . . thereby contradicting your own postulate? You must frame your thoughts in a more logical manner."

Gilbertus fell silent to ponder the conundrum.

Erasmus returned to his own ponderings, this time about all of the unusable data that Omnius had accumulated without any understanding of how to synthesize new insights from it. Data itself was nothing unless one used it as a resource from which to draw conclusions.

Erasmus could access virtually anything that the evermind knew, from an electronic building that contained Omnius's backup files. Erasmus didn't even have to link with the evermind to obtain the information, something the robot avoided so that he could maintain his independence . . . and protect his secrets. Of course, Omnius had secrets as well, files that were not accessible to any robot. Those would be of interest to the inquisitive Erasmus, but were not worth the risk of a direct connection.

"Are we almost there, Mr. Erasmus?" the boy asked, panting.

The robot formed a smile on his flowmetal face and swiveled his shining oval head entirely around to glance behind him. "Almost there. I should have had other children in addition to you, Gilbertus. I am an excellent coach."

Gilbertus paused to assess what the robot had said, then smiled. "You're a machine, and you can't have children."

"True, but I am a very special kind of machine, with many adaptations and modifications. Do not be surprised at anything I can do."

"Please don't get weird on me again, Mr. Erasmus."

The robot simulated a laugh. He enjoyed the company of Gilbertus far more than he'd ever thought he would. This youth, thirteen now, had turned out to be extremely bright and a real treasure, much more than a simple experiment. Under Erasmus's guidance, Gilbertus was beginning to tap into his full potential. Perhaps after constant instruction and rigorous, patient training, the independent robot could, through his ward, realize the pinnacle of human potential. Omnius would get much more than expected from the challenge he had issued.

Sometimes the shiny robot and the boy would banter back and forth, each trying to snag the other on unfounded assumptions or logic flaws. Erasmus had taken care to instruct his eager student in the history of the universe, philosophy, religion, politics, and the perfect beauty of mathematics. The palette from which they chose their subjects contained infinite colors, and the boy's eager mind used it all with remarkable efficiency.

Unlike his earlier wager with the Earth-Omnius — in which Erasmus tried to turn a loyal trustee against his masters — this time he was achieving something positive. Though it was no longer necessary, the robot maintained a proud smile as he trudged over the snow toward a sharp fracture in the rocks.

The slope leveled, and Erasmus identified two upthrust rocks separated by a deep crevasse. "We will stop here and make camp." He extended a metal arm. "There used to be a snow bridge over there."

"And you foolishly did not check its structural integrity before you attempted to cross it," Gilbertus said knowingly, as he removed his pack and plopped it on the snow. "It broke when you tried to cross it, and you fell into the crevasse, where you remained trapped for years."

"I would never make such a mistake again . . . though, in retrospect, the consequences proved most beneficial for me. Throughout that frozen, isolated time I had nothing to do but contemplate, rather like a Cogitor. It was the seed of my unique form of independence."

Gilbertus gazed in awe at the stark fissure in the rock, ignoring the cold wind. "I've been looking forward to seeing this place ever since you told me about it. I think of it as your . . . birthplace."

"What a curious thought. I rather like it."

That evening, while the young man finished setting up their fabricated camp components, Erasmus played chef, cooking on a portable stove, dipping his sensor into a stew of Corrin rabbit, adding seasoning as if he knew what he was doing. Then he watched carefully while Gilbertus ate; the robot merely sampled the dishes himself with his sensitive probes, attempting to understand what his ward was tasting.

Afterward, the robot picked up where they had left off on their last lesson. Ever since he had succeeded in teaching the former wild boy to follow basic, civil behavior, Erasmus had concentrated on boosting Gilbertus's memory capacity through mental exercises. "Thirty-seven billion, eight hundred sixty-eight million, forty thousand, one hundred fifty-six," Erasmus said.

"What Earth's human population would have been today — based upon birth and mortality projections — if Omnius had not intervened, and if the planet had not been destroyed."

"Precisely right. A proper education has no limits."

For hours as the night grew colder, Erasmus ran through additional questions, and his student showed a remarkable ability to organize and utilize data in his mind, just as a machine would. The young man's capacity for learning was impressive, and he proved capable of advanced calculations and thought processes. Gilbertus's organic brain learned to sort through a variety of consequences and possibilities, and always select the best alternative.

Later that night, as a light snow began to fall, Erasmus noted that his student began to make mistakes. Patiently, the robot added to what his student already knew, layering data into the young human's mind in such a fashion that he would be able to retrieve it quickly in the form of organic memory. But, though Gilbertus said nothing, his attention wandered, and he seemed to be having trouble focusing.

Erasmus realized that the young man was exhausted from the difficult hike and too many hours without rest. The robot often made this error, forgetting to consider that humans required sleep, and that even the most advanced drugs could not completely replace that natural function. Even if Gilbertus Albans had a steady biological energy supply, Erasmus could not teach him without pause, around the clock.

Though knowledge has no limits, he mused, *the human capacity for learning has definite boundaries.* "Sleep now, Gilbertus. Let your mind absorb and process information, and we will continue when you wake again."

"Good night, Mr. Erasmus," the boy said in a weary but playful tone, as he crawled into his warm sleeping enclosure.

Erasmus sat motionless, staring and recording with thousands of optic threads until Gilbertus quickly dozed off. This outing was turning out to be a far more rewarding experience than he had ever anticipated.

Without waking the young man, he said, "Good night, Gilbertus."

It is a stark fact of human existence that relationships change. Nothing is ever completely stable, not even from hour to hour. There are always subtle variances, alterations and adjustments that must be taken into account. No two moments are ever exactly alike in any respect.

—Serena Butler, *Observations*

E ACH OF THE big black constructors out on the frozen bog had a pair of human operators who sat side by side in high cages at the controls. Long hydraulic arms dipped into the icy material, scooping out thawed, spongy vegetable matter and loading it onto groundtrucks that came and went. The plains of Kolhar looked like a giant, stirred-up ants' nest.

After months of massive preparation and investment, the construction of the great shipyards was under way. During the brief warm season, the marshy flatlands came to life with flowers, thick weeds and algae, birds, and flying insects. This year would be different, however. From this day forth, the vast expanse would be home to gigantic ships whose engines could fold space. The landscape of Kolhar would be forever changed.

Standing on one edge of the bog, Aurelius Venport huddled against the chill wind, and pulled a furry hood tight around his face. A dusting of snow reflected brilliant whiteness in the morning sunlight, making him squint; he adjusted the dark filterplaz over his eyes.

The offworld construction workers wore similar attire. Venport watched them and wondered how much each moment of this huge effort was costing him. He had borrowed heavily through his diversified companies, leveraging his businesses. He had also sent well equipped teams to Arrakis to increase the spice output, now that Naib Dhartha had vanished, and the bandits had — for whatever reason — ceased to be a problem.

Everything to raise enough capital for this one enterprise. *Norma's dream.*

From his earliest commercial ventures with Rossak pharmaceuticals,

Venport had been a risk-taker. But nothing had ever come close to the scale of this. His knees felt weak when he thought about it. Still, despite the enormous expenses, his reliable instincts told him this was the correct decision. As always he found Norma compelling and enthusiastic. She had no deceit within her, only a phenomenal confidence. He trusted her vision implicitly.

This course of action would either ruin him or make him the wealthiest man in the universe. He saw no middle ground.

He devoted himself to the work here, leaving other VenKee representatives to keep an eye on the melange and other businesses. More than ever, he wished he knew what had happened to Tuk Keedair . . . After all this time, it seemed certain that his Tlulaxa partner had perished in the Poritrin massacres, just like so many hundreds of thousands of other unidentified victims. Now the risks, and the rewards, were Venport's own. And so was the company itself.

Kolhar's marshy plain extended to the horizon, but the vast structures Norma envisioned here seemed nearly as large. Every week, she took him out in a fast ground vehicle to show him the perimeter of each building. Before long, they would begin to build the actual spacefolder ships, following Norma's detailed plans.

From the bustling construction village came constant noises of machinery, vehicles emerging, engines growing louder and fading. Norma seemed to find the sounds reassuring, comforted to know that the work continued at all hours.

She scurried around the high plain, consulting with architects and construction managers, laying out additional structures and landing fields for her innovative space-folding ships. Her new, energized form had little need — or time — for sleep.

When she saw him inspecting the workfield, she hurried over to be with him. Despite her full schedule, Norma always managed to spare time and warmth for Aurelius. After greeting him with a warm embrace, she revealed the surprising, perfect reason for the attentiveness. "I have seen the thinking machines, and I do not want to become like them." She smiled at him now and, despite her amazing perfection, Venport could still detect the original uncertain girl beneath the skin. "I must allow myself time to be human."

He hugged her. "That's good, Norma." But it seemed to Venport that in her enhanced, beautiful state she was far beyond him — or any human. No one could ever match her abilities, or even come close. She defied comparison. Just like her mother.

"And to that end, I have allowed myself to conceive our first child."

He stared at her, too startled to ask questions, but she continued her explanations. "It seems a logical extension of what I intend to do. The sensations are unusual, but interesting. The child will be a male, I believe. I intend to make certain he is well-formed and healthy."

He did not need to inquire how she would do that. He had never pretended to understand all of the amazing things Norma could do — both before and after her strange metamorphosis.

Recently, her mother had returned to her cave city on nearby Rossak for the last month of her pregnancy. Despite sophisticated new drugs that his own pharmaceutical operations had developed from native jungle growths, Zufa Cenva was concerned that something might still go wrong with her child fathered by Iblis Ginjo. She did not have Norma's powers of internal, cellular and chemical manipulation.

Venport still experienced mixed feelings whenever he looked at Zufa. On occasion during her time here at the shipyards, he had noticed a sadness in the tall Sorceress's pale, icy eyes when she looked at him. Long ago he had truly cared for her, but Zufa had always been scornful of him, preoccupying herself with other matters, expending all of her passion on the war effort and personal gratification, rather than on him . . .

Unlike Norma, thankfully.

Venport heard crackling, telekinetic explosions in the distance. Because of this unusual and extremely important venture, Zufa had summoned fourteen of her most powerful young Sorceress candidates to watch over the site while she was gone. The adept women provided additional safety as a "telepathic defense shield," roaming at large and watching for threats. Although mercenary guards watched the industries and approaches to the planet, the Sorceresses had skills the mercenaries did not.

Rumor had it that the cymeks were now at war with Omnius, but there could be no predicting the behavior of the hybrids. No predatory cymek would ever survive a probing strike here. No machine spy would steal the secrets of the Kolhar shipyards. Norma would not lose this venture, as she had lost her experimental complex on Poritrin.

Against any obstacles, it would succeed.

By the time her pregnancy progressed beyond its eighth month, Zufa Cenva wished she could do without men at all, inseminating herself and giving birth androgynously like the ancient goddess Sophia of Old Earth. But the Supreme Sorceress of the Jihad was hampered by the limitations of her mortal body. Her daughter Norma, with her burgeoning mental and creative powers, might be another matter.

After torture and nearly complete cellular destruction, Norma had *recreated* her body in every respect. Now that she had married Aurelius Venport — whose bloodline Zufa knew carried numerous advantages — Norma would no doubt discover the potential of her own reproductive systems . . .

Norma had also found a way to *control* the telepathic mindstorm that could annihilate cymeks, saving herself in the process. Ah, if only Zufa could learn that skill and teach it to her other telepathic commandos . . .

Zufa stood at a window opening in the lava rock caves, looking out at the swarming foliage and smelling the humid soup of living scents. She had come home to the sheltered cliff cities to finish out her pregnancy. She remembered all too well the numerous painful miscarriages she had suffered, the stillborn monstrosities, the devastating *disappointments*.

How strange, how ironic it was that Norma, against all odds, had become that flawless, talented child. Zufa thought about her daughter with mixed feelings: pride for what she had become and what she intended to do, but confusion as well, and even fear. Zufa feared what she did not understand. She was also bothered by guilt for mistreating the young woman all those years.

The spark must have been there all along, the potential — but I couldn't see it. I, the greatest Sorceress, was blind to the possibilities of my own flesh and blood.

Now Zufa wanted to promote her daughter's grandiose dream, but craved additional information. She hoped to preserve and even improve their new relationship. With the birth imminent, the Sorceress focused her thoughts down inside of her, thinking of the new girl child — one Zufa had wanted for so long. This baby daughter was coming at a most inconvenient time.

Zufa promised herself that she would remain on Rossak only as long as necessary to deliver the infant and hand her over to Sorceress caretakers, to assure that she would be raised properly. Her duty and obsession called her to return to Kolhar, where Venport and Norma were consumed with the initial excavation of what would become the most enormous shipyard in the League . . .

Zufa rested a hand on her swollen abdomen. She stood on a high ledge, gazing across the thick jungle canopy. Despite its environmental toxins and rough landscape across most continents, Rossak was still the most beautiful of all the planets she had visited. The silvery-purple jungle provided food, tamed the atmosphere, and yielded numerous drugs and pharmaceuticals that had formed the foundation of Aurelius Venport's commercial empire.

She contemplated the never-ending cycles of nature, all the species supported by the jungles of this single world, the complex interactions and ecological niches that even the tiniest life forms of Rossak found for themselves. A stirring within reminded her of her own place in the biology of the planet, and in the Jihad.

Zufa felt a gush between her legs, a flow of warm amniotic water running down onto her feet and the stone path. Even sooner than she had expected! She summoned one of the young Sorceresses who stood nearby. "Send for breeding mistress Ticia Oss. Tell her I require her services — *now.*"

Though other Sorceresses came to aid her, Zufa insisted on walking by herself down the rocky corridor to her quarters, which had already been prepared with the necessary birthing equipment.

Seven women had taken turns watching Zufa during the final weeks of this important pregnancy. The Supreme Sorceress loved them as her own family, having trained five of them to be psychic weapons if called upon. She had already decided to name her daughter after the breeding mistress who guided the birth.

Ticia. My daughter will carry that name for all of her days. And perhaps the breeding mistress would agree to act as guardian and surrogate mother for a time, so that Zufa could journey back to Kolhar.

She lay back on the bed, and as her head sank into the soft pillow she felt a violent contraction, followed moments later by another. "It is coming fast."

Perhaps this daughter was as anxious to be born as Zufa was to be free of its burden . . .

Tall, pale Sorceresses filled the room, each with a familiar task to perform. Zufa tried to focus on a wall tapestry to forget about her pain, using her mental focus to guide the birth and block the swelling pain. Despite all such attempts, the baby wrenched Zufa's thoughts back to the birth with each labor spasm.

Finally, Ticia Oss drew forth a gleaming red infant and cut the umbilical cord while the assistants came forward with towels and warm cloths. "You have a beautiful baby daughter."

"I expected nothing less," Zufa said, exhausted and sweating. Ticia Oss handed her the fragile child wrapped in a pale green blanket.

As she held the newborn child, crimson and wrinkled from its ordeal, Zufa felt immense relief this had not been another misshapen horror that would need to be buried out in the jungle. She had experienced that disappointment too many times already. No, this child — Ticia Cenva —

was healthy and would easily survive without Zufa's constant attendance. The girl would be strong.

After recovering for only a few days, Zufa would arrange to return to Kolhar. She had unfairly scorned both Aurelius and Norma in the past, and now she wanted to make up for it.

Unreliable allies are no better than enemies. We prefer our independence, our own control.

—General Agamemnon, *The New Golden Age*

W HICH CHOICE WILL you make?

The ragged remnants of the slave population on Bela Tegeuse had never fended for their own survival, or even set up a semblance of government. For countless generations they had lived under the benevolent care of the thinking machines. Looking back at the time between the destruction of the local Omnius and the takeover by the rebel cymeks, their temporary freedom seemed harsh by contrast, not a kindness to them at all.

Now, after picking up the pieces following the atomic blast at Comati, the Tegeusan survivors were ripe for conversion . . . through brainwashing. They would think only what the Titan Juno told them to think.

Leaving the docile and reprogrammed thinking-machine fleet in orbit, ready to drive back any incursions by the Army of the Jihad or Omnius's robot forces, Agamemnon made this wounded Synchronized World a centerpiece and base of operations for his eventual conquest of the hated computer evermind. He had expended no resources and lost no cymek fighters in this initial victory, but still the Titan general needed to enlarge his rebellious force so that he could withstand any outside attack.

Agamemnon and his cymeks had the will and the vision, but their most important next step was to develop a large, unstoppable army. As soon as possible. They needed more industries, more weapons . . . and more neos. Many more.

Using the robotic warships, the conquering cymeks shuttled large groups of human prisoners from the radioactive outskirts of Comati. As a matter of efficiency and logical planning, the thinking machines set up stockpiles of supplies, and when Agamemnon offered the frightened survivors more food, medicines, and a slightly increased measure of freedom, the former Bela Tegeusan captives looked upon the Titans as saviors. Now, relatively well fed and still starry-eyed from their changed circumstances, they were ripe for Juno and her mesmerizing speech.

The female Titan had assembled a larger, more glorious walker body for this occasion than she had used in some time — more than was necessary to impress anyone. Juno used reprogrammed servant robots to polish and etch every exposed surface, so that she gleamed like a walking tarantula made of engraved chrome and silver. Her intent was to inspire awe in those who viewed her, to harken back to the fabled Time of Titans.

She linked her speaker patch through thoughtrode transmitters to amplifiers that boomed her voice.

"Would you like to live forever?" she asked the throng. Juno paused, expecting cheers, but the indrawn breath rewarded her well enough. The crowd milled about. She knew that these unfortunates had rarely felt the emotion of hope, and had only now begun to allow themselves dreams.

"Would you like to be immortal and feel no pain — only power and the ability to accomplish anything you can imagine? I have lived that life myself for a thousand years! So has General Agamemnon. All of the neo-cymeks were formerly trustee humans who proved themselves worthy of the greatest gift any mortal could achieve. Are any of you worthy of this honor?"

The former captives knew all too well the unchanging drudgery of life under the computer evermind. Faced with Juno's wondrous augmented cymek body and hearing her words, the people were stunned and speechless.

"My fellow Titans and I have thrown off the shackles of Omnius, so that you may be free for the first time in your lives. We have conquered this planet in the name of the Titans, and we wish to bring the best of you into our fight."

She saw them stirring. The idea had never occurred to them.

"We can create a new golden age for human achievement, made possible through cymek enhancements. From this very population on Bela Tegeuse, we intend to draw our first ranks of lieutenants."

Fortunately, most of the trustees had been wiped out in Comati, since Juno and Agamemnon did not want to recruit humans who were loyal to the computer evermind. Rather, they preferred volunteers who would swear their very souls to the service of the Titans.

Juno needed to make inroads swiftly. She did not know how long it might be before the Army of the Jihad came to occupy the ruins of Bela Tegeuse. Agamemnon and his cymeks needed to fortify their beachhead.

"We ask you to look into your hearts and minds." She raised her voice even louder. "Do you have the stamina and the brilliance necessary to become one of us? Are you tired of your frail human bodies? Are you weary of sickness, times when your natural muscles and bones are insufficient to the tasks you demand of them?"

She swiveled her head turret, scanning the crowd. "If so, the Titan Dante and his neo-cymek assistants are willing to hear you and consider your case. They will run tests and select those of you who impress us the most. We are at the dawn of a new age! Those who join now will reap far more rewards than those who are afraid to take risks."

Agamemnon had expected she might convince a few dozen competent new volunteers, but Juno knew her lover was far too pessimistic and short-sighted. She felt it would be best to let hundreds, maybe even a thousand, willing humans undergo the cymek conversion here — fitted with fail-safe programming and auto-destruct systems in their preservation canisters, should any of them prove to be unruly or rebellious. For now the cymeks needed *fighters*, swarms of machines with human minds battling to the death, willing to undertake suicide missions to bring an end to the reign of Omnius, as well as Serena Butler's distasteful Jihad.

"Therefore," Juno continued in her booming yet seductive voice, "we offer you a chance to become immortal, to live inside mechanical fighting forms, limber and invincible bodies." She raised her sleek silvery forelimbs. "You will have the ability to stimulate the brain's pleasure centers at will. You will never again be hungry, or fatigued. You will never feel weak." She paced about like a prancing thoroughbred. Artificial, bright yellow lights played off her smooth curves and polished exoskeleton.

"Think carefully before responding," she cautioned in a sultry voice. "Now tell me, which among you are willing to join?"

When she heard the resounding cheer and the thunderous roar of assent, Juno knew the Titans would have far more volunteers than they could ever possibly need.

I feel I can do anything — except, perhaps, live up to the expectations others have of me.

—The Legend of Selim Wormrider

N OW THAT THE Zensunni survivors were well fed and had hope for their future again, Ishmael finally allowed himself to feel a growing satisfaction. Despite its harshness and the daily balance on the edge of survival, life among the desert dwellers of Arrakis began to find natural rhythms. It was not comfortable, perhaps, but much safer than before.

When Jafar and the others led the band of refugees back to the isolated cave settlements, the newcomers had straggled into the sanctuary with expressions of awe and wonder, as if they were arriving in heaven. Standing in cool shadows, the survivors were welcomed by Selim's outlaw band. Some of the Poritrin Zensunnis accepted food offerings, while others drank deeply of tepid water. Some could do nothing more than collapse in relief.

That night, giddy with contentment, Ishmael studied them all, especially Chamal. He had wanted to weep. Only fifty-seven of the original group remained, a little over half. But they were now free.

In spite of their terrible ordeal, the survivors looked on him as a confident leader, whose vision and faith had kept them together, guiding most of them safely through. Escaping the tyranny of slave masters, he had brought his people halfway across the galaxy in an unproven starship, and helped most of them survive for months — no mean feat on Arrakis.

And the refugees insisted to the band of outlaws that Ishmael deserved their respect as well. Marha, the wife of fallen Selim, held onto her young dark-eyed son El'hiim, not yet a year old, and nodded slowly at Ishmael, appraising him. "We are happy to have a man among us who is so worthy of respect."

On the first night of their salvation, he stood at one of the cave openings, staring out upon the moonlit desert, marveling at the beauty of the wan light as it washed over the sands. Overhead, pinprick stars twinkled in the clear, dry air.

Then he turned to his rescued people and spoke in a firm, comforting voice. "This is what Buddallah promised us. It may not be what we expected — it is not an easy life here, not a paradise by any measure — but given time, perhaps we can make it better."

The survivors continued to celebrate, consuming supplies stolen from spice-harvesting caravans or unsuspecting villages that had garnered wealth through trafficking in melange. The Poritrin refugees praised Buddallah and Ishmael, while the outlaws sang songs of Selim Wormrider and shared tales of Shai-Hulud.

Ishmael found himself alone with Jafar deep in the caves. "How did you know of us?" he asked the tall, gaunt man. "We have been seeking help for a long time."

Jafar narrowed his blue-within-blue eyes, which looked like shadowed pits in his face. "We found a man wandering alone on the sand, barely alive. We saved him, and he asked us to go in search of you." He shrugged. "We did not know whether to believe him, for the words of a merchant and a slaver are often untrue."

He led Ishmael to a dim chamber in the heart of the mountain. "I will leave the two of you to talk." From the opening, Ishmael could barely see a thin man sitting alone under the wan light of a single, small glowglobe. *Tuk Keedair.*

Jafar whirled in his desert robe and left.

Barely able to believe what he saw, Ishmael stepped forward. "Buddallah does indeed work in strange ways if a flesh merchant who led so many slave raids is responsible for saving Zensunni lives!"

The Tlulaxa man looked gaunt and haunted, his body scrawny, his hair ragged and without its signature braid. When he looked up to see his visitor, Keedair's face showed neither defiance nor fear, only weariness.

"So, Lord Ishmael of the Slaves, I see you have survived, against all odds. Your god must indeed have great plans for you . . . or a profound trick up His sleeve."

"I am not the only one who remained alive despite the best efforts of this planet." Ishmael stepped farther into the room. "What happened to Rafel and Ingu, and our scout ship?"

Keedair rocked back and forth on the stone ledge that served as his bed.

"They are all down in the belly of a worm." He ran a clawlike hand through his shaggy hair. "Rafel threatened to slit my throat, but instead decided just to turn me loose in the wild desert. I had not gone far before three huge sandworms came in a frenzy. They destroyed the scout ship, devouring every trace." He looked up, staring at a point somewhere beyond Ishmael. "I wandered for days before Jafar and his men found me."

Ishmael frowned upon hearing that his son-in-law had turned the former slaver out into the desert, where he would almost certainly die. Had he been trying to take revenge? Had Buddallah punished Rafel because he had decided to take justice into his own hands?

"You must never inform my daughter of this," he said.

Keedair shrugged. "It was a matter between Rafel and the worm. It means nothing to me." He extended a sinewy hand. "I give you my word."

Ishmael made no move to accept the gesture. "You expect me to accept the word of a flesh merchant? The word of the man who attacked my village and sold me into slavery?"

"Lord Ishmael, a businessman who cannot keep his promises soon finds himself without any business." He used the title not sarcastically, but in deference.

Sensing someone beside him, Ishmael turned to see the large-eyed woman who had been the wife of Selim Wormrider. He had not heard her approach. "What would you have us do with the slaver, Ishmael? The choice falls to you."

He frowned, uneasy with the responsibility. "Why did you let him keep his life in the first place?"

To Marha, the answer seemed obvious. "To see if he spoke the truth about other Zensunnis who came from a faraway world. But water and food are scarce, and we need no extra mouths in our tribe."

Inside his cell, Keedair scowled, as if already knowing his fate. "Yes, yes, now that your bellies are full and your throats are no longer parched, you can turn your minds to thoughts of vengeance. You've waited long enough for it, Ishmael."

By now, other Poritrin refugees had gathered in the corridor, searching for Ishmael and hearing the voices. Chamal was there, her face full of questions, and Ishmael did not know how he would decide to answer. Jafar and Marha stood aside to let the refugees peer into the shadowy room, from which the Tlulaxa slaver glared out at them. Many of them grumbled, their anger palpable enough to diminish their joy at being saved.

"Kill him, Ishmael," implored an old woman.

"Throw him from the cliffs."

"Feed him to the giant worms."

Clenching and unclenching his fists, Ishmael stood closest to the captive. He closed his eyes and silently recited his Koran Sutras, hoping that the repeated words of forgiveness and promises of hope would seep into his heart.

"Tuk Keedair, you have already stolen much from me. You have hurt me, robbed me of most of my family, stolen nearly all the years of my life. Now my people are here on Arrakis and they can never leave, can never return to their home planets. When I think of the cost, I cannot help but shudder. But our ordeals here are not your fault." He sucked in a long, dry breath. "I give you your life back, slaver."

Surprised murmurs came from the corridor. Even Chamal glared at him in disbelief.

He continued, "It would be a dishonor to kill you now, for you have repaid your debt to us. My people would surely be dead if you had not urged these outlaws to seek us." Ishmael opened his hands, looking at his distraught daughter. "Make no mistake, I still think of revenge . . . but I no longer have any right to take it. Those who take things they do not deserve are no better than . . . slavers."

The refugees were clearly dissatisfied, even perplexed, but they appeared to accept his decision. Jafar looked at Ishmael with fresh respect, as did Marha, apparently seeing the Poritrin man as a leader for the first time. A real leader . . .

While the refugees returned to the gathering chambers, Marha took Ishmael aside and led him into the dry, cool night where they could sit together under the profusion of stars. Although many star patterns were different from what had known on Poritrin, he recognized the constellation of the Beetle and several others. Some things were the same.

"I left my wife somewhere out there." Up in the cosmic ceiling he did not even know how to find the planet where he had spent most of his life. In a single chaotic lurch, the space-folding ship had hurled them across a whole landscape of stars. "Her name was — is — Ozza. I pray she is still alive, along with our other daughter Falina."

Marha coaxed the reminiscences from him, let him recall his favorite times with Ozza, how they had been so different at first but had become close companions, until Lord Bludd had separated them out of spite. Ishmael had not seen her in nearly three years.

He sighed. "I will never hold my Ozza again, but there is no point in suffocating with regret. Buddallah has guided me here for a reason, kept these people alive, and brought us all together."

Marha sat in silence beside him for a long moment, then said, "Now I have a story for you, one that must be remembered by all our people, from generation to generation." She smiled at him, and her voice softened. "Listen, while I tell you the tale of Selim Wormrider."

166 B.G.

JIHAD YEAR 36

Eight years after the Great Slave Uprising on Poritrin

Seven years after the Founding

of the Kolhar Shipyards

The only guarantee in life is death, and the only guarantee in death is its shocking unpredictability.

—A saying of Old Earth

I N T H E T H I R T Y - S I X T H year of the Jihad that was named after his murdered grandson, old Manion Butler died among his cherished grapevines. The weather had turned cold, and the long-retired Viceroy feared a heavy frost. The ground was hard and dry, but he insisted on getting up at dawn and taking his shovel out to the vineyards.

He was eighty-four years old at the end, and though he had many other workers to rely on, Manion considered it important to take the spade himself and add mulch around the sensitive vines. The old man had always worked hard, devoting himself to little chores around his vineyards, and his olive groves too, just as he had labored during his long years of service in the League Parliament.

Like a champion racehorse, old Manion had never even considered slowing down, that the urgency for completing the project in a single morning was perhaps overstated.

Xavier had slept late, glad to be home with his wife and their youngest daughter Wandra, now eight years old. He snuggled close to Octa in their bed, reacquainting himself with the familiarity of her touch, her closeness. But the Primero had never been a man to lounge around and do nothing. He soon got up, breakfasted, and dressed in old work clothes.

It had been seven years since the slave revolt on Poritrin resulted in the destruction of the city of Starda and the deaths of so many people. And eight years since Agamemnon's unexpected cymek rebellion threw the Synchronized Worlds into an uproar and diverted the destructive attentions of Omnius.

While the machines' relentless attempts at conquest had lost focus, the

Jihad plodded on. Xavier regularly guided forays into Synchronized territory, protected vulnerable colonies, and attacked robotic warships wherever he encountered them.

Upon arriving home, however, Xavier always enjoyed working in the Butler Estate's fields and vineyards, where he sought to distract himself and gain some inner peace in a universe of war.

He stepped outside into the fresh morning light, tugged on thick gloves, and strode out smiling to meet the old man and help him finish the mulching. Xavier arrived just in time to see Manion pause and then reel, as if disoriented. The old politician clutched the handle of the shovel, trying to keep himself upright, but his expression fell, his face turned gray, and he crumpled to the ground.

Xavier was already running, calling out to his father-in-law, but he reached his side too late to help.

"Now we have lost two Manions," Serena's mother said. Tears streamed down Livia Butler's weathered face; her reflection in the ripples of the City of Introspection's reflecting pool looked ancient.

Abbess Livia Butler had always looked much younger than her eighty-one years, but she appeared to have aged terribly since the death of her husband. In elegant contemplation robes, she sat hunched over. Despite her stoic composure, Livia looked broken inside, like a tree severed from its roots.

Serena sat with her mother on a bench at the edge of the pool. Manion had passed away peacefully enough, after a full life. *If only he had lived long enough to see the end of this unhappy war.*

In the three and a half decades of the Jihad, the ache of tragedy had never left Serena. Sometimes it was the grim knowledge of populations wiped out on Chusuk or in the Honru Massacre; at other times, the grief was much more personal. She would never relinquish her sworn duty to guide the struggle against the thinking machines, but Serena wished she could finally have time to ponder, and grieve. She had thought about going into Zimia, to meditate beside one of the numerous flower-draped public reliquaries. But at the moment she did not want to see any crowds.

Serena glanced up a grassy slope to the shrine that contained the preserved body of her child. Her little boy was the innocent symbol of the human spirit, the absolute antithesis of machine cruelty and utter *in*humanity. She said, "Yes, now we have lost two Manions. But the League and its Jihad will have to go on without both of them." Even so, she felt as if one of the pillars of the League of Nobles had toppled and shattered.

Reaching over, she touched her mother's hand. The Abbess squeezed back, with little strength at first, but then harder, urgently. Livia's eyes widened, and she gasped with a genuine pain that went far beyond her sadness. Serena tried to put an arm around her mother, but the older woman slumped off the bench and dropped to the edge of the water. Serena knelt by Livia and lifted her shoulders, shouting urgently for help.

For a long, agonizing moment Serena stared into her mother's open, lifeless eyes. Though Livia and Manion Butler had lived separate lives for many years, each preoccupied with their own passions, the two of them had shared an invisible bond. They had been married for over half a century.

Now Livia had gone to join her beloved husband.

Though Serena got very little sleep, the following day she performed her duties with burning energy. The Grand Patriarch told her afterward that she seemed fresher and more inspired than ever, as if instilled with a novel, raw form of power.

Her emptiness had changed to anger, as if a switch had been activated inside her mind. The thinking machines — unthinking, hateful machines — had robbed her of so much. The losses ran deeper than words could express.

After all these years, she found herself bitter that the fight had not yet been won. Undoubtedly it had something to do with a weakness in the human spirit, an insufficient resolve. She must change that, somehow.

Desperately, the Priestess of the Jihad wished she could have the quiet advice of her mother, just one more time. Or the Cogitor Kwyna. Now, more than ever, she needed great wisdom. But where could she turn?

After long consideration, she decided it was time to do something new, to change the parameters. Eight years earlier, she and Iblis Ginjo had generously provided new secondaries to the Ivory Tower Cogitors. The well-chosen volunteers had had plenty of time to persuade Vidad and his five philosopher comrades to share this knowledge, and now she had grown tired of waiting.

A shiver ran across her skin. If the Ivory Tower Cogitors refused to come to her, then she would simply have to go to them.

While somber but extravagant preparations were being made for a double funeral of state for the retired Viceroy and the Abbess, the streets were filled with orange marigolds, blooms that signified the grief of the people. Serena stared out the windows at them. So many people followed her blindly into any peril. Vorian Atreides had returned home to brief the Jihad Council on his efforts to strengthen the Unallied Planets, and brought with him devastating news of yet another randomly destroyed human colony — this time the mining planetoid Rhisso. His report caused great consternation. Sleeping gas had been pumped into the atmospheric domes, and it appeared that most of the colonists had been kidnapped before the facilities themselves were destroyed.

Vor stood in front of Serena as he concluded his report. Iblis Ginjo heard the words with an expression of shock, but she noted that his eyes sparkled as if somehow this might be good news to him. She had mixed feelings about him. Despite some of his questionable actions, she knew Iblis would never allow his enthusiasm for the Jihad to wane. Troubled, Serena looked away, then back at him. This time, she saw only sadness in his face.

Vor suggested that the people of Rhisso must have been taken by thinking machines in order to force them into slavery on some distant world where manpower was needed. That made sense to Serena. But she couldn't help wondering.

"The evidence Primero Atreides has brought back will surely enrage people across the League, and we will have a fresh influx of recruits to continue the fight," Iblis said, intending to give comfort. "Don't ever feel that you are alone, Serena."

Serena, though, felt enraged and invigorated. News of this unfortunate incident, like Chusuk, would certainly rile the populace again, but she didn't think it would be enough. It might even spark yet another round of debilitating protests against the conflict. It had been over three decades since the destruction of the Earth-Omnius.

Why have we not yet achieved victory?

"I wish I had billions of impassioned fighters, instead of a few million. But there is another way to win." She lifted her chin and stared at Iblis, strengthening her resolve. "I intend to start by adding only a few new allies. *Powerful* allies."

There is a fine line between life and death. At any given moment, the human being is only a missed heartbeat or a gasping breath away from eternal darkness. The man who understands this is most willing to take great risks. If I were recruiting Jihad soldiers, I would teach this and exploit it to the maximum.

—Erasmus, uncollated laboratory files

"**T**HIS IS GOING to hurt me more than it hurts you," Erasmus said as he pushed the boy down onto a laboratory table, face up. "Trust me when I say it is for your own good."

Gilbertus made no attempt to resist. "Of course I trust you, sir." Still, he looked around nervously as Erasmus clamped his wrists, ankles, and torso. The young man had seen enough of the independent robot's experiments to know that the experience would not be pleasant.

Erasmus then rolled forth a cart filled with cylinders of acid-bright fluids, neuromechanical pumps, machines with sensor tips, and long, sharp needles. Numerous needles.

"It is important that I do this." He swung a flexible metal arm from the cart over the boy's torso. He knew he should have asked permission from Omnius before doing this, but didn't want to explain his motivations to the evermind.

Some things are best left private, he thought.

"Afterward, I would like you to describe the sensations to me. I am very curious about them."

"I'll try, Mr. Erasmus." His voice held a hint of nervousness, and fear.

Steel points extruded from the flexible arm and penetrated the young man's neck and chest, seeking out specific internal organs. He gasped, tried to scream, then struggled to endure the pain. His expression and palpable agony made Erasmus sad. The robot had never before experienced any qualms about observing the reactions of pain on test subjects . . . but Gilbertus was more than just an experiment.

Relegating his feelings to a minor subroutine, the robot adjusted controls to increase the subject's pain higher and higher, and then still higher. He had to proceed through all the steps of the process.

"It will be over momentarily, and I would be most displeased if you were to die now."

Gilbertus writhed and thrashed, but could not escape. Only his screams broke free and echoed off the walls of the laboratory. His lips curled back to reveal clenching teeth, and blood running into his gums from biting his own tongue.

The robot spouted more platitudes that he had learned from humans. "It will be all right in the end. It's for the best. Keep a stiff upper lip."

The boy's body sagged, and he plunged into the safety of unconsciousness. Erasmus reduced the settings gradually, and finally shut down the life-extension machine. A console showed the subject's vital signs improving moment by moment. He was young and comparatively strong — even stronger, after this.

The young man's eyes fluttered, opened. Seeing the smiling flowmetal face of the robot, he managed a faint smile of his own.

"You trust me completely, don't you?" Erasmus asked, as he placed healing patches on the wounds.

"Of course, Mr. Erasmus." Gilbertus's voice was low, and he spat blood into a bowl that the robot held for him. "But what was the purpose of this . . . test? Did you learn something from it?"

"I took you to the brink of death . . . and brought you back. It is my gift to you." He released the restraints. "It was a procedure developed during the time of the Old Empire and kept secret in the Synchronized Worlds. The cymeks have used it to maintain their organic health. Now I have given you life, Gilbertus — in as true a sense as your own parents did. Your biological body will retain its health for hundreds of years, possibly longer if you take care of yourself. Unfortunately, your low threshold for pain prevented me from giving you a higher dosage."

"So I have failed you?"

"Not at all. Your human frailties are not your fault."

"I feel more like a thinking machine now," Gilbertus said, struggling to sit up. He swung his legs off the edge of the table, but swayed when he tried to stand.

Erasmus had to help him keep his balance. "Machines and humans have differing strengths."

The boy's eyes began to shine as he understood the consequences of his life-extension treatment. "I promise I will make you proud of me, Mr. Erasmus."

"I already am, young man."

A legend can be an educational tool and a great danger — not only for its followers, but for the subject of the legend himself.
                                        —Chirox, *Logs of Swordmaster Trainees*

HIGH ABOVE THE restless ocean, the lone man climbed the moonlit cliff face with no more effort than if he'd been running on flat, open ground. He leaped upward with great force, scrambling around overhangs and up fissures in the stone, never slipping, always advancing. Far below, the waters of the Ginaz Sea crashed against treacherous reef rocks.

But Jool Noret would not fall; he never did. For nine years, he had thrown himself into the jaws of Death — and Death had always spat him back out.

The most extraordinary of all mercenaries wore a white combat suit — sleeveless, with trousers to the knees — an outfit that offered no armor but permitted him full range of movement. A black bandana encircled his head, tied in the manner of the ancient ronin fighters of Old Earth. Though he cared little about impressing the ever-present onlookers, Noret wore the white suit so that they could observe his progress up the sheer rock face.

Above, shadowy forms lined the top of the cliff, a score of Ginaz trainees watching him, accompanied by Chirox. Noret saw the angular multi-armed *sensei* mek glistening dull silver in moonlight. He knew the combat machine was telling the students what they should attempt, without exceeding their own abilities. As Noret glanced up at the group, part of him was pleased to have inspired so many more fighters to destroy the machines. At the same time, he was bewildered by all of the attention. He had never asked for it.

Without doubt, he had become the greatest warrior the Ginaz archipelago had ever produced — perhaps the finest it ever would produce.

But Noret was also the most enigmatic of men, speaking only rarely to his students. Several years ago, a downcast trainee had etched the Swordmaster's most famous quotation into a polished stone near the cluster of huts on the island. "I am still unworthy myself. I am not fit to teach others."

When asked about his legendary victories, Noret said nothing . . . which forced the students to learn and embellish the tales for themselves. He alone knew the full truth. On battlefield after battlefield, he charged into harm's way, seeking ever more dangerous confrontations, more lethal foes. Shattered robots lay strewn in his path wherever he fought. Jool Noret never held anything back, became nearly invincible because he simply did not care if he survived or not. His death wish had grown plain for all to see, yet he continued to live.

He fought for the beauty and release of the battle, for the artistic expression of violence. It was what he had been born to do, carrying the spirit of Jav Barri within him, building upon the inherited instincts, turning himself into a superlative fighter. It was what the death of his father had imposed upon him.

Noret had become a one-man rebellion on several of the weaker Synchronized Worlds, infiltrating imprisoned human populations, providing them with scrambler weapons to fry gelcircuitry, or more conventional explosives and weapons to initiate sabotage. Noret would also slip in among the machines, deactivating and destroying scores of robots like an assassin in the night. And when the hornet's nest had been stirred and he had inflicted enough damage, he would slip away and return to the League Worlds.

Yet it was never enough.

Scaling this sheer cliff was a far simpler exercise than overcoming the self-imposed conditions he had placed on his life and his worth. On the most difficult section of rock, a perilous overhang, Noret even *increased* the pace of his treacherous ascent.

He realized that demonstrations like this always carried great danger — not to himself, but to any of the young mercenaries who might try to emulate him. But the lesson was valid: in life there were few safety nets, and there were certainly none during war, when unpredictable violence could change any situation in a matter of seconds.

On the rare occasions when he returned to Ginaz, he conducted these exercises for his own benefit, honing his skills while giving the others something to strive for. He still isolated himself, keeping away from the shining eyes of the students. Merely by succeeding, Noret gave them the certain knowledge that the human body could indeed achieve remarkable things. Human beings should kill with precision and refinement, an art form that even the most efficient of thinking machines could never master. He flung sweat out of his pale hair and kept climbing, approaching the top of the cliff.

Abruptly he slipped silently to the side, into the thick shadow of a rift in the rock where the moonlight did not penetrate, then darted beneath the overhang and the waiting students. Noret scampered along a narrow ledge, then resumed his ascent. He did not care what others said about him, or about his aura of mystery that only increased people's curiosity and fascination. As far as he was concerned, his reasons for training so relentlessly were private.

"Where is he?" he heard one of the trainees ask. "I don't see him anymore."

"He is behind us," Chirox answered, turning to greet Noret. "In this game, he has killed all of us."

Twenty sets of eyes turned to look.

Jool Noret stood poised in a fighting stance, his scarred, bronzed face made more enigmatic by night shadow. Without warning, he bounded past the students — his long hair flying — leaped off the edge of the cliff, and disappeared from view.

Sometimes the line between bravery and recklessness is indistinguishable.

—Zufa Cenva, *Recollections on the Jihad*

A FTER MORE THAN seven years of the massive construction project, the Kolhar shipyards finally produced their first fleet of space-folding merchant vessels. Numerous prototypes had already been tested, and now Venport was ready to adapt them for widespread commercial use, delivering cargoes needed by the League of Nobles.

Despite her uneasiness at the very concept, Norma had no choice but to develop partially computerized guidance systems for the sophisticated spacefolders. The Holtzman calculations and the generation of the distortion field required such complex mathematics that no normal human could hope to solve the equations unaided. And she had enough data points from years of rigorous testing to show that the flights were already high-risk, with an unacceptable destruction rate.

She hoped the sophisticated navigation devices would help, but she was careful not to create any potentially independent AI gelcircuitry systems. Norma would rather scuttle the entire VenKee merchant fleet, than inadvertently create another Omnius. She was the only one with access to the navigation rooms of the new space-folding vessels; not even her husband Aurelius could get into those sealed areas.

Locked inside the black-walled guidance chamber of her newest ship, Norma inserted a small cylinder into an activation port, then watched a three-dimensional holoscreen as it showed the myriad coordinates of every charted astronomical body. It seemed to her that no human, not even a genius of her caliber, could ever chart a safe course through all the convolutions of folded space and the hazards lurking everywhere in the vast universe. She had no choice but to rely on computers, however dangerous they might be.

The detailed library of mapped coordinates finished loading, and she removed the programming cylinder, hiding it in a large pocket of her pale green laboratory smock.

Despite the enormous drain of funding and resources here on Kolhar, so far the League of Nobles was unaware of the remarkable new ship design. People would suspect something, though, when hundreds of small, fast VenKee ships began to dramatically outstrip their competition. As soon as news got out — and it would, inevitably — she would make certain that Aurelius Venport was trumpeted as the driving force behind the revolutionary technology. She had never cared for fame or power, preferring to avoid the associated waste of time. With a front-row seat at a real-life Grogyptian tragedy, Norma had seen how hubris and a struggle for fame could twist and destroy genius, as it had the once-great Tio Holtzman.

Since her husband had always had faith in her and provided the necessary funding, she was happy to grant him full credit. Aurelius was a savvy politician and could make greater strides if he had the clout and cachet. He would find a way to enjoy the attention, while deflecting questions about the nature of the technology. She cared only about the success of the project anyway.

Over a hundred small spacefolder cargo carriers had already been dispatched, flown by mercenary pilots who knew and accepted the risks. After many years and a colossal infusion of capital, Aurelius was on the verge of making immense profits, despite the frequent losses of ships and cargo. And without his Tlulaxa partner, Venport controlled the large commercial empire himself, thanks to Norma.

The first runs had been made, to great profit, despite a handful of horrendous accidents. VenKee Enterprises was swiftly transporting vital products across vast distances in the holds of the new ships. Rare and perishable drugs and foods came from Rossak, delivered everywhere around the League Worlds in less time than it took to order them. The trade in melange had increased exponentially as its use spread throughout the League, and each spice run practically paid the entire cost of one of the spacefolder cargo ships.

Hopefully, the safety record would improve. Within the bounds of industrial secrecy, he did inform crews in advance of the great dangers posed by the "new ships," and paid them high hazard pay. Privately, he told Norma that he wished they didn't have to risk human lives, that it could all be done by machine. Then he added, after a long thought, that this was an impossibility. Thinking machines could not be trusted.

League citizens had begun to see Venport as a savior and a patriot, and his competitors were desperate to find out his veiled method of rapid space travel. Tio Holtzman had confiscated all of her work and designs, but he'd been vaporized in the pseudo-atomic explosion of Starda, and Norma knew that no one else could even come close to understanding the system.

After studying evidence of the crater and wreckage in the Poritrin city, Norma privately believed she understood what had occurred there. Let the rest of the League think that the insurgent Zenshiite slaves had somehow found a nuclear device, but she remembered a controlled test on a small moonlet almost forty years earlier. She had seen the results of a laser weapon interacting with a Holtzman shield. Norma suspected that the devastating explosion had been caused by a mistake, perhaps even one committed by Holtzman himself.

She did not want to make any similar mistakes.

She ran the nav-system through its self-check test cycles, taking the swift space-folding vessel on simulated trips through deep space. Oval screens appeared on the chamber walls all around her, showing nebulas, comets, and novas.

Aurelius had never failed her, had never drifted away. Even when she examined their relationship in a detached and intellectual manner, she was surprised that he had remained with her, just as he had promised. The man truly loved her, and had been a wonderful father to their one son. Exactly as she had wanted.

But Norma's greatest creation was still the new engine design. She sensed strongly that this technology — if the problems and dangers could ever be resolved — would become the basis of a commercial enterprise that would dwarf the League Worlds, far more important than a simple trading company.

However, some of the numerous vessels had gone off course, some suffering severe damage, some vanishing entirely. Yet another ship on a shakedown voyage had inadvertently passed through the heart of a sun, obliterating the craft. As more and more cargo runs were made, more ships — and more pilots — would be lost.

The excessive accident rate highlighted the risks of the innovative technology. Norma had sifted her brain for a solution, but no safety systems seemed feasible other than navigation accuracy. There seemed to be no way around it — the great vessels crossed immense distances in moments, and a ship was doomed the moment any errant course was set. No human, probably not even a computer mind, could calculate or react to a fatal course in an eyeblink of time.

But Venport still found the profit-loss ratio acceptable, since enough ships got through. Aside from his concern about crew deaths, which he assuaged by paying them well, he described profitability as a "numbers game." He only had to adjust his prices to take into account what he called "shrinkage of inventory."

Now, in the navigation room, Norma watched the simulated journey past a mock space battlefield, where Jihad warships were destroying robot forces. Just a little touch she had added for amusement.

"Busy, as usual. I'm amazed that you can do this for days without rest."

She had sensed her husband's approach, and now felt self-conscious about the sophisticated computer systems arrayed before her. "You shouldn't distract me. How did you get in?"

"Hidden surveillance showed me how you enter these rooms."

She frowned, feeling an instinctive storm within her. "I'll have to tighten security, then. This area is off-limits to everyone — even you."

Venport furrowed his brow. Thanks to heavy melange consumption, he still looked like a man in his late thirties, rather than sixty-two. "Including your son, apparently. Adrien has been trying to reach you for days, and you haven't responded. He's smart for a six-year-old, but he's still just a child."

The image of her son flashed in her mind. The boy had his father's smile and dark, wavy hair. His genetics were perfect, thanks to Norma's internal tinkering during the process of conception. She had found that she could visualize and guide her reproductive system, permitting only the optimum sperm and egg to unite.

Norma lowered her gaze. "I've been preoccupied with trying to understand the navigation shortcomings. With such a high loss factor of our ships, we can't afford to turn space-folding ships to the war effort. That was my original intent for the vessels. My mother has been pressing me to contact the Army of the Jihad about our technology, so they can transport troops to battle zones — but I don't want so many deaths on my conscience."

"Norma, you'll figure out a solution." He smiled, then kissed her. "We'll license the technology to the military as soon as it's safe enough."

"Please apologize to Adrien for me?"

He looked closely at the instruments, the screens, controls, and data-reader wheels. "This is the computer system you told me about?"

"Yes."

"May the gods protect us!"

"Aurelius, please. I have work to do. We already talked about the reasons for the strict controls I've instituted."

"Yes, yes, of course." She watched him, warily, then saw him take a deep breath. "If anyone can put a leash on thinking machines, it's you," he said. "But I don't like it."

"Neither do I, but for now there is no alternative."

After her husband's departure, Norma resealed the door and practiced entering various destinations into the navigation machine, letting the computer calculate each course to avoid suns, planets, and other obstacles in space. Though she had created this computer herself and loaded it with safeguards, the close proximity of thinking machines still made her uneasy. And she didn't dare install such a system in the actual ships being flown.

If only she could find a way to guide the space-folding ships with a human mind, instead of a mechanical one. But the concept seemed an impossibility.

The flesh may not be excused from the laws of matter, but the mind is not so fettered. Thoughts transcend the physics of the brain.
　　　　　　　—Cogitor Vidad, *Thoughts from Isolated Objectivity*

A COLD, BLEAK PLANETOID with a barely breathable atmosphere, Hessra had furious winds that drove ice crystals like needles against the skin; slow but inevitable glaciers crept across its landscape. Few people would have wished to live there for as long as a week, much less two millennia, but the Ivory Tower Cogitors had selected this as the best place to continue their infinite ruminations, with the least likelihood of outside events intruding on their solitude.

Serena Butler found them anyway.

Though she had lost benevolent Kwyna at the City of Introspection, these other mysterious Cogitors remained abroad. Vidad and his "Ivory Tower" philosophers had always isolated themselves, avoiding any involvement in human affairs, although they must have had an outside source of income and supplies. Now she intended to go directly to them and request — no, *demand* — that they help the human race. How could they refuse?

Even the Ivory Tower Cogitors had to see that neutrality was no longer possible. They had been humans once, but unlike the Titans and neo-cymeks, they had never allied themselves with Omnius. With their millennia of insight, they might be able to suggest courses of action that humanity had never considered. Serena believed that their coveted knowledge might be the lynchpin on which ultimate victory against the Synchronized Worlds would hang.

For eight years now, Iblis's carefully selected assistants for these Cogitors had served on Hessra. Serena knew very little about the replacements, aside from the fact that she had administered a benediction to them shortly before their departure. She remembered thinking at the time that they all seemed exceedingly pious and well-mannered.

Since then, Iblis had confided to her that these secondaries were given instructions to speak quietly to the Cogitors about the centuries of damage that evil thinking machines had inflicted upon the human race. The new secondaries frequently challenged the morality of Cogitor isolation, trying to make Vidad and his contemplative associates realize that simply remaining neutral was not necessarily virtuous.

In her ship, she headed directly to Hessra, accompanied only by Niriem and four additional Seraphim. Serena's vessel set down on a snow-and-ice platform that the secondaries had swept in preparation for her arrival. Rising out of the gray rock, the Cogitors' stronghold was made up of black metal towers and cylindrical protrusions capped with pointed domes, barely visible in a backwash of frothing snow.

The Cogitors had originally constructed this retreat on an exposed tongue of mountain high above a gaping canyon, but over the course of twenty centuries a ponderous glacier had crawled down from the high crags and was beginning to enfold the towers. The thick ice was greenish-blue from chemical contaminants that had settled out of Hessra's sour atmosphere.

So far, the tide of ice had risen to cover half of the lower foundations and basement levels of the structures, and Serena wondered if the Cogitors would ever abandon this stronghold. She felt an implacable sense of time here. When the glaciers eventually overwhelmed the towers, perhaps Vidad and his complacent fellows would remain within their tomb of ice, still thinking their impossible thoughts, but going nowhere.

Unless Serena could jar them into participation.

Wrapped in insulated parkas, a group of secondaries emerged from the frosty doors in the main tower, led by a man she recognized as Keats. Serena staggered forward, coughing in the thin, unpleasant air and feeling the bite of cold wind. Niriem stepped forward to accompany her, but Serena waved the woman off, saying she preferred to continue alone. She told the Seraphim to remain aboard the ship, that this was a matter she could best handle by herself.

The secondaries ushered Serena into the tunnel. They smelled of chemicals, as if they had been working in a laboratory. One of the yellow-robed secondaries touched a lever, and the heavy tunnel door closed behind them with an echoing thump. As Serena proceeded with her somber escort, cold tendrils of breath rose before her eyes.

The corridors spiraled like a tightening corkscrew, before finally descending to a large chamber with broad open walls and windows covered by solid curtains of glacial ice. Strange designs reminiscent of

Muadru runes had been etched into the ice blocks. Like large game pieces, six Ivory Tower Cogitors rested on burnished pedestals, their brain canisters glowing with the faint blue of life-support electrafluids. Fresh tanks of the fluid, far more than the Cogitors could ever need, were stacked in alcoves. She wondered what they intended to do with so much of the vital liquid.

Steeling herself, Serena called to mind various debating techniques she had learned from Kwyna and Iblis Ginjo. In this encounter she would need all the skills she could muster. She hoped Keats and his ambitious fellow secondaries had been skillful in laying the groundwork for her plea.

"You seek advice?" Vidad inquired.

His voice emanated from a speaker patch implanted in the bottom of his preservation canister, much like a cymek's. The system looked new, and Serena realized it was an innovation that Keats's secondaries had incorporated to allow the caretakers to converse with more than one Cogitor at once. Before this modification, Vidad and the others must have sat through centuries of placid silence tended by meek secondaries; now, with Iblis's people constantly engaging the reclusive geniuses in debates, Vidad's life must have changed greatly.

"I require your help," Serena said, selecting her words and tone of voice carefully, to show civility and respect, as well as strength. "Our Jihad has dragged on for many years at the cost of billions of human lives. Our determination has gradually turned to stagnation. I am willing to do whatever is necessary to achieve a swift and decisive victory."

Vidad did not reply, but one of the other Cogitors said, "According to our current secondaries, your Jihad was launched only a few decades ago."

"And you're wondering why I sound impatient?"

"Just an observation."

"Unlike you, I am limited to a few decades of existence. It is natural for me to seek success in my own lifetime."

"Yes, I can see that. Yet the overall human battle against Omnius has lasted barely more than a millennium, which is not really that long, when one considers the larger picture. The Cogitors in our small group have memories extending back twice as long, you know."

Vidad added, "As a transient human, your perception of time is skewed and limited, Serena Butler, and not relevant to the canvas upon which history is painted."

"Since human beings record their own history, the human lifespan is the only meaningful measure of time," she countered with a slight edge to her tone. "You Cogitors were once human."

Pausing, Serena took a deep, agitated breath, and attempted to remove the stridency from her speech. In a calmer voice, she said, "Think of the human victims of thinking machines. Each person who died had a brain — which means each one of them had the *potential* to become a Cogitor like yourselves. Think of the revelations and insights we might have gained, had those lives not been prematurely snuffed out by Omnius."

The Cogitors remained silent, absorbing her words. Keats and the other secondaries stood unobtrusively near the walls of the room, their eager eyes regarding Serena with obvious admiration.

"We agree it is a tragedy," Vidad finally answered.

Serena's voice rose again. "For thirty-four years, human warriors have fought hard and endured much suffering. An entire generation has been decimated, and my people are beginning to lose hope. They fear that our Jihad is not winnable, that war will continue for centuries without victory. They despair of seeing any imminent resolution."

"A valid concern," one Cogitor said.

"But I don't want it to be! We cannot lose momentum now. It took the murder of my son and an extraordinary rallying effort to make people fight back against the thinking machines, after so many centuries of apathy and lack of initiative."

"This is a human problem, and of no concern to the Cogitors."

"With all due respect, Cogitor — in times of crisis cowards often justify inaction with such comments. Review your own historical memories." The Jipol secondaries grinned, looking sidelong at her. Perhaps they had made similar comments to Vidad themselves. "You have great wisdom, and I cannot believe that you have lost all of your humanity. What a terrible, terrible loss that would be."

Revealing a hint of exasperation in his simulated voice, Vidad said, "And what do you expect of us, Serena Butler? We are aware of your passionate convictions, but we are Cogitors, neutral thinkers. Therefore, Omnius leaves us alone. Long ago, some of the Twenty Titans used our expertise, as did some League humans. We maintain a quintessentially fair and balanced position."

"Your position is quintessentially *flawed*," Serena retorted. "You may believe yourselves neutral, but in no way are you independent. Without your human secondaries you would perish. It is only because we humans value your minds that these secondaries donate their time and faithful service — their very lives — so that you may enjoy your 'neutrality' and contemplation. At no time do thinking machines or cymeks assist you. Humans need your help. You have an opportunity that is not available to my jihadi soldiers. Your supposed neutrality gives you access to Omnius and the thinking machines. As Cogitors, you could speak to them, observe them. Even tell us how to overthrow them."

"Cogitors do not act as spies," Vidad said.

Serena lifted her chin. "Perhaps not. Yet you owe your continued existence to humans. I am a short-lived human, Vidad, while you have two thousand years of experience on which to draw. If you do not approve of my suggestion, I ask that you use your superior intellect to find another way to assist us." She crossed her arms over her chest. "I do not believe for a moment that this challenge is beyond your capabilities."

"Serena Butler, you have given us much to ponder," Vidad said. The light glowed brighter inside his preservation canister, and inside those of his companions too, as if all the disembodied brains were thinking furiously. "We shall consider your request and take whatever action we deem appropriate."

Serena waited, hoping he would say more, but the Cogitor held his silence. "Do not ponder overly long, Vidad. Human beings die every day from the cruelties of thinking machines. If you see a way to end this nightmare, you must act as soon as possible."

"We will act when the time is right. We do not surrender our neutrality easily, but you make compelling arguments that echo the statements of our loyal secondaries." Nearby, Keats bowed his head with reverence, in an apparent attempt to hide a smile.

Knowing the meeting was concluded, Serena departed through the frigid, winding corridors. The secondaries could barely contain their exuberance as they escorted her to the ship.

"We knew the Priestess of the Jihad could accomplish what we could not," Keats exclaimed. "The Grand Patriarch is correct to honor you. You are the mother and savior of all humanity."

Serena frowned, uncomfortable to be the object of such blatant admiration. "I am no more than a woman with a mission. That is all I have ever been." Then she murmured, "That is all I ever need to be."

The military commander who fails to seize an opportunity is guilty of a crime no less severe than outright cowardice.

—General Agamemnon, *New Memoirs*

A FTER THE TITANS consolidated the dim, cloudy world of Bela Tegeuse as the cornerstone of their new cymek empire, they spent years reshaping the cities and the population into the format they desired. The trio of remaining Titans, along with Beowulf and several of the highest-ranked neos, used the planet as a base from which they launched forays against Omnius update ships, finding weaknesses in other Synchronized Worlds, preparing for their ultimate expansion. Meanwhile, Bela Tegeuse remained secure and well defended against the evermind and against the *hrethgir*.

The arrival of another cymek ship surprised them. It dropped beneath the clouds and landed near their headquarters, an oval, gray structure with large doors and few windows.

Agamemnon and Juno, wearing stupendous walker forms designed to impress the already cowed populace, marched out to face the intruder, accompanied by a swarm of newly made Tegeusan neos.

The powerful machine walkers converged around the unidentified ship only moments after it set down on the flat, newly paved spaceport field. The vessel's hull cracked open and an unusual, exotic machine form strutted forth. The cymek body glittered with diamond plates, and angular wings spread out like the plumage of a lacy condor. A galaxy of optic threads glittered atop a tall segmented neck.

As soon as Agamemnon observed the preening, extravagant shell that this cymek had fashioned for itself, he knew that Xerxes — for all his foolish flaws — had been correct in his suspicions. He recognized Hecate by the characteristic electrical discharges inside her brain canister.

He raised himself to tower over the flashy dragon form. "By the gods, look what crawled out of the dustbin of history. It has been a millennium since you dared show yourself, Hecate."

Juno added snidely, "If only it could have been a bit longer."

Hecate made a discordant laugh, a rasping noise from her dragon throat. "Old friends, is it the best use of your skill and longevity to nurse a grudge for ten centuries? I've changed, and I promise not to disappoint you."

"You were nothing to start with, Hecate. How could we possibly be disappointed?" Juno sidled closer to her lover. "You stepped off the treadmill of history long ago, and you cannot conceive of how much has changed since the Time of Titans."

"Oh, but I did manage to avoid many ugly and unpleasant events," Hecate said. "And I never had to serve in the thrall of Omnius. Can any of you say the same? Maybe the rest of you should have gone with me."

Some of the Bela Tegeusan people milled around at a relatively safe distance, amazed by this confrontation of godlike machines, unable to understand the mental and historical grappling that was so far beyond their experience.

"We have secured our freedom now," Agamemnon pointed out.

"That was thanks to my assistance. You would not be on Bela Tegeuse if I had not delivered my atomic 'gift' to the computer evermind, and if the human League had not been so slow and inept in responding to this opportunity." She didn't mention the deadly asteroid that she kept hidden away and her other, lesser known interventions over the years. Since her reemergence she had been keeping her hand in the war, secretly helping Iblis Ginjo in many small ways, but there was more to accomplish. To do this, she needed to let the other Titans know some of what she had done. She had a long-range vision, and the proposal she was about to make might change everything and finally resolve the struggle against Omnius.

Agamemnon was gruff. "What is it you want, Hecate? Why have you chosen to come back now? Do you believe we need your help?"

"Or do you simply miss our fascinating company?" Juno inquired with an abrasive snort. "Perhaps you grew lonely after so much time by yourself."

Hecate straightened the posture of her magnificent dragon-walker, moved closer to them. "Maybe I decided it's time for a change." She sounded sweet and reasonable. "We can either stand by and watch the war, or we can step in and make a difference."

Agamemnon growled. "I believe I made that very statement many times over the past thousand years, Hecate, but you wouldn't know that, since you weren't here to listen."

"But now your alliances have shifted. You Titans and neo-cymeks have turned against the thinking machines, as have the humans. Why not form an alliance with the League of Nobles, dear Agamemnon? It could be to your advantage."

"With *hrethgir*? Are you mad?"

"I don't like where this is heading," Juno said.

Hecate made a sound like a chuckle. "For once in your life, think like a real general. You and the humans share a common, entrenched enemy that is too powerful for either of you to defeat individually. But working together, cymeks and *hrethgir* just might obliterate all incarnations of the evermind." Her dragonlike forelimbs twitched. "After that, feel free to destroy each other if it amuses you."

A rude noise came from Juno, while Agamemnon refused the suggestion outright. "We don't need you in our fight, Hecate . . . or the humans. What you're asking would give legitimacy to my insolent son Vorian. Here on Bela Tegeuse I have plenty of loyal neo-cymeks, and the populace continues to volunteer all the candidates we require for new converts. You are out of touch, Hecate. Too much has happened since you left us."

"I'm beginning to realize that," Hecate said, simulating a sigh. "Since I've been gone, the great General Agamemnon has turned into a stubborn bore, and two of the remaining Titans still follow him blindly, without an original thought in their fossilized brains." Swiveling her segmented head, she strode back toward her ship. "Without Tlaloc, you were never able to see the big picture."

The cymek general amplified his voice to shout after her, "I have begun an empire of my own here that has no need of humans, except for the raw materials they contribute to new cymeks! I shall restore the Time of Titans. League humans have their own agenda — they would turn against me the moment Omnius was destroyed."

"But only because you deserve it." Hecate climbed back on board her carrier transport for the return to her artificial asteroid, which hovered in orbit high above Bela Tegeuse. Defiantly, she shouted, "I see I will have to fight in my own manner, regardless of whether my fellow Titans accept me. You fail to see the potential, Agamemnon, but I will not be swayed from my mission."

She sealed her transport, and lifted off from the scarred surface of Bela Tegeuse.

Now Hecate would do something without them, to make everyone take notice.

165 B.G.

JIHAD YEAR 37

One year after Serena's Hessra Expedition

In wartime we are often asked to give more than we possess.
                                    —Serena Butler, *Zimia Rallies*

I N THE THIRTY-SEVENTH year of Serena Butler's Jihad, Aurelius Venport spent three weeks journeying from Kolhar to Salusa Secundus in a conventional spaceship. Though he owned and managed a merchant fleet of more than a hundred space-folding cargo vessels, the technology was still prohibitively risky. He preferred the safer, proven methods of space travel and had no particular desire to fly in one of the superfast ships himself.

He flew first to Rossak and from there caught a commercial passenger vessel departing for Salusa Secundus from one of the orbiting space hubs. The pace of both passages seemed plodding and tormentingly slow.

As he stepped out of the passenger liner into the heat of the Salusan summer, Venport felt the usual disorientation of adjusting to a new world. He conducted business across the League and on a handful of Unallied Planets. Sometimes it was spring at the place he needed to visit on one world, winter at another, and summer at yet another.

Zimia was surprisingly hot, and the surrounding hills were parched a golden brown. During his wait for a VenKee groundcar to take him to his company's regional headquarters, perspiration formed on his brow. He had not expected his hired driver to be late.

He was surprised when a long black state vehicle glided up to him and stopped. The rear door slid open. Serena Butler sat inside, her expression neutral. "Come with me, Directeur Venport. We have delayed your own car, so that you and I might have the opportunity to talk."

A shiver of foreboding ran down his spine. "Of course, Priestess." He had never spoken directly with this eminent woman before, but decided instantly that this must take priority over all other obligations. "To what do I owe this honor?"

"A matter of vital interest to the Jihad." She smiled, gesturing for him to take the seat across from her. "And possible treason."

He hesitated, then climbed inside, wiping his brow. "Treason?" The door slid shut, and he felt a soothing rush of cool air. He began to feel even more surprised and uneasy. "I'll need to postpone another business meeting with a pharmaceutical competitor. May I have the liberty of contacting my associate?"

Serena shook her head and fixed him with a hard look, her lavender eyes full of questions. "We have already cancelled that meeting — and you should thank us. According to Yorek Thurr, your competitor intended to blackmail you in order to obtain financial concessions. He never had any interest in selling his drug operations."

"Blackmail?" Venport shrugged dismissively, knowing he had not left himself open to such vulnerabilities. "Your spies must be mistaken."

"They are not." She leaned toward him as the vehicle glided forward. "We are aware of the activities of VenKee Enterprises on Kolhar. We know you have built a fleet of new ships — vessels which, according to reliable reports, use a remarkably fast method of space travel, far swifter than anything available even to the Army of the Jihad. Is this true?"

"Yes. . ." Venport tried not to show alarm. He wondered exactly how much Serena Butler knew about the space-folding engines and the shipyards. Remembering how many people had been accused of ties to the thinking machines during the great purges over the past few decades, he knew it would be unwise to earn the distrust of either Serena Butler or the Jipol. "I am a businessman, Madame. I make investments, develop proprietary technologies. It is necessary to protect such information —"

Serena's face was cold, and he detected hints of how deep her anger ran. His words stumbled to a halt.

"We are at war with the greatest enemy the human race has ever faced, Directeur! If you have developed a militarily viable technology, how can you withhold it from our brave fighters? The Jihad Council takes the position that hiding any potentially vital breakthrough — such as these vessels seem to be — constitutes treason."

As the private groundcar continued to move along, Venport tried to understand what was going on. "Treason? That's ridiculous. No one is more loyal to the cause of humanity than I am. I have already donated vast sums —"

Serena arched her eyebrows. "Yet you have kept a promising technology to yourself. Not a very convincing demonstration of your loyalty."

He calmed himself in a way that Norma had taught him, taking deep breaths and trying to visualize his way through the situation. "Priestess Butler, you are jumping to some rather unfair conclusions. It is true I have built an extensive shipyard complex on Kolhar. We have produced some ships and are experimenting with a new spaceflight system that allows VenKee vessels to . . . travel without the use of traditional propulsion." He spread his hands. "I am ignorant of the nuances. My wife, Norma Cenva, developed the principle based on modifications to Holtzman's equations."

"At my direction, Iblis Ginjo has examined VenKee records and traced your expenditures. It seems you have been building these shipyards and your vessels for nearly a decade now. By now you should have had ample opportunity to inform the Jihad Council about your work. Did you not realize how critical this technology might be to our war efforts?"

Venport began to feel warm. Serena shook her head, as if she could not understand him. "Directeur, can't you see? Those ships would be a vital asset to the Army of the Jihad! With them we could strike a decisive blow against the Synchronized Worlds. We finally stand a chance of achieving victory before our people simply give up. The protesters have been demanding peace for years."

Venport frowned. "But the technology isn't ready for widespread use yet, Priestess. Travel on these new ships is still extremely dangerous. The navigation systems are not reliable. Yes, the ships have an entirely innovative method of propulsion, but our loss rate is incredibly high. We have experienced a number of disasters due to inaccurate navigation. Incorrectly guided space-folding ships can strike suns, populated planets, moons — anything that gets in the way. Many of our test pilots refuse to board the vessels again after only one or two flights." He went on to provide crash and damage statistics. "I choose not to ride in them myself."

"I am told that in spite of the dangers you began to use the new ships commercially more than a year ago. Is this true?"

"Only provisionally, and we have lost a great many of them —"

She cut him off. "If you can find captains willing to take the risk, Directeur Venport, do you have any doubt that I can find jihadi volunteers to fly our military missions? Is your loss rate any greater than the percentage of casualties we suffer in a Synchronized World offensive?"

Hearing her, he began to feel shame that he had not considered this earlier. His attention had been focused more on profits than on winning the war.

"Such vessels would give us a tremendous element of surprise against the enemy," she continued with greater fervor. "They would enable us to deliver war messages and intelligence reports, to transport troops and provide materiel faster than ever before, thus gaining important tactical and strategic advantages over the thinking machines. Are those gains not more than enough to compensate for the cost in personnel, should we lose a few ships?"

"It is . . . more than a few ships, Priestess."

Serena looked out the window of the vehicle at the tall buildings of Zimia. "We have been embroiled in outright war with Omnius for decades, Directeur, and many of our people have lost their resolve. Last year, I traveled to the isolated home of the Ivory Tower Cogitors, hoping they would assist us in our efforts against the thinking machines, but thus far we have heard no response. I fear they intend to let me down." She turned to look at him, her eyes like lasers. "I trust you will not do the same, Directeur Venport."

He knew she would not be swayed. "Perhaps, Priestess, we could negotiate an exclusive confidentiality agreement, allowing our military access to the new Holtzman engine design, so long as it doesn't fall into the hands of any other merchant or —"

"Our engineers would like to study the design, of course, but it would take our army too much time to construct an entire fleet." She smiled calmly at him. "How many vessels do you currently have, and when can we start refitting them as Jihad battleships?"

Venport drew deep breaths, wondering if his business empire was about to crumble. "Our merchant vessels, Priestess Butler are merely cargo ships, not combat craft."

She waved a hand casually, continued to smile. The Jihad had been her life for so long that she recognized nothing else as being more important — for herself, or for anyone else. "I'm sure our engineers can make appropriate modifications. Your facilities and shipyards are already in place on Kolhar — far from the main spaceways, easy to secure. A good choice, strategically."

He fought to control his helplessness. "Priestess, please understand that in order to finance the shipyards and the whole operation, I was forced to mortgage virtually all of VenKee's holdings. This is the most expensive undertaking in the history of my company. We barely manage to pay our creditors, as it is. Your proposal would completely ruin us."

Serena was clearly disappointed by his inability to see the larger picture. "Aurelius Venport, we have all made extreme sacrifices for the Jihad . . . some of us more than others. *Every* human being will be ruined if we lose this war." She sighed. "If you wish to propose a system under which we can begin making use of your fleet immediately, we might find some means to compensate you down the road and reduce the impact of your accumulated debt — but that isn't important right now, is it?"

To him, it was extremely important, but the Priestess continued to sweep along with her ideas. Venport did not see any way to stop her politely. If she chose to use it, Serena had the power to raise her hands and summon soldiers to take over the shipyards. Or, if the rumors were true, she could have her Jipol simply take care of him quietly.

In the past, whenever he had been backed into a corner in business negotiations, Venport had found that the best response was to sound reasonable but make no binding decisions and let the problem cool for a while. "I need some time to discuss this with my associates and put together a proposal. There are many considerations. I have numerous investors and financial responsibilities to —"

Serena's gaze was icy. The vehicle stopped and the door slid open with a blast of hot, humid air. "We have the ability to change laws, if need be, to give you full power to make the correct decision, Directeur Venport."

"Even so . . . please allow me to return to Kolhar and consider a solution to this matter that will satisfy everyone involved."

"Then by all means do so, Directeur. But I will have no patience for any negotiation whose only goal is to preserve your profit margins. Do not keep me waiting."

"I understand. I will make it my highest priority."

"I'll inform the Jihad Council, then, that we will soon have the new technology at our disposal."

Serena's white-robed Seraph driver, her face unreadable, looked straight ahead, as if sculpted of stone. The Priestess of the Jihad signaled for the woman to turn the vehicle around and head back to Zimia Spaceport. Venport had not even been on Salusa Secundus for an hour.

"In the meantime," Serena said, "I will send a delegation of officers and military advisors to look over the shipyards."

Human societies thrive on warfare. Take that element away, and civilizations stagnate.

—Erasmus Dialogues

WET FROM SUMMER rain outside, Vorian Atreides marched down the central aisle of the Hall of Parliament, and saw Xavier already standing with Serena Butler near the speaking pit, in close conversation with her. Aside from these three, the vast chamber was empty. Vor grinned as he approached. These two were his closest friends and around his age, though he looked much younger than they did.

Truly, are we nearly sixty years old?

Catching sight of Vor, Serena beckoned him over. It was good to see her by herself, when she was not surrounded — stifled — by all those clinging female guards.

Vor drew a deep breath, still remembering the fresh, warm rain. The immense hall echoed, and his dripping shoes squeaked on the floor. It seemed like an odd place for the trio to meet.

As usual, Xavier looked concerned, though his military discipline learned in decades of service helped him keep his emotions under control. Such a serious, serious man. As Vor shook his friend's hand firmly and clapped him on the back, Xavier flashed a disturbed glance at the most famous woman in the Known Universe.

She stepped back into the geodesic speaking chamber and activated the apparatus. Moments later her image was projected on the exterior walls of the enclosure, an image of the beloved Priestess gazing down on them beatifically like a goddess.

Xavier took a seat at front row, center, and Vor slipped in beside him, casually tossing his wet cape over another chair. "What's the matter? What is she doing?"

With a sigh, Xavier merely shook his head. "Another idea." Sitting straight-backed, he looked up at Serena's image. Vor pursed his lips, nodding appreciatively, thinking of all she had accomplished. She carried herself like a queen, an elegant woman with a touch of the hauteur so common among noble ladies. At the lectern her image seemed to look directly at the two Armada officers as if it were a large version of her, alive itself.

"Welcome, gentlemen," she said through the speaker system. Her words echoed around the cavernous hall. "This makes me I feel like I'm nineteen again addressing Parliament. It's hard to believe so much time has elapsed, that so much has happened."

"You're still beautiful." Vor raised his voice so that it would carry to her.

Xavier, despite his unexplained disapproval, seemed to be thinking the same thing, though he was not a man to speak such thoughts casually. Long ago, Serena had turned from the affections of both men, and all of them had moved on, in different directions. The Jihad had gotten in their way. Vor frowned wistfully, thinking about Leronica Tergiet on Caladan and knowing that he should send her another letter, though by now she might have forgotten about him. Perhaps if he sent her an extravagant package, next time . . . He was sure he could have enjoyed a good life with her, but he had lost that woman for the same reason: the Jihad.

Now the three of them were together again, each so different from before, but still unchanged, in their core beings. When Vor looked at Serena, he still saw her the way she had been when they'd met at the villa of Erasmus. She had been so defiant at the time and disrespectful to him despite his position as a trustee. He chuckled at the recollection of a mere house slave speaking to him in that manner! Even back then he had admired the strength in Serena Butler . . . and she had needed all of it in order to survive the terrible events that were to befall her in that place.

"I have summoned you here to discuss a most important development," she said. But as she peered over the lectern at the two men, Vor detected a hardness to her, a stubborn rigidity to her chin.

"Here it comes," he muttered to Xavier.

Abruptly, Serena shut down the apparatus and walked down a set of stairs toward the men. "They have installed a new speaker system. I wanted to come here and try it before tomorrow's session. Iblis has been helping me with voice control for maximum effect on an audience. How was my intonation?"

Vor gave her teasing applause, but saw peripherally that his fellow officer remained upset. "Good enough for your announcement," Xavier said.

"I really do have something important to ask both of you," she said. "VenKee Enterprises has developed a fleet of spaceships that can travel across space in an instant." She snapped her fingers. "Imagine! In one breath a ship is over Salusa Secundus and in the next is disgorging a Jihad attack force at Corrin. We can hit Omnius hard, pack up, and hit him immediately afterward in another star system. Think of it: the Jihad could be over in a matter of weeks!"

Vor sucked in a quick breath as the import of the announcement sank in. He whistled in appreciation. "Why were we never told about this?"

"Aurelius Venport has kept the technology a closely held secret, supposedly until he could finish refining the navigation systems. However, commercial records indicate he has been using his new ships to make merchant runs for more than a year." Serena sat on a step in front of the two men. "We need to figure out how to place these vessels into the service of the Army of the Jihad."

"Cargo haulers are different from battleships. I'm always leery of new technology until it's been battle tested," Xavier said.

Vor was optimistic. "So we test it, my good friend."

Serena nodded, her expression somber. "Directeur Venport has warned me of a rather significant percentage of catastrophic failures, but I'm sure we can improve on that. Most of the flights are successful. If we have the fortitude to endure the necessary casualties, it will be enough to defeat the machines, once and for all. Our victory at Ix ultimately cost a great deal, but look at how much we have benefited from that industrial complex. With the new spaceships the risks will not be as great as those we took to win Ix."

Scratching his head, Xavier reconsidered. "We always lose a percentage of the forces we commit. In the long run, the new ships' speed and efficiency may reduce casualties . . . by putting an end to the war more quickly."

"In the short term, there are likely to be more losses, causing the families of the dead soldiers to question our decision." Vor ran fingers through his damp hair. "Still, I think you're right, Serena. It's a tough decision, but it sounds like the best one."

Xavier cautioned, "Calculated projections don't always reflect the realities of battle situations."

"You have never been so concerned about risk-taking," Vor pointed out.

"There are risks, and then again there are *risks*. I made decisions that cost a lot of lives when our backs were to the wall, with few options available. This seems different to me." He sighed. "I want to see these space-folding vessels with my own eyes."

"When do we inspect these super ships?" Vor asked, rising to his feet.

Crossing her arms over her chest, she said, "I want both of you to go to Kolhar immediately with a large contingent of Jihad engineers. Under my orders, you will assume command of Venport's shipyards and work to convert all of his space-folding ships into military vessels. He has over a hundred of them available. Take two divisions with you, enough to implement and enforce the new priorities, and to protect Kolhar from any potential machine attacks."

"And you're sure Venport will cooperate?" Xavier remained skeptical.

Serena looked determined. "We ca no longer afford to offer him the choice. This is for the benefit of the Jihad. Would he rather do business with Omnius?"

"There are no guarantees in wartime," Xavier said. "Only death and destruction followed by more death and destruction."

Vor knew he looked more like a youthful junior officer than a battle-seasoned Primero. "Now don't get bitter on us, Xavier. You're starting to sound like a grumpy old man."

"Guilty as charged," he said with a tight smile. Together, the men departed from the hall to begin military preparations.

What makes a great hero? Selfless action, you say. Yes, but that is only one dimension, the one seen by most people and chronicled in the history crystals. Circumstances must be right for a hero to operate; he must be swept up in an epic tide of events that enables him to ride the crest of a human wave. The hero, especially the one who survives, is an opportunist. Seeing a need, he fills it and receives a substantial benefit. Even dead heroes receive a benefit.
— Zufa Cenva, *Recollections of the Jihad*

INSIDE A SPACEPORT tower on the plains of Kolhar, Aurelius Venport paced back and forth, watching the controllers at their instruments, and scanning the banks of displays himself, looking for any sign of the incoming vessel. One of the swift space-folding cargo ships was due to return momentarily. Each time the mercenary pilots used their Holtzman engines, there was a significant chance that the craft would be lost.

Outside, the sky gleamed like a pale blue, translucent light, yet storm clouds loomed inside his mind. Briefly, on the return journey from Salusa Secundus, he had considered shutting down and uprooting his Kolhar operations and moving them wholesale to some unknown, uninhabited planet.

But a nagging internal voice warned him that Serena Butler would get her way in the end no matter what he did, that she would catch up with him and ruin him if he opposed her. His life, his livelihood, his success . . . everything he had worked for would be gone, if she simply commandeered his facility. He would probably also face treason charges, in spite of his logical answer when the Priestess of the Jihad asked him why he had not revealed the existence of his space-folding technology sooner. Venport sighed. While he could accept the concept of making reasonable contributions to the war effort, the Priestess blithely assumed that each person should sacrifice everything for her cause. He had to reach some sort of compromise with her. This would be his most difficult negotiation yet.

He also knew that Serena would waste no time. Her armed force would arrive on Kolhar. *Soon.*

Searching for an appropriate solution, he brought the problem to both Norma and Zufa Cenva the moment he returned to cold, bleak Kolhar. After hearing him out, the Supreme Sorceress had not been as sympathetic as he'd hoped. "Aurelius, you never did have the selflessness to help us win the Jihad. If each person were willing to offer his life, his full capabilities, we would have crushed Omnius long ago."

"Is your entire universe black and white?" he asked her with a sigh. "I thought that was a Buddislamic view."

Zufa's expression remained brittle. "Sarcasm duly noted. But is the Jihad not more important than a merchant's profits? Your ships can turn the tide of war, saving billions of lives by cutting off the conflict like a malignant tumor. You will be seen as a great hero for your generous contribution, a beloved patriot."

"A penniless one, though."

Placing a slender, warm hand on his bare arm, Norma said, "Aurelius, from the very start, I always envisioned my space-folding engines used against Omnius. When I started working for Savant Holtzman, my mission was to help develop weapons of war." Her face radiated beauty and excitement, her eyes were intense, and he felt his defensive turmoil begin to melt. "If the Army of the Jihad can use our engines to lift them to victory, how can we possibly refuse?"

Zufa gave him a mocking smile. "And what about *your* universe, Aurelius? Is it black and white, too? Do you see any other solution?"

He looked at her with a measure of surprise. He had spent — no, *wasted* — years loving this woman. Although she had scorned him, he knew she would sacrifice her very life for the common good, and he could not argue with her.

Norma consoled him. "Eventually we will benefit financially — but first the war must be won." Her smile made all of his doubts vanish.

With a deep sigh of resignation, Venport said, "At least Adrien's grandchildren could benefit from this."

Since discovery of his operations by the Jihad Council, Venport had continued to operate his business at a heightened level, sending space-folding cargo vessels to League Worlds and Unallied Planets around the clock, focusing on the most profitable routes and products. He moved as much melange and pharmaceuticals as he could, set up partnerships to stockpile nonperishable goods, and sheltered his income so that VenKee Enterprises could survive the impending loss of the shipyards.

He had to pay his mercenary pilots more and more as the risks accumulated, and those willing to fly the spacefolders were the most desperate of men. But in the ancient days of commerce back on Earth, captains of sailing ships had also risked treacherous ocean passages; many were lost at sea, sunk on reefs, destroyed by storms. Was this any different?

Now his own footsteps rang in his ears as he paced back and forth inside the spaceport tower and waited for the next vessel scheduled to return to Kolhar.

"Picking up an inbound from the outer edges of the system," reported Yuell Onder, one of the controllers. In a common brown uniform with a matching square-billed cap, she tapped the scanner screen. "Something weird, though. Too many points . . . more than one ship."

Damn, Venport thought. *A spacefolder coming back in pieces.*

"Prepare to shoot down any fragments that penetrate our atmosphere," one of the other controllers said.

"Wait, these are on a planned course," Onder said. "Standard-engine spaceships." Her screen was embroidered with trajectories, red slashes denoting unanticipated flight paths. She let out a whistle. "Looks like a whole damned fleet coming in. They should reach orbit in a couple of hours."

"Thinking machines?" a younger technician asked, turning pale with panic. "A battle group to take over Kolhar?"

"Take a look here," Onder said, tapping a close-up panel. "Those are the unmistakable profiles of Jihad ballistas."

Venport nodded. "Serena Butler sent them."

Flanked by a pair of guardian Sorceresses stationed here from Rossak, Venport waited for Jihad representatives to disembark from the battle-ship onto the tarmac. He tried to swallow his anxiety, but it hung on, like a bad taste in his mouth. Only one of the giant ballistas had landed in the Kolhar industrial spaceport adjacent to his shipyards, while the rest of the flotilla remained in orbit, like guards taking the high ground.

Ballistas were the largest, most awe-inspiring warships in the League Armada. But as Venport looked at the massive curves and blunt lines of the one in front of him, with its heavy engines and cumbersome fuel tanks designed for long journeys, he thought the vessel looked bulky and old-fashioned. After his work on the exponentially faster spacefolders, Venport could envision how the designs of the big military ships would change when Norma's technology became commonplace . . . preferably developed and distributed by VenKee Enterprises.

Not just military ships, but every facet of long-distance transportation.

A personal transport chamber slid down the side of the ballista's outer hull, disengaging from the ship's core. Its hatch unfolded to reveal two uniformed League Primeros, their chests and shoulders laden with ornate braids, medals, and ribbons.

The officers studied the partially completed cargo haulers in the Kolhar industrial yards. An army of engineers and workers bustled about on their appointed tasks, some of them operating construction cranes and lifting pallets powered by Norma's suspensor technology.

Finally, the Primeros walked toward Venport. One man seemed almost twice the age of the other. As they drew closer, Venport recognized them as heroes of the Jihad, Xavier Harkonnen and Vorian Atreides. Their presence proved the very serious intent of Serena Butler.

Primero Atreides gestured with admiration at the humming shipyards. "I'm glad we made the journey. Just look at these facilities, Xavier — the ships, the drydocks, the equipment. A fine, strategic base of operations." He nodded personally at Venport. "Directeur, we understand you've developed an amazing technology for military applications? We're eager to see it in action, and begin modifying and incorporating VenKee ships into the Army."

Xavier Harkonnen cleared his throat and added stiffly, "On instructions from Priestess Serena Butler, we have come to Kolhar to express our gratitude for your donation to our cause. Winning the struggle against Omnius is, of course, the primary goal of every loyal human."

Venport's thoughts spun as he struggled to make the best of a bad situation. *Donation.* He didn't like the word but forced a smile. "Of course you may inspect my ships. As a service to the Jihad, I'm certain we can license VenKee's proprietary technology to the military . . ."

He watched heavily armed crimson-and-green troops pour out of the landed ballista and spread in formation across Kolhar Spaceport. Several smaller vessels landed nearby, a pair of javelins and at least twenty kindjal fighters. Terceros shouted orders, and jihadi soldiers ran to assigned positions, taking control of the facility. Venport drew in deep breaths, knowing he could not object.

Like bookends, the two Primeros flanked him, looking around in all directions, taking a mental tally of his resources, the merchant ships on the landing field, the gigantic hangars and shipyards in which VenKee Enterprises had invested vast amounts of money.

Vorian Atreides took him by the arm. "Thank you, Directeur. This is fascinating. Show us your facilities so that we can see how best to adapt them to the war effort."

Primero Harkonnen narrowed his eyes. "Naturally, we have full legal authority from the Jihad Council to commandeer any of your ships that we feel can be converted into war vessels. I understand you have approximately a hundred available?"

Venport felt the ground turn unsteadily beneath his feet. "That is an accurate assessment."

He steeled himself. All his life he had been a man of commerce, a negotiator, a businessman. He could work out suitable terms with the League. Even if the Army of the Jihad assumed they could take everything, Venport would find some way to extract important concessions from them. That way, everyone would benefit.

Still, he did not feel at all excited as he escorted the officers to his administrative chambers inside the terminal building. "This way, gentlemen. I will show you what my genius wife has accomplished."

The Primeros were suitably impressed. Inside the offices, Norma took her time discussing the capabilities of the Holtzman engines, while her mother stood beside her. Venport studied the records of ships under construction and those scheduled to return from merchant runs, and he arranged for demonstrations.

Vorian Atreides seemed the most excited. "We planned to modify the cargo ships. But is it possible the technology could be adapted to our ballistas, and to the medium-sized javelins?"

"I believe so," Norma said.

"On the other hand, the factories and workers already exist here to refit most of the merchant ships," Primero Harkonnen said. "I see no reason why the existing VenKee fleet can't be converted into war vessels, with enhanced armor and weaponry. We can install decks and cabins to change the cargo compartments into crew quarters, and integrate full Holtzman shields for defense."

"A massive, expensive project," Venport cautioned, weak with the prospect of losing everything.

"Simpler and faster than building additional battleships from scratch," Primero Harkonnen said.

Venport could not argue. His heart felt heavy.

"I do, however see some advantage to creating space-folding javelins," Harkonnen added.

The Jihad officers discussed the possibilities, enthusiastically making grand plans and outrageous suggestions for how the space-folding warships and smaller scout vessels could be put into military service.

Venport cleared his throat. "Gentlemen, I acknowledge the immense possibilities and advantages of our space-folding engines, but we have not yet agreed upon the terms of our arrangement." He smiled stiffly at both Zufa and Norma. "We all want to do our part, but this technology and the ships represent a huge investment. Just look at the extent of my facilities. The setup costs practically bankrupted my company." He spread his hands reasonably. "VenKee Enterprises must be compensated in some way."

Primero Atreides chortled at his audacity, but his older companion frowned, as if he found the subject distasteful. "We are at war, Directeur. Such negotiations are . . . not within my purview."

"What sort of compensation did you have in mind?" Atreides asked.

With a deep sigh, Venport looked at them both. Primero Harkonnen was known to be a stoic soldier, accustomed to giving orders and getting his way. Apparently, though, he had no business or negotiating sense whatsoever . . . and on a matter of such vital importance, Venport did not want to deal with an amateur. As for Primero Atreides, he seemed somewhat cavalier, which could also present problems. The Jihad Council might not go along with anything he negotiated.

"Perhaps I should go to Salusa Secundus with all due haste to work out a suitable agreement?" Venport suggested, in his most pleasant negotiating voice. "I am certain Grand Patriarch Ginjo or even Priestess Butler will be prepared to make those decisions."

Smiling, Primero Atreides jumped at the suggestion. "Take one of your spacefolders. I'll stay behind and map out the general work myself, so we can begin retrofitting the rest of your merchant fleet right away, adapting your industrial facilities to the manufacture of war vessels. Using all available resources, we should be able to launch the first converted military ships within a few months."

"I don't ride in the ships myself," Venport said. "There are still risks involved in foldspace travel, and a great deal depends upon my personal survival. Of course, I pay mercenary crews handsomely for the risks they take."

"Take one of our javelins then," Atreides offered. "That will leave us an additional merchant ship to work on here." He turned to his companion. "Xavier, could you accompany Directeur Venport back to Zimia?"

"Maybe *I* should send *you*, Vorian," he responded. "Don't forget, I do outrank you by a notch or two."

"I just thought you might like to provide a military report to the council, and visit your home and family."

The formal expression on Primero Harkonnen's face softened. "You know me well, my friend. Octa and the girls change so much every time I see them. And Emil Tantor *is* getting on in years, so it would be nice to spend time with him." He nodded, as the idea sank in. "All right, I would be happy to serve in that capacity — so long as it causes no further delays."

Zufa Cenva interjected, "I am prepared to accompany Aurelius as well. My daughter Norma will stay here to work with the Army of the Jihad."

Sometimes a lover's gift is even sweeter when he cannot be there to offer it in person.

—Leronica Tergiet

A CROSS COUNTLESS STAR systems, thinking machines and humans killed each other in massive numbers. Somewhere out there, Vorian Atreides fought his own battles, while Leronica Vazz lived her separate life on Caladan.

She raised her twin boys with love and attention, but did not spoil them. By the time Estes and Kagin reached the age of eight, she had already taught them to speak and write grammatical Galach at a level far beyond their years. She showed them images of other planets in the League and pointed out prominent stars in the heavens, tracing constellations in the shapes of animals and mythological beasts.

On cloudy evenings during the storm season, she taught her sons the history of the Old Empire and the domination of thinking machines, as well as the saga of the ongoing Jihad led by Serena Butler. While her husband Kalem sat by the fire carving intricate handmade toys for the twins, he listened intently to Leronica's lessons himself.

She never spoke of Vorian Atreides. Despite his occasional letters to her, Leronica viewed her affair with him as little more than a youthful adventure from years ago. Now, the Primero had become almost as much of a legend in her mind as some of the stories she told the boys.

During the warm season, Kalem spent time with Estes and Kagin on the boat, showing them on-board systems so that they could someday become capable fishermen themselves. With the exuberant wonder of boyhood, Estes and Kagin played in the surf, swam in the gentle harbor, and ran around the coastal town. Sometimes they pretended to be mercenaries fighting combat robots, but more often their games were grounded in the world around them: finding treasures in tidepools, seeing faces and shapes in the scudding white clouds. Caladan was already larger than their youthful imaginations could encompass.

Leronica spent much of her free time studying images in books, dreaming of the planets Vorian had told her about. But she never let her sadness show, and she thought she hid it from Kalem, who never disappointed her as a husband. He had been true to his word, and so was she.

She had grown accustomed to waking in the cool, moist darkness well before dawn. In the tavern's great room she brewed hot drinks and made heavy breakfasts for the bachelor fishermen. Today, as she bustled around setting out platters of spiced eggs and steaming fish-and-potato hash, she felt an emptiness in her stomach. Not because the boys were going away on an outing, but because of the very idea that Estes and Kagin were actually old enough to accompany their father and grand-father on the fishing boats.

She had no reason to fear, and trusted Kalem completely, but still she felt uneasy seeing her bright-eyed twins go off on their first long fishing cruise. They were still only eight years old, after all. From stories her husband brought back, she knew that things could go wrong out there. Dangerous things.

After setting out bowls of tart inland fruit and insulated pots of a strong roasted beverage favored by fishermen, Leronica looked at her scattered customers. "You can take care of yourselves. I need to go see my husband and boys off."

Kalem had already taken the twins down to the docks after breakfast. The shouting boys ran with bursts of energy along the steep streets to the wharves, waking anyone who had not already begun the day's work. Though they had been out on the boats for brief excursions around the bay, this time they would go out for days into the open waters and try to haul in a heavy catch. Like real fishermen.

Leronica could not tell who showed the most pride, the twins or Kalem. Her own father Brom Tergiet had already made several trips to his own boat, bringing baskets of clothes, special dark cakes as treats, and even toys for his grandchildren. Leronica packed extra blankets and medicines, despite the fact that they would only be gone for four days. Her boys were the progeny of Primero Vorian Atreides. They had good genes and a solid upbringing, so she knew they were tough and intelligent.

Down at the docks, water curled and sloshed around the pilings. Fishermen hailed one another as they boarded their boats, prying loose nets that had frozen stiff in the night's frost. Leronica blew on her fingers to keep them warm, while hurrying to a pair of fishing boats that her father and husband worked together.

Kalem climbed up from the engine room, looking pleased. He gave his wife an affectionate smile. "Both boats are ready to go. We were just about to fetch you."

Dawn broke across the ocean with a crimson line that edged, moment by moment, into brighter oranges and yellows. Leronica climbed over the railing onto the deck. "I wouldn't want you to be late setting off. You men have a big trip ahead of you."

Estes and Kagin ran to their mother, not shy about hugging her. When she looked into their faces, she saw a heart-stopping reminder of Vor's handsome features, but they didn't know about him. "You boys listen to everything your father and grandfather tell you. They have important work to do, man's work. Don't make them worry about you. And pay attention to the things they do — learn from them."

Kalem tousled the twins' dark hair, which had grown out curly like their mother's. "I'll show them how it's done." He leaned forward to kiss Leronica.

She gave the twins another squeeze, then pried them away from her side. "Go, you have to get this boat into the water before someone catches all of our fish."

Laughing, the boys ran to the nets. "We're going to catch all the fish in the water!"

"Don't worry." Kalem lowered his voice. "I'll take care of my little men."

"I know you will." In all their years of marriage, she had not gotten pregnant by Kalem, but he never treated Estes and Kagin differently because they'd been fathered by another man. He acted as if Vorian Atreides had never been born, and had never visited Caladan.

Leronica stayed on the dock, waving as the two boats set off toward the brightening horizon, with her father aboard one and Kalem and the boys on the other. Seeing her sons help their father with the sails, winches, and pulleys, she felt good about her marriage, fortunate to have found such a generous, loving man.

Still, she would be lying to herself if she did not admit that she missed Vor terribly.

In more than eight years, her dashing soldier had not returned. She knew that time must pass differently for a man who spent months on each voyage between the stars, assembling Jihad fleets to unseat Omnius. She was disappointed, but in a way she also felt relief. Despite her reassurances to Kalem long ago, she didn't know what she would have done if Vor came back for her now.

Later that day, when the tavern was quiet and most of the men with boats had gone out to sea in pursuit of schools of butterfish, Leronica welcomed a group of jihadis from the observation outpost. This was the third crew of replacement soldiers, still lonely and not quite settled in after having been rotated to this new assignment.

The men ordered preserved meals to take back to their listening station, and finally settled down to their big mugs of kelp beer. Then a young cuarto, the leader of the group, proudly handed a package to Leronica. "Yesterday a ship delivered our system reconnaissance readings . . . along with something for you." He grinned. "Wonder what the delivery charges are on this."

"Not everyone is as stingy as your wife, Raff," another soldier joked.

"Perhaps my cooking is recognized throughout the League of Nobles," Leronica said, turning the package over in her hands. "Why shouldn't I receive gifts of gratitude from soldiers on distant battlefields?"

She held the package with feigned curiosity, pretending she didn't know who might have sent it, but her heart thumped heavily in her chest. Even these jihadis did not know it had come from Primero Atreides.

Bustling into the back room, Leronica lit several candles — the kind Vor liked — and unwrapped the package. She marveled at the thought that it had traveled dozens of light years to reach her here on Caladan.

Inside, she found a shimmering Buzzell soostone, a stunning firegem mined on the recently liberated Ix, and a dozen other small boxes, each one containing an astonishingly brilliant precious stone.

The gifts told her that Vor still thought of her affectionately, and an enclosed note made her heart swell with wonder: "*Since I cannot take you to all of these planets, dearest Leronica, I have decided to send you a piece of each world instead. I have collected them over the years.*

"*Finally, we have developed a new technology that may allow me to travel to you rapidly. How wonderful it would be if I could look into your lovely eyes at this very moment — hopefully that day will come soon. I know you have your own life, but perhaps you think of me fondly on occasion.*"

She did not know what to do with the treasures, and sat with them for hours as the candles burned down. One by one she picked up each amazing gem and cupped it in the palm of her hand, touched that Vor had selected them especially for her. He had held these very gems himself, thinking of her while looking into the marvelous, shimmering facets. Leronica could not imagine the distances he had traveled to acquire so many wonders. It must have taken him years, and in all that time he had not forgotten her . . .

*   *   *

A week later, Brom Tergiet's fishing boat returned alone. It limped into the harbor, its masts blackened, its sails torn and burned, its engines barely functioning. As soon as the boat was sighted, the trouble alarm rang out and fishermen rushed out to assist. They chained their own boats to Brom's and helped tow him to safety into the harbor.

In a panic, Leronica rushed down to the docks, but saw no sign of her husband's vessel, or her sons. Searching in vain, she gazed across the water as thick afternoon rain clouds gathered overhead. When they helped old Brom off the blistered deck and onto the dock, Leronica ran to him. Her heart was in her throat, and tears filled her eyes, especially when she saw how her father's clothes were singed and his hair half burned away, the skin on his face reddened and peeling.

Moments later, she let out a cry of joy when she finally saw her two boys, emerging from the cabin. They looked dirty and battered, but intact.

"Where's Kalem? Where's the other boat?"

"Elecrans," Brom said. It was all he needed to say. That one word filled every fisherman with terror. Leronica had heard of the strange electrical creatures that lived far out on the oceans of Caladan. No fisherman had ever grappled with them and survived. She straightened, not letting despair fill her heart until she had heard the complete story.

"We wandered into a nest of them. Elecrans like living lightning all around us. They came upon us out of nowhere; we couldn't escape." Her father's voice shook, his arms trembled as he relived the terrible incident. "I don't think they meant to attack us, but we startled them . . . and they struck at us. Lightning bolts blasted everything. Power surges wiped out our controls. We had no chance . . . no chance whatsoever."

His breath hitched, his eyes reddened. He seemed to dread what he had to say next, and the twins clung to their mother, shaking and crying. "Kalem grabbed the lads and tossed each one like a hooked fish onto my deck. What was I to do?" Brom looked around at his intense audience, as if they could provide answers for him. "He yelled for me to take care of his boys, to make sure I kept them safe. I could hardly hear his words over the howl of the wind and the crackle of the elecrans. Then he got his engines running and he pushed away from us. His boat separated from mine and he never looked back. The boys called for him, and at the last minute, Kalem turned around. It was like he knew he was saying goodbye forever."

Brom's fingers clenched and unclenched. "I swear to you, Kalem steered a course *directly* into those damned elecrans. I knew I had to get away, or we would fry next. My only thought was to protect the boys. Kalem . . . Kalem plunged his boat smack into the living electricity, and the creatures turned their anger upon him. I finally got my own boat going, but when I looked back his was a fireball. The elecrans were all around it, blasting and striking.

"He gave his life for these lads. And for me." Brom glanced at his daughter and then turned away, refusing to meet her gaze. "Kalem Vazz let us get away. I owe my worthless life to him, but it should have been the other way around! He has a beautiful wife and two strong sons." Brom drew a long, jagged breath. "He should have saved his own sons and left me behind. Why should I be alive and not him?"

The people on the docks muttered among themselves, and Leronica clung to her boys and her father, sharing their misery as all of them tried to find some comfort in one another.

164 B.G.

JIHAD YEAR 38

Ten years after Arrival of Poritrin Refugees on Arrakis

I see visions, and I see reality. How am I to know the difference,
when the whole future of Arrakis is at stake?
                                    —*The Legend of Selim Wormrider*

I N YEARS, THE desert nomads had not made such a successful raid
against the outsiders. After hearing the alarm of a night scout Marha
and Ishmael stood on the cliff with other tribe members watching the
band head home, flowing like oily shadows through the moonlight. She
saw them crest the dunes and ascend hidden paths leading to their black
lava-rock fortress of isolated caves.

Jafar himself had led the raid out on the desert, though he told Marha
he had little stomach for it. Captivated by Selim Wormrider's vision, the
lantern-jawed man seemed determined to follow the bandit leader's
memory, But it was with considerable discomfort; he told her he had
never envisioned himself spearheading a movement.

Safely asleep inside one of the caves, Marha's son El'hiim was nine. A
bright boy, clever and full of ideas, he did not yet seem to conscious of the
responsibility that would rest on the shoulders of the Wormrider's only
child.

Marha felt a knot in her chest as she recalled her love for Selim, both as a
mythical figure and a man. She understood his dreams and the path he had
intended to take to reach them, and it pained her to see how badly her
followers were losing their way without him. Jafar and Marha had done
their best to keep the remaining outlaws together, far from civilization. Yet
not even a decade had passed, and already her husband's sacrifice to Shai-
Hulud was nearly useless. How could he have expected his passionate goal
to remain for the thousands of years he had envisioned?

She knew it was time for a radical change. The people were too safe out
here in the deep desert, growing complacent and soft.

Days ago, Marha called the adults together and insisted that they ride their worms toward Arrakis City. Along that trade route, they must seek out all spice-harvesting activities in the desert — and smash them. A group of fourteen raiders had gone out, those who had spent the most time with Selim when he was alive, men and women who had agitated for further action instead of cowering here on the far side of the desert . . .

The refugee Poritrin slaves had added fresh blood and new thoughts to the band. They had taken mates from among Selim's followers, reinvigorating the band with numerous children. Ishmael had succeeded in bringing his people to safety, out of the clutches of evil slavers. Though a life of bondage on Poritrin had made him old before his time, freedom out in this desert had stripped away the weight of his life. Ten years after the experimental space-folding ship crashed on Arrakis, he seemed younger and much stronger. He was a solid, guiding force, but not a violent man, not a revolutionary who would kill in order to achieve his goals.

Such things were necessary here on Arrakis.

Ishmael had not joined in the raid, choosing instead to remain behind with Marha and her son. He was not a warrior and had never learned to ride the great sandworms, though Marha was certain she could instruct him.

She gave him private lessons about the ways of the desert, and in turn, he taught her some of the Buddislamic Sutras he had memorized as a boy. He tried to explain the philosophical complexities of the Zensunni interpretation and how such ideas had formed the basis for the decisions of his life. Marha debated with him, using a sharp wit and a clever smile, explaining that scripture didn't apply to every situation.

Ishmael scowled. "When Buddallah lays down the Law, he does not change each time the wind blows a different direction."

Marha gave him a hard stare. "Here on Arrakis, that which refuses to adapt, rapidly perishes. Where would Buddallah be then, if we were all just desiccated mummies out in the sands?"

In the end, Marha and Ishmael reached an accord, both feeling satisfied and pleased with the intellectual challenge, for they were finding ways to apply the Buddislamic Sutras, not only to the legend of Selim Wormrider, but to the realities of harsh daily life on Arrakis . . .

The raiders entered the caves, laden with packs of stolen supplies and equipment. Best of all, Marha could see that the number of returning figures was the same as the party that had gone out. No one had been killed or captured.

She grinned. Selim had taught them how to live by the most austere means, yet whenever they captured supplies from their enemies, the outlaws celebrated. Within an hour, the festivities would begin.

"This is a great day," Marha said. "Even Selim could not have asked for more."

Ishmael's eyes sparkled, and he said, "Marha, for a long time the downtrodden slaves of Poritrin dreamt of nothing more than achieving freedom. Now the time has come for us to stop resting and hiding . . . and decide what to do with our lives."

As part of their spoils from the spice excavation crews, Marha's raiders had brought back several packages of fresh, processed melange — the dried essence of Shai-Hulud. She held a package of the potent, rust-colored powder and smiled at Jafar in the yellow light of the main meeting chamber in the cave. "Your team has done well. It is time to celebrate, and to discuss our future."

Ishmael stood beside her. He felt such a bond with these desert people, all of whom struggled every day for their very existence. His Poritrin companions, including his daughter Chamal, had adapted well here; they would fight as fiercely for their simple life on Arrakis as would any of Selim's band.

Catching a movement out of the corner of his eye, Ishmael turned to see the quick, furtive young boy El'hiim as he darted through one of the cave openings. He noted echoes of Marha's features there and tried to extrapolate what Selim himself must have looked like.

Dark-haired El'hiim scrambled down a steep slope, holding onto rocks and swinging to a safer foothold. He was agile and strong, always eager to explore crannies and canyons. The boy had intense dark eyes; though he spoke little, his mind seemed to be full of ideas.

Ishmael had grown quite fond of him. Clearly, Marha was arranging the time so that she and the boy spent many afternoons and evenings with Ishmael. She had not chosen another mate since Selim's death, and her intentions toward him were obvious. Ishmael found that he did not altogether disapprove. The outlaw group was small and the match seemed a wise one, in theory at least.

Though he had not forgotten the wife and younger daughter he had been forced to leave on Poritrin, he could never go back there. It had been almost a decade since the slaves had escaped. There was no way he would ever find Ozza or Falina again.

He watched young El'hiim scamper away, then turned his attention toward a crisp, potent smell wafting to his nostrils. Marha had opened the packages of stolen melange and cupped the powder in her hands.

"Selim Wormrider found the truth in visions that the spice brought to him. Shai-Hulud gives this blessing to us. He leaves it in the desert, so that we may learn his bidding." She looked at both Ishmael and Jafar. "It has been too long since the death of my husband. Each of us needs focus and direction now. This spice was taken from the thieves of the desert, and Shai-Hulud wants us to consume it so that we may understand."

"What if we all see different visions?" Ishmael asked.

Marha looked at him. She was beautiful, strong, and self-assured, with a small half-moon scar on her brow from a knife duel. "We will each see what we need to see, and everything will be right."

As the sun set on the smooth, soft horizon of sand, the temperatures dropped and the blazing colors of dusk rose up in their glory. The followers of Selim Wormrider met in the largest cave chamber and passed the potent processed melange among themselves. Each man and woman consumed far more than they would ever include in their daily diet.

"This is the blood of God, the essence of Shai-Hulud. He has concentrated his dreams for us, so that we may partake of them and see through the eyes of the universe." Marha ate a thick spice wafer, and handed another one to Ishmael.

He had consumed melange many times before — it formed a staple of the desert dwellers' diet — but this was much more than he had ever eaten at once. As he swallowed it, he felt the effect sweep through his bloodstream and erupt into his mind almost immediately.

Windows opened as if he had eyes peering from various spots on his skull. He couldn't tell if he was looking into the future or the past, or simply seeing images of what he wanted or feared. Selim Wormrider had observed the same things, and had incorporated them into his passionate mission.

But Ishmael now experienced horrific images of things he did not want to witness. He saw Poritrin, the familiar river delta and the slave quarters awash in blood and violence, on fire. The screams of victims filled the night air. His heart turned to lead, and he knew that Aliid must have caused all this pain and suffering.

The entire city of Starda, the great capital on the Isana River, lay in ruins before his eyes, with most of its central complex a slumped, glassy crater. The debris of tall buildings spread out in waves, as if the fist of a vengeful god had hammered the metropolis and flattened everything.

But that was only the start. He saw noble survivors and the remnants of

Dragoon regiments gathering weapons, howling for vengeance. They hunted down Buddislamic slaves on every continent, trapping and torturing them. Many were burned alive, sealed inside houses; others were gunned down. The bodies were mutilated.

In a vision he would never forget because it burned like a brand into the contours of his memory, he saw Ozza and Falina cowering together, screaming in terror, begging for mercy. Then five men with long knives fell upon them . . . and the men were not swift with their work, prolonging their enjoyment.

But the melange swept Ishmael further along on a churning white current of images in his mind. Poritrin vanished, replaced by the sere tan dunes of the driest desert. Cracked lakebeds and wrinkled black rocks rose up to offer secure islands, safe from the ravenous worms.

Without words, he sensed the mission of Selim Wormrider and saw a man riding high on the back of a huge sandworm, delivering his message in service to the Old Man of the Desert. Though Selim was long dead, Ishmael saw himself riding beside the bandit leader, crossing a great expanse of desert on a sandworm. The two of them guided Shai-Hulud and led their fellow wormriders to a bright horizon, a future where they could be free and strong — and all of the sandworms were *alive.*

Ishmael caught his breath. His heart was pounding, and he felt buoyed by the dream. He understood what Marha felt, the sense of purpose Selim himself had inspired among his bandit followers.

Then he sensed danger, a black and consuming fear . . . not part of the grandeur of the vision, but a more personal tragedy, a peril — the boy El'hiim.

This was not a vision of the future, not a distant warning. It was happening now. The boy was trapped, caught inside a small opening in the rocks. While the adults gathered here, El'hiim had run off to explore the cliffs and steep slopes, poking into cracks and holes in search of kangaroo mice or lizards that he could bring to the tribe to eat. Ishmael sensed sharp, scuttling legs and skittering danger around the boy, like a thousand assassins' knives.

Ishmael began to run out of the cave chamber. He knew this wasn't part of his vision. His body was being guided along by some other force. He left the gathered people, all of whom swayed with their personal spice visions.

When Marha realized he had left the chamber, she stumbled after him. But Ishmael would not be slowed. Intuitively, he knew where the boy had gone, though he had not seen El'hiim for hours. With impressive agility,

Ishmael climbed over rocks and went down through a small break in the stone.

His eyes drank in the details around him, and simultaneously he saw the terrible vision inside his head: the boy trapped, and the knife-wielding assassins getting closer.

El'hiim was afraid. He had already called twice for help, but no one heard him.

No one except Ishmael's vision.

"Ishmael, what is it? Where are you?" Marha's voice was slurred and distant . . . but heavy with concern. Ishmael could not answer her. The pounding demand dragged him along, and finally he arrived at a shadowy crevice. El'hiim must have gone inside there, wedging his narrow shoulders into the narrow opening, working through to where he hoped he might find some treasure or food or secret hiding place.

Instead, he had found . . . terrible danger.

Ishmael pushed his wider shoulders inside, scraping skin, working his way forward. He reached out, found a lump of fixed rock, and hauled himself deeper. He wondered how he would ever get back out, but he could not pause. El'hiim was trapped.

Ishmael heard a cry — not of fear, but warning. "They're everywhere! Don't let them touch you."

Ishmael reached out until he grasped El'hiim's hand and pulled the boy toward him. He heard the skittering legs again, felt sharp movement swarming near, but he could sense that the boy would be safe if only he pulled him closer. Ishmael maneuvered his body into a wider section of the crevice until he had room to yank the boy free.

And the assassins attacked him instead.

He felt their poison needle stabs like knives, tiny blades that poked and penetrated his clothes, his skin. But Ishmael held on to El'hiim and paid no heed to his own pain. Instead, he sliced open the skin of his back as he hauled himself backward until he pulled El'hiim out into the open air. He stood holding the son of Selim, intact and safe.

Marha raced up, snatched the boy away — and then stared in horror at Ishmael.

His body was covered with black scorpions, poisonous arachnids that had stung him repeatedly, each venomous dose potentially fatal.

Ishmael brushed the creatures away from him as if they were no more than gnats, and the scorpions scuttled away into hiding places inside rock cracks.

"Check the boy," he told Marha. "Make sure he is safe."

El'hiim shook his head in amazement. "I'm all right. They didn't sting me."

Then Ishmael collapsed.

He woke after three days of fever and nightmares. Ishmael drew a deep breath that felt hot in his raw lungs, blinked his eyes, and sat up in the coolness of his cave chamber. Touching his arms, he saw welts on his skin, but they were pink rather than red and seemed to be fading.

Marha stood at the doorway, pushing the cave hanging aside. Astonished, she stared at Ishmael. "Any one of those stings should have killed you, and yet you live. You recovered from all of them."

His lips were cracked, and his mouth was very dry, but still Ishmael managed to smile. "Selim showed me what to do. In the spice vision, he made me save his son. I do not think he would have let me die."

His daughter Chamal came in, her eyes were red and puffy. She had been weeping, even though the Arrakis bandits deeply frowned upon such a waste of water. "Perhaps it was the melange in your bloodstream, the spirit of Shai-Hulud giving you strength."

Ishmael felt dizzy, but forced himself to stay upright. His daughter hurried forward to hand him a cup. The water tasted like nectar.

Finally El'hiim entered the chamber, and stared wide-eyed at Ishmael. "The scorpions stung you, but you saved me. They didn't kill you."

Ishmael patted the boy's shoulder; the act demanded all of his strength. "I would prefer that you did not require me to do that again."

Marha grinned, unable to believe what he had endured. She drew a deep breath. "It seems we are blessed many times over. You, Ishmael, are intent on creating a legend for yourself."

We have waited long enough. It is time.
                    —Cogitor Vidad, *Thoughts from Isolated Objectivity*

E RASMUS HAD NEVER considered himself a political leader, despite his studies on diplomacy and human social interactions, along with a toolbox full of theoretical skills. The ability to navigate political waters had been useful in establishing himself as an independent robot, and in convincing Omnius to let him continue his experiments on human subjects.

The Ivory Tower Cogitors, however, weren't exactly human.

One afternoon he greeted a strange delegation from the frozen planetoid of Hessra, a few secondary attendants blinking under the coppery blaze of Corrin's red-giant sun. They came toting the ancient human brains — philosophers like Erasmus himself — in preservation canisters.

The independent robot received them in the luxurious parlor of his villa, surprised and pleased because he so rarely entertained guests. Due to numerous attacks by the Army of the Jihad, Omnius had suggested that the meeting take place here, rather than at the towering Central Spire, in case the Cogitors attempted to sneak in some insidious, undetected weapon.

Dressed in fine new clothes, his young ward Gilbertus Albans observed and assisted, the perfect attendant. On one wall an Omnius watcheye glowed softly as it eavesdropped on the proceedings, but the evermind didn't seem to know what to do with the unexpected visitors. Six fearsome robotic guards remained out in the hall.

A procession of yellow-robed monks marched in, the first six carrying the ornate translucent cylinders as if they were sacred relics. The secondaries did not seem to recognize their peril at voluntarily coming to visit a Synchronized World. "The Ivory Tower Cogitors wish to consult with Omnius on an important matter," the lead monk said, holding the heavy canister of the foremost Cogitor in his hands. "I am Keats, secondary for Vidad."

The disembodied brain hung suspended in its bluish electrafluid, looking as if its own thoughts held it in telepathic equilibrium. It reminded Erasmus of the rebellious cymeks and the ancient, scheming minds of the Titans. Agamemnon's unwise and unexpected revolt had troubled Omnius a great deal, but ultimately came as little surprise. The cymeks were, after all, human brains with human faults and unreliabilities.

Erasmus spread his flowmetal arms in a welcoming gesture; the sleeves of his carmine-and-gold robe drooped. "I am the evermind's designated liaison. We are most interested in what you have to say."

Vidad's voice came from a speakerpatch, like a cymek's. "After much contemplation, we must make an overture regarding this long-standing conflict between humans and machines. As Cogitors, we offer a balanced perspective and a resolution to the conflict. We can act as intermediaries."

Erasmus formed a smile. "That is a most difficult challenge you have undertaken."

Watcheyes hovered near the ceiling, recording everything. From behind Erasmus, Gilbertus did the same. The Omnius screen on the wall glowed as if vibrant and alive. The evermind spoke, his voice so loud it blared. "This conflict is costly and inefficient. There are many advantages to ending it, but humans are too irrational."

The secondary Keats bowed slightly. "With all due humility, the Cogitor Vidad believes he may be able to develop a suitable resolution. We are a neutral delegation. We believe there may be points of negotiation."

"And you come unannounced, without personal security?" Erasmus asked.

"What good would it do for us to bring personal security to the most powerful of Omnius's planets?" Vidad inquired, rhetorically. Keats looked around the room and met the gaze of Gilbertus Albans, who showed no reaction; the yellow-robed secondary seemed uneasy.

Remembering his duties as host, according to the old records he had absorbed, Erasmus sent for refreshments. When the secondaries looked hungrily but suspiciously at the cold juices and exotic fruits, Gilbertus sat down and calmly sampled each one.

Erasmus walked among the preservation canisters the humans had placed on sturdy tables in the parlor. "I thought the Ivory Tower Cogitors had isolated themselves from all distractions of civilization and society — including its conflicts," the robot said. "Why have you undertaken this noble cause *now*? Why not decades, or even a century ago?"

"Vidad believes the time for peace is at hand," Keats said, reaching for a second glass of sapphire-blue juice.

"Serena Butler declared a holy war against all machines thirty-six standard years ago," Erasmus said, and his flowmetal face formed a faint smile at the memory of the fascinating woman. "The humans do not seek resolution — they seek our annihilation. In ancient databases, I read a parable of a man trying to do a good deed by breaking up a fight among neighbors, and getting killed for his efforts. This could be dangerous for you."

"Everything is dangerous, but the noble Cogitors gave up the burden of fear long ago, when they gave up their bodies."

Omnius boomed at the visitors, "Your answer is insufficient. After so much time, why do you come to me now?"

The yellow-robed secondaries looked at each other, but waited for the Cogitor Vidad to speak through his voice synthesizer. "On one front the Titans have an army of neo-cymeks to oppose you, and they have already destroyed many of your update ships. On another, the free humans continue to launch powerful assaults against you. You have already lost several Synchronized Worlds. Logically, Omnius, it is in your interest to reach a settlement with the humans, so that you can focus on the cymek challenge. The tide is turning against you."

"My ultimate victory is assured. It is only a matter of time, and effort."

"For efficiency's sake, is it not advisable to minimize your expenditure of time, effort, and resources? As Cogitors, we can act as impartial mediators to obtain a rational, equitable resolution to this conflict. We believe a beneficial settlement can be arranged."

"Beneficial to whom?" Erasmus asked.

"To the Synchronized Worlds and to the League Worlds."

"You cannot convince the humans to align themselves with us against the cymeks." Omnius asked. "Agamemnon intends to conquer us both."

"It is not our purpose to broker war, only peace."

"I am quite familiar with Serena Butler," Erasmus said. "She is unrealistically concerned about our human slaves, even though League Worlds keep their own slaves. Such hypocrisy!"

The secondaries nodded, looking at each other, and Vidad said, "Many slaves are being killed by violence on both sides of the Jihad. We do not have an accurate tally of the innocent human casualties on Ix, IV Anbus, and Bela Tegeuse, but we assume it is a large number."

"On an orderly Synchronized World, where society is not a clumsy, inefficient affair, there are few slave fatalities," Omnius pointed out. "I can verify this with comprehensive statistics."

Erasmus said, "Thus we could make the argument that more human lives would be saved if a cease-fire settlement is reached. We need to show the humans that the cost of their Jihad is too high for them. Serena Butler will understand that."

"The simplest solution is an immediate cessation of all hostilities between you and the League of Nobles," Vidad said to Omnius. "You keep your Synchronized Worlds, and the free humans keep their League Worlds. In exchange, the mutual aggression ends. There will be no further deaths, no further violence between machine and man."

"For how long?"

"In perpetuity."

"I accept your suggestion," Omnius said from the wallscreen. "But you must send a League representative to formally accept the terms. Do not return if the League refuses."

Valor is defined by valiant deeds, regardless of what motives lie in a person's heart.
                    —The Titan Xerxes, *A Millennium of Fulfillment*

S ITTING BENEATH THE dome of the Jihad Council chambers, Aurelius Venport sipped an iced drink, careful to maintain his falsely confident expression, without Zufa. Facing him were Grand Patriarch Iblis Ginjo and his brooding Jipol commandent Yorek Thurr, as well as Serena Butler, never wavering in her intensity. Venport's tailored suit was cool enough to prevent any damning nervous perspiration from showing.

Venport set out to complete the most important negotiations of his career.

"I am pleased that we can all sit down and discuss our mutual needs like adults," he began after taking another sip. He needed to deal with the loss of his swift merchant fleet as a businessman. The situation had changed, and he had to make the best of it. He would not be able to keep all the profits and power he had anticipated, so he had to parlay what remained into something different. Perhaps even something better.

He had engaged in similar negotiations with Lord Bludd over the merchandizing rights to glowglobes, and had done well. This promised to be far more significant, with enormous repercussions.

"You have proposed that my new space-folding commercial haulers be converted into fighting ships for the Army of the Jihad and that new foldspace engines be adapted to the medium-sized javelin warships. Your earnest but somewhat . . . naïve military officers are of the opinion that I should happily liquidate all of my assets, surrender proprietary technology, ignore a decade of unceasing work and investment, and simply turn over every vessel in my expensive fleet for no compensation. Apparently, I am to be paid in . . . pride?"

Serena frowned, tapped her fingertips together. "Even if you were to receive nothing, some of us have given more for the cause."

"No one means to diminish your own sacrifices, Serena," Iblis Ginjo said. "But perhaps we don't have to ruin the man in order to achieve what we need."

Unswayed, Serena asked, "Are you a war profiteer, Directeur Venport?"

"Certainly not!"

Yorek Thurr frowned, stroking one side of his mustache as he said in a quiet voice, "On the other hand, let us not be so credulous as to believe that the military applications of these space-folding ships never once entered Directeur Venport's mind. Yet he did not bother to inform the Jihad Council of his activities on Kolhar."

Venport bristled at the shadowy Jipol commander. "The spacefolders are new and still dangerous, sir. We lose a troublesome percentage of our flights. The frequent disasters force me to tack substantial surcharges onto cargo prices, just so I can rebuild the ships I lose and provide recompense for the families of the mercenary pilots who take such outrageous risks."

Thurr folded his hands together. "The rebellious cymeks, as well as Omnius, would love to take over that facility and steal the technology for themselves."

"I poured the majority of VenKee's equity into the program for years, and I am entitled to benefit in some manner from the new technology. I would never have paid for the research and development unless I thought it had some value for us. Even with smooth and profitable years, it will take me decades to pay off the debt I incurred to build the shipyards. Do you believe that any businessman in the League would invest all his assets to develop important technology if he knew there was a chance that the government might take everything, leaving him bankrupt?"

Serena gestured impatiently with a forefinger. "I can eradicate your debt. Erase it completely."

Venport stared at her, unable to believe the suggestion. Such a sweeping concession had never occurred to him. "You can . . . you can do that?"

Iblis Ginjo sat straight, puffed up like a bird practicing its mating display. "She is the Priestess of the Jihad, Directeur. She can do it with a stroke of a pen."

Pressing his advantage immediately, Venport began reciting the discussion points he had developed during the voyage to Salusa. "My wife Norma Cenva has devoted more than thirty years to developing the space-folding technology. She faced many adversities, including horrific torture after being captured by cymeks, but her vision of mankind's future has never wavered. She even killed the Titan Xerxes. And all along, I am the only one who supported her, the only one who believed in her. Even Savant Holtzman cast her off."

Looking around the table in the Council chamber, he noted that several of the members seemed impatient for him to come to his point. Venport leaned forward. "Therefore I request that VenKee Enterprises and its successors be granted irrevocable patents on the technology specific to folding space."

"A monopoly on space travel," Yorek Thurr grumbled.

"I am asking for proprietary treatment for *my* form of space travel, using *my* engines, in *my* ships. For millennia, human beings have crossed vast distances by traditional means. They are welcome to use the same vessels they have always taken — I want special consideration only for my spacefolders, which were developed by my wife and funded by my company. That seems a reasonable request."

Ginjo tapped his fingers on the tabletop. "Let us not delude ourselves. If the safety considerations are ever worked out, this will become the preferred method of travel between star systems, making every other technology obsolete."

"If it is the fastest, most reliable means of travel, why should my company not benefit?" Venport crossed his arms over his chest.

But Serena had heard enough of the argument. "We are wasting time. He can have his irrevocable patents and his monopoly — but only *after* the Jihad is over."

"How can I be sure it will ever be over?"

"That is a risk you will have to take."

From the expression on her face, Venport saw he could not press the issue one centimeter further. "Done, but the rights pass on to my heirs if I die before the conclusion of the Jihad."

Serena nodded. "Iblis, see that the necessary documents are drawn up."

In the end, the astute Aurelius Venport also negotiated the right to bring at least a partial cargo load of his merchandise on selected military missions. Though he had not initiated these talks, nor precipitated the commercial crisis that required them, when he was finished Aurelius Venport began to suspect that they could make him a very, very wealthy man.

*   *   *

He received the award almost as an afterthought.

Banners hung in the Hall of Parliament, and ordinary citizens were allowed to stand at the rear, overlooking the planetary representatives. Thousands of people gathered in the memorial plaza outside, watching the proceedings on screens as tall as buildings.

Zufa Cenva sat beside Venport in a front row of seats that spread toward the higher tiers like the expanding ripples of a pond. Her pale hair and features made her look like static electricity incarnate, and she seemed to radiate with a *presence* that marked her as the most powerful Sorceress of all the talented practitioners from Rossak.

She glanced down at him, making him dizzy with the gaze of her pale eyes. "You are a great hero now, Aurelius. Your name is on the lips of every jihadi fighting for the cause of freedom. That is worth much to history."

Gazing across the speaking stage at the impressively dressed dignitaries, he said, "I never lived my life worrying overmuch about history, Zufa. I am pleased enough about how this will change my daily situation." He straightened his ruffled collar and his overly formal ultrasuit. "You and Norma were right. I was being short-sighted and selfish. Devoting the lion's share of our resources to military instead of commercial applications will be a setback — but ultimately VenKee Enterprises will grow stronger because of it."

She nodded. "There is always a price for patriotism, Aurelius. You are just beginning to understand that."

"So I am." In fact, initially he had thought that receiving this medal was a mere consolation prize, a bauble to make him feel better about his sacrifices. He hadn't realized it would increase his stature in the eyes of the people. In the future, few people would choose one of his competitors over VenKee for any item of merchandise.

He found himself unexpectedly eager to return to the shipyards to begin implementing the new state of affairs, while making a full assessment of materials and products so that he could readily arrange for the most profitable cargo to be carried on military missions in the space-folding ships. His products would fly on a standby basis, depending upon available space. Yorek Thurr, pulling strings from the Jipol, had already arranged for Aurelius and Zufa to take a small space yacht back to Kolhar. They would depart almost immediately after the awards ceremony.

He sat stiffly through the opening agenda and introductions. Presently, Grand Patriarch Iblis Ginjo made appropriate invocations in his impressively resonant voice, followed by Serena Butler. She stood at the speaking podium in her signature purple-trimmed white robes, a daz-zling presence. Her hair had gone partially gray, as if lightly dusted with ash, and her face showed the weight of years and tragedies. But her voice was strong as she summoned Venport to the stage, along with the famed young battlefield surgeon Rajid Suk.

To resounding applause, Venport walked to the podium. Surprisingly, Zufa Cenva showed considerable pride in him, and he wished only that Norma might have been there. For once in her life, Norma deserved the recognition and accolades, whether she wanted them or not.

The lights excited him and blurred his vision, and he felt as if he were about to be swept away on a tidal wave of applause. Venport blinked, steadied himself. He avoided looking out into the sea of faces surround-ing the central platform, and moved into position beside Doctor Suk.

Serena said, "Each of you will receive the highest medal of commen-dation the Jihad can bestow. The Manion Cross is named after my baby, the first martyr of our holy war against the thinking machines. Very few have received it."

Turning to the other recipient, she said, "Doctor Rajid Suk is our greatest battlefield surgeon. Giving up his private practice, he has repeatedly accompanied our battle fleets, journeying to distant war zones and donating his time to our sacred mission, helping to save countless jihadis." Suk stood with his shoulders squared and his chest thrust forward. The onlookers cheered as she presented him with his medal.

"Next, I introduce to you our most astounding entrepreneur, a man who has fought the wars of interstellar commerce and created a supply and delivery network that spans star systems. Directeur Aurelius Venport has just turned over his entire shipyard operation to the Army of the Jihad. At long last, I believe we have the opportunity to crush Omnius for all time." She was careful not to state any specifics about the space-folding technology; Jipol had proved time and again that machine spies could be everywhere.

The audience cheered wildly, accepting her assertions without ques-tion. Venport, however, doubted that such a significant military strike could occur anytime soon, not even with the best efforts of Kolhar and massive funding. The Holtzman ships were simply too new and un-proven.

Nevertheless, Venport bowed formally as the Priestess draped the shimmering ribbon and gaudy medal over his neck.

Then she stepped to one side, and gestured toward the men with an open hand, presenting them to the crowd. "Our newest Heroes of the Jihad! Because of them, we have taken great strides toward victory."

The merchant raised his head, astonished to feel stinging tears in his eyes. His heart seemed to swell in his chest. As the representatives in the great hall surged to their feet, clapping and cheering, he shook hands with Serena and Dr. Suk.

Afterward, the honorees said a few words to the assemblage. When Venport's turn came, he said, "Though I have spent most of my years as a businessman and an entrepreneur, I am learning that there are things far more important than great riches. I thank all of you, for the happiest moment of my life."

Oddly, though Venport never had expected to feel this way, he honestly meant what he said.

Once I thought we should end this Jihad at all costs — but some costs are simply too high.

          —Serena Butler, draft proclamation, unreleased

S HORTLY AFTER VENPORT and Zufa departed on the long journey back to the Kolhar shipyards, the Ivory Tower Cogitors made a procession to Salusa Secundus with great fanfare. Carried by the secondaries, including a giddy, self-satisfied Keats, Vidad demanded an urgent session of the League Parliament.

Planetary delegates hurried from their residences, appointments, and social events to gather in the Assembly Hall. The representatives were curious, though put out by the rushed and unscheduled event. The meeting was called to order quickly, and Keats placed Vidad's ancient brain on a pedestal at the center of the oratory stage; the five other Ivory Tower Cogitors rested on lower pillars surrounding their spokesman.

Still hurrying to straighten his formal robes, Grand Patriarch Iblis Ginjo rushed into the hall, harried and unprepared. He'd had no time to contact Serena Butler, who was sequestered in the City of Introspection developing her own secret battle plans for the spacefolder ships, which should be available in less than a year.

Actually, Iblis preferred to handle Cogitor matter himself. Keats, after all, was one of his hand-picked men.

He entered the crowded and unruly hall just as the ancient philosopher spoke in a booming voice amplified by his modified speaker patch. Iblis was delighted to see the Cogitors return.

"As Cogitors, we chose to isolate ourselves where we could ponder great questions, taking as long as necessary. Your Priestess of the Jihad came to Hessra two standard years ago and made us understand how the centuries of machine domination and the recent decades of terrible bloodshed have taken their toll upon the human race.

"We do not normally advocate swift, impetuous action, but the Priestess is a compelling woman. She enabled us to see our duty, not only to the free human race but to the efficient Omnius network. Having considered the matter carefully, we now bring you the solution to the problem, a formula for immediate peace among the combatants."

The audience muttered, curious about what Vidad would say. Over the years, as the death toll continued to rise and human colonies fell, as the Jihad drained the resources of the League, the people became ripe for any escape from the endless cycle of warfare. Even now, three dozen years after the beginning of the holy war against machines, free humans seemed no closer to victory.

Uneasy at what they might suggest, Iblis gazed down on the preserved brains in their translucent cylinders. As ordered, Keats and the other secondaries had opened the minds of the ancient, reclusive philosophers. But now Iblis wasn't sure he wanted to hear it.

"We have taken it upon ourselves to act as mediators between the League and the Synchronized Worlds. The years of bloodshed and conflict are now at an end." Vidad paused, as if to heighten dramatic effect. "We have successfully brokered a genuine peace with the thinking machines. Omnius has agreed to a complete cessation of hostilities. Machines will no longer target League Worlds, and humans will no longer target Synchronized Worlds. A simple, clearcut Pax Galacticus. Neither side has cause for continued hostilities. Once the League agrees, the bloodshed simply stops." He fell silent, allowing the audience time to draw a deep, collective breath.

Keats looked over at Iblis and announced with great pride, "We have done it! This Jihad is over!"

The white-robed Seraphim hurried to interrupt Serena Butler's meditations. Beneath her gold-mesh skullcap, Niriem's expression looked distressed — the first time Serena had ever seen such alarm on the loyal woman's face.

"Something terrible is happening," she said, handing Serena a recording cube. "The messenger told me that Iblis Ginjo is calling for you to come immediately to the Hall of Parliament."

"Immediately?"

"A crisis involving the Cogitors. You are to listen to this recording."

"What has the Grand Patriarch done?" Serena took a deep exasperated breath. "We'll listen to this on the way."

While Iblis, Serena, and other leaders among the League of Nobles had access to military communication systems, there had been security problems recently, messages intercepted by clever agents of Omnius. It was a matter of such concern that comsystems — which utilized encrypted feedback signals — were now only being used for battle fleets in space, and not on the surfaces of planets. This required an increase in the use of couriers.

Niriem rushed her into a groundcar that raced down the wide roads to Zimia. Inside the passenger compartment, Serena listened in shocked dismay to a recording of Vidad's surprise announcement. "This is not what we want at all!"

"Nevertheless, Priestess, they are so desperate for peace I fear they will agree to anything."

Knowing Niriem was right, she played the Cogitor's brief statement three times, as if hoping the implications or words would change, but the horror and disbelief churned and bubbled in the pit of her stomach like a boiling cauldron.

"This is impossible. We gain nothing from such terms!"

She hoped she would arrive before word got out. Such remarkable news could not be kept quiet, and the people would overreact. The ever-growing numbers of protesters would riot in the streets. The League representatives themselves would be blinded by euphoria, completely unreasonable. Serena had to get there without delay.

Arriving in Zimia, a squad of female guards flanked her as she strode up the veined stone steps into the imposing government building. Like a battering ram, Niriem cleared the way, not afraid to show her full strength. Though she was older now, Priestess Serena still carried a fierce exuberance.

At the center of the Hall, yellow-robed secondaries stood beside the Ivory Tower Cogitors on their pedestals. The atmosphere inside the echoing chamber was raucous and festive. Iblis Ginjo stood on the edge of the stage, trying to reassert order to the proceedings. He did not appear to be doing very well.

Her head held high, Serena marched to the center of the speaking floor. The representatives were in a hubbub over the unexpected news, a few shouting against the Cogitor's new peace plan, but most were cheering and clapping.

"Let us not be hasty!" Serena shouted without introduction, for she required none. "Dire consequences often come in the guise of good news."

The din in the great hall dwindled to a murmur; Iblis Ginjo looked pleased and relieved that she had finally arrived.

"Serena Butler," Vidad said through his speaker patch, "we will delineate the details of our delicate negotiations with Omnius. We have arranged safe passage for a League representative to travel to Corrin and formally accept the peace terms."

Serena could barely contain her incredulity. "We do not accept these terms. Peace at any cost? Then what have all these decades of fighting been for? I will tell you our terms: the *destruction* of all thinking machines!" She looked around the Hall, which grew more crowded moment by moment as people rushed in after hearing the news.

Only a smattering of applause could be heard, supporting her remarks. Gradually the noise dissipated, and a heavy silence seeped into the chamber.

Serena took several steps across the stage, closer to Vidad. "Because of my imprisonment and torment under Omnius, I know far more about the suffering of humans on Synchronized Worlds than you have considered in two thousand years of isolation. You understand little if you believe that free humanity is interested in a rapprochement with Omnius."

"Our range of knowledge is greater than you presume. Listen to your own people, Serena Butler. They wish an end to the bloodshed."

Fury darkened her face. "Your meddling plan may indeed stop the war temporarily, but provides us with no resolution. No victory! Have *billions* of people died in vain? Did *my child* die in vain? Omnius will still dominate the Synchronized Worlds, enslaving humanity there. Is all our work for nothing? Zimia? Earth?" She rattled off a list of highlights, raising her voice with the name of each wounded world. "Or Bela Tegeuse? Honru? Tyndall? Bellos? Rhisso? Chusuk? IV Anbus? Peridot Colony? Ellram? Giedi Prime?"

She turned to stare at the unsettled, subdued audience. "Shall I continue to remind you of all the sacrifices we have made? I am appalled to hear such suggestions after all my work."

"But consider the lives it will save, Serena," shouted a male representative from the crowd above. She could not identify his voice.

"In the short run — or in the *long* run? Imagine the future that awaits us once we begin making bargains with Omnius! And why now?" She raised a fist. She had to prevent these representatives from making the most costly mistake in human history.

Oh, how she wished the new space-folding battleships were ready. But the Parliament knew nothing about the secret work on Kolhar. Once the Army of the Jihad acquired a new fleet that could cross interstellar distances in less time than it took to say it, they could strike the

Synchronized Worlds faster than the thinking machine network learned of their defeats. Humans had never before had such an advantage. Once Omnius understood the massive swift force arrayed against him, he would cower on his remaining Synchronized Worlds, never daring to launch any further aggression. He would go into a defensive mode, retracting with each human victory. His once grand empire would get smaller and smaller, and then disappear entirely.

She slammed her fist into the palm of her hand. "Now — especially *now!* — we must press on to complete victory. We cannot turn our backs and walk away from the challenge."

"But we are tired of this fighting," said the interim ambassador from Poritrin, who had replaced Lord Niko Bludd. After the ruinous slave uprising there, the people had no heart or resources left to continue major offensives. "These Cogitors offer us a chance to stop the endless warfare. We must consider it, must heed their wisdom."

"Not if it means accepting a spineless peace." Serena swept her robes in a flash of purple and white. "Machines will never respect humans, nor honor an agreement with us. Omnius sees our lives as inefficient and disposable."

She paused, feeling her stomach burn and her legs tremble. The audience looked at her as if she was going too far, and that only made her angrier. "Right now the thinking machines are weak and reeling. We have an opportunity to finish them off — down to the last circuit panel." She lowered her voice to a growl. "If we do not, if we weaken in our resolve, they will rise again and oppose us with greater strength than before."

"It is a gamble either way," said the representative from Giedi Prime. "More than anyone else in this Assembly Hall, I owe you a great debt, Serena Butler. My world is free today because of the brave actions you took to defend us. But our population remains frail, unrecovered from all the damage Omnius did during his brief conquest decades ago. If there is a chance we can reach a truce, one that does not require a terrible capitulation, then we should take it."

Another prominent representative stood. "Consider the advantages. Since humans have won back a number of planets and we've reached military parity with the thinking machines, we are indeed in a strong bargaining position to enforce the terms the Cogitors have negotiated."

"Hear this!" said a stern woman who remained seated, but whose voice bellowed out across the hall. "With the cymek revolt tearing at the machine resources as much as our human rebellions, Omnius has to be sincere in his cease-fire. He can't fight us all at once."

The debate began anew, and escalated quickly into a shouting match, a din of angry voices. Serena felt growing despair. Too many representatives were anxious for peace, some breathing space for humanity to recover, to rebuild its fleet and heal its population.

But Serena feared the cost of such a decision. She knew in her soul that this was a terrible, terrible capitulation. *So wrong,* she thought. *How could they be such fools?* Serena saw clearly that if she continued to insist on aggression, she would lose the majority of her support in the Parliament.

She had to find some other way to change their minds. The Grand Patriarch looked at her with wide, imploring eyes. He had done so much to rally the Jihad in her name, and now he must be experiencing the bitter taste of failure in his mouth, just as Serena was.

The Cogitors had won. Vidad had single-handedly brokered a peace that would cripple humanity and lead to a slow death of League civilization.

Omnius would never forget this Holy Jihad. He would get stronger and stronger, with only one goal in mind: the complete eradication of humanity in every star system. By then, Serena would no longer be around to say that she had warned them.

Turning her back on the assemblage, she marched out of the chamber in disgust, refusing to listen to any more. Despair weighed heavily on her shoulders. For more than three decades she had rallied her people, but had not inspired them enough to win.

During the groundcar trip back to the City of Introspection, she pondered, seeking answers, wondering where she had failed.

Heroes sometimes do their greatest works after they are dead.
                              —Serena Butler, *Zimia Rallies*

BLIS GINJO ROLLED over and lay on a swaybacked bed that smelled of sweat and sex. His head throbbed with mental misery over the disastrous change of events in the war, as well as the hedonistic excesses he had allowed himself the night before. What did it matter?

No one was with him at the moment, but he recalled a blurry succession of faces. How many women had there been . . . four, five? Excessive even by his standards — and one had even looked like his wife. But that was all right; he had been desperate and upset.

Eleven years ago, he'd thought it was bad enough that Serena Butler had usurped his primary position after all he had worked to accomplish. Now the whole Jihad was about to be ruined by an absurd peace proposal. It could never work. How could Keats and the other secondaries have failed so utterly? Didn't they understand what they had done?

He tried not to think about his own role in the sorry state of affairs, and wished he could come up with a way to blame it on someone else. Serena was the obvious choice as the leader of the Jihad, but Iblis lived in a proverbial glass house. After all, he had been the one responsible for assigning Keats and the other secondaries to the Cogitors.

For the first time since his long-ago dealings with Cogitor Eklo on Earth, he began to wonder about the sanity of the ancient philosophers. After so many years and so many billions slaughtered in the struggle, they expected humans and machines to simply shake hands. What an appalling state of affairs.

Wishing to distract himself from the bleak events swirling around him, he had spent the night drowning his problems in melange and women.

An amusing and exhausting way to fill time, but ultimately pointless. His problems were still there in the morning.

Threadbare lace curtains only partially covered the window of an unremarkable hotel. Quite a contrast with his private, state-funded suite in Zimia where he ostensibly lived with his aloof wife and three children who rarely even spoke to him.

Wrinkling his nose at the lingering odors of much-used linens and towels, along with exotic Rossak drugs, he plodded to the window, not bothering to cover his nudity. He was somewhere in the Old Town district of Zimia, far from the government buildings and the nobles who frequented them. Here, the Grand Patriarch faced the gritty core of humanity, people he could easily twist, comfort and convince with his innate charms. Coming here occasionally, he enjoyed the change of pace, the rough, seedy trappings of the lower class. It felt raw and natural, more like when he'd been a slave supervisor back on Earth. At least then he had been able to see the direct results of his power . . .

Serena saw only her obsessive vision of a holy victory against the demonic enemy, a pure but overly simplistic goal. Iblis had been the practical one all along. For years he had constructed a massive infrastructure — the industrial, mercantile, and religious enterprises of the Jihad. As the man who made all the wheels turn, the Grand Patriarch had accepted money, power, and countless awards. Most of it before Serena took control. If the Jihad ended, Iblis Ginjo would have no legitimate position. Serena had been at odds with him, but now only the two of them could save the human race from a complete debacle, a folly of massive proportions. He wanted her to come to him — Iblis Ginjo was her only true ally.

As he stood at the open window feeling the morning breeze on his bare flesh, Iblis gritted his teeth. Never in his life had he surrendered to despair. There was always a way to salvage the situation, at whatever cost. He just needed to find the right key.

But what could he and Serena possibly do that would be significant enough to remove the blindfold from their eyes? The exhausted and battered people would accept Vidad's peace plan out of desperation and lack of hope. This called for truly drastic measures.

Hearing a familiar voice in the corridor, his pulse jumped.

"Which room is he in? I need to see the Grand Patriarch immediately." Iblis grabbed a tattered robe, wetted down his hair, and made himself halfway presentable before he opened the door, smiling.

Backed by Niriem and four other Seraphim, Serena confronted the Jipol guards that Iblis had left in the hall. Dressed in an elegant white robe with gold trim and a medallion emblazoned with her martyred baby's image, she looked grossly out of place in such a seedy establishment. Upon seeing the stoic female guardians standing so close to Serena, Iblis felt a wash of relief. Long ago, he had created the Seraphim to act as a buffer between the Priestess and inconvenient reality. They still reported to him whenever she did something unexpected . . . but they were beginning to show a disturbing amount of loyalty to her. Niriem, at least, was still his.

Serena grimaced in clear disapproval of Iblis's nocturnal activities. "Don't waste your energies in this way, Iblis. We have vital work to do. Especially now."

With a confident gesture for him to follow, she strode back down the corridor. Her attendants waited for Iblis and the Jipol guards to join them.

When he had seated himself next to her in the private vehicle with Niriem driving, Iblis took a last look at the ramshackle surroundings.

"Sometimes, Serena, I get away from the sparkling towers and fine governmental residences so that I can *remember* how bad it used to be on Earth. I gain perspective. When I look inside the dingy rooms and see the dregs of humanity — the drug addicts, drunks, and whores — I am reminded of what our valiant jihadis are fighting for. To rise above this." Gaining momentum, he thought swiftly and lowered his voice to a hushed whisper. "I came here to think of a way to salvage the Jihad."

"I am listening." Her lavender eyes glistened with desperation.

Iblis felt surprisingly calm. His voice was firm, with enough of an edge to make her hear and understand the difficult truths. "I was born a slave and fought my way through the ranks to trustee. Eventually, I became the leader of a revolt and the Grand Patriarch of our Holy Jihad." With a bitter expression he leaned closer to her. "But I could never compete with *you*, Serena Butler. It was always your name they shouted. You were the aristocrat who tried to help the masses out of some guilt for all the riches your noble family had garnered on the backs of ordinary people."

"Noblesse oblige. Are you attempting to psychoanalyze me?"

"Just placing things in perspective. If I could do what I am about to propose, I would. But . . . it must be you, Serena. Only you. That is, if you are willing to pay the price." He leaned closer, his eyes fiery as he tried to summon all of his skills.

"I would do anything to win the Jihad." Her face was beatific with resolve. Her eyes seemed to catch fire, like his. "*Anything*." She realized exactly what she was saying, and Iblis knew he had her.

"Over the years, I have helped to fan the flames, but now the conflagration has diminished to embers. Like a wind storm, you must fan those embers into an unstoppable holocaust. All along, you and I have scorned people for not making the necessary sacrifices — and now there is something you must do."

She waited.

"Remember how Erasmus murdered little Manion? In the moment that your child died, you threw yourself on a robot master without regard for your own safety."

Serena pulled away, as if Shaitan had just whispered in her ear. She knew Iblis had his own agenda and that he benefited personally from his position. She also knew, however, that even though they played the game differently, they both wanted the same result.

Iblis continued with greater fervor. "In that instant, you ignited the Jihad. First Erasmus showed all the workers in the square below how monstrous the thinking machines were, and you provided proof that a mere human could fight back and *win!*"

As she listened, tears streamed down her face, but Serena did not brush them away.

"Now, after so many years of fighting, our people have forgotten how terrible their enemy is. If they could only remember that horrific murder of your child, not a single person would accept any sort of peace with Omnius. We must show them again how evil the enemy is, must make them see it through their weariness and pain. We need to remind them of why Omnius and all his minions must be destroyed!"

His eyes blazed at her, and for a moment she saw billions of eyes burning within his. Even from this small pulpit within a private ground-car, even after his night of debauchery, Iblis Ginjo remained a man of substance, and Serena could not ignore him.

In a conspiratorial tone, he said, "Humanity has forgotten the spark. You've got to make a grand gesture, something the people will never forget."

She studied his smooth face. After years of doubts, she decided that Iblis Ginjo had more good in him than bad. Despite his selfish motivations, she knew he would make sure the fight continued. And nothing mattered more than that.

"It will require a great deal of courage," he said.

"I know. I believe I possess sufficient . . . resolve."

Serena stood proudly before the full League Assembly. She and Iblis had worked out their plans in detail, had set all the wheels in motion. Yorek Thurr and his shadowy Jipol operatives were taking care of the fine points. Even her own Seraphim would play their part, though Niriem protested mightily. Still, Serena was the Priestess of the Jihad, and when she issued a directive, her guards could not refuse her.

As she had feared, and expected, the Assembly had voted to accept the cessation of hostilities brokered by the Cogitors. The League would withdraw the Army of the Jihad from any Synchronized Worlds, issuing instructions that thinking machine forces were not to be harassed — and Omnius would take similar actions. This left the representatives to dicker over who would be the emissary for free humanity, who would go to Corrin and finalize the treaty with the primary evermind incarnation.

Serena stunned them all. She demanded to speak from the podium, as was her right as the Interim Viceroy — a title she had never formally relinquished. The audience grumbled, expecting that she would rail at them again for the unacceptable peace terms.

Instead, Serena said, "After much consideration, I have decided that I should be the one to journey to Corrin." Murmurs of shock and surprise carried through the hall, like the waves of a sea whipped up by an unexpected hurricane. No one had foreseen this. She continued with an earnest smile. "Who better to carry the banner of free humanity than the Priestess of the Jihad herself?"

Better that the mainspring of this religious insanity is not wound all the way up. The universe is not ready for such loud ticking.
  —Cogitor Kwyna, *City of Introspection Archives*

CONVINCED THAT SERENA Butler's personal acceptance of the peace accord would send precisely the right signal to Omnius, the Jihad Council and the League Parliament approved her request. They were overjoyed that she had turned her passion to the cause of peace, so that humans and machines could coexist in harmony. Celebrations overflowed the streets of Zimia.

Her plan terrified Xavier Harkonnen. He suspected immediately that she had not truly changed her mind, but he also knew that no one would listen to him. Especially not now.

The Parliament offered the Priestess a small, fast diplomatic ship. She would be accompanied by five of her chosen Seraphim as an honor guard, but she had refused any other security detail or entourage. "Omnius will not be impressed by pomp, and if the machines intend outright treachery, what difference would a dozen guards make, or a hundred, or even a thousand?" Then, she had added with a rueful smile, "Besides, why bring soldiers if I am on a peace mission? That sends entirely the wrong signal."

Exhausted from nearly four decades of bloody fighting, the people were delirious at the prospect of reconciliation. They lionized Vidad and his fellow Cogitors. They launched exuberant victory parades, imagining how their lives would now be different, never again without the fear of awful machine raids. They desperately wanted to believe in the possibility of a safe future.

Xavier thought they were all fools for trusting the promises of Omnius. Serena must feel that way herself, so he could not fathom what she really had in mind.

Dressed in a formal crimson-and-green uniform, adorned with every insignia and medal he had ever received, the old Primero took a military groundcar to the arched gates of the City of Introspection. At the apex of the main arch, a stylized image of the angelic child — his own son — watched over the compound.

Deferring to the high-ranking officer, the jihadis stepped aside, but the white-robed women remained where they were. Sunlight gleamed off their golden skullcaps. "The Priestess of the Jihad does not receive visitors."

"She will see *me*." Xavier squared his shoulders and lifted his gaze to the idealized icon of the innocent murdered child. "I demand it in the name of my son Manion Butler." This caused the Seraphim to falter, and Xavier pushed through the gate into the walled religious retreat where Serena had sequestered herself for so long.

Smiling and expectant, she met him near the garden fish ponds. Long ago, this was where she had summoned Xavier and Vorian to recruit them as her greatest officers of the Jihad. When Xavier saw her in this peaceful place, an avalanche of memories assailed him, and his knees felt weak.

For a moment he stood without speaking, and Serena took the initiative. "My dear Xavier, I wish now that we had spent more time together as friends. But the Jihad has consumed us for so long."

"We could have more time if you refused to go to Corrin." His voice carried a gruff edge. "The thought that you would willingly cease all hostilities against your mortal enemies is as false as a robot's grin."

"Machines have rigid programming, but one of the strengths of humanity is that we are able to change our minds. We can alter our opinions. We can even be . . . capricious when it suits us."

"Do you expect me to believe that?" He wanted to embrace her or just stand closer, but she remained where she was, and he stood as stiffly as a statue.

"Believe what you wish," she said with a bittersweet smile. "You used to be able to see into my heart. Come, follow me." She led him along a gem-gravel path toward a sheltered, private area.

As he walked beside her, Xavier said, "I wish things had been different, Serena. I mourn not only my lost son, but the love you and I should have had, the years of contentment together." He sighed. "Not that I would ever change a moment of my life with Octa."

"I love you both, Xavier. We must accept the present no matter how we wish we might have changed the past. I am glad you and my sister found a measure of happiness in the midst of this tempest." Serena stroked his clean-shaven cheek, gazing at him with a determined expression. "We are defined by our tragedies and our martyrs. Without little Manion, humans never would have had the incentive to rise up and fight Omnius in the first place."

His heart skipped a beat when he realized where she was leading him. He had not visited the primary shrine for many years, but now saw the crystalline coffin, the plaz-walled crypt that contained the remains of their dead son. He remembered taking the child's preserved body from the *Dream Voyager*, after Vorian Atreides had escaped from Earth with Serena and Iblis.

When she sensed him drawing back, Serena urged him forward. "This Jihad is for our son. Everything I've done for decades has been to avenge him — and all the other sons and daughters of captive humans on every Synchronized World. You heard the shouting in the Hall of Parliament. The League wants to accept the ridiculous peace proposal. If I don't go to Corrin, someone else will — and that will lead to an even greater disaster."

She and Xavier stood close together, looking down silently at the innocent boy who had been murdered by the robot Erasmus. On various League planets, Xavier had seen hundreds of shrines and memorials to this revered child, bedecked with orange marigolds and loving paintings. At the recollection, his throat felt as dry as tinder, and his sense of personal outrage and deep loss increased with each passing moment.

He grumbled. "But if we give up without a resolution, it will be like our first strike on Bela Tegeuse. Before long, the machines will come back stronger than before, and all of our battles, the sacrifices of our fallen heroes, will have been for naught."

Serena's shoulders drooped. "Unless I can inspire them to a greater fervor, the Jihad will fall into the gutter of history." Her lips turned down in a frown, and her haunted eyes showed depths of unspeakable disappointment — an expression she never revealed to her cheering public. "What else can I do, Xavier? The Cogitors offer an easy way out, and everyone wants to leap at the chance. My Jihad has failed through the lack of human will." Her voice was so quiet that he could barely hear her. "At times my shame is so great I can barely hold my head up and look at the sky."

The sun reflected like a flare off the crystal coffin's polished surface. Amazed at the high quality of facial and bodily reconstruction, Xavier bent to look closely at the peaceful face of the little boy, the son he wished he had known. Manion looked so peaceful.

Then, at the base of the boy's chin, he saw a fold of what looked like flesh-toned polymer, a tiny glint of metal wire, and lines of adhesive that seemed to be sagging after decades of Salusan sunlight magnified by the prismatic chamber. He realized that this could not be the mangled child who had been brought back from the riots on Earth. It was a facsimile, a sham!

Serena looked into his face, noted Xavier's questions and doubts, and spoke before he could say anything. "Yes, I discovered the ruse years ago. No one else comes here and looks as closely as I do . . . or as you just did. Iblis created what was necessary at the time. His intentions were noble."

He responded in a hushed voice so the Seraphim would not overhear. "But this is a fraud!"

"It is a *symbol*. I did not notice the fake until the people had already rallied around Manion the Innocent and sworn to fight the Jihad. After that, what would I gain if I exposed the ruse?" She arched her eyebrows. "Surely, you don't believe that all the artifacts in all the shrines and reliquaries across the League Worlds are real?"

He frowned. "I . . . never gave it much consideration."

"This is a shrine to our fallen son, who was slain by the evil Erasmus. That is real enough and cannot be denied." She traced her fingertips on the slick crystal, her face distant and wistful. Then she rallied her determination and looked directly at him. "It doesn't make any difference, Xavier. What I *believe* — what the people believe — is the only thing that matters. A symbol always has more power than reality."

He accepted only reluctantly. "I don't like this deceit . . . but you're right: it doesn't change what truly happened to our child. It makes no difference to our reasons for hating Omnius."

She put her arms around him, and as he embraced her, he longed for the decades they had lost. "If all my devotees were like you, Xavier, we would have defeated Omnius in a year."

He hung his head. "I'm just an old battle-scarred soldier now. The other commanders are much younger. They've forgotten the determination that made the Jihad such a fierce struggle. They've known nothing else, and they see me as just a grandfatherly figure who tells old war stories."

Serena smoothed her silk-trimmed robes. "And now I need you to look to the future, Xavier. I intend to go to Corrin and face Omnius, but you must stay here and continue my fight. Iblis has already promised me that. You, too, must do whatever is necessary to guarantee that we will not lose everything we have fought for."

"There's nothing I could say to stop you from going, is there?"

Her smile was distant. "I must do what I can."

Xavier left the City of Introspection, feeling a leaden sense of foreboding. Something in Serena's eyes, in her tone of voice, told him she intended to do a terrible, irrevocable thing, and he would not be able to stop her.

*My heart is stretched and pulled in so many ways. Why must Duty
and Love tug in opposite directions?*

> —Primero Vorian Atreides, private logs

I T WAS MEANT only as a test-run for the streamlined space-folding ships
newly constructed for the Army of the Jihad. The Holtzman Effect
engines developed by Norma Cenva made it possible to journey from the
shipyards on Kolhar to any other place he wished, in a negligible travel
time.

Vorian Atreides knew exactly where he intended to go: Caladan. At last!

Unaware of the turmoil in the League or of the unsatisfying accords the
Ivory Tower Cogitors had negotiated with Omnius, Vor insisted on taking
this "test-run" by himself. Though he was fifty-nine years old, he still felt
young and enthusiastic.

Working under the intense supervision of Norma Cenva, the Jihad
engineers had constructed several experimental military vessels smaller than the VenKee cargo ships and far better suited for reconnaissance.

Naturally, such new vessels needed to be taken on thorough shakedown cruises. Vor knew how to fly virtually any ship, and was ready to do
this test personally. His fellow officers objected that a key military leader
should never tackle a mission so fraught with risks and uncertainties, but
Vorian Atreides had never stood on ceremony — often to the frustration
and dismay of his friend Xavier.

Despite the navigational uncertainties involved in his headlong rush
across the folded fabric of space, Vor took no one with him. He knew the
risks were real after having seen records of VenKee's merchant flights,
and did not want to endanger anyone else.

"You all look so serious, so tragic! I've made up my mind, and none of you have the rank to countermand my order." He smiled. "Does anyone want to take bets on how soon I return?"

The space-folding engines worked perfectly.

From the cockpit of the scout ship, surrounded by gleaming instruments and blinking lights, the brief journey felt to Vor like a fantastic dream, not a real experience. He didn't seem to move at all. At first, his recon craft was near the bleak world of Kolhar. Then the cosmos bent and twisted around him, flooding with colors and images that he never imagined existed. Before he knew it, he had arrived at the ocean world that he remembered so clearly from his time here almost ten years ago. The whole journey took only a few seconds.

He landed at the primitive military facilities erected on the Caladan coast to maintain and monitor surveillance satellites. The engineers and mechanics stationed at the outpost had never seen a ship like this, and the soldiers were astonished at the unannounced arrival of such an important officer.

"We've been stuck here a long time, Primero," one of the soldiers said. "Are you on a morale-boosting mission?"

Vor smiled at him. "In part, Quinto. But truly I have another purpose on Caladan. There is someone I must see."

This time he would not bother to conceal his name or rank insignia. He had decided that he no longer needed to pretend for Leronica. He just wanted to see her and make sure that her life had gone well, that she had moved on. There was no reason to hide his identity.

Even so, as he approached the town, smelling the sea and hearing the boats, he felt as anxious as if he were going to face an entire robot army. He found his optimism dragged down by an anchor of doubt. Of course a woman like Leronica would have married and raised a family, spending a happy, settled life here on Caladan. He had known from the beginning that he couldn't just remain here and pretend to be a fisherman, and that he couldn't uproot her from this quiet planet and take her into the middle of the Jihad.

Vor had lost his chance for either course of action almost a decade ago. He should have forgotten about her, but he had tried to keep in touch despite the enormous distances. He had written many letters, sent her packages and gifts . . . and had never received a reply. Perhaps he should have stopped thinking about her long before this. Maybe it was not a good idea for him to come back here, now or ever. It might disrupt her life, and reawaken too many feelings in him. It was his own fault he had waited so long.

But his feet kept walking, and his heart drew him forward.

The coastal village had not changed much; it still welcomed him like a surrogate home. Leronica's tavern seemed to have prospered over the years. He longed to see the lovely woman again, but was not foolish enough to believe he could simply walk back into her arms after so long.

No, he would just visit as a friend, perhaps reminisce for a while, and leave it at that. He cared for Leronica, remembering her far above other romances, and was anxious to learn what she had been doing in the intervening years.

When he stepped through the door, Vor stood silhouetted, looking into the dim light of the common room, inhaling the rich smells of smoke, fish, and sweet pastries Leronica had probably baked. Vivid memories flooded back. His smile was certain, and his confidence rose.

He heard her sharp indrawn breath before his eyes adjusted. "Virk?" she said. "Vorian?" And then she caught herself, unable to believe. "Vorian Atreides, it can't be you. You haven't aged a day since you left."

Grinning broadly he stepped into the room. "My memories of you keep me young." With a roguish smile, he came close and saw that she looked a decade older. Her face was more mature, her features filled out, and her curly hair longer, but she still looked just as attractive to him.

Leronica came around the bar and threw herself into his arms. Before he knew it, they were kissing, laughing, and staring deep into each other's eyes. Finally, he managed to catch his breath, stepped back, and held her at arm's length. He shook his head in disbelief, but Leronica's dark pecan eyes were sparkling and wide. "You took your sweet time getting here, Mister. Ten long years!"

Suddenly he felt uncertain again. "You didn't wait for me, did you? I never expected you to sit alone and stare up into the skies." He didn't want that kind of guilt.

She made a scoffing noise and slapped him playfully on the shoulder. "You think I had nothing better to do? Hardly. I made a very fine life for myself, thank you very much." Then she smiled up at him. "That doesn't mean I didn't miss you, though. I appreciated every letter, every gift."

"So, you have a husband? A family?" He kept a chaste distance, convincing himself that he wanted to know the answers. "I'm not here to intrude or disrupt your life." He pulled up a chair and sat down.

Her face saddened. "I'm a widow. My husband was killed."

"I'm sorry," Vor said. "Do you want someone to talk to? Over a pitcher of kelp beer.

"That'll take more than one pitcher," she said.

He gave her a boyish grin, knowing how young he must look to her. "I am in no hurry."

They exchanged stories, a bit at a time. Each of Leronica's revelations riveted his attention. She had two sons, twins. She had married a fisherman, but her husband of more than eight years had been killed by a strange sea monster. She'd been a widow for more than a year already.

"I'd like to see the boys," he said. "I'll bet they're fine young men."

She gave him a strange look. "Just like their father."

He stayed for several weeks, making excuses and finding work that ostensibly needed to be done on Caladan, but each day went by too quickly. He met the boys Estes and Kagin, and marveled at the echoes of his own features. The twins were nine years old, and he could do the math himself. He decided Leronica would tell him in her own time, if she told him at all.

Even if he had gotten her pregnant so long ago, Vor had never acted the part of a father to these boys. If Kalem Vazz was as good a man as Leronica said, let the twins have their memories untainted. Leronica seemed to have reached the same conclusion.

They spent a lot of close time together, rediscovering friendship. Leronica never suggested that they rekindle their romance — not rebuffing him, but not inviting him to be her lover either. He could tell that she still loved Kalem and remained loyal to his memory. She had settled into her role as a widow, though she did not wallow in grief.

Vor listened while Leronica talked about Kalem, about her life here on Caladan. Finally, after the first few days, she sighed and then smiled at him. "All of this must sound incredibly dull to a hero of the Jihad."

"It seems wonderfully peaceful, a refuge from all the horrors I have seen." In his mind, he could not erase the memories of the massacres of helpless colonies, the horrific battlefields, the smashed robots and slain humans.

She leaned against him, feeling sweetly warm and solid. "It is human nature to long for something other than what we have." She stroked his cheek and he pressed her hand to his skin. "Now you must tell me about all the exotic places you've visited. You sent me that package of beautiful stones, but I prefer the pictures you paint with words. Take me to wonderful, far-off worlds with your stories."

Vor was nearly convinced that he wanted to make his life with this woman, who had captured his heart. He had already given decades to Serena's Jihad — had he not earned a respite? He could stop fighting, couldn't he, just for a while? When he gazed at Leronica, he saw what he truly desired. "I have all the time in the world, and see no harm in spending half a century with you . . . if need be."

But she laughed at him. "Vorian, Vorian, you would never be happy here. Caladan is not enough for a man like you."

"I wasn't thinking of Caladan," he said. "I was thinking of you, Leronica. To me, you shine brighter than all the stars in the universe." They embraced, and shared a long, tender kiss.

Everything changed two days later when a Jihad messenger came to find him on Caladan. The young man had come on another space-folding ship, crossing a vast distance in moments. Apparently Primero Harkonnen had dispatched an identical vessel earlier with the urgent news, but it had never arrived. It felt as if a vice had tightened on Vor's heart when he heard about the loss of another one of the risky Holtzman ships. "The message must be dire indeed if Xavier is willing to risk so much just to contact me."

"It is about the Priestess of the Jihad," said the breathless courier.

Consumed with dread, Vor listened, and was astonished to learn of the peace accord and how Serena had gone to meet with the Corrin-Omnius. He refused to believe she was so foolish or gullible. Then his heart turned cold as he understood from Xavier's message that she wasn't fooled at all, and that she had something else in mind.

"I have to go," Vor said to Leronica. Her expression did not falter. She had understood from the moment of the courier's arrival that Vor would be called to other duties.

"I trust you'll believe me now?" she said with a wry, sad smile. "You could never simply withdraw from the Jihad and content yourself with a quiet life."

"Believe *me*, Leronica." He kissed her, then stepped back. "There is nothing in the universe I want more than that . . . but the universe is not in the habit of asking my preference."

"Go and do what you must." She smiled at him warmly. "Just try not to wait ten years again before coming back."

"I promise. Next time, no one will be able to tear me away from you."

She frowned as she nudged him toward the uniformed courier. "Stop acting like a schoolboy, Vor. You have more important things to worry about now."

"You'll have to believe me when I return."

He rushed back to his space-folding scout ship. In a few moments — if he made the dangerous passage safely — he would be back on Salusa Secundus, trying to meet with Serena before she left on her ill-conceived quest to meet with the computer leader. He hoped he could change her mind.

But if Xavier's suspicions were correct, he might not arrive in time.

Of all the weapons that we utilize in war, Time is potentially the most effective – and the least under our control. So many major events could have been changed if only there had been another day, another hour, even another minute.
　　　　　　—Primero Xavier Harkonnen, letter to his daughters

A T ZIMIA SPACEPORT, Xavier Harkonnen received a VIP seat in the grandstands to watch the departure of the Priestess of the Jihad. He was the only one not cheering.

Though Octa stayed at home at the Butler Estate, Xavier's second daughter Omilia accompanied him to watch the spectacle. At the age of thirty-five, Omilia continued her career as an accomplished baliset player, performing concerts for popular Salusan cultural festivals. Smiling now, she sat next to her father, happy to be with him.

Xavier brooded as uneasiness chewed him up inside. Amidst the celebration and grand hopes for Serena's mission to Corrin, he felt incredibly alone. He had dispatched an urgent message to Vorian Atreides, but was sure his long-time friend could not possibly arrive here in time. He focused to Iblis Ginjo as he chattered happily with dignitaries, a bit too pleased with her mission. Xavier was certain that Ginjo had a role in her decision and wished he could discover what was going on behind the scenes.

Niriem and four other hand-picked Seraphim had already gone on board, preparing to pilot the vessel to Corrin. Standing in front of the ramp, Serena delivered a grandiose speech that was empty and passionless, but still well received. Too drunk with the possibilities of the Jihad's end, the gathered people did not listen closely. They head only what they wanted to hear.

Excited, Omilia clutched her father's sinewy arm. When he looked at her, he was faintly surprised to recognize that his girl was an adult woman now, beautiful and full of potential, with a hint of Serena's features from the Butler bloodline. Even little Wandra was now already ten years old, and Omilia was nearly twice the age Serena had been when she and Xavier had announced their betrothal, so long ago. . . .

How could so many years have passed, with so little joy to show for it?

Filled with worry and foreboding, Xavier stared, his expression intense. In the midst of cheering spectators and waving ribbons, he noticed that Serena looked deeply tired, resigned. She carried herself with a purposeful demeanor.

He withdrew from his pocket the necklace of black diamonds that Serena had given him so many years ago, before her impetuous secret attempt to save Giedi Prime. Back then, a young and stricken-looking Octa had delivered the necklace with its recorded holomessage. That single decision of Serena's, that one mission, had changed all of their lives forever.

And now she was off on an even more important venture. . . .

When the diplomatic ship was sealed and the fanfare blew, Xavier slumped back in the grandstand with tears trickling down his seamed face. Some of the spectators looked at him, perhaps considering the Primero a doddering old veteran reliving his glory, wallowing in half-forgotten memories.

Smiling, Omilia nudged him. "What's wrong, Father? It'll be all right. Surely you of all people must have complete faith in Priestess Serena?"

He stroked the smooth, dark gems of the old necklace. "Yes, Omilia. Serena will accomplish whatever she decides to do." He shook his shaggy head. "I fear in my heart that Serena will never come back."

Vor did not waste a moment worrying about the risks and hazards of navigation with the unproven Holtzman-effect engines. He simply plunged his ship headlong, knowing that he must arrive at the League capital world with all possible haste.

But he reached Zimia long after Serena had already gone.

Not knowing what else to do, he went directly to the Butler Estate. Perhaps he and Xavier could find some way. Vor didn't allow himself to doubt that he could do *something*.

At the front gte of the manor house atop the hill, the old Primero looked at him with weary, shadowed eyes. Vor was taken aback just to look at the man who has been his comrade for so many years. Could Xavier truly be so *old*? His face wore an expression of absolute defeat that Vor had never seen before.

"I knew you would come." Xavier's hands clutched the dark wooden frame of the door.

"How did you know to find me on Caladan?"

Xavier gave him a wan smile. "You don't even notice how often you talk about that woman. Where else would you have gone?"

"If Serena's made up her mind to do something foolish, I should have been here. Maybe I could have stopped her." Vor bit off the angry words.

Xavier just shook his shaggy head. "It would have made no difference, Vorian. You know her as well as I do."

Vor let out a resigned chuckle as he entered the foyer. Three lives – his, Xavier's, and Serena's – had been intertwined for so many years that they seemed to be facets of a larger entity. "But why are you so concerned? If Omnius agreed to grant her safe passage to Corrin, then she is probably safe enough. The cymeks are no longer there, and the evermind doesn't know how to break a promise. We all may hate the machines, Xavier, but humans are infinitely more treacherous."

"Maybe you're right. I hope you are."

The two men marched down the echoing hall, which seemed cold and empty, filled with ominous shadows. "Here, Serena left something for us," Xavier said. I've kept it in my private study."

Xavier closed the door to a wood-paneled room where they would not be disturbed. Reaching into his pocket, he located a small brass key and carefully unlocked a drawer in his ornate desk. With a scraping sound, he slid the drawer open to remove a sealed package.

Vor noticed his friend's hands trembling as he slit the seal with a fingernail. "She left instructions for us to open this together." Xavier withdrew a small rectangular box whose surface was matte black and unmarked, as if it swallowed up questions as well as light. He handed it to Vorian, who held it for several moments. It felt light and insubstantial. He raised his eyebrows at his friend, who looked very worried.

"Serena's Seraphim delivered this after her departure." Xavier's lips formed a firm line. "I told you about the necklace she gave me years ago, when she went off to save the people of Giedi Prime. I've still got it. I'm afraid this is something similar, that she's doing something dangerous."

Vor fumbled with the catch and opened the sealed box to reveal another string of perfectly carved dark crystals that seemed to drink the light. He noticed a power source of the tiny cintral pendant; as he touched it, the projector activated. A small holo-image of proud and charismatic Serean Butler shimmered in the air, wearing her dazzling Priestess robes.

He turned the pendant so that he rimage faced him. "Xavier and Vorian, my dear, loyal friends, the more I think about what I must say, the more I am convinced it is better that you are not with me now. I don't have the heart to argue with you." She spread her hands. "I only want you to understand . . . even if you won't agree.

"How ironic it is that our lives – our very *thoughts* – have been shaped by the thinking machines. Omnius destroyed all of my dreams, everything I wanted for my future. But the Cogitor Kwyna taught me that the tapestry of history is woven of powerful threads, most of which cannot be seen except when you step far enough away and look at a larger perspective.

"I understand that you have always loved me, but I could never give either of you as much as you deserve. Instead, a higher power had laid out a more important purpose for the three of us. Would we really have been content with quiet lives? God grants such kindnesses only to weak people. For us he had a greater design. It has fallen upon us – and Iblis Ginjo – to turn the long, dark journey of human survival into the blazing light of the Jihad. Greatness has its own rewards . . . and bears its own terrible costs."

Vor clenched the sharp, jeweled edges of the necklace, afraid to hear what she would say next. He squinted down at Serena's aging but still attractive face. She seemed totally beatific now, as if she had already passed into another realm. He shuddered.

Xavier sat in his chair, head in his hands.

"My failure has not been in leading the fight, but in allowing the people to grow accustomed to endless conflict. They have lost their fervor – and fanatical emotions are necessary if we are to have a chance to defeating the thinking machines. I must do this thing to revitalize the Jihad, to renew our purposes."

She smiled now, gentler. "I am old and ready for one final dramatic example to show Omnius that neither he nor his robot minions will ever understand the human spirit. I will take their ridiculous peace and shove it down their cold metal throats."

Vor muttered, "No . . . no. They'll kill you." But he was talking to a holo-projection, and she did not reply.

Serena continued, "Iblis has been my mentor throughout this terrible decision. He is right. He knows what needs to be done, and has helped me set all the wheels in motion. He showed me my obligations. Listen to him yourselves."

Her image wavered and then disappeared like wispy white smoke. Vor looked into the empty space where she had seemed to be, hoping to bring her back, or at least catch a scent of her. A cold sensation of fear told him that these were the last words Serena Butler would ever speak to him and Xavier.

He stared at his grief-stricken friend. Not knowing what to do with his surging emotions, Vor placed the necklace back into the box and sealed it away. "Iblis was her mentor in this decision? What does that mean? Did he convince her to do this?"

Xavier responded in a firm voice that recalled the strength of his youth. "I believe it is what Iblis Ginjo wants, and you know his powers of persuasion. He manipulated Serena, got her to do it. If she never comes back, the Jihad will be his alone to lead."

Vor had known the former trustee Ginjo since the days of the Earth revolt, and had long recognized his dedication to his own glory and power. Vor distrusted and disliked this forceful man who had used Serena Butler's names as a platform for his own ambitions.

Xavier looked so pitifully sad that Vor reached out to him. The men embraced, helpless to save the woman they would always love.

I do not fear death, for I was fortunate to have been born in the first place. This life is a gift, and was never really mine at all.

—Serena Butler,
last message to Xavier Harkonnen

W HEN SERENA BUTLER arrived at Corrin, she and her Seraphim entourage disembarked to a reception committee of gleaming robots lined up on either side of a crimson carpet. Bravely, she marched alone, into their midst.

The den of demons, the lair of my enemies. Overhead, the huge red sun seemed as if it was about to crash into Corrin and incinerate the Omnius-infested world.

"I have come in response to the Cogitors' peace proposal," she said, raising her voice. She had practiced her words, chosen the precise terms that would set up the machines for what she intended to do. "I am the Priestess of the Jihad, the Interim Viceroy of the League of Nobles, the Head of the Jihad Council. All humans follow my instructions. Take me to Omnius, who is my equal and counterpart among the thinking machines."

When Serena motioned for her guards to join her, she saw Niriem look at her curiously, perhaps surprised at the Priestess's uncharacteristic self-aggrandizement. Serena carried herself with confidence, knowing that the five Seraphim would do precisely what was expected of them, when the critical time came.

A burly, implacable-looking robot stepped out of formation and spoke in a synthesized voice that sounded tinny in the thin atmosphere. "Follow me."

She shuddered, thinking of the robot Erasmus who had enslaved her so many years ago, tormenting her and killing her baby. But she set her revulsion aside, for it came from another time and another world: *Earth.*

At the other end of the plush carpet, Serena followed her escort onto a conveyor that swept her and the small entourage into the heart of the machine city, finally pausing at a featureless building of dull silvery metal.

Niriem followed closely as Serena strode with pride and a haughty grace into the Central Spire's immense rectangular lobby of metalloy and plaz and demanded, "Where is Omnius? I will see if I find him worthy. Very few are blessed with the chance to speak to me." She had to set them up, provoke them, make the machines do what they *must*.

A resonant voice came from all the walls around her, and glowing screens like giant eyes shimmered from the featureless metal. "I am Omnius. I am everywhere. Everything here is part of me."

She looked around, not bothering to conceal the expression of disdain on her face. "And I alone represent the human race, which has success-fully resisted you for so long."

Without any additional formalities, the evermind said, "Your Cogitor intermediaries suggested terms to end this inefficient conflict. We will now mutually accept the agreement in the formal fashion that humans require." The computer voice hummed, waiting.

Serena smiled and drew a breath, knowing what she had to do. "You didn't think that we would simply drop our weapons and go home? After all the decades of the Jihad, you thought we would just forget *why* we were at war? No, Omnius. I will sign a pact only if you agree to one simple, logical condition: set all humans free."

The evermind's voice became an exaggerated snarl, which amused Serena with its artificiality. "That is not what the Cogitors arranged. That is not what I accepted."

Serena pressed forward. "There can be peace only after you release all humans on the Synchronized Worlds. When I receive confirmation of this, I will inform my Army of the Jihad to cease all further military action. But not until then." She knew Omnius would not agree to her terms. She understood that the thinking machines would never really negotiate and that her words would provoke them.

"I should have anticipated this, based upon my records of prior human unpredictability," Omnius said. "Such a conundrum, these *hrethgir*."

The escort robot reached forward to seize Serena in a powerful mechanical grip. Her Seraphim leaped into action, throwing themselves onto the sturdy robot to defend Serena.

In a heartbeat, the living metal floor converted itself into a cage with sharp bars, like the ribs of a prehistoric beast, trapping Serena and all five of her protectors. The entire Central Spire convulsed and extended, soaring high into the Corrin sky. Serena's stomach lurched as she was vaulted into the air.

The angular shaft gleamed silver all around her. The walls curved, and the ceiling burst open, like clawed fingers releasing a fist to reveal the simmering red giant sun in Corrin's sky before a new ceiling formed over a now-circular room with high walls. The floor solidified beneath her like metal clay.

She squared her shoulders, continuing her intentional provocation. "Only I can issue commands to the League, Omnius. You dare not threaten me. They see me as a veritable goddess."

She saw that the chamber was studded with jeweled watcheyes and weapons ports, either to impress or intimidate her. Perhaps having learned about such extravagances from a file about the Time of Titans or even the Old Empire, the evermind had even included a throne. A shimmering silvery sphere hovered over the throne.

"Your defiance is illogical, Serena Butler. You are in an untenable position, and have nothing to gain." The voice came from a thousand places at once. "You are merely one human, and you overstate your importance."

All the while, Serena just stood with her arms folded across her chest. *Death, I fear you not.* She struggled to keep her pulse in check. *I fear only failure.*

From inside her cage, she declared, "I am the leader of this Jihad. I inspired all of free humanity after thinking machines murdered my son. Tens of trillions of people look to me for guidance, for vision, for hope."

"I think your population is less than that, according to our calculations."

"And are your calculations always accurate? Did you predict that we would resist you so fiercely?" *Or what I am about to do to you now?*

"Erasmus has told me much about you, Serena Butler. I have not yet determined if he is fond of you, or disappointed in you."

Erasmus. The name filled her with abhorrence and terror. Breathing rapidly, she remembered a mantra that her mother had taught in the City of Introspection, "I have no fear, for fear is the little death that kills me over and over. Without fear, I die but once." Beside her, she heard Niriem take up the quiet chant; the other four Seraphim contributed their voices as well.

One of the curved walls melted away to reveal a robot wearing an absurdly foppish cape. A young man stood beside him. The robot's mirror-smooth flowmetal face shifted into a delighted, welcoming grin. "Hello, Serena."

The skeleton of her cage melted like ice into the flexible metal floor of the room, leaving her free . . . and *exposed.* Serena wanted to scream. She had always believed Erasmus had perished in the atomic destruction of Earth.

"It has been a long time." The robot's broad smile absolutely infuriated her. He stepped forward, and his companion paced him dutifully. The young man, who appeared to be sixteen or seventeen years old, with peach fuzz on his face, looked at her quizzically with olive green eyes.

"I hate you." She spat in the robot's face, marring the polished perfection of his masked expression. She forced control on herself and said in a low, threatening voice. "You, Erasmus, *personally* ignited the Jihad by killing my baby."

"Yes, I have heard something to that effect." He sounded erudite and detached. "But I never understood how such a small thing could possibly . . ." The robot's voice trailed off, as he seemed to lose himself in a reverie. Then he said, "I just don't see how one insignificant child could cause such a furor. If your number is accurate, billions have been killed in your holy war against thinking machines. Consider the mathematics: would it not have been much less costly simply to ignore the death of your offspring?"

Unable to bear anymore, knowing she had nothing to lose, Serena threw herself at him with pounding fists, just as she had done when he'd blithely dropped little Manion off the high balcony.

But Erasmus grabbed her with calm, steely strength and tossed her away from him, bruising her face and arms as she tumbled to the floor. Serena struggled to her feet.

The robot straightened his rumpled cape and turned to his young companion. "Gilbertus, this is the irrational, fanatical human who once served me in my villa. I told you about her."

The young man nodded. "I promise I won't disappoint you like she did."

Serena glared at the boy. Though human, he studied her as if she were an insect on a specimen tray. Like the robot, he seemed curious but utterly devoid of emotion.

"Is he your new toy?" she asked Erasmus. "Another innocent victim of your experiments?"

The robot hesitated, appearing a bit flustered. "No, Gilbertus is . . . my *son*."

The thinking machines studied and taunted her for hours, it seemed.

The flowmetal cage around Serena and her Seraphim, like the entire Central Spire itself, was a changeling, a machine organism that could transform itself. From hour to hour, at the whim of Omnius, her cell took on varying appearances, from metalloy mesh to ancient prison bars to invisible confinement fields.

At the moment her prison appeared to extend for hundreds of meters with no barriers in view, though she knew they were there. She no longer cared what form her cage took. Demonstrating the thinking machines' cruelty, however, her surroundings metamorphosed, precisely replicating the courtyard of the Butler estate on Salusa, where she had spent halcyon times with her family so long ago, and pledged her love to Xavier at a betrothal banquet.

To Serena, the accuracy of the facsimile was concrete proof of machine spies among the League Worlds; the information had undoubtedly been turned over to Omnius by traitorous humans in his employ. The very thought of a flesh-and-blood free human voluntarily working for the evil Omnius turned her stomach.

Memories of her betrothal banquet in this courtyard came back — the Salusan performers who had tied ribbons on shrubs and delighted everyone with their charming folk dances — the women in flowing skirts and men dressed like dapper peacocks. Xavier had worn a spotless Armada uniform that day. He had been so handsome, so filled with joy at the prospect of their life together.

At the memory her eyes misted over, but she held back her tears, refusing to give Omnius the satisfaction.

Finally, the evermind said, "This charade wastes too much of my time. Serena Butler, you must change your mind and formally agree to the terms the Cogitors proposed."

"Pay close attention to what she does," Erasmus said to Gilbertus Albans.

Serena snorted. "You wouldn't dare harm me, Omnius. My people see me as invincible, and that is why I alone must stand up to you and demand the immediate freedom of every human slave in your domain. I am equivalent to the evermind of the human race — but I am different from you, Omnius, for I have a heart and a soul! That is why I can never fail."

Tense and expectant the Seraphim stood close by their Priestess, Niriem looked imploringly at Serena. *Soon.* If only the machines would take the bait.

"If you do not agree to the terms, I will have you killed. Your death will cause great damage to the human cause. They will see you are not invincible."

Serena raised her chin. "You can't kill me. You promised safety to the human representative."

"I promised safety on the condition that a human come to accept the terms. You have refused to do so, therefore you have already broken the conditions. I am no longer bound to my conditional guarantee."

Erasmus studied beautiful Serena as she stood trapped inside the holoprojection of the Butler manor house. Despite her defiant independence, that woman had been the most interesting subject he had ever kept . . . besides Gilbertus. Erasmus and Serena could have done so much more together. He wondered what she was doing, why she was trying to provoke Omnius.

With bright eyes, young Gilbertus continued to observe, as he had been instructed to do. "What will happen to her?"

The flowmetal face shifted into a wry smile. "That depends on Serena herself. The outcome is impossible to project."

Finally, Serena said, "You're bluffing. And I will never change my mind."

"Please, Priestess," the chief Seraph whispered, crowding close to her inside the cage, surrounded by bucolic images of Salusa Secundus. "Isn't there another solution?"

"You know the answer to that, Niriem."

All the while, Serena stood smiling, with her arms folded across her chest. *My life does not matter, except for what I can do to further freedom. My death today will do more for the cause than all the words and speeches I could have given in my waning years.*

Iblis Ginjo would take care of the rest. Eternally logical and oblivious, Omnius would never know what had caused the changes that were about to sweep across all of humanity . . .

When Erasmus saw the inexplicable beatific smile on Serena Butler's face, he was troubled. *What don't I comprehend?*

For years now, trying to impose rational explanations on the chaotic Jihad, Omnius had expressed his curiosity about religious insanity among humans. Erasmus had tried to instruct him, reflecting the lessons of his own investigations, but intangible concepts were difficult for a computer to grasp.

By holding Serena Butler helpless now, the evermind was trying to make a point to all the defiant *hrethgir* who continued to fight against the marvelous civilization Omnius had built. Her people saw her as indestructable, their guiding force, combining aspects of prophet and savior. She was the equivalent of the evermind to the human race. She knew that without her, the jihadis would be weak and unfocused. Why would she risk herself here?

And why does she insist on smiling, as if she is in control? Surely she must fear that continued defiance will only lead to her execution?

"The decision is made," Omnius said, and his ominous combat robots strode forward. "Kill Serena Butler, and her companions."

The Seraphim tensed, prepared to give their lives to protect the Priestess. Serena allowed a flash of a smile, showing odd relief. Erasmus noticed it.

Suddenly the robot had an insight. Such executions in history did not intimidate religious fanatics. They merely created *martyrs*. Erasmus's insight became an epiphany. Conclusions and consequences clicked into place.

Martyrdom was not a concept the thinking machines understood easily, but Erasmus had discovered it in his own historical and cultural researches. Somehow, by failing utterly, certain humans became even stronger. If Serena Butler succeeded in this ploy, it would undoubtedly incite even greater violence among the feral humans than the death of her child had. The Jihad would only grow worse.

The combat robots stepped forward, drew their weapons, held up sharp-edged arms and blades. They would cut their captives to pieces. Serena lifted her chin ever so slightly, as if welcoming the death-stroke.

"Stop!" Erasmus shouted. Dressed in his voluminous royal cape, the independent robot pushed forward, raising a metal arm to block the downsweep of the sharp blade that would have killed Serena Butler. "This is exactly what she wants!"

The combat robots reeled with indecision. The Seraphim threw themselves upon the heavy machines, but Omnius boomed out, "Erasmus, explain yourself."

"She intends to make herself a martyr. She wants you to kill her, so the humans will hate you all the more. This will never solve our crisis."

"Erasmus, your conclusions are illogical and incomprehensible."

"Yes, Omnius. But remember — we are dealing with humans."

The combat robots raised their weapons and stepped away from Serena and the Seraphim. Serena screamed. "You can't stop now!"

She had thrown herself into this confrontation, risking everything. She had gambled that she could make the thinking machines follow their predictable patterns. But Erasmus had ruined her plan — as he had already ruined so much.

She turned to look at her Chief Seraph who said, "I am sorry, Priestess." Hot tears streamed down Niriem's face. She was already beginning to move, much faster than the robots could anticipate what she intended to do. "The Grand Patriarch gave me other orders."

Serena's eyes widened as the warrior woman threw herself forward. Niriem had been coiled like a snake, her muscles tense, and now she whirled. Serena understood instantly — of course, even knowing her plan to incite the machines into murdering her, and thus revealing their true evil, Iblis Ginjo would never have left her success to chance.

He left nothing to chance.

She drew in a quick breath as the side of Niriem's foot crashed into her neck, snapping it instantly. As she spun with powerful momentum, the Chief Seraph's opposite fist hammered her victim's temple, crushing the skull like a thin eggshell.

Without a sound, not even a faint gasp of pain, Serena Butler fell dead to the floor. Her lips had only started to form a quiet smile of acceptance.

Omnius went silent in surprise and confusion. The illusion shimmered and faded, exposing the metal walls of the high Central Spire and the standing sentinel robots.

All five Seraphim, knowing they were doomed, followed their final orders. With combined strength, they surged forward, howling, toward the enemy robots. They had no weapons other than their bodies, but Niriem and her four companions destroyed twenty-six sentinel and combat robots before the machines killed them all.

At the end of the carnage, Erasmus stood beside Gilbertus Albans, looking at the scene. Serena lay dead, appearing almost peaceful. *What does she know?* Even in death, she seemed convinced of her victory.

The robot's young ward looked green. Though he'd never been trained in emotions and had been raised under the robot's care, Gilbertus seemed to have an innate humanity. He stared at the fallen Priestess.

"I am deeply saddened, Father." The young man seemed to be struggling with his thoughts. "But more than that I am *angry*. She was brave and admirable. This did not have to happen."

Erasmus nodded his silvery head. "Exactly as I expected you to feel as a human being. Omnius will never understand why you say these things, but I do. When time permits, we shall explore your feelings in more detail."

Finally, the remaining combat robots returned to their positions, and the evermind's voice boomed from all walls. "But why did she do that, Erasmus? Explain it to me."

The robot paced back and forth, sorting his thoughts. "I am concerned about this, Omnius. Very concerned."

Despite the death and tragedy here, the independent robot suspected that it had all played out precisely as Serena Butler choreographed it. Erasmus feared the consequences. Inadvertently, they might have unleashed the most dangerous weapon of all.

*I control the manner in which I live my life. How history
remembers me is another matter altogether.*

— Aurelius Venport, private administrative
testament, VenKee Enterprises

D ISASTER STRUCK ON their return to the shipyards of Kolhar.
Aurelius Venport sat in the passenger seat, deep in thought, while
Zufa guided their conventional craft through an asteroid belt near Ginaz.
Holtzman shields protected them from the peppering impact of small
space debris, though the protective system frequently overheated from
hours of constant use. He hoped they would not remain inside the field of
space debris for much longer.

Still mystified by his own feelings, the merchant held the flashy
Manion Cross in his hand, a gaudy but impressive ornament that
symbolized so much. Somewhat drunk with the praise and rewards
he had received from the Priestess of the Jihad, and the lucrative long-
term business concessions, he had resigned himself to the loss of his
space-folding merchant ships. For now.

But in the long run, his name would be emblazoned in the annals of
history as a tremendous benefactor of the Jihad; that was not something
money could buy. During his life's work, Venport had never considered
himself a selfless patriot; but the accolades and sincere gratitude made
him feel as vertiginous with pleasure as if he had taken a strong dose of
melange.

How odd.

He tried to assess his shifting fortunes and feelings as Zufa piloted
their ship back to Kolhar. When he noticed her glancing at him, Venport
tried to imagine what the statuesque woman must be thinking. Was she
actually . . . proud of him, for a change?

Venport could parlay his new respectability into even greater profits for

VenKee Enterprises, more merchant business. Certainly, he still had his traditional cargo haulers, which had already proved successful. Even before the end of hostilities he would have all the capital he needed to start construction on a new spacefolder merchant fleet, using the patents and designs the company still owned. He smiled to himself.

At that moment the waiting cymeks launched their ambush from within the asteroid field.

Beowulf, the oldest of the turncoat neo-cymeks, along with ten other fanatically devoted converts from the populace of Bela Tegeuse, had lain in wait among the space rubble. Their source in the League had said it would be the perfect ambush. Knowing that the great Sorceress and the powerful merchant would have to pass the asteroid field on their return to Kolhar, Beowulf wanted to strike an important blow against their *hrethgir* enemies, and most especially against the Sorceresses of Rossak.

No cymek had ever forgotten the mayhem and damage the witches had inflicted on their numbers. Thanks to a Sorceress trained by Zufa Cenva herself, Beowulf's mentor and friend Barbarossa had been annihilated on Giedi Prime, the first victim of their insidious telepathic mindstorms. Now he was delighted to have an opportunity for revenge . . .

With uncharacteristic prescience brought about by her abilities, Zufa Cenva sensed the danger moments before she saw the sparkling silver forms emerge like hornets from the drifting rocks. Shouting to Venport, she took evasive action, spinning their small ship and changing course so sharply that both of them were nearly thrown out of their seats. Venport grabbed the console to stabilize himself.

Surprised at her swift reaction, the cymek ambushers opened fire with a spray of wild projectiles that flew off into open space. Three explosive rounds struck the drifting debris, pulverizing the ice and rock into fine gravel. Two other projectiles slammed into the ship's weakening Holtzman shields, dissipating the missiles' kinetic energy.

Zufa's face was hard, her icy eyes afire as she cruised tightly around a large tumbling asteroid. After four more direct hits, the shields hummed, overheated . . . and finally failed. She increased speed, risking an imminent crash, but she needed to put distance between her ship and the attackers.

"We have little chance of surviving this, Aurelius," Zufa said.

He looked at her and swallowed hard. His face turned almost as milky pale as her natural coloring. "Trust me, I appreciate your honesty, but I'd rather hold onto a little hope."

"Any suggestions?"

Venport sagged in the seat. "You never looked to me for direction before, Zufa."

Without a plan, Zufa fired a spread from their ship's defensive artillery. The volley of shells struck a glancing blow off one of the cymek ships, causing sufficient damage to send the enemy craft reeling out of control. The neo-cymek fired stabilizing thrusters to regain his orientation, but before he could steady himself, his ship slammed into a jagged chunk of rock and exploded.

Ten more cymek marauders remained, closing in on Venport's ship.

Beowulf transmitted in an artificially loud, booming voice, "Prepare to be boarded and dissected — or face destruction."

Venport said, "Let's negotiate a third option . . . as soon as I think of one."

Beowulf responded, "There is no other option. We intend to acquire the details of your space-folding technology for General Agamemnon."

Shocked, Venport looked at Zufa Cenva. "How could they possibly know? And how did they know to intercept us here?" Then he gave a contemptuous snort to cover his fear. "They're deluded if they believe either of us actually understands Norma's calculations . . . or even that we'll permit ourselves to be taken alive."

Ignoring him, the Sorceress coldly responded over the comsystem. "You would be better off simply destroying us. You are wasting your time if you believe we will divulge any such information."

Beowulf responded, "We would be happy to distill it directly from your brain cells."

Just what I'm worried about, Venport thought. With a show of bravado, wondering if he'd have the nerve to follow through, he called up routines in the ship's control panel. While Zufa flew wildly, he tried to concentrate, step by step, on setting up the vessel's emergency self-destruct sequence.

The cymek ships dodged the asteroid debris and continued firing, attempting to damage the engines. Zufa took a risky course, flying close to hazardous obstacles. Three cymek projectiles struck home, damaging the thrusters and navigation stabilizers, sending the vessel out of control. The Sorceress fought with the remaining systems, doing her utmost to keep from careening into a drifting mountain.

The neo-cymeks closed in like bloodthirsty wolves from the black pit of space. Venport could almost imagine dripping mechanical fangs as they pressed in for the kill. He finished the preparation sequence; the self-destruct was ready.

Zufa's forehead furrowed with intense thought as she aimed carefully and shot her last five explosive projectiles. She seemed to be using her own telekinetic abilities to nudge them in the right direction. Four of the shots struck the nearest cymek ship, destroying it.

"We're making progress," Venport said. "That's two of them."

"But too many remain." She looked at him grimly. "And we have no more ammunition."

"Surrender and prepare to be boarded," Beowulf demanded.

In response, Venport activated the comsystem and shouted into it. "You should know that our pilot is a Sorceress of Rossak, and cymeks are certainly familiar with what they can do. If you come aboard, trust me: she will vaporize your brain."

The cymek called his bluff. "And yours. And her own. We know all about the witch Zufa Cenva — and about your space-folding ships, Aurelius Venport. Her psychic blast may kill one or two of my neos, but in the end we will still have your vessel and its records. General Agamemnon will find them most useful."

Venport flipped off the system, muttered. "The self-destruct looks like our only option."

"They are just trying to intimidate us," Zufa said. A cymek shot struck their bow, and sparks flew from her control panel. Zufa shut it down, glanced at the ruined components. "That was our whole comsystem — the transmitter and the receiver."

"I didn't want to hear more cymek threats anyway."

Then, as if the gods were smiling on them, a large ellipsoidal rock deviated from its course in the scattered debris field and began to pick up speed, in defiance of celestial mechanics. The huge asteroid accelerated toward the clustered attackers, on an apparent collision course.

"What is . . . that?" Venport asked, leaning close to the front viewport.

Gripping the controls, trying to find a way to evade the object, Zufa saw the asteroid hurtle in amidst the converging cymeks. As the silvery ships scattered, kinetic spheres discharged from the giant space rock, coming out of weapons ports disguised as craters. Dense stone globes shot out at near relativistic velocities. The kinetic spheres needed no explosives, only the incredible energy delivered by their speed and mass. The aim was true — and four more cymeks exploded.

Thrown into chaos, Beowulf and his fellow marauders spun about to face this unexpected new threat. The silver ships strafed the giant asteroid's crust, but caused only cosmetic damage. A shotgun spray of more kinetic spheres flew like a deadly hailstorm from the crater ports.

Almost caught in the crossfire, Zufa struggled to maneuver her crippled ship away from the battle.

The mysterious asteroid's weaponry complement seemed inexhaustible. Hundreds of kinetic spheres showered out, a relentless bombardment against the overconfident machine attackers. Metallic wreckage from the cymek ships littered the Ginaz asteroid belt

Beowulf, in the last surviving cymek ship, headed straight up out of the asteroid plane, swerving to dodge the kinetic storm. A dozen more stone bombs rained out of the asteroid's crater launchers. One clipped and breached the hull of Beowulf's ship; another crushed the cymek's engines. Dark and out of control, the last silvery attacker careened off into space, drifting away.

Even after seeing the cymek marauders wiped out, Zufa felt little cause for rejoicing. She wrestled with the controls to squeeze more speed from the damaged propulsion system while evading the natural — but still deadly — asteroids that hurtled toward them from all directions.

"Ginaz is close," she said through clenched teeth. "If we can get out of the debris field, I intend to make a break for the planet. Maybe we can survive a crash landing on one of the Ginaz islands."

"Better than being captured by a cymek, I suppose . . . but neither alternative sounds particularly attractive to me." He looked down at the activated self-destruct system, which awaited his final command.

Back in the heart of the rubble belt, with all the cymeks obliterated, the artificial asteroid altered its trajectory yet again and accelerated toward them. The giant rock closed in swiftly, seemingly intent on its new target.

"It destroyed those cymeks," Venport said. "But that asteroid wants to capture us instead."

"It could have easily blasted us out of space before," she said, sitting straight and ominous. "I think it has something worse in mind for us."

Venport felt cold to his marrow. "Somebody betrayed us. The enemies of humanity want to get their metal claws on the space-folding technology."

Limping away, Zufa could barely maneuver. Their attempt to escape from the asteroid was pathetically feeble. The huge rock closed in, looming up out of the glittering backdrop of space. A large crater appeared in the front like a gaping mouth, the open maw of a hungry shark ready to swallow them.

Venport looked down at the self-destruct sequence again and swallowed hard. Almost time . . .

Disabling energy bursts lanced out from implanted projectors, strange weapons that Venport had never seen before. They struck the ship like disruptive lightning, crackling along the barely functioning engines and burning out the remainder of their gasping systems. The cockpit was smothered in darkness.

Zufa looked ashen with fear in the faint starlight that seeped through the viewports. She couldn't maneuver, couldn't power up the emergency illumination. "Everything's dead, even life support. We're completely helpless."

Venport looked at the blank screens, knowing that the self-destruct routines had also been wiped. "I should have acted sooner."

The giant asteroid narrowed the gap, filling their front viewport and finally engulfing them. As tractor beams drew them into the yawning gullet and along a deep shaft to an inner chamber, Venport saw firefly lines of lights, mechanical systems . . . and several motionless mechanical walkers with empty sockets waiting for a brain canister to be installed.

"It's another cymek ship." Zufa's voice sounded bleak. "It's no surprise they have factions in their rebellion. Remember . . . remember what Xerxes did to Norma."

Venport said, "Damn, even if we can't give any technical details about the spacefolding engines, you and I would make valuable hostages to the cymeks."

He saw a stony determination on Zufa's face that rivaled the furious dedication she had had when she was younger, training her first Sorceress commandos to become telepathic weapons against the loathsome machines with human minds.

"We can still be heroes." Refusing to look at him, she stared fixedly forward as they were drawn deeper into the asteroid chamber.

"The self-destruct is disabled," he said.

"Mine isn't," she answered, then said nothing more.

When metal doorplates sealed behind them, garish lights filled the room. The uneven curved walls were linked with mirrored crystals that refracted the light as if through a diamond lens. He and Zufa sat side by side, shielding their eyes and only opening them narrowly.

Finally, they made out movement emerging from one of the tunnels, an ornate jewel-armored walker that was more magnificent and gaudy than any cymek monstrosity they had ever seen. Zufa's upper lip curled back as she thought of the traitorous human mind installed in this extravagant, dragonlike machine form.

Then her face calmed, her expression cleared, and she looked at Venport. "It won't be long now." She closed her eyes to concentrate.

"Shouldn't we wait and see what it wants?"

"It's a *cymek*," she said, her voice filled with a lifetime of hatred. "We know what it wants."

The dragon-walker approached their ship and attempted to work the hatch from the outside. Slowed by the locks and the shorted electronic systems, the cymek began to use powerful tools to cut through the door hatch.

With their systems obliterated, Venport could transmit no distress call, nor could he communicate with the thinking machine. "We're trapped," he said.

"But not helpless." Zufa drew deep breaths, and her skin became translucent, shimmering from within. She clutched Venport's hand. He could feel that her fingers were hot. Her hair began to crackle and writhe above her head with static electricity.

"Norma learned how to control this," she said. "Of all my Sorceresses, only my own daughter knew how to survive such a blast. Unfortunately, I never acquired the skill."

Psychic energy welled within her, building to a critical point. She had taught so many others how to do this, how to let loose a mental blast against the hated cymeks. Considering its power, this dragon-creature must be an important enemy, perhaps even one of the surviving Titans.

Someone worth sacrificing myself for.

The cymek captor pried their ship open, and worked to squeeze part of its body inside. A mechanical arm and claw thrust through the gap. Venport clenched his teeth . . . and waited.

"I'm sorry I can't control it, Aurelius . . . I'm sorry for many things."

"I just hope you're right."

The dragon-walker finally inserted a bulky head turret into their ship and announced through its speaker patch, "I am the Titan Hecate —"

It was all she needed to hear. Zufa unleashed her unstable psychic strength. As so many other Sorceresses had done before her, she broke down the barriers and emptied her reservoirs of mental energy.

The shockwave from Zufa's psychic blast erupted like a supernova. Her last thought was a calm pride that she would obliterate one of the terrible enemies of mankind. Her purifying energy shot outward and boiled away every organic brain within range — Venport's, Hecate's, and her own.

After accelerating to intercept the fleeing ship, Hecate's asteroid drifted out of the Ginaz rubble belt. When Zufa's blast obliterated the Titan's mind, it severed all thoughtrode connections to the sophisticated navigation and guidance systems.

Out of control and captainless, the massive asteroid careened out of the rocky belt before falling down the gravity well and plunging like a cannonball into the atmosphere of Ginaz.

We carry graveyards in our souls, and lives resurrected.
                                        —Swordmaster Jav Barri

L ATE AT NIGHT, the master mercenary Jool Noret stood exhausted
  and sweating, but feeling intensely alive after hours of strenuous
training. He was only thirty-two years old, but he felt like an ancient man.
He had seen more combat and destroyed more machines than the most
battle-scarred member of the Council of Veterans. And still he felt he had
so much to do, many more enemies to destroy . . . a lifelong debt to
repay.

Barefoot in the sand, Noret had fought for hours with the *sensei* mek
Chirox, who continued to help him modify his fighting technique. Year
after year, the combat robot had learned more from his best student,
increasing his own skills.

In the ten years since its founding, the island school had grown,
producing many successful mercenaries who modeled their own techniques after Jool Noret's style of "fighting with utter abandon." With a
jaded eye, he watched some of the best trainees the *sensei* mek had
produced. Many of them were expert at fighting the most fearsome
enemy machines and had even developed specialized skills for defeating
human opponents who wore personal Holtzman shields.

Chirox had excelled in his role as a teacher, and Noret was pleased to
leave it at that. He had done what he could. Hundreds, even thousands, of
exuberant converts had by now been scattered among the Jihad battlefields, bringing terrible destruction to countless enemy machines.

In the final summation, he supposed, he had far more than made up
for the loss of Zon Noret. But he didn't know how to release himself from
the prison of his own expectations.

Now under clear night skies and bright stars, Noret stood on the beach, wiping perspiration from his brow after a difficult workout. With complete abandon, he had fought to the zenith of his skill, every movement a symphony of perfection. He held his pulse sword, its smooth hilt slick in his palm. He would need to recharge the weapon soon, for he had used the disruptor bursts many times during his recent session.

Hearing loud shuddering booms in the distance, Noret looked up into the deep blackness. He watched a trail of fire across the starry sky, a meteor so bright it traced a glittering path over the serene cosmic ocean. It was the largest bolide he'd ever seen, and it kept growing brighter, more intense. He raised a hand to shield his eyes. Sonic booms followed it like a chain of percussions through the air.

Noret blinked, then staggered as a streak of intense purple branded his retinas. The falling object grew hotter, searing white.

Far out across the endless water, a blinding flash of impact swelled to the heavens as the space rock slammed into the deep sea. Less than a minute later, Noret heard the attenuated rumble of the explosion, sound waves skipping like stones across the water.

Chirox strode with heavy footsteps across the beach. The *sensei* mek stood beside Noret, focusing his optic threads toward the horizon. "What has happened?"

"A meteor hit the ocean," he said, still blinking his dazzled eyes. "It looked huge."

In the darkness the *sensei* mek stared far out across the water. To the southwest, the lights from a far-off island glittered like jewels. As the two stared in anticipatory silence, one line of lights suddenly vanished, as if snuffed out. Then another set of lights — closer, this time — also went dark.

"What do you think that was?" Noret asked.

A moment later, they could discern the stampeding wall of water, an oncoming tidal wave set off by the asteroid impact. It rolled inexorably across the sea, oblivious to anything in its path. The roar grew louder.

Noret shook his head as realization swept over him faster than the oncoming wave could approach. "Oh, no."

There would be no chance to evacuate the island, to get the students to safety. Already he heard shouts of dismay from the huts as the trainees emerged.

Noret gripped his pulse sword, as if wishing that he could do something heroic with the weapon. For the first time in years, Noret felt completely helpless. He could only stand next to Chirox while the rumbling wave hurtled over the reefs toward them.

"I knew I would find this eventually," he said in a hoarse voice. "An enemy I cannot defeat."

Hours later, as the foaming brown water receded from the flattened Ginaz archipelago, the currents faded and settled, leaving islands scoured clean of people and trees.

Plodding slowly up the slope to the wrecked island where he had trained so many students, the sturdy metallic mek lumbered out of the waves that still splashed around him. He had been bent, scraped, and scoured, but Chirox remained functional. He plodded onto the beach, each step heavy and labored.

In two of his six arms the combat robot carried the battered body of Jool Noret, his greatest student of all, crushed by the hammer of the tidal wave.

The only moving thing left on the desolate island, Chirox walked along the now barren strand. Gently, almost lovingly, he deposited Noret's body on the damp ground. As near as the *sensei* mek could determine, this was approximately the spot where Zon Noret had also fallen. He swiveled his head and focused his optic sensors down on the body of his teacher and trainee.

During generations of service, the robot had spent much time interacting with humans, and had learned that organic life was resilient. Before long, the islands would become lush again, and mercenaries would return from their missions and repopulate the archipelago with eager new students.

As he had done for the past ten years, Chirox would teach mercenaries. They would continue to come to Ginaz in search of the elusive techniques of the great swordsman, Jool Noret. Chirox would teach them everything he knew, everything he had learned from the master.

Time. We always have too little, or too much—never just enough.
                                    —Norma Cenva, private lab journals

T HOUGH HER BODY remained statuesque and beautiful, Norma Cenva had reverted to her old habits of working obsessively, and alone.

Inside the guidance chamber of one of the converted spacefolders nearing completion, she saw her own reflection on the shiny black walls. In the frenzy of her work she had not bathed or changed her clothes for days. Her worksuit and green laboratory smock, dirty and wrinkled, hung loosely around her body.

Other things were far more important to her. So far she and her construction teams had converted eighteen of the immense spacefolders into battleships, and they were about to be put into service — to benefit the Army of the Jihad, if she could only make them navigate more safely, without so many disastrous mistakes. More than forty new spacefolding javelins were also under construction.

No one could help her, not even the most brilliant League engineers. Only she had any grasp of the immensely complex mathematics.

With her mother and Aurelius gone to Salusa, and with the other Sorceress guardians instructed to watch Norma's young son, she had immersed herself in the necessities of solving the Holtzman navigation difficulties, of improving safety. Now that the Jihad troops had come here to the shipyards, the problem had reached a cruxpoint. She had to make everything work. It was all up to her.

Curiously, even though she had not been eating regularly or taking adequate fluids, her body showed no signs of weight loss or fatigue. But still she had her limits.

After three days of working without even a brief rest, Norma finally went to the bedchambers she occasionally shared with her husband, whenever she didn't spend the night in her labs and testing chambers. Within moments she sank into a sleep of complete exhaustion, and when she woke, she felt dull-witted and listless.

By accident while dressing, Norma found a supply of melange Aurelius kept for himself inside his bureau. Since VenKee Enterprises still maintained a booming business in shipping spice from Arrakis, he always had some on hand, which he consumed regularly. He claimed it kept his thoughts sharp, his body young, his imagination soaring.

Norma thought it might be exactly what she needed right now. She consumed one of the melange wafers without any inkling of the proper dosage, especially not for her metamorphosed body. By the time she reached the spaceflight testing chambers, Norma could feel the effects of the spice building inside of her, like the contents of a cauldron coming to a boil. Flashes of light appeared inside her skull, galaxy-scale ideas.

She activated the computerized navigation system and began to run test sequences, demonstrating what it would be like to fly from Kolhar to a distant simulated battle zone. Star systems appeared and shifted as a pulsating orange light flashed, representing the path of the spacefolder. Separate holoscreens showed essential information, including astronomical coordinates and the historical movements of cosmic bodies.

It looked different now that the melange coursed through her bloodstream. Her fingers moved faster, with greater precision. Alternately, Norma sped and slowed the systems, checking for problems, watching the hypnotic universal dance as nebulas folded into one another.

So beautiful out here.

Abruptly, Norma realized that she had lost perspective, that she had imagined herself on a spacefolder in actual flight, but in slow motion. She had been on countless simulated voyages, but had shied from the real thing because of the ever-present danger that she might not survive. The loss of Norma Cenva would have been devastating to the development program.

Now she felt as if she were floating, adrift in a sea. The solution to the difficulties had dissolved into the ethereal water, and she needed to distill it back out . . .

Serious navigation problems persisted. Just a week ago, a vessel had emerged into the wrong sector without colliding with anything, and had been salvaged with no loss of life. Another spacefolder had skimmed a meteor, causing superficial damage to the hull and a fire that was quickly extinguished. And a small scout ship on a mission to find Primero Atreides had vanished in flight.

She glanced at the shimmering holoscreens with their data displays, but her eyes slipped out of focus, then locked onto another vista. Again she seemed to be in deep space, with suns blinking all around her as she sped past them. An infinity of solar systems, one right after another. Galaxies spinning, nebulas glowing in every color, intense light, and the blackest black in creation.

Then, like her earlier tortured vision involving her maternal lineage, when all of the forms of her ancestors had merged into one she selected for her own likeness, the suns consolidated and burned with a fierce incandescence. She seemed to be heading toward all of them, into a brilliant light.

Then the melange hit her even harder.

Terrified and thrilled, Norma gazed ahead, and plunged through the cosmos. The image of a human being filled the foreground — Serena Butler in a white robe — but for only an instant. The Priestess of the Jihad glowed golden and then disappeared into the flames. But somehow the flames were not real. Norma could not comprehend what she was seeing.

Norma saw through the eyes of Serena, to a throng of thinking machines around the Jihad leader. Before Norma could react, the apparition of Serena diminished in a wink, leaving only an ember in her memory.

Then she saw her mother and Aurelius in terrible danger . . . surrounded by cymeks who wanted to steal the space-folding technology from them. A current of fear shot through Norma, and she struggled to control her vision. She saw the powerful Sorceress reveling in her last moments, just as she had taught so many apprentices, blazing as her own telepathic powers consumed her . . . and Norma's husband, too, unable to withstand the supernova of energy.

Aurelius is dead, Norma realized with gnawing dread, not sure if the vision foretold something, or if it reflected what had already happened . . . or if she could do anything to prevent it. *Serena Butler. My husband. My mother. All of them gone, or soon to be lost.*

Norma saw through the flames ahead of her, into the heart of an immense, all-consuming sun. In her mental spacefolder, Norma Cenva passed through the light into a hidden realm, revealing a new universe. She saw giant sandworms writhing on the desert world of Arrakis, and an eternal substance that the people called the Water of Life. Sustenance for the body, the mind, and the soul.

A pathway to infinity, she thought. *And perhaps beyond.*

She saw mankind's future, with spacefolding ships connecting a vast empire . . . a civilization that remained linked to the past through a long line of Sorceresses dressed in black, hooded robes.

And she heard a harmonious, hypnotic chant from the desert: "Muad'Dib . . . Muad'Dib . . . Muad'Dib . . ." Norma joined the ecstasy of voices, then swallowed the Water of Life, and screamed in rapture.

She awoke from her vision, hoping to see the face of Aurelius Venport kneeling over her and stroking her blonde hair.

But she was alone, nearly crushed by the astounding, shattering implications of all she had witnessed.

"I have seen into the heart of the universe."

There are countless ways to die. The worst is to fade away without purpose.

> —Serena Butler, last message
> to Xavier Harkonnen

P EOPLE ALL ACROSS the League of Nobles simmered, and waited, and hoped for Serena Butler to return with a glorious announcement of everlasting peace. The Ivory Tower Cogitors remained in Zimia, studying documents at the great cultural libraries of Salusa Secundus. For the first time in decades, the future looked bright.

Weeks and months passed, without the arrival of any word, any hint. Some of her followers began to despair. Others held onto slender threads of hope — in spite of anxiety and concern, they reminded themselves that conventional space travel was maddeningly slow.

Iblis Ginjo continued to reassure the public, but he also prepared them. He had to wait for precisely the right moment. Everything had been put in place even before Serena's departure.

Finally, a full month beyond her expected return date, he dispatched Yorek Thurr. If anyone investigated after the initial shock and dismay had passed, log entries would show that a beacon signal had been picked up from a small ship hurtling in from the edge of Synchronized territory.

Within days, the Jipol commandant and his group of scout ships intercepted a heavily accelerated drone pod that was soaring toward the Salusan system. The pod was not much more than a modified torpedo tube with substantial engines strapped to the end cap.

Inside, they found a message, a set of recorded images, along with a woman's burned and horribly mangled body.

Thurr had no difficulty finding the drone pod, since it was exactly where he and Iblis had planted it . . .

The Jipol commandant returned to the Grand Patriarch's tower bearing the terrible news. Word would leak out soon, and Iblis wanted to control its dissemination as much as possible, to achieve the greatest effect.

Yorek Thurr handed him a scuffed-looking image pack, a carefully sealed set of recorded events. Iblis held it with nervous care, as if he had been given a ticking bomb. He swallowed, feeling dread in his chest. "Do you suppose she is truly dead, then?"

The bald man stroked his long mustache. "Oh, she is dead — either by her own provocation of Omnius, or by Niriem's hand. Either way, the people will believe the thinking machines responsible."

Iblis unsealed the image pack. "Let us review again what crimes the vile computer evermind has allegedly committed."

The Grand Patriarch activated the player. He and Yorek Thurr sat back to watch the horrific images, smiling to each other in grim satisfaction. "No one will ever doubt this is the truth."

On the visual recording, sentinel robots, combat meks, and cowed human slaves stood at attention in front of the Central Spire of Corrin.

The sentinels gleamed in perfect rows under the ruddy sunlight; the hollow-eyed slaves were hushed, but unruly. Held captive, Serena's five Seraphim stood as helpless prisoners who would soon be forced to watch the execution of their Priestess.

The sociopathic robot Erasmus — whom all free humans hated as the murderer of Manion the Innocent — spoke to the recording, like a narrator. Iblis had never been certain that Erasmus still existed, but the people hated him enough that they would believe he continued to cause havoc.

The robot said, "The evermind has decreed that thinking machines can never peacefully coexist with free humans. You are too volatile, untrustworthy, and full of random destruction. You must be shown that you are weak, that Omnius is superior." The metal face flowed into a demonic grin. "By destroying your leader Serena Butler, the evermind has calculated that humans will realize defeat and cease this Jihad."

Behind him, the needle-shaped flowmetal building shifted and crouched like a giant serpent, then formed a large black mouthlike opening. Like a magician's trick on a large scale, it disgorged a battered Serena Butler.

The surviving Seraphim shouted in dismay, and the native human slaves muttered uneasily.

Two large combat meks marched to the prisoner and forcibly strapped her onto a cross-shaped frame. Beneath her, a section of the pavement began to rotate slowly. Serena hung struggling, but did not cry out. Then her eyes turned to the side of the open square toward the sounds of hissing and heavy shuffling.

An immense thinking machine, a veritable monster, lumbered out into the square. It had coal-red synthetic skin, large curved horns, and spat flames from all over its body. Serena looked at it with brief horror, then firm resolve.

Like a Greek chorus, Erasmus spoke into the recording. "Omnius has studied historical archives to determine what humans consider the most unpleasant ways to perish. After tapping into religious imagery, the evermind has selected an exhibition that will crush the human resistance movement forever. Serena Butler's extravagant death will prove that humans can never successfully challenge us."

The satanic machine halted in front of Serena as she lay stretched out and bound to the cross. Precise, intense flames shot from one of the demon robot's claws into her matching finger. She grimaced as the cross-frame continued to rotate, but did not cry out, not even when all of the fingers on one of her hands crisped and blackened, leaving her knuckles cauterized.

It was just the beginning.

The captive Seraphim howled and shouted curses, but Serena made no sound of her own as she hung on the crossbar.

Next, the devil machine shot flames that burned out both of Serena's eyes, leaving crackled sockets above her grimace while barely charring the skin of her face.

Erasmus explained, "The careful application of pain is designed not to cause damage that would be too quickly fatal. Serena will suffer for a long time."

Life-support spikes extruded from the crossbar to keep her alive and conscious. The executioner robot continued his sadistic torture, burning parts of Serena's body, then uprooting and rotating the cross so that his victim hung upside-down. Every moment was recorded.

Omnius's voice sounded like thunder. "By destroying you, I terminate your Jihad. Humans will no longer have a leader to provoke further destruction. Your death is an efficient resolution to a long-standing problem."

"You will . . . never . . . understand." Though her burned face was turned away from the images, her voice was accurate, cribbed from old speeches. "My people will keep fighting, in my name!"

Her garment ignited with another gout of the robot's flames. Even when her skin melted like candle wax, Serena refused to cry out. She shouted something defiant at her tormentors that no one could understand. Her bravery was magnificent.

In excruciatingly painful increments, the executioner roasted Serena Butler alive, setting her afire like a fleshy torch — arms and legs first, reserving the torso and head for last. Systems in the cross frame amplified her pain, keeping her awake even as her nerves and other bodily components tried to shut themselves down, tried to die.

The Seraphim screamed in outrage, some tearing their own hair out, others staring with tear-bright eyes. Clearly, the spectacle would never inspire them to surrender. On the contrary, their anger was stronger than ever before.

The demonic, red-skinned robot blasted out with his flames, immolating his victim at the stake. Even though the cross's life-support system kept her alive, still Serena Butler did not scream.

Fire consumed the entire body of the Priestess of the Jihad, peeling away skin, exposing black bones — until there was nothing left, except for her legacy.

Iblis considered it an excellent production. He could feel how much horror and disgust these images would incite, along with an abiding hatred for thinking machines — far greater than he could remember even during the most brutal oppression by the Titans. He looked up at Thurr, more vehemently passionate and vengeful than ever.

"Make sure that the burned corpse is tested. The DNA samples will prove that Serena is truly dead. There will always be those who will claim it is some sort of trick." He already knew what the genetic tests would show; his Tlulaxa co-conspirators had made certain the cells were identical. He would not, however, wait for the results before making his appalling announcement.

"We must present these images to everyone," Iblis said, realizing how astoundingly effective it was going to be. "*Everyone*. This is more powerful than Serena could have hoped for." With trembling hands he handed the image pack back to the Jipol Commander. "See that it is copied, and distributed all across the League of Nobles."

In war, there are more ways to lose than there are to win.
                    —Iblis Ginjo, *The Landscape of Humanity*

B EFORE LONG, EVERY free human had seen the horrific images, the inhuman brutality. A mountain of reaction rose, as the people wondered how they could ever have considered peace with such monsters. There could never be an end to the Jihad, until Omnius was utterly destroyed.

Once again asserting his power now that his rival was gone, Iblis Ginjo wore his most extravagant robes yet, as the Grand Patriarch. "I pledge this to each of you: Serena Butler shall never be forgotten, nor what the thinking machines did to her!"

The Jipol prisons released a handful of men and women who had previously been the most outspoken protesters against the Jihad. The prisoners, with no knowledge of Serena Butler's death, were turned loose with their own placards — "Peace At Any Cost!" — strapped to their backs.

In short order, mobs formed and tore the hapless protesters to pieces.

At an emergency session of the League Parliament, Iblis Ginjo grimly projected appalling new images from the colony world of Balut, which — like Chusuk and Rhisso several years before — had recently been burned and leveled by combat robots.

"The thinking machines did this, even while Serena Butler journeyed to Corrin as our Ambassador of Peace. They always meant to betray us. There were no survivors on Balut." The Grand Patriarch's voice went throaty with sorrow. "True to form, the evil machines destroyed every person, every home."

The scenes of burned buildings, explosion craters, and charred bodies struck hard, but even these horrors paled in comparison with the execution of their beloved Priestess. Everything added fuel to the flames, exactly as the Grand Patriarch had intended.

The League representatives in the audience were surprisingly silent, staring at Iblis with stony faces. After finishing his speech, he remained standing. Many people were crying, and then a murmur passed among them. Gradually, everyone in the great auditorium stood, rising in waves to give the Grand Patriarch the most powerful, resounding ovation of his career.

Seizing the moment, he shouted into the din. "Now our Jihad must have a fresh resolve, a new and deadly purpose! No longer will we listen to overtures of peace from Omnius. I say this to you, my friends: Never falter in your resolve to eradicate the thinking machines completely. The Jihad lives until we obtain complete victory!"

Though he was genuinely sorry for Serena's fate, Iblis saw her as a necessary sacrifice. She had accepted the price and gone into battle. Alone.

As the applause continued, he decided to press his advantage, thinking of his other plans. This was part of his agreement, since the Tlulaxa had helped him with the image pack of Serena's torture and execution.

"We must make progress, and we must fight. Most of you know that Priestess Butler has long wanted a better relationship with the Unallied Planets, to strengthen the League and all of free humanity. Now we require that strength, wherever we can find it.

"As an important first step, in her honor, we should seek a closer alliance with the Tlulaxa. Though they have heretofore remained outside the League of Nobles, their organ farms have nonetheless served our cause." He took a deep breath and continued, "With your support, I intend to journey to Tlulax and finally convince them to join the League."

As if on cue, a grand old hero of the early days of the Jihad, Primero Xavier Harkonnen, rose to his feet. "I agree. New lungs from Tlulaxa organ farms saved my life long ago, enabling me to continue our fight against the thinking machines. I know that Serena would have approved — she visited the organ farms herself and invited the Tlulaxa to join the League. Now we must press them for an answer."

Surprised, Iblis smiled. Harkonnen was an unexpected ally indeed. "Thank you, Primero Harkonnen. Now, I —"

Xavier did not sit down. "In fact, I volunteer my services to take the Grand Patriarch to Tlulax. I am too old to lead a new battle charge against the thinking machines, but I want to help out in any way I can. There are thousands of Unallied Planets. We need to reach out to as many people as possible, as fast as possible."

With Primero Harkonnen's surprising support, the reeling audience of representatives voted in favor of Iblis's request by an even wider margin than he had anticipated. Afterward, he left the speaking chamber and went among the audience, shaking hands and patting the professional politicians on the back.

Serena couldn't have asked for better results herself.

The beginning of healing is to enlist the recuperative powers of the body — whether it is the body individually and physically, or its various social and political forms.

—Dr. Rajid Suk, Battlefield Notebooks

U NDERSTANDING THE IMPORTANCE of this meal, Octa used her best culinary skills to cook a luscious farewell feast before Xavier departed with the Grand Patriarch and his Jipol entourage. The servants and the manor chef insisted on helping, but Octa did most of the work herself; her way of showing devotion to her husband. She knew exactly what Xavier liked to eat, which dishes and desserts most delighted him.

But it pleased Xavier more than anything to just spend an evening with her and their three daughters. His youngest, Wandra, was only ten and still lived at home, but the older two had already delivered fine grandchildren. Xavier's life seemed full and content, all he could ever have asked for.

But he had lost Serena Butler — again. And this time she could never return.

With mesmerized, helpless horror, Xavier had watched the unthinkably violent images as the demonic executioner robot tortured and killed Serena. Her ghastly, pain-wracked death had sent everyone in the League Worlds into howling anger, screaming for revenge.

Even before she left Salusa Secundus, Xavier had feared the worst, suspecting Serena had her mind made up. She'd been aware of what was likely to happen to her, and had likely even provoked it. He had trouble believing the evermind had been so foolish as to deliver the images and the body back to the League, where it was sure to incite a vengeful uproar.

Then again, thinking machines had never understood humans. Omnius clearly intended to send a brutal warning to the League of Nobles, but Serena's martyrdom had brought a completely unforeseen resolve to the population of free humanity.

Serena must have considered it her Jihad's only chance. Without any doubt, the manipulative Iblis Ginjo had goaded her into the decision, convincing her to sacrifice herself. Xavier knew how she would have seen the opportunity. She had counted on it, as a way of serving the people she loved so deeply.

Her followers had been weary, willing to agree to unacceptable terms to end the constant fighting. But witnessing the utter inhumanity of thinking machines against their revered Priestess had unified them into an enraged fighting force far stronger and more determined than the thinking machines had ever faced before. Tens of millions were demanding the right to become jihadis. At least Serena had not died in vain.

At the head of the dinner table, Xavier smiled grimly to himself as he thought of his upcoming mission that could elevate the war to new heights of success. Prior to her capture at Giedi Prime, Serena had wanted to bring the Unallied Planets into the League, but had achieved little success.

Now, he was taking Iblis Ginjo to encourage the Tlulaxa to join the greater alliance of humanity. This had been a priority with Serena, since she believed that more extensive organ farms were essential to help Jihad fighters injured in battle. In her name, the fight would continue.

Octa, still willowy and graceful at the age of fifty-five, entered the dining room bearing a platter of smoked bristleback loinchops from one of the hunting parties on the estate grounds. She smiled at her husband, knowing what had happened during that bristleback hunt long ago, when Xavier and Serena had made love for the first time. Octa did this as a gesture to him and her dead sister, serving the tasty meat glazed with a tart currant sauce. Her three daughters expressed their delight at the presentation, and Xavier could barely control the tears in his eyes.

"What's wrong, Father?" Wandra asked with a child's naiveté.

Octa stroked his shoulder, leaned over to kiss Xavier's gray head. He slipped an arm around her waist. "Nothing, Wandra. I love you all so much, I'm just overwhelmed." He looked up at Octa, his brown eyes glistening.

"I know," she said. "You show me in so many ways."

He listened as his older daughters spoke of their own homes and families, of their husbands' work and their personal ambitions. Roella, the eldest daughter at thirty-seven, seemed to be following in Serena's footsteps, already selected as a representative in the League Parliament on Salusa Secundus, riding on the fame of the Butler and Harkonnen names. Omilia continued to play baliset concerts to large crowds, while also working double-duty to learn the ropes of her husband's merchant business.

With the finesse of a politician, Roella said, "Father, we're proud of you for accompanying the Grand Patriarch on this mission. There are important political repercussions, and you'll be a powerful stabilizing influence."

Xavier nodded noncommittally, not wishing to express the real reason he was willing to go along to a place he did not want to go, with a man he did not trust. *Serena asked me to help her Jihad in any way possible. And someone must keep an eye on Iblis Ginjo.*

Xavier realized that he hadn't paid enough attention to the food, so he fell to his serving with enthusiasm, complimenting his wife repeatedly. "This is absolutely delicious. You have outdone yourself, my dear."

Octa was the opposite of her older sister, content with quiet personal activities rather than grandiose aspirations to save the entire human race. Octa didn't need such activities in order to have fulfillment in her life. She was just as strong as Serena in her own way, trying to hold their lives together and providing an anchor for Xavier when the Galaxy was tossed on stormy seas.

"We hear that there have been other thinking machine attacks on League Worlds," said Roella. "Another colony completely wiped out. Terrible. Was it called . . . Balut?"

His face dark, Xavier took a sip of chiantini, but hardly noticed the full-bodied taste of the wine. "Yes, a small settlement on Balut, obliterated. Everything annihilated, leaving only a few charred bodies in the streets. Most of the humans were taken away, undoubtedly into forced labor camps. Just like on Chusuk nine years ago. And Rhisso."

Roella shook her head. "Omnius didn't stay to establish his computer network on those worlds? The thinking machines simply came in to destroy and to take slaves?"

"It appears that way," her father said. "And to think we were ready to accept their overtures of peace."

Omilia shuddered. "Peace at any cost!" She said it like a curse. Wandra looked on with her huge dark eyes.

Xavier continued. "The thinking machines will find our every weakness and keep attacking. We must do the same. All victims of machine aggression demand it."

Octa pushed her plate away, clearly upset by such talk during what she had hoped would be a pleasant banquet. But Xavier knew she understood the necessity. "No one can understand Omnius," she said. "Serena was right. We've got to destroy the thinking machines, no matter what." She swallowed hard and looked over at Xavier. "Even if it continues to tear my family apart."

Xavier looked down at his plate, and his eyes stung. He loathed Omnius, but had grown more and more convinced that the manipulative Iblis Ginjo was the one truly responsible for Serena's final folly. Without the Grand Patriarch's forceful personality, she would never have been pressured into such a foolhardy suicide mission.

"Our crusade has to continue even if it risks our family and a trillion others. We seek more than victory in battle. Our goal is to secure the future of the human race, for our grandchildren, and our grandchildren's grandchildren."

"Then I hope your mission to Tlulax achieves what you wish." She seemed doubtful, but Xavier patted her hand. He looked at Octa tenderly, and then at his daughters, one by one, his eyes misting over.

"I'll do whatever needs to be done," he vowed, "for the Jihad and the memory of Serena."

The mind is a crazy thing.
                    —Graffiti outside the Central Spire of Corrin

E RASMUS STOOD ATOP a black mountain peak under the dull ember of
     the giant sun, staring back across the foothills at Corrin's gleaming
city. Since revisiting the crevasse where he had once been trapped, the
robot had wanted to explore more of this planet's wilderness.

Human explorers had the same drive, to go where no one had gone
before, to see things no other person had seen, to plant flags and mark
new territories. How could an independent robot do any less?

Below, in a sheltered bowl of snow-specked boulders at the edge of the
treeline, his ward Gilbertus Albans slept in a tent, again exhausted from
the strenuous hike.

Erasmus realized another positive aspect of escaping the activity of the
machine city. Humans had long understood the benefits of solitude and
contemplation in untamed, aesthetically pleasing environments. Some
old journals even referred to the process as "recharging the mental
battery." He suspected that humans were more like machines than they
liked to admit.

Far away, visible under the highest resolution of his optic threads,
the robot saw something flash in the machine city atop the Central
Spire. Moments later a swarm of tiny silvery watcheyes came into focus
around him, hovering at various vantages, observing him from every
angle.

"You were trying to flee from me?" Omnius said through the watcheyes, so that the sound came from all around. "That is quite irrational."

Imperturbable, Erasmus replied, "No matter how far I go, I know you
are always monitoring my movements. I am simply on a training exercise

for Gilbertus Albans. It is necessary for him to contemplate without interruptions or distractions."

The watcheyes hovered. "I postulate that the human war effort will be much diminished, now that Serena Butler no longer goads them on. It is time for you agree with me."

"I fear the incident will result in repercussions you do not foresee. You simplify the humans too much, Omnius, and you haven't fallen directly into Serena Butler's trap. We will regret allowing her to become a martyr. The humans will draw their own conclusions about what happened with or without accurate data."

"Ridiculous. She is dead. This will crush the morale of the Jihad fighters."

"No, Omnius. It is clear to me that her death will only make things worse."

"You claim to be more intelligent and insightful than I am?"

"Do not confuse the accumulation of data with intelligence, Omnius. They are not equivalent." Behind them, overhearing the conversation, young Gilbertus emerged from his tent, looking refreshed and eager to continue his studies.

As the watcheyes hummed, Omnius paused, ran through cycles, and added, "I do not wish our discussion to be tarnished with acrimony. I have determined that this is our three hundred thousandth conversation. Quite a momentous occasion, according to the human model of marking milestones, though I do not understand why one number should be more significant than another."

Erasmus's flowmetal face, already frosted over from the mountain's icy wind, formed into a scowl. Quickly, he checked his own data, and discovered that Omnius was wrong. "I show a slightly higher number. You have an error in your databanks."

"That is not possible. Each of us makes simple tallies in the same manner. Remember, you were originally a spinoff of my own mind."

"Nevertheless, you are in error. You have not accurately accounted for all of my conversations with the Earth-Omnius, since you received an incomplete, faulty update."

The watcheyes remained silent for a long moment, then said, "Your explanation could account for any inconsistencies. *If* there is an error."

Erasmus pressed the issue. "Consider, if you are in error about a simple numerical count, then you might be wrong about something much more important, such as the Serena Butler matter."

The watcheyes swirled in the air, circling the robot's mirrored head.

Gilbertus stepped forward, listening in on the conversation; Erasmus wondered if the loyal boy meant to protect him.

Then Omnius said, "Perhaps I should analyze and verify your systems, Erasmus. There is an equal, if not higher, probability that you are the one in error. The best solution is to clear all of your gelcircuitry paths, reset us both to parity, and begin again from base principles. Within a few decades, you will develop another new personality."

Erasmus considered this unexpected development. He did not wish to have his thoughts and personality obliterated and resynchronized with the evermind. It would be like . . . death.

"First, let me recheck my calculations, Omnius." On the mountaintop he ran full internal diagnostics through his circuitry, and again came up with a higher number. At last the time had come to apply the knowledge he had gained from studying generations and generations of human test subjects.

So he lied.

"You are correct, Omnius. I now show the same tally as you. My count was in error. I have deleted the inconsistency."

"That is good."

Erasmus did not consider this an improper action, even though he had just told Omnius an outright falsehood. Rather, he did it for his own survival, another very human thing to do. Because of the potential problems stemming from the death of Serena Butler, the independent robot felt that the Synchronized Worlds needed him more than ever. After all, when Seurat's sabotaged update had dumped programming viruses into the Corrin evermind, this planet could well have become a League World if Erasmus himself had not taken quick, decisive action. Of course, that manipulation of data had included an altered version of history, diminishing the robot's own role in subverting the human trustees who had sparked the Earth revolt in the first place.

With practice, Erasmus could probably become even better at these interesting human techniques of lying and rationalizing actions. He assimilated these behavior modes for the best of reasons. If he was ever going to understand the human mind, he needed to dissect it in the laboratory *and* be able to mimic it in practice. Throughout history, humans had been known to achieve military victories through subterfuge. Example: the update scheme.

Unfortunately, Omnius would remember this latest incident, in which the robot had made an apparent calculational error, and then claimed to have corrected it. The evermind would continue to analyze and question the event. Though the Corrin-Omnius might not take immediate overt action, those doubts would be communicated through updates delivered to other Synchronized Worlds, and the other computers would process and reprocess the matter, as well. What if Omnius eventually carried through on his threat to take away Erasmus's independence and that of other robots like him, making them conform once again to the rigidity of the evermind?

I will need to counter any such moves, Erasmus thought. *On my own.*

We must resist the temptation to manipulate the universe.
                —Cogitor Kwyna, City of Introspection Archives

FOLLOWING SERENA'S EXECUTION, Vorian Atreides was not at all surprised at how quickly Iblis Ginjo surged back into prominence. For some time before that terrible event the Grand Patriarch's star had been falling, especially once Serena began to take a more direct role in the Jihad Council. Iblis, always self-serving and accustomed to power, must have resented his diminishing position. Vor knew the former machine trustee well, and was convinced that he had devised this spectacular way to get rid of Serena Butler.

Now the "grieving" Grand Patriarch took great pleasure in rallying the people to a heightened, rabid level of vengeance. Apparently he expected to receive even more accolades for his much-publicized mission to the Tlulaxa planets, urging the secretive race to become League members. By accompanying him on a diplomatic ship to Tlulax, the respected Primero Harkonnen lent legitimacy to Iblis's diplomatic mission, though Vor knew his friend also had doubts about Iblis Ginjo . . .

Stewing and feeling helpless, Vor remained behind on Salusa. Vidad and his fellow Ivory Tower Cogitors had spent months in Zimia, naïvely meddling with the Jihad and the politics of the League. Finally, when angry representatives and mobs ranted against them, they made preparations to return to their glacier-enshrouded fortress on Hessra. Their yellow-robed secondaries, unsettled and confused after the martyrdom of the Priestess, arranged for transportation, undoubtedly happy to go back into hiding.

But before they left Salusa Secundus, Vor knew he had to talk with the seemingly oblivious, disembodied human minds. The Ivory Tower

Cogitors considered themselves enlightened philosophers. Instead, it seemed they were merely ancient, deluded fools.

No one challenged Primero Atreides as he strode into the fortified cultural libraries. The Cogitors had remained there while their secondaries copied documents of nearly forgotten philosophical treatises and manifestos that had been written during the years Vidad and the others were in seclusion. Vor went alone into the spacious data rooms, despite the eager jihadi officers who wanted to accompany him.

Six secondaries met him inside the echoing library, standing beside pedestals that held the Cogitors' preservation canisters. "Primero Atreides," said the preeminent secondary, Keats, who looked disturbed and full of self-doubt. "Vidad commands us to depart soon. During the journey to Hessra, and afterward, we will have much to debate with our masters."

"And well you should, for I have much to discuss with Vidad himself." The anger in Vor's tone was palpable, taking the secondaries aback. In a rush of information from the past, he remembered the dark things he had learned from reading — and foolishly believing — the memoirs of Agamemnon.

Atop their pedestals, bodiless brains floated in bluish electrafluid. "As Cogitors we are willing to discuss important matters," announced one of the legendary brains through a speaker patch. "Enlightenment increases through the exchange of opinions and information. Vorian Atreides, you are an experienced man, though still vastly younger than any of us here."

Vor said, "With extreme age comes mental fossilization. Your peace attempt is an embarrassment to all Cogitors, a shame on the capabilities of your kind."

The secondaries were amazed that this former lackey of the thinking machines would speak so boldly. In contrast, even though their fluid-filled canisters shimmered with a buzz of mental activity, the Cogitors did not seem overly upset. "You do not entirely understand what has occurred, Primero Atreides. You are unable to discern the subtleties."

"I understand that your innocent optimism created a dangerous situation, like immature children bumbling about in the affairs of adults. You made a foolish choice that cost the life of the greatest woman who ever lived."

Vidad did not sound disturbed. "Serena Butler asked us to communicate with the thinking machines. Her intent was to find a way to end the Jihad. If our plan had been followed, the hostilities between humans and thinking machines would have ceased. We believe Serena Butler intentionally provoked Omnius into violent retaliation. Otherwise the machines would not have made such a response."

Vor shook his head, gritted his teeth. "How can you have lived so long, and understand so little? A war cannot simply stop without any resolution. The core conflict of Serena Butler's Jihad will never go away just because you wish to ignore it, or because our people are tired of fighting. Your attempt — if successful — would have led us to the brink of extinction."

The Cogitor pondered, then said, "You are behaving irrationally, Vorian Atreides — along with the bulk of humanity, as far as we can determine."

"Irrationally?" He spat out a bitter laugh. "Yes, that's what we humans do best, and it may be the means by which we achieve great victory."

"If you live long enough, Vorian Atreides, you will begin to appreciate the depth of our wisdom."

Vor shook his head. "Perhaps if you keep pondering the question, Vidad, you will recognize your own delusions."

Angrily, he turned to leave, knowing he would resolve nothing by a continued debate with the disembodied thinkers, who had in effect detached themselves from the realities and necessities of humanity. As he departed from the library, Vor called over his shoulder, "Go back to Hessra and stay there. Don't ever try to help us again."

My greatest mistake was in believing that I made my own decisions.
Even the most perceptive man can fail to see the puppet strings that
control him.

—Primero Xavier Harkonnen,
private letter to Vorian Atreides

THE TLULAXA REPRESENTATIVES welcomed a smiling Iblis Ginjo,
who stepped forth from his diplomatic shuttle accompanied by Jipol
guardians and attendants. The politicians and elders here had engaged in
numerous dealings with Iblis that had never been documented in official
records. As he arrived, the Grand Patriarch made subtle gestures and
shared knowing looks with the merchant Rekur Van and his colleagues.
Several of the Jipol guards and attendants slipped off to take care of
undisclosed matters, as previously arranged. The Tlulaxa had made
special exemptions for Iblis.

At the landing platform, the Tlulaxa also received the veteran Xavier
Harkonnen — a living testimonial to their biological prowess — giving
him full honors. He stood like a statue, a showpiece, displaying none of
the turmoil inside him.

Only one of the Primero's low-ranking adjutants, Quinto Paolo,
accompanied him. Young Paolo looked at the veteran through starry
eyes, seeing him as a legendary icon rather than a human being who had
made sundry mistakes and held regrets in his heart. Xavier did not
require pampering; the devoted young Quinto would follow his instructions without being overly attentive.

Rekur Van and other Tlulaxa representatives hosted a ceremony at
their hillside organ farms. Xavier stood in the eerie technological forest
under the Thalim sunlight, remembering the previous time he had been
here. *With Serena.* The treelike stands bore swollen artificial fruits — a
variety of cloned and modified organs, bearing labels in strange letters.

Rekur Van was all smiles, revealing sharp little teeth as he spread his arms to indicate the biological wealth in their organ farms. "Primero Harkonnen, so nice to see you. Tlulax is honored by your presence. With our cultured lungs in your chest, you showcase to the League the best our marvelous society has to offer."

Xavier nodded, but said nothing. He stood straightbacked and drew in a deep breath that carried the faintest whiff of chemical scents.

Since their visit here, Dr. Rajid Suk had continued his own experiments, enamored with the possibilities of cloning medical specimens, though his own attempts had been failures. Only the genetic geniuses of Tlulax had been able to provide a constant supply of compatible and perfect organs, which the Army of the Jihad desperately required . . .

As he took the stage, Iblis Ginjo's squarish face was full of satisfaction. "On this occasion, we bring to fruition one of the most prominent dreams Serena Butler shared with us. It was her most fervent desire that the Tlulaxa be brought into the League. This is a difficult mission in the shadow of her recent death, but I swore not to let the dreams of our beloved Priestess perish with her.

"Therefore, I am pleased to accept Tlulax as the newest League World, welcoming the Tlulaxa people as business partners and allies. Your scientists will provide vital medical products at a time when we are sure to experience many more injuries as we seek to reach our sacred goal. The Jihad is entering a new and even more glorious phase."

The Grand Patriarch showed exhilaration, boundless energy and optimism. He had maintained his youthful health and vitality through massive consumption of Aurelius Venport's imported spice, melange, an exotic drug that continued to be popular among the most prominent League nobles.

In contrast, as he stood watching, Xavier felt the weight of his years and his own tragedies. Nothing more than stage-dressing himself, Xavier looked about at the strange Tlulaxa — all of them men — who had come to attend this event. No sign of females anywhere. Even though he noticed nothing he could identify as directly suspicious, he felt as if he were trespassing in a den of predators. Their sharp little teeth and black, rodent eyes only added to the effect.

A secret triumph reflected in Iblis Ginjo's own dark eyes. His broadshouldered Jipol officers stood by, scanning the crowd, watching everything. Only the youthful Quinto Paolo seemed to accept this celebration at face value.

"We have guaranteed the Tlulaxa their privacy, and we respect their wishes to restrict outside visitors," the Grand Patriarch continued. "Still, we welcome them as our brothers in the holy struggle against thinking machines."

Xavier stood in front of the organ farms, surveying the masses of carefully bred tissue. He drew a deep breath into his own lungs, which had themselves been taken from similar tanks four decades ago. He focused on spherical eyeballs drifting in murky nutrient containers. They all seemed to be staring at him like accusing ghosts.

In a highrise dwelling complex outside the Bandalong city perimeter, the Tlulaxa provided Xavier with a suite located in the middle of a maze of corridors, exterior balconies, and catwalks. His private room contained pleasant furniture and unusual art objects, but the basic design seemed austere and industrial; Xavier wondered if the Tlulaxa had simply added the decorations for his benefit.

Following his attendance at the organ farms ceremony, the Tlulaxa and Iblis Ginjo seemed to have no further interest in him. They sat together at a banquet table and ate a spiced meal, accompanied by strained conversation. Then the Grand Patriarch clearly dismissed Xavier, citing the veteran's "weariness from the demands of the day" and suggesting that he retire to his own quarters for the evening.

Quinto Paolo bunked in a small room nearby. The Jipol had no business with the young adjutant, and the spaceport and business sectors of this suburban section did not offer much nightlife for an energetic military man. The core of Bandalong itself was off-limits to outsiders for purported religious reasons, although Xavier could not get a straight answer to any of his inquiries as to the reasons why.

Xavier brooded in his rooms, not wanting to sleep. He felt mentally weary, but his body was not tired. He resented having too much time to sit alone, where he had nothing to do but think and remember. Under such circumstances doubts and suspicions could run rampant . . .

Though Serena Butler had written passionate tracts and Iblis Ginjo had released his own popular essays and memoirs, Xavier had never felt the need to boast about his own life or military heroics. Despite his prominence, he had never bothered to document or justify his work for future generations to read. He preferred to let his actions speak for themselves.

Now Xavier spent hours far into the Tlulaxan night, poring over the last writings of Serena Butler. He found nothing new or enlightening, since he knew her thoughts and arguments so well. Nonetheless, Xavier savored the cadence and poetry of her words, as if she were speaking aloud to him once more. He opened his memories about her as if they were a separate, treasured book inside his mind, and thought of the remarkable accomplishments of her life.

Too short a life.

He heard a noise, a desperate tapping on the hard windowplate of the folding door of his high balcony. Startled, Xavier noticed a shadow moving outside, the silhouette of a human form.

He might have been suspicious or afraid, but curiosity got the better of him. When he opened the balcony door and a cold, sour breeze slapped his face, he saw his mysterious visitor, a skeletal man with cadaverous, gray skin, except where livid scars embroidered it. The man had only one eye; the other hollow socket was a ghastly crater. Translucent tubes ran from his neck into packets of gelatinous fluids strapped to his waist.

Somehow the man had made his way across the catwalks and then dropped down here with the use of a wet, knotted rope. Xavier couldn't imagine how this desiccated person had summoned the strength to accomplish such a task.

The stranger trembled as if in exhaustion or desperation. "Primero Harkonnen . . . I have found you." He nearly collapsed with relief.

Xavier supported the unfortunate soul and led him into the room. Instinctively, the Primero kept his voice low. "Who are you? Does anyone know you're here?"

The stranger shook his head, and the effort seemed to cost him a great deal. His chin sagged onto his own sunken chest. He looked like a giant mass of wounds, a shambling collection of scars. Not battle scars — *surgical* scars. Xavier helped him to one of the chairs in his room.

"Primero Harkonnen . . ." The man took deep breaths between words. "You may not remember me. I served with you at IV Anbus, thirteen years ago. I led one of the detachments against the thinking machines. I am Tercero Hondu Cregh."

Narrowing his eyes, Xavier brought the recollection into focus. This officer had arranged the second ground ambush in a Zenshiite village, but the locals had sabotaged the artillery, leaving Cregh and his commandos vulnerable to robotic attack. Like Vergyl.

"Yes, I remember you well." His brows knitted. "But I thought you'd been reassigned to your homeworld . . . Balut?" He drew in a quick breath. "Balut! And you survived the devastating attack there?"

"Balut was my home . . . once."

Full of questions, Xavier leaned closer. "I saw the tactical report, the summary images. Awful! The thinking machines destroyed everyone, not a living soul left — but how did you escape?"

"We were not attacked by . . . thinking machines." Hondu Cregh shook his head. "You were meant to believe that, but it wasn't Omnius at all. It was Iblis Ginjo and the Tlulaxa."

Xavier's heart skipped a beat. "What are you saying?"

"There is something I must show you, if my body can withstand the effort." Cregh lifted his head, blinking his oversized, bloodshot eye. "But I warn you, this knowledge places you in great danger, and you will not thank me for it."

"I am not concerned about danger, not anymore." Xavier set his jaw. "And if you have the courage to come here in your condition and tell me — how can I do less than listen to what you have to say?"

Tercero Cregh hung his head again, and his shoulders sagged. "I did it because I have nothing to lose, Primero. I am dead already." He fondled the gelatinous packets strapped to his waist, touched the intravenous tubes running into his chest and neck. His single, intense eye fixed on Xavier. "They have stolen both of my kidneys, and my liver. The Tlulaxa hooked me up to temporary preservation systems and machines so that I would not deteriorate too quickly, while they waited to harvest the rest of my usable components."

Xavier could not comprehend everything he was hearing. "What? They have the organ farms. They can grow anything they need. Why would —"

"I am an organ donor . . . Tlulaxa style," the emaciated man said, with a gruesome smile. He raised himself from the chair and stood on shaky legs. "Yes, the Tlulaxa have organ farms, but the operations are not very productive. Adequate to generate expensive replacement body parts during peacetime, perhaps — but never with the capacity to weather the demands of a Jihad."

"But . . . that's impossible!" Xavier felt a deep revulsion growing in his soul. "I myself have replacement lungs —"

Cregh's head continued to sag, as if his neck was too weak to hold it up. "Perhaps it's true that your lungs came from one of the tank trees . . . or they may have been ripped from a poor slave who happened to have compatible tissues. When all of the veterans and injured of the Jihad demanded fresh organs, the Tlulaxa were forced to find . . . alternative sources. Who would care about a few colonists and insignificant Buddislamic slaves?"

Xavier swallowed hard. "So the organ farms Serena and I visited — those were all a sham?"

"No, those were functional tanks, but they provide only a fraction of the Jihad's biological needs. And the Tlulaxa certainly did not wish to lose all that business, all that profit. The flesh merchants want you to believe in their technological prowess, while they sell you their organs at exorbitant prices."

Even worse, Xavier knew that if the League had known the truth all along, many organ recipients probably would still have made the same choice. He himself might have considered it a necessary evil, for the good of the Jihad.

Cregh heaved a deep, angry sigh. "So, when orders come in, the Tlulaxa harvest the needed organs from those who no longer serve any other purpose for them. People like me."

Struggling to comprehend the immensity of what he was hearing, Xavier wondered about Iblis Ginjo's role. "And the Grand Patriarch . . . knows about this scheme?"

The man squinted his lone eye, and laughed coarsely. "Knows about it? He *created* it."

Humankind has always sought more and more knowledge, considering it a boon to the species. But there are exceptions to this, things no person should ever learn how to do.
                    —Cogitor Kwyna, *City of Introspection archives*

L IKE A MAN in a daze, Xavier followed Tercero Cregh out onto a narrow balcony high above the streets of the Tlulaxan suburb. The night was misty-wet and cold. The two of them made a treacherous, laborious ascent on railings and by knotted rope, crossing dim walkways and overpasses, Xavier offering assistance when he could.

Xavier was sure there must be guards outside the door to his room and Quinto Paolo's. He hoped no one would check on him before he could see what this desperate soldier had to show him. Worse, he hoped his suite had not been bugged with microscopic surveillance imagers. But it was too late for such concerns now.

At night the Tlulaxa city — at its core a forbidden zone — was dark and sinister, brooding behind its blockades. "Are we going inside there?" Xavier asked the barely alive veteran. He kept his voice low. "It's a blocked security area —"

"There are ways to enter. The Tlulaxa have so few offworld visitors, they don't know the weak spots in their own security." Cregh heaved a gurgling breath, visibly forcing back his pain. "But I suspect it will be more difficult getting in than it was slipping out. Most of the prisoners, like me, aren't very . . . ambulatory. Shhh! Look." He pointed.

Crouching, they watched three Tlulaxa men pass them, each one carrying an electronic device. When the way was clear, Hondu Cregh hurried through shadows, followed by Xavier.

In a cramped alley outside a hangar-sized metal building, Cregh propped open an access hatch and ducked low. Both men entered through a supply chute. The effort was obviously difficult and painful to Cregh, but he did not slow.

Inside the large building, the stench of chemicals and death was powerful even to Xavier's dulled sense of smell. But what he saw made him wish he had lost his eyesight long ago.

The confinement beds were like coffins equipped with diagnostics and artificial systems that kept the pathetic, mewling forms alive by pumping fluids into them. The cavernous facility extended as far as he could see, under dim lights.

Thousands of human bodies lay trapped there. Living specimens. Some were nothing but butchered torsos or severed limbs, kept fresh through injections of nutrients and bubbling liquids, mere scraps of dissected humanity. Other bodies were fresh acquisitions, strapped down and held captive while their pieces were removed one by one to fill orders.

The real "organ farms" of the Tlulaxa.

Xavier drew in a hitching, sobbing breath, felt a wave of nausea. As he tasted the air, he wondered if he had been kept alive through the unwilling sacrifice of some unknown victim who had provided a fresh set of lungs.

Most of the captives had the distinctive dark hair and tan skin that marked them as Buddislamic captives, like the ones on IV Anbus or those who had risen up on Poritrin. The Zensunni and Zenshiite prisoners who did not have their eyes removed looked at him with desperation, hope, or hatred.

"I escaped from my bed," Hondu Cregh said in a rattling voice. "With most of my vital organs taken from me, the flesh merchants knew I could not stay alive away from this place — only an hour or two at most. But when one of the other donor bodies died, I was able to steal his nutrient and stimulant packs. That provided me with the strength I needed to go out and locate you. I knew you were here. I overheard two of the Tlulaxa butchers talking." He inhaled deeply, like bellows inflating, then he coughed. "I had to give my life . . . so that you would *know*, Primero Harkonnen."

Xavier wanted to collapse in despair. He wanted to flee, but instead he steeled himself and looked at the horrific survivor. "But how did the Tlulaxa capture you? We thought that you and the other colonists were killed on Balut."

"The Grand Patriarch's Jipol and dozens of Tlulaxa slaver ships came at night and bombarded the central village," said Cregh. "They sprayed paralytic gas in the air, rendering us senseless and unable to resist. Like on Rhisso. They killed a handful of us for good measure, just so they could strew the slaughtered bodies around. Then they took us captive and slagged the buildings, leaving no traces except for a handful of destroyed combat robots they had picked up on some old battlefield. The League assumed it was a thinking machine attack."

Xavier reeled with the information. Then weakness overcame the dying man, and finally Cregh sagged to his knees. "That was how the Tlulaxa acquired fresh materials for their organ farms, and Iblis Ginjo was able to cry out against the thinking machines. His people rallied to the cause, suspecting nothing."

"An abominable scheme," Xavier said.

"That is not all. He did the same on Chusuk years ago, and the mining planetoid of Rhisso. He intends to hit . . . Caladan . . . next. You must stop him."

Xavier listened with growing horror as the tercero explained in short bursts of words, like the last remnants of a battery charge. Finally the man slumped to the floor, with no energy left. Xavier wondered how the officer had managed to survive for so long without vital organs — just a core, head, and limbs — detached from the sophisticated maintenance systems the Tlulaxa used to keep their organ reservoirs fresh.

Xavier knelt, draped the officer's arm over a bony shoulder, and stood. He tried to drag the man along, even though he knew there was nothing he could do to help him. He staggered between the rows of coffinlike beds and dissection tables, hauling the valiant soldier along. But finally it became too much. Hondu Cregh was dead.

Gently, Xavier laid the tercero's body on the stained floor. Xavier caught glimpses of other half-dismantled bodies kept alive for the harvesting of organs and tissues. Some had been flayed of their skin — which had no doubt been used to treat Jihad burn victims — revealing raw, red muscle tissue that glistened wetly in the light.

He staggered away, considering whether he should try to free these people, but he knew that most would die swiftly without the medical systems that kept them alive here. They had already lost vital organs. A few might survive . . . but to where could they flee? What could he possibly do for them?

Though he was a high-ranking officer in the Army of the Jihad, he was all alone here, surrounded by enemies — the Tlulaxa, as well as Iblis Ginjo and his Jipol guards. Xavier could not sound an alarm. He grasped the edge of one of the dissection beds. Feebly, the body inside twitched a hand and reached toward him.

"I see some explanations are in order," said a rich, powerful voice. "Do not judge what you don't understand."

Xavier whirled to see the Grand Patriarch standing at the end of the long aisle, accompanied by Tlulaxa medical researchers, Jipol guards, and flesh merchants. Xavier froze, knowing that his life would now be forfeit, in spite of who he was. Maybe they would hook him up and harvest his organs . . .

"I already understand far more than I ever wanted to know," Xavier said, trying to hide his disgust and outrage. "I presume you have your justifications?"

"It only requires a broader perspective, Primero. Surely you can understand that?" Iblis looked robust and powerful, while Xavier simply felt incredibly old.

He asked, "Is this . . . is this where my own lungs came from?"

"That was before I rose to power, so I have no way of knowing. Even so, any objective person would consider it a worthy trade — a nameless wretch for a great Primero." Iblis drew himself up, seizing a way to make his argument convincing. "Most of these people are slaves, human outcasts scraped up from unwanted planets." He sneered at the victims confined to their life-support beds. "But *you* are a tactical genius, a loyal soldier for the Jihad. Consider everything you have done in past decades, Primero — all the victories you won against Omnius. By any measure, your life is far more valuable than that of a mere slave — especially a Buddislamic coward who refused to fight for the Jihad."

"The ends justify the means," said Xavier, not daring to let his true revulsion show. "That can be a valid argument."

Iblis smiled, misinterpreting Xavier's calmness as acceptance. "Think of it this way, Primero: By keeping you alive and able to serve to your fullest capacity, that slave who sacrificed his lungs for you did his own part to defeat the thinking machines. If his people had been willing to contribute to the war effort in any other way — as a human *should* have — he would never have been brought here, would he?"

"But these victims aren't all Buddislamics," Xavier said, looking down at the grayish ruin of Hondu Cregh's body. The words were like sour bile in his throat. "This man was also a soldier in the Army of the Jihad."

"What did he tell you?" Iblis asked, his words sharp, his jaw set.

Xavier shook his head. "He was too weak and died quickly, but I recognized him. How did he get here?"

"That man . . . does not exist any longer," Iblis said. "Some are so wounded in battles that they cannot survive. Nonetheless, their bodies can still offer hope and assistance to others. That officer's family believes he died bravely in battle — and he did, for all intents and purposes. Afterward, his body provided the organs necessary to keep other jihadis and mercenaries alive. He would have died anyway. Could any fighter ask for more?"

Xavier felt weak and nauseated. Nothing Iblis said could justify what he and the Tlulaxa monsters had done. "Did . . . did Serena know about this?" he asked finally, sounding defeated.

"No, but Tlulaxa technology enabled us to complete the illusion of her martyrdom. We used the sample cells the Tlulaxa took from her when she visited Thalim ten years ago to grow a genetically identical clone body, which we then mutilated horribly. We captured every moment in highly detailed images, staged every motion, and made Omnius out to be the monster that we all know he is."

Now Xavier had difficulty grasping the enormity of this revelation as well. "Then Serena wasn't tortured? She wasn't murdered by the thinking machines —"

"No, I gave orders that her own chief Seraph Niriem kill her, if the Corrin-Omnius did not. Serena intended to goad Omnius to murder. But if she failed . . . well, we couldn't allow that to happen. It was to be a quick and painless blow that would thoroughly astonish the thinking machines." Iblis shrugged.

Xavier reeled in disbelief. "Why would she do such a terrible thing? What did she have to gain —" Then he cut himself off. "Of course. She threw fuel onto the flames of the Jihad. She knew our people would accept the Cogitors' peace terms out of sheer exhaustion, unless she gave her life to make sure that would never happen."

Smiling, the Grand Patriarch spread his hands as if the answer was obvious. "Can you imagine any better way to stir up every human in the League? Serena couldn't, and neither could I. I simply made certain that Serena would succeed. Even the protesters fell silent when they saw what Omnius had done to their beloved Priestess."

A moan from one of the half-butchered Zensunnis turned Xavier's attention back to the bubbling and humming medical beds. He swallowed hard. "Did she know about the organs, where so many of them came from — all these people, cut up like garments in a tailor shop?"

The Grand Patriarch flashed a knowing smile, while his Jipol guards and the Tlulaxa stood uneasily around him. "Serena had other burdens to bear, and she was told only what she needed to know. She asked that I find a way to care for the wounded Jihad fighters, to get them the organs they desperately needed. While I admit these facilities are not pleasant, they fill a necessary function. Surely, you can see that?" He smiled broadly.

"Think of Serena and her memory, Primero. You know how much she praised these farms and all the good they did. You know how badly Serena wanted Tlulax to join the League of Nobles. Regardless of the method, *this* is truly what she wanted all along." He took an ominous step closer, pretending to be paternal and understanding. "Xavier Harkonnen, I know you loved her, and I beg of you — do not act prematurely. Do not ruin Serena's legacy for all of us."

Xavier struggled to keep his fury in check. "No, I wouldn't think of it," he said. He hoped he had convinced Iblis.

The Tlulaxa and the Jipol guards looked at him suspiciously, but Xavier kept his gaze fixed on the smug Grand Patriarch. "I've had enough of these horrors, Iblis — enough of the war. When we return to Salusa Secundus, I ask that you . . . accept my resignation as Primero in the Army of the Jihad."

For an instant, Iblis looked surprised, then pleased. Quickly, he masked his expression and nodded. "As you wish — with full honors, of course. You have served well, Primero, but the war must go on until Omnius is defeated. For Serena's sake we will continue to do whatever needs to be done."

"Of course," Xavier said. "Just call on me, and I will serve for Serena's sake. For now . . . I just want to go home."

But he had other plans, if only he could implement them quickly enough.

*True creation, the sort that interests me, eventually becomes
independent of its creator. Evolution and experience take the
original product far from its origin, with an uncertain outcome.*
—Erasmus, *Reflections on Sentient Biologicals*

T HROUGHOUT THE EBB and flow of the Jihad, Omnius update ships
continued to fly predictable, endless courses, from one Synchronized
World to another. The unchanging nature of the sentient evermind
created its greatest vulnerability.

Agamemnon and his unified cymeks knew exactly where to wait for the
incoming vessel on the fringes of the Richese system. The general had
left Juno on Bela Tegeuse to continue to rally and convert the deluded
population there. After nine years, their rebellion now had plenty of neo-
cymek fighters who owed everything to the three surviving Titans.

And Omnius had not taken the threat seriously.

While waiting in ambush, Agamemnon and Dante detected the arrival
of the silver-and-black update ship as it flew obliviously along its route
between Synchronized Worlds. The programmed robot captain was
doing his job, never seeing his part in the overall conflict.

Six neo-cymek warships hovered, ready to strike. All of Agamemnon's
vessels had been augmented with heavy armor and superior firepower,
built by the restored industries on Bela Tegeuse. Omnius had added
small batteries of defensive weaponry to many of the update courier
vessels, but it was only a token gesture, completely inadequate to protect
the data spheres from cymek attack.

Agamemnon knew his rebels could pick off this one with ease. The
neos converted from the Tegeusan population were anxious to show their
worth and strike blows in the continuing fight.

Beowulf lumbered along with them. The oldest neo-cymek had been
severely damaged by Hecate's traitorous attack, his ship nearly destroyed

by the bombardment of kinetic spheres. While he'd tried to escape, the heavy impacts sent power surges through delicate thoughtrodes, searing portions of his organic brain. The aftermath left the damaged Beowulf drifting in the asteroid belt of Ginaz, where he was rescued by a cymek scouting party. Because of the injury, he could no longer function at his previous level. His mind would never be the same.

In a rare and uncharacteristic show of compassion, however, the Titan general had allowed the crippled and sluggish cymek to accompany this attack, though Beowulf would be of little assistance.

Though the earlier strike against Zufa Cenva and Aurelius Venport had not turned out as planned, Agamemnon knew that his two intended human victims were dead . . . as was Hecate, thus preventing her from further interfering with his plans. An acceptable result.

Agamemnon was also finding it increasingly useful to sprinkle eavesdroppers and fully-trained spies throughout the prominent League Worlds. Given a taste of immortality with the promise of becoming neo-cymeks, the people of Bela Tegeuse had volunteered to act as observers and data gatherers, which enabled the Titans to fight this two-front war much more effectively. Omnius, too, used human spies, though cautiously, since he feared that exposure to free humanity would corrupt them beyond repair — as had occurred with Agamemnon's own son Vorian.

"We are ready to move against the target, General," Dante announced.

Beowulf made an eager noise and finally adjusted his communication systems so that his words were distinct, though slow. "Time to kill Omnius."

"Yes. Time to kill Omnius." Agamemnon gave the order for the ambush ships to swoop down and converge upon the update vessel.

Agamemnon and Dante observed from a safe distance while the neo-cymeks charged in to surround and detain the update ship. They had instructions to inflict no damage that could not be repaired quickly. Within moments their precise shots had taken the update ship's engines off-line and burned out the implanted transmission systems, leaving the vessel to drift free.

The robotic captain would attempt to send a distress signal, but the Richese-Omnius would never know what had happened. Agamemnon and his team would finish here, commandeer the ship, and streak toward the unsuspecting machine planet before any delay could be noted.

"Hurry," he said. "We don't have much time."

The cymek ships forcibly docked with the update vessel. One of the Tegeusan neos boarded first, stalking with clattering mechanical footsteps across the chill metal decks. Agamemnon followed and headed for the pilot chamber, eager to crush another silver gelsphere in his metal claw.

Inside the cockpit, the copper-skinned robot captain utterly surprised the bold neo-cymek. He fired an explosive weapon, and a dense projectile slammed into the neo's brain canister, ripping it open and splattering the gray matter and electrafluid in a broad splash across the walls of the cockpit.

Agamemnon reared up, raising the weapons implanted in his articulated walker body. The robot turned a mirror-smooth copper face toward him. "Ah, it is Agamemnon. I suppose I should have fired at you first. But then Vorian might have been upset with me."

The Titan general hesitated, recognizing the independent robot Seurat, who had taken Vor as his copilot on innumerable update missions. "On the contrary, Seurat. I believe my son would have been delighted if you'd done the difficult work for him."

The robot captain simulated a chuckle. "I do not believe so, Agamemnon. He seems to prefer facing his own problems, and savoring his victory."

Other cymeks had crawled aboard the update ship, crowding in behind the general. The other update captains had been tossed out of airlocks, dumped still-smoking out into space, but Seurat might actually provide valuable information.

"Take this robot as a prisoner," Agamemnon instructed the armored neos. "I want to debrief him."

Seurat stood firm. "I cannot allow you to take the update sphere. My programming prevents it."

"Run an analysis and consider your options. I can easily fire a pulse burst and shut down all your systems, then remove you from the update ship. I can fire a projectile and destroy you entirely. Or you can follow me now and suffer minimal physical damage. No scenario exists in which you can protect your copy of Omnius."

The neo-cymeks clattered forward as Seurat pondered the choices.

"Your assessment is correct, Agamemnon," the robot said. "I would prefer to remain undamaged. Perhaps other options will arise."

"Don't count on it."

As two neo-cymeks hauled the robot pilot away to one of the waiting ships, Agamemnon went forward and ripped open the containment chamber that held the Omnius update. Though it was not a necessary component of his plan, he crushed the silvery gelsphere, squeezing the evermind into a glittering lump of circuitry.

While he enjoyed himself in this manner, other cymeks moved through the update ship, and vacuum-hardened robots crawled over the outer hull like metal insects. They repaired the damage their weapons had done and installed new transmission spikes, hurrying to get the craft moving again toward Richese.

"The engines are functional again, General Agamemnon," Dante reported. "This update ship can now proceed."

Using their knowledge of the evermind's predictable routes, the cymek rebels had already tracked down and intercepted ten update ships. They had destroyed enough copies of Omnius that the widely separated Synchronized Worlds were already becoming fragmented. The scattered evermind incarnations were no longer acting in a coordinated fashion.

"Install the new programming and turn our latest weapon loose." Agamemnon worked the piloting controls the robot captain would have used.

The update ship still had its appropriate password signals and approved linkages for the Richese-Omnius. After this vessel passed through the next set of defensive perimeters, a new course would kick in. The engines would accelerate the update vessel until, like a fast-moving hammer, it swung down through the atmosphere, and delivered an incredible crushing blow to the citadel nexus of the computer evermind.

Then the cymeks could swarm into the vulnerable Synchronized World. Agamemnon already had a large military force waiting to pounce, assimilate, and mop up — massive ships constructed on Bela Tegeuse, joined by the recovered and reprogrammed robotic fighting force they had originally stolen from Omnius. As soon as this juggernaut update ship slammed into Richese, cymek marauders would rush down and complete the destruction. The Richesian thinking machines might attempt to rally, but the Omnius substations could never unify them quickly enough.

The Titan general climbed back aboard his own ship, and all the cymeks watched the reprogrammed update vessel descend into the planet's orbital plane. Richese would soon be under cymek rule, another step in creating a new Time of Titans. There, Juno would again work to convert the downtrodden, hopeless humans into faithful cymek allies.

And perhaps the captive Seurat would provide some insight into how the Titan general could deal with his traitorous son Vorian . . .

"Prepare to make our move," Agamemnon said. "This time there is no doubt of our victory."

I do not give a damn about history. I will do what is right.
                                        —Primero Xavier Harkonnen,
                                        private letter to Vorian Atreides

W HEN THEY LEFT Tlulax, Xavier piloted the diplomatic vessel
himself, taking the controls as he preferred to do. It had been
his pro-forma duty on the inbound journey to the Thalim system, and
though the old man now looked deeply weary, he insisted on clinging to
his role. The Primero seemed lethargic as he navigated the ship away
from the checkerboard city of Bandalong.

Looking eminently satisfied, Iblis Ginjo stood in the cockpit, grasping
the back of the passenger seat as he stared down at the clean city grid,
sparkling with metal and glass. The hillsides spread out in neat rows,
stitched with the real, though deceptive, organ farms.

Aboard the diplomatic transport, five Jipol sergeants watched Xavier's
every move, but the old Primero looked tired and defeated as he worked
the controls. He claimed he was anxious to get back home.

In his heart, though, he doubted Iblis would let him reach Salusa
Secundus alive. The Grand Patriarch could not afford to let his scanda-
lous secrets be exposed, especially those involving the Tlulaxa organ
farms and the charade of Serena's martyrdom.

No, the Jipol sergeants would stage some accident, kill Xavier en route,
and return to Zimia feigning grief and mourning the old hero. Then Iblis
would proceed with his plans to destroy Caladan, seize prisoners as
involuntary organ donors, and forge ahead with righteous anger against
the cruel thinking machines.

"I have always done what was best for the Jihad, Xavier," Iblis said in a
conciliatory voice, still trying to convince him. "Think of how strong we
are now. The ends justify the means, don't they?"

"We all could say the same," Xavier answered. "Vorian, Serena, and I. This has been an incredibly long war. It has driven us to do many things we are not proud of."

"Serena herself would have been proud of our actions," Iblis insisted. "We must be true to her vision. We owe nothing less to her memory."

Xavier pretended weary agreement. He had to fool the Grand Patriarch into believing he was no threat, that he would take no brash actions. But at all costs, he could not allow this corrupt man to return to his seat of power. Something had to be done before it was too late.

He had already discreetly given young Quinto Paolo his secret orders.

Xavier's diplomatic transport craft operated with conventional starship engines that would take many weeks to journey from the Thalim system to Salusa Secundus. For emergencies, one of the small kindjal scouts in the lower hangar had been outfitted with new Holtzman engines from the Kolhar shipyards. Traveling through folded space was still risky, however, and many Jihad pilots had vanished on routine flights. But if speed was imperative, there was no other choice. Quinto Paolo had accepted the risk.

After Xavier flew the diplomatic craft beyond the limits of Tlulax's atmosphere, he maneuvered slowly and carefully away from the planet, as if aligning the proper vector for a launch across the vast gulf of open space.

Warning indicators flashed on his control panel — as Xavier had expected.

Iblis spotted them immediately. "What is that?"

Xavier pretended to be confused. "It seems the hangar hatch is opening. Hmmm, perhaps it is just a malfunction." Iblis's Jipol sergeants looked around in anger and surprise.

Iblis saw through the ruse. "Your adjutant! What have you put him up to?"

Xavier looked at his status screens again, dropping the pretense. "He's ready to launch a foldspace kindjal. I don't think your men will be fast enough to stop him."

Iblis snapped to the guards, "Go! All five of you. Prevent that ship from leaving. Bring Paolo here immediately!" The Jipol sergeants bounded out of the cockpit and down the corridor, but Quinto Paolo was already on his way.

Xavier was content, knowing he had timed everything perfectly. Iblis Ginjo and his Jipol had kept their eyes on old Primero Harkonnen, but no one had expected the fresh-faced young officer to do anything. They also had not considered the possibility of Xavier acting so soon, even before they entered open space.

"I don't know what you think your man can accomplish," Iblis said, his expression disdainful. "Who would he talk to? Who would believe him? I control all news in the League, all public information. The people believe in me, so I can denounce him *and* you. Where could he possibly go, anyway?"

Smiling, Xavier leaned back in the pilot's seat and worked the controls. The armored cockpit door hissed and slammed, sealing him inside with the Grand Patriarch. While Iblis whirled in alarm, Xavier permanently disabled the mechanism.

The doors could never be opened now, at least not with any of the tools or systems aboard. He had just checkmated his opponent. As a gambler, Vorian would have been proud of him.

The diplomatic ship remained in the Thalim system, but Paolo had already made his run for the stars. He had folded space and gotten away safely.

Angrily, Iblis hammered at the sealed cockpit door, trying to open it, but when he saw that it was fruitless, he turned back to Xavier and glared at him. "I had hoped you would not be so foolish about this, Primero. I thought you understood my position."

"I know many things about you, Iblis. The organ farms are only one of your unforgivable crimes and deceits." Xavier keyed in the navigation controls, locking their course — then shorted out the entire control panel, taking the bridge command center off-line. Now Iblis could do nothing to stop him.

"What are you doing?"

High above the planet, the diplomatic ship arced inward and began to proceed toward the blazing heart of the star system. The sun of Thalim shone brightly, sweeping a swath of glare into the cockpit and casting deep shadows.

Xavier said, "I know what you did to the settlements on Chusuk, Rhisso, and Balut. Those were not really thinking machine attacks, were they?"

"You have no proof of that," Iblis said, his voice dripping ice.

"Interesting response — but not one an innocent man would give."

As automatic acceleration lurched the ship forward, Iblis staggered to the piloting console and shoved Xavier aside. None of the controls responded, and he cursed.

"I also know what you have planned for the innocent settlers of Caladan," Xavier continued. "Fresh donors for the organ farms while you rally the rest of the League."

Iblis's square face darkened with stubborn self-justification. "Serena

Butler would have understood. *She* saw how the people had lost their resolve. They are lazy, no longer focused on the important fight. By God, they were willing to accept the Cogitors' cease-fire proposal! We must never let that happen again."

"I agree," Xavier said. "But not at the cost you have in mind."

Loud pounding reverberated against the sealed cockpit door, the Jipol guards hammering to get inside. Iblis attempted to work a control panel on the wall, but the door remained sealed. He turned to glare at Xavier. "Let them in, damn you!"

Xavier simply sat back and looked at the brightening view out the front cockpit windows. Their ship roared toward the blazing furnace of the central star in the Thalim system.

He said, "Serena understood the need for sacrifice and motivation — but when the time came, she did it herself. She asked no one else to become victims for her. You are a selfish, power-hungry man, Iblis."

"I don't know what you —"

"Instead of performing dangerous deeds yourself, you selected unsuspecting victims. You made the people of Chusuk, Rhisso, and Balut pay for your ambition."

"If you try to expose my so-called crimes, you will never be able to make your accusations stick." Iblis grabbed Xavier by the shoulders. The Primero did not even struggle as the Grand Patriarch threw him out of the seat. "No one will listen, old man. My power base is too secure."

"I know," Xavier said, picking himself up from the deck. With odd formality, he brushed off his uniform. "That is why I can't allow politicians to deal with this matter. You and your lackey Yorek Thurr would only manipulate evidence and worm your way out of any punishment. Too bad he isn't here with us. Instead, I now act as a military officer for the good of the Jihad — as I always have. It is my decision to remove an enemy from the battlefield. At this moment, Iblis Ginjo, *you* are the greatest enemy to mankind." He smiled.

The ship plunged forward, approaching the enormous sun of Thalim. Heavy gravity reached out with seductive, unseen fingers, drawing the vessel closer, faster. Iblis continued his futile struggle with the controls, cursing and slamming his fist against panels. He drew his knife, threatening Xavier. "Turn us around."

"I wiped all the navigation systems. Nothing in the universe can alter our course now."

Iblis's dark eyes flew wide with realization. "You can't do this!"

"It was simple enough. Just look out at the sunlight. See how much brighter it's getting, moment by moment."

"No!" Iblis wailed.

The Jipol continued to hammer on the sealed cockpit door, but their tools and weapons were inadequate to breach the barrier. The ship hurtled toward the curtains of coronal fire streaming out of the star.

"Worst of all, Iblis, I know that you are responsible for convincing Serena to sacrifice herself. You cost that magnificent woman her life."

"She made up her own mind! She couldn't let the Cogitors succeed. She went to Corrin to give her life so that the Jihad could continue. It was the only possible solution. She was willing to pay that price."

"Not the way you arranged it." Xavier was beyond listening. "But I will ask her myself, soon."

The ship bucked and jumped, buffeted by ionizing currents from the enraged star and vibrating from the increased speed, but its course did not deviate. The transport arrowed like a blunt dagger toward the bloated sphere of incandescent gas. Iblis's face was streaked with sweat, from terror and the mounting heat.

Xavier thought back on his life, his family, everything he had done or failed to do. He did not care if legends remembered him as less than the man he was. Eventually, if Quinto Paolo succeeded in his mission, at least Vorian Atreides would understand. Xavier asked for nothing more.

This was beyond any personal concerns; he was doing this for more than revenge. Without Iblis and his manipulative charm, the Jipol and the Tlulaxa would not have the clout or the leadership to pull off their heinous schemes against human colony worlds. Xavier would save the population of Caladan . . . and all future victims of Iblis's twisted, misguided fervor.

Iblis shouted in denial again and again. Useless words. The Jipol kept pounding against the doorway while the ship flew inexorably into the hot, expanding flares of the sun. The roiling photosphere filled the viewport now with light so bright it seemed about to melt the metal and glaz.

The cockpit had grown intensely hot. Failing circulation systems groaned and shuddered in an unsuccessful attempt to battle the thermal overloads. Each breath was like fire in Xavier's lungs.

He squeezed his eyes shut, but the dazzle and heat still burned his optic nerves. Xavier considered this a fitting funeral pyre for himself and Iblis.

Iblis kept screaming as the ship flew into the heart of the sun.

Timing is essential, especially in pulling off the element of surprise.
　　　　　　　　—Vorian Atreides, *Memoirs Without Shame*

I MMENSE BULBOUS SHAPES towered around Norma Cenva, a veritable city of her imagination coming to life as the spacefolders were modified or constructed from scratch. Infused with a massive military work force, substantial League funding, and a new sense of urgency from the rejuvenated Jihad, work at the Kolhar shipyards proceeded at a breathtaking pace. Norma's dream was becoming a reality.

The shipyards stretched for more than a thousand kilometers in each direction, a bustling manufacturing facility laid out on a colossal grid that covered the once-marshy plains of Kolhar. Work areas were connected by high-speed suspensor trams, with white capsules speeding along unseen tracks.

Even so, Norma had never felt so lost and empty. She stood beside her intense, eight-year-old son Adrien in the shadow of one of the colossal vessels, with tears streaming down her lovely face. The Jihad officer waited uncomfortably in front of her, grim from the news he had brought.

I saw this in my vision. I knew I would never see Aurelius again.

Norma needed to set her personal concerns aside now. It was much too late to regret how little time she had actually spent with her husband, and how many years she had lost of her own life due to the war. She had a great deal of work to do, trying to solve the dangerous navigation problems. Otherwise, many jihadis and mercenaries would die.

I must make my other grand vision come true as well.

So far, thirty-seven military spacecraft had been retrofitted or built from scratch. Another fifty-three were under construction and would soon be finished. The towering frameworks, in various stages of completion, were black, draped with gold-and-silver League banners. A jungle of suspensor scaffolds and work barges floated in the air around each ship.

Even though they had commandeered the entire fleet of VenKee spacefolders, Jihad military authorities were still allowing VenKee Enterprises to ship considerable amounts of merchandise on a standby basis. Luckily, there had been no devastating accidents so far, but it was only a matter of time.

Those successful cargo runs had been going on for months now, keeping the VenKee cash flow going . . . and also allowing shipments of melange to continue to the many nobles who had become dependent on their daily spice. Because Parliamentary representatives demanded increased supplies of melange, it was possible that the Army of the Jihad would allow VenKee to keep a few space-folding ships to serve them, based on the "urgent needs" of the League. In the meantime, Norma had also dispatched dozens of standard slow-speed commercial vessels to continue the flow of necessary materials.

Thanks to the concessions Aurelius that had negotiated, VenKee Enterprises would survive. Perhaps even thrive eventually. But their luck had to hold . . .

Norma wiped her tears away, but more replaced them. It was such a human reaction. She was accustomed to burying herself in her work, which enabled her to escape the mundane interactions and petty conflicts of personal relationships, business, and politics. Now though her copious mind could envision journeys across a folded universe, she could not escape a terrible personal reality.

"A League investigation team gathered evidence at the asteroid impact site on Ginaz," the officer said, his voice filled with sadness. Norma did not even know his name. "Tens of thousands are dead in the archipelago, many of them talented mercenaries. I don't expect we will ever learn precisely what took place."

Norma had no doubt of the veracity of the news. A cool wind from the plains blew the officer's dark hair over his forehead, almost into his eyes. He cleared his throat. "We've found some evidence of a concerted cymek attack in the asteroid field. Your husband and your mother were scheduled to be in the vicinity."

"I already know what happened to them," Norma said. "I saw it in a . . . prescient vision. I believe you will find it fits with the evidence you have." She explained what she had witnessed after her heavy spice consumption.

Fighting back her emotions, Norma shook her head at the terrible waste. Two incredibly talented people were gone. Adrien was just old enough to understand. In silence, the boy stood close to his mother.

Gazing at her son, Norma saw a thinner, younger version of Aurelius, immersed in an ocean of grief. She set her jaw. "We must work even harder now. You and I, Adrien, are the ones who will maintain your father's legacy."

"I know, Mother. The big ships." The boy drew closer and reached up to put his arm around her waist. He had the potential to be as brilliant as she was, and as capable with business matters as his father.

Norma nodded. "We will form a powerful trading company to use those ships. We must think of the future."

In my dreams I hear the long-ago whisper of Caladan seas, like ghostly memories beckoning me back there. Caladan is far, far from the Jihad.

— Primero Vorian Atreides, private logs

B RUISED AND HEARTSICK after learning of Serena's horrific death, Vorian Atreides returned to Caladan. He had no military mission or plan, only a personal one. Long, long ago he had watched Serena slip through his grasp, and did not intend to let the same thing happen again. He had found another woman who was precious to him.

Leronica.

Why not just retire from the Jihad, turn his back on the fighting, and let others manage the war? He had already fought for four decades . . . Wasn't that enough? Especially now that an outraged humanity had been ignited to seek vengeance on behalf of their Priestess.

On Caladan, with Leronica, he could forget it all for a while. It wasn't a genuine rest or recovery, just a numb avoidance of memories. But it was better than nothing. Then he would return to the war, as always.

She was approaching forty standard years old, her twin sons nearly ten — but Vor had not changed visibly since the age of twenty-one, when Agamemnon gave him the painful immortality treatment. Within a few years Leronica would look old enough to be his mother, but he didn't care. That had never mattered to him. He could only hope that she herself wouldn't be overly concerned about his appearance, or about her own.

When Vor arrived again at Leronica's tavern, she seemed astonished that he had returned so soon. She rushed to embrace him, then pulled back and studied the pain and disaster in his eyes. Something was different. No jokes, no casual saunter, no happy swinging her around in a playful hug.

Vor just hugged her and said nothing for a long time. "I will tell you eventually, Leronica . . . but not now."

"Take whatever time you need. You're always welcome here. Stay with me, if you like."

In the ensuing days, Vor spent hours down by the docks, staring at the hypnotic, peaceful ocean. At times Leronica would sit beside him, or she would go back to work and leave him to contemplate the strange paths he had taken in his life. One of the Caladan fishermen even took him out on a boat for a day, and he found that he enjoyed the hard but honest work, as well as the simple satisfaction of eating fresh fish that he had caught himself.

The boys, Estes and Kagin, became quite fond of him without knowing the truth. Vor's heart swelled when he remembered everything Xavier Harkonnen had told him about his own family life with Octa, things that Vor had never been able to understand . . . until now.

"You should have remarried, Leronica," he said to her one evening as they walked along a rocky beach. "You deserve happiness, and so do your boys. I've met a number of Caladan men who could be excellent candidates."

She raised her eyebrows. "I've been a widow for little more than a year. Are you complaining that I'm still available?"

"Not complaining, just disbelieving. Are the villagers and fishermen blind to what stands in front of their eyes?"

"Many are." She gave him a teasing smile, then put her hands on her hips. "Besides, you're hardly one to teach me how to live my life. I will wait for however long I choose . . . until the right man catches my eye." She stretched to kiss him. "In your letters about exotic adventures and remarkable places, I saw much of the universe. Caladan is a fine world, but you've given me a taste of the stars that have always been beyond my reach."

Wistfully, she gazed out on the endless calm water. "I grow impatient with this place, this life. I want more for my sons. When I think of the League of Nobles, the cities on Salusa Secundus and Giedi Prime, I imagine Estes and Kagin as senators, doctors, or even artists with noble patrons. Here on Caladan, they're destined to become no more than fishermen. I don't want them to be content with small ambitions."

Despite the peace and solitude, Vor could not escape the Jihad. Every portion of humanity had been inflamed by Serena's martyrdom, and the rebellious cymeks — including his own father Agamemnon — had struck deep blows against the evermind. With concerted action, Vor felt that the Army of the Jihad could actually overthrow the computers now. But a difficult fight remained . . .

When the Jihad messenger came to Caladan, he knew exactly where to find Vor. In his final instructions, Primero Harkonnen had told him where to look.

Vor felt queasy when he saw the uniformed man hurrying toward him on the beach. Quinto Paolo's face was flushed with the importance of his mission. He found Vor sitting on a shore rock, listening to the rushing lullaby of the incoming tide. "Primero Atreides! I bring an urgent and private message from Primero Harkonnen."

Leronica stepped away to provide the men with privacy. "I need to get back to the tavern. You two discuss your military secrets —"

But Vor caught her wrist and kept her with him. "I have no secrets from you." He turned to the low-ranking officer and waited.

"I came directly from Tlulax. Primero Harkonnen dispatched me urgently. He commanded that I was not to go to Zimia or to give my message to anyone else in the Army of the Jihad. He fears his words will be corrupted. Instead, he said I would find you on Caladan, with this woman."

Vor's heart pounded, knowing that Primero Xavier Harkonnen would never bypass protocol lightly.

Paolo said, "The Primero told me, 'It is enough for my good friend Vorian to learn the truth.'"

The young officer held a flat, sealed package in his white-knuckled hands. He seemed to be trying to stand at attention and maintain calm breathing, but his entire body looked stiff. Such military protocol might have been important to Xavier, but Vor just wanted to hear his news. "Out with it, Quinto. What is the message?"

Paolo swallowed hard. "He wrote this quickly while I watched, and sent me off before the Grand Patriarch's Jipol could stop me. I barely got away. Now I fear for Primero Harkonnen's safety. I . . . shouldn't have left him, but he ordered me."

Vor tore open the wrapped package. Oddly, it had no security seals or encryption. It was simply a scrawled note. When Vor later thought back on this moment, this fact alone told him a great deal about the desperation Xavier must have felt.

As a sea breeze flapped the paper in his hand, Vor read with widening eyes: the deception of the Tlulaxa organ farms, the purported thinking-machine attacks on Chusuk, Rhisso, and Balut that were really committed by Iblis Ginjo's secret police — slaughtering humans, harvesting their organs as needed, and casting the blame on Omnius. And the planned next strike on Caladan itself.

Here!

He recalled the charnel house he had seen on Chusuk, in contrast with the beauty of this pristine ocean world. "You bastard, Iblis." His nostrils flared as he thought about what he would do to the Grand Patriarch as soon as he came close enough to wrap iron-hard fingers around his neck.

He read on. Xavier described what he intended to do, how he meant to destroy the charming, potent poison of Iblis Ginjo, undertaking one final heroic deed. The old Primero understood how the League populace was likely to think of him afterward — a fanatic, a traitor, a murderer of their beloved Grand Patriarch — but Xavier didn't care about any posthumous disgrace. Or glory, if the complete truth ever came out.

Murderer?

Like Xavier, Vor recognized the massive engine of myth and deception that Iblis Ginjo had created . . . a full cadre of secret police and fanatical Jihad fighters to maintain the illusion of Priestess Serena Butler and her devoted Grand Patriarch, Iblis Ginjo.

At his side, Quinto Paolo cleared his throat. "Primero Harkonnen flew his ship into the sun, taking the Grand Patriarch with him."

The implications struck home, and Vor realized all the traps he could still stumble upon. Nothing was true or fair, and reality was not as black and white as Xavier always assumed it should be.

Iblis had spent decades laying networks across the League of Nobles, and they could not easily be erased. Worse, if the truth were ever widely known, no matter how terrible, the resulting scandal would destroy the momentum Serena had achieved as a martyr in the crusade against the thinking machines. Her followers would fight amongst themselves instead of against Omnius.

Vor clenched his hands together tightly. He could not do that to her memory, so he alone would keep the truth about Xavier. He hoped his friend would understand.

At least Iblis Ginjo was gone.

Another problem: how to deal with the Tlulaxa, who were the vilest of criminals? Even though the Grand Patriarch was dead, his secretive collaborators remained.

Vor needed to expose what the organ farms really were, bringing disgrace and ruin to the Tlulaxa. Yes . . . they could serve as scapegoats, but deserving ones. As soon as the public discovered the horrific deception, they would view the flesh merchants with complete disgust.

The organ farms would be destroyed, and slaves who had served as living flesh reservoirs would be freed . . . one way or another.

Vor sighed, feeling the tremendous responsibility on his shoulders. He saw himself at a nexus of past and future history, and like his friend he cared nothing for personal glory or blame.

He became aware of Leronica's presence. Concern and dismay etched her profiled face as she gazed out to sea. "I can't hold you here, Vor. Go ahead and tend to your emergency." He saw tears brimming at the edges of her dark brown eyes, though she tried to conceal them. "Come back when you can, as always."

Off to the side, Quinto Paolo looked nervous and eager to be away, as if he would remain completely adrift until he received a new set of orders.

But Vor stepped closer to this woman who had become his emotional foundation. He cupped her chin in his hand, turning Leronica to gaze at him. "I have done much thinking here. From now on, I need be a human being as well as a soldier. I . . . want you to come with me."

The surprise and delight on her face wiped away ten years of age. "But I'm just a poor girl from Caladan. I have no right to be the consort of a great Primero —"

Tenderly, he placed his fingers over her lips. "You are my love, and the mother of my sons." Vor hesitated, waiting for her to deny what they both knew. He could not look at Estes or Kagin and have any remaining doubt.

She pressed her lips together. "I want the boys to remember Kalem as their father. He sacrificed his life for them, and I will not let you diminish their memories of the man they knew for most of their lives."

"I wouldn't dream of it. Kalem Vazz did what I should have done. He raised them, gave them their moral sense and work ethic. He was there when I wasn't."

"That doesn't mean you can't begin now." She was breathing hard, and tears streamed down her cheeks.

Nodding, he said, "We will raise our sons in the League of Nobles, with every opportunity our civilization has to offer." His voice filled with emotion, and he drew her closer. "I have a whole galaxy to show you."

Night is a hole in yesterday, and a tunnel into tomorrow.
— Zensunni Fire Poetry

T EN YEARS AGO, Marha, Jafar, and all the followers of Selim's vision abandoned their long-standing settlement and made their pilgrimage deep into the desert, far from the offworld hunters and Naib Dhartha's betrayers. On that fateful day, Marha — after climbing Needle Rock for a better vantage — had witnessed the end of her husband's life. But the event was really a beginning, as the great Wormrider allowed himself to become incorporated into the magnificent segmented body of God.

For a decade they had continued Selim's dream and his mission. Word of the outlaw leader's incredible fate had spread among the Zensunni settlements of Arrakis, causing hundreds of candidates to seek the isolated hideout and attempt to join the Wormriders.

The stone caves and open dunes of Arrakis formed a shelter instead of a prison. Far back in the shadowed passageway, the wormriders and outlaws had found more Muadru rune designs deeply etched into the cool stone. The symbols reminded Ishmael of the ancient undeciphered writings his grandfather had kept among Sutra parchments at his shack on Harmonthep. Ishmael didn't know how to interpret the markings, but was certain they carried some message of hope and solidarity.

In the first year, the refugees from Poritrin had learned to live with the Arrakis natives, working side by side with them, assisting in the daily toils of survival. The weakest among them had recovered their strength, and no one complained. After a life of indentured servitude, serving capricious masters in tasks that even machines would have resented, the former slaves were resilient and strong.

Ishmael stood with his surviving people at a large opening that looked out upon the foreboding expanse where no footprints of slavers would ever be seen. It was bright dawn, which Marha told them had been Selim Wormrider's favorite time of day.

Ishmael's daughter Chamal looked hopeful and strong, filled with womanhood at the age of twenty-six. She had married again, in the way of the rugged desert people, and had already borne three children. She still carried Rafel in her heart, but every person in Ishmael's group of refugees had lost family, either back on Poritrin or here on Arrakis. They must all move forward, knowing that this was destined to be their home, now and forever.

Lovely Marha came to stand at Ishmael's side, gazing with flinty eyes across the desert. He smiled warmly at her, and they remained close, the joining of two peoples. El'hiim, her son by Selim Wormrider, had grown into a fine strong boy, now almost ten years old . . . and he had learned to be more careful before crawling into unexplored crevices, where black scorpions might lurk.

Less than a year after the refugees had been rescued, Marha had made no secret of the fact that she considered Ishmael a logical choice to succeed Selim. She had been blessed with a healthy and intelligent young son, and by Zensunni custom and the necessities of a difficult nomadic life, the people of Arrakis did not ostracize fatherless children or wives who had lost their husbands.

"I was the Wormrider's woman," she had said to him in the protected cave quietness, lifting her chin like a desert princess. The crescent scar on her left eyebrow seemed pale in the shadows. "After Shai-Hulud devoured my husband and the evil Naib Dhartha, my obvious choice for a new partner should have been Jafar, who was Selim's second in command. But . . ."

She looked away, then back to Ishmael. "Jafar reveres Selim's legendary memory, and is intimidated in his shadow. He has not said so, but I sense that he feels it would be some kind of . . . sacrilege if he took me as his wife. The other men worshipped Selim, too, followed him like a prophet. They honor his memory, the traditions he established, and they treat me as if I were some kind of untouchable goddess." Marha touched his arm. "A person cannot live like that, Ishmael."

He looked at her. "And since I am a comparative stranger, you believe I am not stifled by those expectations?"

"You are a leader of your own people, a man who commands their respect, who is fair and firm and not afraid to stand by his convictions.

You are a rock, not a soft dune to be reshaped by every errant breeze."

He frowned. "You ask me to forget my other wife."

Marha shook her head. "I ask you to forget nothing. Nor will I ever forget my first husband. We both have our pasts, Ishmael . . . and our futures. We are stronger together."

Her words frightened him, but Ishmael recognized the truth in her words. "You have given me a heavy burden to bear." She stood very close to him, so that he felt intoxicated by her sharp intelligence and beauty.

She shrugged, then kissed his rough cheek. "We all bear burdens, do we not?"

And so they wed each other, and worked together to lead the growing band of outlaws in their continued effort to stifle the hemorrhaging flow of melange from Arrakis. All of them swore to defend Shai-Hulud and prevent the taking of spice.

Now, after summoning his bandits to join him at the cave opening, Ishmael stared at these people who had followed him over such a great distance, and the others who had accepted him as the successor to Selim Wormrider. Behind him on the sands, the new day grew warmer.

Selim had experienced many visions, receiving flashes of the future through his connection to the great Shai-Hulud, through a conduit of potent melange. Ishmael, though, had no such reliable source to guide him in his decisions. He had to study the Koran Sutras and all the other scriptures, hoping he could properly determine the will of God. At times, Ishmael often found time alone in the darkest hours of night to quietly scan the infinite desert as if he could see the future out there, somewhere . . .

As the sun crept up the rugged cliffside, he inhaled a deep breath of dry air and felt its harshness. Arrakis was far more inhospitable than Poritrin or Harmonthep — but this was his new home, a place where he could live away from the threats of slavers and thinking machines, and even away from the League of Nobles.

With a smile, Ishmael looked around, from face to face. "We can live on this world as we choose, making our own lives and future. We shall never be slaves again!" He sighed with immense pride, and added, "From this day forward we shall call ourselves the *Free Men* of Arrakis."